博士研究生入学考试辅导用书

考博英语阅读理解

精粹 100 篇

第 7 版

博士研究生入学考试辅导用书编审委员会　编著

机 械 工 业 出 版 社

英语考试在博士研究生入学考试中占有举足轻重的地位，而阅读理解是英语考试中的"重中之重"。本书选材系统、全面，具体内容涉及科学技术、经济管理、教育文化、社会生活、环境生态、政治历史、医学保健、宗教信仰、新闻艺术等诸多方面，可以让考生系统见证考博英语阅读理解材料，强化英语背景知识，在阅读理解考试中轻松取得高分。

本书适合参加博士研究生入学考试的广大考生使用，同时也可以作为参加普通研究生入学考试的广大考生的自学辅导书。

图书在版编目（CIP）数据

考博英语阅读理解精粹100篇/博士研究生入学考试辅导用书编审委员会编著. —7版. —北京：机械工业出版社，2012.3（2012.6 重印）

博士研究生入学考试辅导用书

ISBN　978-7-111-37621-7

Ⅰ. ①考… Ⅱ. ①博… Ⅲ. ①英语—阅读教学—研究生—入学考试—自学参考资料 Ⅳ. ①H319.4

中国版本图书馆 CIP 数据核字（2012）第 035317 号

机械工业出版社（北京市百万庄大街22号 邮政编码100037）
策划编辑：郑文斌　　　　　责任编辑：罗政军
责任印制：乔　宇

三河市国英印务有限公司印刷

2012 年 6 月第 7 版第 2 次印刷
184mm×260mm・23 印张・500 千字
标准书号：ISBN　978-7-111-37621-7
　　　　　　ISBN　978-7-89433-360-5（光盘）
定价：50.00 元（含 1CD）

凡购本书，如有缺页、倒页、脱页，由本社发行部调换

电话服务　　　　　　　　　网络服务
社 服 务 中 心：(010)88361066
销 售 一 部：(010)68326294　　门户网：http://www.cmpbook.com
销 售 二 部：(010)88379649　　教材网：http://www.cmpedu.com
读者购书热线：(010)88379203　　**封面无防伪标均为盗版**

第 7 版前言

我国自 1981 年建立学位制度以来，全国博士招生人数增长速度较快，2008 年全国博士招生人数突破了 6 万人，今后国内博士生招收人数还将略有增加。从整体上看，由于博士生招生形势的不断发展，各院校博士研究生入学考试的难度也越来越大，对考生的外语要求也将越来越高，特别是听说能力。

目前，我国博士研究生英语入学考试采取的是各招生院校自行命题、自行组织考试的办法，各个院校的考试重点、命题特点有相当大的不同。目前国内没有统一的考试大纲，主要是由于国内没有对博士研究生入学英语考试采取统考形式。外语成绩一直是衡量考生能否入选博士研究生的最重要的尺度，因此英语考试是考生参加博士研究生入学考试道路上最大的障碍和挑战。

许多考生有几年的工作经历，但并非在英语环境中工作，所以对英语有几分生疏，英语考试也就很自然地成为了一大难题。

许多考生并非由于专业课，而是英语考试未达到所报考学校的最低录取分数线，因此与自己理想的学校失之交臂。

博士研究生入学考试中的英语考试是重头戏，而阅读理解又是英语考试中的"重中之重"，该部分在整个试卷中的分值最高，且阅读理解能力也是做好其他部分的基础。在复习英语时，把阅读理解作为考试的切入点可以"一箭双雕"，对于提高考生的整体英语水平具有重要的意义。为此，我们在第 6 版的基础上认真修订了这本《考博英语阅读理解精粹 100 篇》，更换了部分陈旧或过时的阅读题材，更正了本书前面各版次的疏漏之处，使本书更加臻于完善，更加符合考生的复习需要。

本书由三部分组成，遵循了由易到难、循序渐进的原则，从难度适中、篇幅较短的基础技能训练，到难度逼近真题或者略高于真题的实战演练。考生经过这 100 篇的系统强化训练之后，对于考博英语阅读理解应该是胜券在握了。

第一部分为基础训练 40 篇，可以作为考生复习的基础训练阅读材料。这部分的总体特点可以概括为选题广泛、话题新颖、注解全面。在选编文章题材、体裁方面尽可能拓展空间，广泛涉猎，包括社会科学、自然科学等各个领域的知识，可以让考生系统见证考博英语阅读理解材料，强化英语背景知识。

第二部分为模拟提高 40 篇，其内容难度较大，是考生在复习提高阅读理解能力阶段磨炼思路、熟悉题型、扩充词汇的最佳练习材料，有利于解题能力的迅速提高。

第三部分为冲刺演练 20 篇，本部分阅读理解材料仿真度极高，供考生在最后冲刺阶段进行热身演练。

广泛的阅读可以提高考生的阅读理解能力，也可以巩固和提高语言应用能力，达到事半功倍的目的。考生在备考阶段应该熟记相关词汇、透彻理解文章，对题目解析和长难句分析应该细心揣摩，领悟考博阅读类题目的出题思路和解题技巧。编撰此书的初衷就是力求提高考生的应试水平和阅读理解能力，不辜负考生的期望和追求知识的挚诚。

本书在编写过程中曾几易其稿，如今已经是第6次修订，希望能尽量满足读者的需求。然而限于作者水平，纰漏之处在所难免，敬请同行和读者批评指正。

参加本书编写的除了马阿婷、李铁红、周槐雄外，还有李雪、樊鹏、成芬、涂振旗、方志仁、姜宝静、黎兴刚、王欢、王宇、董亮、赵娜、张永艳、刘爽、刘仕文、高鹏、苗红宜、李自杰、王德军、陈明慧、孟楠。另外，国外的朋友 Michael Anderson 对本丛书的审订工作付出了很多艰辛的劳动，在此一并表示感谢。

博士研究生入学考试辅导用书编审委员会

目　录

第7版前言

第一部分　基础训练40篇

第二部分　模拟提高40篇

第三部分　冲刺演练 20 篇

第一部分 基础训练 40 篇

Unit 1

Text 1

Much of the language used to describe monetary policy, such as "steering the economy to a soft landing" or "a touch on the brakes", makes it sound like a precise science. Nothing could be further from the truth. The link between interest rates and inflation is uncertain. And there are long, variable lags before policy changes have any effect on the economy. Hence the analogy that likens the conduct of monetary policy to driving a car with a blackened windscreen, a cracked rear view mirror and a faulty steering wheel.

Given all these disadvantages, central bankers seem to have had much to boast about of late. Average inflation in the big seven industrial economies fell to a mere 2.3% last year, close to its lowest level in 30 years, before rising slightly to 2.5% this July. This is a long way below the double digit rates which many countries experienced in the 1970s and early 1980s.

It is also less than most forecasters had predicated. In late 1994 the panel of economists which *The Economist* polls each month said that America's inflation rate would average 3.5% in 1995. In 1995, in fact, it fell to 2.6% in August, and expected to average only about 3% for the year as a whole. In Britain and Japan inflation is running half a percentage point below the rate predicted at the end of last year. This is no flash in the pan; over the past couple of years, inflation has been consistently lower than expected in Britain and America.

Economists have been particularly surprised by favorable inflation figures in Britain and the United States, since conventional measures suggest that both economies, and especially America's, have little productive slack. America's capacity utilization, for example, hit historically high levels earlier this year, and its jobless rate (5.6% in August) has fallen below most estimates of the natural rate of unemployment — the rate below which inflation has taken off in the past.

Why has inflation proved so mild? The most thrilling explanation is, unfortunately, a little defective. Some economists argue that powerful structural changes in the world have up-ended the old economic models that were based upon the historical link between growth and inflation.

1. From the passage we learn that _____.
   A. there is a definite relationship between inflation and interest rates
   B. economy will always follow certain models
   C. the economic situation is better than expected

    D．economists had foreseen the present economic situation

2．According to the passage, which of the following is true?

    A．Making monetary policies is comparable to driving a car.

    B．An extremely low jobless rate will lead to inflation.

    C．A high unemployment rate will result from inflation.

    D．Interest rates have an immediate effect on the economy.

3．The sentence "This is no flash in the pan" (Line 5, Paragraph 3) means that _____．

    A．the low inflation rate will last for some time

    B．the inflation rate will soon rise

    C．the inflation will disappear quickly

    D．there is no inflation at present

4．The passage shows that the author is _____ the present situation.

    A．critical of   B．puzzled by   C．disappointed at   D．amazed at

核心词汇注释

steer [stɪə(r)] *v.* 驾驶，掌舵

brake [breɪk] *n.* 闸，刹车

    v. 刹车

lag [læg] *n.* 落后；囚犯；迟延；桶板，
防护套

    vi. 缓缓而行，滞后

    vt. 落后于；押往监狱；加上外套

analogy [əˈnælədʒɪ] *n.* 类似，类推

liken [ˈlaɪkən] *vt.* 把……比做

blacken [ˈblækən] *v.* 使变黑；诽谤

slack [slæk] *n.* 松弛，静止；淡季，闲散；
家常裤

    adj. 松弛的，不流畅的；疏忽的；软弱的；
漏水的；呆滞的，懒散的

    adv. 马虎地；缓慢地

    vt. 使松弛，使缓慢；马虎从事

    vi. 松懈，减弱，松弛

defective [dɪˈfektɪv] *adj.* 有缺陷的，（智商
或行为有）欠缺的

    n. 有缺陷的人；不完全变化动词

长难句剖析

【文章难句】Average inflation in the big seven industrial economies fell to a mere 2.3% last year, close to its lowest level in 30 years, before rising slightly to 2.5 % this July.

【结构分析】本句中，主干是 "Average inflation fell to 2.3%"，后面的两个分句都是补充、修饰这句话的。close to 意思是 "接近于"，before 在这里的意思是 "之后"，即 "后来到了 7 月份就稍稍上升了"。

【参考译文】去年七大工业国经济的平均通货膨胀率降到了仅 2.3%，接近 30 年以来的最低水平，一直到今年 7 月份才稍稍上升到 2.5%。

【文章难句】Economists have been particularly surprised by favorable inflation figures in Britain and the United States, since conventional measures suggest that both economies, and especially America's, have little productive slack.

【结构分析】本句由一个附带原因状语从句的复合句组成。在后面的分句当中，"and

especially America's"做插入语，that 引导的是宾语从句。

【参考译文】特别让经济学家感到惊讶的是，英、美两国的通货膨胀率带来的是有利结果，因为传统的衡量办法表明两国经济，尤其是美国的经济几乎没有出现生产萧条的现象。

全文参考译文

许多描述金融政策的词语，像"指导经济软着陆"或"经济刹车"使人听起来觉得它是一门精确的科学。事实上远非如此。利率与通货膨胀之间的联系是不确定的。政策变化对经济产生任何影响之前，有一段时间长且易变的滞后期。因此，人们将执行金融政策比作驾驶一辆挡风玻璃黑暗、后视镜破碎而且方向盘失灵的汽车。

尽管有这么多不利因素，但近来中央银行的银行家们好像有许多可以夸耀的东西。去年七大工业国经济的平均通货膨胀率降到了仅 2.3%，接近 30 年以来的最低水平，一直到今年 7 月份才稍稍上升到 2.5%，这比许多国家 20 世纪 70 年代和 80 年代早期经历的两位数通货膨胀率低很多。

这也要低于大多数预测人员所预测的。每月都要邀请一些经济专家座谈的《经济学家》，在 1994 年底邀请的经济专家们说，1995 年美国的平均通货膨胀率将达到 3.5%。事实上，在 1995 年 8 月份就降到了 2.6%，而且，预期全年的平均通货膨胀率仅为 3%左右。在英国和日本通货膨胀率比去年年底预测的低零点五个百分点。这不是暂时的现象，在过去两年里，英国和美国的通货膨胀率一直比预计的要低。

特别让经济学家感到惊讶的是，英、美两国的通货膨胀率带来的是有利结果，因为传统的衡量办法表明两国经济，尤其是美国的经济几乎没有出现生产萧条的现象。比如，在今年早期，美国的产能利用率达到历史新高，而失业率（8 月份为 5.6%）却比大多数人预测的自然失业率要低——过去，失业率低于此，通货膨胀率就会上升。

为什么通货膨胀如此和缓呢？遗憾的是，最令人振奋的解释也是不完善的。某些经济学家认为，世界强大的结构变化已结束了原有的基于经济增长和通货膨胀的历史联系的经济模式。

题目答案与解析

1. 我们从本文可以了解到 _____。
   A．通货膨胀和利率有明确的关系　　　B．经济将总是遵循特定的模式
   C．经济形势比预期的好　　　　　　　D．经济学家早已预见了现在的经济形势

【答案】C

【解析】从文章第 1 段的内容可知，过去被用来描述金融政策的许多术语使得金融政策听起来像是一门严谨的科学，实际情况可能远非如此，利率与通货膨胀之间的联系并不稳定，政策变动对经济产生影响之前，有一段时间长且易变的滞后期。因此，出现了这样的类比——将执行金融政策比作驾驶一辆挡风玻璃已经发黑、后视镜已经破裂并且方向盘已经失灵的汽车。从文章第 2 段的内容可知，尽管有这些不利条件，但是最近中央银行的银行家似乎有不少值得夸耀的东西：七大工业国家的平均通货膨胀率下降了，接近 30 年来的最低水平，比许多国家

20 世纪 70 年代和 80 年代早期经历过的两位数的通货膨胀率要低很多。从文章第 3 段的内容可知，这一数字也比大多数预测人员预测的要低：在英国和日本，通货膨胀率比去年年底预测的要低零点五个百分点；英国和美国的通货膨胀率一直比预测的低。从文章第 4 段的内容可知，英、美两国的通货膨胀率带来的是有利结果，两国的经济，尤其是美国的经济，几乎没有出现生产萧条的现象。文章在最后一段总结出：为什么通货膨胀如此和缓呢？一些经济学家认为，旧的经济模式以经济增长和通货膨胀的历史联系为基础，但是世界经济结构所引起的巨大变化已经打破了这种模式。据此可知，英、美两国目前的经济形势比预计的状况要好。C 项的"经济形势比预期的好"与文章的意思相符；A 项"通货膨胀和利率有明确的关系"与文章第 1 段第 3 句话的意思不符；B 项不正确，依据是文章最后一段的最后一句话"旧的经济模式以经济增长和通货膨胀的历史联系为基础，但是世界经济结构所引起的巨大变化已经打破了这种模式"；D 项明显与文章第 3、4 段第 1 句话的意思不符。综上所述，只有 C 项为正确答案。

2．依据本文的观点，以下说法中正确的是哪项？

　　A．制定金融政策类似于开车。　　　　B．极低的失业率将引发通货膨胀。

　　C．通货膨胀将导致高失业率。　　　　D．利率对经济有直接影响。

【答案】B

【解析】本题中，A 项不正确，文章第 1 段最后一句话只是将执行金融政策比作驾驶汽车，并不是说制定金融政策就像开车；C 项明显不符合文章的意思；D 项不正确，从文章第 1 段的第 3、4 句话可知，利率与通货膨胀之间的联系并不稳定，政策变动对经济产生影响之前，有一段时间长且易变的滞后期；从文章第 4 段的最后一句话可知，今年早些时候，美国的生产力利用率达到历史新高，它的失业率已经低于大多数正常失业率的预计——过去，如果低于这个失业率，通货膨胀率就已经上升。据此可知，如果失业率低，就会导致通货膨胀。B 项的"极低的失业率将引发通货膨胀"，这与文中"the rate below which inflation has taken off in the past（过去，如果失业率低于此，通货膨胀率就会上升）"的意思相符，因此 B 项为正确答案。

3．句子"This is no flash in the pan"（第 3 段第 5 行）意思是指 _____。

　　A．低通货膨胀率将持续一段时间　　　B．通货膨胀率不久将上升

　　C．通货膨胀将很快消失　　　　　　　D．目前没有通货膨胀

【答案】A

【解析】本题中，B 项"通货膨胀率不久将上升"和 C 项"通货膨胀将很快消失"之意明显与文章的意思不符。D 项不正确，文中只是说"通货膨胀率低"，并没有说没有通货膨胀。从文章第 3 段的内容可知，通货膨胀率也比大多数预测人员预测的要低；由经济学家组成的专门研究小组说，美国 1995 年的通货膨胀率将平均达到 3.5%，而实际上，通货膨胀率 8 月份就降到了 2.6%，并且全年的通货膨胀率有望达到大约 3% 的平均水平；在英国和日本，通货膨胀率比去年年底预测的要低 0.5%。这不是昙花一现。过去几年，英国和美国的通货膨胀率一直比预测的低。据此可知，英、美两国的通货膨胀率低并不是偶然现象，而是一直比预测的比率低，并且可能持续一段时间。A 项的"低通货膨胀率将持续一段时间"与文章的意思相符，因此 A 项为正确答案。

4．本文显示出作者对目前的形势 _____。

A．持批评态度 　　　B．感到困惑 　　　C．感到失望 　　　D．感到惊讶

【答案】D

【解析】本题中，A 项 "持批评态度" 和 C 项 "感到失望" 之意明显与文章的意思不符。B 项不正确，文中是说对良好的通货膨胀率感到惊异，并不是说感到困惑。从文章第 2 段的内容可知，通货膨胀率比许多国家 20 世纪 70 年代和 80 年代早期经历过的两位数的通货膨胀率要低很多；从文章第 4 段的内容可知，英、美两国良好的通货膨胀率尤其令经济学家感到惊异，两国的经济，尤其是美国的经济，几乎没有停滞；从文章最后一段的内容可知，为什么通货膨胀如此和缓呢？不幸的是，即使最令人振奋的解释也不怎么完美。据此可知，作者认为当前的经济形势出人意料。D 项的 "感到惊讶" 与文中 "Economists have been particularly surprised by favorable inflation figures（尤其令经济学家感到惊异的是有利的通货膨胀率）" 的意思相符，因此 D 项为正确答案。

Text 2

The Internet can make the news more democratic, giving the public a chance to ask questions and seek out facts behind stories and candidates, according to the head of the largest U.S. online service.

"But the greatest potential for public participation is still in the future," Steven Case, Chairman of America Online, told a recent meeting on Journalism and the Internet sponsored by the Freedom Forum（论坛）. However, some other experts often say the new technology of computers is changing the face of journalism, giving reporters access to more information and their readers a chance to ask questions and turn to different sources.

"You don't have to buy a newspaper and be confined to the four corners of that paper any more," Sam Meddis, online technology editor at *USA Today*, observed about the variety of information available to computer users.

But the experts noted the easy access to the Internet also means anyone can post information for others to see. "Anyone can say anything they want, whether it's right or wrong," said Case. Readers have to determine for themselves who to trust. "In a world of almost infinite voices, respected journalists and respected brand names will probably become more important, not less," Case said.

"The Internet today is about where radio was 80 years ago, or television 50 years ago or cable 25 years ago," he said. But it is growing rapidly because it provides people fast access to news and a chance to comment on it.

1. The main topic of this passage is _____.
   A. the development of journalism
   B. the rapid development of the Internet
   C. the effect the Internet has on journalism
   D. the advantages of the Internet

2. It can be inferred from this passage that the fact that _____ may NOT be regarded as an advantage of the Internet.
   A. the news can be made more democratic
   B. the public can turn to different sources

C. the public can get a chance to ask questions

D. anything can be posted on the Internet for others to see

3. The correct order for the appearance of the four technologies is _____.

A. Internet-cable-television-radio

B. radio-television-cable-Internet

C. radio-cable-television-Internet

D. television-radio-cable-Internet

4. Which of the following statements is true?

A. Only respected journalists can post information on the Internet for others to see.

B. Respected journalists will probably become more important than before.

C. Everyone is using the Internet now.

D. The greatest potential of public participation of the Internet is in the near future.

核心词汇注释

democratic [ˌdeməˈkrætɪk] *adj.* 民主的，民主主义的，民主政体的，平民的

candidate [ˈkændɪdɪt] *n.* 候选人，投考者

participation [pɑːˌtɪsɪˈpeɪʃən] *n.* 分享，参与

journalism [ˈdʒɜːnəlɪz(ə)m] *n.* 新闻业，报纸杂志

sponsor [ˈspɒnsə(r)] *n.* 发起人，保证人，主办人

vt. 发起，主办

v. 赞助

confined [kənˈfaɪnd] *adj.* 被限制的，狭窄

的；分娩的

access [ˈækses] *n.* 通路；访问；入门

vt. 存取；接近

infinite [ˈɪnfɪnɪt] *n.* 无限的东西（如空间、时间）；[数]无穷大

adj. 无穷的，无限的，无数的，极大的

journalist [ˈdʒɜːnəlɪst] *n.* 新闻记者，从事新闻杂志业的人

comment [ˈkɒment] *n.* 注释，评论，意见

vi. 注释，评论

长难句剖析

【文章难句】The Internet can make the news more democratic, giving the public a chance to ask question and seek out facts behind stories and candidates, according to the head of the largest U.S. online service.

【结构分析】本句中，主干是 The Internet can make the news more democratic，后面的现在分词结构 giving the public…candidates 做主句的状语，表示方式。"according to… " 是整个句子的插入语成分。

【参考译文】据美国一家最大的在线服务商的总裁说，互联网可以通过给公众机会提问并找出事件和候选人背后的事实，而让新闻更加民主。

【文章难句】The Internet today is about where radio was 80 years ago, or television 50 years ago or cable 25 years ago.

【结构分析】本句是一个主系表结构，The Internet today 做主语，is 是系动词，where 引导的从句做表语。表语是由三个从句构成的，后两个从句采用了省略形式。

【参考译文】现在的互联网处于起步阶段，就像是 80 年前的收音机、50 年前的电视机或 25 年前的有线电视一样。

【文章难句】"You don't have to buy a newspaper and be confined to the four corners of that paper any more," Sam Meddis, online technology editor at USA Today, observed about the variety of information available to computer users.

【结构分析】本句中，主干是 Sam Meddis…observed，介宾短语 about…users 做动词 observed 的状语。引号中的句子是直接引语。

【参考译文】《今日美国》的在线技术编辑 Sam Meddis 对电脑使用者可获得各种各样的信息评论道，"你再也没必要买报纸了，你的信息不再局限于四四方方的报纸上。"

全文参考译文

据美国一家最大的在线服务商的总裁说，互联网可以通过给公众机会提问并找出事件和候选人背后的事实，而让新闻更加民主。

"不过公众参与的最大潜力还有待挖掘，"在最近由自由论坛发起的讨论关于新闻和互联网的会议上，"美国在线"的主席 Steven Case 这样说道。然而，其他一些专家常说这种电脑新科技正在改变新闻的面貌，它让记者们能够得到更多的信息，公众也有机会提出疑问并能求助于不同的信息来源。

《今日美国》的在线技术编辑 Sam Meddis 对电脑使用者可获得各种各样的信息评论道，"你再也没必要买报纸了，你的信息不再局限于四四方方的报纸上。"

但是专家注意到，互联网的便捷也意味着任何人都可以发布信息供他人阅读。Case 说："任何人可以想说什么就说什么，不管他的言论是否正确。"读者必须自行决定应该相信谁。"在一个充满着无限种声音的世界里，受人尊重的记者和品牌将有可能变得更加重要，"Case 又说。

他说："现在的互联网正处于起步阶段，就像是 80 年前的收音机、50 年前的电视机或 25 年前的有线电视一样。"但因为它可以给人们提供快捷的信息和参与评论的机会，互联网正在飞速发展。

题目答案与解析

1. 本文的主旨是 _____。
   A．新闻业的发展
   B．互联网的快速发展
   C．互联网对新闻业产生的影响
   D．互联网的优势
   【答案】C
   【解析】综观全文，这篇文章主要是讲互联网对新闻的影响，因此 C 项为正确答案。

2. 从文中可以推断出，_____ 因素不能认为是互联网的优点。
   A．新闻可以变得更加民主
   B．公众可以求助于不同的信息来源
   C．公众有提出问题的机会
   D．任何东西都可以发布在互联网上让别人看
   【答案】D
   【解析】本题的依据句是文章的第 4 段 "Anyone can say anything they want, whether it's right or wrong," said Case. Readers have to determine for themselves who to trust. 从中可知 D

项为正确答案。

3．四种技术出现的正确次序是　　　　　。
　　A．互联网——有线电视——电视机——收音机
　　B．收音机——电视机——有线电视——互联网
　　C．收音机——有线电视——电视——互联网
　　D．电视机——收音机——有线电视——互联网
　　【答案】B
　　【解析】本题可参照文章的最后一段，从中可知正确的次序是B项。

4．以下各项陈述中，哪一项是正确的？
　　A．只有受尊敬的记者才可以在互联网上发布信息给别人看。
　　B．受尊敬的记者将可能比以前更加重要。
　　C．现在每个人都在使用互联网。
　　D．互联网公众参与所产生的巨大潜力将在不久的将来显现出来。
　　【答案】B
　　【解析】本题可参照文章的第4段，从中可知B项为正确答案。

Text 3

There is a range of activities which require movements of about one to four or five miles. These might be leisure activities, such as moving from home to swimming pool, tennis club, the theater or other cultural centers, or to a secondary or more advanced school, or they might be movements associated with work and shopping in the central areas of cities. The use of cars capable of carrying five people at 80 mph for satisfying these needs is wasteful of space and most productive of disturbance to other road users.

The use of the bicycle, or some more modern derivative of it, is probably worth more consideration than has recently been given to it. The bicycle itself is a remarkably efficient and simple device for using human muscular energy for transportation. In pure energy terms, it is four to five times as efficient as walking, even though human walking itself is twice as efficient as the movement of effective animals such as dogs or gulls. It is still widely used, not only in some developing countries where bicycles are major means of people and goods, but in a few richer towns such as Amsterdam in Holland and Cambridge in England.

It usually gives inadequate protection from the weather, is not very suitable for carrying goods, and demands considerable muscular work to make progress against wind or uphill. It also offers its rider no protection against collisions with other vehicles. All these difficulties could, however, be greatly eliminated, if not removed, with relatively small changes in design. The whole machine could be enclosed in a plastic bubble which would provide some protection in case of accidents. It would be easy to add a small petrol or electric motor. A wide variety of designs would be possible. As in rowing, we might employ the power of the arms or the general body musculature, as well as those of the legs; more muscular exercise would be good for the health of many people in cities, and a wide use of bicycle like muscle-powered vehicles would be a useful way to ensure this. It could also provide ample opportunities for showing off by the young and vigorous.

1. The main idea of the first paragraph is that the car _____.

    A. can satisfy the demand for speed

    B. causes waste of space

    C. produces disturbance to other road users

    D. is far from perfect for short range movements

2. More attention should be given to the bicycle as a means of transport because it is _____.

    A. a very efficient and simple device

    B. much cheaper than a car

    C. widely used in Amsterdam and Cambridge

    D. still used by rich people

3. Enclosing the bicycle in a plastic bubble would _____.

    A. make it easier to use

    B. save muscular energy

    C. provide protection from the weather

    D. prevent it from colliding with other vehicles

4. Which of these is untrue for the present bicycle?

    A. It is far more efficient than the movement of animals.

    B. It offers its rider no protection.

    C. It is not very suitable for carrying goods.

    D. It can hardly be improved on.

核心词汇注释

leisure [ˈleʒə(r)] *n.* 空闲，闲暇，悠闲，安逸

associate [əˈsəuʃɪet] *vt.* 使发生联系，使联合
vi. 交往，结交
n. 合伙人，同事；准会员
adj. 联合的，联盟的，合伙的；准的

disturbance [dɪˈstɜːbəns] *n.* 骚动，动乱；打扰，干扰，骚扰，搅动

derivative [dɪˈrɪvətɪv] *adj.* 引出的，系出的
n. 派生的事物，派生词

muscular [ˈmʌskjulə(r)] *adj.* 肌肉的，强健的

inadequate [ɪnˈædɪkwət] *adj.* 不充分的，不适当的

collision [kəˈlɪʒ(ə)n] *n.* 碰撞，冲突

eliminate [ɪˈlɪmɪneɪt] *vt.* 排除，消除
v. 除去

bubble [ˈbʌb(ə)l] *n.* 泡沫，幻想的计划
vi. 起泡，潺潺地流

musculature [ˈmʌskjulətʃə(r)] *n.* 肌肉组织

长难句剖析

【文章难句】The use of cars capable of carrying five people at 80 mph for satisfying these needs is wasteful of space and most productive of disturbance to other road users.

【结构分析】本句的主干是 The use of cars…is wasteful of space and most productive, cars 的后置定语是形容词短语 capable of …at 80 mph, for satisfying these needs 短语做主语 use 的目的状语。

【参考译文】开一辆时速 80 英里的、能载 5 个人的汽车去满足这些需要是对空间的浪费，而且会对其他的道路使用者产生干扰。

【文章难句】The use of the bicycle, or some more modern derivative of it, is probably worth more consideration than has recently been given to it.

【结构分析】本句的主干是 The use…is probably worth more consideration, or…it 与 bicycle 并列。consideration 后面是由 than 引导的定语从句。在英语语法中 than 不仅可以作比较副词，还可以用来引导定语从句，它在定语从句中的成分是关系代词。

【参考译文】骑普通的或是更加现代化的自行车或许更值得我们考虑。

【文章难句】It is still widely used, not only in some developing countries where bicycles are major means of people and goods, but in a few richer towns such as Amsterdam in Holland and Cambridge in England.

【结构分析】本句的主干是 It is still widely used，后接由 not only in…but in 引导的地点状语。在第一个地点状语中，developing countries 后面接的是 where 引导的定语从句。在第二个地点状语中，a few richer towns 后面的 such as 引导的短语做补语。

【参考译文】自行车仍然被广泛使用着，不仅一些发展中国家把自行车当做主要的交通和运输工具，而且少数几个较为富裕的城市，像荷兰的阿姆斯特丹和英格兰的剑桥也是如此。

全文参考译文

有一系列的活动需要大约一至四五英里的运动。这些运动可能是些休闲活动，比如从家到游泳池、网球俱乐部、剧院或其他的文化中心，或者是要去一所中学或大学，或者可能与去市中心工作和购物活动有关。开一辆时速 80 英里、能载 5 人的汽车去满足这些需要是对空间的浪费，而且会对其他的道路使用者产生干扰。

骑普通的或是更加现代化的自行车或许更值得我们考虑。自行车本身是一种可以把人的体能转化为运输的非常有效的简单装置。从纯粹的能量上讲，骑车的效率是步行的 4 到 5 倍，虽然人类步行的效率已经比像狗或海鸥这样行动有效的动物要高一倍。自行车仍然被广泛使用着，不仅一些发展中国家把自行车当做主要的交通和运输工具，而且少数几个较为富裕的城市，像荷兰的阿姆斯特丹和英格兰的剑桥也是如此。

自行车通常无法不受天气的影响，也不是很适合携带物品，而且刮风和上坡的时候需要相当的体能才能前进。与其他交通工具相撞时骑车人得不到任何防护。但是所有这些困难即使无法根除也能得到很好的解决，只要在设计上做些小小的改变。整辆车可以用塑料防护罩包起来，这样一旦发生事故可以提供一些防护。加一台汽油或电发动机也很容易。各种各样的设计都是可行的。在骑车过程中，我们不仅要使用双腿的力量，还要使用手臂和全身肌肉的力量；对于很多在城市中生活的人来说，更多的肌肉练习有益健康，广泛地把自行车当做肌肉练习的工具使用，将会是保证这一点的有效方法。这也可以给年轻又有活力的人提供大量的机会炫耀自己。

题目答案与解析

1. 第 1 段的主题是汽车 _____。
   A. 可以满足速度的需求
   B. 造成空间的浪费
   C. 对其他的道路使用者产生干扰
   D. 很不适合小范围的运动

   【答案】D

   【解析】本题的依据句是第 1 段的最后一句话 The use of cars capable of carrying five people at 80 mph for satisfying these needs is wasteful of space and most productive of disturbance to other road users. 从中可知，A、B、C 三项都不能完整地表达第 1 段的中心思想，只有 D 项涵盖了前三项的意思，因此是正确答案。

2. 作为交通工具，自行车应该被给予更多的重视，因为自行车 _____。
   A. 是非常有效并且简单的装置
   B. 比汽车要便宜得多
   C. 在阿姆斯特丹和剑桥都广泛使用
   D. 仍然被富人使用

   【答案】A

   【解析】本题的依据句是文章第 2 段的第 2 句话 The bicycle itself is a remarkably efficient and simple device for using human muscular energy for transportation. 从中可知 A 项为正确答案。

3. 把自行车装入塑料防护罩里将 _____。
   A. 使其更容易使用
   B. 节省肌肉能量
   C. 避免坏天气
   D. 防止与其他车辆相撞

   【答案】D

   【解析】本题的依据句是文章第 3 段的 The whole machine could be enclosed in a plastic bubble which would provide some protection in case of accidents. 从中可知 D 项为正确答案。

4. 关于现在的自行车，以下各项中哪一项是错误的？
   A. 它比动物运动的效率要高得多。
   B. 它无法为骑车人提供保护。
   C. 它不适合运载货物。
   D. 无法对它再进行改良了。

   【答案】D

   【解析】本题可参照文章的第 2 段。第 2 段介绍了如何通过改造来克服自行车的缺点，因此 D 项为正确答案。

Text 4

Telecommuting—substituting the computer for the trip to the job—has been hailed as a solution to all kinds of problems related to office work. For workers it promises freedom from the office, less time wasted in traffic, and help with child-care conflicts. For management, telecommuting helps keep high performers on board, minimizes lateness and absenteeism by eliminating commuters, allows periods of solitude for high-concentration tasks, and provides scheduling flexibility. In some areas, such as Southern California and Seattle, Washington, local governments are encouraging companies to start telecommuting programs in order to reduce rush-hour traffic and improve air quality.

But these benefits do not come easily. Making a telecommuting program work requires careful planning and an understanding of the differences between telecommuting realities and popular images. Many workers are seduced by rosy illusions of life as a telecommuter. A computer programmer from New York City moves to the quiet Adirondack Mountains and stays in contact with her office via computer. A manager comes in to his office three days a week and works at home the other two. An accountant stays home to care for her sick child; she hooks up her telephone modem connections and does office work between calls to the doctor.

These are powerful images, but they are a limited reflection of reality. Telecommuting workers soon learn that it is almost impossible to concentrate on work and care for a young child at the same time. Before a certain age, young children cannot recognize, much less respect, the necessary boundaries between work and family. Additional child support is necessary if the parent is to get any work done. Management, too, must separate the myth from the reality. Although the media has paid a great deal of attention to telecommuting, in most cases it is the employee's situation, not the availability of technology, that precipitates a telecommuting arrangement.

That is partly why, despite the widespread press coverage, the number of companies with work-at-home programs of policy guidelines remains small.

1. What is the main subject of the passage?
    A. Business management policies.
    B. Driving to work.
    C. Extending the workplace by means of computers.
    D. Computers for child-care purposes.

2. Which of the following is NOT mentioned as a problem for employers that is potentially solved by telecommuting?
    A. Employees' lateness for work.
    B. Employees' absence from work.
    C. Employees' need for time alone to work intensively.
    D. Employees' conflicts with second jobs.

3. Which of the following does the author mention as a possible disadvantage of telecommuting?
    A. Small children cannot understand the boundaries of work and play.
    B. Computer technology is never advanced enough to accommodate the needs of every situation.
    C. Electrical malfunctions can destroy a project.
    D. The worker often does not have all the needed resources at home.

4. Which of the following is an example of telecommuting as described in the passage?
    A. A scientist in a laboratory developing plans for a space station.
    B. A technical writer sending via computer documents created at home.
    C. A computer technician repairing an office computer network.
    D. A teacher directing computer-assisted learning in a private school.

核心词汇注释

telecommute [ˌtelɪkə'mjuːt] *vi.*（在家里通过使用与工作单位连接的计算机终端）远距离工作

hail [heɪl] *n.* 冰雹；致敬；招呼；一阵
vt. 向……欢呼；致敬；招呼；猛发
vi. 招呼；下冰雹
int. 万岁，欢迎

conflict ['kɒnflɪkt] *n.* 斗争，冲突
vi. 抵触，冲突

minimize ['mɪnɪmaɪz] *vt.* 将……减到最少
v. 最小化

absenteeism [ˌæbsən'tiːɪz(ə)m] *n.* 旷课，旷工

solitude ['sɒlɪtjuːd] *n.* 孤独

seduce [sɪ'djuːs] *v.* 诱使

hook [hʊk] *n.* 钩，吊钩
v. 钩住，沉迷，上瘾

precipitate [prɪ'sɪpɪtət] *n.* 沉淀物
vt. 猛抛；使陷入；促成；使沉淀
vi. 猛地落下
adj. 突如其来的，陡然下降（或下落）的，贸然轻率的

长难句剖析

【文章难句】Telecommuting — substituting the computer for the trip to the job — has been hailed as a solution to all kinds of problems related to office work.

【结构分析】本句主干是 Telecommuting…has been hailed as a solution。破折号之间的部分 substituting the computer for the trip to the job 是动名词结构，做 telecommuting 的同位语。to all kinds of problems 是介宾短语，修饰 solution。related to office work 是 problems 的后置定语。

【参考译文】远程办公——用计算机代替上班——已经被誉为一种能解决所有办公室相关问题的方法。

【文章难句】In some areas, such as Southern California and Seattle, Washington, local governments are encouraging companies to start telecommuting programs in order to reduce rush-hour traffic and improve air quality.

【结构分析】本句主干是 local governments are encouraging companies to。in some areas, such as…Washington 做地点状语。to start telecommuting programs 做 companies 的补足语。in order to…quality 是主句的目的状语。

【参考译文】在有些地区，像南加州、西雅图、华盛顿，为了缓和高峰期的交通，改善空气质量，地方政府正在鼓励公司开展远程办公项目。

【文章难句】Although the media has paid a great deal of attention to telecommuting, in most cases it is the employee's situation, not the availability of technology, that precipitates（加速……来临）a telecommuting arrangement.

【结构分析】本句是一个主从复合句。主句是 it is the employee's situation，用 not the availability…arrangement 来强调主语 situation。由 although 引导的是让步状语从句。

【参考译文】尽管媒体非常关注远程办公，但大多数情况下是员工们的处境，而不是技术的可能性加速远程办公安排的来临。

全文参考译文

远程办公——用计算机代替上班——已经被誉为一种能解决所有办公室相关问题的措施。对于工作者来说，它可以将他们从办公室的束缚中解脱出来，减少在交通上浪费的时间，而且有助于解决工作和照顾孩子不能兼顾的矛盾。对于管理者来说，远程办公有助于保持高出勤率，通过取消通勤把迟到和旷工减到最少，它允许你有单独的时间处理需要注意力高度集中的任务，而且提供灵活的日程安排。在有些地区，像南加州、西雅图、华盛顿，为了缓和高峰期的交通，改善空气质量，地方政府正在鼓励公司开展远程办公项目。

但以上所述的好处并不是轻而易举的。要使远程办公项目真正能运作起来，必须有周密的计划并理解远程办公的现状和公众的印象之间存在距离。很多员工因幻想当一个远程办公人员的美好生活而着迷。一位从纽约搬到安静的 Adirondack 山脉的计算机程序员，通过计算机与公司保持联系。一位经理一周内只有三天去办公室，其他两天在家办公。一位会计师在家里照顾生病的孩子，她用电话线连通网络，在同医生通话之余完成办公室的工作。

这些是很突出的例子，但并不足以反映现实情况。远程办公人员很快就知道，投入工作和照顾孩子几乎不可能同时进行。不到一定年纪的小孩不会意识到，更不会尊重工作和家庭之间必要的界线。如果父母要完成工作，孩子们额外的支持是必要的。管理者也必须把神话和现实区分开来。尽管媒体非常关注远程办公，但在大多数情况下是员工们的处境，而不是技术的可能性加速远程办公安排的来临。

这就是尽管媒体的报道铺天盖地，而实行在家办公计划的公司却很少的部分原因。

题目答案与解析

1. 本篇文章的主题是什么？
   A．企业管理制度。　　　　　　　　　　B．开车去上班。
   C．通过计算机扩展工作地点。　　　　　D．计算机用来照看孩子。
   【答案】C
   【解析】综观全文，本文主要讲的是利用计算机在家里工作的利和弊。因此 C 项为正确答案。

2. 作为远程办公可能解决的问题，下面哪一项没有涉及？
   A．员工对工作的惰性。　　　　　　　　B．员工旷工。
   C．员工对独自办公的强烈需求。　　　　D．员工与第二个工作的冲突。
   【答案】D
   【解析】本题可参照文章的第 1 段。从中可知，只有 D 项未被提及，因此 D 项为正确答案。

3. 在远程办公可能的不利之处中作者提到了下列哪一项？
   A．小孩子们不能理解工作与玩耍的区别。
   B．计算机技术还没有发展到足够适应各种场合的需要。
   C．电力故障可能会破坏整个工程。
   D．员工家里可能没有所需的全部资源。
   【答案】A

【解析】本题的依据句是文章第 3 段的 Before a certain age, young children cannot recognize, much less respect, the necessary boundaries between work and family. 从中可知，小孩子分不清工作和家庭的界限。因此 A 项为正确答案。

4. 以下各项中，哪项是文章中提到的远程办公的例子？

A．科学家在实验室里开发空间站计划。

B．技术作者通过计算机发送在家里写好的稿件。

C．计算机技术员修理办公室网络。

D．教师在私人学校指导计算机辅助学习。

【答案】B

【解析】本题的依据句是文章第 2 段中间的 A computer programmer from New York City moves to the quiet Adirondack Mountains and stays in contact with her office via computer. 因此 B 项为正确答案。

Unit 2

Text 1

The payroll register constitutes the treasurer department's authority to pay the employees. Payment is usually made in the form of a check drawn on the company's regular bank account. Pre-numbered payroll checks should be used, and there should be independent verification of the agreement of the checks with the payroll register in detail and in total.

Payroll checks should be distributed directly to employees, on proper identification, by treasurer's department personnel. The checks should not be returned to payroll for distribution since the payroll department would then have control over both preparing and paying the payroll. Alternatively, payroll checks may be deposited directly in the employee's checking account.

Payment of employees in cash is the exception rather than the rule. This form of payment is more easily influenced by errors, irregularities, and robbery than payment by check. Following payment, check numbers are entered on the register, the preparation and payment of the payroll are programmed on a computer.

A termination notice should be issued by the personnel department on the completion of an individual's employment with the company. Copies of the termination authorization should be sent to the employee's supervisor and to payroll, and a copy should be filed in the employee's personnel record. The proper execution of this function is vital in preventing terminated employees from continuing on the payroll. The subsequent diversion of such payroll checks to an unauthorized individual has been responsible for many payroll cheat through the years.

Every company is expected to fulfill the legal requirements relevant to the filing of payroll tax returns and the payment of the resulting taxes. Ordinarily, the payroll department prepares the tax returns and a check is issued through the guarantor system in payment of the taxes. The responsibility for the filing of returns before due dates should be assigned to a payroll department supervisor. Furthermore, there should be independent verification within that department of the accuracy and completeness of the return. Effective control over tax returns is necessary to avoid penalties for late or incorrect filings.

1. According to the passage employees should be paid _____.

   A. monthly in cash   B. weekly by bank   C. regularly by check   D. properly in time

2. Payroll checks should be _____.

   A. identified by treasurer's department personnel

   B. distributed to employees by the company's bank

   C. sent to employees directly and responsibly by post

   D. deposited regularly in the employee's account

3. Which of the following statements may NOT be the weakness of payment in cash?

    A. It's easily affected by mistakes.   B. It may be distributed irregularly.

    C. There is possibility of robbery.   D. It can be done conveniently.

4. When an employee stops working in the company, all of the following should be done except _____.

    A. a termination notice should be issued by the personnel department

    B. a copy of the termination authorization should be given to the employee personally

    C. a copy of the termination authorization should be sent to the employee's supervisor

    D. a copy of the termination authorization be delivered to the payroll register

核心词汇注释

treasurer ['treʒərə(r)] *n.* 司库，财务员，出纳员

distributed [dɪ'strɪbjutɪd] *adj.* 分布式的，分配的

identification [aɪˌdentɪfɪ'keɪʃ(ə)n] *n.* 辨认，鉴定，证明，视为同一

alternatively [ɔː'tɜːnətɪvlɪ] *adv.* 作为选择地，二者选一地

deposit [dɪ'pɒzɪt] *n.* 堆积物；存款，押金，保证金；存放物

vt. 存放；堆积

vi. 沉淀

irregularity [ɪˌregjʊ'lærɪtɪ] *n.* 不规则，无规律

termination [ˌtɜːmɪ'neɪʃ(ə)n] *n.* 终止

diversion [daɪ'vɜːʃ(ə)n] *n.* 转移，转换，牵制；解闷，娱乐

filing ['faɪlɪŋ] *n.* 整理成档案，文件归档；锉

penalty ['penəltɪ] *n.* 处罚，罚款

长难句剖析

【文章难句】The checks should not be returned to payroll for distribution since the payroll department would then have control over both preparing and paying the payroll.

【结构分析】本句是一个主从复合句。主句是 The checks should not be returned to payroll for distribution，后面是一个由 since 引导的原因状语从句。since 引导的原因状语从句不如 because 引导的从句强烈，因此常常被放在主句之后。

【参考译文】这些支票不能返回作为工薪额再来分发，因为工薪管理部门要控制工薪的准备和支付。

【文章难句】Every company is expected to fulfill the legal requirements relevant to the filing of payroll tax returns and the payment of the resulting taxes.

【结构分析】本句主干是 Every company is expected to fulfill the legal requirements。relevant to 引起形容词短语，做后置定语。

【参考译文】每个公司都应履行把工薪所得税申报表归档并交纳相应税款的有关法律责任。

【文章难句】The responsibility for the filing of returns before due dates should be assigned to a payroll department supervisor.

【结构分析】本句主干是 The responsibility…should be assigned to a payroll department supervisor。for...dates 做主语的后置定语。

【参考译文】在规定日期前应将所得税申报表归档的责任指派给工薪发放部门主管人。

全文参考译文

工薪分录账是财务部门向员工支付工薪的权威。一般来说，工薪是在公司普通银行存款账目下以支票形式发放的。应采用预先填写数目的工薪支票，而且应该独立验证这些支票与工薪分录账的明细与总额是否符合。

依据正确的身份证明，财务部门人员应将工薪支票直接发放给员工。这些支票不能返回作为工薪再分发，因为工薪管理部门要控制工薪的准备和支付。作为选择，可以将工薪支票直接存入员工的账户。

用现金发放员工的工薪不是惯例而是特例。这种工薪支付方式比支票支付更容易受到失误、无规律和抢劫的影响。支票支付后，其数额记入工薪分录账，而工薪的准备和支付则由计算机进行编程。

当一名员工的雇佣期结束时，公司人事部门应该发出一份终止通知。终止授权书应发给该员工的主管和工薪发放部门，并归入员工的人事档案。这种职能的妥善执行，对于防止离职员工再领工薪是至关重要的。最近几年出现的许多工薪诈骗事件，都和这种工薪支票随后转入非许可的人有关。

每个公司都应履行把工薪所得税申报表归档并交纳相应税款的法律责任。通常，这项工作由工薪发放部门负责，通过担保人体系交纳税款。在规定日期之前应将所得税申报表归档的责任指派给工薪发放部门的主管。此外，该部门必须独立验证申报表的准确性和完整性。所得税申报表的准确控制是必要的,这样可以避免因延迟或错误归档而受到的处罚。

题目答案与解析

1. 根据文章的内容，员工工薪的支付方式应是 _____。
   A．按月给现金   B．由银行按周发放 C．定期给支票   D．很及时
   【答案】C
   【解析】本题的依据句是文章第 1 段中的 Payment is usually made in the form of a check drawn on the company's regular bank account. 从中可知 C 项为正确答案。
2. 薪资支票应 _____。
   A．由财务部门人员进行身份确认   B．由公司的银行发放给员工
   C．直接邮给员工并以同样的方式回复   D．定期存入员工的账户
   【答案】A
   【解析】本题的依据句是文章第 2 段的第 1 句话 Payroll checks should be distributed directly to employees, on proper identification, by treasurer's department personnel. 从中可知 A 项为正确答案。
3. 以下陈述中，哪一项不是现金支付工资的缺点？
   A．它很容易出错。   B．它可能不定期地发放。
   C．有被抢劫的可能。   D．它发放比较方便。

【答案】D

【解析】本题的依据句是文章第 3 段的第 2 句话 This form of payment is more easily influenced by errors, irregularities, and robbery than payment by check. 从中可知 D 项为正确答案。

4.　当员工停止在公司工作时，下面四项中除 _____ 都应该做。

　　A．终止通知书应由人事部门发放　　　　B．应该给员工本人一份终止授权书

　　C．应该给员工的主管一份终止授权书　　D．应该把终止授权书送至工薪分录账

【答案】B

【解析】本题可参照文章第 4 段。从中可知，员工的雇佣期结束时，公司的人事部门应该发出一份终止通知。终止授权书应该发给该员工的主管和工薪发放部门，并归入员工的人事档案。因此 B 项为正确答案。

Text　2

Tight-lipped elders used to say, "It's not what you want in this world, but what you get." Psychology teaches that you do get what you want if you know what you want and want the right things.

You can make a mental blueprint of a desire as you would make a blueprint of a house, and each of us is continually making these blueprints in the general routine of everyday living. If we intend to have friends to dinner, we plan the menu, make a shopping list, decide which food to cook first, and such planning is an essential for any type of meal to be served.

Likewise, if you want to find a job, take a sheet of paper, and write a brief account of yourself. In making a blueprint for a job, begin with yourself, for when you know exactly what you have to offer, you can intelligently plan where to sell your services.

This account of yourself is actually a sketch of your working life and should include education, experience and references. Such an account is valuable. It can be referred to in filling out standard application blanks and is extremely helpful in personal interviews. While talking to you, your could-be employer is deciding whether your education, your experience, and other qualifications will pay him to employ you and your "wares" and abilities must be displayed in an orderly and reasonably connected manner.

When you have carefully prepared a blueprint of your abilities and desires, you have something tangible to sell. Then you are ready to hunt for a job. Get all the possible information about your could-be job, make inquiries as to the details regarding the job and the firm. Keep your eyes and ears open, and use your own judgement. Spend a certain amount of time each day seeking the employment you wish for, and keep in mind: Securing a job is your job now.

1.　What do the elders mean when they say, "It's not what you want in this world, but what you get"?

　　A．You'll certainly get what you want.

　　B．It's no use dreaming.

　　C．You should be dissatisfied with what you have.

D. It's essential to set a goal for yourself.

2. A blueprint made before inviting a friend to dinner is used in this passage as_____.

A. an illustration of how to write an application for a job

B. an indication of how to secure a good job

C. a guideline for job description

D. a principle for job evaluation

3. According to the passage, one must write an account of himself before starting to find a job because _____.

A. that is the first step to please the employer

B. that is the requirement of the employer

C. it enables him to know when to sell his services

D. it forces him to become clearly aware of himself

4. When you have carefully prepared a blueprint of your abilities and desires, you have something_____.

A. definite to offer   B. imaginary to provide

C. practical to supply   D. desirable to present

核心词汇注释

tight-lipped *adj*. 紧闭嘴巴的，几乎不讲话的

blueprint ['bluːprɪnt] *n*. 蓝图，设计图，计划 *vt*. 制成蓝图，计划

routine [ruːˈtiːn] *n*. 例行公事，常规，日常事务，程序

likewise ['laɪkwaɪz] *adv*. 同样地，照样地，又，也 *n*. 同样地

intelligent [ɪnˈtelɪdʒ(ə)nt] *adj*. 聪明的，伶俐的，有才智的，[计]智能的

ware [weə(r)] *n*. 陶器，器皿；[*pl*.]商品

tangible ['tændʒɪb(ə)l] *adj*. 有形的；切实的

regarding [rɪˈɡɑːdɪŋ] *prep*. 关于

secure [sɪˈkjʊə(r)] *adj*. 安全的，可靠的，放心的，无虑的 *v*. 保护；得到

长难句剖析

【文章难句】Psychology teaches that you do get what you want if you know what you want and want the right things.

【结构分析】本句的主干是一个宾语从句，psychology 做主语，teach 做谓语，that 引导的是一个宾语从句。在这个宾语从句中，"what you want" 做动词 get 的宾语从句，if 引导的是个条件状语从句。

【参考译文】心理学教育人们，如果你知道你想要什么，并且你想要的东西又合乎情理，那么你一定能得到你想要的东西。

【文章难句】While talking to you, your could-be employer is deciding whether your education, your experience, and other qualifications will pay him to employ you and your "wares" and abilities must be displayed in an orderly and reasonably connected manner.

【结构分析】本句中，主句为由 and 连接的两个并列句构成，could-be 是复合形容词，用来修饰 employer；"whether your education，your experience，and other qualifications will pay him to employ you" 是分句中的宾语从句，后半句中使用的是带有情态动词的被动语态，介词短语 "in an orderly and reasonably connected manner" 做方式状语。前面的 "while talking to you" 为时间状语从句。

【参考译文】在与你交谈时，你未来的雇主就在考虑，你所受的教育、工作经历和其他条件是否值得他雇佣你，你的"商品"和能力必须要条理分明地依次展示出来。

全文参考译文

说话谨慎的老人过去常说："这个世界上不是你想要什么，而是你能得到什么"。心理学教育人们，如果你知道你想要什么，并且你想要的东西又合乎情理，那么你一定能得到你想要的东西。

你可以在心里描绘一张愿望蓝图，就像绘制一间房屋的蓝图。事实上，在普通的日常生活中我们每一个人都在不断描绘着这些蓝图。如果我们想邀请朋友吃饭，我们就要计划菜谱，制定购物清单，决定先做哪些菜。这样的计划对准备任何类型的一顿饭都是必要的。

同样地，如果你想找到一份工作，就拿一张纸，写下自己的简单说明。在制定找工作蓝图时，你要从自己开始，因为当你确切知道你能提供什么时，你才能明智地计划到哪儿去谋职。

这种自我描述实际是你工作生活的概括，应当包括所受教育、工作经验和推荐信。这种描述是有价值的。填写标准申请表时可以作为参考，个人面试时尤其有用。在与你交谈时，你未来的雇主就在考虑，你所受到的教育、工作经历和其他条件是否值得他雇佣你。你的"商品"和能力必须条理分明地依次展示出来。

当你精心地准备了你的能力与愿望的蓝图之后，你就有切实的东西可以推销了。这就为你找工作做好了准备。收集关于要选择的工作的所有可能的信息，调查关于这个工作和公司的细节。眼观六路，耳听八方，做出自己的判断。每天花一定时间找你希望的工作，记住：要找的工作就是你现在的工作。

题目答案与解析

1. 当年长者说 "It's not what you want in this world，but what you get" 时，他们的意思是指什么？

   A．你肯定会得到你想要的东西。　　　　B．梦想没有用。

   C．你应该不满足于你所拥有的东西。　　D．为你自己确定一个目标很有必要。

   【答案】B

   【解析】本题中，A 项"你肯定会得到你想要的东西"之意与文章第 2 段的意思不符；在文中没有提到 C 项的"你应该不满足于你所拥有的东西"之意；D 项不正确，"为你自己确定一个目标很有必要"之意是本文作者提倡的观点，不是年长者说这句话的意思。从文章第 1 段的内容可知，出言谨慎的年长者过去常说：在这个世界上，重要的不是你想要什么，而是你能得到什么；从第 2 段的内容可知，心理学教育人们，如果你知道你想要什么，并且你想要的东西又合乎情理，那么你肯定会得到它。据此可知，年长者们说这句话的意思应该是：要面对现实，不要想那些不合乎情理的东西。B 项中说"梦想没有用"与文章的意思相符，因此 B 项为正确答案。

2. 本篇文章中，请朋友吃饭前所制定的计划被用来_____。

A．写求职申请的例证
B．如何获得一份好工作的暗示
C．描述工作的方针
D．评估工作的原则

【答案】A

【解析】本题中，B 项"如何获得一份好工作的暗示"不是作者使用该例子的目的。本文作者提倡的是"要现实，不要想那些不合乎情理的东西"。C 项"描述工作的方针"不是作者使用该例子的目的，文中没有描述过工作。D 项"评估工作的原则"之意不是作者使用该例子的目的，文中并没有评估过工作。从文章第 3 段的内容可知，如果我们想请朋友吃饭，我们就要定菜谱，列购物清单，并决定先做哪道菜；对于要招待的任何一种饭局来说，这样的计划都是必要的；从第 4 段的内容可知，同样，如果你想找到一份工作，你就应该取一张纸，写下你的自我简介。据此可知，作者列举请朋友吃饭前所制订的计划这个例子，是为了说明找工作时应该怎样制订计划这个问题。A 项的"如何写求职申请的例证"与文章的意思相符，因此 A 项为正确答案。

3. 依照本文的观点，一个人在开始找工作之前必须写一份自我简介，原因是_____。

A．那是取悦雇主的第一步
B．那是雇主的要求
C．自我简介能够使他知道何时推销自己的服务
D．自我简介促使他清楚地了解他自己

【答案】D

【解析】本题中，A 项"那是取悦雇主的第一步"和 B 项"那是雇主的要求"两项之意明显与文章的意思不符；C 项的"自我简介能够使他知道何时推销自己的服务"之意不对，文中是说"你才能明智地计划到哪儿去求职"，不是说何时去求职。从文章第 4 段的内容可知：同样，如果你想找到一份工作，你就应该取一张纸，写下你的自我简介；为寻找工作制订计划时，应该以自己的实际情况为出发点，因为，只有当你确切地知道你可以提供什么时，你才能明智地计划到哪儿去求职。据此可知，找工作前之所以要写自我简介，是因为自我简介可以让你清楚地了解你自己。D 项的"自我简介促使他清楚地了解他自己"与文中的"when you know exactly what you have to offer, you can intelligently plan where to sell your services（只有当你确切地知道你可以提供什么时，你才能明智地计划到哪儿去求职）"的意思相符，因此 D 项为正确答案。

4. 当你认真地准备好一份有关你的才能和愿望的计划时，你就已经有了_____。

A．确切的东西可以提供
B．虚构的东西可以提供
C．实际的东西可以提供
D．令人满意的东西可以提供

【答案】A

【解析】本题中，B、C、D 三项都与文意不符。从文章最后一段的内容可知，精心制定好了你的才干和愿望计划后，你就有了具体的东西可推销了；这样，你就可以寻找工作了。据此可知，制定好了自己的才干和愿望计划后，你就可以向可能的雇主提供确切的东西了。A 项的"确切的东西可以提供"与文中的"you have something tangible to sell（有了具体的东

西可推销了）" 的意思相符，因此 A 项为正确答案。

Text 3

The stability of the U.S. banking system is maintained by means of supervision and regulation, inspections, deposit insurance, and loans to troubled banks. For over 50 years, these precautions have prevented banking panics. However, there have been some close calls. The collapse of Continental Illinois Bank & Trusted Company of Chicago in 1984 did not bring down the banking system, but it certainly rattled some windows.

In the late 1970s, Continental soared to a leadership position among Midwestern banks. Parts of its growth strategy were risky, however. It made many loans in the energy field, including $1 billion that it took over from Penn Square Bank of Oklahoma City. To obtain the funds it needed to make these loans, Continental relied heavily on short term borrowing from other banks and large 30-day certificates of deposit — "hot money", in banking jargon. At least one Continental officer saw danger signs and wrote a warning memo to her superiors, but the memo went unheeded. Although the Comptroller of the Currency inspected Continental on a regular basis, it failed to see how serious its problems were going to be.

Penn Square Bank was closed by regulators in July 1982. When energy prices began to slip, most of the $1 billion in loans that Continental had taken over from the smaller banks turned out to be bad. Other loans to troubled companies such Chrysler, International Harvester, and Braniff looked questionable. Seeing these problem，"hot money" owners began to pull their funds out of Continental.

By the spring of 1984, a run on Continental had begun. In May, the bank had to borrow $3.5 billion from the Fed to replace overnight funds it had lost. But this was not enough. To try to stem the outflow of deposits from Continental, the FDIC agreed to guarantee not just the first $100,000 of each depositor's money but all of it. Nevertheless, the run continued.

Federal regulators tried hard to find a sound bank that could take over Continental — a common way of rescuing failing banks. But Continental was just too big for anyone to buy. By July, all hope of a private sector rescue was dashed. Regulators faced a stark choice: Let Continental collapse, or take it over themselves.

Letting the bank fail seemed too risky. It was estimated that more than 100 other banks had placed enough funds in Continental to put them at risk if Continental failed. Thus, on a rainy Thursday at the end of July, the FDIC in effect nationalized Continental Illinois at a cost of $4.5 billion. This kept the bank's doors open and prevented a chain reaction. However, in all but a technical sense, Continental had become the biggest bank failure in U.S. history.

1. In the spring of 1984, Continental experienced _____.
   A. a fast growth period   B. a stability period
   C. a run   D. an oil price decrease
2. By July, all hope of a private sector rescue was _____.
   A. destroyed   B. absurd   C. desperate   D. damaged
3. The nationalization of Continental _____.

    A. saved it

    B. made "hot money" owners continue to pull their funds out of Continental

    C. almost brought down the banking system

    D. fired many high-ranking officers

4. Banking panics may be prevented by means of _____.

    A. deposit insurance   B. growth strategy

    C. long-term borrowing   D. warning memo

核心词汇注释

stability [stə'bɪlɪtɪ] *n.* 稳定性

precaution [prɪ'kɔːʃ(ə)n] *n.* 防范措施或方法

panic ['pænɪk] *n.* 惊慌，恐慌，

soar [sɔː(r)] *v.* 高飞，高耸；滑翔；剧增，昂扬

    n. 高飞范围，高涨程度

strategy ['strætɪdʒɪ] *n.* 策略

jargon ['dʒɑːgən] *n.* 行话

unheeded [ʌn'hiːdɪd] *adj.* 未被注意的，被忽视的

comptroller [kəmp'trəʊlə(r)] *n.* 审计员

stem [stem] *n.* 茎，干；茎干，词干

    v. 滋生，阻止

estimate ['estɪmeit] *v.* 估计，估价，评估

    n. 估计，估价，评估

nationalize ['næʃ(ə)nəlaɪz] *v.* 国有化，公有化

长难句剖析

【文章难句】The stability of the U.S. banking system is maintained by means of supervision and regulation, inspections, deposit insurance, and loans to troubled banks.

【结构分析】本句的主干是 The stability… is maintained。

【参考译文】美国银行业系统的稳定是通过监管、调控、查账、存款保险以及给经营困难的银行提供贷款这些手段来维持的。

【文章难句】To obtain the funds it needed to make these loans，Continental relied heavily on short term borrowing from other banks and large 30-day certificates of deposit — "hot money", in banking jargon.

【结构分析】本句主干是 Continental relied heavily on。不定式 to obtain 构成的词组做句子的目的状语。funds 后面的 it needed to…loans 是定语从句。

【参考译文】为了获得放贷所需的资金，大陆银行过度依赖从其他银行借来的短期借款和 30 天大额定期存单——银行业的行话称为"热钱"。

【文章难句】When energy prices began to slip，most of the $1 billion in loans that Continental had taken over from the smaller banks turned out to be bad.

【结构分析】本句是主从复合句。主句是 most of…bad。most of the $1 billion in loans 做主语，谓语是 turned out to be bad，that 引导的定语从句修饰主语。when 引导的是时间状语从句。

【参考译文】当能源价格开始下跌时，大陆银行从这些小银行手中接管的 10 亿美元贷款中的大部分都成了坏账。

全文参考译文

　　美国银行业系统的稳定是通过监管、调控、查账、存款保险以及给经营困难的银行提供贷款这些手段来维持的。50多年以来，这些防范措施已经防止了一些银行业危机。不过还是有很危急的时候。1984年的伊利诺大陆银行和芝加哥信托公司的倒闭虽然没有导致银行业系统的崩溃，但是影响也不小。

　　大陆银行20世纪70年代末期快速成为中西部银行中的领头雁。可它的一些发展策略是很危险的。该银行在能源领域发放了很多贷款，包括从Oklahoma市的Penn Square银行接管10亿美元。为了获得放贷所需的资金，大陆银行过度依赖从其他银行借来的短期贷款和30天大额定期存单——银行业的行话称为"热钱"。至少有一位大陆银行官员看到了危险征兆并给她的上级写了备忘录，但并未受到重视。尽管货币监理经常对大陆银行进行检查，但也没能发现问题的严重性。

　　Penn Square银行在1982年7月被执法人员关闭。当能源价格开始下跌时，大陆银行从这些小银行手中接管的10亿美元贷款中的大部分都成了坏账。除此之外，提供给Chrysler、International Harvester和Braniff等经营不善的公司的贷款似乎也是问题重重。鉴于这些问题，"热钱"的持有者开始从大陆银行抽回资金。

　　到1984年春天，大陆银行开始出现挤兑。5月，该银行不得不从联邦银行借款35亿美元来弥补一夜之间流失的资金，但是这还不够。为了尽量防止大陆银行的存款外流，美国联合存款保险公司同意保证储户所有的钱，而不是最初的每人10万美元。但是，挤兑仍然在继续。

　　联邦管理部门试图找到一家好的银行接管大陆银行，这是一种拯救衰落银行的普遍方式。可对于任何一个买主来说，大陆银行都太大了。到了7月，所有私营机构的拯救希望都破灭了。管理部门面临着痛苦的选择：是让大陆银行破产，还是自己接管过来。

　　让大陆银行破产太过冒险。按照估计，若是让其倒闭，大约有100家其他银行在大陆银行存放的资金足以使他们自己濒临险境。所以在7月底一个阴雨的星期四，美国联合存款保险公司以45亿美元的代价让伊利诺大陆银行国有化。这使得银行可以继续营业，避免了连锁反应。但严格来说，大陆银行已经成为了美国银行业历史上最大的败笔。

题目答案与解析

1.　大陆银行在1984年春天经历了＿＿＿＿＿。
　　A．一段快速成长期　B．一段稳定时期　　　C．一场挤兑风波　　D．油价下跌
　　【答案】C
　　【解析】本题的依据是文章第四段的第一句话By the spring of 1984, a run on Continental had begun，从中可知，C项为正确答案。

2.　到了7月，所有私营机构的拯救希望都＿＿＿＿＿。
　　A．破灭了　　　　　　　B．是荒谬的　　　　C．孤注一掷　　D．被损坏
　　【答案】A
　　【解析】本题可参照文章第五段。依据是第五段的第三句话By July, all hope of a private sector rescue was dashed. Regulators faced a stark choice: Let Continental collapse, or take it over themselves. 从句中的collapse（垮台，崩溃）一词可看出事态的严重性，因此A项为正确答案。

3．大陆银行的国有化 _____。

 A．拯救了大陆银行

 B．使"热钱"所有者继续从大陆银行抽回资金

 C．几乎摧毁了整个银行业系统

 D．解雇了很多高层官员

【答案】A

【解析】本题的依据是最后一段的第三句话 Thus, on a rainy Thursday at the end of July, the FDIC in effect nationalized Continental Illinois at a cost of $4.5 billion. This kept the bank's doors open and prevented a chain reaction. 从中可知，将 Continental 国有化后，该银行能继续开门营业。因此 A 项为正确答案。

4．可以通过 _____ 方法来防止银行业危机。

 A．存款保险   B．成长策略   C．长期借款   D．警示备忘录

【答案】A

【解析】本题的依据是第一段第一句话的 banking system is maintained by means of supervision and regulation, inspections, deposit insurance, and loans to troubled banks，从中可知，四个选项中只有 A 项为正确答案。

Text　4

If sustainable competitive advantage depends on work-force skills, American firms have a problem. Human resource management is not traditionally seen as central to the competitive survival of the firm in the United States. Skill acquisition is considered as an individual responsibility. Labor is simply another factor of production to be hired or rented at the lowest possible cost much as one buys raw materials or equipment.

The lack of importance attached to human resource management can be seen in the corporation hierarchy. In an American firm the chief financial officer is almost always second in command. The post of head of human resource managements is usually a specialized job, often at the edge of the corporate hierarchy. The executive who holds it is never consulted on major strategic decisions and has no chance to move up to Chief Executive Officer (CEO). By way of contrast, in Japan the head of human resource management is central— usually the second most important executive, after the CEO, in the firm's hierarchy.

While American firms often talk about the vast amounts spent on training their work-forces, in fact they invest less in the skill of their employees than do the Japanese or German firms. The money they do invest is also more highly concentrated on professional and managerial employees. And the limited investments that are made in training workers are also much more narrowly focused on the specific skills necessary to do the next job rather than on the basic background skills that make it possible to absorb new technologies.

As a result, problems emerge when new breakthrough technologies arrive. If American workers, for example, take much longer to learn how to operate new flexible manufacturing stations than workers in Germany (as they do), the effective cost of those stations is lower in Germany than it is in the United Stated. More time is required before equipment is up and running at capacity, and the need for extensive retraining generates costs and creates bottlenecks that limit the speed with which new equipment can be employed. The result is a slower pace of technological change. And in the end the skills of the bottom half of the population affect the wages of the top half. If the bottom half can't effectively staff the processes that have to be operated, the management and professional jobs that go with these processes will disappear.

1. Which of the following applies to the management of human resources in American companies?

   A. They hire people at the lowest cost regardless of their skills.

   B. They see the gaining of skills as their employees own business.

   C. They attach more importance to workers than to equipment.

   D. They only hire skilled workers because of keen competition.

2. What is the position of the head of human resource management in an American firm?

   A. He is one of the most important executives in the firm.

   B. His post is likely to disappear when new technologies are introduced.

   C. He is directly under the chief financial executive.

   D. He has no authority in making important decisions in the firm.

3. The money most American firms spend in training mainly goes to _____.

   A. workers who can operate new equipment

   B. technological and managerial staff

   C. workers who lack basic background skills

   D. top executives

4. What is the main idea of the passage?

   A. American firms are different from Japanese and German firms in human resource management.

   B. Extensive retraining is indispensable to effective human resource management.

   C. The head of human resource management must be in the central position in a firm's hierarchy.

   D. The human resource management strategies of American firms affect their competitive capacity.

核心词汇注释

sustainable [səˈsteɪnəbl] *adj.* 可以忍受的，足可支撑的，养得起的，能长期维持的，能持续的

survival [səˈvaɪv(ə)l] *n.* 生存，幸存，残存，幸存者，残存物

acquisition [ˌækwiˈziʃən] *n.* 获得，获得物

attach [əˈtætʃ] *v.* 依附，附加，随着，相联系

hierarchy [ˈhaɪərɑːkɪ] *n.* 层次，等级制度

strategic [strəˈtiːdʒɪk] *adj.* 战略的，战略上的

contrast [kənˈtrɑːst] *v.*

　vt. 使与……对比，使与……对照

　vi. 和……形成对照

['kɒntrɑ:st] *n.* 对比，对照，（对照中的）   **generate** ['dʒenəreɪt] *vt.* 产生，发生
差异   **bottleneck** ['bɒtlnek] *n.* 瓶颈
breakthrough ['breɪkθru:] *n.* 突破

长难句剖析

【文章难句】The lack of importance attached to human resource management can be seen in the corporation hierarchy.

【结构分析】本句的主干是 The lack of importance…can be seen。attached to human resource management 做 importance 的后置定语。

【参考译文】可以看到，在公司等级制度中人力资源管理没有受到相应的重视。

【文章难句】By way of contrast, in Japan the head of human resource management is central— usually the second most important executive，after the CEO，in the firm's hierarchy.

【结构分析】本句是一个简单句。破折号后面的成分是对表语 central 的进一步解释，句首的 By way of contrast 是方式状语。

【参考译文】与之相反，在日本，人力资源主管是核心——在公司等级中通常是位于 CEO 之后的第二号执行者。

【文章难句】While American firms often talk about the vast amounts spent on training their work-forces，in fact they invest work less in the skill of their employees than do the Japanese or German firms.

【结构分析】本句是一个主从复合句。主句中使用了一个比较结构，than 后的 do 指代前面出现的谓语动词 invest。while 引导时间状语从句，其中过去分词短语 spent on training their work-forces 是 the vast amounts 的后置定语。

【参考译文】虽然美国公司经常谈论他们在培训员工上所花费的大量资金，但事实上，与日本或德国的公司相比，他们在员工技能上的投入却少得多。

全文参考译文

如若可持续的竞争优势依靠劳动力的技能，美国公司就有麻烦了。美国公司一贯不把人力资源管理看作生存竞争的核心问题。技能的获得被认为是个人的责任。劳动力和原材料及设备一样，只是另外一种以尽可能低的成本雇佣或租赁的生产要素。

可以看到，在公司的等级制度中人力资源管理没有受到相应的重视。财务主管在美国公司中几乎总是第二个发号施令的人。人力资源主管常常是一种专业化的工作，处于公司等级边缘。在作出重大决策的过程中，没有人去咨询人力资源主管的意见，并且他也没有机会升职为 CEO。与之相反，在日本，人力资源主管是核心——在公司等级中通常是位于 CEO 之后的第二执行官。

虽然美国公司常常谈论他们在培训员工上所花费的大量资金，但事实上，与日本或德国的公司相比，他们在员工技能上的投入却少得多。他们所投入的资金更多地集中在专业人员和管理层员工身上。用于培训工人的有限投入也更加局限于进行下一项工作所必需的具体技能，而不是用于可能吸收新技术的一些基础的背景技术。

结果，当新的技术突破到来时就出现了问题。比如，美国的工人与德国的工人相比，要花

费更长时间来掌握怎样操作新型的、灵活的制造设备，那么这些岗位在德国的有效成本就比美国低。设备正常运转起来需要更长时间，需要广泛的再培训，这会提高成本并产生瓶颈，限制新设备生产的速度。结果导致技术改造步伐缓慢，最终这些下层工人的技术会影响上层人员的工作。若下半层工人不能有效地融入到生产流程中去，与之共生的管理职业将会消失。

题目答案与解析

1. 下面哪一种指的是美国公司的人力资源管理方法？
   A. 他们以最低价雇用应聘者，不考虑其技能。
   B. 他们将技能的获得看做员工自己的事情。
   C. 他们认为工人比设备更加重要。
   D. 因为竞争激烈，所以他们只雇用熟练工人。

   【答案】B

   【解析】本题的依据是文章第 1 段第 3 句话 Skill acquisition is considered as an individual responsibility，从中可知 B 项为正确答案。

2. 人力资源主管在美国公司里的地位如何？
   A. 他是公司最重要的主管之一。   B. 当引入新的技术时他的职位很可能消失。
   C. 他是财务主管的直接下级。   D. 他在公司里没有权力作出重要决定。

   【答案】D

   【解析】本题可参照文章第 2 段中的第 3 句、第 4 句话。从中可知，在美国的公司里人力资源部门的主管在管理层中没有什么地位，在重大决策中没有发言权。因此 D 项为正确答案。

3. 美国公司用来培训的钱主要分配给 _____。
   A. 操作新设备的工人   B. 技术和管理人员
   C. 缺乏基础背景技术的工人   D. 高层主管

   【答案】B

   【解析】依据文章第 3 段第 2 句话 The money they do invest is also more highly concentrated on professional and managerial employees，选项 B 符合文章的内容，是本题的正确答案。

4. 这篇文章的主旨是什么？
   A. 在人力资源管理方面美国公司与德国和日本的公司不同。
   B. 对有效的人力资源管理来说，广泛的再培训是必不可少的。
   C. 在公司等级中，人力资源主管一定要处于核心位置。
   D. 美国公司的人力资源管理战略影响了他们的竞争力。

   【答案】D

   【解析】综观全文，只有 D 项能概括文章的中心思想，A、B、C 三个选项只能概括文章部分段落的内容。因此正确答案为 D。

Unit 3

Internet is a vast network of computers that connects many of the world's businesses, institutions, and individuals. The internet, which means interconnected network of networks, links tens of thousands of smaller computer networks. These networks transmit huge amounts of information in the form of words, images, and sounds.

The Internet was information on virtually every topic. Network users can search through sources ranging from vast databases to small electronic "bulletin boards", where users form discussion groups around common interests. Much of the Internet's traffic consists of messages sent from one computer user to another. These messages are called electronic mail or e-mail. Internet users have electronic addresses that allow them to send and receive e-mail. Other uses of the network include obtaining news, joining electronic debates, and playing electronic games. One feature of the Internet, known as the World Wide Web, provides graphics, audio, and video to enhance the information in its documents. These documents cover a vast number of topics.

People usually access the Internet with a device called a modem. Modems connect computers to the network through telephone lines. Much of the Internet operates through worldwide telephone networks of fiber optic cables. These cables contain hair thin strands of glass that carry data as pulses of light. They can transmit thousands of times more data than local phone lines, most of which consist of copper wires.

The history of the Internet began in the 1960s. At that time, the Advanced Research Projects Agency (ARPA) of the United States Department of Defense developed a network of computers called ARPAnet. Originally, ARPAnet connected only military and government computer systems. Its purpose was to make these systems secure in the event of a disaster or war. Soon after the creation of ARPAnet, universities and other institutions developed their own computer networks. These networks eventually were merged with ARPAnet to form the Internet. By the 1990s, anyone with a computer, modem, and Internet software could link up to the Internet.

In the future, the Internet will probably grow more sophisticated as computer technology becomes more powerful. Many experts believe the Internet may become part of a larger network called the information superhighway. This network, still under development, would link computers with telephone companies, cable television stations, and other communication systems. People could bank, shop, watch TV, and perform many other activities through the network.

1. This passage is about the _____ of the Internet.
   A. future
   B. general introduction
   C. use
   D. history

2. Which of the following statements about the Internet is true?

    A. ARPA was the first net used by American universities and institutions.

    B. The history of the Internet can be traced back to fifty years ago.

    C. The purpose of the Internet is to protect the world in the event of war.

    D. ARPAnet formed the foundation of the Internet nowadays.

3. The Internet enables people to do all the following things EXCEPT _____ .

    A. sending email   B. obtaining news

    C. exchanging modem   D. internet related chat (IRC)

4. According to the last paragraph, in the future _____ .

    A. it may be hard to predict the development of the Internet

    B. the Internet will become an indispensable superhighway

    C. the Internet will be applied more

    D. the Internet will combine cable stations

核心词汇注释

interconnect [ˌintə(:)kə'nekt] *vt.* 使互相连接

debate [dɪ'beɪt] *v.* 争论，辩论　*n.* 争论，辩论

graphics ['græfiks] *n.*（做单数用）制图法，制图学，图表算法，图形

pulse [pʌls] *n.* 脉搏，脉冲

copper ['kɒpə(r)] *n.* 铜；警察

merge [mɜ:dʒ] *v.* 合并，并入，结合；吞没，融合

sophisticated [sə'fɪstɪkeɪtɪd] *adj.* 诡辩的，久经世故的；复杂的，精密的

superhighway ['su:pəˌhaɪweɪ] *n.* 高速公路

长难句剖析

【文章难句】Network users can search through sources ranging from vast databases to small electronic "bulletin boards", where users form discussion groups around common interests.

【结构分析】本句主干是 Network users can search through sources。现在分词短语 ranging from … "bulletin boards" 做后置定语，修饰 sources。where 引导的非限制性定语从句用来修饰 bulletin boards。

【参考译文】从大型数据库一直到小型的电子公告板，都可以成为互联网用户搜索信息的来源，用户们常常在电子公告板上围绕着某个共同兴趣形成讨论小组。

【文章难句】One feature of the Internet, known as the World Wide Web, provides graphics, audio, and video to enhance the information in its documents.

【结构分析】本句主干是 One feature of the Internet, …provides graphics, audio, and video to…。过去分词短语 known as the World Wide Web 做 Internet 的后置定语。后面的不定式 to enhance…做目的状语。

【参考译文】互联网也称为万维网。它的一个特点是，提供了图形、音频和视频以增强文档的信息。

【文章难句】They can transmit thousands of times more data than local phone lines, most of which consist of copper wires.

【结构分析】本句主干是 They can transmit…data…，句中还出现了倍数比较级 thousands of times more…than…。which 引导的非限制性定语从句修饰 local phone lines。

【参考译文】这样的光缆就能够以比由铜线组成的电话线快数千倍的速度传递数据。

全文参考译文

互联网是一个巨大的计算机网络，它把世界上许多公司、机构团体和个人连接起来。互联网，即网络相互连接形成的网络，连接了数以万计的更小的计算机网络。这些网络以文字、图像和声音的形式传输大量的信息。

事实上，互联网上几乎有关于所有主题的信息。从大型数据库一直到小型的电子公告板，都可以成为互联网用户搜索信息的来源，网民们经常在电子公告板上围绕着某个共同兴趣形成讨论小组。互联网上大量的通信由从一台计算机送往另一台计算机的消息组成。这些消息被称为电子邮件。互联网用户有用来收发电子邮件的邮件地址。此外，网络功能还包括获取新闻、参与网上辩论、玩电子游戏等。互联网也称为万维网。它的一个特点是，提供了图形、音频和视频以增强文档的信息。这些文档涵盖了大量的主题。

通常人们使用调制解调器接入互联网。调制解调器通过电话线将计算机连接到网络。互联网通过全世界的光缆电话网络运转。这些光缆包含多股细如发丝的玻璃纤维，它能够以光脉冲的形式携带数据。这样的光缆能够以比由铜线组成的电话线快数千倍的速度传递数据。

互联网诞生于 20 世纪 60 年代。美国国防部高级研究计划署（ARPA）那时发展了名为 ARPAnet 的计算机网络。ARPAnet 最初只用于连接军用和政府计算机系统。其目的是：若发生灾祸或者战争，ARPAnet 能够保证这些系统的安全。在创造 ARPAnet 不久，很多大学和一些公共机构发展了自己的计算机网络。这些网络最终同 ARPAnet 相融合形成了互联网。到 20 世纪 90 年代，任何人只要有计算机、调制解调器和互联网软件就能够连接到互联网上。

将来，随着计算机技术的发展，互联网或许会越来越成熟。很多专家相信，互联网可以成为被称为"信息高速公路"的更大的网络的一部分。信息高速公路尚在发展阶段，它能将计算机同电话公司、有线电视台以及其他信息系统连接起来。人们能够通过网络办理银行业务、购物、看电视，也可以进行其他的活动。

题目答案与解析

1. 这篇文章是关于互联网的 _____。
   A．未来　　　　B．一般介绍　　　　C．用途　　　　D．历史

【答案】B

【解析】综观全文，可以了解到什么是互联网，互联网的应用以及它的发展过程和未来的预期应用，因此 B 项是正确答案。

2. 以下关于互联网的描述中，哪一项是正确的？
   A．ARPA 是第一个被美国大学和研究所使用的网络。
   B．互联网的历史可以追溯到 50 年以前。

C. 互联网的目的是为了在战时保护世界。

D. ARPA 网构成了现代互联网的基础。

【答案】D

【解析】本题可以参照文章的第 4 段，即 Internet 的历史。从中可知 A、B、C 三项都和原文有悖，因此 D 项是正确答案。

3. 除了 _____ 之外，互联网能让人们做以下这些事。

A. 发电子邮件　　　　　　　　　　B. 获取新闻

C. 交换调制解调器　　　　　　　　D. 网络聊天

【答案】C

【解析】本题可参照文章的第 2 段。从中可知，互联网的应用包括电子公告板、大型数据库、电子邮件、游戏、获取新闻、参与网上辩论等有关功能，只有交换调制解调器没有被提到，因此 C 项为正确答案。

4. 根据文章的最后一段，未来 _____。

A. 预测互联网的发展将会很困难　　B. 互联网将成为不可缺少的超级高速公路

C. 互联网将得到更广泛的应用　　　D. 互联网将和有线电视相连接

【答案】C

【解析】从最后一段可知，未来随着科学技术的发展，网络会变得愈加成熟，而且文中提到了网络还可以和电话公司、有线电视台和其他信息系统连接起来，给人们提供更方便的服务，因此 C 项是正确答案。

Text 2

Sex prejudices are based on and justified by the ideology that biology is destiny. According to this ideology, basic biological and psychological differences exist between the sexes. These differences require each sex to play a separate role in social life. Women are the weaker sex both physically and emotionally. Thus, they are naturally suited, much more so than men, to the performance of domestic duties. A woman's place, under normal circumstances, is within the protective environment of the home. Nature has determined that women play caretaker roles, such as wife and mother and homemaker. On the other hand, men are best suited to go out into the competitive world of work and politics, where serious responsibilities must be taken on. Men are to be the providers; women and children are "dependents".

The ideology also holds that women who wish to work outside the household should naturally fill these jobs that are in line with the special capabilities of their sex. It is thus appropriate for women, not men, to be employed as nurses, social workers, elementary school teachers, household helpers, and clerks and secretaries. These positions are simply an extension of women's domestic role. Informal distinctions between "women's work" and "men's work" in the labor force, according to the ideology, are simply a functional reflection of the basic differences between the sexes.

Finally, the ideology suggests that nature has worked her will in another significant way. For the human species to survive over time, its members must regularly reproduce. Thus, women must, whether at home or in the labor force, make the most of their physical appearance.

So goes the ideology. It is, of course, not true that basic biological and psychological differences between the sexes require each to play sex-defined roles in social life. There is ample evidence that sex roles vary from society to society, and those role differences that to exist are largely learned.

But to the degree people actually believe that biology is destiny and that nature intended for men and women to make different contributions to society, sex-defined roles will be seen as totally acceptable.

1. Women's place, some people think, is within the protective environment of the home because _____.

    A. women can provide better care for the children

    B. women are too weak to do any agricultural work at all

    C. women are biologically suited to domestic jobs

    D. women can not compete with men in any field

2. According to the author, sex roles _____.

    A. are socially determined

    B. are emotionally and physically determined

    C. can only be determined by what education people take

    D. are biologically and psychologically determined

3. The author points out that the assignments of women's roles in work _____.

    A. are determined by what they are better suited to

    B. row out of their position inside the home

    C. reflect a basic difference between men and women

    D. are suitable to them, but not to men

4. Which of the following is NOT true according to the passage?

    A. The division of sex-defined roles is completely unacceptable.

    B. Women's roles in work are too limited at present.

    C. In one society, men might perform what is considered women's duties by another.

    D. Some of the women's roles in domestic duties can not be taken over by men.

核心词汇注释

prejudice ['predʒudɪs] *n.* 偏见，成见；损害，侵害
    v. 损害

ideology [ˌaɪdɪ'ɒlədʒɪ, ɪd-] *n.* 意识形态

destiny ['destɪnɪ] *n.* 命运，定数

psychological [ˌsaɪkə'lɒdʒɪkəl] *adj.* 心理（上）的

domestic [də'mestɪk] *adj.* 家庭的，国内的；与人共处的，驯服的

caretaker ['keəteɪkə(r)] *n.* 管理者，看管

者，看守者

elementary [ˌelɪ'mentərɪ] *adj.* 初步的，基本的；[化] 元素的，自然力的

distinction [dɪ'stɪŋkʃ(ə)n] *n.* 区别，差别，级别；特性；声望，显赫

significant [sɪg'nɪfəkənt] *adj.* 有意义的，重大的，重要的

contribution [ˌkɒntrɪ'bjuːʃ[n]ne] *n.* 捐献，贡献，投稿

长难句剖析

【文章难句】On the other hand, men are best suited to go out into the competitive world of work and politics, where serious responsibilities must be taken on.

【结构分析】本句主干是 men are best suited to go out into the competitive world of work and politics。where 引导的非限制性定语从句修饰 the competitive world。

【参考译文】另一方面，男人最适合外面充满竞争的政治与工作世界，在那里他们必须承担严肃的责任。

【文章难句】The ideology also holds that women who wish to work outside the household should naturally fill these jobs that are in line with the special capabilities of their sex.

【结构分析】本句主语是 the ideology，谓语动词为 holds，由 that 引导的从句做宾语。在宾语从句中，who 引导的定语从句修饰从句的主语 women，that 引导的定语从句修饰宾语 these jobs。

【参考译文】这种观念也认为，那些希望出外工作的女性应当从事那些符合她们性别特点的工作。

【文章难句】It is, of course, not true that basic biological and psychological differences between the sexes require each to play sex defined roles in social life.

【结构分析】本句因为主语结构太复杂，所以用 it 做形式主语。that 后面的成分才是真正的主语。

【参考译文】当然，认为性别间基本的生理和心理差异需要不同性别在社会生活中扮演其由性别决定的角色的想法也是错误的。

全文参考译文

生理就是命运的观念是性别偏见的根据和理由。按照这种思想，两性之间存在着基本的生理和心理差别。这种差别要求两性在社会生活中扮演不同的角色。不论在生理上，还是心理上，女性都是弱者。这样，她们自然就比男性更适合承担家庭义务。通常情况下，一个女人的位置是在家庭这种受到保护的环境中。天性决定了女性要扮演照顾他人的角色，比如做个妻子、母亲或者全职太太；另一方面，男人最适合外面充满竞争的政治与工作世界，在那里男人必须承担严肃的责任。男人是要养家糊口的，女人和孩子则是"被抚养者"。

这种观点也认为，那些希望外出工作的女性应当从事那些符合她们性别特点的工作。因而女性比男性更适合做护士、社工、小学教师、保姆、职员和秘书等工作。这些职位只是女性家庭角色的延伸。按照这种想法，"女性工作"和"男性工作"非正式的区分在劳动力中只是性别基本差异的功能反映。

这种观念最后认为，自然用另一种重要的方式实施它的意愿。因为人类要世代生存下去，其成员必须繁衍后代。因而无论是在家中，还是外出工作，女性都必须充分展示自己的身体外表特征。

这种观念就是这样。当然，认为性别间基本的生理和心理差异需要不同性别在社会生活中扮演其由性别决定的角色的想法同样是错误的。有充分的证据可以说明在不同的社会中性别的角色也不尽相同。所存在的角色差别也大多是后天习得的。

但是在一定程度上人们深信生理就是命运，大自然让男人和女人对社会作出不同的贡献。由性别决定的角色完全被认为是可以接受的。

题目答案与解析

1. 某些人认为，女性的位置应该是在家庭环境的保护之下，因为 _____。
   A．女性可以给予孩子们更好的照料　　B．女性太弱了，根本不能干农活
   C．女性天生就适合家务劳动　　　　　D．女性在任何领域都无法和男性竞争
   【答案】C
   【解析】本题可参照文章的第 1 段。题目中的 some people think 和原文第 1 段第 2 句话中的 According to this ideology…是对应的。第 5 句话作者又归因到 Thus, they are naturally suited, much more so than men, to the performance of domestic duties，从中可知 C 项是正确答案。

2. 按照作者的观点，性别角色 _____。
   A．是由社会决定的　　　　　　　　　B．是由情感和身体决定的
   C．只取决于受到的教育　　　　　　　D．是由生理和心理决定的
   【答案】A
   【解析】本题的依据是文章第 6 段的 So goes the ideology. It is, of course, not true that basic biological and psychological differences between the sexes require each to play sex defined roles in social life. 根据上下文可知，作者是不同意这种观念的，因此 A 项是正确答案。

3. 作者指出，在工作中女性角色的分配 _____。
   A．取决于她比较适合于做什么　　　　B．是她们在家庭中角色的延伸
   C．反映了男性和女性的根本不同　　　D．适合女性，不适合男性
   【答案】B
   【解析】这道题与文章的第 2 段有关。作者在这一段的倒数第 2 句话中指出 These positions are simply an extension of women's domestic role. 从中可知 B 项是正确答案。

4. 根据本文，以下各项中哪一项是错误的？
   A．按照性别定义的角色划分是完全不可接受的。
   B．现代女性在工作中的角色太有限了。
   C．在一个社会中，男性可能从事另一个社会认为的女性的工作。
   D．在家庭责任中，某些女性角色不可能由男性代替。
   【答案】A
   【解析】本题可参照文章的最后一段。从中可知，这种性别角色在不同的社会里差异很大，但人们还是愿意接受这种男女之间的差异是天生的观念。因此 A 项为正确答案。

Text　3

In a sense, the new protectionism is not protectionism at all, at least not in the traditional sense of the term. The old protectionism referred only to trade restricting and trade expanding devices, such as the tariff or export subsidy. The new protectionism is much broader than this;

it includes interventions into foreign trade but is not limited to them. The new protectionism, in fact, refers to how the whole of government intervention into the private economy affects international trade. The emphasis on trade is still there, thus came the term "protection". But what is new is the realization that virtually all government activities can affect international economic relations.

The emergence of the new protectionism in the Western world reflects the victory of the interventionist, or welfare economy over the market economy. Jab Tumiler writes, "The old protectionism…coexisted, without any apparent intellectual difficulty with the acceptance of the market as a national as well as an international economic distribution mechanism. Indeed, protectionists as well as (if not more than) free traders stood for laissez faire. Now, as in the 1930s, protectionism is an expression of a profound skepticism as to the ability of the market to distribute resources and incomes to societies satisfaction."

It is precisely this profound skepticism of the market economy that is responsible for the protectionism. In a market economy, economic change of various colors implies redistribution of resources and incomes. The same opinion in many communities apparently is that such redistributions often are not proper. Therefore, the government intervenes to bring about a more desired result.

The victory of the welfare state is almost complete in northern Europe. In Sweden, Norway, Finland, Denmark, and the Netherlands, government intervention in almost all aspects of economic and social life is considered normal. In Great Britain this is only somewhat less true. Government traditionally has played a very active role in economic life in France and continued to do so. Only West Germany dares to go against the tide towards excessive interventionism in Western Europe. It also happens to be the most successful Western European economy.

The welfare state has made significant progress in the United States as well as in Western Europe. Social security, unemployment insurance, minimum wage laws, and rent control are by now traditional welfare state elements on the American scene.

1. This passage is primarily concerned with discussing _____.
   A. the definition of the new protectionism
   B. the difference between new and old protectionism
   C. the emergence of the new protectionism in the Western world
   D. the significance of the welfare state

2. Which of the following statements is NOT a characteristic of a welfare state mentioned in this passage?
   A. Free education is available to a child.　　B. Laws are made to fix the minimum wage.
   C. A jobless person can be insured.　　D. There are regulations for rent.

3. Which of the following inferences is true, according to this passage?
   A. The economy developed faster in welfare states than in non-welfare states.
   B. In the 1930s, protectionism began to rise.
   C. The new protectionism is so called mainly because it is the latest.

D. Government plays a more active role in economic life in Northern Europe than in Great Britain.

4. The passage supplies information for answering which of the following questions?
   A. When did the new protectionism arise?
   B. Why is the new protectionism so popular in northern European countries?
   C. Does the American government play a more active role in economic life than the British government?
   D. Why does the government intervene in economic life?

核心词汇注释

protectionism [prə'tekʃ(ə)nɪz(ə)m] *n.* 保护主义

tariff ['tærɪf] *n.* 关税，关税表，税则；（旅馆、饭店等的）价目表、价格表 *vt.* 课以关税

subsidy ['sʌbsɪdɪ] *n.* 补助金，津贴

emergence [ɪ'mɜːdʒəns] *n.* 浮现，露出；（植物）突出体；出现

interventionist [ˌɪntə'venʃənɪst] *n.* 干涉主义者 *adj.* 干涉主义的

coexist [ˌkəʊɪg'zɪst] *vi.* 共存

laissez faire [leɪ'seɪ'feər] *n.* 放任，自由主义

skepticism ['skeptɪsɪz(ə)m] *n.* 怀疑论

redistribution [ˌriːdɪstrɪ'bjuːʃ(ə)n] *n.* 重新分配，再区分

excessive [ɪk'sesɪv] *adj.* 过多的，过分的，额外的

长难句剖析

【文章难句】But what is new is the realization that virtually all government activities can affect international economic relations.

【结构分析】本句是一个典型的主系表结构，what 引导的名词性从句做主语，表语是 realization。that 引导的从句是 realization 的同位语成分。

【参考译文】但是意识到所有的政府行为都能影响国际经济关系却是最近的事情。

【文章难句】The old protectionism…coexisted, without any apparent intellectual difficulty with the acceptance of the market as a national as well as an international economic distribution mechanism.

【结构分析】本句的主干是 The old protectionism…coexisted, …with the acceptance。谓语动词的方式状语是 without…difficulty。as a national as well as…mechanism 做 market 的补足语。

【参考译文】古老的经济保护主义……同接受市场作为国内国际经济分配体制的做法看似合理地并存着。

【文章难句】Now, as in the 1930s, protectionism is an expression of a profound skepticism as to the ability of the market to distribute resources and incomes to societies satisfaction.

【结构分析】本句的开头是时间状语。主干是 protectionism is an expression。as to…satisfaction 短语是句子的条件状语。

【参考译文】现在跟 20 世纪 30 年代一样，保护主义表达了一种对市场作为资源和收入配置方式的能力能否获得社会认同的深刻怀疑。

全文参考译文

新的保护主义在某种意义上不完全是保护主义，至少不是传统意义上的保护主义。传统的保护主义只涉及贸易限制（trade-restricting）或贸易推广（trade-expanding）措施，例如关税和出口补贴。新的保护主义则比这个广泛得多。它包括对外国贸易的干涉，但不仅限于此。事实上，新保护主义涉及整个政府是如何干预私有经济从而影响国际贸易的。因为它依然强调贸易，才有"保护主义"一词。但是意识到所有的政府行为都能影响国际经济关系却是最近的事情。

西方社会新保护主义的出现反映了干涉主义者的胜利，或者说福利经济胜过了市场经济。Jab Tumiler 写到："古老的经济保护主义……同接受市场作为国内国际经济分配体制的做法看似合理地并存着。实际上，保护主义者同自由贸易者一样，甚至比他们更加支持放任政策。现在跟 20 世纪 30 年代一样，保护主义表达了一种对市场作为资源和收入配置方式的能力能否获得社会认同的深刻怀疑。"

保护主义出现的原因正是这种对市场经济的深刻怀疑。各种经济变化在市场经济中意味着资源和收入再分配。显然，很多社会一致认为，这样的再分配通常是不合理的。所以，政府实施干预以期获得更加令人满意的结果。

北欧国家的福利政策几乎取得了完全胜利。在瑞典、挪威、芬兰、丹麦和荷兰，人们认为政府对经济和社会生活各个领域的干预是很正常的事情。英国稍微有点不一样。法国政府一如既往地在经济生活中起着积极作用而且会继续做下去。只有前西德敢于逆过度干预的潮流行事。而它恰恰是西欧经济最成功的国家。

在美国和西欧，福利都取得了显著进步。现在社会保险、失业保险、最低工资法规和租金控制是美国社会中一些传统的福利条件。

题目答案与解析

1. 本篇文章主要讨论的是关于 _____。
   A. 新保护主义的定义　　　　　　　　B. 新、旧保护主义的区别
   C. 西方国家新保护主义的出现　　　　D. 福利国家的重要性
   【答案】A
   【解析】综观全文，只有 A 项较全面地概括了文章的中心思想，是四个选项中的最佳选项，因此 A 项为正确答案。

2. 以下各项中，哪一项不是本文中提及的福利国家的特点？
   A. 儿童可接受免费教育。　　　　　　B. 制定法律，规定最低工资。
   C. 失业人员可享受保险。　　　　　　D. 租金控制。
   【答案】A
   【解析】本题可参照文章的最后一段。从中可知，B、C、D 三项在这一段中均已提及，只有 A 项没有提到，因此 A 项是正确答案。

3. 依据本文，以下各项推论中哪一项是正确的？

A. 福利国家的经济发展速度比非福利国家快。

B. 20世纪30年代，保护主义开始出现。

C. 所谓新保护主义是因为它是最近出现的。

D. 北欧国家政府在经济生活中扮演的角色比英国政府更活跃。

【答案】D

【解析】本题可参照文章的第4段。从中可知，A项不对，这一段讲述的情况与A项相反。B项与第2段最后一句话有关，这是对的，但文章已有明确表示，不属于推理。C项无法判断，所以也应排除。只有D项可根据第4段推理得出，因此D项是正确答案。

4. 本文提供的信息可以回答下列哪个问题？

A. 新保护主义为什么出现？

B. 新保护主义为什么在北欧国家如此流行？

C. 在经济生活中，美国政府比英国政府扮演的角色更加积极吗？

D. 为什么政府要干预经济生活？

【答案】D

【解析】综观全文，只有D项与全文关系较密切，因为在文章的第2段回答了这一问题，而第3段是承上启下，十分重要。因此D项为正确答案。

Text 4

It has been argued that where schools become bureaucratized, they become bound up with the techniques and implementation of the managerial process, and may concentrate on concern with position and self-advancement. In so doing, they may neglect the purpose for which they were set up.

Thus, they do not facilitate the development of those who are part of the school community, and tend to neglect the desires of children, parents and society at large.

It is because of such criticisms that there has been an increasing influence in political rhetoric and legislation of free-market theories of organization and society. Such theories suggest that a much more market-oriented, competitive approach is required so that schools reorient themselves towards their "clients". By so doing, it is claimed, not only do they once again address the needs of those with whom they should be primarily concerned, but such an approach also unleashes the benefits of individual responsibility, freedom of choice, and reward.

Though much of this sounds attractive, it has its roots as much in an economic body of thought as in social and political theory, and this must raise the question of whether it can be viably transferred to an educational context. Indeed, if by "educational" we mean the development of all within the school community, then free-market theory may miss the mark by concentrating on only one section, "the consumers". If teachers are seen as part of this community, then their development is just as important.

If bureaucratic forms of management face the problem of explaining how their values can be objective when they are in fact the product of a particular value orientation, the forms of management derived from free-market theories, suggesting an openness to the adoption of different sets of values, are subject to the charge of relativism. In other words, free-market theories, granted that they are arguing that individuals should be allowed to pursue their own ends, must explain why any set of values, including their own, is preferable to another.

1. According to the author, criticism of schools arises from _____.

   A. concerns that schools deliberately neglect students

   B. the high cost of education due to bureaucracy

   C. a perception of them as self-serving and bureaucratic

   D. a misunderstanding of schools officials

2. The "school community" (Line 4 Para. 4) the author refers to would probably include _____.

   A. students   B. students and parents

   C. students, parents and teachers   D. teachers and students

3. The transfer of free market ideas to the schools may fail because _____.

   A. schools have no real clients

   B. they concentrate only on the consumer and do not include teachers

   C. schools are totally different from the free market

   D. they have no solid purpose in their aims

4. According to the text, criticism of free market solutions in education arise from the fact that _____.

   A. they do not explain why their set of values are better than others

   B. their values are too subjective

   C. their values are too different from those within an educational context

   D. the educational context is not a free market

5. The "charge of relativism" mentioned in the last paragraph is meant to show _____.

   A. the values are too narrow-minded   B. the values are not specific enough

   C. the values are too self-serving   D. the values are not strongly held

核心词汇注释

bureaucratize [bjʊəˈrɒkrətaɪz] *v.* 使官僚主义化

implementation [ˌɪmplɪmənˈteɪʃən] *n.* 执行

managerial [ˌmænəˈdʒɪəriəl] *adj.* 管理的

facilitate [fəˈsɪlɪteɪt] *vt.*（不以人作主语的）使容易，使便利，推动，帮助，促进

rhetoric [ˈretərɪk] *n.* 讨论；修辞学；花言巧语

legislation [ˌledʒɪsˈleɪʃ(ə)n] *n.* 立法，法律的制定（或通过）

reorient [ˌriːˈɔːrɪent] *vt.* 使适应；再教育

unleash [ʌnˈliːʃ] *v.* 释放

orientation [ˌɔːriənˈteɪʃ(ə)n] *n.* 方向，方位，定位；倾向性

relativism [ˈrelətɪvɪzəm] *n.* 相对论，相对主义

长难句剖析

【文章难句】Though much of this sounds attractive, it has its roots as much in an economic body of thought as in social and political theory.

【结构分析】本句为主从复合句，主干是 it has its roots as much…as。though 引导让步状语从句。主句为同级比较句型。this 指代上一段的观点。as much A as B 表示同等程度，可以理解为"不仅 B 而且 A"。

【参考译文】尽管这种理论听起来很有吸引力，但是其根源不仅在于社会政治理论，而且在于经济思想体系。

【文章难句】The forms of management derived from free-market theories, suggesting an openness to the adoption of different sets of values, are subject to the charge of relativism.

【结构分析】本句为简单句。主干是 The forms of management…are subject to the charge of relativism。derived…和 suggesting…为两个分词短语，修饰主语 the forms of management。

【参考译文】源自于自由市场理论、表明采用各种不同价值体系的管理形式会被人指责为相对主义。

【文章难句】In other words, free-market theories, granted that they are arguing that individuals should be allowed to pursue their own ends, must explain why any set of values, including their own, is preferable to another.

【结构分析】本句为主从复合句。主干是 free-market theories…must explain why…。why 引导宾语从句。that 引导让步状语从句，在句中作插入语，表示补充说明，意为"即使"。

【参考译文】换言之，自由市场理论，即使认为应该允许个人追求自己的目标，也必须解释清楚为什么某个价值体系，包括自己的价值体系，比另一个更可取。

全文参考译文

一些人认为，学校变得官僚机构化，热衷于管理过程的方法和执行，专注于对职位和自我发展的考虑。这样他们也许就忽视了当初建校的目的。

因而他们并没有为学校群体成员的发展提供便利，而很可能忽视孩子、家长以及整个社会的愿望。

这种指责在政治性的文章中和社会机构关于自由市场理论的立法中的影响越来越大。这种理论认为，学校需要采取一种更加面向市场的、更有竞争意识的态度，以便自我调整，面向"顾客"。据称，这样做学校不仅又一次满足了应主要关注的那部分人的需要，而且这种态度也可以使人得到个人责任、自由选择以及奖励所带来的好处。

虽然这种理论听起来很有吸引力，但是其根源不仅在于社会政治理论，而且在于经济思想体系，这必然会引起能否成功地转用于教育领域的问题。事实上，如果我们把"教育"理解为学校群体内所有成员的发展，那么自由市场理论可能因为只关注于一个部分，即"消费者"而达不到目的。如果教师被视为该群体的一部分，那么他们的发展则同样重要。

若官僚机构化的管理形式面临着这样的问题：在它们事实上是一个特定价值取向产物的时候去解释其价值观念如何客观，那么这种源自于自由市场理论，却表明采用各种不同价值体系的管理形式会被人指责为相对主义。换句话说，自由市场理论，即使认为应该允许个人追求自己的目标，也必须解释清楚为什么某个价值体系，包括自己的价值体系，比另一个更可取。

题目答案与解析

1. 按照作者的观点，对学校的批评来自 _____。
   A．对学校故意忽视学生问题的关注　　B．因官僚作风而产生的高额教育经费
   C．对他们自私自利和官僚政治的了解　　D．对学校官员的误解

   【答案】C

   【解析】本题的依据是原文的 It has been argued that where schools become bureaucratized, they become bound up with the techniques and implementation of the managerial process, and may concentrate on concern with position and self-advancement. C 项中的 self-serving 对应 concentrate on concern with position and self-advancement；bureaucratic 对应 bureaucratized。

2. 作者引用的 "school community"（第 4 段第 4 行）可能包括 _____。
   A．学生　　　　B．学生和父母　　　C．学生、父母和老师　　D．老师和学生

   【答案】C

   【解析】本题的依据是原文的 "Indeed, if by 'educational' we mean the development of all within the school community, then free-market theory may miss the mark by concentrating on only one section, 'the consumers'. If teachers are seen as part of this community, then their development is just as important"。从中可知，school community 包括 consumers 和 teachers。根据全文语境判断，consumers 指 students 和 parents。

3. 将自由市场的思想用在学校上可能失败的原因是 _____。
   A．学校没有真正的消费者　　　　　B．他们只关注消费者而忽视教师
   C．学校与自由市场是完全不同的　　D．在他们的目标中没有一致的目的性

   【答案】B

   【解析】本题属于事实细节题。本题的依据句与上题相同。从中可知 B 项为正确答案。

4. 依照本文，对用自由市场解决教育方案的批评来自于 _____ 这个事实。
   A．他们无法解释自己的价值体系优越于其他价值体系
   B．他们的价值体系太主观
   C．他们的价值体系与那些存在于与教育领域内部的价值体系区别太大
   D．教育领域不是自由市场

   【答案】A

   【解析】本题的依据句是全文的结尾句。依据本段主题—— 自由市场管理形式以偏概全、妄自尊大，可知本句表明自由市场管理形式无法解释自己的价值体系优越于其他价值体系。因此 A 项为正确答案。

5. 在最后一段中提及的 "charge of relativism" 是用来表明 _____。
   A．这种价值太狭隘　　　　　　　　B．这种价值不够明确
   C．这种价值太自私　　　　　　　　D．这种价值不能被坚定地保持

   【答案】C

   【解析】本题可参照上题。原文中词组 in other words 后的 "free-market theories, granted that they are arguing that individuals should be allowed to pursue their own ends, must explain why any set of values, including their own, is preferable to another" 是具体阐释。

Unit 4

Text 1

Shoppers who have flocked to online stores for their holiday shopping are losing privacy with every mouse click, according to a new report.

The study by the Washington-based Electronic Privacy Information Center scrutinized privacy policies on 100 of the most popular online shopping sites and compared those policies with a set of basic privacy principles that have come to be known as "fair information practices".

The group found that none of the 100 sites met all of the basic criteria for privacy protection, which include giving notice of what information is collected and how it is used, offering consumers a choice over whether the information will be used in certain ways, allowing access to data that give consumers a chance to see and correct the information collected, and instituting the kind of security measures that ensure that information won't fall into the wrong hands.

"This study shows that somebody else, other than Santa, is reading your Christmas list," said Jeff Chester, executive director of the Center for Media Education, which also worked on the survey.

The online privacy of children is protected by Federal Trade Commission rules, but adults do not share the same degree of privacy protection. The movement, like the online shopping industry, favors self-regulation over imposition of further movement restrictions on electronic commerce.

Marc Rosenberg, executive director of the privacy group, said the study shows that self regulations have failed, "We need legislation to enforce fair information practices," he said, "Consumers are at greater risk than they were in 1997," when the group released its first report.

The survey also asked whether the 100 sites used "profile-based" advertising, and whether the sites incorporate "cookies" technology, which gives Websites basic information on visitors. Profiling is the practice of gathering in then used to create targeted advertising on Websites.

All but 18 of the top shopping sites did display a privacy policy, a major improvement over the early days of electronic commerce, when such policies were scarce. But that did not satisfy the privacy group. "Companies are posting privacy policies, but these policies are not the same thing as fair information practices," Rosenberg said.

The sites also did not perform well by other measures, the group said it found that 35 of the sites feature profile-based advertising, and 87 percent use cookies. The group concluded that the phonies that were posted "are typically confusing, incomplete, and inconsistent". The report, "Surfer Beware III: Privacy Policies Without Privacy Protection, " is the third such survey by the group. It called for further development of technologies that help consumers protect their privacy and even anonymity when exploring the Internet.

1. What does the sentence "This study shows that somebody else, other than Santa, is reading your Christmas list" mean?

  A．The study shows that someone else would buy consumers a gift for Christmas

  B．The study shows that consumers'privacy is being invaded.

  C．The study shows that companies want to make a Christmas list for children.

  D．The study shows that Santa would not bring the Christmas gifts this year.

2．Which of the following is not in the list of the basic criteria of privacy protection mentioned in paragraph 3?

  A．Give notice of what information is collected and how it is used to consumers.

  B．Allow access to data that give consumers a chance to see and correct the information collected.

  C．Make consumers believe that the information provided by the sites is surely correct.

  D．Institute the kind of security measures that ensure that the information won't fall into the wrong hands.

3．It could be drawn from the passage that _____.

  A．the Washington-based Electronic Privacy Information Center has released at least 3 reports concerning the online privacy

  B．adults cannot get any online privacy protection

  C．both the online privacy of children and that of adults are not protected by FTC rules

  D．only 18 of the top shopping sites displayed a privacy policy nowadays

4．What does the passage mainly talk about?

  A．Marc Rosenberg's study on self-regulation.

  B．Some online problems found by a privacy group's study.

  C．Adults and children are different.

  D．Online security measures.

核心词汇注释

flock [flɒk] *n.* 羊群，（禽、畜等的）群 *v.* 聚结

scrutinize ['skru:tɪnaɪz] *v.* 细察

criteria [kraɪ'tɪərɪə] *n.* (*pl.*) 标准

imposition [ˌɪmpə'zɪʃ(ə)n] *n.* 强迫接受

enforce [ɪn'fɔ:s] *vt.* 强迫，执行，坚持，加强

release [rɪ'li:s] *n.* 释放，让渡，豁免；发行的书；释放证书；版本；发布 *vt.* 释放，解放，放弃，让与，免除，发表

incorporate [ɪn'kɔ:pəreɪt] *adj.* 合并的，结社的，一体化的 *vt.* 合并，使组成公司；具体表现，[律]结社，使成为法人组织 *vi.* 合并，混合；组成公司

phony ['fəʊnɪ] *adj.* 假冒的 *n.* 假冒者

anonymity [ˌænə'nɪmɪtɪ] *n.* 匿名，作者不明（或不详）

长难句剖析

【文章难句】The study by the Washington-based Electronic Privacy Information Center scrutinized privacy policies on 100 of the most popular online shopping sites and compared those policies with a set of basic privacy principles that have come to be known as "fair information practices".

【结构分析】本句主干是 The study…scrutinized privacy policies…and compared those policies with。by 引导的介词短语修饰主语 study；on…sites 是一个地点状语；a set of basic privacy principles 后面是 that 引导的定语从句。

【参考译文】位于华盛顿的电子隐私信息中心仔细审查了 100 个最受欢迎的购物站点上的隐私条款并将这些条款和名为"公平信息准则"的一套基本隐私保护条例进行了比较。

【文章难句】The group found that none of the 100 sites met all of the basic criteria for privacy protection, which include giving notice of what information is collected and how it is used, offering consumers a choice over whether the information will be used in certain ways, allowing access to data that give consumers a chance to see and correct the information collected, and instituting the kind of security measures that ensure that information won't fall into the wrong hands.

【结构分析】本句主干是 The group found that none…met all of the basic criteria…which include。which 引导的非限制性定语从句修饰 the basic criteria。在这个从句中，谓语动词 include 的宾语是由几个并列的动名词构成的：giving…used，offering…ways，allowing…collected 和 instituting…hands。

【参考译文】这个中心发现 100 个站点中没有一个可以达到隐私保护的所有基本标准。这些标准的内容包括通知收集用户信息的内容和使用方式，让消费者决定其信息是否能以某些方式使用，允许消费者有机会进入数据库修改被收集的个人信息，并使用能够保证信息不会被滥用的安全措施。

【文章难句】All but 18 of the top shopping sites did display a privacy policy, a major improvement over the early days of electronic commerce, when such policies were scarce.

【结构分析】本句主干是 All but 18 of the top shopping sites did display a privacy policy。主句后面的部分实际上是前面整个句子的同位语。the early days of electronic commerce 后是 when 引导的非限制性定语从句。

【参考译文】除 18 家网站外，所有大型购物站点均显示了隐私保护条款，在电子商业发展早期，这样的隐私保护条款极为少见，相比之下，这是一个很大的进步。

全文参考译文

一份新近的报告表明，那些蜂拥到网上商店进行假日购物的消费者每次点击鼠标的时候都在泄漏个人的隐私。

位于华盛顿的电子隐私信息中心仔细审查了 100 个最受欢迎的在线购物站点上的隐私条款并将这些条款和名为"公平信息准则"的一套基本隐私保护条例进行了比较。

这所中心发现，在 100 个站点中，没有一个能够达到隐私保护的所有基本标准。这些标准的内容包括通知收集用户信息的内容和使用方式，让消费者决定其信息是否能以某些方式使用，允许消费者有机会进入数据库查看并修改被收集的个人信息，并使用能够保证信息不会被滥用的安全措施。

"这项研究显示，除了圣诞老人以外还有人看到了你的圣诞节购物清单。"媒体教育中心的执行总裁 Jeff Chester 这样说道。这家中心也在进行此项调查。

儿童的网上隐私受联邦商务委员会有关规定的保护，而成人却没有享受同样的隐私保护。

像在线购物这样的行业，更倾向于自我管理而不是被强制要求接受电子商业的约束条款。

当隐私保护机构发布第一份报告的时候，执行理事 Rosenberg 认为，研究显示了自我管理的方式是行不通的。他说："我们需要通过立法来加强公平的信息准则，消费者比他们在1997年面临着更大的风险。"

调查也询问了这 100 个站点是否使用了"基于特征分布"的广告宣传和是否集成了cookies 技术——这项技术能让站点知道访问者的基本信息。特征分布方法是通过跟踪消费者的在线活动来收集他们的兴趣信息。这些信息接下来就用于制作网站上有针对性的广告。

除18家网站外，所有大型购物站点均显示了隐私保护条款。这样的隐私保护条款在电子商业发展的早期是极为少见的，相比之下，这已经是一个很大的进步了。不过这依然不能让隐私保护机构满意，Rosenberg 说："公司公布隐私保护条款，但这些条款和公平信息准则不是一回事。"

隐私保护机构声称，这些站点也没有采取其他措施来进行更完善的隐私保护。他们发现其中的 35 家站点采用了基于特征分布的广告宣传，同时，87%的站点使用了cookies。由此得出结论：这些站点贴出的隐私保护条款通常是模糊的、不完善的和自相矛盾的。一篇名为《网上冲浪须知三：没有隐私保护的隐私保护条款》的报告，是这个机构开展的第三次这样的调查。报告呼吁进一步发展技术，帮助消费者在浏览网站时保护自己的隐私，甚至匿名浏览。

题目答案与解析

1. "这项研究显示除了圣诞老人以外还有人看到了你的圣诞节购物清单"这句话是什么意思？
   A．这项研究显示其他人将为消费者购买圣诞礼物。
   B．这项研究显示消费者隐私受到侵犯。
   C．这项研究显示公司希望为孩子们做一个圣诞节购物清单。
   D．这项研究显示圣诞老人今年不会带来圣诞礼物了。
   【答案】B
   【解析】本题可参照文章的第 4 段。前 3 段已经讲到网上购物极易暴露购物者的隐私。第 4 段中说读你圣诞购物清单的不一定就是圣诞老人。这是在举例说明文章前三段的内容。所以正确答案为 B。

2. 下面哪一项不在第 3 段提到的隐私保护基本标准列表中？
   A．通知收集信息的内容和使用方式。
   B．允许消费者有机会进入数据库查看并修改被收集的个人信息。
   C．让消费者确信网站提供的信息是绝对正确的。
   D．制订能够保证信息不会被滥用的安全措施。
   【答案】C
   【解析】本题可参照文章第 3 段的 the basic criteria for privacy protection, which include giving…offering…allowing…and instituting…，从中可知只有 C 项没有列出，因此 C 项为正确答案。

3. 从这篇文章中可以得出 _____ 。
   A．以华盛顿为基地的电子隐私信息中心至少发表了三份关于网上隐私的报告
   B．成人无法享受任何的隐私保护

C．成人和儿童的网上隐私都无法受到联邦商务委员会有关规定的保护

D．现在，所有大型购物站点中，只有 18 家显示了隐私保护条款

【答案】A

【解析】本题的依据是文章最后一段倒数第 2 句话 The report…is the third such survey by the group，从中可知 A 项是正确答案。

4．本篇文章主要讨论的是什么？

A．Marc Rosenberg 关于自律的研究。　　B．隐私研究团体发现的一些网上的问题。

C．成人与儿童是不同的。　　　　　　　D．网上的安全措施。

【答案】B

【解析】综观全文，A、C、D 三项与文章无关或者关系不大。只有 B 最合适，因此正确答案为 B。

Text 2

Suppose you go into a fruiterer's shop, wanting an apple — you take up one, and on biting it you find it is sour; you look at it, and see that it is hard and green. You take up another one, and that, too, is hard, green, and sour. The shopman offers you a third; but, before biting it, you examine it, and find that it is hard and green, and you immediately say that you will not have it, as it must be sour, like those that you have already tried.

Nothing can be more simple than that, you think; but if you will take the trouble to analyze and trace out into its logical elements what has been done by the mind, you will be greatly surprised. In the first place you have performed the operation of induction. You find that, in two experiences, hardness and greenness in apples went together with sourness. It was so in the first case, and it was confirmed by the second. True, it is a very small basis, but still it is enough from which to make an induction; you generalize the facts, and you expect to find sourness in apples where you get hardness and greenness. You found upon that a general law, that all hard and green apples are sour; and that, so far as it goes, is a perfect induction. Well, having got your natural law in this way, when you are offered another apple which you find it hard and green, you say, "all hard and green apples are sour; this apple is hard and green; therefore, this apple is sour." That train of reasoning is what logicians call a syllogism, and has all its various parts and terms — its major premises, its minor premises, and its conclusion. And by the help of further reasoning, which, if drawn out, would have to be exhibited in two or three other syllogisms, you arrive at your final determination, "I will not have that apple." So that, you see, you have, in the first place, established a law by induction, and upon that you have founded a deduction, and reasoned out the special particular case.

Well now, suppose, having got your conclusion of the law, that at some times afterwards, you are discussing the qualities of apple with a friend; you will say to him, "It is a very curious thing, but I find that all hard and green apples are sour!" Your friend says to you, "But how do you know that?" You at once reply, "Oh, because I have tried them over and over again, and have always found them to be so." Well, if we are talking science instead of common sense, we should call that an experimental verification. And, if still opposed, you go further, and say, "I have heard from people, in Somerset shire and Devon shire, where a large number of apples are grown, and in London, where many apples are sold and eaten, that they have observed the same thing." It is also found to be the case in Normandy, and in North America. In short, I find it to be the universal experience of mankind wherever attention has been directed to the subject. Whereupon, your friend, unless he is a very unreasonable man, agrees with you, and is convinced that you are quite right in the conclusion you have drawn. He believes, although perhaps he does not know he believes it, that the more extensive verifications have been made, and results of the same kind arrived at — that the more varied the conditions under which the same results are attained, the more certain is the ultimate conclusion, and he disputes the question no further. He sees that the experiment has been tried under all sorts of conditions, as to time, place, and people, with the same result; and he says with you, therefore, that the law you have laid down must be a good one, and he must believe it.

1. Apples are used _____.

   A. in order to convince the reader that fruit has no intellect

   B. to illustrate the subject of the passage

   C. to give color to the story

   D. to show how foolish logic is

2. The term "natural law " as it appears in the text refers to _____.

   A. common sense   B. the result of an induction

   C. the order of nature   D. a scientific discovery

3. If you find a hard and green apple that is not sour, you should _____.

   A. try more apples to see if the natural law has changed

   B. eat the rest of the apple at once

   C. reject the law stating that hard and green apples are usually sour

   D. conduct further investigations and make adjustments to the law of apples as necessary

4. The writer is probably _____.

   A. French   B. English   C. American   D. None of the above

核心词汇注释

fruiterer [ˈfruːtərə] *n.* 水果商贩

trace [treɪs] *n.* 痕迹，踪迹，迹线；微量；缰绳

vt. 描绘，映描，画轮廓；追踪，回溯，探索

vi. 上溯，沿路走

induction [ɪnˈdʌkʃ(ə)n] *n.* 感应，感应现象；

generalize [ˈdʒenərəlaɪz] *vt.* 归纳，概括；推广，普及

logician [ləʊˈdʒɪʃ(ə)n] *n.* 逻辑学家

syllogism [ˈsɪlədʒɪz(ə)m] *n.* [逻]三段论法，推论法，演绎

premise [ˈpremɪs] *n.* [逻][法]前提，（企业、机构等使用的）房屋连地基

vt. 提论，预述；假定

vi. 作出前提

deduction [dɪˈdʌkʃ(ə)n] *n.* 减除，扣除，减除额；推论，演绎

verification [ˌverɪfɪˈkeɪʃən] *n.* 验证，确认，查证，作证；[律]诉状结尾的举证声明

长难句剖析

【文章难句】Well, having got your natural law in this way, when you are offered another apple which you find it hard and green, you say, "All hard and green apples are sour; this apple is hard and green; therefore, this apple is sour."

【结构分析】本句主干是 you say。引号中的句子是直接引语，做 say 的宾语。现在分词 having…way 做伴随状语；when 引导时间状语；another apple 后面是由 which 引导的定语从句。

【参考译文】那么，你既已经通过这种方式得到了一条自然规律，如果再有人给你苹果，而你发现它又硬又绿，你就会说："所有既硬又绿的苹果都是酸的，这个苹果又硬又绿，所以它是酸的。"

【文章难句】And, by the help of further reasoning, which, if drawn out, would have to be exhibited in two or three other syllogisms, you arrive at your final determination.

【结构分析】本句主干是 you arrive at your final determination。介词 by 引导的短语做方式状语。further reasoning 后面的 which 引导非限制性定语从句。if drawn out 做定语从句中的条件状语，省略主语。

【参考译文】通过进一步推理的帮助（如果把这部分推理分开来，大家就会看到它又是两三个三段论推理），你作出了最终的决定。

【文章难句】I have heard from people, in Somerset shire and Devon shire, where a large number of apples are grown, and in London, where many apples are sold and eaten, that they have observed the same thing.

【结构分析】本句主干是 I have heard from people…, that…。in…shire…and in London 做地点状语。这两个地点状语都是由 where 引导的非限制性定语从句修饰。另外，主句谓语动词的宾语是一个 that 从句。

【参考译文】我听别人说过，在苹果广泛种植的 Somerset 和 Devon 郡以及在苹果销量和消费量都很大的伦敦，他们都发现了同样的规律。

全文参考译文

假设你进入一家水果店，想要买苹果。你尝了第一个，发现它是酸的，你看了看它，发现它又青又硬。你又拿起了另一个，发现它也是又青又硬又酸。店主给你拿来了第三个，而你在咬它之前先仔细观察了一下，发现它又硬又青，于是你立刻说你不要了，因为你认定它是酸的，和你刚才尝的那几个一样。

你认为这再简单不过了。不过当你不怕麻烦深入分析和探索你的大脑作出这样的反应的逻辑因素时，你就会大吃一惊。首先，你进行了归纳。你发现，在前两个事例中，苹果的"硬"和"青"这两个特征都是和"酸"同时出现的。在第一个例子里是如此，而这又被第二个例子所证实了。当然，这是一个很弱的基础条件，但是从中做出一个归纳已经足够了。你归纳

了这些事实，并设想在具有"硬"和"青"这两个特性的苹果身上就具有"酸"这个性质。你就发现了一条普遍规律：所有又硬又青的苹果都是酸的。并且到目前为止，这还是个完美的结论。那么，你既已经通过这种方式得到了一条自然规律，如果再有人给你苹果，而你发现它又硬又青，你就会说："所有既硬又青的苹果都是酸的，这个苹果又硬又青，所以它是酸的。"这种推理链在逻辑学中叫做三段论法，并有它独特的结构和术语——它的大前提、小前提和结论。那么，通过进一步推理的帮助（如果把这部分推理分开来，大家就会看到它又是两三个三段论推理），你作出了最终的决定："我不要那个苹果。"因此你首先通过归纳建立了一条规律，然后在这条规律的基础上进行演绎，推出某个特定情况。

假如现在你已经总结出了规律，当以后某个时间你正在和你的一个朋友讨论苹果的质量的时候，你会对他说，"有件事情很有趣，我发现所有又硬又青的苹果都是酸的。"你的朋友对你说，"可你是怎么知道的？"你马上回答说："哦，因为我已经品尝了很多次，发现它们总是如此。"那么，如果我们是讲科学而不是常识，我们应该说这是一个经实验证实的结论。如果你的朋友仍旧不同意，你可以进一步这样说"我听别人说过，在苹果广泛种植的 Somerset 和 Devon 郡以及在苹果销量和消费量都很大的伦敦，他们都发现了同样的规律。在诺曼底和北美也是如此。总之，我发现几乎所有关心这个问题的地方人们都发现了这条规律。"

因此，只要你的朋友不是一个非常不讲道理的人，他就会赞成你的观点，而且会相信你所得到的结论是正确的。他相信尽管也许他自己都没有意识到，但他相信经过越广泛的验证，就会得到越多相同的结论，就是说，得到相同的结论的环境越多样化，最终的结论就越确定，而且他也不会再争论这个问题。他发觉实验在所有条件下都得到了验证。虽然是不同的时间、不同的地点、有不同的人，但都出现同样的结果；所以他会和你一样认为，你所断言的规律一定是一条正确的规律，他必须相信。

题目答案与解析

1. 举出苹果的例子是 _____。
   A. 为了使读者确信苹果是没有智力的　　B. 用来解释文章的主题
   C. 为了给故事增加一些色彩　　　　　　D. 为了显示逻辑是多么愚蠢
   【答案】B
   【解析】本题表面上问的是吃苹果这一例子，实际上问的是文章的主要内容。从文中内容可知，通过吃苹果的事例讲解了逻辑上的归纳法和演绎法。因此 B 项为正确答案。

2. 在文章中出现的术语"自然法则"与 _____ 有关。
   A. 常识　　　　　B. 归纳的结果　　　　C. 自然的秩序　　　D. 科学的发现
   【答案】B
   【解析】本题可参照第 2 段中间的一句话 Well, having got your natural law in this way, when…。而这一句前面有这样一句话：True, it is a very small basis, but still it is enough from which to make an induction. 从中可知 B 项为正确答案，即 the result of an induction。

3. 如果你发现一个又硬又青的苹果不是酸的，你就应该 _____。
   A. 尝试更多的苹果，看看自然法则是否发生了改变
   B. 立即吃掉其余的苹果

C. 抛弃又硬又青的苹果是酸的这条法则

D. 进行深入调查，对苹果法则做出必要的调整

【答案】D

【解析】本题的目的是让读者理解上下文，搞清演绎法的含义。四个选项中 B 和 C 明显错误。D 项比 A 项更为全面，因此 D 项是正确答案。

4. 作者也许是 _____。

    A. 法国人　　　　　B. 英国人　　　　　C. 美国人　　　　　D. 以上都不是

【答案】B

【解析】本题可参照文章倒数第 2 段。从中可知作者引用了地名 Somerset shire and Devon shire, London, Normandy 和 North America, 由此可以看出作者是英国人。因此 B 项为正确答案。

Text　3

Government is not made in virtue of natural rights, which may and do exist in total independence of it, and exist in much greater clearness, and in a much greater degree of abstract perfection; but their abstract perfection is their practical defect. By having a right to everything, men want everything. Government is a contrivance of human wisdom to provide for human wants. Men have a right that these wants should be provided for by this wisdom. Among these wants is to be reckoned the want, out of civil society, of a sufficient restraint upon their passions. Society requires not only that the passions of individuals should be subjected, but that even in the mass and body, as well as in the individuals, the inclinations of men should frequently be thwarted, their will controlled, and their passions brought into subjection. This can only be done by a power out of themselves; and not, in the exercise of its function, subject to that will and those passions which is its office to bridle and subdue. In this sense, the restraints on men, as well as their liberties, are to be reckoned among their rights. But because the liberties and the restrictions vary with times and circumstances, and admit to infinite modifications, they cannot be settled upon by any abstract rule; and nothing is so foolish as to discuss them upon that principle.

The moment you abate anything from the full rights of men, each to govern himself, and suffer any artificial, positive limitation upon those rights, from that moment the whole organization of government becomes a consideration of convenience. This is which makes the constitution of a state, and the due distribution of its powers, a matter of the most delicate and complicated skill. It requires a deep knowledge of human nature and human necessities, and of the things that facilitate or obstruct the various ends, which are to be pursued by the mechanism of civil institutions. The state is to have recruits to its strength, and remedies to its distempers. What is the use of discussing a man's abstract right to food and medicine? The question is upon the method of procuring and administering them. In that deliberation, I shall always advise to call in the aid of the farmer and the physician, rather than the professor of metaphysics.

1. According to the author, government _____.

A. is made by men
B. is made in virtue of natural rights
C. has a right to everything
D. wants everything

2. The author states that the will and the passions of the people _____.
   A. can be effectively controlled by the people themselves
   B. should determine government policies
   C. can be controlled only by a power that exists apart from the people and is not subject to that will and those passions
   D. cannot be controlled

3. The restraints on men as well as the liberties of men _____.
   A. are matters for individual concern
   B. are rights of men
   C. should be of no concern to the government
   D. cannot be tolerated by people

4. Besides a deep knowledge of human nature and human necessities, establishing a constitution of a state and deciding upon its powers require a knowledge of _____.
   A. the liberties and restrictions on man's rights
   B. the things which facilitate or obstruct the ends pursued by the mechanism of civil institutions
   C. the will of all the people
   D. the constitutions of many nations

核心词汇注释

contrivance [kən'traɪvəns] *n.* 发明，发明才能；想出的办法，发明物

reckon ['rekən] *vt.* 计算，总计，估计，猜想 *vi.* 数，计算，估计；依赖，料想

restraint [rɪ'streɪnt] *n.* 抑制，制止，克制

thwart [θwɔːt] *adj.* 横放的 *vt.* 反对，阻碍，横过 *adv. prep.* 横过 *n.* [船]横坐板

bridle ['braɪdl] *n.* 马勒，缰绳 *v.* 上笼头，昂首（表示傲慢、愤怒等）；抑制

subdue [səb'djuː] *v.* 征服

abate [ə'beɪt] *vt.* 使（数量、程度等）减少，减轻，除去，缓和，打折扣 *vi.* （数量、程度等）减少，减轻，失效，缓和；（法令等）被废除

distemper [dɪ'stempə(r)] *n.* 大瘟热，不高兴，病异状 *vt.* 用胶画颜料画；使发狂

metaphysics [ˌmetə'fɪzɪks] *n.* 形而上学，玄学；纯粹哲学，宇宙哲学

长难句剖析

【文章难句】Government is not made in virtue of natural rights, which may and do exist in total independence of it, and exist in much greater clearness, and in a much greater degree of abstract perfection.

【结构分析】本句主干是 Government is not made in virtue of natural rights。which 引导的非限制性定语从句用来修饰 natural rights。在这个从句中有两个并列的谓语动词和三个 in 引导的介词短语做方式状语。

【参考译文】政府不是借助于自然权利而成立的，自然权利或许而且肯定是完全不依赖于政府而存在的；并且它们存在于更为纯粹的状态和更加抽象化的完美阶段。

【文章难句】Among these wants is to be reckoned the want, out of civil society, of a sufficient restraint upon their passions.

【结构分析】本句中，the want of a sufficient restraint upon their passions 是主语；谓语动词则是 is to be reckoned out of civil society。Among these wants 修饰主语。

【参考译文】其中对人类感情进行充分限制的需要是被排除于市民社会之外的。

【文章难句】It requires a deep knowledge of human nature and human necessities, and of the things that facilitate or obstruct the various ends, which are to be pursued by the mechanism of civil institutions.

【结构分析】本句主干是 It requires a deep knowledge。两个并列的 of 短语做 knowledge 的后置定语。在第二个 of 短语中，that…ends 是定语从句修饰 the things。在这个从句中还包含一个由 which 引导的非限制性定语从句，用来修饰 ends。

【参考译文】它需要对人性和人类的需求、促进或阻碍各种各样事物发展的因素深入了解，而这些都由民间机构来研究。

【文章难句】Society requires not only that the passions of individuals should be subjected, but that even in the mass and body, as well as in the individuals, the inclinations of men should frequently be thwarted, their will controlled, and their passions brought into subjection.

【结构分析】本句中，主语是 society，谓语动词是 requires，宾语是由 not only…but 连接在一起的两个 that 从句。在第二个 that 从句中有三个并列的句子，第一个是 the inclinations…thwarted，第二和第三个都省略了被动语气中的 be。

【参考译文】社会要求不仅要使个人的感情服从，而且从整个社会来讲，人类不应随心所欲，他们的意愿应受节制，他们的感情也应该变得屈从。

全文参考译文

政府不是借助于自然权利成立的，自然权利或许而且肯定是完全不依靠政府而存在的；并且它们存在于更为纯粹的状态和更加抽象化的完美阶段；但是自然权利抽象化的完美正是它们实际的缺陷。人类对一切事物都有权利，因此想得到一切。政府是人类智慧的发明，用来满足人类的需要。人类有权利让这种智慧满足他们的需要。其中对人类感情进行充分限制的需要是被排除于市民社会之外的。社会要求不仅要使个人的感情服从，而且从整个社会来讲，人类不应随心所欲，他们的意愿应受到节制，他们的感情也应该变得屈从。只有人类自身能力之外的力量才能做到这点，而不会在发生作用的过程中被政府所要抑制和征服的那种意愿和感情支配。从这个意义上讲，对人类及其自由的限制应被算作他们的一种权利。但因为自由和限制总是随着时间和条件在变化，而且需要不断地改进，它们难以用抽象的条文形式确定下来，所以按照规则讨论自由和限制是再愚蠢不过的事情了。

　　在你减少人类所有权利中的任何一项时，人人都开始控制自己并忍受这些人为地加于权利之上的但正当的限制。从那一刻开始，整个政府机构都成为一种便利的因素。正是这一点促使一个国家宪法的产生，及其权利的正当分配，这是一个最棘手和最复杂的技巧问题。它需要对人性和人类的需求、促进或阻碍各种各样事物发展的因素深入了解，而这些都由民间机构来研究。国家通过增加生力军，消除社会动荡。谈论一个人有得到食物和医疗的抽象权利究竟有何用处？这个问题超出了食品和药物采购与管理方法的范畴。鉴于此，我永远建议去援助农民和医生而不是那些形而上学的教授。

题目答案与解析

1.　按照作者的观点，政府 _____。
　　A．是人类发明的　　　　　　　　　B．是借助自然权利创造的
　　C．对所有事物拥有权利　　　　　　D．想得到一切
　　【答案】A
　　【解析】本题的依据是文章第 1 段的第 3 句话 Government is a contrivance of human wisdom to provide for human wants，从中可知 A 项是正确答案。

2.　作者认为，人类的意愿和感情 _____。
　　A．可以由人类自己有效控制
　　B．应该决定政府的政策
　　C．只能够被人类自身能力之外的力量所控制，那种力量不屈服于人类的意愿和感情
　　D．无法控制
　　【答案】C
　　【解析】本题的依据是第 1 段中间的几句话：Society requires not only that the passions of individuals should be subjected, but that even in the mass and body, as well as in the individuals, the inclinations of men should frequently be thwarted, their will controlled, and their passions brought into subjection. This can only be done by a power out of themselves. 从中可知 C 项是正确答案。

3.　对人类及对人类自由的限制 _____。
　　A．与个人利害相关　　　　　　　　B．是人类的权利
　　C．和政府无关　　　　　　　　　　D．人们无法忍受
　　【答案】B
　　【解析】本题的依据是第 1 段倒数第 2 句话 In this sense, the restraints on men, as well as their liberties, are to be reckoned among their rights，因此 B 项是正确答案。

4.　制定一个国家宪法并决定宪法的权限，除了需要对人性和人类的需求有深刻的了解外，还需要了解 _____。
　　A．人类权利的自由和限制
　　B．由民间机构来研究的促进或阻碍各种各样事物发展的因素
　　C．所有人民的意愿
　　D．许多国家的宪法

【答案】B

【解析】本题的依据是文章第 2 段中间的一句话 It（指制定宪法、决定宪法的权限等）requires a deep knowledge of human nature and human necessities, and of the things that facilitate or obstruct the various ends, which are to be pursued by the mechanism of civil institutions，从中可知 B 是正确答案。

Text 4

Habits are a funny thing. We reach for them mindlessly, setting our brains on auto-pilot and relaxing into the unconscious comfort of familiar routine. "Not choice, but habit rules the unreflecting herd," William Wordsworth said in the 19th century. In the ever-changing 21st century, even the word "habit" carries a negative connotation.

So it seems antithetical to talk about habits in the same context as creativity and innovation. But brain researchers have discovered that when we consciously develop new habits, we create parallel synaptic paths, and even entirely new brain cells that can jump our trains of thought onto new, innovative tracks.

Rather than dismissing ourselves as unchangeable creatures of habit, we can instead direct our own change by consciously developing new habits. In fact, the more new things we try—the more we step outside our comfort zone—the more inherently creative we become, both in the workplace and in our personal lives.

But don't bother trying to kill off old habits, once those ruts of procedure are worn into the brain, they're there to stay. Instead, the new habits we deliberately ingrain into ourselves create parallel pathways that can bypass those old roads.

"The first thing needed for innovation is a fascination with wonder," says Dawna Markova, author of *The Open Mind*. "But we are taught instead to 'decide,' just as our president calls himself 'the Decider'." She adds, however, that "to decide is to kill off all possibilities but one. A good innovational thinker is always exploring the many other possibilities."

All of us work through problems in ways of which we're unaware, she says. Researchers in the late 1960s discovered that humans are born with the capacity to approach challenges in four primary ways: analytically, procedurally, relationally (or collaboratively) and innovatively. At the end of adolescence, however, the brain shuts down half of that capacity, preserving only those modes of thought that have seemed most valuable during the first decade or so of life.

The current emphasis on standardized testing highlights analysis and procedure, meaning that few of us inherently use our innovative and collaborative modes of thought. "This breaks the major rule in the American belief system—that anyone can do anything," explains M. J. Ryan, author of the 2006 book *This Year I Will*...and Ms. Markova's business partner. "That's a lie that we have perpetuated, and it fosters commonness. Knowing what you're good at and doing even more of it creates excellence." This is where developing new habits comes in.

1. In Wordsworth's view, "habits" is characterized being _____.

A. casual　　　　B. familiar　　　　C. mechanical　　　D. changeable

2. Brain researchers have discovered that the formation of new habits can be _____.

A. predicted　　　B. regulated　　　　C. traced　　　　D. guided

3. The word "ruts"(Line 1 , Paragraph 4) is closest in meaning to _____.

A. tracks　　　　B. series　　　　　C. characteristics　　D. connections

4. Dawna Markova would most probably agree that _____.

A. ideas are born of a relaxing mind　　　B. innovativeness could be taught

C. decisiveness derives from fantastic ideas　D. curiosity activates creative minds

5. Ryan's comments suggest that the practice of standardized testing _____.

A. prevents new habits from being formed

B. no longer emphasizes commonness

C. maintains the inherent American thinking mode

D. complies with the American belief system

核心词汇注释

bypass/by-pass　['baɪpɑːs,-pæs] *n.*（绕地市镇的）旁道，迂回道；分流术，旁通管 *vt.* 绕过，绕……走；越过，置……于不顾

foster　['fɒstə] *vt.* 促进，助长；培养；养育（非亲生子）；照顾

deliberate　[de'lɪberate] *adj.* 故意的；深思熟虑的 *v.* 仔细考虑

paradoxical　[ˌpærə'dɒksɪkəl] *adj.* 事与愿违的；出乎意料的；怪诞的；自相矛盾的，似是而非的

perpetuate　[pə(ː)'petjueɪt] *vt.* 使永存；使人记住不忘；使不朽 *v.* 使永久化；使持久化；使持续

fascination　[ˌfæsɪ'neɪʃ(ə)n] *n.* 魅力；有魅力的东西；迷恋，陶醉，入迷

adolescence　[ˌædəʊ'lesəns] *n.* 青春期（一般指成年以前由 13 至 15 的发育期），青春

长难句剖析

【文章难句】But brain researchers have discovered that when we consciously develop new habits, we create parallel paths, and even entirely new brain cells, that can jump our trains of thought onto new, innovative tracks.

【结构分析】本句主干是 But brain researchers have discovered。that when we consciously…部分为宾语。该宾语从句中，以 when 引导的从句为时间状语，而第二个以 that 引导的从句 that can jump our brains of thought onto new, innovative tracks 为定语从句，修饰先行词 paths and brain cells。

【参考译文】但研究大脑的人员发现，当我们有意识地形成新的习惯时，我们的大脑就开创了平行但又相互关联的路线。我们甚至还能创造全新的脑细胞，这能使我们思想的列车跳跃到新颖而创新的轨道上。

【文章难句】Rather than dismissing ourselves as unchangeable creatures of habit, we can instead direct our own change by consciously developing new habits.

【结构分析】本句主干是 we can instead direct our own change。by consciously developing new habits 为方式状语，修饰谓语 direct（指导）一词。而句首的 rather than 意为"而不是（而

非）……"，该词置于句首、句中、句末均可。

【参考译文】我们不用拒绝承认自己是一成不变拥有习惯的生物，相反我们可以通过发展新的习惯来有意识地改变。

【文章难句】In fact, the more new things we try—the more we step outside our comfort zone—the more inherently creative we become, both in the workplace and in our personal lives.

【结构分析】本句句型结构为："the+比较级……，the+比较级……"，意为 "越……，越……"。第三个 the more 结构为本句主句，第一个 the more 结构为从句，而第二个 the more 结构（即破折号中间的内容）为从句的同位语，对从句进一步加以解释说明。

【参考译文】事实上，我们对新事物尝试得越多，就会离自己的舒适地带越远，在工作场所及个人生活中就会变得越来越有创造性。

全文参考译文

习惯是个有意思的现象。我们毫无意识就会形成一种习惯，将大脑设置成自动驾驶，不知不觉就会进入一种日常的舒适状态。19 世纪的威廉·华兹华斯这样说道："是习惯而不是选择支配着不会思考的人们。"在不断变化的 21 世纪，即使是"习惯"这个词语也有负面含义。

因此，在此种情形下把习惯等同于创造力和创新似乎有些矛盾。但研究大脑的人员发现，当我们有意识地形成新的习惯时，我们的大脑就开创了平行但又相互关联的路线。我们甚至还能创造全新的脑细胞，这能使我们思想的列车跳跃到新颖而创新的轨道上。

我们不用拒绝承认自己是一成不变拥有习惯的生物，相反我们可以通过发展新的习惯来有意识地改变。事实上，我们对新事物尝试得越多，就会离自己的舒适地带越远，在工作场所及个人生活中就会变得越来越有创造性。

不过，无需为努力改掉旧习惯而烦恼。一旦那些旧惯例的轨迹被磨成辙痕，它们就停留在那里了。相反，当我们慎重地将新习惯深深植入心中时，这些新习惯就会创造出相似的道路，并能绕过那些旧的道路。

道娜·马克耶维奇是《敞开的心灵》的作者，她说："创新首要的就是想象的魅力"。她还补充道："但是我们被教育要学会'作决定'，正像我们的总裁称呼他自己为'决策者'一样。"然而，"作决定意味着除了保留一个外，其他所有的可能性都被扼杀。而一位优秀的创新思维者总是探索其他方面的多种可能性。"

她还说"我们所有人都是在以自己并不了解的方式来处理问题。在 20 世纪 60 年代末，据研究人员所述，人生来就具有应对挑战的能力，主要表现在四个方面：分析、程序、联系（或者合作）和创新。然而在青春期，大脑关闭了那些能力中的一半，只保留了思维方式。在生命最初 10 年左右的时间里，这些思维方式看来是最珍贵的。

目前，标准化测试强调突出了分析和程序，这意味着很少有人运用创新和合作的思维方式。《今年我将……》一书的作者兼马克耶维奇女士的商业合伙人 M. J. 赖安说道："这打破了美国人信仰体系中的主要规则——任何人都能做到，这是一个我们一直铭记在心的谎言，而且它鼓励了共性。了解你所擅长的事物并且完善它，这样才能创造卓越。"这就是培养新习惯的原因。

题目答案与解析

在华兹华斯看来，"习惯"的特点是_____。

1. A. 随意的 B. 熟悉的 C. 机械的 D. 易变的

【答案】C

【解析】本题的依据句是文章第1段的第2句话：Not choice, but habit rules the unreflecting herd.从中可知，C项为正确答案。

2. 大脑研究人员已发现，新习惯的形成可以_____。

A. 预言 B. 调整

C. 追踪 D. 引导

【答案】D

【解析】本题的依据句是文章第2段第2句话和第3段的第1句话：But brain researchers have discovered that when we consciously develop new habits, we create parallel synaptic paths, and even entirely new brain cells, that can jump our trains of thought onto new, innovative tracks. Rather than dismissing ourselves as unchangeable creatures of habit, we can instead direct our own change by consciously developing new habits.从中可知，D项为正确答案。

3. "ruts"该词（第4段，第1行）与下面_____意义最为接近。

A. 踪迹 B. 系列

C. 特点 D. 联系

【答案】A

【解析】本题的依据句是文章第4段：But don't bother trying to kill off old habits, once those ruts of procedure are worn into the brain, they're there to stay. Instead, the new habits we deliberately ingrain into ourselves create parallel pathways that can bypass those old roads.从中可知，A项为正确答案。

4. 道娜·马尔科娃最可能赞同的是_____。

A. 想法产生于放松状态下的大脑 B. 创新可以传授

C. 果断来自于新奇想法 D. 好奇心激发创新思维

【答案】D

【解析】本题的依据句是文章第5段："The first thing needed for innovation is a fascination with wonder,"…A good innovational thinker is always exploring the many other possibilities."从中可知，D项为正确答案。

5. 赖安的评论表明：标准化测试的实行_____。

A. 阻止新习惯的形成

B. 不再注重平庸

C. 保持美国人固有的思维方式

D. 与美国人信仰体系相一致

【答案】A

【解析】本题可参照文章第7段。从中可知，标准化测试的推行对思维方式的创新是一种打击，阻碍了新习惯的形成。因此A项为正确答案。

Unit 5

Text 1

A little more than a century ago, Michael Faraday, the noted British physicist, managed to gain audience with a group of high government officials, to demonstrate an electro-chemical principle, in the hope of gaining support for his work.

After observing the demonstrations closely, one of the officials remarked bluntly, "It's a fascinating demonstration, young man, but just what practical application will come of this?"

"I don't know," replied Faraday, "but I do know that 100 years from now you'll be taxing them."

From the demonstration of a principle to the marketing of products derived from that principle is often a long, involved series of steps. The speed and effectiveness with which these steps are taken are closely related to the history of management, the art of getting things done. Just as management applies to the wonders that have evolved from Faraday and other inventors, so it applied some 4,000 years ago to the working of the great Egyptian and Mesopotamian import and export firms…to Hannibal's remarkable feat of crossing the Alps in 218 B.C. with 90,000 foot soldiers, 12,000 horsemen and a "conveyor belt" of 40 elephants…or to the early Christian Church, with its world-shaking concepts of individual freedom and equality.

These ancient innovators were deeply involved in the problems of authority, divisions of labor, discipline, unity of command, clarity of direction and the other basic factors that are so meaningful to management today. But the real impetus to management as an emerging profession was the Industrial Revolution. Originating in 18-century England, it was triggered by a series of classic inventions and new processes; among them John Kay's flying Shuttle in 1733, James Hargrove's Spinning Jenny in 1770, Samuel Compton's Mule Spinner in 1779 and Edmund Cartwright's Power Loom in 1785.

1. The anecdote about Michael Faraday indicates that _____.
   A. politicians tax everything
   B. people are skeptical about the values of pure research
   C. government should support scientists
   D. he was rejected by his government

2. Management is defined as _____.
   A. the creator of the Industrial Revolution B. supervising subordinates
   C. the art of getting things done   D. an emerging profession

3. Management came into its own _____.
   A. in the Egyptian and Mesopotamian import and export firms

B. in Hannibal's famous trip across the Alps

C. in the development of early Christian Church

D. in the eighteenth century

4. A problem of management NOT mentioned in this passage is _____.

A. the problem of command　　　　　B. division of labor

C. control by authority　　　　　　　D. competition

核心词汇注释

blunt [blʌnt] *adj.* 钝的，生硬的

fascinating [ˈfæsɪneɪtɪŋ] *adj.* 迷人的，醉人的，着魔的

evolve [ɪˈvɒlv] *v.* （使）发展，（使）进展，（使）进化

feat [fi:t] *n.* 技艺，功绩，武艺，壮举，技艺表演

　　　 adj. 漂亮的，合适的

Alps [ælps] *n.* 阿尔卑斯山

convey [kənˈveɪ] *vt.* 搬运，传达，转让

innovator [ˈɪnəuveɪtə(r)] *n.* 改革者，革新者

impetus [ˈɪmpɪtəs] *n.* 推动力，促进

originate [əˈrɪdʒɪneɪt] *vt.* 引起，发明，发起，创办

　　　 vi. 起源，发生

trigger [ˈtrɪgə(r)] *vt.* 引发，引起，触发

　　　 n. 扳机

长难句剖析

【文章难句】A little more than a century ago, Michael Faraday, the noted British physicist, managed to gain audience with a group of high government officials, to demonstrate an electro-chemical principle, in the hope of gaining support for his work.

【结构分析】本句主干是 Michael Faraday…managed to gain audience with。A little more than a century ago 是时间状语，the noted British physicist 是主语的同位语，不定式 to demonstrate 短语做目的状语，而最后的介词词组 in the hope of…是句子的伴随状语。

【参考译文】100 多年前，英国著名的物理学家 Michael Faraday 邀请到一些政府高级官员，为他们演示一种电化原理，以期获得工作上的支持。

【文章难句】The speed and effectiveness with which these steps are taken are closely related to the history of management, the art of getting things done.

【结构分析】本句主干是 The speed and effectiveness…are closely related to the history of management。主语后面紧接着是一个介词 with 前置的定语从句，the art of…做 the history of management 的同位语。

【参考译文】每一步发展的效果与速度都与管理的历史密切相关，管理就是将事情办好的艺术。

【文章难句】So it applied some 4,000 years ago to the working of the great Egyptian and Mesopotamian import and export firms…to Hannibal's remarkable feat of crossing the Alps in 218 B.C. with 90,000 foot soldiers, 12,000 horsemen and a "conveyor belt" of 40 elephants…or to the early Christian Church, with its world-shaking concepts of individual freedom and equality.

【结构分析】本句主干是 it applied…to the working…to Hannibal's remarkable feat…or to the early Christian Church。Some 4,000 years ago 是时间状语。和 apply 搭配的介词 to 后面分别有三个并列的宾语，第一个是动名词结构 the working of…firms，第二个是一个名词词组…feat，后面由 of 加动名词修饰，最后是一个名词词组 the…church，后面的 with…做它的后置定语。

【参考译文】它同样适用于大约 4000 年前由伟大的埃及和美索不达米亚人民所开办的进出口公司里的工作方式……也适用于汉尼拔在公元前 218 年带领 9 万名步兵，12000 个骑兵和一条由 40 头大象组成的"传送带"翻越阿尔卑斯山脉的壮举……或是适用于早期传播举世皆惊的个人自由平等理念的基督教。

全文参考译文

100 多年以前，英国著名的物理学家 Michael Faraday 邀请了一些政府高级官员，为他们演示一种电化原理，以期获得工作上的支持。

仔细观察完演示之后，一位官员很生硬地说道"年轻人，这是一场精彩的演示，可这能带来什么实际应用啊？"

Faraday 回答说："我不知道，不过我知道 100 年后你们将向它征税。"

从原理演示到以此原理为基础的产品在市场上销售常常是一个长期而复杂的发展过程。每一步发展的效果与速度都与管理的历史密切相关，管理就是将事情办好的艺术。就像管理适用于从 Faraday 和其他发明家发展而来的奇迹一样，它同样适用于大约 4000 年前由伟大的埃及和美索不达米亚人民所开办的进出口公司里的工作方式……也适用于汉尼拔在公元前 218 年带领 9 万名步兵、12000 个骑兵和一条由 40 头大象组成的"传送带"翻越阿尔卑斯山脉的壮举……或是适用于早期传播举世皆惊的个人自由平等理念的基督教。

这些古代的革新者就十分关注权威问题、劳动力分配问题、纪律问题、命令统一问题、明确方向问题和其他的基本因素。这些对现代管理仍然很有意义，但是真正推动管理成为一种新兴职业的是工业革命。追溯到 18 世纪的英国，一系列杰出的发明和新工序触发管理的兴起，1733 年 John Kay 的飞梭、1770 年 James Hargrove's 的珍妮纺织机、1779 年 Compton 的骡梭和 1785 年 Cartwright's 动力织布机均包括在其中。

题目答案与解析

1. 有关 Michael Faraday 的故事说明了 _____。
   A. 政客们对所有的东西都征税　　　　B. 人们对纯粹学术研究的价值持怀疑态度
   C. 政府应该支持科学家　　　　　　　D. 他被政府抵制
   【答案】B
   【解析】本题可参照第二段。第二段中一官员问实验虽然精彩，但有什么用？从这句话不难看出人们对于科学新发现都是持怀疑态度的。因此 B 项为正确答案。

2. 管理被定义为 _____。
   A. 工业革命的缔造者　　　　　　　　B. 管理下属
   C. 将事情办好的艺术　　　　　　　　D. 一种新兴职业

【答案】C

【解析】本题的依据是文章第四段的第二句话…are closely related to the history of management, the art of getting things done，从中可知 C 项为正确答案。

3. 管理成为一种独立职业是 _____。

    A．在埃及和美索不达米亚进出口公司里   B．在汉尼拔翻越阿尔卑斯山脉时

    C．在早期基督教的发展时期   D．在 18 世纪

【答案】D

【解析】本题的依据是文章最后一段的 But the real impetus to management as an emerging profession was the Industrial Revolution，从中可知 D 项是正确答案。

4. 本文中未提到的管理问题是 _____。

    A．命令的问题   B．劳动力的分工   C．权威控制   D．竞争

【答案】D

【解析】本题的依据是文章最后一段的 the problems of authority, divisions of labor, discipline, unity of command, clarity of direction，从中可知，提到了管理学上的政令、分工、权威等因素，但没提到竞争。因此 D 项为正确答案。

Text 2

By education, I mean the influence of the environment upon the individual to produce a permanent change in the habits of behavior, of thought and of attitude. It is in being thus susceptible to the environment that man differs from the animals, and the higher animals from the lower. The lower animals are influenced by the environment but not in the direction of changing their habits. Their instinctive responses are few and fixed by heredity. When transferred to an unnatural situation, such an animal is led astray by its instincts. Thus the "ant-lion" whose instinct implies it to bore into loose sand by pushing backwards with abdomen, goes backwards on a plate of glass as soon as danger threatens, and endeavors, with the utmost exertions to bore into it. It knows no other mode of flight, "or if such a lonely animal is engaged upon a chain of actions and is interrupted, it either goes on vainly with the remaining actions (as useless as cultivating an unsown field) or dies in helpless inactivity". Thus a net-making spider which digs a burrow and rims it with a bastion of gravel and bits of wood, when removed from a half finished home, will not begin again, though it will continue another burrow, even one made with a pencil.

Advance in the scale of evolution along such lines as these could only be made by the emergence of creatures with more and more complicated instincts. Such beings we know in the ants and spiders. But another line of advance was destined to open out a much more far-reaching possibility of which we do not see the end perhaps even in man. Habits, instead of being born ready-made (when they are called instincts and not habits at all), were left more and more to the formative influence of the environment, of which the most important factor was the parent who now cared for the young animal during a period of infancy in which vaguer instincts than those of the insects were molded to suit surroundings which might be considerably changed without harm.

This means, one might at first imagine, that gradually heredity becomes less and environment more important. But this is hardly the truth and certainly not the whole truth. For although fixed automatic responses like those of the insect-like creatures are no longer inherited, although selection for purification of that sort is no longer going on, yet selection for educability is very definitely still of importance. The ability to acquire habits can be conceivably inherited just as much as can definite responses to narrow situations. Besides, since a mechanism — is now, for the first time, created by which the individual (in contradiction to the species) can be fitted to the environment, the latter becomes, in another sense, less not more important. And finally, less not the higher animals who possess the power of changing their environment by engineering feats and the like, a power possessed to some extent even by the beaver, and preeminently by man. Environment and heredity are in no case exclusive but always-supplementary factors.

1. Which of the following is the most suitable title for the passage?
   A. The Evolution of Insects.
   B. Environment and Heredity.
   C. Education: The Influence of the Environment.
   D. The Instincts of Animals.
2. What can be inferred from the example of the ant-lion in the first paragraph?
   A. Instincts of animals can lead to unreasonable reactions in strange situations.
   B. When it is engaged in a chain actions it cannot be interrupted.
   C. Environment and heredity are two supplementary factors in the evolution of insects.
   D. Along the lines of evolution heredity becomes less and environment more important.
3. Based on the example provided in the passage, we can tell that when a spider is removed to a new position where half of a net has been made, it will probably _____.
   A. begin a completely new net   B. destroy the half-net
   C. spin the rest of the net   D. stay away from the net
4. Which of the following is true about habits according to the passage?
   A. They are natural endowments to living creatures.
   B. They are more important than instincts to all animals.
   C. They are subject to the formative influence of the environment.
   D. They are destined to open out a much more far-reaching possibility in the evolution of human beings.

核心词汇注释

susceptible   [sə'septɪb(ə)l] *adj.* 易受影响   astray   [ə'streɪ] *adv.* 迷途地，入歧途地
的，易感动的；容许……的   endeavor   [ɪn'devə(r)] *n.* 努力，尽力
n. （因缺乏免疫力而）易得病的人   *vi.* 尽力，努力

exertion [ɪgˈzɜːʃ(ə)n] *n.* 尽力，努力，发挥，行使，运用

mold [məuld] *n.* 模子，铸型
vt. 浇铸，塑造

purification [ˌpjuərɪfɪˈkeɪʃən] *n.* 净化

conceivable [kənˈsiːvəb(ə)l] *adj.* 可能的，想得到的，可想象的

contradiction [ˌkɒntrəˈdɪkʃ(ə)n] *n.* 反驳，矛盾

beaver [ˈbiːvə(r)] *n.* 海狸（毛皮）

preeminent [priːˈemɪnənt] *adj.* 卓越的

长难句剖析

【文章难句】It is in being thus susceptible to the environment that man differs from the animals, and the higher animals from the lower.

【结构分析】本句是一个强调句，正常的语序应该是 man differs from the animals, and the higher animals from the lower in...susceptible...environment。被强调的部分 in being thus susceptible to the environment 做句子的方式状语。

【参考译文】能够如此容易受到环境的影响，这正是人区别于动物的地方，也是高等动物区别于低等动物的不同之处。

【文章难句】Thus the "ant-lion" whose instinct implies it to bore into loose sand by pushing backwards with abdomen, goes backwards on a plate of glass as soon as danger threatens, and endeavors, with the utmost exertions to bore into it.

【结构分析】本句主干是 the "ant-lion"..., goes backwards on a plate of glass...and endeavors。whose 引导的定语从句是用来修饰主语 the "ant-lion" 的，"as soon as...threatens" 作时间状语，最后的 with 短语做伴随状语修饰谓语动词 endeavor。

【参考译文】正如"蚁狮"的本能让它利用腹部努力地向后移动，以钻入松散的细沙，然而却不知面临着很大的危险，而一步步地在玻璃板上后退，尽最大的努力钻进去。

【文章难句】Advance in the scale of evolution along such lines as these could only be made by the emergence of creatures with more and more complicated instincts.

【结构分析】本句主干是 Advance...could only be made by the emergence of creatures。介宾短语 in...在主语 advance 后面做后置定语，along...these 是作为 evolution 的后置定语，with...短语用来修饰 creatures。

【参考译文】生物具有越来越复杂的本能，它们的出现促使这些意义上的进化的发展。

全文参考译文

　　通过教育，我的意思是经由环境的影响，对个体形成一种持久的行为上、思想上乃至心态上的习惯的改变。能够如此易受环境的影响正是人区别于动物的地方，也是高等动物区别于低等动物的不同之处。低等动物会受环境的影响，但不会直接引起习惯的改变。它们（低等动物）的本能反应极少而且固定地由遗传决定。当换到一个非自然的环境中时，这种动物就会被它们的本能带入歧途。正如"蚁狮"的本能让它利用腹部蠕动努力地向后移动，以钻入松散的细沙，而当它处于一块玻璃之上，它仍试图用老办法，尽最大的努力以图钻到玻璃之内，而这却给它带来了致命的危险。它们找不到任何其他方式去逃脱险境，"或者说，这样一种孤独的动物，在忙碌于一系列的动作中时，一旦被打断，那么它要么徒劳地完成剩余的

动作（就像在一片没有播种的土地上耕作），要么死于无助的静止状态"。因此当蜘蛛挖了一个地洞并且在地洞边缘用砂砾和木片修建蛛网时，如果它离开了已经结了一半的网，则无论如何也不会再从头开始，尽管它也许会继续挖另一个洞穴，甚至是用铅笔作为原料，但也不会重复以前的工作。

生物具有越来越复杂的本能，它们的出现促使这些意义上的进化的发展。就我们所知，这种生物有蚂蚁和蜘蛛。但是另一种意义上的发展却注定会开辟出一种更有深远意义的可能性，即使是在人类身上，我们也没有看到这种可能性的结果。习惯，并不是生来就有的（有时它们被叫做本能而不是习惯），它们已经越来越受到环境的影响了。而环境影响中最重要的因素是我们的父母，他们照料在婴儿期的幼小生命，在这个期间，那些比昆虫的本能还要模糊一些的本能就会作出相当大的无害的变化以适应环境的需要。

这样我们首先会想到，这意味着环境的影响愈加重要，而遗传的作用却在减小。可是很难说这就是正确的，不过肯定不是完全正确的。因为尽管像昆虫一样的固定的机械式的反应已经不再是遗传所致，尽管物种进化选择已经不复存在，但是关于可塑性的选择显然还是非常重要的。正如对于恶劣的环境可以作出积极的回应一样，获得习性的能力的确可以遗传。另外，一些新的机制产生。利用这些机制，个体（相对于物种而言）就可以很好地适应环境。这样一来，环境的影响就显得不那么重要了。最后，高等动物可以通过类似工程技艺等的东西来改变环境。从某种程度上说，海狸就具有这种能力，而人类在这方面具有卓越的能力。环境与遗传绝不是相互排斥的因素，而永远都是相辅相成的因素。

题目答案与解析

1. 以下各项中"_____"最适合作为本文的标题？
   A. 昆虫的进化   B. 环境与遗传   C. 教育：环境的影响   D. 动物的本能
   【答案】B
   【解析】从文中内容可知，作者是在讲外部环境和遗传是互补的因素。四个选项中，只有B项包含了外部环境和遗传两个方面，因此B项为正确答案。

2. 我们可以从第1段蚁狮的例子中推断出什么？
   A. 动物的本能会导致陌生环境下的不合理反应。
   B. 当它进行一系列动作时不能被打断。
   C. 在昆虫的进化过程中，环境和遗传只是辅助因素。
   D. 沿着进化的路线，遗传的重要性降低，而环境的重要性提高
   【答案】B
   【解析】本题可参照第1段中间一句话 if such a lonely animal is engaged upon a chain of actions and is interrupted, it either goes on vainly with the remaining actions…or dies in helpless inactivity，从中可知，蚁狮会执著地作出本能的反应。因此B项为正确答案。

3. 根据本文提供的例子，我们知道如果蜘蛛被移至一个已经有一个织了一半的网的新地方时，它最可能_____。
   A. 开始做一个新网   B. 破坏那半张网
   C. 继续织网的剩余部分   D. 离开那张网
   【答案】D

【解析】本题可参照第 1 段的 when removed from a half finished home, will not begin again。因此 D 项是正确答案。

4．根据文中内容，下面关于习性的句子中哪一句是正确的？

    A．习性是自然给予活着的动物的馈赠。

    B．对于所有动物来讲，习性比本能更重要。

    C．习性受到环境发展的影响。

    D．习性注定可以揭示人类进化过程中存在更加广泛的可能。

【答案】C

【解析】本题可参照文章第 2 段的 Habits, instead of being born ready-made…were left more and more to the formative influence of the environment. 从中可知 C 项为正确答案。

Text 3

It is a wise father that knows his own child, but today a man can boost his paternal (fatherly) wisdom — or at least confirm that he's the kid's dad. All he needs to do is shell out $ 30 for paternity testing kit (PTK)at his local drugstore — and another $ 120 to get the results.

More than 60,000 people have purchased the PTKs since they first become available without prescriptions last years, according to Doug Fog, chief operating officer of Identigene, which makes the over-the-counter kits. More than two dozen companies sell DNA tests directly to the public, ranging in price from a few hundred dollars to more than $ 2500.

Among the most popular: paternity and kinship testing, which adopted children can use to find their biological relatives and latest rage a many passionate genealogists — and supports businesses that offer to search for a family's geographic roots.

Most tests require collecting cells by swabbing saliva in the mouth and sending it to the company for testing. All tests require a potential candidate with whom to compare DNA.

But some observers are skeptical, "There is a kind of false precision being hawked by people claiming they are doing ancestry testing," says Trey Duster, a New York University sociologist. He notes that each individual has many ancestors — numbering in the hundreds just a few centuries back. Yet most ancestry testing only considers a single lineage, either the Y chromosome inherited through men in a father's line or mitochondrial DNA, which a passed down only from mothers. This DNA can reveal genetic information about only one or two ancestors, even though, for example, just three generations back people also have six other great-grandparents or, four generations back, 14 other great-great-grandparents.

Critics also argue that commercial genetic testing is only as good as the reference collections to which a sample is compared. Databases used by some companies don't rely on data collected systematically but rather lump together information from different research projects. This means that a DNA database may have a lot of data from some regions and not others, so a person's test results may differ depending on the company that processes the results. In addition, the computer programs a company uses to estimate relationships may be patented and not subject to peer review or outside evaluation.

1. In paragraphs 1 and 2, the text shows PTK's _____.
   A. easy availability
   B. flexibility in pricing
   C. successful promotion
   D. popularity with households

2. PTK is used to _____.
   A. locate one's birth place
   B. promote genetic research
   C. identify parent-child kinship
   D. choose children for adoption

3. Skeptical observers believe that ancestry testing fails to _____.
   A. trace distant ancestors
   B. rebuild reliable bloodlines
   C. fully use genetic information
   D. achieve the claimed accuracy

4. In the last paragraph, a problem commercial genetic testing faces is _____.
   A. disorganized data collection
   B. overlapping database building
   C. excessive sample comparison
   D. lack of patent evaluation

5. An appropriate title for the text is most likely to be _____.
   A. Fors and Againsts of DNA Testing
   B. DNA Testing and It's Problems
   C. DNA Testing Outside the Lab
   D. Lies behind DNA Testing

核心词汇注释

boost [buːst] *v.* 提升，增加，提高
　　n. 提升，增加，提高
paternity [pəˈtəːniti] *n.* 父亲的身份〔地位〕
prescription [priˈskripʃən] *n.* 处方；命令，法规
kinship [ˈkinʃip] *n.* 亲属关系；（因起源或态度相似而产生的）亲切感
saliva [səˈlaivə] *n.* 唾液，口水
swab [swɔb] *n.* （医用的）药签；（用拭子取下的）化验标准
　　vt. 用拭子拭抹或擦净；（用拖把、抹布等）擦洗

长难句剖析

【文章难句】It is a wise father that knows his own child, but today a man can boost his paternal (fatherly) wisdom — or at least confirm that he's the kid's dad.

【结构分析】本句由两个并列句构成，连接词为 but。第一个分句为强调句，句型结构为："It is(was)+强调部分+ that +剩余部分"，强调该句的主语为 a wise father；转折部分句子主干

为 a man can boost or confirm that，其中 that 引导的宾语从句在此处充当 confirm 的宾语。

【参考译文】了解自己孩子的父亲才是明智的，但是如今的男人能够增进做父亲的智慧——或者至少能够确定他是孩子的父亲。

【文章难句】This DNA can reveal genetic information about only one or two ancestors, even though, for example, just three generations back people also have six other great-grandparents or, four generations back, 14 other great-great-grandparents.

【结构分析】本句主干是 This DNA can reveal genetic information。even though 引导让步状语从句。此从句包括两个由 or 连接的部分：people also have six other great-grandparents or, four generations back, (people have)14 other great-great-grandparents，三者为并列成分，省略了动词 have。

【参考译文】这种 DNA 只能显示出一两个祖先的遗传信息。即便如此，举例来说，就在三代人之前人们也有六个曾祖父母，或者四代人之前有十四个曾曾祖父母。

【文章难句】Critics also argue that commercial genetic testing is only as good as the reference collections to which a sample is compared.

【结构分析】本句主干是 Critics also argue that...。that 引导宾语从句。从句的主干为 commercial genetic testing is as good as...，as good as 为比较结构。

【参考译文】评论家们有争议，商业基因鉴定仅相当于将样本与收集的数据作比较。

【文章难句】Databases used by some companies don't rely on data collected systematically but rather lump together information from different research projects.

【结构分析】本句句子主干：Databases don't rely on data...but rather...。

【参考译文】一些公司使用的数据库并不依赖于系统的数据收集，而是把不同研究机构收集的信息合在一起。

全文参考译文

了解自己孩子的父亲才是明智的，但是如今的男人能够增进做父亲的智慧——或者至少能够确定他是孩子的父亲。他所需要做的就是花上 30 美元在本地药房买套亲子鉴定工具，然后再花 120 美元以获得鉴定结果。

自从去年不需要处方就可购买亲子鉴定工具后，现已有 6 万多人购买了。该消息出自遗传基因公司的首席运营官道阁·福格之口，该公司制造柜台出售的全套亲子鉴定工具。直接向公众提供基因检测的公司超过 24 家，价格在几百美元到 2500 多美元之间。

被收养的孩子可以通过亲子鉴定和亲属关系鉴定来找到和他具有血缘关系的亲属，但最近这种鉴定是许多热心的谱系学家的时尚做法，从技术上支持那些为探寻一个家族的祖籍提供亲子鉴定的公司。

多数鉴定需要通过采集口腔的唾液来收集细胞，然后将样本送到公司去鉴定。所有的鉴定都需要有一个潜在的、与被测的 DNA 相比较的对比者。

但是一些观察人员对此持怀疑态度。"那些声称正在做祖先鉴定的人们所宣扬的（祖先鉴定）精确度其实是虚假的，"纽约大学的社会学家特洛伊·达斯特如是说道。他指出了几个世纪前，在某些郡中每个人都有很多祖先编排方式。然而，多数祖先鉴定只考虑了一个单独的谱系，或者是从父系那里遗传来的 Y 染色体，或者只是从母系那里遗传来的线粒体 DNA。

这种 DNA 只能显示出一两个祖先的遗传信息。即便如此，举例来说，就在三代人之前人们也有六个曾祖父母，或者四代人之前有十四个曾曾祖父母。

评论家们有争议，商业基因鉴定仅相当于将样本与收集的数据作比较。一些公司使用的数据库并不依赖于系统的数据收集，而是把不同研究机构收集的信息合在一起。这就意味着处理数据的公司不同，所用的 DNA 数据库也会不同。另外，一个公司使用的鉴定亲属关系的电脑程序可能被申请专利，因此不受同级评审或者外界评估的影响。

题目答案与解析

1. 第一、二段中，文章表明亲子鉴定工具包 _____。

    A．容易获得   B．价格灵活

    C．成功促销   D．受家庭追捧

【答案】A

【解析】本题的依据句是文章第 1 段的最后 1 句话和第 2 段的第 1 句话：All he needs to do is shell out $ 30 for paternity testing kit (PTK) at his local drugstore — and another $ 120 to get the results. More than 60,000 people have purchased the PTKs since they first become available without prescriptions last years. 从中可知，A 项为正确答案。

2. 亲子鉴定工具包被用于 _____。

    A．点明出生地   B．加快基因研究

    C．确认亲子关系   D．选择孩子领养

【答案】C

【解析】本题可参照文章第 3 段。从中可知，基因检测有助于被领养的孩子寻找生物学上的亲属，而家庭可以用它来寻找孩子的下落。它是谱系学家最流行的做法，还能帮助寻找家族地理根源。因此 C 项为正确答案。

3. 持怀疑态度的观察家认为家谱检测无法 _____。

    A．追溯年代久远的祖辈   B．重建可信赖的血统谱系

    C．使基因信息得到充分利用   D．达到所称精准度

【答案】D

【解析】本题的依据句是文章第 5 段的前两句话：But some observers are skeptical, "There is a kind of false precision being hawked by people claiming they are doing ancestry testing," says Trey Duster, a New York University sociologist. He notes that each individual has many ancestors — numbering in the hundreds just a few centuries back. 从中可知，D 项为正确答案。

4. 在文章最后一段中，商业基因检测所面临的一个问题是 _____。

    A．数据收集乱无章法   B．数据建设部分重复

    C．过度比较样本   D．缺乏专利评估

【答案】A

【解析】本题的依据句是第 6 段的第 2 句话：Databases used by some companies don't rely on data collected systematically but rather lump together information from different research projects. 从中可知 A 项为正确答案。

5. 本文最为合适的标题可能是 _____。

A．DNA 检测之利与弊
B．DNA 检测与其问题
C．实验室外的 DNA 检测
D．DNA 检测背后的谎言

【答案】B

【解析】本题可参照全文内容。文章开篇即以名人名言引出话题，然后介绍 DNA 检测的特征、用途、要求，再针对 DNA 检测的精确性、数据库的系统性以及计算机系统可的靠性提出质疑。因此 B 项为正确答案。

Text 4

The truly incompetent may never know the depths of their own incompetence, a pair of social psychologists said on Thursday. "We found again and again that people who perform poorly relative to their peers tended to think that they did rather well," Justin Kruger, co-author of a study on the subject, said in a telephone interview.

Kruger and co-author David Dunning found that when it came to a variety of skills — logical reasoning, grammar, even sense of humor — people who essentially were inept never realized it, while those who had some ability were self-critical.

"It had little to do with innate modesty," Kruger said, "but rather with a central paradox: Incompetents lack the basic skills to evaluate their performance realistically. Once they get those skills, they know where they stand, even if that is at the bottom."

"Americans and Western Europeans especially had an unrealistically sunny assessment of their own capabilities," Dunning said by telephone in a separate interview, "while Japanese and Koreans tended to give a reasonable assessment of their performance. In certain areas, such as athletic performance, which can be easily quantified, there is less self-delusion, the researchers said. But even in some cases in which the failure should seem obvious, the perpetrator is blithely unaware of the problem."

This was especially true in the areas of logical reasoning, where research subjects — students at Cornell University, where the two researchers were based — often rated themselves highly even when they flubbed all questions in a reasoning test.

Later, when the students were instructed in logical reasoning, they scored better on a test but rate themselves lower, having learned what constituted competence in this area.

Grammar was another area in which objective knowledge was helpful in determining competence, but the more subjective area of humor posed different challenges, the researchers said.

Participants were asked to rate how funny certain jokes were, and compare their responses with what an expert panel of comedians thought. On average, participants overestimated their sense of humor by about 16 percentage points.

This might be thought of as the "above-average effect", the notion that most Americans would rate themselves as above average, a statistical impossibility.

The researchers also conducted pilot studies of doctors and gun enthusiasts. The doctors overestimated how well they had performed on a test of medical diagnoses and the gun fanciers thought they knew more than they actually did about gun safety.

So who should be trusted: The person who admits incompetence or the one who shows confidence? Neither, according to Dunning.

"You can't take them at their word. You've got to take a look at their performance," Dunning added.

1. Why do incompetent people rarely know they are inept?
    A. They are too inept to know what competence is.
    B. They are not skillful at logical reasoning, grammar, and sense of humor.
    C. They lack the basic skills to evaluate their performance realistically.
    D. They have some ability to over criticize themselves.

2. Which of the following statement is NOT true, according to the passage?
    A. Students at Cornell University often rated themselves highly even when they flubbed all questions in a reasoning test.
    B. Grammar was an area in which objective knowledge was helpful in determining competence.
    C. Participants in the test estimated their sense of humor by about 16 percentage points.
    D. Students scored better on a logical reasoning test but rated themselves lower.

3. What do you know about "above-average effect" based on the passage?
    A. Most Americans assess themselves as above average.
    B. American doctors overestimated how well they had performed on a test of medical diagnoses.
    C. American gun enthusiasts thought they knew more than they actually did about gun safety.
    D. All of the above.

核心词汇注释

peer [pɪə(r)] *n.* 同等的人，贵族
 vi. 凝视，窥视
 vt. 与……同等，封为贵族

inept [ɪ'nept] *adj.* 不适当的，无能的，不称职的

innate [ɪ'neɪt] *adj.* 先天的，天生的

paradox ['pærədɒks] *n.* 似非而是的论点，自相矛盾的话

self-delusion ['selfdɪ'luːʒ(ə)n] *n.* 自欺

blithe [blaɪð] *adj.* 愉快的，高兴的

flub [flʌb] *vt.* 搞坏，把……搞得一团糟，做得不好，弄糟
 vi. 搞错，瞎搞
 n. 失策

comedian [kə'miːdɪən] *n.* 喜剧演员

diagnose ['daɪəgnəuz] *v.* 诊断

fancier ['fænsɪə(r)] *n.* 空想家，培育动物（或植物）的行家，爱好者

长难句剖析

【文章难句】We found again and again that people who perform poorly relative to their peers tended to think that they did rather well.

【结构分析】本句主干是 We found…that people…tended to think that they did rather well.

people 后面是 who 引导的定语从句。

【参考译文】我们一次又一次地发现，那些相对于同等人表现很差的人，往往认为他们做得相当好。

【文章难句】Kruger and co-author David Dunning found that when it came to a variety of skills — logical reasoning, grammar, even sense of humor — people who essentially were inept（无能的，愚蠢的）never realized it, while those who had some ability were self-critical.

【结构分析】本句中，that 引导的宾语从句中一开始是由 when 引导的时间状语从句，破折号中间的部分是进一步解释前面的 a variety of skills，后面出现了主句的主语 people，紧接着是由 who 引导的定语从句修饰 people，while 是个连词，连接了宾语从句中两个并列的主句。

【参考译文】Kruger 和合作者 David Dunning 发现当说到各种技巧，如逻辑推理、语法，甚至是幽默感的时候，那些无能之辈总是不知深浅，而那些有能力的人则是进行自我批评。

【文章难句】Later, when the students were instructed in logical reasoning, they scored better on a test but rate themselves lower, having learned what constituted competence in this area.

【结构分析】本句是一个主从复合句，主句是 they…lower；when 引导的是时间状语从句；现在分词结构 having learned…area 做原因状语。

【参考译文】稍后，当学生们接受逻辑推理辅导的时候，他们考试成绩有所提高，但对自己的评价却降低了，因为他们知道这一方面的能力包含什么内容。

全文参考译文

两位社会心理学家在这个星期四说，真正没有能力的人也许永远不知道他们无能到何种程度。这一课题研究的合作者 Justin Kruger 在一次电话访谈中说："我们一再地发现那些相对于同等人表现很差的人，往往认为他们做得相当好。"

Kruger 和合作者 David Dunning 发现，当说到各种技巧，如逻辑推理、语法，甚至是幽默感的时候，那些没有能力的人总是不知深浅，而那些有能力的人则是进行自我批评。

"这和天性谦虚没有什么关系，" Kruger 说，"不过却和一句自相矛盾的话有关：无能的人缺乏实际评估自己表现的基本技巧。一旦他们获得这样的技巧，他们就知道他们所在的位置，即使是处于最落后的位置。"

在一次单独采访中 Dunning 通过电话说："尤其是美国人和西欧人对他们自己能力的评价高得不切实际，而日本人和韩国人常常对自己的表现进行合理的评价。研究者认为有些方面，像运动中的表现，可以轻易得到量化，这样自我欺骗就会比较少。但甚至在有些失败已是显而易见的情况下，事主仍然乐呵呵地没有意识到问题。"

这种情况在逻辑推理方面更是如此，在逻辑推理研究中，康奈尔大学是这两位研究人员的基地。作为研究受试者，那里的学生经常对自己评价过高，即便他们在逻辑推理考试中把所有问题都答得一团糟。

当学生们随后接受逻辑推理辅导的时候，他们考试成绩有所提高但对自己的评价却降低了，因为他们知道这一方面的能力包含什么内容。

研究人员说，在语法这个领域中能力取决于客观知识，但在幽默这个更主观的领域，情况就不同了。

　　参与人员被要求评价某些笑话的有趣程度，接着把他们的答案与喜剧演员专家组的想法进行比较。参与者对自己的幽默感通常高估了 16%。

　　这可能被认为是"中等偏上效果"，这个观点认为大多数美国人对自己的评价高于平均水平，在统计学上这是不可能的事情。

　　研究人员对医生和枪支迷进行了初步研究。医生都过高地估计他们在医学诊断考试中的成绩，枪支爱好者认为自己对枪支安全很了解，但事实上不是这样。

　　那么应该相信谁：那些承认自己无能的人，还是表现自信的人？根据 Dunning 的观点，两者都不能相信。

　　Dunning 补充说："你不能相信他们的话。你应该看看他们的表现。"

题目答案解析

1. 没有能力的人很少能认识到他们无能的原因是什么？

   A．因为他们太过无能，以至于不知道能力是什么。

   B．他们不擅长逻辑推理、语法和幽默感。

   C．他们缺乏评价自己实际表现的基本技能。

   D．他们有过度指责自己的能力。

   【答案】C

   【解析】本题可参照文章的第 4 段。从 It had little to do with innate modesty 和 Incompetents lack the basic skills to evaluate their performance realistically 可知 C 项是正确答案。

2. 根据本篇文章，以下哪一项陈述是错误的？

   A．康奈尔大学的学生经常对自己评价过高，即使他们在逻辑推理考试中把所有问题都答得一团糟。

   B．在语法这个领域中客观知识对能力有益。

   C．参与者对自己的幽默感估计为 16%。

   D．学生逻辑推理考试成绩有所提高但对自己的评价却降低了。

   【答案】C

   【解析】本题中，A、B、D 三项在文中都曾提及，并与原文相符。C 项与文章第 8 段的最后一句话 participants overestimated their sense of humor by about 16 percentage points 内容相悖，因此 C 项是正确答案。

3. 根据本篇文章，你对于"中等偏上效果"如何理解？

   A．大多数美国人评价自己为中等偏上。

   B．美国医生高估了自己在医学诊断测试中的表现。

   C．美国枪支爱好者认为他们了解的枪支的安全性知识比他们实际上了解的要多。

   D．以上所有。

   【答案】D

   【解析】本题可参照文章的第 9 段。从中可知，the notion that most Americans would rate themselves as above average。而接下来的一段作者又举了两个例子，一个是美国的医生，还有一个是枪支迷，因此 D 项是正确答案。

Unit 6

Text 1

Less than 40 years ago in the United States, it was common to change a one-dollar bill for a dollar's worth of silver. That is because the coins were actually made of silver. But those days are gone. There is no silver in today's coins. When the price of the precious metal rises above its face value as money, the metal will become more valuable in other uses. Silver coins are no longer in circulation because the silver in coins is worth much more than their face value. A silver firm could find that it is cheaper to obtain silver by melting down coins than by buying it on the commodity markets. Coins today are made of an alloy of cheaper metals.

Gresham's Law, named after Sir Thomas Gresham, argues that "good money" is driven out of circulation by "bad money". Good money differs from bad money because it has higher commodity value.

Gresham lived in the 16th century in England where it was common for gold and silver coins to be debased. Governments did this by mixing cheaper metals with gold and silver. The governments could thus make a profit in coinage by issuing coins that had less precious metal than the face value indicated. Because different mixings of coins had different amounts of gold and silver, even though they bore the same face value, some coins were worth more than others as commodities. People who dealt with gold and silver could easily see the difference between the "good" and the "bad" money. Gresham observed that coins with a higher content of gold and silver were kept rather than being used in exchange, or were melted down for their precious metal. In the mid-1960s when the U.S. issued new coins to replace silver coins, Gresham's law went right in action.

1. Why was it possible for Americans to use a one-dollar bill for a dollar's worth of silver?
    A. Because there was a lot of silver in the United States.
    B. Because money was the medium of payment.
    C. Because coins were made of silver.
    D. Because silver was considered worthless.

2. Today's coins in the United States are made of_____.
    A. some precious metals
    B. silver and some precious metals
    C. various expensive metals
    D. some inexpensive metals

3. What is the difference between "good money" and "bad money"?
    A. They are circulated in different markets.
    B. They are issued in different face values.
    C. They are made of different amounts of gold and silver.
    D. They have different uses.

4. What was the purpose of the governments issuing new coins by mixing cheaper metals with

gold and silver in the 16th century?

A. They wanted to reserve some gold and silver for themselves.

B. There was neither enough gold nor enough silver.

C. New coins were easier to be made.

D. They could make money.

核心词汇注释

circulation [ˌsɜːkjʊˈleɪʃ(ə)n] *n.* 循环，流通，发行额

melting [ˈmeltɪŋ] *adj.* 熔化的，融化的，溶解的，混合的

commodity [kəˈmɒdɪtɪ] *n.* 日用品

alloy [ˈælɔɪ] *n.* 合金
vt. 使成合金，减低成色

argue [ˈɑːgjuː] *vi.* 争论，辩论
vt. 说服

differ [ˈdɪfə(r)] *vi.* 不一致，不同

debase [dɪˈbeɪs] *vt.* 贬低，降低

coinage [ˈkɔɪnɪdʒ] *n.* 造币；货币制度；创造；新造的字及词语等

content [ˈkɒntent] *n.* 内容，容量；目录；满足
adj. 满足的，满意的，愿意的
vt. 使满足

replace [rɪˈpleɪs] *vt.* 取代，替换，代替；把……放回原处

长难句剖析

【文章难句】A silver firm could find that it is cheaper to obtain silver by melting down coins than by buying it on the commodity markets.

【结构分析】本句中，主语是 A silver firm，谓语动词是 find, that 引导的从句做宾语。在宾语从句中应用了比较级，方式状语 "by…" 是比较的部分。

【参考译文】银制品公司会发现通过熔化银币获得银比从市场上购买要便宜。

【文章难句】Gresham's Law, named after Sir Thomas Gresham, argues that "good money" is driven out of circulation by "bad money".

【结构分析】本句主干是 Gresham's Law…argues that…。过去分词 named after…做主语的后置定语，谓语动词 argue 后接由 that 引导的宾语从句。

【参考译文】以托马斯·格雷欣爵士的名字命名的格雷欣法则，认为"良币"被"劣币"驱逐出流通领域。

【文章难句】Because different mixings of coins had different amounts of gold and silver, even though they bore the same face value, some coins were worth more than others as commodities.

【结构分析】本句是一个主从复合句。主句是 some…commodities，从句是由 because 引导的原因状语从句，even though 引导的是让步状语从句。

【参考译文】因为混合方法不同，金银含量也不同，所以即使钱币上标示的面值一样，有些钱币也比其他的钱币商品价值高。

全文参考译文

30 多年前，在美国，把一美元钞票换成价值一美元的银币是很平常的事情。不过这

种日子一去不复返了。现在硬币中已经不含银了。当这种珍贵金属的价值升到高于它作为货币的面值后，它作为其他用途就更有价值了。因为钱币中的银比它的面值值钱得多，所以银币不再出现在流通领域。银制品公司会发现通过熔化银币获得银比从市场上购买要便宜。现在钱币都是用便宜的金属合金铸造的。以托马斯·格雷欣爵士的名字命名的格雷欣法则，认为"良币"被"劣币"驱逐出流通领域。良币有更高的商品价值是良币与劣币的区别。

格雷欣生活在 16 世纪的英格兰。当时降低金币或银币的成色是很普遍的。政府将廉价的金属和金银混合在一起降低钱币成色。这样，政府就可以通过发行珍贵金属含量低于面值的钱币获取利益。因为混合方法不同，金银含量也不同，因此即便钱币上标示的面值一样，有些钱币也比其他的钱币商品价值高。用金银做交易的人很容易看出"良币"和"劣币"的差异。格雷欣观察到了金银含量高的钱币更多地被保存了下来，而不是用来交换，或者被熔化以提取贵重金属。20 世纪 60 年代中期，美国发行了新的钱币取代银币，格雷欣法则正式开始实施。

题目答案与解析

1. 美国人可以用 1 美元钞票兑换成价值 1 美元银币的原因是什么？
   - A．因为美国当时有大量的银。
   - B．因为钱是付款的中介物。
   - C．因为硬币是由银制成的。
   - D．因为银被认为是没有价值的。

   【答案】C

   【解析】本题可参照文章第 1 段的 it was common to change a one-dollar bill for a dollar's worth of silver。从中可知，以前用一美金钞票兑换价值一美元的银币是很平常的事情，紧接着作者给出了原因——银币在当时的确是由银制作的。因此 C 项是正确答案。

2. 美国现在的硬币是由 _____ 制作的。
   - A．一些珍贵的金属
   - B．银和一些珍贵的金属
   - C．各种昂贵的金属
   - D．一些便宜的金属

   【答案】D

   【解析】本题的依据是文章第 1 段最后一句话 Coins today are made of an alloy of cheaper metals。因此 D 项为正确答案。

3. "良币"和"劣币"之间有什么区别？
   - A．他们在不同的市场流通。
   - B．他们发行的面值不同。
   - C．他们的金银含量不同。
   - D．他们有不同的用途。

   【答案】C

   【解析】本题可参照文章第 2 段的第 2 句话，从中可知良币和劣币的差别在于他们有不同的商品价值，而第 3 段中又提到政府使用便宜的金属和金银混合以降低货币的实际价值，而且做金银交易的人可以分别出两种货币的不同，因此 C 项为正确答案。

4. 16 世纪政府发行用廉价金属和金银混制成的新型硬币的目的是什么？
   - A．他们想私自把金银保存起来。
   - B．没有足够的金和银。
   - C．新硬币容易制作。
   - D．他们可以赚钱。

   【答案】D

【解析】本题的依据是文章最后一段的第 3 句话 The governments could thus make a profit in coinage by issuing coins that had less precious metal than the face value indicated. 从中可知 D 项为正确答案。

Text 2

By the mid-nineteenth century, the term "ice-box" had entered the American language, but ice was still only beginning to affect the diet of ordinary citizens in the United States: The ice trade grew with the growth of cities. Ice was used in hotels, taverns, and hospitals, and by some forward-looking city dealers in fresh meat, fresh fish, and butter. After the Civil War (1861-1865), as ice was used to refrigerate freight cars, it also came into household use. Even before 1880, half the ice sold in New York, Philadelphia, and Baltimore, and one-third of that sold in Boston and Chicago, went to families for their own use. This had become possible because a new household convenience, the icebox, a precursor of the modern refrigerator, had been invented.

Making an efficient icebox was not as easy as we might now suppose: In the early nineteenth century, the knowledge of heat, which was essential to a science of refrigeration, was rudimentary. The commonsense notion that the best icebox was one that prevented the ice from melting was of course mistaken, for it was the melting of ice that performed the cooling. Nevertheless, early efforts to economize ice included wrapping the ice in blankets, which kept the ice from doing its job. Not until near the end of the nineteenth century did inventors achieve the delicate balance of insulation and circulation needed for an efficient icebox.

But as early as 1803, an ingenious Maryland farmer, Thomas Moore, had been on the right track. He owned a farm about twenty miles outside the city of Washington, for which the village of Georgetown was the market center. When he used an icebox of his own design to transport his butter to market, he found that customers would pass up the rapidly melting stuff in the tubs of his competitors to pay a premium price for his butter, still fresh and hard in neat, one-pound bricks. One advantage of his icebox, Moore explained, was that farmers would no longer have to travel to market at night in order to keep their produce cool.

1. What is the main idea of this passage?
    A. The influence of ice on the diet.   B. The transportation of goods to market.
    C. The development of refrigeration.   D. Sources of the term "ice-box".
2. According to the passage, when did the word "ice-box" become part of the American language?
    A. In 1803.   B. Around 1850.
    C. During the Civil War.   D. Before 1880.
3. The word "rudimentary" in Paragraph 2 is closest in meaning to _____.
    A. basic   B. sufficient
    C. necessary   D. undeveloped
4. The sentence "Thomas Moore, had been on the right track". (Para. 3) indicates that _____.
    A. Moore's farm was not far away from Washington

  B.　Moore's farm was on the right road

  C.　Moore's design was completely successful

  D.　Moore was suitable for the job

核心词汇注释

diet ['daɪət] *n.* 通常所吃的食物

tavern ['tæv(ə)n] *n.* 酒馆，客栈

Baltimore ['bɔ:ltɪmɔ:(r)] *n.* 巴尔的摩（美国马里兰州的一所城市）

precursor [,pri:'kɜ:sə(r)] *n.* 先驱

rudimentary [,ru:dɪ'mentərɪ] *adj.* 根本的，未发展的

commonsense [,kɒmən'sens] *adj.* 具有常识的

economize [ɪ'kɒnəmaɪz] *v.* 节约，节省；有效地利用

insulation [,ɪnsjʊ'leɪ[n](ə)n] *n.* 绝缘

ingenious [ɪn'dʒi:nɪəs] *adj.* 机灵的；有独创性的；精制的；具有创造才能的

premium ['pri:mɪəm] *n.* 额外费用；奖金，奖赏；保险费；（货币兑现的）贴水

长难句剖析

  【文章难句】Even before 1880, half the ice sold in New York, Philadelphia, and Baltimore, and one-third of that sold in Boston and Chicago, went to families for their own use.

  【结构分析】本句是一个简单句。主干是…half the ice…and one-third of that…went to families…。even before 1880 是时间状语，过去分词结构 sold in New York…做后置定语，for their own use 做目的状语。

  【参考译文】甚至在 1880 年前，半数在纽约、费城、巴尔的摩销售的冰，三分之一在波士顿和芝加哥销售的冰进入家庭供使用。

  【文章难句】The commonsense notion that the best icebox was one that prevented the ice from melting was of course mistaken, for it was the melting of ice that performed the cooling.

  【结构分析】本句主干是 The commonsense notion…was of course mistaken。that 引导的从句做主语 notion 的同位语成分，for 引导的短语做原因状语。原因状语中使用了强调句，被强调的部分是这个从句的主语 the melting of ice。

  【参考译文】那种认为最好的冰盒就是阻止冰融化的常识自然是错误的，因为正是冰的融化才导致冷却。

  【文章难句】Not until near the end of the nineteenth century did inventors achieve the delicate balance of insulation and circulation needed for an efficient icebox.

  【结构分析】本句是倒装结构。主干是 did inventors achieve，时间状语是 not until…century。否定副词放到句首，后面的主谓要不完全倒装，即把助动词提前。

  【参考译文】直到近 19 世纪末期，发明家们才完成了有效冰盒所必需的隔热与循环的精确平衡。

全文参考译文

  冰盒这个词到 19 世纪中期就已经进入美国语言中了，不过冰只是开始影响美国普通市

民的饮食。伴随着城市的发展，冰的交易也增多了。在宾馆、酒馆、医院，冰被一些有远见的城市商人用在鲜肉、鲜鱼和黄油上面。美国内战后，当冰被用在冷藏车上时，它也进入了家庭。甚至在 1880 年以前，半数在纽约、费城、巴尔的摩销售的冰，1/3 在波士顿和芝加哥销售的冰进入家庭供使用。这些之所以成为可能，都是因为一种新的家庭设备——冰盒，即现代冰箱的前身，被发明了出来。

　　制作一个有效的冰盒并不像我们现在想象的那么容易。作为制冷科学关键因素的热学在 19 世纪早期还没有得到发展。那种认为最好的冰盒就是阻止冰融化的常识自然是错误的。因为导致冷却的正是冰的融化。然而，早期节约冰的努力也包括将冰包裹起来阻止冰的融化。直到近 19 世纪末期，发明家们才完成了有效冰盒所必需的隔热与循环的精确平衡。

　　但早在 1803 年时，一个天才的马里兰农夫——Thomas Moore，就曾经找到了方法。他拥有华盛顿城外的一个 20 英里的农场，乔治镇是这个地区的中心市场。当他用自己设计的冰盒往市场运送黄油时，他发现顾客们会拒绝购买他的竞争对手们那些快速融化的黄油，而会给他的仍然新鲜干爽的、一磅重的黄油块出高价。Moore 揭示，他冰盒的优点之一是农夫们无需为了要保持他们产品的低温天不亮就到市场上来。

题目答案与解析

1. 本文的主旨是什么？
　　A．冰对人们饮食的影响。　　　　　　　B．货品向市场的运输。
　　C．冷藏技术的发展。　　　　　　　　　D．"冰盒"一词的来源。
　　【答案】C
　　【解析】从文中内容可知，作者一开始谈到冰盒在美国出现，逐渐进入美国家庭，后面又提到人们一直都在尝试着更有效的利用冰来保鲜。从中可知 C 项为正确答案。

2. 根据本文，在美国语言中 "ice-box" 一词是什么时候出现的？
　　A．1803 年。　　　　　　　　　　　　B．1850 年左右。
　　C．在美国内战期间。　　　　　　　　　D．1880 年前。
　　【答案】B
　　【解析】本题的依据是文章的第 1 句话 By the mid-nineteenth century, the term "ice-box" had entered the American language，从中可知 B 项为正确答案。

3. 和第 2 段中 "rudimentary" 这个词的意思最接近的是 _____。
　　A．基本的　　　　B．足够的　　　　C．必要的　　　　D．发展不充分的
　　【答案】D
　　【解析】本题可参照第 2 段的第 2 句话。这句话的意思是"在 19 世纪早期，作为制冷科学关键因素的热学知识还没有……"，而紧接着的一句"那种认为最好的冰盒就是阻止冰融化的常识自然是错误的"，从这句话可以判断当时人们对热学并不了解，引申这个意思的话就可以知道 rudimentary 的意思肯定是负面的，因此 D 项是正确答案。

4. "Thomas Moore，就曾经找到了方法"这句话（第 3 段）说明了什么？
　　A．Moore 的农场离华盛顿不远。　　　　B．Moore 的农场就在路边。
　　C．Moore 的设计很成功。　　　　　　　D．Moore 适合这项工作。

【答案】C

【解析】本题可参照第 3 段。从中可知，穆尔是一个天才的农夫，他设计了一个冰盒并应用于黄油的储存上，因而让自己的产品卖到好价钱，因此 C 项为正确答案。

Text 3

Today, the computer has taken up appliance status in more than 42 percent of households across the United States. And these computers are increasingly biting wired to the Internet. Online access was up more than 50 percent in just the past year. Now, more than one quarter of all U.S. households can surf in cyberspace.

Mostly, this explosive growth has occurred democratically. The online penetration and computer ownership increases extend across all the demographic levels — by race, geography, income, and education.

We view these trends as favorable without the slightest question because we clearly see computer technology as empowering. In fact, personal growth and a prosperous U.S. economy are considered to be the long-range rewards of individual and collective technological power.

Now for the not-so-good news. The government's analysis spells out so-called digital divide. That is, the digital explosion is not booming at the same pace for everyone. Yes, it is true that we are all plugged in to a much greater degree than any of us have been in the past. But some of us are more plugged in than others and are getting plugged in far more rapidly. And this gap is widening even as the pace of the information age accelerates through society.

Computer ownership and Internet access are highly classified along lines of wealth, race, education, and geography. The data indicates that computer ownership and online access are growing more rapidly among the most prosperous and well educated: essentially, wealthy white people with high school and college diplomas and who are part of stable, two-parent households. The highest income bracket households, those earning more than $ 75,000 annually, are 20 times as likely to have access to the Internet as households at the lowest income levels, under $10,000 annually. The computer-penetration rate at the high-income level is an amazing 76.56 percent, compared with 8 percent at the bottom end of the scale.

Technology access differs widely by educational level. College graduates are 16 times as likely to be Internet surfers at home as are those with only elementary-school education. If you look at the differences between these groups in rural areas, the gap widens to a twenty-six-fold advantage for the college-educated.

From the time of the last study, the information-access gap grew by 29 percent between the highest and lowest income groups, and by 25 percent between the highest and lowest education levels.

In the long run, participation in the information age may not be a zero sum game, where if some groups win, others must lose. Eventually, as the technology matures we are likely to see penetration levels approach all groups equally. This was true for telephone access and television ownership, but eventually can be cold comfort in an era when tomorrow is rapidly different from today and unrecognizable compared with yesterday.

1. How many U.S. households have linked to Internet today?
    A. More than 25 percent.   B. By 29 percent.
    C. More than 42 percent.   D. More than 50 percent.

2. According to the text, the computer used by the high-income level is _____ that by the lowest income levels.
    A. 8 percent more than   B. 76.56 percent more than
    C. nearly 10 times as many as   D. about 20 times as many as

3. According to the author, which of the following prevents people from gaining access to the Internet?
    A. Income level.   B. Poor education and low-income level.
    C. Participation in the information age.   D. Telephone access and television ownership.

4. Judging from the context, what does "digital divide" (Para. 3) probably mean?
    A. The government's analysis.
    B. The divide between the poor and the rich.
    C. The pace of the information age.
    D. The gap between people's access to the computer.

核心词汇注释

explosive [ɪkˈspləʊsɪv] *adj.* 爆炸（性）的，爆发（性）的，暴露的
   n. 爆炸物，炸药

democratically [ˌdeməˈkrætɪklɪ] *adv.* 民主地，民主主义地

penetration [ˌpenɪˈtreɪʃ(ə)n] *n.* 穿透，渗透，突破

demographic [ˌdeməˈgræfɪk] *adj.* 人口统计学的

empower [ɪmˈpaʊə(r)] *v.* 授权，使能够

prosperous [ˈprɒspərəs] *adj.* 繁荣的

plug [plʌg] *vt.* 堵，塞；插上，插栓
   n. 塞子，插头，插销

diploma [dɪˈpləʊmə] *n.* 文凭，毕业证书，证明权力、特权、荣誉等的证书，奖状

mature [məˈtjʊə(r)] *adj.* 成熟的，充分考虑的；（票据等）到期的
   vt. 使成熟
   vi. 成熟，到期

长难句剖析

【文章难句】The data indicates that computer ownership and online access are growing more rapidly among the most prosperous and well educated：essentially, wealthy white people with high school and college diplomas and who are part of stable, two-parent households.

【结构分析】本句中，the data 是主语；indicates 是谓语动词；宾语是 that 从句。在宾语从句中，主干是 "computer ownership and online access are growing more rapidly"，among 短语做句子的地点状语，冒号后面的部分是对前面内容的进一步解释。

【参考译文】数据显示计算机的拥有和互联网的接入在最富裕的、教育良好的，即拥有

高中和大学文凭的富裕白人和那些稳定的双亲家庭中增长更迅速。

【文章难句】The highest income bracket households, those earning more than $75,000 annually, are 20 times as likely to have access to the Internet as households at the lowest income levels, under $ 10,000 annually.

【结构分析】本句主干是 The highest income bracket households…are 20 times as likely to have access to the Internet as households at the lowest income levels。those earning more than $ 75,000 annually 做主语的同位语成分。句中还出现了 as…as 结构，在这个结构前面有倍数 20 times。

【参考译文】最高收入阶层的家庭，即年收入高于 75,000 美元的家庭访问互联网的可能性是那些低收入阶层，即年收入低于 10,000 美元的家庭的 20 倍。

【文章难句】In the long run, participation in the information age may not be a zero sum game, where if some groups win, others must lose.

【结构分析】本句主干是 participation in the information age may not be a zero sum game。宾语 a zero sum game 后面是由 where 引导的非制定性定语从句，其中还有一个 if 引导的条件状语。

【参考译文】从长远看，加入信息时代可能不是一个平局游戏，在这里一些团体赢了，另一些一定会输。

全文参考译文

如今在全美 42%以上的家庭里，计算机已经占据了家电的地位。而且这些计算机还在越来越多地接入互联网。仅仅在过去一年中在线访问量就提高了 50%。现在，超过 1/4 的美国家庭可以上网。

在多数情况下，这种爆炸式增长很民主地出现。不论什么样的人种、地理位置、收入及受教育程度，网络连接和计算机保有量的增长扩展到人口的各个层面。

我们认为这种趋势无疑是使人高兴的，因为我们明确地认为计算机技术造成了这种趋势。实际上，个人的发展和繁荣的美国经济被认为是个人和集体技术力量的长期发展的结果。

现在还有一些不太好的消息。政府的分析清楚地说明了所谓的数字分水岭。即对于每个人来说，数字化发展的速度并不相同。的确，现在我们所有人都比过去更频繁地接触网络。但是，与其他人相比，我们其中的一些人同网络的接触更频繁，速度也更快。即使当信息时代在全社会加速前进的时候，这种差距也还在加大。

根据财富、种族、教育、地域的不同，计算机的拥有程度和互联网的接入规模有很大差别。数据表明，计算机的拥有程度和互联网的接入规模在最富裕的、教育良好的，即拥有高中和大学文凭的富裕的白人和那些稳定的双亲家庭中增长更迅速。最高收入阶层的家庭，即年收入高于 75,000 美元的家庭访问互联网的可能性是那些低收入阶层，即年收入低于 10,000 美元的家庭的 20 倍。高收入家庭使用计算机的比例高达 76.56%，但与之相比，低收入家庭只有 8%。

根据教育水平的不同，互联网的访问情况也有很大不同。大学毕业生在家里上网的可能性是那些只有小学教育水平的人的 16 倍。如果在乡村观察这些群体的不同，受教育者的优势差别扩大到 26 倍。

最高收入和最低收入人群之间的信息访问差距自上一次研究开始已经增大了 29%，在最高教育水平和最低教育水平之间差距增长了 25%。

从长远来看，加入信息时代也许不是一个平局游戏，在这里一些团体赢了，另一些一定会输。最后随着技术的成熟，我们也许将会看到每个团体都能达到同一水平。电话的使用和电视机的拥有就是如此。但是在这个日新月异的时代，计算机最终会自然而然的被普及。

题目答案与解析

1. 如今有多少美国家庭已接入互联网？
   A. 多于 25%。　　　　B. 29%。　　　　C. 多于 42%。　　　　D. 多于 50%。
   【答案】A
   【解析】本题的依据是文章第 1 段的最后一句话 Now, more than one quarter of all U.S. households can surf in cyberspace。据此可知 A 项为正确答案。

2. 按照本篇文章，高收入阶层对计算机的使用是低收入阶层的 _____。
   A. 多于 8%　　　B. 多于 76.56%　　　C. 将近 10 倍　　　D. 将近 20 倍
   【答案】C
   【解析】本题可参照第 5 段的 The computer-penetration rate at the high-income level is an amazing 76.56 percent, compared with 8 percent at the bottom end of the scale. 从中可知，在高收入阶层中，计算机渗透率是惊人的 76.56%，而在这个比例的最底端仅有 8%。拿前者的 76.56% 与后者的 8% 相比，前者正好是后者的将近 10 倍，因此 C 项是正确答案。

3. 按照作者的观点，下面哪种因素使人们无法接入互联网？
   A. 收入水平。　　　　　　　　B. 受教育太少和低收入水平。
   C. 参与信息时代。　　　　　　D. 电话的使用和电视的拥有。
   【答案】B
   【解析】本题的依据是文章第 5 段的第 1 句话 Computer ownership and Internet access are highly classified along lines of wealth, race, education, and geography. 在接下来的几段里，作者分别从教育和收入的角度对这种差别进行了比较分析，因此 B 项是正确答案。

4. 联系上下文能够判断，"digital divide" 可能指的是什么？
   A. 政府的分析。　　　　　　　B. 贫富的分界。
   C. 信息时代的前进步伐。　　　D. 人们在计算机使用上的差距。
   【答案】D
   【解析】本题可参照文章第 4 段。从第 1 句话中可知，政府的分析清楚地说明了所谓的数字分水岭。即数字爆炸发展的速度对于每个人是不同的。而这里的数字爆炸明显是指计算机的使用，因为在文章第 2 段的第 1 句话里就说到了这种爆炸式的增长，如果和第 1 段联系起来，爆炸式的增长指的就是计算机的使用。因此正确答案为 D 项。

Text 4

Just over a year ago, I foolishly locked up my bicycle outside my office, but forgot to remove the pannier. When I returned the pannier had been stolen. Inside it were about ten of the little red notebooks I take everywhere for jotting down ideas for articles, short stories, TV shows and the like.

When I lost my notebooks, I was devastated; all the ideas I'd had over the past two years were contained within their pages. I could remember only a few of them, but had the impression that those I couldn't recall were truly brilliant. Those little books were crammed with the plots of award-winning novels and scripts for radio comedy shows that were only two-thirds as bad as the ones on at the moment.

That's not all, though. In my reminiscence, my lost notebooks contained sketches for many innovative and incredible machines. In one book there was a design for a device that could turn sea water into apple cider; in another, plan for an automatic dog; in a third, sketches for a pair of waterproof shoes with television screens built into the toes. Now all of these plans are lost to humanity.

I found my notebooks again. It turns out they weren't in the bike pannier at all, but in a bag in my spare room, where I found six months after supposedly losing them. And when I flipped through their pages, ready to run to the patent office in the morning, I discovered they were completely full of rubbish.

Discovering the notebooks really shook me up. I had firmly come to believe they were brimming with brilliant, inventive stuff—and yet clearly they weren't. I had deluded myself.

After surveying my nonsense, I found that this halo effect always attaches itself to things that seem irretrievably lost. Don't we all have a sneaking feeling that the weather was sunnier, TV shows funnier and cake-shop buns bunnier in the not-very-distant pasty.

All this would not matter much except that it is a powerful element in reactionary thought, this belief in a better yesterday. After all, racism often stems from a delusion that things have deteriorated since "they" came. What a boon to society it would be if people could visit the past and see that it wasn't the paradise they imagine but simply the present with different hats.

Sadly, time travel is impossible.

Until now, that is. Because I've suddenly remembered I left a leather jacket in an Indonesian restaurant a couples of years ago, and I'm absolutely certain that in the inside pocket there was a sketch I'd made.

1. By "only two-thirds as bad as the ones on at the moment" the author means _____.
   A. better than
   B. as bad as
   C. worse than
   D. as good as
2. As soon as the author read the lost notebooks, he _____.
   A. reported the fact
   B. found it valueless
   C. registered the inventions
   D. was very excited
3. Which of the following would the author most probably agree with?
   A. Yesterday is better.
   B. Yesterday is no better than today.
   C. Self-delusion sometimes is necessary.
   D. Things today have deteriorated.

核心词汇注释

pannier [ˈpænɪə(r)] *n.* 笊，筐，背篓，撑
裙，（自行车的）挂篮

devastate [ˈdevəsteɪt] *vt.* 毁坏

cider [ˈsaɪdə(r)] *n.* 苹果酒

patent [ˈpeɪt(ə)nt] *n.* 专利权，执照，专利品
adj. 特许的，专利的；显著的；明白的；
新奇的
vt. 取得……的专利权

brim [brɪm] *n.*（杯，碗等的）边，边缘，
（河）边
vt. 注满，使满溢
vi. 满溢

delude [dɪˈluːd] *vt.* 迷惑，蛊惑

irretrievable [ˌɪrɪˈtriːvəb(ə)l] *adj.* 不能挽
回的，不能复原的

delusion [dɪˈluːʒ(ə)n] *n.* 错觉

deteriorate [dɪˈtɪərɪəreɪt] *v.*（使）恶化

boon [buːn] *n.* 恩惠，实惠，福利

长难句剖析

【文章难句】Inside it were about ten of the little red notebooks I take everywhere for jotting down ideas for articles, short stories, TV shows and the like.

【结构分析】本句是一个完全倒装句。主语是 about...the like，系动词是 were，表语是 inside it。在主语中还有一个定语从句 I take everywhere for...the like，做 notebook 的后置定语。

【参考译文】挂篮中有大约十几本我随身携带的红色小笔记本，是用来记录我对文章、短故事、电视秀等的想法。

【文章难句】Those little books were crammed with the plots of award-winning novels and scripts for radio comedy shows that were only two-thirds as bad as the ones on at the moment.

【结构分析】本句中，that...moment 是修饰 radio comedy 的定语从句。

【参考译文】这些小本子里写满了许多得奖小说的情节和比当时正在上演的那些要稍好一点的广播喜剧剧本。

【文章难句】What a boon to society it would be if people could visit the past and see that it wasn't the paradise they imagine but simply the present with different hats.

【结构分析】本句是一个感叹句。主干是 What a boon to society it would be...if 引导的是条件状语从句，这个条件状语用的是虚拟语气，表示和现实情况相反。

【参考译文】如果人们可以拜访过去，看看过去并不是他们想象中的天堂，而仅仅是戴着不同帽子的现实，那对社会来说是一种多大的恩惠啊。

全文参考译文

就在一年前，我做了件蠢事，我把自行车锁在办公室外面，而忘了拿下挂包。当我回来时挂包已经被偷走了。挂包中有大约十几本我随身携带的红色小笔记本，上面记录了我对文章、短故事、电视秀等的想法。

丢失笔记本后，我一下子蒙了。我两年以来所拥有的想法都包含在笔记本中。我只能记起很少的一点，但是我却认为那些不能回忆起来的东西才是真正的闪光点。这些小本子

里写满了许多得奖小说的情节和比当时正在上演的那些要稍好一点的广播喜剧剧本。这还不算完，在我的回忆中，我丢失的笔记本中包括了许多创新的、令人难以置信的机器草图。在一个本子中，有一个可以将海水变成苹果酒的机器设计，在另一个本里是自动狗的计划，第三个里有一张脚趾头嵌入电视机屏幕的防水鞋的草图。现在，所有的这些计划都丢失在茫茫人海之中了。

我再一次找到了我的笔记本。好像是它们根本没有在自行车篮里，而是在我休息室的小背包里。在我认为丢失了 6 个月后我从那里找到了它。而当我翻看笔记本准备一大早就跑到专利局去时，我发现它们完全是一堆垃圾。

发现笔记本让我震惊。我曾经坚定地认为它们是充满智慧的、创造性的素材，但显然不是。我感到迷惑。

看完我的废话之后，我发现这种晕轮效应总是伴随着一些看起来一去不复返的东西而出现。我们不是都有一种内心的感觉——没多久以前，天气更好，电视秀更有趣，蛋糕店的圆面包更圆吗？

相信过去更好除了在复古思想中是一种强大因素外，在其他方面都不要紧。毕竟，种族主义经常孳生于一种错觉，即自从"他们"来了以后，所有的事情都变糟了。如果人们可以拜访过去，看看过去并不是他们想象中的天堂，而仅仅是戴着不同帽子的现实，那对社会来说是一种多大的恩惠啊。

不幸的是，时间旅行是不可能的。至少到现在为止是不可能的。因为我猛然记起来几年前我曾经把一件皮夹克丢在了印度尼西亚的饭店里，而且我完全肯定在里面的口袋里有一幅我画的草图。

题目答案与解析

1. 作者用 "only two-thirds as bad as the ones on at the moment" 这句话的意思是什么？

   A．更好。 B．一样糟糕。 C．更糟糕。 D．一样好。

   【答案】A

   【解析】本题可参照文章的第 2 段。从中可知，作者在丢失了笔记本之后感到非常可惜，而且认为自己丢失的都是精华，所以题干前面提到的笔记本里记载的广播剧剧本应该是比现在上演的要好，而且题干直译的话就是：只是正在上演的那些剧目的 2/3 糟，也就是说过去记载的要稍好一点。因此 A 项为正确答案。

2. 作者一阅读失而复得的笔记本就 _____。

   A．公布了事实 B．发现它没有价值

   C．注册了发明 D．非常兴奋

   【答案】B

   【解析】本题的依据是第 4 段的最后一句话 when I flipped through their pages, ready to run to the patent office in the morning, I discovered they were completely full of rubbish，从中可知 B 项为正确答案。

3. 作者最有可能赞同下面哪种观点？

   A．昨天更好。 B．昨天不比今天好。

C. 自己产生的错觉有时是必要的。　　　　D. 现在的情况已经恶化了。

【答案】B

【解析】本题可参照文章的最后 4 段。作者对于自己在丢失笔记本后和重新找到后出现的思想变化进行了分析，从作者的分析中我们可以看出，他已经意识到人类对过去的、丢失的东西特别珍爱，而且与现有的东西比，人们总认为过去的和丢失的好，那么从文章倒数第 3 段的第 1 句话：相信过去更好除了在复古思想中是一种强大因素外，在其他方面都不要紧。从中可知作者并不赞同这一观点，因此 B 项为正确答案。

Unit 7

To us it seems so natural to put up an umbrella to keep the water off when it rains. But actually the umbrella was not invented as protection against rain. Its first use was as a shade against the sun.

Nobody knows who first invented it, but the umbrella was used in very ancient times. Probably the first to use it were the Chinese, way back in the eleventh century B.C.

We know that the umbrella was used in ancient Egypt and Babylon as a sunshade. And there was a strange thing connected with its use: it became a symbol of honor and authority. In the Far East in ancient times, the umbrella was allowed to be used only by royalty or by those in high offices.

In Europe, the Greeks were the first to use the umbrella as a sunshade. And the umbrella was in common use in ancient Greece. But it is believed that the first persons in Europe to use the umbrella as protection against rain were the ancient Romans.

During the Middle Ages, the use of the umbrella practically disappeared. Then it appeared again in Italy in the late sixteenth century. And again it was considered a symbol of power and authority. By1680, the umbrella appeared in France and later on in England.

By the eighteenth century, the umbrella was used against rain throughout most of Europe. Umbrellas have not changed much in style during all this time, though they have become much lighter in weight. It wasn't until the twentieth century that women's umbrellas began to be made in a whole variety of colors.

1. The first use of umbrella was as _____.
   A. protection against rain   B. a shade against the sun
   C. a symbol of power   D. a symbol of honor
2. _____ were the people who first used umbrellas.
   A. Chinese   B. Romans   C. Greeks   D. Egyptians
3. The umbrella was used only by royalty or by those in high offices _____.
   A. in Europe in the 18th century   B. in ancient Egypt and Babylon
   C. in the Far East in ancient times D. during the Middle Ages
4. According to the passage, which of the following is not true?
   A. Women enjoy using umbrellas with varied kinds of colors nowadays.
   B. The inventor of the umbrella is unknown.
   C. Once ordinary people had no right to use umbrellas.
   D. Umbrellas were popular and cheap in ancient times.
5. Which of the following is the best title of the passage?
   A. When Was the Umbrella Invented?   B. The History of Umbrella

C. Umbrella — A Symbol of Honor   D. Who Used Umbrella First?

核心词汇注释

umbrella [ʌmˈbrelə] *n.* 伞，雨伞；庇护

ancient [ˈeɪnʃənt] *adj.* 远古的，旧的

Egypt [ˈiːdʒɪpt] *n.* 埃及

Babylon [ˈbæbɪlən] *n.* 巴比伦；奢华淫靡的城市，任何大的富庶的或罪恶的城市

sunshade [ˈsʌnʃeɪd] *n.* 遮阳伞，帽遮；天棚

Greek [griːk] *adj.* 希腊的，希腊人的，希

腊语的　*n.* 希腊人，希腊语

disappear [ˌdɪsəˈpɪə(r)] *vi.* 消失，不见

symbol [ˈsɪmb(ə)l] *n.* 符号，记号，象征

throughout [θruːˈaut] *prep.* 遍及，贯穿　*adv.* 到处，始终，全部

variety [vəˈraɪəti] *n.* 变化，多样性；品种，种类

长难句剖析

【文章难句】But it is believed that the first persons in Europe to use the umbrella as protection against rain were the ancient Romans.

【结构分析】本句中，真正的主语是由 that 引导的名词性从句，而这个名词性从句是一个主系表结构，the first persons in Europe 是主语，不定式 to use…是定语，系动词是 were，表语是 the ancient Romans。it 做形式主语。

【参考译文】但我们认为在欧洲最初用伞防雨的是古罗马人。

【文章难句】It wasn't until the twentieth century that women's umbrellas began to be made in a whole variety of colors.

【结构分析】本句是由 it 引导的强调句，转换成正常语序应是 Women's umbrellas did not begin to be made in a whole variety of colors until the twentieth century。原句中的 not until the twentieth century 做句子的时间状语。

【参考译文】直到 20 世纪，女士们的伞才开始被做成各种各样的颜色。

全文参考译文

对我们来说，下雨时打伞防雨是很自然的事情。可是事实上伞并不是为了防雨而发明的。它最初的用途是遮阳。

没人知道第一个发明伞的人是谁，但伞在远古时代就已被使用。可能早在公元前 11 世纪中国人就开始使用伞。

我们知道在古埃及和古巴比伦伞被用来遮阳。并且有一件奇怪的事情和伞的使用相关：它成为荣誉和权利的象征。在古时的远东地区，只有贵族或那些身居高位的人才能使用伞。

在欧洲，最早使用伞遮阳的是希腊人。并且伞在古希腊被广泛使用。可我们认为在欧洲最初用伞防雨的人是古罗马人。

伞的使用在中世纪事实上消失了。后来在 16 世纪晚期它又重现在意大利。并且又一次被视为权利和权威的象征。到 1680 年，伞出现在法国，而后是英格兰。

到了 18 世纪，在欧洲的多数地区，人们用伞来防雨。一直以来，虽然伞的重量越来越轻，但伞在样式上没有太大的改变。直到 20 世纪，女士们的伞开始被做成各种各样的颜色。

题目答案与解析

1. 最初伞被用做 _____。

   A．防雨 　　　B．遮蔽阳光 　　　C．权利的象征 　　　D．荣誉的象征

   【答案】B

   【解析】本题的依据是第 1 段的最后一句话 Its first use was a shade against the sun。因此 B 项为正确答案。

2. 最早使用伞的人是 _____。

   A．中国人 　　　B．罗马人 　　　C．希腊人 　　　D．埃及人

   【答案】A

   【解析】本题的依据是文章第 2 段的最后一句话 Probably the first to use it were the Chinese，因此 A 项为正确答案。

3. 在 _____ 只有贵族或高官才可以使用伞。

   A．18 世纪欧洲 　　　　　　　　B．埃及和古巴比伦

   C．古时的远东地区 　　　　　　　D．中世纪

   【答案】C

   【解析】本题的依据是文章第 3 段的最后一句话：In the Far East in ancient times, the umbrella was allowed to be used only by royalty or by those in high offices。因此 C 项为正确答案。

4. 按照本篇文章，下面哪一项是错误的？

   A．女士现在喜欢使用各种颜色的伞。　　　B．伞的发明者现在还不为人知。

   C．普通人曾经没有使用伞的权利。　　　　D．在古代伞既便宜又普遍。

   【答案】D

   【解析】综观全文，只有 D 项文中并未提及，因此 D 项是正确答案。

5. 下面哪一项是本文最好的标题？

   A．伞是什么时候发明的？　　　　　B．伞的历史

   C．伞—— 荣誉的象征 　　　　　　D．谁最早使用伞？

   【答案】B

   【解析】从文中内容可知，作者是在按照时间顺序讲述伞的历史，因此 B 项是正确答案。

Text 2

Adam Smith, writing in the 1770s, was the first person to see the importance of the division of labor and to explain part of its advantages. He gives as an example the process by which pins were made in England.

"One man draws out the wire; another strengthens it; a third cuts it; a fourth points it; a fifth grinds it at the top to prepare it to receive the head. To make the head requires two or three operations. To put it on is a separate operation, to polish the pins is another. And the important business of making pins is, in this manner, divided into about eighteen operations, which in some factories are all performed by different people, though in others the same man will sometimes perform two or three of them."

Ten men, Smith said, in this way, turned out twelve pounds of pins a day or about 4,800 pins per worker. But if all of them had worked separately and independently without division of labor, none of them could have made twenty pins in a day and perhaps not even one.

There can be no doubt that division of labor is an efficient way of organizing work. Fewer people can make more pins. Adam Smith saw this but he also took it for granted that division of labor is in itself responsible for economic growth and development and that it accounts for the difference between expanding economies and those that stand still. But division of labor adds nothing new; it only enables people to produce more of what they already have.

1. According to the passage, Adam Smith was the first person to _____.
   A. take advantage of the division of labor
   B. introduce the division of labor into England
   C. understand the effects of the division of labor
   D. explain the causes of the division of labor
2. Adam Smith saw that the division of labor _____.
   A. enabled each worker to make pins more quickly and more cheaply
   B. increased the possible output per worker
   C. increased the number of people employed in factories
   D. improved the quality of pins produced
3. Adam Smith mentioned the number 4,800 in order to _____.
   A. show the advantages of the division of labor
   B. show the advantages of the old craft system
   C. emphasize how powerful the individual worker was
   D. emphasize the importance of increased production
4. According to the writer, Adam Smith's mistake was in believing that division of labor _____.
   A. was an efficient way of organizing work
   B. was an important development in methods of production
   C. certainly led to economic development
   D. increased the production of existing goods
5. Which of the following could serve as an appropriate title for the passage?
   A. Adam Smith, the English Economist
   B. The Theory of Division of Labor
   C. Division of Labor, an Efficient Way of Organizing Work
   D. Adam Smith, the Last Discoverer of Division of Labor

核心词汇注释

division [dɪ'vɪʒ(ə)n] *n.* 分开，分割，区分；除法；公司；（军事）师；分配；分界线

pin [pɪn] *n.* 钉，销，栓，大头针，别针；腿

vt. 钉住，别住；阻止，扣牢，止住，牵制

strengthen ['streŋθ(ə)n] *v.* 加强，巩固

point [pɔɪnt] *n.* 点，尖端；分数；要点

vt. 削尖，指向，指出，瞄准，加标点于

vi. 指，指向，表明

grind [graɪnd] *v.* 磨（碎），碾（碎），折磨

polish [ˈpɒlɪʃ] *n.* 磨光，光泽；上光剂；优雅，精良

vt. 擦亮，发亮，磨光，推敲

vi. 发亮，变光滑

divide [dɪˈvaɪd] *v.* 分，划分，分开，隔开

separately [ˈsepərətlɪ] *adv.* 个别地，分离地

still [stɪl] *n.* 寂静，剧照，照片

adj. 静止的，静寂的

adv. 还，仍，更，还要，尽管如此，依然

enable [ɪˈneɪb(ə)l] *vt.* 使能够，授予权利或方法

长难句剖析

【文章难句】Adam Smith saw this but he also took it for granted that division of labor is in itself responsible for economic growth and development and that it accounts for the difference between expanding economies and those that stand still.

【结构分析】本句是两个并列句。Adam Smith saw this 是第一个句子，第二个句子则是 but 引出的转折部分，其中 he 是主语，took it for granted 是谓语动词，it 是形式宾语，而真正的宾语是后面由 that 引导的两个并列从句。第一个从句是主系表结构，主语是 division of labor，系动词是 is，in itself 做状语，表语则是 responsible for economic growth and development；第二个从句是主谓宾结构，it 做主语，谓语动词是 accounts for，宾语是 the difference, between expanding economies and those that stand still 做后置定语，其中还有一个修饰 those 的由 that 引导的定语从句。

【参考译文】亚当·斯密看到这一点，但他想当然地认为劳动分工是经济增长和发展的根本原因，而且可以解释扩张的经济和停滞不前的经济之间存在的不同。

【文章难句】There can be no doubt that division of labor is an efficient way of organizing work.

【结构分析】本句是 there be 结构，no doubt 是做表语，that 引导的从句是 no doubt 的同位语从句。从句中主语是 division of labor，表语是 an efficient way of organizing work。

【参考译文】劳动分工无疑是组织工作的一种有效方式。

全文参考译文

亚当·斯密是最先看到劳动分工的重要性并解释了其部分优点的人。他在 18 世纪 70 年代的著作中举出英国大头针的生产过程这个例子来进行说明。

"一人拉出铁丝，另一人拉紧；第三个人把它割断；第四个人把它弄尖；第五个人在它的一端打磨，这样可以让它准备好接头。制作针头需要两或三个工序。把头安上是一个单独的工序，磨光这些针是另一个工序。照这样，制作大头针的重要工作被分成大约 18 个工序，在有些工厂都是由不同的工人分别完成的，虽然在其他的厂家同一个人有时要完成两或三个工序。"

斯密说，10 个人用这样的方法一天可以生产 12 磅大头针，即大约每名工人生产 4 800 个。但是若全部的工人单独工作而不进行劳动分工的话，一天之中，没有人可以制作出 20 个大头针，甚至有可能一个都没有。

劳动分工无疑是组织工作的一种有效方式。较少的人可以制作更多的大头针。亚当·斯

密看到这一点，但他想当然地认为劳动分工是经济增长和发展的根本原因，而且可以解释扩张的经济和停滞不前的经济之间存在的不同。但是劳动分工并未增添新的东西，它只是让人们能够生产出更多的原有产品来。

题目答案与解析

1. 按照本篇文章，亚当·斯密是第一个 _____ 的人。
   A. 利用劳动分工
   B. 把劳动分工引入英国
   C. 理解劳动分工的作用
   D. 解释劳动分工的由来

   【答案】C

   【解析】本题的依据是文章第 1 段的第 1 句话…was the first person to see the importance of the division of labor and to explain part of its advantages。C 项中的 understand 等于原文中的 see，因此 C 项为正确答案。

2. 亚当·斯密看到劳动分工 _____。
   A. 使工人们生产大头针速度更快，成本更低
   B. 增加了每名工人的可能产量
   C. 增加了工厂雇佣工人的数量
   D. 提高了大头针的生产质量

   【答案】B

   【解析】本题可参照文章的第 3 段。从中可知，通过分工合作工人们能极大地提高产量。因此正确答案为 B 项。

3. 亚当·斯密说起 4,800 这一数字的目的是 _____。
   A. 显示劳动分工的优势
   B. 显示旧的工艺系统的优势
   C. 强调工人个体是多么强大
   D. 强调产量增长的重要性

   【答案】A

   【解析】本题可参照此句的下一句 without division of labor, none of them could have made twenty pins in a day and perhaps not even one。从中可知，作者用这一数字显示分工的优越性。因此 A 项为正确答案。

4. 按照作者的观点，亚当·斯密的错误是他认为分工问题 _____。
   A. 是组织工作的有效方式
   B. 是生产方式的重要发展
   C. 一定会导致经济的发展
   D. 增加了现有货品的产量

   【答案】C

   【解析】本题的依据是文章最后一段的第 3 句话 Adam Smith saw this but he also took it for granted that 和文章的最后一句话 But division of labor adds nothing new; it only enables people to produce more of what they already have。因此 C 项是正确答案。

5. 下面哪一个题目最适合本篇文章？
   A. 亚当·斯密，英国经济学家
   B. 劳动分工原理
   C. 劳动分工，一种有效的劳动组织方式
   D. 亚当·斯密，劳动分工的最后发现者

   【答案】C

   【解析】从文中内容可知，A 项不够全面，作者并非是在介绍这位经济学家。B 项不适

合，文章主要是讲分工，但重点不在理论研究方面，而是用实例说明分工怎样提高了劳动效率。D 项是明显错误的，因为文章说 Adam Smith 是第一个提出分工理论的人，而不是最后一个。因此 C 项是正确答案。

Text 3

With the start of BBC World Service Television, millions of viewers in Asia and America can now watch the Corporation's news coverage, as well as listen to it.

And of course in Britain listeners and viewers can tune in to two BBC television channels, five BBC national radio services and dozens of local radio station. They are brought sport, comedy, drama, music, news and current affairs, education, religion, parliamentary coverage, children's programmes and films for an annual licence fee of 83 pounds per household.

It is a remarkable record, stretching back over 70 years — yet the BBC's future is now in doubt. The Corporation will survive as a publicly-funded broadcasting organization, at least for the time being, but its role, its size and its programmes are now the subject of a nation-wide debate in Britain.

The debate was launched by the Government, which invited anyone with an opinion of the BBC—including ordinary listeners and viewers — to say what was good or bad about the Corporation, and even whether they thought it was worth keeping. The reason for its inquiry is that the BBC's royal charter runs out in 1996 and it must decide whether to keep the organization as it is, or to make changes.

Defenders of the Corporation — of whom there are many — are fond of quoting the American slogan "If it ain't broke, don't fix it." The BBC "ain't broke" , they say, by which they mean it is not broken (as distinct from the word 'broke', meaning having no money), so why bother to change it?

Yet the BBC will have to change, because the broadcasting world around it is changing. The commercial TV channels — TV and Channel 4 — were required by the Thatcher Government's Broadcasting Act to become more commercial, competing with each other for advertisers, and cutting costs and jobs. But it is the arrival of new satellite channels — funded partly by advertising and partly by viewers' subscriptions — which will bring about the biggest changes in the long term .

1. The world famous BBC now faces _____.
   A. the problem of new coverage
   B. an uncertain prospect
   C. inquiries by the general public
   D. shrinkage of audience

2. In the passage, which of the following about the BBC is not mentioned as the key issue?
   A. Extension of its TV service to Far East.
   B. Programmes as the subject of a nation-wide debate.
   C. Potentials for further international co-operations.
   D. Its existence as a broadcasting organization.

3. The BBC's "royal charter" (Line 4, Paragraph 3) stands for _____.
   A. the financial support from the royal family

B. the privileges granted by the Queen

C. a contract with the Queen

D. a unique relationship with the royal family

4. The foremost reason why the BBC has to readjust itself is no other than _____.

A. the emergence of commercial TV channels

B. the enforcement of Broadcasting Act by the government

C. the urgent necessity to reduce costs and jobs

D. the challenge of new satellite channels

核心词汇注释

tune [tju:n] n. 曲调，调子，合调；和谐 vt. 调音，调整，拨收，收听，知道或察觉他人所说的话或表现的情绪

comedy [ˈkɒmədɪ] n. 喜剧，喜剧性的事情

drama [ˈdrɑ:mə] n.（在舞台上演的）戏剧，戏剧艺术

parliamentary [ˌpɑ:ləˈmentərɪ] adj. 议会的

stretch [stretʃ] v. 伸展，伸长

n. 一段时间，一段路程；伸展

charter [ˈtʃɑ:tə(r)] vt. 租，包（船、车等） n. 宪章

quote [kwəut] vt. 引用，引证，提供，提出，报（价）

slogan [ˈsləugən] n. 口号，标语

satellite [ˈsætəlaɪt] n. 人造卫星

subscription [səbˈskrɪpʃ(ə)n] n. 捐献；订金；订阅；签署；同意；[医]下标处方

长难句剖析

【文章难句】The debate was launched by the Government, which invited anyone with an opinion of the BBC — including ordinary listeners and viewers — to say what was good or bad about the Corporation, and even whether they thought it was worth keeping.

【结构分析】本句中，主干是"the debate was launched by the Government"，which 引导的是一个非限定性定语从句，定语从句中的"including ordinary listeners and viewers"起到补充解释作用。what was good or bad about the Corporation，"and even whether they thought it was worth keeping"是动词 say 的两个并列的宾语从句。

【参考译文】辩论是由政府发起的，政府请任何对英国广播公司有看法的人（包括普通听众和观众）对公司的好坏情况发表意见，他们甚至可以就"公司是否值得继续办下去"这种话题发表自己的观点。

全文参考译文

伴随着英国广播公司电视节目的开播，亚洲和美洲数以百万观众现在不仅可以收听而且还可以观看它的新闻报道。

当然，英国听众和观众能收到两个电视频道，五个全国广播服务和几十个地方无线电台。每户每年交 83 英镑费用即可看到体育、喜剧、戏剧、音乐、新闻和时事、教育、宗教、议会

报道、儿童频道和电影节目。

过去的 70 年间，英国广播公司成就辉煌，但它的未来现在还是个未知数。公司将作为公众资助的广播机构而存在，至少目前如此，但它所扮演的角色、它的规模和它的节目如今在英国成了广泛争论的话题。

争论是由政府发起的。它邀请了每一位对英国广播公司有看法的人——包括普通听众和观众——讨论公司好坏所在，甚至说出他们认为该公司是否值得继续存在下去。这样做的原因是英国广播公司持有的皇家特许证到 1996 年终止。政府必须决定对该公司维持原状还是进行改革。

他们中很多的公司辩护人喜欢引用美国的一个广告口号："如果还没坏，就不要修理它"。他们这样说意思是英国广播公司还没有"broke（垮掉）"（与表示"破产"的"broke"——意味着没钱——含义不同），所以为什么要找麻烦去改变它呢？

但英国广播公司将不得不改革，因为它周围的广播界正在发生变化。商业电视频道——独立电视公司和四频道——按撒切尔政府的广播法案要求更加商业化，互相竞争广告业务，削减成本并裁员。但是，新增加的卫星频道，其资金部分来自广告收入，部分来自用户收视费，它的到来从长远看将会带来最大的变化。

题目答案与解析

1. 世界著名的英国广播公司如今面临着 _____。
   A．新闻报道范围的问题
   B．不确定的前途
   C．普通大众的质询
   D．观众人数的减少

【答案】B

【解析】从文章第一段的内容可知，随着 BBC（英国广播公司）国际电视服务节目的开播，亚洲和美洲数以百万计的人不仅可以收听还可以收看到该公司新闻报道，据此可知 A 项的"新闻报道范围的问题"和 D 项"观众人数的减少"不是 BBC 现在面临的问题。C 项不正确，文中第四段提到了"调查、质询"，但那是政府为了解普通大众的意见所采取的行动，并不是 BBC 现在面临的问题。从文章第三段的内容可知，不过，如今的 BBC 前途悬而未决。据此可知，现在的 BBC 前途不确定。B 项的"不确定的前途"与文中的"the BBC's future is now in doubt.（如今，BBC 的前途悬而未决）"的意思相符，因此 B 项为正确答案。

2. 本篇文章中，下面有关 BBC 的说明中，哪项没有被作为关键问题提到？
   A．把其电视覆盖范围拓展到远东。
   B．节目成为全国争论的话题。
   C．进一步加强国际合作的潜力。
   D．作为广播机构的存在。

【答案】C

【解析】本题中，C 项的"进一步加强国际合作的潜力"有文中没有提到。从文章第三段的第二句话可知，该公司将作为政府基金资助的广播机构而幸存，至少目前是这样，但是它的作用、规模以及它的节目成为现阶段整个英国争论的话题。据此可知，BBC 的生存方式、作用、规模以及它的节目都是目前的关键问题。这说明 A 项"把其电视覆盖范围拓展到远东"、B 项"节目成为全国争论的话题"和 D 项"作为广播机构的存在"三项之意都是文中所说的关键问题。因此正确答案为 C。

3. BBC 的"royal charter"（第四段第四行）意指 _____。
   A．来自皇室的财政资助
   B．女王授予的特权

C．与女王签订的合约　　　　　　　D．与皇室的独特关系

【答案】C

【解析】本题中，A、B、D 三项都与文意不符。从文章第四段的最后一句话可知，政府做这样的调查的原因是——BBC 持有的皇家合约将于 1996 年到期，政府必须决定是维持该公司的原状呢，还是实行改革。据此可知，"royal charter" 应该是指 "BBC 与皇家签订的合约"。C 项的 "指的是与女王签订的合约" 与文中 "the BBC's royal charter runs out（BBC 持有的皇家契约将到期）" 的意思相符，因此 C 项为正确答案。

4. ＿＿＿＿＿正是 BBC 不得不重新自我调整的主要原因。

A．商业电视频道的出现　　　　　　B．政府加大《广播法》的执法力度

C．降低成本、裁减员工的迫切需要　D．新卫星频道的挑战

【答案】D

【解析】本题中，A、B、C 三项都不是主要原因。从文章最后一段的内容可知，然而 BBC 将不得不实行改革，因为其周边的广播业正在发生变革；撒切尔政府的广播法要求商业电视频道更加商业化，要它们互相竞争广告商，要它们降低成本，裁减员工；但是，从长远来看，正是新卫星频道的出现——部分资金来自于广告收入，部分来自于用户的收视费，才会带来最大的变革。据此可知，BBC 不得不重新自我调整的主要原因是新卫星频道的出现。D 项的 "新卫星频道的挑战" 与文中的 "the arrival of new satellite channels will bring about the biggest changes in the long term（从长远来看，新卫星频道的出现会带来最大的改变）" 的意思相符，因此 D 项为正确答案。

Text 4

The United States is a country made up of many different races. Usually they are mixed together and can't be told from one another. But many of them still talk about where their ancestors came from. It is something they are proud of.

The original Americans, of course were the Indians. The so-called white men who then came were mostly from England. But many came from other countries like Germany and France.

One problem the United States has always had is discrimination. As new groups came to the United States they found they were discriminated against. First it was the Irish and Italians. Later it was the blacks. Almost every group has been able to finally escape this discrimination. The only immigrants who have not are the blacks. Surprisingly enough the worst discrimination today is shown towards the Indians.

One reason the Indians are discriminated against is that they have tried so hard to keep their identity. Of course they are not the only ones who have done so. The Japanese have their Little Tokyo in Los Angeles and the Chinese a Chinatown in New York. The Dutch settlement in Pennsylvania also stays separate from other people. Their towns are like something from the 19th century. They have a different reason from the other groups for staying separately. They live separately for religious reasons rather than keep together in a racial group.

Although some groups have kept themselves separate and others have been discriminated against, all groups have helped make the United States a great county. There is no group that has not helped in some way. And there is no group that can say they have done the most to make it a great country.

Many people still come from other countries to help the United States grow. A good example is the American project that let a man walk on the moon. It was a scientist from Germany who was most responsible for doing that. It is certain that in the future the United States will still need the help of people from all racial groups to remain a great country.

1. Which of the following statements can best describe the main idea of this passage?

   A. The United States is a country made up of many different races.

   B. Discrimination is the most serious problem in the United States.

   C. All races in the United States have helped make the country a great one.

   D. The prosperity of the United States is mainly due to the hard work of the most discriminated races.

2. In the first paragraph the word "told" means _____.

   A. separated   B. distinguished   C. revealed   D. made known

3. This passage implies that discrimination is a problem which _____.

   A. many races in the United States have experienced

   B. will still be very serious in the United States in the future

   C. has already been solved in the United States

   D. is strongly opposed by many different races in the United States

4. The main reason why the Indians are most discriminated against is that _____.

   A. they have tried hard to keep their religions

   B. they have tried hard to live together to keep their Indian customs

   C. they are the only ones who have tried to keep their identity

   D. they discriminate many other races

5. The Dutch live separately in Pennsylvania _____.

   A. to escape discrimination   B. to keep together in a racial group

   C. to enjoy themselves in their own towns   D. for religious reasons

核心词汇注释

race [reɪs] *n.* 种族，种族气质，种族特征；赛跑；急流；姜根
vi. 赛跑，疾走
vt. 与……赛跑，使空转

ancestor ['ænsəstə(r)] *n.* 祖先，祖宗

original [ə'rɪdʒɪn(ə)l] *adj.* 最初的，原始的，独创的，新颖的
n. 原物，原作

Indian ['ɪndɪən] *adj.* 印度的，印度人的，印第安人的

n. 印度人，印第安人，印第安语

discrimination [dɪsˌkrɪmɪ'neɪʃ(ə)n] *n.* 辨别，区别；识别力，辨别力；歧视

Irish ['aɪərɪʃ] *n.* 爱尔兰人，爱尔兰语，爱尔兰
adj. 爱尔兰的，爱尔兰人的

immigrant ['ɪmɪɡrənt] *adj.* （从外国）移来的，移民的，移居的
n. 移民，侨民

identity [aɪ'dentɪtɪ] *n.* 同一性；身份；一致；特性；恒等式

Pennsylvania [ˌpensɪl'veɪnɪə] *n.* 宾夕法尼亚州（美国州名）

racial ['reɪʃ(ə)l] *adj.* 人种的，种族的，种族间的

长难句剖析

【文章难句】One reason the Indians are discriminated against is that they have tried so hard to keep their identity.

【结构分析】本句的主干是 one reason is…, the Indians are discriminated against 前面省略了关系代词 that，做主语 one reason 的后置定语从句。is 后接表语从句，这个表语从句的结构是 they…tried to keep…。

【参考译文】印第安人被歧视的一个原因是他们努力保持自己的特性。

【文章难句】It is certain that in the future the United States will still need the help of people from all racial groups to remain a great country.

【结构分析】本句的主干是 It is certain that…the United States will still need…to…。真正的主语是由 that 引导的主语从句，it 只是形式主语。to remain a great country 在主语从句中做目的状语。

【参考译文】毫无疑问，美国要想在未来继续保持其大国的地位，仍然需要来自各个种族的人的支持和帮助。

全文参考译文

美国是一个由众多不同种族构成的国家。他们通常融合在一起不易区分。不过他们中的很多人始终在谈论他们的祖先来自何方。这是他们引以为豪的事情。

印第安人自然是最初的美国人，以后来到美国的所谓的白人大多数来自英国。但也有很多来自其他的国家，比如德国和法国。

美国一直以来都存在歧视问题。当新的种族来到美国，他们发现自己受到歧视，刚开始是爱尔兰人和意大利人，以后是黑人。差不多每个种族最终都能够摆脱歧视。

唯一未能摆脱歧视的移民是黑人，使人惊讶的是印第安人受到了最严重的歧视。印第安人被歧视的一个原因是他们努力保持自己的特性。当然他们不是唯一这样做的种族。日本人在洛杉矶有他们的小东京，中国人在纽约有唐人街。在宾西法尼亚州的荷兰人聚居地也是和其他人分开的。他们的小镇有着一些 19 世纪的特色。他们单独居住的原因不同于其他种族。他们和其他种族分开居住是因为宗教而不是为了族群的聚居。

即便一些人群分开居住，还有一些受到歧视，但所有的种族都帮助美国成为了一个伟大的国家。每个种族都以某种方式提供帮助。任何一个种族都不能说他为美国的繁荣富强作出了最大贡献。

始终有许多不同国家的人来帮助美国成长。一个很好的例子就是美国的登月计划。主要负责这个计划的是一位来自德国的科学家。毫无疑问，美国要想在未来继续保持其大国的地位，仍然需要来自各个种族的人的支持和帮助。

题目答案与解析

1. 以下哪一项是对本文中心思想的最好描述？
   A. 美国是由许多不同种族构成的。

B．歧视是美国最严重的问题。

C．所有的种族都为美国成为一个伟大国家做出了贡献。

D．美国的繁荣主要来自大多数受歧视种族的努力工作。

【答案】C

【解析】本题可参照文章的第 5 段。从中可知，美国所有的种族都为建设美国作出了贡献，体现了文章的中心思想，因此 C 项为正确答案。

2．第 1 段中单词"told"的意思是 _____。

　　A．分离　　　　　　B．区别　　　　　　C．揭示　　　　　　D．让……知道

【答案】B

【解析】文中原句是 Usually they are mixed together and can't be told from one another. told 是 tell 的过去分词，常与 can, could, be able to 连用，意思是"辨别，分辨，认出"。因此 B 项为正确答案。

3．本篇文章暗示歧视是一个 _____ 的问题。

　　A．美国许多种族都经历过　　　　　　　B．在美国将来仍然会十分严重

　　C．在美国已经解决了　　　　　　　　　D．在美国被许多不同种族强烈反对

【答案】A

【解析】本题的依据是文中第 3 段的 As new groups came to the United States they found they were discriminated against。First…Later…Almost every group has been able to finally escape this discrimination。因此 A 是正确答案。

4．印第安人最受歧视的原因是 _____。

　　A．他们努力试图保持自己的宗教信仰

　　B．他们努力试图住在一起并保持他们的风俗习惯

　　C．只有他们试图保持自己特色

　　D．他们歧视许多其他种族

【答案】C

【解析】本题的依据是第 4 段的第 1、2 句话 One reason the Indians are discriminated against is that they have tried so hard to keep their identity. Of course they are not the only ones who have done so，从中可知 C 项为正确答案。

5．住在宾州的荷兰人自成一体的目的是 _____。

　　A．逃避歧视　　　　　　　　　　　　　B．在种族团体中住在一起

　　C．喜欢住在他们自己的城镇里　　　　　D．出于宗教原因

【答案】D

【解析】本题的依据是第 4 段的最后一句话：They live separately for religious reasons rather than keep together in a racial group。从中可知，荷兰人自成一体是出于宗教的原因，因此 D 项为正确答案。

Unit 8

Text 1

Fear and its companion pain are two of the most useful things that men and animals possess, if they are properly used. If fire did not hurt when it burnt, children would play it until their hands were burnt away. Similarly, if pain existed but fear did not, a child would burn itself again and again, because fear would not warn it to keep away from the fire that had burnt it before. A really fearless soldier— and some do exist— is not a good soldier because he is soon killed; and a dead soldier is of no use to his army. Fear and pain are therefore two guards without which men and animals might soon die out.

In our first sentence we suggested that fear ought to be properly used. If, for example, you never go out of your house because of the danger of being knocked down and killed in the street by a car, you are letting fear rule you too much. Even in your house you are not absolutely safe： an airplane may crash on your house, or ants may eat away some of the beams in your roof so that the latter falls on you, or you may get cancer!

The important thing is not to let fear rule you, but instead to use fear as your servant and guide. Fear will warn you of dangers; then you have to decide what action to take. In many cases, you can take quick and successful action to avoid the danger. For example, you see a car coming straight towards you; fear warns you, you jump out of the way, and all is well.

In some cases, however, you decide that there is nothing that you can do to avoid the danger. For example, you cannot prevent an airplane crashing onto your house. In this case, fear has given you its warning; you have examined it and decided on your course of action, so fear of this particular danger is no longer of any use to you, and you have to try to overcome it.

1. Children would play with fire until their hands were burnt away if _____.

  A. they were given no warning beforehand B. they had never burnt themselves

  C. they had no sense of pain D. they were fearful of the fire

2. A really fearless soldier _____.

  A. is of little use to the army B. is without equal

  C. is nothing but a dead soldier D. easily gets killed in a battle

3. Fear should be used properly because _____.

  A. an airplane may crash on your house

  B. you may get cancer

  C. fear can only be used as a servant and guide

  D. men are now letting fear rule them too much

4. People sometimes succeed in timely avoiding danger because _____.

    A. they have gained experience

    B. they jump out of the way in time

    C. they are calm in face of danger

    D. they are warned of the danger and can take quick action

5. Which of the following statements is implied but not stated?

    A. Fear is always something helpful.

    B. Too much fear is harmful.

    C. Fear ought to be used as a servant and guide.

    D. Fear is something unprofitable.

核心词汇注释

companion [kəmˈpænɪən] *n.* 同伴，共事者

fearless [ˈfɪəlɪs] *adj.* 不怕的，大胆的，勇敢的，无畏的

exist [ɪgˈzɪst] *vi.* 存在，生存，生活；继续存在

knock [nɒk] *v.* 敲，敲打，敲击；（使）碰撞 *n.* 敲，击，敲打

absolutely [ˈæbsəluːtlɪ] *adv.* 完全地，绝对地

airplane [ˈeəpleɪn] *n.* 飞机

crash [kræʃ] *n.* 碰撞，坠落，坠毁；撞击声，爆裂声

v. 碰撞，坠落，坠毁；（指商业公司、政府等）破产，垮台

beam [biːm] *n.* 梁，桁条；（光线的）束，柱，电波；横梁 *v.* 播送

latter [ˈlætə(r)] *adj.* 后面的，（两者中）后者的，较后的，近来的

cancer [ˈkænsə(r)] *n.* 癌，毒瘤

servant [ˈsɜːvənt] *n.* 仆人

course [kɔːs] *n.* 过程，经过，进程；方针；路线；跑道；课程；一道菜；学业 *v.* 追猎；急行，运行；流动

长难句剖析

【文章难句】Similarly, if pain existed but fear did not, a child would burn itself again and again, because fear would not warn it to keep away from the fire that had burnt it before.

【结构分析】本句主干是 if pain…a child…burn…because…，a child…是主句，if 引导条件状语，because 引导原因状语，

【参考译文】如果只有痛苦而没有恐惧，一个孩子会一次又一次地用火烧自己，因为恐惧不会警告他远离曾经烧到自己的火。

【文章难句】Fear and pain are therefore two guards without which men and animals might soon die out.

【结构分析】本句主干是 Fear and pain are therefore two guards，其中 fear 和 pain 是并列主语。without 在从句中和 which 一起做条件状语，which 引导的定语从句用来修饰 two guards。

【参考译文】因此恐惧和痛苦是两位保镖，没有它们，人类和动物就会很快灭亡。

【文章难句】If, for example, you never go out of your house because of the danger of being knocked down and killed in the street by a car, you are letting fear rule you too much.

【结构分析】本句主干是 If you...because of...you...，其中 if 引导的是条件状语，because of...是 if 从句中的原因状语，并不修饰主句。

【参考译文】如果因为害怕被车撞倒，横尸街头，而从不走出家门，那你就受到了恐惧过分的束缚。

全文参考译文

如果得到恰当的使用，恐惧和与之相伴的痛苦会是人类和动物所拥有的最有用的两样东西。如果孩子们没有疼痛感，他们会一直玩火直到烧掉双手。相同的道理，如果只有痛苦而没有恐惧，一个孩子会一次又一次地用火烧自己，因为恐惧不会警告他远离曾经烧到他自己的火。一个真正无畏的士兵——的确存在一些这样的人——不是一个好士兵，因为他很快就会被杀死，而一个死掉的士兵对他的军队没有任何用处。所以恐惧和痛苦是两位保镖，人类和动物没有它们就会很快灭亡。

在本文第一句当中我们提到恐惧应当得到恰当的使用。例如，若因为害怕被车撞倒，横尸街头，而从不走出家门，那你就受到了恐惧过分的束缚。即便在家中你也不是完全安全的：一架飞机可能会撞到你的房子，或者蚂蚁吃光了你家房顶大梁的某一部分，结果木头掉下来砸到你身上，或者你有可能得癌症！

重要的不是让恐惧控制你，而是要把恐惧当做你的仆人和向导来驾驭。恐惧会警告你危险，接下来你必须决定采取何种行动。你在多数情况下能够采取快速而又成功的行动，避免危险发生。比如，你看到一辆车向你直接开过来：恐惧警告你，你跳开了，则一切平安无事。

但你在有些情况下发现，对于危险你避免不了，无能为力。比如，你无法防止一架飞机撞上你家房子。在这种情况下，恐惧已经向你发出警告，你对此考虑后决定你要采取的一系列行动，所以因为这种特别的危险而产生的恐惧不再对你有任何用处，你必须尽力克服它。

题目答案与解析

1. 假如 _____，孩子们会一直玩火到烧掉双手。
   A. 他们没有事先得到警告　　　　B. 他们永远不会烧到自己
   C. 他们没有疼痛感　　　　　　　D. 他们怕火

   【答案】C

   【解析】本题的依据是文章第一段的第二句话：If fire did not hurt when it burnt。从中可知 C 项为正确答案。

2. 一个真正勇敢无畏的士兵 _____。
   A. 对军队没什么用　　　　　　　B. 是无敌的
   C. 仅仅是一个死士兵而已　　　　D. 在战斗中很容易被打死

   【答案】D

   【解析】本题的依据是文章第一段倒数第二句话：A really fearless soldier...is not a good soldier because he is soon killed...从中可知 D 项为正确答案。A 项似乎很有道理，但只要与第

一段倒数第二句话的后半部分仔细比较一下,就会发现 A 项的主语是 A really fearless soldier,而原句后半部分的主语是 a dead soldier。所以不能选择 A 项。

3. 应该合理利用恐惧,因为 _____。

    A. 飞机可能在你的房子上坠毁   B. 你可能得癌症

    C. 恐惧只能用来作为仆人和向导   D. 人类正在被恐惧紧紧束缚

【答案】C

【解析】本题的依据是文章第三段的第一句话:The important thing is not to let fear rule you, but instead to use fear as your servant and guide。从中可知 C 项是正确答案。

4. 有时人们能够成功逃脱危险,原因是 _____。

    A. 他们获得了经验   B. 他们及时跳离了道路

    C. 他们在危险面前保持平静   D. 他们得到了危险警告并迅速做出反应

【答案】D

【解析】本题可参照第四段。从中可知 D 项为正确答案。

5. 本文中隐含但没有陈述的意思是哪一项?

    A. 恐惧总是有帮助的。   B. 太多的恐惧有害。

    C. 恐惧应该被用来作为奴仆和向导。 D. 恐惧是没用的东西。

【答案】B

【解析】综观全文,只有 B 项是文章隐含的意思,为本题正确答案。A 项中有 always 这个副词,使该项所表达的意思走向极端,与原文"如果能正确对待恐惧的话"意思不符。C 项是文章直接表达的思想,而不是隐含的意思。D 项与文章的中心思想相反。

> **Text 2**

Thirty-one million Americans are over 60 years of age, and twenty-nine million of them are healthy, busy, productive citizens. By the year 2030, one in every five people in the United States will be over 60. Elderly people are members of the fastest-growing minority in this country. Many call this the "graying of America".

In 1973, a group called the "Gray Panthers" was organized. This group is made up of young and old citizens. They are trying to deal with the special problems of growing old in America. The Gray Panthers know that many elderly people have health problems: some cannot walk well, others cannot see or hear well. Some have financial problems; prices are going up so fast that the elderly can't afford the food, clothing, and housing they need. Some old people are afraid and have safety problems. Others have emotional problems. Many elderly are lonely because of the death of a husband or a wife. The Gray Panthers know another fact, too. Elderly people want to be as independent as possible. So, the Gray Panthers are looking for ways to solve the special problems of the elderly.

The president of the Gray Panthers is Maggie Kuhn, an active woman in her late 70s. She travels across the United States, educating both young and old about the concerns of elders. One of the problems she talks about is where and how elders live. She says that Americans do not encourage elders to live with younger people. As far as Maggie Kuhn is concerned, only elders who need constant medical care should be in nursing homes.

Maggie Kuhn knows that elders need education, too. She spends lots of time talking to groups of older Americans. She encourages them to continue to live in their own houses if it is possible. She also tells them that it is important to live with younger people and to have children around them. This helps elders to stay young at heart.

1. What health problems do many elderly have?
    A. They feel lonely.   B. They are suffering from cancer.
    C. They cannot walk or see or hear well.   D. They have got heart problems.

2. Nursing homes _____.
    A. are good for elders who need constant medical care
    B. help keep elders young
    C. are set up for training nurses
    D. are places where small children are taken care of

3. Maggie Kuhn travels across the United States in order to _____ elders.
    A. collect money for   B. show concerns for
    C. find houses for   D. educate people to help

4. One of the problems Maggie Kuhn talks about is _____.
    A. why elders should be taken care of   B. where and how elders live
    C. who needs medical care   D. how to improve education in the USA

5. Maggie Kuhn encourages elders to _____.
    A. live in nursing homes   B. travel more
    C. live with younger people   D. do some house work

核心词汇注释

productive [prə'dʌktɪv] *adj.* 生产性的，生产的；能产的，多产的

minority [maɪ'nɒrɪtɪ] *n.* 少数；少数民族

panther ['pænθə(r)] *n.* 豹，黑豹

elderly ['eldəlɪ] *adj.* 过了中年的，稍老的

financial [faɪ'nænʃ(ə)l] *adj.* 财政的，金融的

emotional [ɪ'məʊʃən(ə)l] *adj.* 情绪的，情感的

solve [sɒlv] *vt.* 解决，解答

concern [kən'sɜːn] *vt.* 涉及，关系到 *n.* （利害）关系；关心，关注

encourage [ɪn'kʌrɪdʒ] *vt.* 鼓励，怂恿 *v.* 鼓励

nursing ['nɜːsɪŋ] *n.* 看护，养育

长难句剖析

【文章难句】She travels across the United States, educating both young and old about the concerns of elders.

【结构分析】本句的主干是 She travels across the United States。现在分词短语 educating… elders 做主句的目的状语。

【参考译文】她到美国各地，教育年轻人和老年人，告诉他们老人们的问题。

【文章难句】One of the problems she talks about is where and how elders live.

【结构分析】本句是主系表结构，one of the problems 是主语，where 和 how 引导的是表语从句。she talks about 是定语从句，修饰主语。

【参考译文】她所谈到的问题之一就是老人在哪儿居住和怎样生活。

全文参考译文

已年逾 60 的美国公民有 3 100 万，其中 2 900 万身体健康，忙碌而又能干。到 2030 年美国人口的 1/5 将超过 60 岁。在这个国家当中，老人将是增长最快的一个少数群体。许多人把这称之为"美国的灰色化"。

一个名为 Gray Panthers 的团体于 1973 年成立了。这个团体的成员既有年轻的又有年老的。他们正尝试着解决美国日益增加的老人所存在的特殊问题。Gray Panthers 了解许多老人有健康问题：有些人行动不便，有些人眼神和听力都不太好。有些老人经济困难；物价上涨以至于老人负担不起他们必需的食品、衣服和栖身之所。有些老人害怕并且有安全隐患。其他一些老人还有情感问题。许多鳏寡老人很孤单。Gray Panthers 也了解另外一个情况：老人们都想尽可能的独立。所以 Gray Panthers 正在寻找能够解决这些老人的特殊问题的方法。

Maggie Kuhn 是 Gray Panthers 的主席，她是一位年届七旬，但仍很活跃的女士。她到美国各地，教育年轻人和老年人，告诉他们老人们的问题。其中她所谈到的一个问题就是老人在哪儿居住而且怎样生活。她说美国人不鼓励老人和年轻人住在一起。在她看来，只有那些需要长期医疗护理的老人才应该住在敬老院。

Maggie Kuhn 懂得老人也需要教育。她用了大量的时间和很多群体的美国老年人交流。她鼓励他们尽可能继续在自己的家里生活。她也告诉他们，和年轻人一起生活，和孩子们在一起，这很重要。这可以帮助老人保持一颗年轻的心。

题目答案与解析

1. 很多老年人在健康方面有什么问题？
   A．他们感到孤独。　　　　　　　　B．他们受到癌症的折磨。
   C．他们不能走路、看或者听。　　　D．他们的心脏有问题。

   【答案】C

   【解析】本题的依据是文章第 2 段的第 4 句话：The Gray Panthers know that many elderly people have health problems: some cannot walk well, others cannot see or hear well. 从中可知 C 项是正确答案。

2. 养老院 _____。
   A．对经常需要医疗保健的老年人有益　B．有助于让老年人保持年轻
   C．是为培训护士创建的　　　　　　　D．是照看小孩的地方

   【答案】A

   【解析】本题的依据是文章第 3 段的最后一句话：...only elders who need constant medical care should be in nursing homes. 从中可知 A 项为正确答案。

3．Maggie Kuhn 走遍整个美国目的是 _____。

    A．为老人筹款　　　　　　　　B．对老人表示关心

    C．为老人找房子　　　　　　　　D．教育人们给予老人帮助

【答案】D

【解析】本题的依据是文章第 3 段的第 2 句话：…educating both young and old about the concerns of elders. 从中可知，Maggie Kuhn 走遍整个美国的目的是为了教育不同年龄层次的人去关心、帮助老年人。因此 D 项为正确答案。

4．Maggie Kuhn 谈及的众多问题之一是 _____。

    A．为什么老人们需要被照看　　　B．老人们生活在哪里，怎样生活

    C．谁需要医疗保健　　　　　　　D．怎样改善美国的教育水平

【答案】B

【解析】本题的依据是第 3 段的第 3 句话：One of the problems she talks about is where and how elders live. 从中可知 B 项为正确答案。

5．Maggie Kuhn 鼓励老年人 _____。

    A．住在养老院　　B．多去旅游　　　C．和年轻人住在一起　　D．做一些家务

【答案】C

【解析】本题的依据是最后一段的第 3、4 句话：She encourages them to continue to live in their own houses if it is possible. She also tells them that it is important to live with younger people and to have children around them. 从中可知，Maggie Kuhn 鼓励老年人与年轻人和小孩子共同生活。因此 C 项为正确答案。

Text 3

How men first learnt to invent words is unknown; in other words, the origin of language is a mystery. All we really know is that men, unlike animals, somehow invented certain sound to express thoughts and feelings, actions and things, so that they could communicate with each other; and that later they agreed upon certain signs, called letters, which could be combined to represent those sounds, and which could be written down. Those sounds, whether spoken or written in letters, we call words.

The power of words, then, lies in their associations — the things they bring up before our minds. Words become filled with meaning for us by experience; and the longer we live, the more certain words recall to us the glad and sad events of our past; and the more we read and learn, the more the number of words that mean something to us increases.

Great writers are those who not only have great thoughts but also express these thoughts in words which appeal powerfully to our minds and emotions. This charming use of words is what we call literary style. Above all, the real poet is a master of words. He can convey his meaning in words which sing like music, and which by their position and association can move men to tears. We should therefore learn to choose our words carefully and use them accurately, or they will make our speech silly and dull.

1. The origin of language is _____.
   A. a legend handed down from the past
   B. a matter that is hidden secretly
   C. a question difficult to answer
   D. a problem not yet solved

2. One of the reasons why men invented certain sounds to express thoughts and actions was that _____.
   A. they could agree upon certain signs
   B. they could write them down
   C. they could communicate with each other
   D. they could combine them

3. What is true about the words?
   A. They are used to express feelings only.
   B. They can not be written down.
   C. They are simply sounds.
   D. They are mysterious.

4. In expressing their thoughts, great writers are able _____.
   A. to confuse the readers
   B. to move men to tears
   C. to move our actions
   D. to puzzle our feelings

5. Which of the following statements about the real poet is NOT true?
   A. He is no more a master of words than an ordinary person.
   B. He can convey his ideas in words which sing like music.
   C. He can move men to tears.
   D. His style is always charming.

核心词汇注释

unknown [ʌn'nəʊn] *adj.* 不知道的，未知的，不知名的

mystery ['mɪstərɪ] *n.* 神秘，神秘的事物

association [ə,səʊsɪ'eɪʃ(ə)n] *n.* 协会；联合；结交；联想

event [ɪ'vent] *n.* 事件；事变；结果；活动；精力；竞赛

increase [ɪn'kriːs] *n.* 增加，增大，增长
vt. 增加，加大
vi. 增加，繁殖

appeal [ə'piːl] *n.* 请求，呼吁；上诉；吸引力；要求
vi. 求助，诉请，要求
vt. 控诉

charming ['tʃɑːmɪŋ] *adj.* 迷人的，娇媚的

literary ['lɪtərərɪ] *adj.* 文学（上）的，从事写作的，文艺的，精通文学的，书本的

poet ['pəʊɪt] *n.* 诗人

convey [kən'veɪ] *vt.* 搬运，传达，转让

长难句剖析

【文章难句】All we really know is that men, unlike animals, somehow invented certain sound to express thoughts and feelings, actions and things, so that they could communicate with each other; and that later they agreed upon certain signs, called letters, which could be combined to represent those sounds, and which could be written down.

【结构分析】本句是主系表结构，all we really know 是主语，系动词是 is, that 引导的从句作表语。在表语从句中，主干是 men…invented… so that they could communicate…and that later they agreed upon…which…，主语是 men，谓语动词是 invented certain sound，接下来的不定式 to…做目的状语，后面 so that 引导的是两个并列的目的状语从句，其中第二个从句中，which 引导的非限制性语从句修饰名词 letters。

【参考译文】我们只知道，人类不像动物，人类设法创造了某个音来表达思想感情、行为和事物，因此他们能够互相交流；并且后来他们对某些符号达成一致意见，这些符号被称作字母，它们可以连在一起代表那些音，而且可以用笔记录下来。

【文章难句】The longer we live, the more certain words recall to us the glad and sad events of our past.

【结构分析】本句是 "the more…the more…" 结构。

【参考译文】而且我们活得越长，就有更多的一些词让我们回想起过去的悲伤与快乐。

【文章难句】Great writers are those who not only have great thoughts but also express these thoughts in words which appeal powerfully to our minds and emotions.

【结构分析】本句的主干是 Great writers are those…，who 引导的定语从句修饰 those，在这个定语从句中，which 引导的关系从句用来修饰 in 的宾语 words。

【参考译文】伟大的作家是那些不但有伟大的思想而且能用强烈感染我们思想感情的词语把它表达出来的人。

全文参考译文

最开始时人类是如何学会创造词语的尚未可知，换句话说，语言的起源是个谜。我们只知道，人类不像动物，人类设法创造了某个音来表达思想感情、行为和事物，以便他们能够互相交流；并且后来他们对某些符号达成一致意见，这些符号被称为字母，它们可以连在一起代表那些音，而且可以用笔记录下来。这些音，不管是口述的还是用字母写下来的，我们都称之为词。

词的力量存在于它们的联想——它们能使我们的大脑回忆起事物。随着经验的增长，对于我们来说词充满意义，而且我们活得越长，就有更多的一些词让我们回想起过去的悲伤与快乐；我们读得越多，学得越多，就会知道更多对我们有意义的词。

伟大的作家是那些不但有伟大的思想而且能用强烈感染我们思想感情的词语把它表达出来的人。我们把这种对词语巧妙的使用称之为文学风格。总而言之，真正的诗人是语言大师。他可以用那些读起来像音乐般的词语表达他的意思，这些词语被安置的位置以及它们所带来的联想能让人感动地落泪。因此我们应该学会慎重地选择我们所用的词语并准确地使用它们，不然的话，它们会让我们的谈吐变得愚蠢而又无聊。

题目答案与解析

1. 人类语言的起源是 _____。
   A. 从过去流传下来的传说
   B. 秘密隐藏起来的事情
   C. 一个难于回答的问题
   D. 一个还没得到解决的问题

【答案】D

【解析】本题的依据是文章第 1 段的第 1 句话：How men first learnt to invent words is unknown; in other words, the origin of language is a mystery。从中可知 D 项是正确答案。

2. 人类发明用某种声音表达思想和行动的原因之一是 _____。
    A. 他们可以就某些信号达成一致   B. 他们可以写下来
    C. 他们可以互相交流   D. 他们可以将他们结合起来

【答案】C

【解析】本题可参照第 1 段的第 2 句话，从 so that 所引导的状语从句 so that they could communicate with each other 可知，C 项为正确答案。

3. 下面关于"词"的表述中哪个正确？
    A. 他们仅仅被用来表达感情。   B. 他们不能被写下来。
    C. 他们仅仅是声音。   D. 他们是神秘的。

【答案】C

【解析】本题的依据是第 1 段的最后一句话：Those sounds, whether spoken or written in letters, we call words。从中可知，C 项为正确答案。A 项不对，因为原文提过 express thoughts and feelings, actions and things。B 项中的 not 使这一选项与文中的事实相反，D 项文中没有提及，原文只说过语言的起源是 mystery，而不是语言本身。

4. 当表达他们思想的时候，伟大的作家能 _____。
    A. 使读者迷惑   B. 使人们感动得流泪
    C. 改变我们的行动   D. 迷惑我们的感觉

【答案】B

【解析】本题可参照文章的最后一段。从中可知，一位真正的诗人（the real poet）能把我们普通人感动得流泪，因此 B 项为正确答案。

5. 以下关于一位真正诗人的描述中不正确的是 _____。
    A. 与其说他是个语言大师，不如说他是个普通人
    B. 他可以用那些音乐般的词语表达他的意思
    C. 他可以使人感动得流泪
    D. 他的风格总是很迷人

【答案】A

【解析】本题可参照文中最后一段的第 3 句话 Above all, the real poet is a master of words。而 A 项与之不符。因此 A 项为正确答案。

Text 4

Today is the anniversary of that afternoon in April a year ago that I first saw the strange and appealing doll in the window of Abe Sheftel's toy shop on Third Avenue near Fifteenth Street, just around the corner from my office, where the plate on the door reads: Dr. Samuel Amory. I remember just how it was that day: the first hint of spring floated across the East River, mixing with the soft-coal smoke from the factories and the street smells of the poor neighborhood.

As I turned the corner on my way to work and came to Sheftel's, I was made once more aware of the poor collection of toys in the dusty window, and I remembered the approaching birthday of a small niece of mine in Cleveland, to whom I was in the habit of sending modest gifts. Therefore, I stopped and examined the window to see if there might be anything suitable, and looked at the confusing collection of unappealing objects — a red toy fire engine, some lead soldiers, cheap baseballs, bottles of ink, pens, yellowed envelopes, and advertisements for soft drinks. And thus it was that my eyes eventually came to rest upon the doll stored away in one corner, a doll with the strangest, most charming expression on her face. I could not wholly make her out, due to the shadows and the film of dust through which I was looking, but I was aware that a tremendous impression had been made upon me as though I had run into a person, as one does sometimes with a stranger, with whose personality one is deeply impressed.

1. What made an impression on the author?
   A. The doll's unusual face.
   B. The collection of toys.
   C. A stranger he met at the store.
   D. The resemblance of the doll to his niece.
2. Why does the author mention his niece?
   A. She likes dolls.
   B. The doll looks like her.
   C. She lives near Sheftel's.
   D. He was looking for a gift for her.
3. Why did the author go past Sheftel's?
   A. He was on his way to work.
   B. He was looking for a present for his niece.
   C. He wanted to buy some envelopes.
   D. He liked to look in the shop windows.
4. The story takes place in the _____.
   A. early summer   B. early spring   C. midsummer   D. late spring
5. Most of the things in the store window were _____.
   A. expensive   B. appealing   C. neatly arranged   D. unattractive

核心词汇注释

anniversary [ˌænɪˈvɜːsərɪ] *n.* 周年纪念

doll [dɒl] *n.* 洋娃娃，玩偶；美丽但无头脑的女子；<俚>美男子

hint [hɪnt] *n.* 暗示，提示，线索

floater [ˈfləʊtə(r)] *n.* 漂浮者，漂浮物，浮子；游民，临时工；（公司筹办的）筹资开办人

neighborhood [ˈneɪbəhʊd] *n.* 附近，邻近

approach [əˈprəʊtʃ] *n.* 接近，逼近，走进；方法，步骤；途径，通路
   vt. 接近，动手处理
   vi. 靠近

rest [rest] *n.* 休息，静止；支持物，台，架；

[音]休止符；其余，其他
   vi. 休息，睡眠，静止；依靠，搁在；保持；取决于
   vt. 使休息，使静止，睡眠；依靠，搁在

tremendous [trɪˈmendəs] *adj.* 极大的，巨大的

run [rʌn] *n.* 跑，赛跑，奔跑；运转，趋向
   vi. 跑，奔，逃跑；竞选；跑步；蔓延；进行，行驶
   vt. 使跑，参赛；追究；管理；运行，开动
   adj. 熔化的，融化的，浇铸的
   run 的过去式和过去分词

长难句剖析

【文章难句】The first hint of spring floated across the East River, mixing with the soft-coal smoke from the factories and the street smells of the poor neighborhood.

【结构分析】本句主干是…hint…floated across the East River，现在分词 mixing with…做伴随状语。

【参考译文】春天里最早的一丝气息从东河对岸飘过来，和工厂里燃烧烟煤排放出的浓烟及附近街道上贫穷的气息混杂在一起。

【文章难句】As I turned the corner on my way to work and came to Sheftel's, I was made once more aware of the poor collection of toys in the dusty window, and I remembered the approaching birthday of a small niece of mine in Cleveland, to whom I was in the habit of sending modest gifts.

【结构分析】本句主干是…I was made once more aware of…and I remembered the approaching birthday…。as 引导时间状语从句，在第二个并列主句的后面接有一个由 whom 引导的非限制性定语从句用来修饰 of 的宾语 a small niece。

【参考译文】当我从上班的路上转过拐角处来到 Sheftel's 玩具店的时候，我立刻就注意到在积满灰尘的橱窗里的那几个玩具，然后我想起在 Cleveland 我的一个小侄女就要过生日了，我习惯给她送一些便宜的礼物。

【文章难句】And thus it was that my eyes eventually came to rest upon the doll stored away in one corner, a doll with the strangest, most charming expression on her face.

【结构分析】本句是一个强调句型。rest upon 的宾语是被强调成分，因为这个宾语接有过去分词做定语，而且还有一个同位语，因此没有直接放到 it was 后面。

【参考译文】就这样我的目光最终落到那个放在角落里的玩具娃娃身上，这个娃娃的脸上带着一种最奇怪、最有魅力的表情。

全文参考译文

一年前的今天，4月的一个下午，我在第五大街附近的第三大街上一家名为 Abe Sheftel's 玩具店的橱窗里，首次见到这个奇怪而又很吸引人的玩具娃娃。这家玩具店距离我门上写着"Samuel Amory 医生"的办公室非常近。我仍记得当时的情形：春天里最早的一丝气息从东河对岸飘过来，和工厂里燃烧烟煤排放出的浓烟及附近街道上贫穷的气息混杂在一起。

当我从上班的路上转过拐角处来到 Sheftel's 玩具店时，我立刻就注意到在积满灰尘的橱窗里的那几个玩具，然后我记起在克里夫兰我的一个小侄女就要过生日了，我习惯给她送一些便宜的礼物。所以我停下来仔细瞧瞧橱窗里是否有什么适合的东西，但看到了一堆莫名其妙并不招人喜爱的东西——一件红色的玩具打火机、一些铅制的士兵、廉价的棒球、一瓶瓶墨水、钢笔、发黄的信封，还有软饮料的广告。就这样我的目光最后落到那个放在角落里的玩具娃娃身上。这个娃娃的脸上带着一种最奇怪、最有魅力的表情。由于是透过橱窗上一层灰尘观看并且光线阴暗，我无法完全辨认出她来。但是我意识到这个娃娃给我留下了深刻的印象，就像是我撞倒了一个人，就像有时候一个人对一个有着鲜明个性的陌生人所产生的深刻印象。

题目答案与解析

1. 什么给作者留下了印象？
   A．娃娃奇怪的脸。　　　　　　　　　　B．一堆礼物。

C．他在店里遇到的陌生人。　　　　　　D．娃娃和他侄女的脸的相同之处。

【答案】A

【解析】本题的依据是文章最后一段中的两句话 a doll with the strangest, most charming expression on her face…a tremendous impression had been made upon me。因此 A 项为正确答案。

2．作者提及他的侄女的原因是什么？

A．她喜欢娃娃。　　　　　　　　　　B．娃娃看上去像她侄女。

C．她住在 Sheftel's 玩具店附近。　　　D．他正在为她寻找礼物。

【答案】D

【解析】本题可参照文章的第 2 段。开始时作者说在上班的路上路过那家玩具店，而且当时碰巧想起每年要给自己的侄女买件生日礼物，而且他知道侄女喜欢不太贵的玩具，因此才停下来看看有没有合适的。这里提到侄女应该是作者为自己下一步的举动做出的一个铺垫。因此 D 项为正确答案。

3．作者经过 Shefte's 玩具商店门口的原因是什么？

A．他在去上班的路上。　　　　　　　B．他在给他侄女寻找礼物。

C．他想买点信封。　　　　　　　　　D．他喜欢看橱窗。

【答案】A

【解析】本题可参照文章的第 2 段。开始时作者说在上班的路上路过那家玩具店，从中可知作者并非专门去玩具店买东西，只不过是路过而已。因此 A 项为正确答案。

4．本篇故事发生在 _____。

A．早夏　　　　　B．早春　　　　　C．仲夏　　　　　D．晚春

【答案】B

【解析】从文中第 1 行中间的 in April 和第 4 行的 the first hint of spring 可知，B 项为正确答案。

5．在玩具店橱窗中多数的东西 _____。

A．昂贵　　　B．吸引人　　　C．安排得很整洁　　　D．不引人注意

【答案】D

【解析】本题的依据是文章第 2 段的 And looked at the confusing collection of unappealing objects。unappealing 和 D 项中的 unattractive 一样，意思都是"不吸引人的"，因此 D 为正确答案。

Unit 9

Text 1

The United States is often considered a young nation, but in fact it is next to the oldest continuous government in the world, and the reason is that its people have always been willing to accommodate themselves to change. It should be realized, however, that sharing benefits of our achievements was the result of trial and error. Unprincipled businessmen had first to be restrained by government before they came to learn that they must serve the general good in pursuing their economic interests. Thus, although early statesmen strongly believed in private enterprise, they chose to make the post office a government monopoly and to give the schools to public ownership. Since then, government has broadened its activities in many ways including preventing monopolies from taking over the economy.

Increased growth by acquisition by our largest corporations has resulted in a situation where virtually independent economic giants will dominate the American economy. Growth of these vast corporate structures, even though accompanied by an increase in the number of much smaller and less powerful companies that operate under their control, foretells the creation of monopoly — like structures throughout American business. In general, the major acquisitions by the sample companies were corporate organizations that were profitable and successful before acquisition. The main effect of the merger or acquisition was to transfer control and management of an already successful enterprise to a new group. Profitability ratios indicate that, in most instances, the acquired companies operated less efficiently after acquisition.

Americans hold with Lincoln that "the legitimate object of government is to do for a community of people whatever they need to have done but cannot do at all, or cannot do so well for themselves, in their separate and individual capacities." Clearly merger restriction is one example of legitimate government intervention.

1. It is implied that the main quality of the United States stressed is its _____.
   A. youth   B. shared wealth   C. trial and error   D. flexibility
2. The term "general good" (Line 5, Para. 1) refers to _____.
   A. efficient practices   B. ethical practices
   C. common well-being   D. profitable decisions
3. The creation of U.S. post office monopoly is cited as an example of a _____.
   A. replacement of the existing economic order
   B. restraint of unprincipled businessmen
   C. flexible view of government
   D. system of shared profits

4. From the text we learn that when mergers occurred, the added companies had _____.
   A. low profitability ratios
   B. management difficulties
   C. poor productivity
   D. achieved success

5. The author's view of mergers is _____.
   A. critical
   B. cautious
   C. qualified
   D. favorable

核心词汇注释

accommodate [əˈkɒmədeɪt] *vt.* 供应，供给；使适应，调节；和解；向……提供，容纳；调和
vi. 适应

unprincipled [ʌnˈprɪnsɪp(ə)ld] *adj.* 不道德的，无原则的，不合人道的

restrained [rɪˈstreɪnd] *adj.* 受限制的，拘谨的，有限的

monopoly [məˈnɒpəlɪ] *n.* 垄断，垄断者；专利权，专利事业

acquisition [ˌækwɪˈzɪʃ(ə)n] *n.* 获得；获得物

dominate [ˈdɒmɪneɪt] *v.* 支配，占优势

foretell [fɔːˈtel] *v.* 预言，预示，预测

merger [ˈmɜːdʒə(r)] *n.* 合并，归并

ratio [ˈreɪʃɪəʊ] *n.* 比，比率；[财政]复本位制中金银的法定比价

legitimate [lɪˈdʒɪtɪmət] *adj.* 合法的；合理的；正统的
v. 合法

长难句剖析

【文章难句】Increased growth by acquisition by our largest corporation has resulted in a situation where virtually independent economic giants will dominate the American economy.

【结构分析】本句主干是 Increased growth…has resulted in a situation…。situation 后面的 where 引导的是定语从句。两个 by 中，第一个 by 表示方式，第二个 by 表示施动者。

【参考译文】我们的最大型企业通过收购得以继续发展，这样导致的情况是，几个几乎独立的经济巨头将支配美国经济。

【文章难句】Growth of these vast corporate structures, even though accompanied by an increase in the number of much smaller and less powerful companies that operate under their control, foretells the creation of monopoly — like structures throughout American business.

【结构分析】本句主干是 Growth…foretells the creation…，even though 引导的状语做插入语，that 引导定语从句，修饰 companies。their 指代 these vast corporate structures。

【参考译文】尽管与此同时规模小得多、实力弱得多、在其控制下运作的公司数量也在增长，但是这些庞大企业结构的发展预示了美国商业界类似垄断的结构会产生。

全文参考译文

美国常常被认为是一个年轻的国度，但实际上，它差不多是世界上连续执政时间最长的政府，原因是美国人民总是愿意适应变化。然而，应意识到，能共享我们成就所带来的好处是反复尝试的结果。不讲道德的商人必须首先由政府加以约束才能逐渐认识到，在追求经济利益的同时，自己必须服务于公益。所以虽然早期政治家坚定地认为企业应该私有，但他们

情愿让邮政为政府垄断，使学校为公共所有。自此以后，政府在诸多方面扩展了活动范围，包括防止垄断控制经济。

我们的大型企业通过收购得到了发展，但是这样做的结果事实上将是这些独立的经济巨头控制美国经济。尽管与此同时规模小得多、实力弱得多、在其控制下运作的公司数量也在增长，但是这些庞大企业结构的发展预示了美国商业界类似垄断的结构会产生。通常来说，典型公司的主要收购是收购之前赢利的成功企业组织。合并或收购的主要影响在于，将一个业已成功企业的调控和管理转移到一个新的集团。赢利比率表明，在多数情况下，被收购的公司在收购后运作效率降低。

美国人赞成林肯的观点："政府的合理目标是，为作为群体的民众去做他们需要做到的，但以公民各自独立之力不能做到，或者不能做好的事情。"很明显，限制合并是政府合理干预的一个例证。

题目答案与解析

1. 文中暗示了美国所强调的主要特征是它的 _____。
   A．年轻 B．财富共享 C．反复试验 D．灵活变通
   【答案】D
   【解析】从文章的首句可知，美国政府之所以几乎是世界上连续执政时间最长的政府，其原因在于美国人民总是愿意适应变化，据此可推知，D 项为正确答案。

2. 词语"general good"（第 1 段第 5 行）指的是 _____。
   A．有效的实践 B．道德的实践 C．公共福利 D．有利的决定
   【答案】C
   【解析】本题的依据是原文的 they must serve the general good in pursuing their economic interests，根据后续提示可知，general good 的词义一定与 their economic interests 相反。因此 C 项为正确答案。

3. 引用美国邮政垄断这个例子是用来说明 _____。
   A．现有经济秩序的替代 B．对不道德商人的约束
   C．政府的灵活政策 D．共享利润制度
   【答案】B
   【解析】本题考查逻辑关系。可以通过关联词语判定，该例前有 thus，说明是承接上文。上文讲的是美国乐于适应变化。据此推断，举出该例是为了说明政府自由的观念。

4. 从文中我们了解到，公司之间进行合并时，被合并的公司 _____。
   A．利润低 B．管理困难 C．生产力低下 D．已获得成功
   【答案】D
   【解析】本题的依据是原文的 In general, the major acquisitions by the sample companies were corporate organizations that were profitable and successful before acquisition，从中可知，被合并的公司在收购前是运作成功的。

5. 作者对合并所持的观点是 _____。
   A．批评的 B．谨慎的 C．有资格的 D．赞成的

【答案】A

【解析】从本文的第 2 段可知，作者先后指出，最大型企业的收购带来的最终结果是经济巨头垄断美国经济，而且收购后的公司运作效率不如以前，可见作者对合并持批判态度。

Text 2

Around the world more and more people are taking part in dangerous sports and activities. Of course, there have always been people who have looked for adventure — those who have climbed the highest mountains, explored unknown parts of the world or sailed in small boats across the greatest oceans. Now, however, there are people who seek an immediate excitement from a risky activity which may only last a few minutes or even seconds.

I would consider bungee jumping to be a good example of such an activity. You jump from a high place (perhaps a bridge or a hot-air balloon) 200 meters above the ground with an elastic rope tied to your ankles. You fall at up to 150 kilometers an hour until the rope stops you from hitting the ground. It is estimated that two million people around the world have now tried bungee jumping. Other activities which most people would say are as risky as bungee jumping involve jumping from tall buildings and diving into the sea from the top of high cliffs.

Why do people take part in such activities as these? Some psychologists suggest that it is because life in modern societies has become safe and boring. Not very long ago, people's lives were constantly under threat. They had to go out and hunt for food, diseases could not easily be cured, and life was a continuous battle for survival.

Nowadays, according to many people, life offers little excitement. They live and work in comparatively safe environment; they buy food in shops; and there are doctors and hospitals to look after them if they become ill. The answer for some of these people is to seek danger in activities such as bungee jumping.

1. A suitable title for the passage is _____.
   A. Dangerous Sports: What and Why?
   B. The Boredom of Modern Life
   C. Bungee Jumping: Is It Really Dangerous?
   D. The Need for Excitement

2. More and more people today _____.
   A. are trying activities such as bungee jumping
   B. are climbing the highest mountains
   C. are close to death in sports
   D. are looking for adventures such as exploring unknown places

3. People probably take part in dangerous sports nowadays because _____.
   A. they have a lot of free time
   B. they can go to hospital if they are injured
   C. their lives lack excitement
   D. they no longer need to hunt for food

4. The writer of the passage has a (n) _____ attitude towards dangerous sports.
   A. positive   B. negative   C. objective   D. subjective

核心词汇注释

adventure [əd'ventʃə(r)] *n.* 冒险，冒险经历
  v. 冒险

sail [seɪl] *v.* 航行（于）
  vi. 起航，开船
  n. 帆，篷；航行

elastic [ɪ'læstɪk] *adj.* 弹性的

ankle ['æŋk(ə)l] *n.* [解]踝

involve [ɪn'vɒlv] *vt.* 包括，笼罩；潜心于；
使陷于

diving ['daɪvɪŋ] *n.* 潜水，跳水

cliff [klɪf] *n.* 悬崖，绝壁

survival [sə'vaɪv(ə)l] *n.* 生存，幸存，残存；
幸存者，残存物

comparatively [kəm'pærətɪvlɪ] *adv.* 比较
地，相当地

长难句剖析

【文章难句】There have always been people who have looked for adventure — those who have climbed the highest mountains, explored unknown parts of the world or sailed in small boats across the greatest oceans.

【结构分析】本句主干是 There have always been people....。people 后面是 who 引导的定语从句，破折号后面的 those 指 people，它后面也接有一个由 who 引导的定语从句，climbed, explored, sailed 是这个定语从句中的三个并列的谓语动词。

【参考译文】总是有人寻求冒险—— 他们攀登最高的山峰，在世界未知的领域探险或是乘小舟跨越大洋。

【文章难句】Other activities which most people would say are as risky as bungee jumping involve jumping from tall buildings and diving into the sea from the top of high cliffs.

【结构分析】本句主干是 Other activities...involve jumping...and diving...。which 引导的定语从句修饰句子的主语 other activities。在这个定语从句中，主干是 which are as risky as bungee jumping, most people would say 做插入语成分。

【参考译文】大多数人认为的和蹦极一样冒险的其他活动包括从高楼跳下和从悬崖顶跳入海里。

【文章难句】You jump from a high place (perhaps a bridge or a hot-air balloon) 200 meters above the ground with an elastic rope tied to your ankles.

【结构分析】本句主干是 You jump from a high place。200 meters...ground 是 a high place 的定语成分，而 with 短语则是整个句子的伴随状语。

【参考译文】你从离地面 200 米的高处（有可能是一座桥或是一个热气球）跳下，脚踝上绑着一条有弹性的绳子。

全文参考译文

世界各地愈来愈多的人正在参加危险的体育活动。当然，总是有人寻求冒险——他们攀登最高的山峰，在世界未知的领域探险或是乘小舟跨越大洋。但是，现在有人可以从持续时间只有几分钟甚至几秒钟的冒险活动中获取即时的刺激。

我认为蹦极就是这样一种典型的活动。你从离地面 200m 的高处（有可能是一座桥或是

热气球）跳下，一条有弹性的绳子绑在脚踝上。你以高达 150 公里的时速落下，快接近地面时再被绳子拉起。估计世界各地有 200 万人现在已经尝试了蹦极。其他大多数人认为和蹦极一样冒险的活动包括从高楼跳下和从悬崖顶跳入海里。

为什么人们会参加这样的活动呢？某些心理学家认为原因就是现代的生活已经变得安全无趣。从前人们的生命时时受到威胁，他们不得不外出觅食，疾病也很难治愈，生活就是一场无休止的生存战斗。

对于很多人来说，现在的生活缺乏刺激。他们在相对安全的环境中生活和工作；他们可以在商店里购买食物；如果生病了，有医生和医院照料他们。在蹦极这样的活动中寻求危险就是他们中一些人的排解方法了。

题目答案与解析

1. _____ 是适合本文的题目。
   A. 危险体育运动：是什么？为什么？　　B. 对现代生活的厌倦
   C. 蹦极：真的危险吗？　　　　　　　　D. 刺激的需要

【答案】A

【解析】从文中内容可知，第 1 段讲到全世界有越来越多的人参加各种危险的运动和活动。第 2 段以蹦极为例加以说明。第 3、4 两段主要在解释人们参加这类活动的原因。只有 A 项能概括全文，因此正确答案。

2. 如今愈来愈多的人 _____。
   A. 正在尝试像蹦极这样的运动　　　　　B. 正在攀登最高的山峰
   C. 在运动中接近死亡　　　　　　　　　D. 正在寻找冒险，例如探索未知地区

【答案】A

【解析】从文中内容可知，第 1 段第 1 句话就讲到全世界有越来越多的人参加各种危险的运动和活动。第 2 段以蹦极为例加以说明。只有 A 项符合文章的意思，为本题的正确答案。

3. 如今人们参加危险运动的原因可能是 _____。
   A. 他们有太多的空闲时间　　　　　　　B. 如果受伤可以去医院
   C. 他们的生活缺乏刺激　　　　　　　　D. 他们不再需要寻找食物

【答案】C

【解析】本题可参照文章的第 3、4 段。从 Nowadays, according to many people, life offers little excitement 可知，C 项为正确答案。

4. 对危险运动，本文作者所持的态度是 _____。
   A. 肯定的　　　　B. 否定的　　　　C. 客观的　　　　D. 主观的

【答案】C

【解析】本题应在理解全文的基础上来进行判断。综观全文，作者的态度是较为客观的，因此 C 项为正确答案。

Text　3

When they advise your kids to "get an education" if you want to raise your income, they tell you only half the truth. What they really mean is to get just enough education to provide man power for your society, but not too much that you prove an embarrassment to your society.

Get a high school diploma, at least. Without that, you are occupationally dead, unless your name happens to be George Bernard Shaw or Thomas Alva Edison and you can successfully drop out in grade school.

Get a college degree, if possible. With a B. A., you are on the launching pad. But now you have to start to put on the brakes. If you go for a master's degree, make sure it is an MBA, and only from a first-rate university. Beyond this, the famous law of diminishing returns begins to take effect.

Do you know, for instance, that long-haul truck drivers earn more a year than full professors? Yes, the average 1977 salary for those truckers was $24,000, while the full professors managed to average just $23,930.

A Ph.D is the highest degree you can get, but except in a few specialized fields such as physics or chemistry, where the degree can quickly be turned to industrial or commercial purposes, you are facing a dim future. There are more Ph.Ds unemployed or underemployed in this country than in any other part of the world by far.

If you become a doctor of philosophy in English or history or anthropology or political science or languages or—worst of all—in philosophy, you run the risk of becoming overeducated for our national demands. Not for our needs, mind you, but for our demands.

Thousands of Ph.Ds are selling shoes, driving cabs, waiting on tables and filling out fruitless applications month after month. And then maybe taking a job in some high school or backwater college that pays much less than the janitor earns.

You can equate the level of income with the level of education only so far. Far enough, that is, to make you useful to the gross national product, but not so far that nobody can turn much of a profit on you.

1. According to the writer, what the society expects of education is to turn out people who _____.
   A. will not be a shame to the society
   B. will become loyal citizens
   C. can take care of themselves
   D. can meet the demands as a source of manpower

2. Many Ph.Ds are out of job because _____.
   A. they are wrongly educated
   B. they are of little commercial value to the society
   C. there are fewer jobs in high schools
   D. they prefer easy jobs to more money

3. The nation is only interested in people _____.
   A. with diplomas
   B. specialized in physics and chemistry
   C. valuable to the gross national product
   D. both A and C

4. Which of the following is NOT true?

A. Bernard Shaw didn't finish high school, nor did Edison.

B. One must think carefully before going for a master's degree.

C. The higher your educational level, the more money you will earn.

D. If you are too well educated, you'll make things difficult for the society.

核心词汇注释

diploma [dɪ'pləumə] n. 文凭，毕业证书；证明权力、特权、荣誉等的证书；奖状

launching ['lɔ:ntʃɪŋ] n. 下水

pad [pæd] n. 垫，衬垫；便笺簿

v. 加上衬垫

brake [breɪk] n. 闸，刹车   v. 刹车

diminish [dɪ'mɪnɪʃ] v. （使）减少，（使）变小

return [rɪ'tɜ:n] n. 回来，返回；来回票；利润；回答

adj. 返回的，回程的；报答的；反向的；重现的

vi. 回返，归还

vt. 归还，回报；报告，获得；回答；返回

dim [dɪm] adj. 暗淡的，模糊的，无光泽的；悲观的，怀疑的

vt. 使暗淡，使失去光泽

n. <美俚>笨蛋，傻子

anthropology [ˌænθrə'pɒlədʒɪ] n. 人类学

overeducate [ˌəuvər'edju:keɪt] vt. 使接受（超过职业需要的）过多教育

fruitless ['fru:tlɪs] adj. 不结果实的

backwater ['bækwɔ:tə(r)] n. 死水，停滞不动的状态或地方

janitor ['dʒænɪtə(r)] n. 看门人

长难句剖析

【文章难句】What they really mean is to get just enough education to provide man power for your society，but not too much that you prove an embarrassment to your society.

【结构分析】本句是主系表结构。what 引导的名词从句做主语，系动词是 is, to do 不定式做表语。在这个不定式中，动词 get 的宾语有两个，一个是 enough education…，一个是 not too much…，而 enough education 的宾语补足语是 to provide man power for your society。

【参考译文】他们真正的意思是受到足够的教育可以为社会提供劳力，但不要过度，不然你就只能在社会中困窘不堪。

【文章难句】Without that, you are occupationally dead, unless your name happens to be George Bernard Shaw or Thomas Alva Edison and you can successfully drop out in grade school.

【结构分析】本句主干是 you are occupationally dead。without that 是一个条件状语，后面也是一个由 unless 引导的条件状语从句，这个条件状语是由两个并列的句子构成的。

【参考译文】至少应该有中学文凭，不然你会没有工作，除非你碰巧是大名鼎鼎的萧伯纳或是爱迪生，可以从中小学辍学并取得成功。

【文章难句】A Ph. D. is the highest degree you can get, but except in a few specialized fields such as physics or chemistry, where the degree can quickly be turned to industrial or commercial purposes, you are facing a dim future.

【结构分析】本句的主干是 A Ph. D. is the highest degree…but…you are facing a dim future。

在第一个分句中，you can get 是定语从句，修饰前面的 degree。在第二个分句中，except 引导的介宾短语做条件状语，in…做 except 的宾语。在英语语法中，常见到介词后面接介词短语的情况。physics or chemistry 后面是关系副词 where 引导的非限制性定语从句。

【参考译文】你能获得的最高学位是博士学位，但除了在少数能将学位快速转化成工业或商业用途的专门领域内，比如物理或化学，你的前途会很黯淡。

全文参考译文

如若你要提高收入，他们就会建议你的孩子去"受些教育"，他们这样只说对了一半。他们真实的意思是受到足够的教育可以为社会提供劳力，但不要过度，否则你就只能在社会中困窘不堪。

至少应该获得中学文凭，否则你会没有工作，除非你碰巧是大名鼎鼎的萧伯纳或是爱迪生，可以从中小学辍学并取得成功。

若可能的话，要取得大学文凭。拥有了大学文凭，你就像上了"发射台"。不过此时，你就应该"刹车"了。如果你想申请硕士学位，那最好是一流大学的 MBA。否则，再往后，著名的报酬递减率就会起作用了。

举例来说，你知道长途运输司机的年收入比教授高吗？没错，1977 年长途运输司机的平均收入是 24,000 美金，而教授的平均收入是 23,930 美金。

你能获得的最高学位是博士学位，但除了在少数能将学位快速转化成工业或商业用途的专门领域内，比如物理或化学，你的前途会很黯淡。到目前为止，这个国家里失业或大材小用的博士多于世界其他国家。

假如你成为一名研究英语、历史、人类学、政治、语言或最糟糕的哲学的博士，你就有受到超出了国家需要的过度教育的危险。提醒你，不是超出了我们自身的需要，而是超出了我们的需求。

成千上万的博士或者卖鞋、开出租车，或者月复一月地坐在办公桌旁填写一些没用的表格，也可能在一些中学或没有前途的大学当差，挣的钱比看门人还要少得多。

你可以将收入的高低和受教育的高低对等起来，即让你能够为提高国民生产总值有点用处的教育就已足够，而不要受过度的教育以至于没有人能够从你身上得到利润。

题目答案与解析

1. 按照作者的观点，提供 _____ 的人是社会对教育的期望。
   A. 不会成为社会羞耻 　　　 B. 将成为忠诚的城市人
   C. 能够自我照顾 　　　　　 D. 可以满足人力资源需求
   【答案】D
   【解析】本题的依据是第 1 段的最后一句话 just enough education to provide man power for your society。因此 D 项为正确答案。
2. 很多博士生无法找到工作的原因是 _____。
   A. 他们受到了错误的教育 　 B. 他们对社会缺乏商业价值
   C. 高校中的工作职位太少 　 D. 他们更喜欢简单的工作，而不是更多的钱

【答案】B

【解析】本题的依据是第5段的第1句话 A Ph. D. is the highest degree you can get, but except in a few specialized fields such as physics or chemistry, where the degree can quickly be turned to industrial or commercial purposes，据此可知他们的学识不能很快应用在工业或商业上。因此B项为正确答案。

3. 这个国家仅仅对_____人感兴趣。

    A. 有学位的   B. 物理或化学专业的

    C. 对国民生产总值有用的   D. A 和 C

【答案】D

【解析】本题可参照文章的第2段和第3段。这两段告诉我们社会对有文凭的人感兴趣。但我们不能选择A项，因为文中也提到有些学历太高的人，社会也不需要，有的是卖鞋、开出租车和填无用的表格的博士。再参照最后一段，对国民生产总值有价值的人才能获得较高的收入，因此C项也对。所以D项为正确答案。

4. 下面各项中不正确的是哪项？

    A. 萧伯纳和爱迪生都没有上完高中。

    B. 申请硕士学位前必须仔细考虑一下。

    C. 受到的教育水平越高，赚的钱越多。

    D. 如果你受了过度教育，你将给社会制造麻烦。

【答案】C

【解析】从文中内容可知，你有可能受教育过度。对国民生产总值有价值的人才能获得较高的收入。又根据第4段里讲到的例子——长途运输司机的收入比教授的高，因此C项为正确答案。

Text 4

I wonder if you realize just how many others share your problem. It is so common for people to distort the truth about themselves. Sometimes it's just an invented excuse when you're late for something or a pretence that you like someone you don't. These white lies don't usually harm anyone and indeed often help smooth over difficult social situations. They certainly are embarrassing if exposed but, on the whole, they're easily forgiven.

What you describe is a habit of lying that is more serious than this. I suspect that the lies you tell are ways of defending an idea you have of your own worth. People who have doubts about their own self-esteem often worry that others will judge them as harshly as they feel they deserve because of a secret idea that they are pretty worthless. In other words, they create a false picture of themselves, a picture of someone who meets all the expectations they think others have of them, And as you say, that causes problems — since they have to keep living up to that image. At the same time, they have to tell further lie to cover the stories they have already told. According to some authorities, this is particularly among women especially those who have few opportunities to develop an adequate sense of self-worth.

I suggest you give yourself one day during which you stick solidly to the truth about yourself.

Give yourself a small treat at the end of the day if you have managed to keep it up. Wait a week and then try it again. Once you have achieved three separate lie-free days, see if you can cope with three days running, then extend it to a whole week. Don't make a promise to yourself that you will never lie again because almost certainly you will——it's too much to take on at once. Try to change things little by little, by setting yourself manageable targets. After a while, you'll wonder why you ever had the problem at all.

1.　This passage is a reply to someone who _____.

　　A．keeps a habit of lying for vain reasons

　　B．works hard to meet others' expectations

　　C．does not know the truth about himself and is too sure of himself

　　D．does not know how to make a realistic plan for himself

2.　Which of the following statements is true according to the passage?

　　A．White lies often cause embarrassment in social situations.

　　B．It is important for women to have an adequate sense of self-worth.

　　C．It takes a little time to get rid of your habit.

　　D．Take exercise like running if you are free and keep it up.

3.　The expression "living up to" in the second paragraph can best be replaced by _____.

　　A．growing up with　　B．living with　　　C．seeking　　　　D．sticking to

4.　In the last paragraph the writer implies that _____.

　　A．you will solve the problem with patience and a strong will

　　B．you must be hard on yourself to accomplish something

　　C．your problem lies in the fact that you hasten to make promises

　　D．you must set different targets at different stages of your life

核心词汇注释

distort [dɪ'stɔ:t] *vt.* 弄歪；扭曲，歪曲；误报

pretence [prɪ'tens] *n.* 伪装

lie [laɪ] *n.* 谎言
　v. 躺卧；说谎

describe [dɪ'skraɪb] *vt.* 描写，记述，形容
　v. 描述

self-esteem [ˌself'sti:m] *n.* 自尊，自负，自大，自尊心

harshly ['hɑ:ʃlɪ] *adv.* 严厉地，苛刻地

deserve [dɪ'zɜ:v] *vt.* 应受，值得
　v. 应受

adequate ['ædɪkwət] *adj.* 适当的，足够的

stick [stɪk] *n.* 棍，棒，手杖
　v. 粘住，粘贴
　vt. 刺，戳

cope [kəʊp] *vi.* （善于）应付，（善于）处理

长难句剖析

【文章难句】Sometimes it's just an invented excuse when you're late for something or a pretence that you like someone you don't.

【结构分析】本句主干是 it's just an invented excuse...or a pretence。when 引导的是时间状语。a pretence 后面是 that 引导的同位语从句。

【参考译文】有时候只是迟到的时候编造理由或是假装喜欢一个其实并不喜欢的人。

【文章难句】People who have doubts about their own self-esteem often worry that others will judge them as harshly as they feel they deserve because of a secret idea that they are pretty worthless.

【结构分析】本句主干是 People...worry that...because of...。people 后面是 who 引导的定语从句，that 从句在主句的谓语动词 worry 后面做宾语。在这个宾语从句中，as harshly as they feel they deserve 作为状语成分修饰动词 judge。最后是由 because of 引导介词短语做原因状语。

【参考译文】那些怀疑自己尊严的人经常担心他人会苛刻地评价他们，正像他们因心里认为自己一文不值而感到自己应得的那样。

【文章难句】Don't make a promise to yourself that you will never lie again because almost certainly you will—it's too much to take on at once.

【结构分析】本句是一个祈使句，主干是 Don't make a promise。that 引导同位语从句，修饰 a promise。because...will 是原因状语成分；破折号后面是对这个原因进行进一步的解释。

【参考译文】不要对自己许诺不再说谎，因为毫无疑问你会说谎——立刻付诸实施太难。

全文参考译文

　　我不知道你是否意识到和你有着同样问题的人有多少。人们歪曲有关自己的事实是非常普遍的事情。有时候只是迟到的时候编造理由或是装着喜欢一个其实并不喜欢的人。这些善意的谎言通常不会伤害任何人而且的确会有助于缓和一些困窘的社交处境。如果被揭穿，这些谎言当然很令人尴尬，不过总体上，这些谎言轻易就会得到人们的原谅。

　　你所描述的是一种说谎的习惯，比起上面那种情况要严重得多。我不相信你说的谎是捍卫自己价值观的方式。那些怀疑自己尊严的人经常担心他人会苛刻地评价他们，正像他们因心里认为自己一文不值而感到自己应得的那样。换句话说，他们对自己的认识是错误的。他们认为自己是一个能够满足他人所有期望的人。就像你所说的，这会造成问题——因为他们必须不负众望。同时，他们还要说更多的谎来圆说过的谎。一些专家认为这种情况在女性当中极其普遍，尤其是那些没有机会充分认识自身价值的女性。

　　我建议你将一天的时间给自己，在这一天内你完全坚持做真正的自己。若你能够坚持到底，在一天结束时给自己一个小小的奖励。待下一周再尝试一次。一旦你可以成功尝试了三个不连续的无谎日，看看你是否能够连续三天做到这一点，接下来把它延长到一个星期。不要对自己许诺不再说谎，因为无疑你会说谎——立刻付诸实施太难。通过树立可达到的目标，一点一滴地努力改变情况。一阵子之后，你就会纳闷为什么你曾经有过这种问题。

题目答案与解析

1. 本篇文章是对什么人的回应？

　　A．因为虚荣而把撒谎当做习惯的人。　　B．努力工作以达到别人期望的人。

C. 不了解自己，自视过高的人。 D. 不知道如何为自己制定现实计划的人。

【答案】A

【解析】综观全文，这是一篇劝人改变习惯，不再说谎的文章。从文章的第 2 段可知，这部分着重解释了说谎的种种原因，其中很多原因都与虚荣有关。因此，文章是给因为虚荣而有说谎习惯的人写的。因此 A 项为正确答案。

2. 按照本篇文章，以下各项叙述中哪项是正确的？

   A. 善意的谎言通常会导致令人尴尬的社交处境。

   B. 对女性来说，对自我价值有足够的认识是很重要的。

   C. 改掉习惯要花一点时间。

   D. 空闲时间进行跑步之类的锻炼并且坚持下去。

【答案】B

【解析】本题的依据是文章第 2 段的最后一句话：According to some authorities, this is particularly among women especially those who have few opportunities to develop an adequate sense of self-worth. 从中可知 B 项是正确答案。

3. 在第 2 段中，"living up to" 用 _____ 代替最为适宜？

   A. 和······一起成长 B. 和······一起生活

   C. 寻找 D. 不放弃，不改变，相符

【答案】D

【解析】本题中，living up to 的意思是"符合"，与 D 项意思一致。因此 D 项为正确答案。

4. 在文章最后一段，作者暗示 _____。

   A. 有耐心和坚强的意志，就能解决问题

   B. 如果要完成事情必须要坚强

   C. 你的问题在于许诺太快

   D. 你必须在生命的不同阶段定下不同的目标

【答案】A

【解析】本题可参照文章最后一段的最后两句话，从中可以推知，要改变说谎的习惯需要时间、耐心和意志。因此 A 项是正确答案。

Unit 10

The London Stock Exchange has been famous as a place for men only, and women used to be strictly forbidden to enter. But the world is changing day by day, and even the Stock Exchange, which seemed to be a men's castle, is gradually opening its doors to the other sex. On 16th November 1971, a great decision was taken. The Stock Exchange Council (the body of men that administers the Stock Exchange) decided that women should be allowed onto the new trading floor when it opened in 1973. But the "castle" had not been completely conquered. The first girls to work in "The House" were not brokers or jobbers. They were neither allowed to become partners in stock broking firms, nor to be authorized dealers in stocks and shares. They were simply junior clerks and telephone operators.

Women have been trying to get into the Stock Exchange for many years. Several votes have been taken in "The House" to see whether the members would be willing to allow women to become members, but the answer has always been "No". There have been three refusals of this kind since 1967. Now women are admitted, although in a very junior capacity. Two forms of jobbers made an application to the Stock Exchange Council to be allowed to employ girl clerks. Permission was finally given. A member of the Stock Exchange explained after this news had been given, "The new floor is going to be different from the old one. All the jobbers will have their own stands, with space for a telephone and typewriters, therefore there will have to be typists and telephone operators. So women must be allowed in." This decision did not mean a very great victory in the war for equal rights for women. However, it was a step in the right direction. The Chairman of the new building will eventually lead to women being allowed to have full membership of the Stock Exchange. It is only a matter of time; it must happen.

1. The London Stock Exchange is famous _____.
   A. for its favorable location
   B. for its policy of opening its doors to women
   C. because it has been a place for men only
   D. because women are now beginning to enter its doors to work

2. Several votes have been taken in "The House" _____.
   A. to see if women were willing to become members
   B. to decide when women would be allowed into "The House"
   C. to find out whether the members were willing to allow women to become members
   D. to decide when to allow women onto the new trading floor

3. Which of the following is true?
   A. Since 1973 women have been allowed to work with the London Stock Exchange.
   B. Women have always been refused participation in stock trading.

C. Women were never officially allowed to enter the Stock Exchange.

D. Men have been trying to get into the Stock Exchange.

4. What is this article about?

A. Women's place in society.

B. How the London Stock Exchange functioned in 1971.

C. How women have been struggling for full membership of the Stock Exchange.

D. How women were gradually allowed to work in the Stock Exchange.

核心词汇注释

castle [ˈkɑːs(ə)l] *n.* 城堡

conquer [ˈkɒŋkə(r)] *vt.* 征服，战胜，占领，克服

broker [ˈbrəʊkə(r)] *n.* 掮客，经纪人

jobber [ˈdʒɒbə(r)] *n.* 临时工，做散工者；批发商；股票经纪人

dealer [ˈdiːlə(r)] *n.* 经销商，商人

share [ʃeə(r)] *n.* 共享，参与；一份，部分，份额；参股
vt. 分享，均分，共有，分配
vi. 分享

vote [vəʊt] *n.* 投票，选举；选票，选举权；表决，得票数
vi. 投票，选举
vt. 投票选举，投票决定，公认，<口>建议，使投票

refusal [rɪˈfjuːz(ə)l] *n.* 拒绝，推却；优先取舍权，优先取舍的机会

junior [ˈdʒuːnɪə(r)] *n.* 年少者，晚辈；下级，（年龄、职位等）较低者；大学三年级学生
adj. 年少的；下级的；后进的

membership [ˈmembəʃɪp] *n.* 成员资格，成员人数

长难句剖析

【文章难句】The London Stock Exchange has been famous as a place for men only, and women used to be strictly forbidden to enter.

【结构分析】本句是个并列句。在前面的分句中，be famous as 的意思是"作为……而出名"。

【参考译文】伦敦证券交易所曾以它只为男人开放而女人谢绝入内而闻名于世。

【文章难句】The Stock Exchange Council (the body of men that administers the Stock Exchange) decided that women should be allowed onto the new trading floor when it opened in 1973.

【结构分析】本句主干是 The Stock Exchange Council...decided that...。括号中内容是对主语的解释。that 引导的宾语从句接在谓语动词 decided 后。在这个宾语从句中含有一个由 when 引导的时间状语从句。

【参考译文】证券交易委员会（一个管理证券交易的男性团体）做出一个重要决定，那就是1973年开市时女性应该被允许进入交易所。

全文参考译文

伦敦证券交易所曾以它的只为男人开放而女人谢绝入内而闻名于世。但世界也在逐渐

地变化，即使是证券交易所，一座男人们的城堡，也正渐渐向异性敞开大门。证券交易委员会（一个管理证券交易的男性团体）于 1971 年 11 月 16 日做出一个重要决定，那就是 1973 年开市时女性应该被允许进入交易所。但是这个"城堡"还没有被完全征服。第一批在交易所里工作的女孩不是经纪人或股票经纪人。她们既不能成为证券经纪公司的股东，也不能成为经授权的股票和证券交易商。她们只是低等职员和电话接线员。

　　多年以来，女性一直在努力进入证券交易所。交易所内举行了几次投票表决来看看成员们是否愿意允许女性的加入，可是答案总是"不"。自从 1967 年以来，就已遭到三次这样的反对。现在女性被允许进入，尽管在数量上很少。两种股票经纪人向证券交易委员会申请允许雇佣女性职员，最终得到了批准。在消息发布后，一位委员会的成员解释说："新的场地和旧的完全不同，以后所有的股票经纪人将会有自己的位置，有放置电话和打字机的空间。因此，就需要打字员和电话接线员，所以不得不允许女性进入。"这个决定并不意味着在女性争取平等权利的战争中取得了伟大的胜利。但是这是向正确的方向迈进了一步。新交易所的主席最终同意让女性取得股票交易的正式成员资格。这仅仅是时间问题，一定能够实现。

题目答案与解析

1. 伦敦证券交易所因 _____ 而著名。
   A．它的好位置
   B．它向女性开放的制度
   C．它是男性的专属领地
   D．女性开始进门工作

【答案】C

【解析】本题的依据是文章的第 1 句话 has been famous as a place for men only. 因此 C 项为正确答案。

2. 在交易所内进行了几次投票，目的是为了 _____ 。
   A．看看女性是否希望成为其会员
   B．决定什么时候允许女性进入交易所
   C．看看其成员是否愿意允许女性成为交易所成员
   D．决定什么时候允许女性进入这个新的交易场所

【答案】C

【解析】本题的依据是第 2 段的第 2 句话…to see whether the members would be willing to allow，从中可知 C 项为正确答案。

3. 下面哪一项是正确的？
   A．自从 1973 年，女性被允许在伦敦证券交易所工作。
   B．女性以前总是被拒绝参加股票交易。
   C．女性从来没有被正式允许进入股票交易领域。
   D．男性曾经试图进入股票交易领域。

【答案】A

【解析】本题可参照第 1 段中间的一句话 The Stock Exchange Council… 1973，从中可知 A 项为正确答案。

4. 本文是关于什么的？

　　A. 女性的社会地位。

　　B. 伦敦证券交易所是怎样在 1971 年成立的。

　　C. 女性是怎样努力争取成为伦敦证券交易所正式成员的。

　　D. 女性是如何一步一步被允许在伦敦证券交易所工作的。

【答案】D

【解析】从文中内容可知，A、B 两个选项与文章无关，应首先排除。C 项应排除，本文重点并不是讲述妇女如何斗争，如何争取进入证券交易所，而是讲述证券交易所的理事会怎样阻挠妇女进入证券交易所，但同时又不得不逐步退让，让妇女进入交易所工作。只有 D 项为正确答案。

Text 2

When we talk about intelligence, we do not mean the ability to get a good score on a certain kind of test, or even the ability to do well in school. By intelligence we mean a style of life, a life, a way of behaving in various situations. The true test of intelligence is not how much we know how to do, but how we behave when we don't know what to do.

The intelligent person, young or old, meeting a new situation or problem, opens himself up to it. He tries to take in with mind and senses everything he can about it. He thinks about it, instead of about himself or what it might cause to happen to him. He grapples with it boldly, imaginatively, resourcefully, and if not confidently, at least hopefully; if he fails to master it, he looks without fear or shame at his mistakes and learns what he can from them. This is intelligence. Clearly its roots lie in a certain feeling about life, and one's self with respect to life. Just as clearly, unintelligence is not what most psychologists seem to suppose, the same thing as intelligence, only less of it. It is an entirely different style of behavior, arising out of entirely different set of attitudes.

Years of watching and comparing bright children with the not-bright, or less bright, have shown that they are very different kinds of people. The bright child is curious about life and reality, eager to get in touch with it, embrace it, unite himself with it. There is no wall, no barrier, between himself and life. On the other hand, the dull child is far less curious, far less interested in what goes on and what is real, more inclined to live in a world of fantasy. The bright child likes to experiment, to try things out. He lives by the maxim that there is more than one way to skin a cat. If he can't do something one way, he'll try another. The dull child is usually afraid to try at all. It takes a great deal of urging to get him to try even once; if that try fails, he is through.

Nobody starts off stupid. Hardly an adult in a thousand, or ten thousand could in any three years of his life learn as much, grow as much in his understanding of the world around him, as every infant learns and grows in his first three years. But what happens, as we grow older, to this extraordinary capacity for learning and intellectual growth? What happens is that it is destroyed, and more than by any other one thing, it is destroyed by the process that we misname education — a process that goes on in most homes and schools.

1. The writer believes that intelligence is _____.
   A. doing well in school
   B. doing well on some examinations
   C. a certain type of behavior
   D. good scores on tests

2. The writer believes that "unintelligence" is _____.
   A. similar to intelligence
   B. less than intelligence
   C. the common belief of most psychologists
   D. a particular way of looking at the world

3. Why does the writer say that education is misnamed?
   A. Because it takes place more in homes than in school.
   B. Because it discourages intellectual growth.
   C. Because it helps dull children with their problems.
   D. Because it helps children understand the world around them.

4. In the paragraphs which follow the above passage, the writer probably discusses _____.
   A. how education destroys the development of intelligence
   B. how bright children differ from dull children
   C. how intelligence is inherited
   D. how the child's intellectual capacity grows at home and school

核心词汇注释

grapple ['græp(ə)l] v. 格斗

bold [bəuld] adj. 大胆的
　　n. 粗体

imaginative [ɪ'mædʒɪnətɪv] adj. 想象的，虚构的

resourceful [rɪ'sɔ:sful] adj. 资源丰富的，足智多谋的

embrace [ɪm'breɪs] vt. 拥抱，互相拥抱；包含；收买；信奉

vi. 拥抱
n. 拥抱

barrier ['bærɪə(r)] n.（阻碍通道的）障碍物，栅栏，屏障

inclined [ɪn'klaɪnd] 倾向……的

fantasy ['fæntəsɪ] n. 幻想，白日梦

maxim ['mæksɪm] n. 格言，座右铭

misname [ˌmɪs'neɪm] vt. 叫错……名字；给……取名不当

长难句剖析

【文章难句】When we talk about intelligence, we do not mean the ability to get a good score on a certain kind of test, or even the ability to do well in school.

【结构分析】本句主干是 When… we do not mean the ability…or even the ability…when 引导的是时间状语从句，主句中谓语动词 mean 的宾语是由两个并列的成分构成的，它们是 the ability to…test 和 or 以后的部分。

【参考译文】当我们谈及智慧时，我们指的不是在某种考试中取得高分的能力，也不是学习好的能力。

【文章难句】The true test of intelligence is not how much we know how to do, but how we behave when we don't know what to do.

【结构分析】本句是主系表结构，The true test of intelligence 是主语，系动词是 is，后面是两个由 how 引导的并列的表语从句。在第二个从句中，when 引导的是时间状语从句，疑问代词 what 引导的不定式做 know 的宾语。

【参考译文】真正的智力测验不是测试我们知道怎样去做，而是测试当我们不知道做什么的时候会怎样做。

【文章难句】Years of watching and comparing bright children with the not-bright, or less bright, have shown that they are very different kinds of people.

【结构分析】本句主干是 Years of watching and comparing…have shown…介宾短语 of 加动名词 watching 和 comparing…构成了 years 后面的定语部分，谓语动词 show 的宾语是一个 that 从句。

【参考译文】对聪明的孩子和不聪明或不太聪明的孩子多年来的比较和观察显示，他们是截然不同类型的人。

全文参考译文

当我们谈及智慧，我们指的不是在某种考试中取得高分的能力，也不是学习好的能力。我们所谈的智慧指的是一种生活风格，一种生活，一种在各种情况下的行为方式。真正的智力测验不是测试我们知道怎样去做，而是测试当我们不知道做什么的时候会怎样做。

不论年老年少，有才智的人遇到新的情况或问题时，都会豁达地面对。他努力用心和感觉去尽可能地掌握所有细节。他考虑问题，而不是考虑他自己或是这将给他带来什么后果。他大胆地、富有想象力地、机智地，而且如果算不上信心十足，至少是充满希望地去解决问题；假如他无法圆满解决，对自己的错误他也并不害怕或是感到惭愧，而且尽量从中吸取教训，这就是智慧。很明显，它源于一种对生活的感情和自身对生活的尊重。同样，愚蠢并不是大多数心理学家认为的只是缺乏智慧。它是一种完全不同的行为风格，源自截然不同的一类态度。

对聪明的孩子和不聪明或不太聪明的孩子多年来的比较和观察显示，他们是截然不同类型的人。聪明的孩子对生活和现实充满好奇，渴望与之接触、拥抱，合二为一。他和生活之间没有任何障碍。另一方面，迟钝的孩子对周围发生的事情和现实情况不怎么好奇和感兴趣。他们更愿意生活在幻想的世界。聪明的孩子喜欢做试验，对事物进行验证。他的生活格言就是"给猫剥皮的方法不止有一种"。如果他不能用一种方法做某件事，他会尝试另一种。迟钝的孩子通常害怕尝试。甚至让他试一次都需要不停地敦促；如果这次尝试失败了，他就不干了。

没有人开始就是愚蠢的。一千个或是一万个成人当中，几乎没有人能在他生命中的任意三年里，能够在对周围世界的领悟过程中和每个婴儿最初三年学到的东西和成长的速度一样多，一样快。随着我们长大，这种非凡的学习能力和智慧增长到底发生了什么改变呢？那就是它遭到了破坏，它是被我们误称为教育的过程—— 一个在大多数家庭和学校进行的过程破坏的，这要比任何其他的事物的破坏严重得多。

题目答案与解析

1. 作者认为"智慧"是 _____。
   - A. 在学校成为好学生
   - B. 测试成绩优秀
   - C. 一种行为
   - D. 考了高分

   【答案】C

   【解析】本题的依据是文章第 1 段的第 2 句话 By intelligence we mean a style of life, a life, a way of behaving in various situations，从中可知 C 项为正确答案。

2. 作者认为"愚蠢"_____。
   - A. 和聪明类似
   - B. 不如聪明
   - C. 是心理学家的普遍信条
   - D. 是一种观察世界的特殊方式

   【答案】D

   【解析】本题的依据是第 2 段的最后两句话：Just as clearly, unintelligence is not what most psychologists seem to suppose, the same thing as intelligence, only less of it. It is an entirely different style of behavior, arising out of entirely different set of attitudes. 从中可以推知 D 项为正确答案。

3. 作者说教育名不副实的原因是什么？
   - A. 因为它在家里发生的次数比学校多。
   - B. 因为它阻碍了智力的成长。
   - C. 因为它对迟钝孩子有益。
   - D. 因为它帮助孩子们理解周围世界。

   【答案】B

   【解析】本题可参照文章的最后一段。从最后两句话可知，作者认为人们学习和智力增长的能力被"教育"破坏了。因此 B 项为正确答案。

4. 作者在文章下面的段落中最可能讨论的是 _____。
   - A. 教育如何摧毁智力的发展
   - B. 聪明的孩子和迟钝的孩子有何区别
   - C. 智力如何遗传
   - D. 孩子的智力才能在家里和学校如何增长

   【答案】A

   【解析】从文章最后一段的内容可知，后面几段会讲述教育怎样破坏智力的发展。因此 A 项为正确答案。

Text 3

An upsurge of new research suggests animals have a much higher level of brainpower than previous thought. Before defining animals' intelligence, scientists defined what is not intelligence. Instinct is not intelligence. It is a skill programmed into an animal's brain by its genetic heritage. Rote conditioning or cuing, in which animals learn to do or not to do certain things by following outside signals is also not intelligence, since tricks can be learned by repetition, but no real thinking is involved. Scientists believe insight, the ability to use tools, and communications using human language are effective measures.

When judging animal intelligence, scientists look for insight, which they define as a flash of sudden understanding. When a young gorilla could not reach fruit from a tree, she noticed crates scattered about the lawn, piled them and then climbed on them to reach her reward. The gorilla's insight allowed her to solve a new problem without trial and error. The ability to use tools is also an important sign of intelligence. Crows use sticks to pry peanuts out of cracks. The crow exhibits intelligence by showing it has learned what a stick can do. Likewise, otters use rocks to crack open crab and, in a series of complex moves, chimpanzees have been known to use sticks to get at favorite snack-termites. Many animals have learned to communicate using human language. Some primates have learned hundreds of words in sign language. One chimp can recognize and correctly use more than 250 abstract symbols on a keyboard and one parrot can distinguish five objects of two different types and can understand the difference between numbers, colors, and kinds of object.

The research on animal intelligence raises important questions. If animals are smarter than once thought, would that change the way humans interact with them? Would humans stop hunting them for sport or survival? Would animals still be used for food or clothing or medical experimentation? Finding the answer to these tough questions makes a difficult puzzle even for a large-brained, problem-solving species like our own.

1. According to the text, which is true about animals communicating through the use of _____ human language?

   A. Parrots can imitate or repeat a sound.

   B. Dolphins click and whistle.

   C. Crows screech warnings to other crows.

   D. Chimps have been trained to use sign language or word symbolizing geometric shapes.

2. The word "upsurge", (Line 1, Para 1), most nearly means _____.

   A. an increasingly large amount   B. a decreasing amount

   C. a well-known amount   D. an immeasurable amount

3. The chimpanzee's ability to use a tool illustrates high intelligence because _____.

   A. he is able to get his food

   B. he faced a difficult task and accomplished it

   C. he stored knowledge away and called it up at the right time

   D. termites are protein-packed

4. The concluding paragraph of this text infers _____.

   A. there is no definitive line between those animals with intelligence and those without

   B. animals are being given opportunities to display their intelligence

   C. research showing higher animal intelligence may fuel debate on ethics and cruelty

   D. animals are capable of untrained thought well beyond mere instinct

5. Which of the following is NOT a sign of animal intelligence?

   A. Shows insight.   B. Cues.   C. Uses tools.   D. Makes a plan.

核心词汇注释

upsurge [ˈʌpsɜːdʒ] n. 高潮   **brainpower** [ˈbreɪnpaʊə] n. 智能，智囊，

智囊团

program ['prəʊɡræm] *n.* 节目；程序；纲要，计划 *vt.* 规划，拟……计划；安排……入节目 *vi.* 安排节目；编程序

rote [rəʊt] *n.* 死记硬背，机械的做法，生搬硬套

conditioning [kən'dɪʃənɪŋ] *n.* [心]条件作用，训练

pry [praɪ] *v.* 探查

chimpanzee [ˌtʃɪmpən'ziː] *n.* [动]非洲的小人猿，黑猩猩

termite ['tɜːmaɪt] *n.* [昆]白蚁

primate ['praɪmeɪt] *n.* 首领，大主教，灵长类的动物

chimp [tʃɪmp] *n.*（非洲）黑猩猩

interact [ˌɪntər'ækt] *vi.* 互相作用，互相影响

长难句剖析

【文章难句】Rote conditioning or cuing, in which animals learn to do or not to do certain things by following outside signals is also not intelligence, since tricks can be learned by repetition, but no real thinking is involved.

【结构分析】本句主干是 Rote conditioning or cuing…is also not intelligence。介词 in+which 引导定语从句，修饰主语。since 引导原因状语从句，其中包括两个并列复合句，由 but 连接。

【参考译文】动物通过遵从外界信号，学会做或者不做某些事情，这种机械的条件作用或者提示也不是智能，因为技巧可以通过重复而学会，但并不涉及真正的思考。

全文参考译文

大量新的研究表明，动物的智能比人们以前所认为的要高得多。科学家们在给动物智能下定义之前界定了什么不是智能。本能不是智能。它是通过遗传设置在动物大脑中的一种技能。动物通过遵从外界信号，学会做或者不做某些事情，这种机械的条件作用或者提示也不是智能，因为技巧可以通过重复而学会，并不涉及真正的思考。科学家们认为，有效的标准是悟性、使用工具的能力以及用人类语言交流。

科学家们在判断动物智力时，在寻找一种洞察力，他们将其定义为灵光一现。当一只年幼的大猩猩够不到树上的果实，看到草坪上散放着板条箱，于是把箱子堆在一起，然后爬上去得到自己想要的东西。大猩猩的悟性让自己一次性地解决了新问题。同样是智能的一个重要标志是使用工具的能力。乌鸦使用木棍从裂缝中撬出花生。乌鸦通过表明自己已经了解木棍的功能来展示智能。同样地，水獭使用石块砸开螃蟹。根据了解，黑猩猩做出一系列复杂的动作。使用木棍够到爱吃的白蚁作为快餐。许多动物学会使用人类语言进行交流。有些灵长目动物学会了数百个手势语词汇。一只黑猩猩能识别并正确使用 250 多个抽象的键盘符号。一只鹦鹉能区分属于两个不同类型的五个物体，并能理解数字之间的差别、颜色以及物体的类别。

有关动物智能的研究引出了重要的问题。假如动物比人们从前所认为的更为聪明，这将改变人类与它们相互作用的方式吗？人类会不再为了娱乐或者生存而捕杀它们吗？还会将动物用于食物、服装或者医学实验吗？找到这些疑难问题的答案，即使对于像我们人类这样一个高智能、善于解决问题的物种来说，也是一个难题。

题目答案与解析

1. 依照本文，有关动物使用人类语言进行交流的说法正确的是哪项？
   A. 鹦鹉能够模仿或重复某种声音。
   B. 海豚发出滴答声和口哨声。
   C. 乌鸦发出尖叫声来警告其他的乌鸦。
   D. 训练黑猩猩使用手势语或象征几何形状的词语。

   【答案】D

   【解析】本题中，A、B、C 三项或违背原文信息，或原文未经提到。只有 D 项为正确答案。

2. 与单词"upsurge"（第 1 段第 1 行）最相近的意思是 _____ 。
   A. 急剧增长的数量   B. 渐少的数量
   C. 清楚明白的数量   D. 不可估量的数量

   【答案】A

   【解析】本文中，单词 upsurge 的意思是"急剧增长的数量"。

3. 黑猩猩使用工具的能力证明了它们具有高智能，因为 _____ 。
   A. 它能得到食物   B. 它面对困难的任务并能够完成这项任务
   C. 它积累知识并在恰当的时间使用   D. 白蚁含有蛋白质

   【答案】C

   【解析】根据黑猩猩能做出一系列复杂的动作，并使用木棍够到白蚁，说明它们能积累经验，加以利用，证明它们具有智能。因此 C 项为正确答案。

4. 从本文结束段落可推断出 _____ 。
   A. 有智能的动物和没有智能的动物之间没有明确的分界线
   B. 给动物们机会来展现它们的智能
   C. 调查显示高智能动物可能会引起有关伦理、残酷方面的辩论
   D. 动物能够不经训练地思考不只是出于本能

   【答案】C

   【解析】本文的最后一段提出一系列人类与动物关系的问题，涉及人类对动物的残酷，据此可推断出，对动物较高智能的研究可能引发有关伦理、残酷方面的辩论。因此 C 项为正确答案。

5. 下面不属于动物智能的表现的是哪项？
   A. 显示悟性   B. 发出信号
   C. 使用工具   D. 制订计划

   【答案】B

   【解析】本题中，动物智能包括悟性、使用工具和制订计划。cues（发出信号）不属于动物智能的表现。因此 B 项为正确答案。

Text 4

There are increasingly fraught relationships that adults are having with children — in all walks of life, from the police and politicians, within the public sector and within communities themselves. The fear of young people has changed the way society is policed, how pupils are treated in schools and how insecure adults relate to children on their estates. Rather than children and young people becoming more violent and anti-social, it is adults who have changed, having fewer relationships with young people and becoming less confident in their dealings with them.

We must explore the role that crime and safety initiatives have on the outlook of the public. The attempt by government, council departments, the police and many others to reduce the fear within communities by developing safety initiatives is having the opposite effect, resulting in the institutionalization of this fear. Curfews have increased adults'fear of young people and reduced the amount of time young children are allowed out to play. They have raised the level of insecurity amongst parents about the safety of their children and ultimately reduced the contact between generations within this community. It is not far from the truth to say that "youth" no longer exists — if by youth we mean the freedom loving rebelliousness. The outcome of this process is breeding a generation of young people who are if anything more fragile and fearful than their grandparents.

Finally, as well as exploring the fear of young people, we must look at the insecurity that parents have for their children. There has been a reduction in play, and specifically in "free play", and the effect of this more regulated environment on children's lives is yet to be determined and not something we can continually ignore in our rush to protect society from children.

1. The author is mainly directing his message towards _____.
   A. adults in general   B. the younger generation
   C. law enforcement authorities   D. parents
2. The first paragraph is mainly about _____.
   A. the way younger people have changed
   B. the change in attitude and treatment towards youth
   C. the fewer relationships between youth and adults
   D. the fear that youth and adults have towards each other
3. The author sees safety initiatives as part of the problem because _____.
   A. they actually cause more rebelliousness
   B. they are unpopular with young people
   C. they worsen relationships and create more fear
   D. they reduce the play young people can use to expend energy
4. The author believes it's possible to say youth no longer exists because _____.
   A. youth have no more rebellion and freedom
   B. youth are indistinguishable in character from their grandparents
   C. they are not allowed to voice their opinions
   D. they do not love freedom the way they should
5. To correct the problem the author discusses we are advised to _____.
   A. stop being so insecure towards children   B. let children play more
   C. study the roots and effects of our fear   D. stop regulating children's lives

核心词汇注释

fraught [frɔːt] *adj.* 充满……的；担心的，焦虑的

insecure [ˌɪnsɪˈkjʊə(r)] *adj.* 不可靠的，不安全的

estate [ɪˈsteɪt] *n.* 状态；不动产；时期；阶层；财产

initiative [ɪˈnɪʃɪətɪv] *n.* 主动

curfew [ˈkɜːfjuː] *n.*（中世纪规定人们熄灯安睡的）晚钟声，打晚钟时刻；宵禁令（时间）

rebelliousness [rɪˈbelɪəsnɪs] *n.* 造反，难以控制

breeding [ˈbriːdɪŋ] *n.* 饲养，教养

fragile [ˈfrædʒaɪl] *adj.* 易碎的，脆的

reduction [rɪˈdʌkʃ(ə)n] *n.* 减少；缩影，变形；缩减量，缩小，降低；缩图，缩版

长难句剖析

【文章难句】The fear of young people has changed the way society is policed, how pupils are treated in schools and how insecure adults relate to children on their estates.

【结构分析】本句是主从复合句，主干是 The fear…has changed the way…how…and how… 。三个并列的宾语在动词 changed 之后。当 police 用作动词时，意思是"维持治安"。词组 relate to 的意思是"交往"。

【参考译文】对年轻人的恐惧已改变了社会治安，改变了学生在学校的待遇，改变了局促不安的成人在住宅区和孩子的交往。

【文章难句】Rather than children and young people becoming more violent and anti-social, it is adults who have changed, having fewer relationships with young people and becoming less confident in their dealings with them.

【结构分析】本句为强调句型，主干是 it is adults who have changed，强调的是 adults。rather than 引起的短语做状语。由 having 和 becoming 引出的两个并列的状语修饰 change。

【参考译文】孩子和年轻人并没有变得更加充满暴力和反对社会，而是成年人变了，和年轻人的交往减少，在与年轻人的交往中信心不足。

【文章难句】The attempt by government, council departments, the police and many others to reduce the fear within communities by developing safety initiatives is having the opposite effect, resulting in the institutionalization of this fear.

【结构分析】本句主干是 The attempt…is having the opposite effect。主语之后有三个短语，第一个 by 表示 attempt 的施动者，不定式短语 to reduce…表示 attempt 的内容；第二个 by 表示不定式动词的方式。resulting in…是动词现在分词短语做状语。

【参考译文】政府、市政各部门、警方以及众多其他机构通过推出安全措施，试图减少社区内部的恐惧，但适得其反，使这种恐惧制度化。

全文参考译文

包括警方和政界、公共部门以及社区自身在内的社会各界，对于成人和孩子之间的关系愈发担忧。对年轻人的恐惧已改变了社会治安，改变了学生在学校的待遇，改变了局促不安的成人在住宅区和孩子的交往。孩子和年轻人并没有变得更充满暴力和反对社会，而是成年

人变了，和年轻人的交往减少，在与年轻人的交往中信心不足。

我们必须研究犯罪和安全措施对公众看法的影响。通过推出安全措施，政府、市政各部门、警方以及众多其他机构试图减少社区内部的恐惧，结果适得其反，这些措施却使这种恐惧制度化。宵禁增加了成年人对年轻人的恐惧，减少了小孩子允许出门玩耍的时间，加大了父母对子女安全问题的忧虑，最终减少了社区内部两代人之间的交往。完全可以说，假如我们把青春期理解为喜欢桀骜不驯的自由，那么青春期已不复存在。这一过程的结果是，培养出比祖父母更为脆弱、更加胆怯的一代年轻人，假如有不同的话。

最后，除了研究对年轻人的恐惧之外，我们还必须考察父母对子女的担心。孩子玩耍，特别是"自由玩耍"减少了。这种更加受到制约的环境对孩子生活的影响有待于确定，在将孩子同社会隔开的狂潮中，我们不能一直对这种影响视而不见。

题目答案与解析

1. 作者写作的主要对象是 _____。
   A. 全体成年人
   B. 年轻的一代
   C. 法律强制性权威
   D. 父母
   【答案】A
   【解析】综观全文，本文话题主要涉及成年人对年轻人的恐惧，因此作者的写作对象是全体成年人。A 项为正确答案。

2. 第 1 段主要讲的是关于 _____。
   A. 年轻人改变的方式
   B. 对待青少年的态度和方式方面的改变
   C. 年轻人和成年人之间的关联很少
   D. 年轻人和成年人之间的恐惧
   【答案】B
   【解析】从第 1 段的内容可知，成年人对待青少年的态度和方式方面发生了改变。因此 B 项为正确答案。

3. 作者将安全措施问题看作问题的一部分，因为 _____。
   A. 它们实际上引发了更多的反叛
   B. 它们在年轻人当中不受欢迎
   C. 它们使关系恶化并造成了更多的恐惧
   D. 它们减少了年轻人发泄精力的方式
   【答案】C
   【解析】从第 2 段的内容可知，作者指出安全措施适得其反，紧接着讲到安全措施加重了问题，造成成年人对年轻人更多的恐惧，前后信息应为因果关系。因此 C 项为正确答案。

4. 作者认为，可以说年轻人不再存在的原因是 _____。
   A. 年轻人没有更多的反叛和自由
   B. 年轻人和祖父母在性格上没有区别
   C. 他们不被允许表达见解

　　D．他们不喜欢应该有的自由方式

【答案】B

【解析】本题应参照第 2 段的结尾一句。作者指出，如果年轻人和祖父母有区别的话，则是更为脆弱、更加胆怯。这说明年轻人和祖父母在性格上没有区别。因此 B 项为正确答案。

5.　为了纠正这个问题，作者建议我们应该 _____。

　　A．停止对孩子们的不安全感　　　　B．让孩子们更多地玩耍

　　C．研究我们恐惧的根源和影响　　　D．停止对孩子们生活的控制

【答案】C

【解析】综观全文，本文探讨了社会各界对年轻人恐惧的根源和影响。因此 C 项为正确答案。

第二部分　模拟提高 40 篇

Unit　11

Text　1

Everybody loves a fat pay rise. Yet pleasure at your own can vanish if you learn that a colleague has been given a bigger one. Indeed, if he has a reputation for slacking, you might even be outraged. Such behaviour is regarded as "all too human", with the underlying assumption that other animals would not be capable of this finely. But a study by Sarach Brosnan and Frans de Waal of Emory University in Atlanta, Georgia, which has just been published in *Nature*, suggests that it is all too monkey, as well.

The researchers studied the behaviour of female brown capuchin monkeys. They look cute. They are good-natured, cooperative creatures, and they share their food readily. Above all, like their female human counterparts, they tend to pay much closer attention to the value of "goods and services" than males.

Such characteristics make them perfect candidates for Dr. Brosnan's and Dr. de Waal's study. The researchers spent two years teaching their monkeys to exchange tokens for food. Normally, the monkeys were happy enough to exchange pieces of rock for slices of cucumber. However, when two monkeys were placed in separate but adjoining chambers, so that each could observe what the other was getting in return for its rock, their behaviour became markedly different.

In the world of capuchins, grapes are luxury goods (are much preferable to cucumbers). So when one monkey was handed a grape in exchange for her token, the second was reluctant to hand hers over for a mere piece of cucumber. And if one received a grape without having to provide her token in exchange at all, the other either tossed her own token at the researcher or out of the chamber, or refused to accept the slice of cucumber. Indeed, the mere presence of a grape in the other chamber (without an actual monkey to eat it) was enough to induce resentment in a female capuchin.

The researchers suggest that capuchin monkeys, like humans, are guided by social emotions. In the wild, they are a cooperative, group-living species. Such cooperation is likely to be stable only when each animal feels it is not being cheated. Feelings of righteous indignation, it seems, are not the preserve of people alone. Refusing a lesser reward completely makes these feelings abundantly clear to other members of the group. However, whether such a sense of fairness evolved independently in capuchins and humans, or whether it stems for the common ancestor that the species had 35 million years ago, is, as yet, an unanswered question.

1. In the opening paragraph, the author introduces his topic by _____.
   A. posing a contrast
   B. justifying an assumption
   C. making a comparison
   D. explaining a phenomenon

2. The statement "it is all too monkey" (Last line, Para. 1) implies that _____.
   A. monkeys are also outraged by slack rivals
   B. resenting unfairness is also monkeys' nature
   C. monkeys, like humans, tend to be jealous of each other
   D. no animals other than monkeys can develop such emotions

3. Female capuchin monkeys were chosen for the research most probably because they are _____.
   A. more inclined to weigh what they get
   B. attentive to researchers' instructions
   C. nice in both appearance and temperament
   D. more generous than their male companions

4. Dr. Brosnan and Dr. de Waal have eventually found in their study that the monkeys _____.
   A. prefer grapes to cucumbers
   B. can be taught to exchange things
   C. will not be co-operative if feeling cheated
   D. are unhappy when separated from other

5. What can we infer from the last paragraph?
   A. Monkeys can be trained to develop social emotions.
   B. Human indignation evolved from an uncertain source.
   C. Animals usually show their feelings openly as humans do.
   D. Cooperation among monkeys remains stable only in the wild.

核心词汇注释

vanish ['vænɪʃ] *vi.* 消失，突然不见；[数] 成为零
n. [语]弱化音

slack [slæk] *n.* 松弛，静止；淡季；闲散；家常裤
adj. 松弛的；不流畅的；疏忽的；软弱的；漏水的；呆滞的；懒散的
adv. 马虎地；缓慢地
vt. 使松弛；使缓慢；马虎从事
vi. 松懈；减弱；松弛

outrage ['aʊtreɪdʒ] *n.* 暴行；侮辱；愤怒
vt. 凌辱；引起义愤；强奸

capuchin ['kæpjʊʃɪn] *n.* 僧帽猴；教会修士

[C-]（天主教）圣方济

counterpart ['kaʊntəpɑːt] *n.* 地位或作用相似的人或物

token ['təʊkən] *n.* 表示；象征；记号；代币
adj. 象征的；表意的

preferable ['prefərəb(ə)l] *adj.* 更可取的；更好的，更优越的

reluctant [rɪ'lʌktənt] *adj.* 不顾的；勉强的；难得到的；难处理的

toss [tɒs] *v.* 投，掷

indignation [ˌɪndɪg'neɪʃ(ə)n] *n.* 愤慨，义愤

长难句剖析

【文章难句】However, whether such a sense of fairness evolved independently in capuchins and humans, or whether it stems from the common ancestor that the species had 35 million years ago, is, as yet, an unanswered question.

【结构分析】本句中，两个由 whether 引导的主语从句用 or 连接，句子的谓语用第三人称单数。在第二个主语从句中，由 that 引导的定语从句修饰 ancestor。

【参考译文】然而这种公平意识究竟是僧帽猴和人类自身独立演化形成的，还是源于 3,500 万年前他们的共同祖先，至今仍然是一个"悬而未解"的问题。

全文参考译文

每个人都喜欢丰厚的加薪。但是，如果你了解到某个同事的薪水比你增加得更多的话，你的这份欣喜就可能消失了。实际上，如果这位同事还有懒散的名声的话，你甚至可能会感到很愤怒。这样的行为被看成是"人之常情"，这种说法包含一个假设，即其他的动物不可能很好地做到这一点。然而，一项由佐治亚州亚特兰大市 Emory 大学的 Sarach Brosnan 和 Frans de Waal 所做的研究表明，这种行为也极具"猴性"—— 这项研究刊登在《自然》杂志上。

研究人员研究了雌性棕色僧帽猴的行为。这些猴子看上去很灵敏。它们是温和、协作的动物，很愿意分享食物。最重要的是，如同人类女性一样，它们往往比雄性更注重"物品和服务"的价值。

这些特征使得它们成为 Brosnan 博士和 de Waal 博士理想的研究对象。两位研究人员花了两年时间教他们研究的猴子用代币来换取食物。通常，猴子们非常愿意用石块换取黄瓜片。但是，当两个猴子被放在隔开但相邻的猴舍时，每个猴子就都可能观察另一个猴子用石块换取什么，它们的行为就变得明显不同。

比较黄瓜而言，僧帽猴更喜欢葡萄，葡萄可以说是它们的奢侈品。于是，当研究人员递给一只猴子一颗葡萄以换取它的代币时，另一只猴子就不情愿拿它的代币只换取一片黄瓜。如果一只猴子不用交换代币就能获得一颗葡萄，那么另一只猴子要么把它的代币掷给研究人员，要么把代币扔出室外，要么拒绝接受那片黄瓜。的确，只要一颗葡萄出现在另一个猴舍，就足以导致雌性僧帽猴的怨气。

研究人员指出，僧帽猴和人类一样，也受社会情感的支配。在野外，它们是协作、群居的物种。只有在每个动物都觉得它没有受到欺骗时，这种协作才有可能稳定。如此看来，正当的愤怒感并非人类所特有的。完全拒绝较小的奖励使得群体的其他成员非常清楚这些情感。然而，这种公平意识究竟是僧帽猴和人类自身独立演化形成的，还是源于 3,500 万年前他们的共同祖先，至今仍然是一个未解之谜。

题目答案与解析

1. 在本文的第 1 段，作者引出他的主题是通过 _____。

    A. 提出一个对照   B. 证明一种假设的正确性

    C. 进行比较   D. 解释一种现象

【答案】C

【解析】从文章的第 1 段内容可知，人人都喜欢丰厚的加薪。然而，如果你了解到某个同事的薪水增加得更多的话，你的这份欣喜就可能消失了；事实上，如果这位同事还有懒散的名声的话，你甚至可能会怒不可遏。这样的行为被看成是"人之常情"。隐藏其中的假设是，其他动物不可能很好地做到这一点。但是，一项研究却显示，这种行为也极具"猴性"。由此可知：作者是通过比较来引出自己的主题的。因此 C 项为正确答案。

2. 所陈述的 it is all too monkey（第 1 段最后一行）暗示了_____。
   A. 懒惰的竞争者也会使猴子怒不可遏
   B. 对不公平现象的不满也是猴子的本性
   C. 与人一样，猴子也往往相互嫉妒
   D. 除了猴子，没有其他动物能够培养这样的情感

【答案】B

【解析】从文中第 1 段的内容可知，人人都喜欢丰厚的加薪。然而，如果你了解到某个同事的薪水增加得更多的话，你的这份欣喜就可能消失了。事实上，如果这位同事还有懒散的名声的话，你甚至可能会怒不可遏。这样的行为被看成是"人之常情"。其他动物不可能很好地做到这一点。但是，一项研究却显示，这种行为也极具"猴性"。据此可知，动物也会对不公平的事情感到愤怒。因此 B 项为正确答案。

3. 选雌性僧帽猴来做这项研究，最有可能是因为它们_____。
   A. 更倾向于重视它们所得到的东西　　B. 专注于研究人员的指令
   C. 外表和性情都很得体　　　　　　　D. 比它们的雄性同伴更大方

【答案】A

【解析】本题可参照文章的第 2 段。从中可知，研究人员研究了雌性棕色僧帽猴的行为；这些猴子看上去很聪明，它们是温和、协作性动物，乐意分享食物。最重要的是，如同人类女性一样，它们往往比雄性更注重"物品和服务"的价值。由此可知：雌性僧帽猴之所以被选来做这项研究，主要是因为它们注重"物品和服务"的价值。A 项与文章的意思相符。因此 A 项为正确答案。

4. 在研究中，Brosnan 博士和 de Waal 博士最终发现：猴子_____。
   A. 更喜欢葡萄而不是黄瓜　　　　　　B. 可以被教会交换物品
   C. 如果觉得受到欺骗，就不会合作　　D. 如果同其他猴子分开就会不高兴

【答案】C

【解析】本题可参照文章的第 3、4 段。从中可知，两位研究人员花了两年时间教猴子用代币换取食物。正常情况下，猴子们非常乐意用石块换取黄瓜片；然而，当两个猴子被安置在隔开但相邻的猴舍时，每只猴子就都可能观察另一个猴子在用石块换取什么，它们的行为就变得明显不同。当研究人员递给一只猴子一颗葡萄以换取它的代币时，另一只猴子就不情愿拿它的代币只换取一片黄瓜。如果一只猴子不用交换代币就能获得一颗葡萄，那么另一只猴子要么把它的代币掷给研究人员，要么把代币扔出室外，要么拒绝接受那片黄瓜。由此可知：当猴子觉得受骗时，它们就不会同研究人员合作。C 项与文章的意思相符。因此 C 项为正确答案。

5. 我们可以从最后一段推知什么？
   A. 猴子可以被训练去培养社会情感。
   B. 人类的愤怒是从一种不确定的因素演变而来的。
   C. 同人类一样，动物也通常公开显露自己的情感。

D. 猴子之间的协作只有在野外才保持稳定。

【答案】B

【解析】根据文章的最后一段可知，研究人员指出，僧帽猴与人类一样，也受社会性情感的支配。在野外，它们是协作、群居的物种。只有在每个动物都觉得它没有受到欺骗时，这种协作才有可能稳定。看起来，正当的愤怒感并非人类所特有的。完全拒绝较小的奖励使得群体的其他成员非常清楚这些情感。然而，这种公平意识究竟是僧帽猴和人类自身独立演化形成的，还是源于他们共同祖先，至今仍是一个有待回答的问题。据此可知，现在还不清楚人类和猴子的愤怒感源于什么因素。B 项与文章的意思相符。因此 B 项为正确答案。

Text 2

Do you remember all those years when scientists argued that smoking would kill us but the doubters insisted that we didn't know for sure? That the evidence was inconclusive, the science uncertain? That the antismoking lobby was out to destroy our way of life and the government should stay out of the way? Lots of Americans bought that nonsense, and over three decades, some 10 million smokers went to early graves.

There are upsetting parallels today, as scientists in one wave after another try to awaken us to the growing threat of global warming. The latest was a panel from the National Academy of Sciences, enlisted by the White House, to tell us that the Earth's atmosphere is definitely warming and that the problem is largely man-made. The clear message is that we should get moving to protect ourselves. The president of the National Academy, Bruce Alberts, added this key point in the preface to the panel's report: "Science never has all the answer. But science does provide us with the best available guide to the future, and it is critical that our nation and the world base important policies on the best judgments that science can provide concerning the future consequences of present actions."

Just as on smoking, voice now come from many quarters insisting that the science about global warming is incomplete; that it's OK to keep pouring fumes into the air until we know for sure. This is a dangerous game: by the time 100 percent of the evidence is in, it may be too late. With the risks obvious and growing, a prudent people would take out an insurance policy now.

Fortunately, the White House is starting to pay attention. But it's obvious that a majority of the president's advisers still don't take global warming seriously. They continue to press for more research, a classic of "paralysis by analysis".

To serve as responsible stewards of the planet, we must press forward on deeper atmospheric and oceanic research. But research alone is inadequate. If the Administration won't take the legislative initiative, Congress should help to begin fashioning conservation measures. A bill by Democratic Senator Robert Byrd of West Virginia, which would offer financial incentives for private industry, is a promising start. Many see that the country is getting ready to build lots of new power plants to meet our energy needs. If we are ever going to protect the atmosphere, it is crucial that those new plants be environmentally sound.

1. An argument made by supporters of smoking was that _____.
   A. there was no scientific evidence of the correlation between smoking and death
   B. the number of early deaths of smokers in the past decades was insignificant
   C. people had the freedom to choose their own way of life
   D. antismoking people were usually talking nonsense

2. According to Bruce Alberts, science can serve as _____.
   A. a protector   B. a judge   C. a critic   D. a guide

3. What does the author mean by "paralysis by analysis" (Last line, Para. 4) ?
   A. Endless studies kill action.   B. Careful investigation reveals truth.
   C. Prudent planning hinders progress.   D. Extensive research helps decision-making.

4. According to the author, what should the Administration do about global warming?
   A. Offer aid to build cleaner power plants.   B. Raise public awareness of conservation.
   C. Press for further scientific research.   D. Take some legislative measures.

5. The author associates the issue of global warming with that of smoking because _____.
   A. they both suffered from the government's negligence
   B. a lesson from the latter is applicable to the former
   C. the outcome of the latter aggravates the former
   D. both of them have turned from bad to worse

核心词汇注释

antismoking [ˌæntɪˈsməʊkɪŋ] n. &
adj. 反对吸烟（的），禁止吸烟（的）

lobby [ˈlɒbɪ] n. 大厅，休息室，<美>游说
议员的团体
vi. 游说
vt. 对（议员）进行疏通

panel [ˈpæn(ə)l] n. 面板，嵌板，仪表板；
座谈小组；全体陪审员
vt. 嵌镶板

enlist [ɪnˈlɪst] v. 征募；谋取；应募；赞助；
支持；征召；参军

preface [ˈprefəs] n. 序文，绪言，前言
vi. 作序；写前言
vt. 为……写序言；开始

quarter [ˈkwɔːtə(r)] n. 四分之一；（常 pl.）
方向；地区；方面；季；季度；一刻钟
num. 四分之一；刻

prudent [ˈpruːdənt] adj. 谨慎的

press [pres] n. 压，按；印刷；压力；拥挤，
紧握；新闻
vt. 压，压榨；紧抱；逼迫
vi. 压；逼迫；拥挤；受压

paralysis [pəˈrælɪsɪs] n. 瘫痪；麻痹

steward [ˈstjuːəd] n.（轮船、飞机等）乘
务员；干事

incentive [ɪnˈsentɪv] n. 动机
adj. 激励的

长难句剖析

【文章难句】But science does provide us with the best available guide to the future，and it is critical that our nation and the world base important policies on the best judgments that science can provide concerning the future consequences of present actions.

【结构分析】本句是一个由 and 连接的并列复合句。前面的分句结构简单。后面的分句结构略显复杂，其形式主语是 it，第 1 个 that 引导的从句是实际主语。第 2 个 that 引导的是定语从句，修饰 judgements。concerning 引导的现在分词短语作状语，意思是"就……而言，针对……而做的"。

【参考译文】但是，科学的确为我们提供了通向未来的最佳指导。现在至关重要的是，我们的国家和整个世界将自己的重要政策置于最佳判断之上，这些判断是科学界针对人类目前行为的未来后果所能提出的。

全文参考译文

还记得以前的那些岁月吗？当时科学家认为吸烟会使我们丧命，而怀疑者则坚持认为我们不能肯定这种观点。证据不充分，科学对此也不确定，反对吸烟的游说团体就要破坏我们的生活方式了，政府应该不闻不问吗？许多美国人相信这种毫无道理的说法，30 年来，大约有 1000 万吸烟者因为吸烟过早去世。

现在，由于科学家一次又一次地试图唤醒我们正视全球逐渐变暖的威胁，令人忧虑的相似景象又卷土重来。最近，美国科学院里一个由白宫指定的专家小组表示，地球的气候肯定在变暖，而且这个问题主要是人为的。确凿的信息表明我们应当行动起来保护自己。美国科学院院长 Bruce Alberts 在该小组的报告前言上加了这一重要观点："科学永远不会找到所有答案。但是，科学的确为我们提供了走向未来的最佳指导，现在至关重要的是，我们的国家和整个世界将自己的重要政策基于那些最佳判断，而这些判断是科学界针对人类目前的行为的未来后果所能提供的。"

如同吸烟的问题一样，一些不同的观点坚持认为，有关全球变暖的科学资料还不完整，我们可以继续向空气中排放烟雾，直到我们确实了解其后果。这是一种危险的游戏：等到有了 100% 的证据时就可能太晚了。由于风险明显并且在不断增长，一个谨慎的民族现在就应该购买一份保单。

所幸的是，白宫已经开始关注此事。但是，很显然总统的大多数顾问仍然没有认真对待全球变暖这个问题。他们继续要求进行更深入的研究——一种"被分析而麻痹"的杰作。

要想担任这个星球负责任的管理者，我们就必须坚持进行更深入的大气和海洋研究。但是，只是研究还不够。如果政府不在立法上采取主动的话，国会就应当开始帮助制定保护措施。来自西弗吉尼亚州的民主党参议员 Robert Byrd 提出的一个法案是个大有前途的开端，该法案将为私营产业提供财政奖励。很多人都注意到，我们国家正在准备修建大量新电站，以满足我们的能源需求。如果我们要保护大气层的话，那么最重要的是这些新电站必须是环保的。

题目答案与解析

1. 由支持吸烟者提出的一种论点是 _____。
   A. 没有科学证据证实吸烟与死亡之间的相互关系
   B. 过去几十年，过早死亡的吸烟者人数忽略不计
   C. 人们有选择他们自己的生活方式的自由

D．反对吸烟的人们通常是在胡说八道

【答案】C

【解析】本题可参照文章的第 1 段：还记得以前的那些岁月吗？当时，科学家认为吸烟会使我们丧命，而怀疑者则坚持认为我们不能肯定这种观点。反对吸烟的游说团体就要破坏我们的生活方式了，政府应该袖手旁观吗？据此可知，支持吸烟者认为，人们有权选择他们自己的生活方式。C 项与文章的意思相符。因此 C 项为正确答案。

2．按照 Bruce Alberts 的观点，科学可以用来充当 _____。

    A．一个保护者   B．一名法官

    C．一名评论家   D．一个向导

【答案】D

【解析】本题可参照文章的第 2 段。从中可知，美国科学院院长 Bruce Alberts 在一个小组的报告前言上附加了这个要点：科学永远不会找到所有答案；但是，科学的确为我们提供了通向未来的最佳指导。现在至关重要的是，我们的国家和整个世界依据做出的最佳判断来制定重要政策，而这些判断是科学界针对人类目前的行为的未来后果所能提供的。据此可知，Bruce Alberts 认为，科学能为我们作指引。D 项与文章的意思相符。因此 D 项为正确答案。

3．作者用 paralysis by analysis（第 4 段最后一行）表达什么意思？

    A．无止境的研究扼杀行动。   B．仔细的调查揭示真理。

    C．谨慎的计划阻碍进步。   D．深入的研究有助于作出决定。

【答案】A

【解析】本题可参照文章的第 4 段：幸运的是，白宫已经开始关注此事；但是，很显然总统的大多数顾问仍然没有认真看待全球变暖这个问题。他们继续要求进行更深入的研究——一种"被分析而麻痹"的杰作。据此可知，作者说这句话的意思是太多的研究阻碍人们采取行动。A 项与作者的观点相符。因此 A 项为正确答案。

4．按照作者的观点，政府对于全球变暖问题应该做什么？

    A．提供援助，帮助修建更清洁的电站。   B．唤起公众的保护意识。

    C．继续要求进行进一步的科学研究。   D．采取一些立法措施。

【答案】D

【解析】本题可参照文章的最后一段。从中可知，要想充当这个星球负责任的管理者，我们就必须坚持更深入地研究大气和海洋。如果政府不在立法上采取主动，国会就应当开始帮助制定保护措施。据此可知，作者认为政府应该在立法上采取行动。D 项与作者的观点相符。因此 D 项为正确答案。

5．作者将全球变暖问题与吸烟问题结合起来的原因是 _____。

    A．这两个问题都受到政府的忽视

    B．从吸烟问题吸取的教训适用于全球变暖问题

    C．吸烟问题产生的后果加剧了全球变暖问题的后果

    D．这两个问题都越来越严重

【答案】B

【解析】文中讲道：还记得以前的那些岁月吗？当时，科学家认为吸烟会使我们丧命，

而怀疑者则坚持认为我们不能肯定这种观点。证据并不充分，科学对此也不确定。如今，由于科学家一轮又一轮地试图唤醒我们正视全球逐渐变暖的威胁，令人忧虑的相似景象又卷土重来。最近，美国科学院里一个由白宫指派人员的小组告诉我们，地球的气候肯定在变暖，而且这个问题主要是人为的。正如有关吸烟问题一样，来自于不同角度的观点坚持认为，有关全球变暖的科学还不完善，继续向空气中排放烟雾没有关系，直到我们确实了解其后果。据此可知，作者认为吸烟引发的问题与全球变暖问题很相似。B 项与文章的意思相符。因此 B 项为正确答案。

Text 3

Of all the components of a good night's sleep, dreams seem to be least within our control. In dreams, a window opens into a world where logic is suspended and dead people speak. A century ago, Freud formulated this revolutionary theory that dreams were the disguised shadows of our unconscious desires and fears; by the late 1970s, neurologists had switched to thinking of them as just "mental noise" — the random byproducts of the neural -repair work that goes on during sleep. Now researchers suspect that dreams are part of the mind's emotional thermostat, regulating moods while the brain is "off-line". And one leading authority says that these intensely powerful mental events can be not only harnessed but to help us sleep and feel better. "It's your dream, " says Rosalind Cartwright, chair of psychology at Chicago's Medical Center, "If you don't like it, change it. "

Evidence from brain imaging supports this view. The brain is as active during REM (rapid eye movement) sleep — when most vivid dreams occur — as it is when fully awake, says Dr. Eric Nofzinger at the University of Pittsburgh. But not all parts of the brain are equally involved; the limbic system (the "emotional brain") is specially active, while the prefrontal cortex (the center of intellect and reasoning) is relatively quiet. "We wake up from dreams happy or depressed, and those feelings can stay with us all day," says Stanford sleep researcher Dr. William Dement.

The link between dreams and emotions shows up among the patients in Cartwright's clinic. Most people seem to have more bad dreams early in the night, progressing toward happier ones before awakening, suggesting that they are working through negative feelings generated during the day. Because our conscious mind is occupied with daily life we don't always think about the emotional significance of the day's events — until, it appears, we begin to dream.

And this process need not be left to the unconscious. Cartwright believes one can exercise conscious control over recurring bad dreams. As soon as you awaken, identify what is upsetting about the dream. Visualize how you would like it to end instead; the next time it occurs, try to wake up just enough to control its course. With much practice people can learn to, literally, do it in their sleep.

At the end of the day, there's probably little reason to pay attention to our dreams at all unless they keep us from sleeping or "we wake up in panic, " Cartwright says. Terrorism, economic uncertainties and general feelings of insecurity have increased people's anxiety. Those suffering from persistent nightmares should seek help from a therapist. For the rest of us, the brain has its ways of working through bad feelings. Sleep — or rather dream — on it and you'll feel better in the morning.

1. Researchers have come to believe that dreams _____.
    A. can be modified in their courses
    B. are susceptible to emotional changes
    C. reflect our innermost desires and fears
    D. are a random outcome of neural repairs
2. By referring to the limbic system, the author intends to show _____.
    A. its function in our dreams
    B. the mechanism of REM sleep
    C. the relation of dreams to emotions
    D. its difference from the prefrontal cortex
3. The negative feelings generated during the day tend to _____.
    A. aggravate in our unconscious mind
    B. develop into happy dreams
    C. persist till the time we fall asleep
    D. show up in dreams early at night
4. Cartwright seems to suggest that _____.
    A. waking up in time is essential to the ridding of bad dreams
    B. visualizing bad dreams helps bring them under control
    C. dreams should be left to their natural progression
    D. dreaming may not entirely belong to the unconscious
5. What advice might Cartwright give to those who sometimes have bad dreams?
    A. Lead your life as usual.
    B. Seek professional help.
    C. Exercise conscious control.
    D. Avoid anxiety in the daytime.

核心词汇注释

suspend [sə'spend] *vt.* 吊；悬挂
　v. 延缓
neurologist [ˌnjʊə'rɒlədʒɪst] *n.* 神经学者，神经科专门医师
by-product ['baɪprɒdʌkt] *n.* 副产品
thermostat ['θɜːməstæt] *n.* 自动调温器，温度调节装置
harness ['hɑːnɪs] *n.* （全套）马具；系在身上的绳子；甲胄
　vt. 上马具；披上甲胄；利用（河流、瀑布等）产生动力（尤指电力）
limbic ['lɪmbɪk] *adj.* 边的，边缘的
generate ['dʒenəreɪt] *vt.* 产生，发生
visualize ['vɪʒjʊəlaɪz] *vt.* 形象；形象化；想象
　vi. 显现
terrorism ['terərɪz(ə)m] *n.* 恐怖主义；恐怖统治；恐怖行动
therapist ['θerəpɪst] *n.* 临床医学家

长难句剖析

【文章难句】Most people seem to have more bad dreams early in the night, progressing toward happier ones before awakening, suggesting that they are working through negative feelings generated during the day.

【结构分析】本句主干是 Most people seem to have more bad dreams early in the night，progressing toward happier ones before awakening 做状语，表示梦发展的过程。现在分词 suggesting 引导的短语对主句内容作了概括性说明。

【参考译文】大多数人似乎在晚上睡眠初期做噩梦，随着睡眠加深直至醒来，人们会逐

渐做更快乐的梦。这意味着他们在力图消除白天产生的不良情绪。

全文参考译文

一夜好觉的所有因素中，梦似乎是最不好控制的因素。在梦境中，一扇窗户开启，将我们带入了这样一个世界：在那里，逻辑被置之不理，死者开口说话。一个世纪前，弗洛伊德阐述了这样的革命性理论：梦是我们潜意识愿望和恐惧的被伪装的阴影；到了 20 世纪 70 年代末期，神经病理学家改变了想法，开始认为梦不过是"精神噪音"——睡眠期间进行的神经修复过程中产生的随机副产品。现在，研究人员怀疑，梦是大脑情感调节装置的一部分，在大脑处于"脱机"状态时调节情绪。一位权威人士说，这些强有力的心理事件不仅可以得到利用，而且还能帮助我们获得更好的睡眠和感觉。芝加哥医疗中心的心理学主任 Rosalind Cartwright 说："梦是你自己的。如果你不喜欢，你就换一个。"

大脑影像的证据支持了这种观点。匹兹堡大学的 Eric Nofzinger 博士说，在 REM（快速眼动）睡眠期间——这时大多会做栩栩如生的梦，大脑十分活跃，正如在完全清醒时一样。但是，并非大脑的所有部分都是这样；脑边缘系统情感大脑相对活跃，而前额皮质（智力和理智的中心）就相对平静。"无论我们从梦中醒来时是高兴还是沮丧，那些情感都可能整天伴随我们。"斯坦福大学睡眠研究员 William Dement 博士说。

梦与情感之间的联系在 Cartwright 门诊部的患者中得到体现。在夜里早些时候，大多数人似乎会做更多噩梦，在睡醒前逐渐转为较愉快的梦，这表示他们正在化解在白天产生的消极情感。因为我们的意识被日常琐事占据，所以我们并不总是考虑白天所发生事情对情绪的影响，直到我们开始做梦，这种影响似乎才出现。

我们不应该把这个过程看成是潜意识的。Cartwright 认为，一个人可以经过练习，有意识地控制反复出现的噩梦。你一醒来就应该确定梦中有什么在困扰你。想象一下你想要如何终止这个梦；当它出现的时候，你应该尽力醒来，以便控制它的进程。实际上，经过大量的练习后，人们可以学会在梦中做到这点。

可能很少有什么理由使我们晚上关注自己的梦，除非那些梦使我们无法睡眠，或者使"我们在恐慌中惊醒"，Cartwright 说。恐怖主义、经济上的不确定性以及通常的不安全感加重了人们的焦虑。那些持续遭受噩梦折磨的人应当寻求治疗专家的帮助。对其余的人来说，大脑有它自己化解恶劣情绪的办法。放心地睡觉——或者尽管去做梦，早上醒来时你会感觉好一些。

题目答案与解析

1. 研究人员开始认为梦 _____。
   A. 在其进程中可以改变　　　　　B. 容易受到情感变化的影响
   C. 反映了我们内心深处的愿望和恐惧　　D. 是神经修复过程中的一个随机产物
   【答案】A
   【解析】本题可参照文章的第 1 段。从中可知，一个世纪前，弗洛伊德阐述了这样的革命性理论——梦是我们潜意识欲望和恐惧的伪装阴影；到了 20 世纪 70 年代末期，神经病理学家改变了想法，开始认为梦不过是睡眠期间进行的神经修复过程中产生的随机副产品；现在，研究人员怀疑，梦是大脑情感调节装置的一部分，在大脑处于"脱机"状态时调控情绪；

一位权威人士说，这些心理事件不仅可以得到利用，而且还能帮助我们获得更好的睡眠和感觉。Cartwright 说，"梦是你自己的，如果你不喜欢，你就换一个。"据此可知，研究人员认为梦可以改变。A 项与文章的意思相符。因此 A 项为正确答案。

2. 作者通过谈论脑边缘系统是想揭示 _____ 。

  A. 其在我们梦境中的作用   B. REM 睡眠的机制

  C. 梦与情感的关系   D. 它与前额皮层的区别

【答案】C

【解析】本题可参照文章的第 2 段。从中可知，Eric Nofzinger 博士说，在 REM（眼睛快速运动）睡眠期间，大脑十分活跃，正如在完全清醒时一样。但是，并非大脑的所有部分都是这样；脑边缘系统（情感大脑）就相对平静。"无论我们从梦中醒来时是高兴还是沮丧，那些情感都可能整日伴随我们，"William Dement 博士说。据此可知，作者提到脑边缘系统是想说明做梦与情感之间的联系。C 项与作者的意图相符。因此 C 项为正确答案。

3. 白天产生的消极情绪会趋向于 _____ 。

  A. 加剧我们的无意识情绪   B. 演变成愉快的梦

  C. 一直延续到我们入睡为止   D. 出现在夜里早些时候的梦境中

【答案】D

【解析】本题可参照文章的第 3 段。从中可知，梦与情感之间的联系在 Cartwright 门诊部的患者中得到体现。在夜里早些时候，大多数人似乎会做更多噩梦，在睡醒前逐渐转为较愉快的梦，这表示他们正在化解在白天产生的消极情感。因为我们的意识被日常生活占据，所以我们并不总是考虑白天所发生事件的情感意义。据此可知，白天产生的消极情绪往往会在夜里早些时候的梦境中出现。D 项与文章的意思相符。因此 D 项为正确答案。

4. Cartwright 像是在提示 _____ 。

  A. 及时醒来对于摆脱噩梦至关重要 B. 使噩梦形象化有助于控制噩梦

  C. 梦应该被看成是自然的进程   D. 做梦可能不完全属于无意识行为

【答案】D

【解析】本题可参照文章的最后两段。从中可知，这个过程不应该被看成是潜意识的。Cartwright 认为，一个人可以经过练习，有意识地控制反复出现的噩梦。你一醒来就应该确定梦中有什么在困扰你。想象一下你想要如何终止这个梦；当它出现的时候，你应该尽力醒来，以便控制它的进程。晚上可能很少有什么理由使我们关注自己的梦，除非那些梦使我们无法睡眠，或者使"我们在恐慌中惊醒"，Cartwright 说。恐怖主义、经济的不确定性以及通常的不安全感加重了人们的焦虑。据此可知，Cartwright 认为人们做梦可能不完全是无意识的行为。D 项与文章的意思相符。因此 D 项为正确答案。

5. Cartwright 对那些有时做噩梦的人可能会提出什么建议？

  A. 像平常一样生活。   B. 寻求专业人员的援助。

  C. 练习控制意识。   D. 避免在白天焦虑。

【答案】A

【解析】本题可参照文章的最后一段。从中可知，可能很少有什么理由使我们关注自己的梦，除非那些梦使我们无法睡眠，或者"我们在恐慌中惊醒"，Cartwright 说。恐怖主义、经济的不确定性以及通常的不安全感加重了人们的焦虑。那些持续遭受噩梦折磨的人应当寻求治疗专家的帮助。对其余的人来说，大脑有它自己化解恶劣情绪的办法。放心地睡觉——或者尽管去做梦，早上醒来时你会感觉好一些。据此可知，Cartwright 认为不经常做噩梦的人没有必要担心。A 项与 Cartwright 的观点相符。因此 A 项为正确答案。

Text 4

Americans no longer expect public figures, whether in speech or in writing, to command the English language with skill and gift. Nor do they aspire to such command themselves. In his latest book, *Doing Our Own Thing, The Degradation of Language and Music and Why We Should, Like, Care,* John Mc Whorter, a linguist and controversialist of mixed liberal and conservative views, see the triumph of 1960s counter-culture as responsible for the decline of formal English.

Blaming the permissive 1960s is nothing new, but this is not yet another criticism against the decline in education. Mr. McWhorter's academic speciality is language history and change, and he sees the gradual disappearance of "whom", for example, to be natural and no more regrettable than the loss of the case-endings of Old English.

But the cult of the authentic and the personal, "doing our own thing", has spelt the death of formal speech, writing, poetry and music. While even the modestly educated sought an elevated tone when they put pen to paper before the 1960s, even the most well regarded writing since then has sought to capture spoken English on the page. Equally, in poetry, the highly personal genre is the only form that could claim real liveliness. In both oral and written English, talking is triumphing over speaking, spontaneity over craft.

Illustrated with an entertaining array of examples from both high and low culture, the trend that Mr. McWhorter documents is unmistakable. But it is less clear, to take the question of his subtitle: Why We Should, Like, Care. As a linguist, he acknowledges that all varieties of human language, including nonstandard ones like Black English, can be powerfully expressive — there exists no language or dialect in the world that cannot convey complex ideas. He is not arguing, as many do, that we can no longer think straight because we do not talk proper.

Russians have a deep love for their own language and carry chunks of memorized poetry in their heads, while Italian politicians tend to elaborate speech that would seem old-fashioned to most English speakers. Mr. McWhorter acknowledges that formal language is not strictly necessary, and proposes no radical educational reforms—he is really grieving over the loss of something beautiful more than useful. We now take our English on "paper plates instead of china". A shame, perhaps, but probably an inevitable one.

1. According to McWhorter, the decline of formal English_____.
   A. is inevitable in radical education reforms
   B. is but all too natural in language development
   C. has caused the controversy over the counter-culture
   D. brought about changes in public attitudes in the 1960s
2. The word "talking" (Line 5, Para. 3) denotes _____.

　　A. modesty　　　　　　B. personality　　　　　C. liveliness　　　　D. informality

3. To which of the following statements would McWhorter most likely agree?

　　A. Logical thinking is not necessarily related to the way we talk.

　　B. Black English can be more expressive than standard English.

　　C. Non-standard varieties of human language are just as entertaining.

　　D. Of all the varieties, standard English can best convey complex ideas.

4. The description of Russians' love of memorizing poetry shows the author's_____.

　　A. interest in their language　　　　　　B. appreciation of their efforts

　　C. admiration for their memory　　　　　D. contempt for their old-fashionedness

5. According to the last paragraph, "paper plates" to "china" is as_____.

　　A. "temporary" to "permanent"　　　　　B. "radical" to "conservative"

　　C. "functional" to "artistic"　　　　　　D. "humble" to "noble"

核心词汇注释

aspire [ə'spaɪə(r)] *vi.* 热望；立志

controversialist [ˌkɒntrə'vɜːʃəlɪst] *n.* 争论者；好争论者

triumph ['traɪəmf] *n.* 胜利，成功

　　v. 获得胜利

elevated ['elɪveɪtɪd] *adj.* 提高的；严肃的；欢欣的

genre ['ʒɒrə] *n.* 类型；流派

spontaneity [ˌspɒntə'neɪəti] *n.* 自发性

array [ə'reɪ] *n.* 排列；编队；军队；衣服；大批

　　vt. 部署；穿着；排列

dialect ['daɪəlekt] *n.* 方言；语调

chunk [tʃʌŋk] *n.* 大块；矮胖的人或物

elaborate [ɪ'læbərət] *adj.* 精心制作的；详细阐述的；精细的

　　vt. 精心制作；详细阐述

　　v. 详细描述

长难句剖析

【文章难句】As a linguist, he acknowledges that all varieties of human language, including nonstandard ones like Black English, can be powerfully expressive — there exists no language or dialect in the world that cannot convey complex ideas.

【结构分析】本句是一个复合句。主干是 he acknowledges that，第一个 that 引导的是宾语从句。在这个从句中，all varieties of human language 是主语，can be powerfully expressive 是谓语。破折号后面的句子对主句表达的意思作进一步说明，第二个 that 引导的定语从句修饰 language or dialect。

【参考译文】作为语言学家，他承认所有类型的人类语言，包括黑人英语那样的不标准语言，都能极具表现力——世界上还不存在不能表达复杂思想的语言或方言。

全文参考译文

　　无论是在演说中还是在写作中，美国人都不再期望公众人物在应用英语时有技巧和天分。他们也不渴望自己应用英语时也是如此。John McWhorter 是一位语言学家，也是一位掺

杂自由和保守观点的有争议的人物。在其最近出版的名为《自行其是：语言和音乐的退化及我们为什么应当喜欢和在乎》的书中，他指出 20 世纪 60 年代反文化的胜利应该对正式英语的衰退负责任。

责备放任的 20 世纪 60 年代并不是什么新鲜事，但是，这还算不上对教育衰退的另一种批评。McWhorter 先生的研究方向是语言的历史和演变，比如，他认为，whom 一词的逐渐消失是很自然的事情，同古代英语中格的消失一样并不令人遗憾。

然而，狂热崇尚真实和个性化以及 "自行其是" 已经导致正式演说、写作、诗歌以及音乐的死亡。在 20 世纪 60 年代以前，那些受教育程度不太高的人在动笔写东西时都在寻求高雅的语调，而从那以后，连那些最受尊敬的写作都寻求应用口头英语。同样，在诗歌中，只有高度个性化的诗歌类型才可以称得上真正具有活力的诗歌。在口头和书面语中，随意言谈胜过正式演说，自发性胜过技巧。

通过大量的高雅和粗俗文化的有趣事例，McWhorter 先生证实的趋势一目了然。但是，对其新书副标题中的问题—— 我们为什么应当喜欢和在乎的答案则不那么清楚。作为一名语言学家，他认为所有类型的人类语言，包括像黑人英语那样的不标准语言，都可以极具表现力——世界上还不存在不能表达复杂思想的语言或方言。如许多人一样，他不是在争论，说因为无法恰当地交谈，而使我们不能有条理地思考。

俄罗斯人深爱自己的语言，他们的脑海中记录着大量的诗歌，而意大利的政客们往往向大多数讲英语者详细阐述他们似乎老掉牙的演说。McWhorter 先生认为，正式语言不是确实需要的，他没有建议进行激进的教育改革—— 他确实在为失去某些美好而非有用的东西感到悲伤。我们现在把英语放在 "纸盘而不是瓷盘" 上。也许这是一种遗憾，但是一种无法避免的遗憾。

题目答案与解析

1. 按照 McWhorter 的观点，正式英语的衰退_____。

　　A．在激进的教育改革过程中是不可避免的

　　B．只不过是语言发展过程中的自然现象

　　C．已经引发人们有关反文化的争论

　　D．导致 20 世纪 60 年代公众态度的变化

　　【答案】B

　　【解析】本题可参照文章的第 1 段。从中可知，John McWhorter 是一位语言学家，也是一位掺杂自由和保守观点的有争议人物。在其最近出版的书中，他认为，20 世纪 60 年代反文化的胜利应该对正式英语的衰退负责任。McWhorter 先生的研究方向是语言的历史和演变，比如，他认为，whom 一词的逐渐消失是很自然的事情，同古代英语中格的消失一样并不令人遗憾。据此可知，McWhorter 认为正式英语的衰退是非常自然的现象。B 项与 McWhorter 的观点相符。因此 B 项为正确答案。

2. 单词 talking（第 3 段第 5 行）意为 _____。

　　A．谦逊　　　　B．个性　　　　C．活泼　　　　D．非正式

　　【答案】D

　　【解析】本题可参照文章的第 3 段。从中可知，20 世纪 60 年代以前，那些受过适当教育

的人在动笔写东西时都在寻求高雅的语调，但那以后，连那些最受尊敬的写作都寻求应用口头英语。同样，在诗歌中，只有高度个性化的诗歌类型才可以称得上真正具有活力的诗歌。在口头和书面英语中，随意言谈胜过正式演说，自发性胜过技巧。据此可知，该单词的意思是"随意言谈"。D 项与文章的意思相符。因此 D 项为正确答案。

3．下面各项中，McWhorter 最有可能赞同的说法是哪一项？

　　A．逻辑思维不一定与我们的谈话方式有关。

　　B．黑人英语可能比标准英语更具表现力。

　　C．非标准类型的人类语言只是有趣。

　　D．在所有类型中，标准英语能够最恰当地表达复杂思想。

【答案】A

【解析】本题可参照文章的文章第 4 段。从中可知，通过大量来自于高雅和粗俗文化的有趣例子，McWhorter 先生证实的趋势一目了然。但是，对其新书副标题中的问题——我们为什么应当喜欢和在乎，则不那么清楚。作为一名语言学家，他认为，所有类型的人类语言，包括像黑人英语那样的不标准语言，都可以极具表现力——世界上还不存在不能表达复杂思想的语言或方言。如许多人一样，他不是在争论，说因为无法恰当地交谈，而使我们不能有条理地思考。据此可知，McWhorter 认为，人们的思维方式与人们的交谈方式没有多大关系。A 项与文章的意思相符。因此 A 项为正确答案。

4．对俄罗斯人喜爱记忆诗歌的描述表现出作者 ＿＿＿＿＿＿。

　　A．对他们的语言有兴趣　　　　　　B．赞赏他们做出的努力

　　C．赞赏他们的记忆力　　　　　　　D．蔑视他们过时的风格

【答案】B

【解析】本题可参照文章的最后一段。从中可知，俄罗斯人深爱他们自己的语言，他们的脑海中记录着大量诗歌，而意大利的政客们往往向大多数讲英语者详细阐述他们似乎老掉牙的演说。据此可知，作者钦佩俄罗斯人的努力。B 项与文章的意思相符。因此 B 项为正确答案。

5．按照本文的最后一段，比较"纸盘"与"瓷盘"就像比较 ＿＿＿＿＿＿。

　　A．"暂时的"与"永久的"　　　　　B．"激进的"与"保守的"

　　C．"实用的"与"艺术的"　　　　　D．"粗俗的"与"高雅的"

【答案】C

【解析】从文章的最后一段可知，McWhorter 先生认为，正式语言不是确实需要的，他没有建议进行激进的教育改革——他确实在为失去某些美好而非有用的东西感到悲伤。我们现在把英语放在"纸盘而不是瓷盘"上。也许这是一种遗憾，但是一种无法避免的遗憾。据此可知，把"纸盘子"与"瓷器"相比是在比较美观和用途。C 项与文章的意思相符。因此 C 项为正确答案。

Unit 12

Text 1

Hunting for a job late last year, lawyer Gant Redmon stumbled across Career Builder, a job database on the Internet. He searched it with no success but was attracted by the site's "personal search agent". It's an interactive feature that lets visitors key in job criteria such as location, title, and salary, then e-mail them when a matching position is posted in the database. Redmon chose the key words *legal, intellectual property,* and *Washington, D. C.* Three weeks later, he got his first notification of an opening. "I struck gold," says Redmon, who e-mailed his resume to the employer and won a position as in-house counsel for a company.

With thousands of career-related sites on the Internet, finding promising openings can be time consuming and inefficient. Search agents reduce the need for repeated visits to the databases. But although a search agent worked for Redmon, career experts see drawbacks. Narrowing your criteria, for example, may work against you, "Every time you answer a question, you eliminate a possibility," says one expert.

For any job search, you should start with a narrow concept what you think you want to do— then broaden it. "None of these programs do that," says another expert. "There's no career counseling implicit in all of this." Instead, the best strategy is to use the agent as a kind of tip service to keep abreast of jobs in a particular database; when you getan e-mail, consider it a reminder to check the database again. "I would not rely on agents for finding everything that is added to a database that might interest me," says the author of a job-searching guide.

Some sites design their agents to tempt job hunters to return. When Career Site's agent sends out messages to those who have signed up for its service, for example, it includes only three potential jobs—those it considers the best matches. There may be more matches in the database; job hunters will have to visit the site again to find them—and they do. "On the day after we send our messages, we see a sharp increase in our traffic," says Seth Peets, vice president of marketing for Career Site.

Even those who aren't hunting for jobs may find search agents worthwhile. Some use them to keep a close watch on the demand for their line of work or gather information on compensation to arm themselves when negotiating for a raise. Although happily employed, Redmon maintains his agent at Career Builder. "You always keep your eyes open," he says. Working with a personal search agent means having another set of eyes looking out for you.

1. How did Redmon find his job?
   A. By searching openings in a job database.
   B. By posting a matching position in a database.

  C.　By using a special service of a database.

  D.　By e-mailing his resume to a database.

2.　Which of the following can be a disadvantage of search agents?

  A.　Lack of counseling.　　　　　　B.　Limited number of visits.

  C.　Lower efficiency.　　　　　　　D.　Fewer successful matches.

3.　The expression "tip service" (Line 4, Para. 3) most probably means _____.

  A.　advisory　　　　B.　compensation　　　　C.　interaction　　　　D.　reminder

4.　Why does Career Site's agent offer each job hunter only three job options?

  A.　To focus on better job matches.　　B.　To attract more returning visits.

  C.　To reserve space for more messages.　D.　To increase the rate of success.

5.　Which of the following is true according to the text?

  A.　Personal search agents are indispensable to job-hunters.

  B.　Some sites keep e-mailing job seekers to trace their demands.

  C.　Personal search agents are also helpful to those already employed.

  D.　Some agents stop sending information to people once they are employed.

核心词汇注释

stumble　['stʌmb(ə)l] *v.* 绊倒；使困惑；蹒跚；结结巴巴地说话；踌躇
　n. 绊倒；错误

counsel　['kaʊns(ə)l] *n.* 讨论；商议；辩护律师
　vt. 劝告；忠告

promising　['prɒmɪsɪŋ] *adj.* 有希望的；有前途的

consuming　[kən'sjuːmɪŋ] *adj.* 强烈的

agent　['eɪdʒənt] *n.* 代理（商）

drawback　['drɔːbæk] *n.* 缺点；障碍；退税（指进口货物再出口时退还其进口时的关税）

abreast　[ə'brest] *adv.* 并肩地，并排地

worthwhile　[wɜːθ'waɪl] *adj.* 值得做的，值得出力的

长难句剖析

　　【文章难句】I would not rely on agents for finding everything that is added to a database that might interest me.

　　【结构分析】本句主干是 I would not rely on agents，介词短语 for finding everything 做状语。rely on 的意思是 "依赖，指望"。第一个 that 引导的是定语从句，修饰 everything，第二个 that 引导的也是定语从句，修饰 database。

　　【参考译文】我不会依赖求职代理在添加到数据库的所有内容中逐一寻找令我感兴趣的东西。

全文参考译文

　　去年年底，一位名叫 Gant Redmon 的律师在寻找工作的时候，偶然发现了互联网上一个叫做 Career Builder 的求职数据库。在该数据库里，他没有找到合适的工作，但网上一项称之为 "个人求职搜索代理" 的服务吸引了他。这项服务的互动特性使访问者可以键入求职标准，

如地点、职务和薪金，而当数据库中有与之匹配的职位时，就会通过电子邮件通知访问者。Redmon 选择了以下关键词：法律、知识产权和华盛顿。三周以后，他第一次得到了职位空缺的通知。"我如愿以偿。"Redmon 说。他把他的简历通过电子邮件发送到那家公司，并获得了那家公司内部律师的职位。

　　互联网上有数以千计的与职位有关的网站，寻找有希望的职位空缺可能是很耗时的，效率很低的。搜索代理减少了重复访问数据库的必要性。尽管搜索代理为 Redmon 找到了工作，求职专家还是看到了它们的不足之处。例如，缩小你的工作标准，可能会对你不利。"你每多回答一个问题，你就减少了一个可能性。"一位专家说。

　　对于任何求职搜索，你应从想干什么的狭窄概念开始，然后再加以扩展。"这些程序里没有一个这么做，"另一位专家说，"在整个过程中，没有隐含任何求职咨询。"与此相反，最佳策略就是把这种代理看做一种提示服务，与某个特定数据库中的职位信息保持同步。当你收到电子邮件时，把它作为再次检查该数据库的一种提示。"我不会依赖求职代理在添加到数据库里的所有内容中逐一寻找令我感兴趣的东西。"一位求职搜索指南的作者说。

　　一些网站设计它们的代理服务吸引求职者再次访问。例如，当 Career Site 网的代理向那些注册了它的服务的用户发送信息时，它只提供三个它认为最可能匹配的岗位。数据库中可能有更多的工作匹配；求职者不得不再次访问这个网站去寻找它们——他们的确这么做了。"我们哪天发出职位信息，就会看到我们的访问量急剧增加。"Career Site 网市场部副经理 Seth Peets 说。

　　甚至那些不求职的人也能发现求职搜索代理的价值。一些人利用搜索代理密切关注本行业的工作需求，或者收集有关工薪的信息为增薪谈判做好准备。虽然已找到满意的工作，但 Redmon 仍保留他在 Career Builder 网站的代理服务。他说，"你必须永远保持关注。"拥有一个个人搜索代理意味着你有另一双眼睛看这个世界。

题目答案与解析

1. Redmon 是如何找到工作的？
   A. 通过在一个求职数据库中搜寻职位空缺。
   B. 通过在一个数据库中寻找合适的职位。
   C. 利用一个数据库的特殊服务。
   D. 通过电邮向数据库发送简历。
   【答案】C
   【解析】本题可参照文章的第 1 段。从中可知，去年年底在找工作时，Redmon 偶然发现了互联网上的一个求职数据库。网站的"个人求职搜索代理"吸引了他。这种服务具有互动特征——让访问者输入求职标准，然后，当数据库贴出一个合适的职位时，就通过电子邮件给聘职方寄去你的相关资料。Redmon 通过这种方式找到了一份工作。据此可知，Redmon 是通过一种新型的服务找到工作的。C 项与文章的意思相符，因此 C 项为正确答案。
2. 下面各项中，哪项可能是求职搜索代理的缺陷？
   A. 缺乏咨询。　　　　　　　　　　　B. 访问者数量有限。
   C. 较低的效率。　　　　　　　　　　D. 较少的成功匹配。
   【答案】A

【解析】根据文章第 2 段的最后一句话可知，严格标准可能对你产生不利影响。根据第 3 段的第 3 句话可知，另一名专家说这些程序中没有隐含任何求职咨询。根据第 4 段的第 2 句话可知，代理人给那些登录需要服务的人们发送信息时，所发送的信息只包括三种可能的工作。综上所述，没有提供求职建议是一种不利条件。A 项与文章的意思相符，因此 A 项为正确答案。

3. 短语 tip service（第 3 段第 3 行）的意思最可能是 _____。

   A. 忠告   B. 补贴   C. 互相作用   D. 提示

   【答案】D

   【解析】本题可参照文章的第 3 段。从中可知，最佳策略是把求职搜索代理看成是密切关注一个特定数据库中的职业提示者；你收到电子邮件时，把它看成是再次检查该数据库的提示。据此可知，tip service 与 reminder（提示）同义。D 项与文章的意思相符。因此 D 项为正确答案。

4. 为什么 Career Site 的求职搜索代理只给每名求职者提供三种工作选择？

   A. 为了关注更合适的工作。   B. 为了吸引更多的人回访。

   C. 为了给更多的信息保留空间。   D. 为了提高成功率。

   【答案】B

   【解析】本题可参照文章的第 4 段。从中可知，Career Builder 网站的搜索代理服务给那些登录需要其服务的人们发送信息时，所发送的信息只包括三种可能的工作。数据库中可能有更多相似的工作。求职者只得再次访问该网站以便找到它们——他们也这样做了。据此可知，代理人只给每名求职者提供三种工作选择的原因是为了吸引求职者再次访问该网站。B 项与文章的意思相符，因此 B 项为正确答案。

5. 依照本文的观点，以下哪一项是正确的？

   A. 对于求职者来说，个人求职搜索代理必不可少。

   B. 一些网站不停地给求职者发电子邮件以便跟踪他们的要求。

   C. 对于已经找到工作的人来说，个人求职搜索代理也有帮助。

   D. 一旦人们找到工作，一些求职搜索代理就会停止给他们发送信息。

   【答案】C

   【解析】本题可参照文章的最后一段。从中可知，甚至那些不求职的人也能发现求职搜索代理的用武之地。一些人利用它们密切关注本行业的工作需求，或者收集有关工薪的信息为增薪谈判作好准备。使用求职搜索代理意味着有另一双眼睛在为你留心。据此可知，无论你是否求职，个人求职搜索代理都对你有帮助。C 项与文章的意思相符，因此 C 项为正确答案。

Text 2

Over the past century, all kinds of unfairness and discrimination have been condemned or made illegal. But one insidious form continues to thrive: alphabetism. This, for those as yet unaware of such a disadvantage, refers to discrimination against those whose surnames begin with a letter in the lower half of the alphabet.

It has long been known that a taxi firm called AAAA cars has a big advantage over Zodiac cars when customers thumb through their phone directories. Less well known is the advantage that

Adam Abbott has in life over Zoe Zysman. English names are fairly evenly spread between the halves of the alphabet. Yet a suspiciously large number of top people have surnames beginning with letters between A and K.

Thus the American president and vice-president have surnames starting with B and C respectively; and 26 of George Bush's predecessors (including his father) had surnames in the first half of the alphabet against just 16 in the second half. Even more striking, six of the seven heads of government of the G7 rich countries are alphabetically advantaged (Berlusconi, Blair, Bush, Chirac, Chretien and Koizumi). The world's three top central bankers (Greenspan, Duisenberg and Hayami) are all close to the top of the alphabet, even if one of them really uses Japanese characters. As are the world's five richest men (Gates, Buffett, Allen, Ellison and Albrecht).

Can this merely be coincidence? One theory, dreamt up in all the spare time enjoyed by the alphabetically disadvantaged, is that the ret sets in early. At the start of the first year in infant school, teachers seat pupils alphabetically from the front, to make it easier to remember their names. So shortsighted Zysman junior gets stuck in the back row, and is rarely asked the improving questions posed by those insensitive teachers. At the time the alphabetically disadvantaged may think they have had a lucky escape. Yet the result may be worse qualifications, because they get less individual attention, as well as less confidence in speaking publicly.

The humiliation continues. At university graduation ceremonies, the ABCs proudly get their awards first; by the time they reach the Zysmans most people are literally having a ZZZ. Shortlists for job interviews, election ballot papers, lists of conference speakers and attendees: all tend to be drawn up alphabetically, and their recipients lose interest as they plough through them.

1. What does the author intend to illustrate with AAAA cars and Zodiac cars?
   A. A kind of overlooked inequality.　　　　B. A type of conspicuous bias.
   C. A type of personal prejudice.　　　　　D. A kind of brand discrimination.

2. What can we infer from the first three paragraphs?
   A. In both East and West, names are essential to success.
   B. The alphabet is to blame for the failure of Zoe Zysman.
   C. Customers often pay a lot of attention to companies' names.
   D. Some form of discrimination is too subtle to recognize.

3. The 4th paragraph suggests that _____.
   A. questions are often put to the more intelligent students
   B. alphabetically disadvantaged students often escape from class
   C. teachers should pay attention to all of their students
   D. students should be seated according to their eyesight

4. What does the author mean by "most people are literally having a ZZZ" (Line 2, Para.5)?
   A. They are getting impatient.　　　　B. They are noisily dozing off.
   C. They are feeling humiliated.　　　　D. They are busy with word puzzles.

5. Which of the following is true according to the text?
   A. People with surnames beginning with N to Z are often ill-treated.

B. VIPs in the Western world gain a great deal from alphabetism.

C. The campaign to eliminate alphabetism still has a long way to go.

D. Putting things alphabetically may lead to unintentional bias.

核心词汇注释

insidious [ɪnˈsɪdɪəs] *adj.* 阴险的

thrive [θraɪv] *v.* 兴旺，繁荣；茁壮成长；旺盛

zodiac [ˈzəudɪæk] *n.* [天] 十二宫图，黄道带

halves [hɑːvz] *pl.* half

ret [ret] *vt.* 浸水使柔软
vi. 受潮湿腐烂

humiliation [hjuːˌmɪlɪˈeɪʃən] *n.* 羞辱；蒙耻

shortlist [ˈʃɔːtlɪst] *n.* <英>供最后挑选（或考虑）用的候选人名单

ballot [ˈbæləd] *n.* 选举票；投票；票数
vi. 投票

attendee [æˌtenˈdiː] *n.* 出席者，参加者，在场者

recipient [rɪˈsɪpɪənt] *adj.* 容易接受的，感受性强的
n. 容纳者，容器

长难句剖析

【文章难句】This, for those as yet unaware of such a disadvantage, refers to discrimination against those whose surnames begin with a letter in the lower half of the alphabet.

【结构分析】本句主干是 This… refers to discrimination。for those as yet unaware of such a disadvantage 做状语；as yet 的意思是到目前为止（仍），现在还，至今。against those whose surnames begin with a letter in the lower half of the alphabet 是修饰 discrimination 的定语，由 whose surnames 引导的定语从句修饰 those。

【参考译文】对于那些尚未意识到这种不利因素的人来说，它指的是对那些姓氏首字母排在字母表后半部分的人的一种歧视。

全文参考译文

在过去的一个世纪，所有的不平等和歧视都受到谴责或被视为违法。但一种歧视却潜伏下来，继续蔓延：字母歧视。对于那些尚未意识到这种不利因素的人来说，它指的是对那些姓氏字母排在字母表后半部分的人的一种歧视。

很久之前人们就知道，当客户在翻看他们的电话簿时，AAAA Cars 出租车公司比 Zodiac Cars 公司有更大的优势。人们不太知晓的是，Adam Abbott 这个名字在生活中比 Zoe Zysman 更具有优势。英语名字按字母表相当均匀地分布。但难以置信的是很多杰出的上层人士，其姓氏是以 A～K 的字母开头的。

同样美国的总统和副总统的姓氏分别以 B 和 C 开头；在乔治·布什的前任总统（包括他父亲）中，有 26 人其姓氏字母是以字母表前半部分开头的，姓氏首字母排在字母表后半部分的仅有16人。更惊人的是，西方七大工业国政府首脑有 6 位的姓氏有字母表顺序优势（Berlusconi，Blair，Bush，Chirac，Chretien 和 Koizumi）。世界三大中央银行家（Greenspan，Duisenberg 和 Hayami）的姓氏都以字母表前面的字母开头，即使他们中有一人用的是日本字

符。世界上的五大富翁（Gates，Buffett，Allen，Ellison 和 Albrecht）的姓氏也是如此。

这仅是巧合吗？由姓氏处于字母表不利位置的人在空闲时间构思出的一种理论认为，在幼儿园第一年的开始阶段，老师按学生姓氏的字母表顺序由前往后安排座位，这样比较容易记住学生的名字。所以眼睛近视的 Zysman 只能坐在后排，并且很少被那些感觉迟钝的老师问一些有质量的问题。那时，那些不具备姓氏字母优势的学生可能觉得他们幸运逃避了提问。但结果可能更糟，因为他们很难得到个人关注，同时在公共场合讲话时也缺乏自信。

这种耻辱继续着。在大学毕业典礼上，姓氏以 A、B、C 等前面字母开头的学生可以首先自豪地得到奖励，轮到 Zysman 时，大多数人都在打瞌睡了。求职者面试的最后名单、投票选举名单、会议演讲者和出席者的名单，往往都会按字母顺序制作的，当他们的收件人查看这些名单时，他们会慢慢失去兴趣。

题目答案与解析

1. 作者用 AAAA Cars 和 Zodiac Cars 汽车公司为例意欲说明什么？
   A. 一种被人们忽视的不平等。　　　B. 一种显而易见的偏见。
   C. 一种个人偏见。　　　　　　　　D. 一种少见的歧视。
   【答案】A
   【解析】本题可参照文章的第 1 段和第 2 段。从文章的第 1 段可知，一种隐秘的不公平和歧视继续盛行——按字母排序。第 2 段接着讲到，人们早就知道，当客户通过电话本叫出租车时，名为 AAAA Cars 的出租车公司就比名为 Zodiac Cars 的公司更具优势。人们不太知晓的是，Adam Abbott 这个名字在生活中比 Zoe Zysman 有优势。据此可知，作者举 AAAA Cars 和 Zodiac Cars 出租车公司为例是为了说明——人们忽视了一种隐秘的不公平和歧视。A 项与文章的意思相符，因此 A 项为正确答案。
2. 我们从文章的前 3 段中可以推知什么？
   A. 不管是在东方还是在西方，姓名对于成功至关重要。
   B. 人们指责字母表导致姓氏靠后者的失败。
   C. 消费者通常非常注重公司的名字。
   D. 某种歧视太细微因而难以辨别。
   【答案】D
   【解析】从文章的第 1、2、3 段的内容可知，过去各种各样的不公平和歧视受到人们的谴责或是被视为违法；但是，一种隐秘的不公平和歧视继续盛行。人们早就知道，当客户通过电话本叫出租车时，名为 AAAA Cars 的出租车公司就比名为 Zodiac Cars 的公司更具优势；人们不太知晓的是，Adam Abbott 这个名字在生活中比 Zoe Zysman 有优势。然后举例说明，指出有些人有姓氏字母方面的优势。据此可知，由于某些隐秘的不公平和歧视太细微，所以难以被人们关注。D 项与文章的意思相符，因此 D 项为正确答案。
3. 第 4 段暗示了 _____。
   A. 更聪明的学生经常被提问　　　　B. 不具备姓氏字母优势的学生经常逃课
   C. 老师应该关注所有学生　　　　　D. 应该根据学生的视力来给他们排座位
   【答案】C

【解析】文章第 4 段讲道，这仅是巧合吗？一种理论认为，这种情况早就存在。在幼儿园的开始阶段，老师按学生姓氏字母顺序从前到后排座位。一些近视的、姓氏靠后的幼儿不得不坐在后排，那些感觉迟钝的老师很少向这些幼儿提一些有助于提高的问题。那时，那些不具备姓氏字母优势的人可能认为他们幸运逃避了提问。但结果可能更糟。据此可知，老师不应该忽视那些没有姓氏字母优势的学生。C 项与文章的意思相符，因此 C 项为正确答案。

4. 作者说 most people are literally having a ZZZ（第 5 段第 2 行）的含义是什么？
   A. 他们变得不耐烦。 B. 他们已鼾声大作。
   C. 他们觉得丢脸。 D. 他们忙于做字谜游戏。

【答案】B

【解析】从文章第 5 段的内容可知，在大学的毕业典礼上，那些姓氏字母靠前者首先获得奖品；等到该姓氏字母靠后者获奖时，大多数人都在打瞌睡。求职面试的最后名单、投票选举名单、会议演讲者以及出席者名单，往往都是根据字母顺序制作的。当收件人查看这些名单时，他们的兴趣也随之消失了。据此可知，该句话的意思应该是——大多数人都在打鼾。B 项与文章的意思相符，因此 B 项为正确答案。

5. 依照本文的观点，以下选项中哪一项是正确的？
   A. 以 N 到 Z 为姓氏的人经常受到虐待。
   B. 西方世界的重要人物从字母排序的做法中获得极大的好处。
   C. 消除以字母先后排序的运动仍然任重道远。
   D. 以字母排序的做法可能会导致无心的偏见。

【答案】D

【解析】从文章第 1 段的内容可知，过去，各种各样的不公平和歧视受到人们的谴责或是被视为违法。但是，有一种隐秘的不公平和歧视继续盛行——按字母排序。从第 2 段的内容可知，人们早就知道，当客户通过电话本叫出租车时，名为 AAAA Cars 的出租车公司就比名为 Zodiac Cars 的公司更具优势；但是，人们不太知晓的是：Adam Abbott 这个名字在生活中比 Zoe Zysman 有优势。第 3 段举例说明。第 4 段接着讲到，这能算是巧合吗？跟着举例指出：在幼儿园，老师按学生姓氏的字母表顺序从前到后排座位，可能会造成更严重的后果，因为这些人受到的关注更少，他们也更缺乏公开表达自己信心的机会。从文章的最后一段内容可知，这种使人蒙羞的情况还在继续。据此可知，根据字母排序的做法可能无意中导致偏见。D 项与文章的意思相符，因此 D 项为正确答案。

Text 3

When it comes to the slowing economy, Ellen Spero isn't biting her nails just yet. But the 47-year-old manicurist isn't cutting, filing or polishing as many nails as she'd like to, either. Most of her clients spend $12 to $50 weekly, but last month two longtime customers suddenly stopped showing up. Spero blames the softening economy. "I'm a good economic indicator," she says. "I provide a service that people can do without when they're concerned about saving some dollars. " So Spero is downscaling, shopping at middle-brow Dillard's department store near her suburban Cleveland home, instead of Neiman Marcus. "I don't know if other clients are going to abandon me, too," she says.

Even before Alan Greenspan's admission that America's red-hot economy is cooling, lots of working folks had already seen signs of the slowdown themselves. From car dealerships to Gap outlets, sales have been lagging for months as shoppers temper their spending. For retailers, who last year took in 24 percent of their revenue between Thanksgiving and Christmas, the cautious approach is coming at a crucial time. Already, experts say, holiday sales are off 7 percent from last year's pace. But don't sound any alarms just yet. Consumers seem only mildly concerned, not panicked, and many say they remain optimistic about the economy's long-term prospects even as they do some modest belt-tightening.

Consumers say they're not in despair because, despite the dreadful headlines, their own fortunes still feel pretty good. Home prices are holding steady in most regions. In Manhattan, "There's a new gold rush happening in the $ 4 million to $10 million range, predominantly fed by Wall Street bonuses," says broker Barbara Corcoran. In San Francisco, prices are still rising even as frenzied overbidding quiets. "Instead of 20 to 30 offers, now maybe you only get two or three," says John Tealdi, a Bay Area real-estate broker. And most folks still feel pretty comfortable about their ability to find and keep a job.

Many folks see silver linings to this slowdown. Potential home buyers would cheer for lower interest rates. Employers wouldn't mind a little fewer bubbles in the job market. Many consumers seem to have been influenced by stock-market swings, which investors now view as a necessary ingredient to a sustained boom. Diners might see an upside, too. Getting a table at Manhattan's hot new Alain Ducasse restaurant used to be impossible. Not anymore. For that, Greenspan & Co. may still be worth toasting.

1. By "Ellen Spero isn't biting her nails just yet" (Line 1, Para. 1), the author means _____.
    A. Spero can hardly maintain her business   B. Spero is too much engaged in her work
    C. Spero has grown out of her bad habit   D. Spero is not in a desperate situation
2. How do the public feel about the current economic situation?
    A. Optimistic.   B. Confused.   C. Carefree.   D. Panicked.
3. When mentioning "the $4 million to $10 million range" (Line 3, Para. 3), the author is talking about _____.
    A. gold market   B. real estate   C. stock exchange   D. venture investment
4. Why can many people see "silver linings" to the economic slowdown?
    A. They would benefit in certain ways.
    B. The stock market shows signs of recovery.
    C. Such a slowdown usually precedes a boom.
    D. The purchasing power would be enhanced.
5. To which of the following is the author likely to agree?
    A. A new boom, on the horizon.   B. Tighten the belt, the single remedy.
    C. Caution all right, panic not.   D. The more ventures, the more chances.

核心词汇注释

manicurist [ˈmænɪˌkjʊərɪst] *n.* 指甲修饰师

indicator [ˈɪndɪkeɪtə(r)] *n.* 指示器，[化] 指示剂

lagging [ˈlægɪŋ] *n.* 绝缘层材料

temper [ˈtempə(r)] *n.* （钢等的）韧度，回火；性情，脾气，情绪，心情；调剂，趋向
v. （冶金）回火，锻炼；调和，调节

retailer [ˈriːteɪlə(r)] *n.* 零售商人，传播的人

belt-tightening [ˈbeltˌtaɪtənɪŋ] *n.* 强制性节约
adj. 节约的，节省开支的

bonus [ˈbəʊnəs] *n.* 奖金，红利

frenzied [ˈfrenzɪd] *adj.* 狂热的，激怒的，狂乱的

lining [ˈlaɪnɪŋ] *n.* 加衬里，内层，衬套

ingredient [ɪnˈɡriːdɪənt] *n.* 成分，因素

长难句剖析

【文章难句】I provide a service that people can do without when they're concerned about saving some dollars.

【结构分析】本句主干是 I provide a service, that 引导的定语从句修饰 service。在定语从句中，that 做 do without 的宾语。when they're concerned about saving some dollars 为句子的状语从句。

【参考译文】人们手头紧时，我提供的服务对他们来说就是可有可无的了。

全文参考译文

谈到速度减缓的经济，Ellen Spero 现在还不是面临紧要关头。但这位 47 岁的指甲修饰师也不再能修剪、锉或打磨像她所期望的那么多的指甲了。她的大多数客户每周花费 12～50 美元修指甲，但上个月，两个老客户突然不再来了。Spero 埋怨这疲软的经济。"我是一盏很好的经济指示灯，"她说，"人们手头紧时，我提供的服务对他们来说就可有可无了"。所以 Spero 正在缩小规模，减少消费。她现在去她在克利夫兰郊区住所附近的一般的 Dillard 商店购物，而不去 Neiman Marcus。"我也不知道其他客户是否会放弃我。"她说。

甚至在艾伦·格林斯潘承认美国的红热经济正在冷却之前，许多工作的人们已看到了经济滑坡的迹象。从汽车的经销到汽油的出口，由于购买者调整了他们的支出，销售已滞后了几个月。对于零售商人来说，去年他们在感恩节和圣诞节期间的销售收入占了全年总收入的 24%，现在又到了这个关键时期，他们应谨慎对待。专家报告说，假期销售比去年低了 7%。但还没有发出任何警告。消费者看上去也只是适度关注，并不恐慌，并且许多人都说，尽管他们会适度地勒紧腰带，但他们对经济发展的长期前景保持乐观态度。

消费者说他们并不绝望，因为，他们觉得他们自己的运气还相当好。房地产价格在大多数地区保持稳定。在曼哈顿岛，"出现了一种新的在 400 万～1 000 万范围之内的淘金热，主要有华尔街的红利资助。"经纪人 Barbara Corcoran 说。在旧金山，尽管狂热的叫价已平静下来，但价格仍在上涨。"以前你能拿到 20～30 个报价，而现在也许只会得到两三个报价。"一位"海湾地区"的不动产经纪人 John Tealdi 说。大多数人相信他们有能力找到工作和保持原来的工作。

许多人从这种经济减缓过程中看到了有利的一面。潜在的购房者将会为比较低的利率欢

呼。雇佣者不会介意工作市场上出现些许小小的泡沫。许多消费者似乎受到股票市场波动的影响，而投资者把它看成维持繁荣的一个必要因素。在餐馆就餐的人可能也看到了利好的一面。在曼哈顿岛的一家新开的生意红火的 Alain Ducasse 餐厅寻找一个位子过去常常是不可能的，现在不再这样了。正因为那样，格林斯潘公司仍值得夸耀。

题目答案与解析

1. 作者通过说"Ellen Spero isn't biting her nails just yet"（第 1 段第 1 行）的意思是 _____。
   A．Spero 几乎维持不了她的生意　　　　B．Spero 太忙于她的工作了
   C．Spero 已经改掉了她的不良习惯　　　D．Spero 没有陷入令人绝望的境地
   【答案】D
   【解析】从文章第 1 段的内容可知，谈到速度减缓的经济，Ellen Spero 现在还不是面临紧要关头；但这位修指甲师也不再修剪、锉或是打磨她所期望的那么多的指甲了；上个月，她的两名老顾客突然不光顾了；所以，Spero 正在缩减规模；她说："我不知道其他顾客是否也会抛弃我。"据此可知，该句话的意思应该是——Spero 现在还没有遇到极大的困难。D 项与文章的意思相符，因此 D 项为正确答案。

2. 公众对当前的经济形式感觉如何？
   A．乐观。　　　　B．迷惑不解。　　　　C．无忧无虑。　　　　D．恐慌。
   【答案】A
   【解析】本题可参照文章的第 2 段。从中可知，就在艾伦·格林斯潘承认美国过热的经济正在降温之前，许多工薪族已经看到了经济减速的迹象；几个月来，销售一直在衰减，因为消费者在削减开支；但是，现在还不用发出任何警告；消费者似乎只是稍微有点担心，并没有恐慌，许多人说他们对于经济的长期繁荣持乐观态度。据此可知，公众对目前的经济持乐观态度。A 项与文章的意思相符，因此 A 项为正确答案。

3. 作者提及 the $ 4 million to $10 million range（第 2 段第 3 行）是在谈论 _____。
   A．黄金市场　　　B．房地产　　　C．股票交易　　　D．风险投资
   【答案】B
   【解析】从文章第 3 段的内容可知，在大多数地区，房产的价格一直稳定；在曼哈顿，在 400 万到 1 000 万美元的范围内，正在出现一股新的寻金热，主要是由于华尔街的红利助长起来的；在旧金山，价格仍然在上涨；"以前你能拿到 20～30 个报价，而现在你也许只会得到两三个报价，"约翰·泰尔迪说，他是"海湾地区"房地产公司的经纪人。据此可知，作者在提到该短语时，是在说房地产方面的事情。B 项与文章的意思相符，因此 B 项为正确答案。

4. 许多人能够看到走出经济衰退的"希望"的原因是什么？
   A．他们会通过某些方法获得好处。　　　B．股票市场显现了复苏的迹象。
   C．经济繁荣之前通常有这样的减速。　　D．购买力将会提高。
   【答案】A
   【解析】本题可参照文章的第 4 段。从中可知，许多人看到了走出这场经济衰退的希望；接着举例道：潜在的住房购买者将会为更低的利率而欢呼；雇主也不会在意就业市场中的一些小的波动；许多消费者似乎受到股票市场波动的影响——现在，投资者认为这是保持繁荣必不

可少的要素；以前到曼哈顿新开的生意红火的 Alain Ducasse 餐厅找个座位就餐是不可能的，现在再也不会有这种事了。据此可知，由于人们认为他们可能从目前的经济中得到好处，所以他们认为他们看到了走出经济衰退的"希望"。A 项与文章的意思相符，因此 A 项为正确答案。

5. 作者也许会赞成下面哪项？

A．一场新的经济繁荣即将来临。　　B．紧缩开支是唯一的补救方法。

C．谨慎是应该的，但不必恐慌。　　D．风险越多，机会也就越多。

【答案】C

【解析】从文章第 1 段的内容可知，谈到速度减缓的经济，Spero 现在还不是面临紧要关头；从第 2 段的内容可知，就在艾伦·格林斯潘承认美国过热的经济正在降温之前，许多工薪族已经看到了经济减速的迹象；几个月来，销售一直在衰减，因为消费者在削减开支；但是，现在还不用发出任何警告；消费者似乎只是稍微有点担心，并没有恐慌，许多人说他们对于经济的长期繁荣持乐观态度；从第 3 段的内容可知，消费者说，他们并没有感到绝望，因为，他们还是觉得他们仍然很富足；在大多数地区，房产的价格一直稳定；大多数人仍相信，他们能够找到并保住一份工作；从文章最后一段的内容可知，许多人看到了走出这场经济衰退的希望。据此可知，作者也许会认为，没有必要对目前的经济形势感到恐慌。C 项与文章的意思相符，因此 C 项为正确答案。

Text 4

Americans today don't place a very high value on intellect. Our heroes are athletes, entertainers, and entrepreneurs, not scholars. Even our schools are where we send our children to get a practical education — not to pursue knowledge for the sake of knowledge. Symptoms of pervasive anti-intellectualism in our schools aren't difficult to find.

"Schools have always been in a society where practical is more important than intellectual,"says education writer Diane Ravitch. "Schools could be a counterbalance. " Ravitch' s latest book, *Left Back: A Century of Failed School Reforms*, traces the roots of anti-intellectualism in our schools, concluding they are anything but a counterbalance to the American distaste for intellectual pursuits.

But they could and should be. Encouraging kids to reject the life of the mind leaves them vulnerable to exploitation and control. Without the ability to think critically, to defend their ideas and understand the ideas of others, they cannot fully participate in our democracy; "Continuing along this path," says writer Earl Shorris. "We will become a second-rate country. We will have a less civil society. "

"Intellect is resented as a form of power or privilege," writes historian and professor Richard Hofstadter in *Anti-Intellectualism in American Life*, a Pulitzer-Prize winning book on the roots of anti-intellectualism in U.S. politics, religion, and education. From the beginning of our history, says Hofstadter, our democratic and populist urges have driven us to reject anything that smells of elitism. Practicality, common sense, and native intelligence have been considered more noble qualities than anything you could learn from a book.

Ralph Waldo Emerson and other Transcendentalist philosophers thought schooling and rigorous book learning put unnatural restraints on children: "We are shut up in schools and college recitation rooms for 10 or 15 years and come out at last with a bellyful of words and do not know a thing. " Mark Twain's *Huckleberry Finn* exemplified American anti-intellectualism. Its hero avoids being civilized — going to school and learning to read — so he can preserve his innate goodness.

Intellect, according to Hofstadter, is different from native intelligence, a quality we reluctantly admire. Intellect is the critical, creative, and contemplative side of the mind. Intelligence seeks to grasp, manipulate, re-order, and adjust, while intellect examines, ponders, wonders, theorizes, criticizes, and imagines.

School remains a place where intellect is mistrusted. Hofstadter says our country's educational system is in the grips of people who "joyfully and militantly proclaim their hostility to intellect and their eagerness to identify with children who show the least intellectual promise".

1. What do American parents expect their children to acquire in school?

A. The habit of thinking independently.

B. Profound knowledge of the world.

C. Practical abilities for future career.

D. The confidence in intellectual pursuits.

2. We can learn from the text that Americans have a history of _____.

A. undervaluing intellect   B. favoring intellectualism

C. supporting school reform   D. suppressing native intelligence

3. The views of Ravitch and Emerson on schooling are _____.

A. identical   B. similar   C. complementary   D. opposite

4. Emerson, according to the text, is probably _____.

A. a pioneer of education reform   B. an opponent of intellectualism

C. a scholar in favor of intellect   D. an advocate of regular schooling

5. What does the author think of intellect?

A. It is second to intelligence.   B. It evolves from common sense.

C. It is to be pursued.   D. It underlies power.

核心词汇注释

entertainer [ˌentəˈteɪnə(r)] *n.* 款待者；表演娱乐节目的人，演艺人员

enterprising [ˈentəpraɪzɪŋ] *adj.* 有事业心的，有进取心的；有魄力的，有胆量的

distaste [dɪsˈteɪst] *n.* 讨厌，嫌恶

elitism [eɪˈliːtɪz(ə)m] *n.* 杰出人物统治论；高人一等的优越感

transcendentalist [ˌtrænsenˈdentəlɪst]

adj. [哲] 先验论者的；超越论者的

recitation [ˌresɪˈteɪʃ(ə)n] *n.* 朗诵，背诵；叙述；背诵的东西

bellyful [ˈbelɪful] *n.* 满腹

contemplative [kənˈtemplətɪv] *adj.* 沉思的，冥想的，[宗]祈祷的

manipulate [məˈnɪpjuleɪt] *vt.* （熟练地）操作；使用；操纵；利用；应付；假造 *vt.* （熟练地）操作；巧妙地处理

长难句剖析

【文章难句】Hofstadter says our country's educational system is in the grips of people who "joyfully and militantly proclaim their hostility to intellect and their eagerness to identify with children who show the least intellectual promise".

【结构分析】本句的结构为间接引语。在间接引语中，主干是 our country's educational system is in the grips of people，who 引导的定语从句修饰 people，并在从句中做主语。从句中的 who 引导的也是定语从句，修饰 children。句中的第一个 to 为介词，第二个 to 为动词不定式做定语。

【参考译文】Hofstadter 说我们国家的教育系统在这些人的掌握之中，"他们欢快而有斗智地显露出他们对才智的敌对态度，并积极认同那些智力最差的孩子"。

全文参考译文

如今的美国人并不把智力看得很重。我们崇拜的都是体育明星、娱乐明星和企业家，而不是学者。甚至我们把自己的孩子送去学校接受实践教育也不是为了求知而追求知识。我们在学校中也不难发现普遍的反智主义的现象。

"学校总是处于一个实践重于智慧的社会中。"教育作家 Diane Ravitch 说。"学校可能成为一种均衡力。"Ravitch 的最近一部著作，《一个世纪教育改革的失败》，探究了这种反理智主义在我们学校的产生根源，得出的结论是，这些现象绝不是美国人由于对才智追求的厌恶而寻找平衡造成的。

但是他们可以而且应该那样。鼓励孩子拒绝思考会使得他们易受剥削和控制。如果没有批判地思考问题的能力，不能坚持自己的观点，不能理解其他人的想法，他们就不可能完全参与到我们的民主政治中。"长此以往，"作家 Earl Shorris 说，"我们将会变成一个二流国家。社会的文明程度也会降低。"

"才智作为力量或特权的一种形式而遭到人们怨恨。"历史学家和教授 Richard Hofstadter 在他的《美国生活中的反智主义》一书中写道。这本关于美国政治、宗教和教育中的反理智主义根源的书为他赢得了普利策奖。Hofstadter 说，从美国的历史开始之时起，我们的民主和平民的愿望驱使我们抵制任何带有精英政治味道的东西。实用性、常识和与生俱来的智能被认为比你从书本上学到的任何东西都高贵。

爱默生和其他先验论哲学家认为学校教育和僵化的书本学习会抑制孩子们的天性。"我们被禁闭在中小学和大学的背诵室里 10～15 年，最后带着满腹经纶出来，却不懂任何东西。"马克·吐温的《哈克贝利·费恩历险记》可以作为美国人反理智主义的例证。它里面描述的英雄没有去学校学习和读书从而变成文明人，所以能够保持他天生的善良本性。

根据 Hofstadter 所说，才智与先天的智能不同，后者是人们勉强赞赏的一种素质。才智是批判的、创造性的，是心灵的沉思。智能试图把握、操纵、重新定位、调节，然而才智却是检测、深思、好奇、理论化、批判和想象。

学校成为一个才智受到猜疑的地方。Hofstadter 认为，我们国家的教育系统控制在这样一群人手中："他们欢快而又富有斗志地显露出他们对才智的敌对态度，并积极地认同那些智力最差的孩子"。

题目答案与解析

1. 美国的父母期待他们的孩子从学校学到什么？
   A. 独立思考的习惯。　　　　　　　　B. 深刻地认识世界。
   C. 为将来谋职的实用本领。　　　　　D. 追求智慧的信心。

   【答案】C

   【解析】从文章第 1 段的内容可知，美国人现在不太重视才智了。我们崇拜的是运动员、演员和企业家，而不是学者。甚至我们的学校也是一个我们送孩子去接受实用教育的场所。在我们的学校，不难发现普遍的反才智主义的现象。从第 2 段的内容可知，作家 Diane Ravitch 说，"学校总是处于一个实践重于智慧的社会之中。"据此可知，美国人期待他们的孩子在学校学到实际本领。C 项与文章的意思相符，因此 C 项为正确答案。

2. 依照本篇文章，我们能了解到美国人有 _____ 的历史。
   A. 轻视才智　　　　　　　　　　　　B. 赞成才智主义
   C. 支持学校改革　　　　　　　　　　D. 压制天赋

   【答案】A

   【解析】从文章第 1 段的内容可知，美国人现在不太重视才智了；从文章第 4 段的内容可知，"才智受到人们的憎恶，"历史学家 Hofstadter 教授指出；他说，自美国的历史开始之时，美国的民主和平民的愿望就促使我们抵制任何带有精英政治味道的东西；实用性、常识以及天赋被看成是比你能够从书本中学得的任何东西都崇高的本领。据此可知，美国人有不重视才智的历史。因此 A 项为正确答案。

3. 有关学校教育，Ravitch 与爱默生所持的观点是 _____。
   A. 相同的　　　　B. 相似的　　　　C. 互补的　　　　D. 相反的

   【答案】D

   【解析】从文章第 2 段的内容可知，"学校总是处于一个实践重于智慧的社会环境之中，"作家 Diane Ravitch 说。"学校可能成为一种平衡力。"Ravitch 的最新作品探究了我们的学校中反才智主义的根源，并得出结论——学校根本就不是美国人反感智慧追求的一种抗衡力；从文章第 5 段的内容可知，爱默生和其他先验论哲学家认为，学校教育和严谨的书本知识学习刻意限制了孩子——我们被禁闭在中小学和大学的背诵室里 10～15 年，最后带着满腹经纶出来，却不懂任何东西。据此可知，这两者的观点大不相同。D 项与文章的意思相符，因此 D 项为正确答案。

4. 依照本文的观点，爱默生大概是 _____。
   A. 一名教育改革的先驱　　　　　　　B. 一名才智主义的反对者
   C. 一名支持才智的学者　　　　　　　D. 一名常规教育的倡导者

   【答案】B

   【解析】本题可参照文章的第 5 段。从中可知，爱默生和其他先验论哲学家认为，学校教育和严谨的书本知识学习不正常地限制了孩子——我们被禁闭在中小学和大学的背诵室里 10～15 年，最后带着满腹经纶出来，却不懂任何东西；马克·吐温的《哈克贝利·费恩历险记》一书再现了美国人的反才智主义现象：书中的主人公逃避接受教育，所以他能够保持他天生的美德。据此可知，爱默生可能是反才智主义的。B 项与文章的意思相符，因此 B 项为正确答案。

5. 作者对才智怎样看待？

    A．它仅次于智慧。   B．它是由常识演变而来的。

    C．它应当受到人们的追求。   D．它是权利的基础。

【答案】C

【解析】本题可参照文章的第 1 段。从中可知，美国人现在不太重视才智了。在我们的学校，不难发现普遍的反才智主义的现象。从第 3 段的内容可知，学校能够也应该成为反才智主义的平衡力。由于缺乏严谨思考的能力，缺乏捍卫自己的思想、理解他人思想的能力，这些孩子不可能完全融入我们的民主生活。如果继续这样发展下去，我们的国家将会成为二流国家，我们的社会的文明程度也会降低。据此可知，作者认为，由于才智非常重要，我们应该追求才智。C 项与作者的观点相符，因此 C 项为正确答案。

Unit 13

Text 1

Wild Bill Donovan would have loved the Internet. The American spymaster who built the Office of Strategic Services in the World War II and later laid the roots for the CIA was fascinated with information. Donovan believed in using whatever tools came to hand in the "great game" of espionage — spying as a "profession". These days the Net, which has already remade pastimes as buying books and sending mail, is reshaping Donovan's vocation as well.

The last revolution isn't simply a matter of gentlemen reading other gentlemen's e-mail. That kind of electronic spying has been going on for decades. In the past three or four years, the World Wide Web has given birth to a whole industry of point-and-click spying. The spooks call it "open source intelligence", and as the Net grows, it is becoming increasingly influential. In 1995 the CIA held a contest to see who could compile the most data about Burundi. The winner, by a large margin, was a tiny Virginia company called Open-Source Solutions, whose clear advantage was its mastery of the electronic world.

Among the firms making the biggest splash in the new world is Straitford, Inc., a private intelligence-analysis firm based in Austin, Texas. Straitford makes money by selling the results of spying (covering nations from Chile to Russia) to corporations like energy-services firm McDermott International. Many of its predictions are available online at *www.straitford.com*.

Straiford president George Friedman says he sees the online world as a kind of mutually reinforcing tool for both information collection and distribution, a spymaster's dream. Last week his firm was busy vacuuming up data bits from the far corners of the world and predicting a crisis in Ukraine. "As soon as that report runs, we'll suddenly get 500 new internet sign-ups from Ukraine," says Friedman, a former political science professor. "And we'll hear back from some of them." Open-source spying does have its risks, of course, since it can be difficult to tell good information from bad. That's where Straitford earns its keep.

Friedman relies on a lean staff with twenty in Austin. Several of his staff members have military- intelligence backgrounds. He sees the firm's outsider status as the key to its success. Straitford's briefs don't sound like the usual Washington back-and-forthing, whereby agencies avoid dramatic declarations on the chance they might be wrong. Straitford, says Friedman, takes pride in its independent voice.

1. The emergence of the Net has _____.
    A. received support from fans like Donovan B. remolded the intelligence services
    C. restored many common pastimes   D. revived spying as a profession
2. Donovan's story is mentioned in the text to _____.

A．introduce the topic of online spying
B．show how he fought for the U.S.
C．give an episode of the information war
D．honor his unique services to the CIA

3．The phrase "making the biggest splash" (Line 1, Para. 3) most probably means _____.
A．causing the biggest trouble
B．exerting the greatest effort
C．achieving the greatest success
D．enjoying the widest popularity

4．It can be learned from Paragraph 4 that _____.
A．Straitford's prediction about Ukraine has proved true
B．Straitford guarantees the truthfulness of its information
C．Straitford's business is characterized by unpredictability
D．Straitford is able to provide fairly reliable information

5．Straitford is most proud of its _____.
A．official status
B．nonconformist image
C．efficient staff
D．military background

核心词汇注释

spymaster [ˈspaɪˌmɑːstə(r)] n. 间谍组织的首脑

espionage [ˈespɪənɑːʒ] n. 间谍，侦探

pastime [ˈpɑːstaɪm] n. 消遣，娱乐

reshape [riːˈʃeɪp] vt. 改造；再成形；采用新方针

spook [spuːk] n. 鬼，幽灵
vt. 鬼怪般地出没于；惊吓
vi. 逃窜

compile [kəmˈpaɪl] vt. 编译；编辑；汇编

margin [ˈmɑːdʒɪn] n. 页边的空白；（湖、池等的）边缘；极限；利润；差数；（时间、金额等的）富余
vt. 加边于；加旁注于

prediction [prɪˈdɪkʃ(ə)n] n. 预言，预报

reinforce [ˌriːɪnˈfɔːs] vt. 加强；增援；补充；增加……的数量；修补；加固
vi. 求援；得到增援
n. 加固物

vacuum [ˈvækjʊəm] n. 真空；空间；真空吸尘器
adj. 真空的；产生真空的；利用真空的
vt. 用真空吸尘器打扫

长难句剖析

【文章难句】The American spymaster who built the Office of Strategic Services in the World War II and later laid the roots for the CIA was fascinated with information.

【结构分析】本句主干是 The American spymaster was fascinated with information. the American spymaster 后面是由 who 引导的定语从句，定语从句中包含两个由 and 连接的并列句。

【参考译文】这位曾经在第二次世界大战当中建立战略服务室而且后来为中央情报局打下基础的美国谍报大师对情报收集非常痴迷。

全文参考译文

狂热的 Bill Donovan 一定会爱上互联网。这位曾经在二次世界大战中建立战略服务室而

且后来为中央情报局打下基础的美国谍报大师对情报收集非常痴迷。Donovan 认为在职业间谍活动这一"伟大事业"中可以利用任何可以利用的工具。互联网已彻底改变了人们的一些日常消遣活动，比如买书、发送邮件，如今它也正在重新塑造着 Donovan 的事业。

近来的变化不仅仅局限于侦读他人的电子邮件。电子间谍活动至今已经有数十年的历史。在过去三四年里，万维网已经衍生了全方位的点击式间谍活动。间谍们称之为"公开来源的情报"。随着互联网的发展，它的影响力也越来越大。1995 年，美国中央情报局举行了一场比赛，看谁能搜集到最多的关于布隆迪的情报。弗吉尼亚州的一家叫做"开源信息咨询公司"的小公司以绝对优势胜出，它的明显优势是对电子世界的把握。

在这片新天地里，最引人注目的就是 Straitford 公司，坐落在得克萨斯州奥斯汀市的一家私人情报分析公司。Straitford 公司通过向如 McDermott International 之类的能量服务公司销售（从智利到俄罗斯等国家的）情报来获得利润。它的许多预测可以在它的网站 www.straitford.com 在线查到。

Straitford 公司的总裁 George Friedman 说，他把在线世界看作是一种信息收集和发布的互动工具，是超级间谍的天堂。上个星期，他的公司正忙于整理来自世界偏僻角落的信息以便预测乌克兰的一场危机。曾是政治学教授的 Friedman 说："只要那报道一出现，我们将立刻得到 500 条来自乌克兰的最新的网上消息，然后从中进行筛选。"的确，公开来源的情报侦察也担有风险，因为难以把有价值的信息和无价值的信息加以区分，然而，这也正是 Straitford 公司生存发展的立足点。

Friedman 在奥斯汀仅依靠一个只有 20 人的团队来进行工作。他的工作人员中有几位具有军事谍报的背景。他把公司的局外人地位视为成功的关键因素。Straitford 公司的情报简讯通常不像华盛顿的那样扑朔迷离，这些官方机构总是以此来避免发表惹人注目的言论，以防出错。Friedman 说，Straitford 公司为其不为人左右的声音而引以为豪。

题目答案与解析

1. 网络的出现已经 _____。
   A. 得到像 Donovan 这样的爱好者的支持　　B. 改变了智能服务
   C. 恢复了许多普通娱乐游戏　　　　　　　D. 使情报行业复兴
   【答案】B
   【解析】本题可参照文章的第 1 段。从中可知，美国的间谍头子 Donovan 对收集情报非常痴迷。他认为，在职业间谍活动这一伟大事业中，可以利用任何可以利用的工具；互联网已经彻底改变了人们的一些日常消遣活动，比如买书、发送邮件，如今它也正在重新塑造着 Donovan 的事业。据此可知，网络改变了其智能服务。B 项与文章意思相符，因此 B 项为正确答案。

2. 文中提到 Donovan 的故事是为了 _____。
   A. 介绍网上刺探情报这一话题　　　　　B. 表明他如何为美国而战
   C. 给信息战增添一个插曲　　　　　　　D. 赞扬他为中央情报局所做出的独特贡献
   【答案】A
   【解析】本题可参照文章的第 1 段。从中可知，Donovan 一定会喜欢互联网，这位在第二次世界大战中建立了战略情报局且后来又为中央情报局的建立奠定基础的美国间谍头子对收集情报非常痴迷；Donovan 认为，在这种间谍活动——刺探情报作为一种"职业"——的"绝妙游戏"中，应该利用可以利用的一切手段。据此可知，文中提到 Donovan 的故事是为了介绍在网上从事间谍活动这一话题。A 项与文章的意思相符，因此 A 项为正确答案。

3．短语 making the biggest splash（第 3 段第 1 行）最可能的意思是 _____。

A．造成最大的麻烦　　　　　　　　B．尽最大的努力

C．取得最大的成功　　　　　　　　D．受到最广泛的欢迎

【答案】C

【解析】从文章第 2 段的后半部分可知，1995 年，中央情报局曾经举办过一次比赛，结果以绝对优势赢得比赛的是弗吉尼亚的一家小公司，名叫"开源信息咨询公司"，它的明显优势就是对电子世界的把握；从第 3 段的内容可知，在这个领域中最成功的公司之一是 Straitford 有限公司，这是一家位于得克萨斯州奥斯汀市的私营情报分析公司，它通过向一些公司出售间谍情报谋取利润。据此可知，making the biggest splash 最可能的意思应该是——"成就最大的"。C 项与文章的意思相符，因此 C 项为正确答案。

4．从第 4 段中可以了解到：_____。

A．Straitford 有关乌克兰的预言被证实是正确的

B．Straitford 保证其所提供情报的真实性

C．Straitford 的经营特征是不可预知性

D．Straitford 能够提供非常可靠的信息

【答案】D

【解析】从文章第 4 段的内容可知，Straitford 公司总裁 George Friedman 把网络世界看成是一种信息收集和发布的互动工具，是超级间谍的天堂；上周，他的公司就忙着从世界各地收集信息，以便预测乌克兰可能发生的危机；"一旦情报传播开，我们将立刻得到 500 条来自乌克兰的最新的网上消息，然后从中进行筛选，"曾是政治学教授的 Friedman 说。当然，这种公开渠道的间谍活动也担有风险，因为很难区分情报的真假，而这正是 Straitford 公司生存发展的立足点。据此可知，Straitford 能够兴旺的原因就是它能够辨别并提供真实的信息。D 项与文章的意思相符，因此 D 项为正确答案。

5．最让 Straitford 感到骄傲的是它的 _____。

A．官方的地位　　　B．不落俗套的形象　　C．效率高的员工　　D．军事背景

【答案】B

【解析】本题可参照文章的最后一段。从中可知，Friedman 依靠的是奥斯汀的 20 名员工中的少数几个人。他的员工中有几名有军事情报背景。他把公司"局外人"的状况看成是其成功的关键。Straitford 公司的情报简讯不像华盛顿的那样扑朔迷离，因为政府机构避免发表惹人注目的言论，以防出错；Friedman 说，Straitford 公司以其与众不同的言论而自豪。由此可知：Straitford 引以为豪的就是它不受约束。B 项与文章的意思相符，因此 B 项为正确答案。

Text　2

To paraphrase 18th-century statesman Edmund Burke, "All that is needed for the triumph of a misguided cause is that good people do nothing." One such cause now seeks to end biomedical research because of the theory that animals have rights ruling out their use in research. Scientists need to respond forcefully to animal rights advocates, whose arguments are confusing the public and thereby threatening advances in health knowledge and care. Leaders of the animal rights movement target biomedical research because it depends on public funding, and few people understand the process of health care research. Hearing allegations of cruelty to animals in research settings, many are perplexed that anyone would deliberately harm an animal.

For example, a grandmotherly woman staffing an animal rights booth at a recent street fair was distributing a brochure that encouraged readers not to use anything that comes from or is tested in animals — no meat, no far, no medicines. Asked if she opposed immunizations, she wanted to know if vaccines come from animal research. When assured that they do, she replied, "Then I would have to say yes." Asked what will happen when epidemics return, she said, "Don't worry, scientists will find some way of using computers." Such well-meaning people just don't understand.

Scientists must communicate their message to the public in a compassionate, understandable way — in human terms, not in the language of molecular biology. We need to make clear the connection between animal research and a grandmother's hip replacement, a father's bypass operation, a baby's vaccinations, and even a pet's shots. To those who are unaware that animal research was needed to produce these treatments, as well as new treatments and vaccines, animal research seems wasteful at best and cruel at worst.

Much can be done. Scientists could "adopt" middle school classes and present their own research. They should be quick to respond to letters to the editor, lest animal rights misinformation go unchallenged and acquire a deceptive appearance of truth. Research institutions could be opened to tours, to show that laboratory animals receive humane care. Finally, because the ultimate stakeholders are patients, the health research community should actively recruit to its cause not only well-known personalities such as Stephen Cooper, who has made courageous statements about the value of animal research, but all who receive medical treatment. If good people do nothing there is a real possibility that an uninformed citizenry will extinguish the precious embers of medical progress.

1. The author begins his article with Edmund Burke's words to _____.
    A. call on scientists to take some actions
    B. criticize the misguided cause of animal rights
    C. warn of the doom of biomedical research
    D. show the triumph of the animal rights movement
2. Misled people tend to think that using an animal in research is _____.
    A. cruel but natural   B. inhuman and unacceptable
    C. inevitable but vicious   D. pointless and wasteful
3. The example of the grandmotherly woman is used to show the public's _____.
    A. discontent with animal research   B. ignorance about medical science
    C. indifference to epidemics   D. anxiety about animal rights
4. The author believes that, in face of the challenge from animal rights advocates, scientists should _____.

A. communicate more with the public   B. employ hi-tech means in research

C. feel no shame for their cause   D. strive to develop new cures

5. From the text we learn that Stephen Cooper is _____.

A. a well-known humanist   B. a medical practitioner

C. an enthusiast in animal rights   D. a supporter of animal research

核心词汇注释

setting ['setɪŋ] *n.* 安置；安装；（太阳）落山；（固定东西的）框架；底座

perplexed [pə'plekst] *adj.* 困惑的，不知所措的

brochure [brəʊ'ʃə(r)] *n.* 小册子

immunization [ˌɪmjʊnɪ'zeɪʃn] *n.* 使免除；使免疫

vaccine ['væksiːn] *adj.* 疫苗的；牛痘的 *n.* 疫苗

molecular [mə'lekjʊlə(r)] *adj.* [化]分子的；由分子组成的

hip [hɪp] *n.* 臀；蔷薇果；忧郁 *adj.* 熟悉内情的 *vt.* 使忧郁；给（屋顶）造屋脊 *int.* 喝彩声

recruit [rɪ'kruːt] *n.* 新兵；新分子；新会员 *vt.* 使恢复；补充；征募 *vi.* 征募新兵；复原

extinguish [ɪk'stɪŋgwɪʃ] *vt.* 熄灭；消灭；压制；使黯然失色；偿清

ember ['embə(r)] *n.* 灰烬；余烬

长难句剖析

【文章难句】All that is needed for the triumph of a misguided cause is that good people do nothing.

【结构分析】本句中，all 是主语。前面由 that 引导的 that is needed for the triumph of a misguided cause 是定语从句修饰 all，后面的 that good people do nothing 是表语从句。

【参考译文】只要好人不作为，受误导的思想就会成功。

全文参考译文

18 世纪的政治家 Edmund Burke 说道："误导之所以得逞，是因为好人无所作为。"现在有这样一种误导的情形能够说明这一名言：生物医学研究将被中止。因为，有一种观点认为，动物有权利拒绝当做人类的研究对象。科学家需要对动物权利的倡导者做出有力的回答，因为这些人的观点正在混淆视听，阻碍了保健知识和医疗的发展。由于生物医学的研究占用公共资金，而医学研究的方法又鲜为人知，于是动物权利运动领导人便把矛头指向生物医学研究上。听说在研究中对动物很残忍，许多人就会感到困惑，以为任何人都会故意伤害小动物。

譬如，在街道上，动物权利保护协会的一位老太太正在分发小册子，鼓励读者不要使用任何动物或在动物身上试验过的任何食品或制品——包括肉类、药品或毛皮。如果问她是否反对免疫，她想知道疫苗是否来自动物试验。当得到的答案是肯定时，她说："那么，我会反对的。"当问到如果发生传染病怎么办时，她说："不必要担心，科学家将会用计算机找到一些解决办法。"这样的好心人根本就不明白其中的道理。

科学家应该用富有感情的、通俗易懂的方式向民众传达信息，即用通俗的语言而不是用分子生物学的语言来讲话。我们需要弄清楚动物研究与祖母的髋骨置换术、父亲的旁道管手术、孩子的免疫接种甚至宠物的防疫注射之间的联系。对于那些不了解只有通过动物研究才能研制出治疗方案、才能开发出新方案和新疫苗的人来说，动物研究说得好听一些是浪费，说得难听一些是残酷。

有许多事情是我们力所能及的。科学家可以借用中学的课堂来介绍自己的研究。他们应该对读者来信作出迅速回复，以免动物权利组织的错误信息没有受到质疑，使人们误将其当做真理。研究机构可以对旅游者开放，以此显示供研究用的动物得到了仁慈的照料。最后，最有利害关系的是病人，保健研究团体不仅要接纳像 Stephen Cooper 这样著名的人物，因为他敢于说出关于动物研究的价值，也要接纳任何愿意接受治疗的人。如果好人不作为，有可能真会使不明就里的人们扑灭医学进步中珍贵的火种。

题目答案与解析

1. 在文章开始时作者引用了 Edmund Burke 的话，是为了 _____。
   A. 号召科学家采取某些行动
   B. 批评被误导的维护动物权利运动
   C. 警告生物医学研究的厄运
   D. 表明动物权利运动的胜利

   【答案】A

   【解析】本题可参照文章的第 1 段。从中可知，18 世纪的政治家 Edmund Burke 说，"误导之所以得逞，是因为好人无所作为。"现在，就有这样的运动寻求终止生化研究，其依据是动物有权要求人们在研究活动中不再使用动物的理论；科学家应该对动物权利倡导者做出有力的反击，因为这些人的观点正在蛊惑公众，从而威胁到了保健知识与医疗的发展。据此可知，作者引用 Edmund Burke 的话是希望科学家对动物权利倡导者进行反击。A 项与文意相符，因此 A 项为正确答案。

2. 被误导的人们常常认为，用动物进行研究 _____。
   A. 残忍但正常
   B. 不人道，不可接受
   C. 不可避免但不道德
   D. 没有意义，纯属浪费

   【答案】B

   【解析】本题可参照文章的第 1 段。从中可知，听说在研究中对待动物很残忍，许多人就会感到困惑，以为任何人都会故意伤害动物。从第 3 段的最后一句话可知，对于那些不了解只有通过动物研究才能研制出治疗方案、才能开发出新方案和新疫苗的人来说，动物研究说得好听一点是浪费，说得难听一点是残忍。据此可知，被误导的人们认为研究中使用动物残忍、不可接受。B 项与文章的意思相符，因此 B 项为正确答案。

3. 举出老太太的例子是用来表示公众 _____。
   A. 对动物研究不满
   B. 不了解医疗科学
   C. 对流行病漠不关心
   D. 担心动物的权利

   【答案】B

   【解析】本题可参照文章的第 2 段。从中可知，在最近的一次街头集市上，一位在动物权利保护协会服务的老太太在分发小册子，鼓励读者不要使用任何来自于动物或在动物身上做过实验的任何东西——包括肉类、药品或皮毛；当问及她是否反对免疫接种时，她说她想知道疫苗是否来自于动物实验；当确信疫苗是来自于动物实验时，她回答说，"那么，我得说我反对。"当问及如果流行病发作该怎么办时，她说，"不用担心，科学家会利用计算机找到某种解决办法的。"这样的好心人只是不了解情况。据此可知，老太太的例子是用来表示许多人根本不了解动物研究。B项与文章的意思相符，因此B项为正确答案。

4. 面对来自动物权利倡导者的挑战，作者认为科学家应该 _____。

   A. 多与公众交流　　　　　　　　　B. 在研究中采用高科技手段
   C. 不要因为他们的运动感到羞愧　　D. 努力研发新的治疗方法

【答案】A

【解析】从文章第2段的最后一句话可知，这样的好心人只是不了解情况；从第3段的内容可知，科学家必须用一种富于同情、易于理解的方式将信息传递给公众；我们必须澄清动物研究与祖母的髋骨置换、父亲的旁道管手术、孩子的免疫接种甚至宠物的防疫注射之间的关系；对于那些不了解只有通过动物研究才能研制出治疗方案、才能开发出新方案和新疫苗的人来说，动物研究说得好听一点是浪费，说得难听一点是残忍；从第4段的内容可知，科学家可以"走进"中学课堂，介绍他们的科研活动；他们应尽快答复读者的来信，以免动物权利组织的错误信息没有引起质疑，从而获得真理的假象；研究机构也应该向游客开放，以表明实验室的动物受到了人道的对待；最后，医学研究界不仅要邀请像Stephen Cooper那样的知名人士来支持自己的事业，还要邀请所有接受过医疗的人来支持自己。据此可知，作者认为科学家应该多与公众交流，让公众了解真实情况。A项与文章的意思相符，因此A项为正确答案。

5. 我们从文中可了解到Stephen Cooper是 _____。

   A. 一位著名的人道主义者　　　　　B. 一名医生
   C. 一名动物权利的热心支持者　　　D. 一名动物研究的支持者

【答案】D

【解析】本题可参照文章的第4段。从中可知，科学家应尽快答复读者的来信，以免动物权利组织的错误信息没有受到质疑，使人们误将其当做真理；研究机构也应该向游客开放，以表明实验室的动物受到了人道的对待；最后，因为最有利害关系者是病人，所以，医学研究界不仅要邀请像Stephen Cooper那样的知名人士来支持自己的事业，他已经勇敢地声明动物研究的价值，还要邀请所有接受过医疗的人来支持自己；如果好人再不采取行动，不明就里的公众真可能会扑灭医疗发展的宝贵火种。据此可知，Stephen Cooper敢于对动物研究的价值发表无所畏惧的言论，说明他支持动物研究。D项与文章意思相符，因此D项为正确答案。

Text 3

In recent years, railroads have been combining with each other, merging into super systems, causing heightened concerns about monopoly. As recently as 1995, the top four railroads accounted for under 70 percent of the total ton-miles moved by rails. Next year, after a series of mergers is completed, just four railroads will control well over 90 percent of all the freight moved by major rail carriers.

Supporters of the new super systems argue that these mergers will allow for substantial cost reductions and better coordinated service. Any threat of monopoly, they argue, is removed by fierce competition from trucks. But many shippers complain that for heavy bulk commodities traveling long distances, such as coal, chemicals, and grain, trucking is too costly and the railroads therefore have them by the throat.

The vast consolidation within the rail industry means that most shippers are served by only one rail company. Railroads typically charge such "captive" shippers 20 to 30 percent more than they do when another railroad is competing for the business. Shippers who feel they are being overcharged have the right to appeal to the federal government's Surface Transportation Board for rate relief, but the process is expensive, time consuming, and will work only in truly extreme cases.

Railroads justify rate discrimination against captive shippers on the grounds that in the long run it reduces everyone's cost. If railroads charged all customers the same average rate, they argue, shippers who have the option of switching to trucks or other forms of transportation would do so, leaving remaining customers to shoulder the cost of keeping up the line. It's theory to which many economists subscribe, but in practice it often leaves railroads in the position of determining which companies will flourish and which will fail. "Do we really want railroads to be the arbiters of who wins and who loses in the marketplace?" asks Martin Bercovici, a Washington lawyer who frequently represents shipper.

Many captive shippers also worry they will soon be hit with a round of huge rate increases. The railroad industry as a whole, despite its brightening fortunes, still does not earn enough to cover the cost of the capital it must invest to keep up with its surging traffic. Yet railroads continue to borrow billions to acquire one another, with Wall Street cheering them on. Consider the 1.02 billion bid by Norfolk Southern and CSX to acquire Conrail this year. Conrail's net railway operating income in 1996 was just 427 million, less than half of the carrying costs of the transaction. Who's going to pay for the rest of the bill? Many captive shippers fear that they will, as Norfolk Southern and CSX increase their grip on the market.

1. According to those who support mergers railway monopoly is unlikely because _____.

    A. cost reduction is based on competition

    B. services call for cross-trade coordination

    C. outside competitors will continue to exist

    D. shippers will have the railway by the throat

2. What is many captive shippers' attitude towards the consolidation in the rail industry?

    A. Indifferent.   B. Supportive.   C. Indignant.   D. Apprehensive.

3. It can be inferred from Paragraph 3 that _____.

    A. shippers will be charged less without a rival railroad

    B. there will soon be only one railroad company nationwide

    C. overcharged shippers are unlikely to appeal for rate relief

    D. a government board ensures fair play in railway business

4. The word "arbiters" (Line 6, Para. 4) most probably refers to those _____.

    A. who work as coordinators   B. who function as judges

    C. who supervise transactions   D. who determine the price

5. According to the text, the cost increase in the rail industry is mainly caused by _____.

    A. the continuing acquisition   B. the growing traffic

    C. the cheering Wall Street   D. the shrinking market

核心词汇注释

heighten [haɪtən] *v.* 提高，升高

monopoly [mə'nɒpəlɪ] *n.* 垄断；垄断者；专利权；专利事业

merger ['mɜːdʒə(r)] *n.* 合并，归并

consolidation [kənˌsɒlɪ'deɪʃən] *n.* 巩固；合并

captive ['kæptɪv] *n.* 俘虏；被美色或爱情迷住的人
  adj. 被俘的；被迷住的

consuming [kən'sjuːmɪŋ] *adj.* 使人着迷的

subscribe [səb'skraɪb] *v.* 捐款；订阅；签署；赞成；预订

flourish ['flʌrɪʃ] *vi.* 繁荣；茂盛；活跃；手舞足蹈；兴旺；处于旺盛时期
  vt. 挥动；夸耀
  n. 茂盛；兴旺；华饰；繁荣

arbiter ['ɑːbɪtə(r)] *n.* 仲裁者；判优器

ton-mile 吨；英里（货物运输计量单位）

surge [sɜːdʒ] *n.* 汹涌，澎湃
  vi. 汹涌，澎湃；振荡；滑脱；放松
  vt. 使汹涌奔腾

Conrail ['kɒnreɪl] *n.* <美>联合铁路公司，联铁（美国一家接受联邦资助的私营公司，主要经营范围在东北部）

长难句剖析

【文章难句】If railroads charged all customers the same average rate, they argue, shippers who have the option of switching to trucks or other forms of transportation would do so, leaving remaining customers to shoulder the cost of keeping up the line.

【结构分析】本句为虚拟语气，主干是 shippers would do so, if railroads charged all customers the same average rate 为条件状语从句，they argue 为插入语，who 引导的定语从句修饰 shippers，现在分词结构 leaving remaining customers to shoulder the cost of keeping up the line 做结果状语。

【参考译文】他们争论道：如果铁路对所有顾客收取一样的费用，那些可以选择卡车或者其他交通工具的托运人就会选择这样做，结果让其他的顾客来承担路线价位上涨的费用。

全文参考译文

近年来，各个铁路公司都一直在进行合并而成为超级系统，这引起了人们对垄断的日益关注。在 1995 年四条最大的铁路运输量不到总吨英里数的 70%。明年，经过一系列的合并之后，这四条铁路将控制主要货运公司全部运输货物的 90%以上。

支持新超级铁路的人们认为，这些合并有助于大幅降低费用，更好地协调货运服务。他们认为，任何来自垄断的威胁都可以通过来自汽车的激烈竞争进行消除。然而，许多托运人

却抱怨说，对于远途大宗货物如煤、化肥和粮食等而言，汽车货运的运费太昂贵，因此铁路解决了这一难题。

铁路业的大规模合并意味着托运人服务的铁路公司仅此一家。这样，一般铁路会比有竞争对手时向"受制"的托运人多收 20%～30%的费用。那些觉得运费过高的人有权向联邦政府地面运输委员会投诉，要求给予运费补贴。然而，这个过程既耗时，又费钱，而且只有在极端的情况下才能如此。

从长远来看，费率的差别降低了各个客户的成本，所以铁路方面认为路方收费差别是合理的。如果铁路对所有客户都平均收费，那些可以选择卡车或其他运输方式的客户就会去选择卡车或其他运输方式。如此一来，剩余的客户就要承担保持铁路运转的费用。对于这一理论，许多经济学家都赞成。但是，这样常常使铁路处于决定哪些公司该继续发展，哪些公司该倒闭的地位。经常作为托运方代理人的华盛顿律师 Martin Bercovici 问道："难道我们真的要让铁路成为市场上判断谁输谁赢的仲裁人吗？"

许多受控制的托运人也担心费用大幅度增加，他们害怕遭受打击。就整个铁路业来说，尽管财源大有希望，其收入仍然不足以支付为维持运量日益增加而投入的资本。然而，由于有华尔街为其鼓气，铁路方面仍然贷款数十亿元去修建一条又一条的铁路。今年 Norfolk Southern 和 CSX 公司出资 10.2 亿美元购得联合铁路公司。而 1996 年联合铁路公司的铁路纯收入仅为 4.27 亿美元，还不到收购成本的一半。那么这笔账的另一半由谁来买单？许多受束缚的托运人担心像 Norfolk Southern 和 CSX 一样，联合铁路公司也会加强对市场的掌控。

题目答案与解析

1. 按照那些支持合并者的观点，铁路垄断不可能发生的原因是 _____。

    A．成本的降低以竞争为基础　　　　B．服务需要跨行业的协调

    C．来自外面的竞争者将继续存在　　D．托运人将控制铁路运输

【答案】C

【解析】本题可参照文章的第 2 段。从中可知，支持这种新型的超级铁路的人宣称，这些合并会考虑大幅度降低成本，并更好地协调货运服务。他们认为，任何来自垄断的威胁都可以通过来自于汽车运输的激烈竞争而消除。据此可知，支持铁路合并的人认为，来自于外面的激烈竞争会消除垄断的局面。C 项与文意相符，因此 C 项为正确答案。

2. 对铁路部门合并这件事，很多受控制的托运人的态度是什么？

    A．漠不关心。　　　B．支持。　　　C．愤怒。　　　D．担心。

【答案】D

【解析】本题可参照文章的第 3 段。从中可知，典型的情况是，在没有竞争对手时，铁路公司一般向这样的"受制的"托运人多收取 20%～30%的费用。从文章第 5 段的内容可知，许多受制的托运人也担心将受到又一轮费用大幅度增加的打击；就整个铁路行业来说，其收入仍不足以支付它必须用于维持日益增加的运输而投入的资金；而且，铁路公司仍在借贷资金以相互兼并；今年，Norfolk Southern 和 CSX 公司投入了 10.2 亿美元兼并了联合铁路公司；许多受制的托运人担心，随着 Norfolk Southern 公司和 CSX 对市场的控制力加强，托运人将承担余下的费用。据此可知，受控制的托运人担心铁路部门的合并。D 项与文章的意思相符，因此 D 项

为正确答案。

3. 从第 3 段可以推知 _____。
   A. 如果没有竞争对手，铁路公司向托运者索取的费用将少一些
   B. 不久，全国将只剩下一家铁路公司
   C. 被索价过多的托运人不可能上诉减少费率
   D. 政府部门保证在铁路经营中实行公平竞争
   【答案】C
   【解析】本题可参照文章的第 3 段。从中可知，铁路业规模空前的合并意味着，大多数托运人将由唯一的一家铁路公司提供服务；铁路公司向这样的"受制的"托运人收取的费用比有别的铁路公司竞争时多 20%～30%；那些觉得被索价过高的托运人有权向联邦政府的水陆运输委员会投诉，要求降低费率，但是这种过程费用高，也费时间，只有在极端情况下才有效。据此可知，托运人上诉的可能性不大。C 项与文章的意思相符，因此 C 项为正确答案。

4. 单词 arbiters（第 4 段第 6 行）最可能意指那些 _____。
   A. 像协调员一样的工作者   B. 行使法官职能者
   C. 监督交易者   D. 决定价格者
   【答案】B
   【解析】本题可参照文章的第 4 段。从中可知，这是一种许多经济学家都赞成的理论，但实际上，这使得铁路公司可以决定哪些公司兴旺，哪些公司倒闭。经常为托运人做代理的华盛顿律师问道："难道我们真的要让铁路公司成为决定市场上谁兴谁衰的仲裁人吗？"据此可知，arbiters 的意思应该是"裁决者"。B 项与文章的意思相符，因此 B 项为正确答案。

5. 依照本文的观点，铁路业的成本增加主要是由 _____ 引起的。
   A. 持续的合并   B. 日益繁忙的运输
   C. 令人鼓舞的华尔街股市   D. 萎缩的市场
   【答案】A
   【解析】本题可参照文章的最后一段。从中可知，许多受制的托运人也担心将受到又一轮费用大幅度增加的打击。就整个铁路行业来说，尽管出现好的转机，但其所赚得的仍不足以支付它必须用于维持日益增加的运输而投入的资金。而且，铁路公司仍在借贷数十亿的资金以相互兼并，华尔街则在旁边为他们打气。接着举例说：Norfolk Southern 公司和 CSX 投入了 10.2 亿美元兼并了联合铁路公司，而联合铁路公司在 1996 年的净运营收入只有 4.27 亿美元，还不到交易成本的一半，那么，谁来支付余下的费用呢？许多受制的托运人担心，随着 Norfolk Southern 公司和 CSX 对市场的控制力加强，托运人将承担余下的费用。据此可知，铁路部门成本增加的主要原因是进一步的合并。A 项与文章意思相符，因此 A 项为正确答案。

Text 4

It is said that in England death is pressing, in Canada inevitable and in California optional. Small wonder. Americans' life expectancy has nearly doubled over the past century. Failing hips can be replaced, cataracts removed in a 30-minutes surgical procedure. Such advances offer the aging population a quality of life that was unimaginable when I entered medicine 50 years ago. But not even a great health-care system can cure death, and our failure to confront that reality now threatens this greatness of ours.

Death is normal; we are genetically programmed to disintegrate and perish, even under ideal conditions. We all understand that at some level, yet as medical consumers we treat death as a problem to be solved. Shielded by third-party payers from the cost of our care, we demand everything that can possibly be done for us, even if it's useless. The most obvious example is late-stage cancer care. Physicians — frustrated by their inability to cure the disease and fearing loss of hope in the patient — too often offer aggressive treatment far beyond what is scientifically justified.

In 1950, the U.S. spent $12.7 billion on health care. In 2002, the cost will be $ 1,540 billion. Anyone can see this trend is unsustainable. Yet few seem willing to try to reverse it. Some scholars conclude that a government with finite resources should simply stop paying for medical care that sustains life beyond a certain age — say 83 or so. Former Colorado governor Richard Lamm has been quoted as saying that the old and infirm "have a duty to die and get out of the way", so that younger, healthier people can realize their potential.

I would not go that far. Energetic people now routinely work through their 60s and beyond, and remain dazzlingly productive. At 78, Viacom chairman Sumner Redstone jokingly claims to be 53. Supreme Court Justice Sandra Day O'Connor is in her 70s, and former surgeon general C. Everett Koop chairs an Internet start-up in his 80s. These leaders are living proof that prevention works and that we can manage the health problems that come naturally with age. As a mere 68-year-old, I wish to age as productively as they have.

Yet there are limits to what a society can spend in this pursuit. As a physician, I know the most costly and dramatic measures may be ineffective and painful. I also know that people in Japan and Sweden, countries that spend far less on medical care, have achieved longer, healthier lives than we have. As a nation, we may be overfunding the quest for unlikely cures while underfunding research on humbler therapies that could improve people's lives.

1. What is implied in the first sentence?

   A. Americans are better prepared for death than other people.

   B. Americans enjoy a higher life quality than ever before.

   C. Americans are over-confident of their medical technology.

   D. Americans take a vain pride in their long life expectancy.

2. The author uses the example of cancer patients to show that _____.

   A. medical resources are often wasted

   B. doctors are helpless against fatal diseases

   C. some treatments are too aggressive

   D. medical costs are becoming unaffordable

3. The author's attitude toward Richard Lamm's remark is one of _____.

   A. strong disapproval   B. reserved consent

   C. slight contempt   D. enthusiastic support

4. In contrast to the U.S., Japan and Sweden are funding their medical care _____.

A. more flexibly
B. more extravagantly
C. more cautiously
D. more reasonably

5. The text intends to express the idea that _____.
   A. medicine will further prolong people's lives
   B. life beyond a certain limit is not worth living
   C. death should be accepted as a fact of life
   D. excessive demands increase the cost of health care

核心词汇注释

cataract [ˈkætərækt] *n.* 大瀑布；奔流；白内障

surgical [ˈsɜːdʒɪk(ə)l] *adj.* 外科的；外科医生的；手术上的
n. 外科病房；外科手术

disintegrate [dɪsˈɪntɪɡreɪt] *vt.* （使）分解；（使）碎裂

perish [ˈperɪʃ] *vi.* 毁灭；死亡；腐烂；枯萎
vt. 毁坏；使麻木

shield [ʃiːld] *n.* 防护物；护罩；盾；盾状物
vt. (from) 保护；防护
v. 遮蔽

physician [fɪˈzɪʃ(ə)n] *n.* 医师；内科医师

routine [ruːˈtiːn] *n.* 例行公事；常规；日常事务；程序

dazzling [ˈdæzlɪŋ] *adj.* 眼花缭乱的；耀眼的

therapy [ˈθerəpɪ] *n.* 治疗

长难句剖析

【文章难句】Shielded by third-party payers from the cost of our care, we demand everything that can possibly be done for us, even if it's useless.

【结构分析】本句主干是 we demand everything，分词结构 Shielded by third-party payers from the cost of our care 做状语，everything 后面是 that 引导的定语从句，even if 引导让步状语从句。

【参考译文】由于有第三方为我们支付医疗费用，我们通常会要求别人为我们做一切可能的事情，尽管有时候是徒劳的。

全文参考译文

有人说：在英国，死亡是无法抗拒的；在加拿大，死亡是不可避免的；在加利福尼亚州，死亡则是可以选择的。其实这种说法不足为怪。在过去的一个世纪里，美国人的平均寿命增加了一倍。有缺陷的髋骨可以置换，白内障30分钟即可手术摘除。这些成就为老年人提供了高质量的生活。50年以前我刚从医时，这种生活是难以想象的。然而，目前还没有任何一种医疗手段能使人不死。面对死亡而无能为力是对我们这个伟大时代的极大嘲讽。

死亡属于正常的现象。从遗传学的角度来说，即使在最理想的条件下，人们也是注定要衰老直至死亡的。我们多少都懂得这一点，然而，有病时我们却把死亡看成是可以解决的问题，因为有第三方为我们支付医疗费用，我们要求别人为我们做一切可能的事情，尽管有时是徒劳。对晚期癌症的治疗是超出科学根据最明显的例子。由于不能治愈癌症又害怕病人对生活失去希望，医生常常给予过于积极的治疗方法。

1950 年，美国用于医疗的费用是 127 亿美元。2002 年达到 15,400 亿美元。大家都知道这种趋势不应继续下去，然而似乎没有几个人愿意设法扭转这种趋势。一些学者认为，资源有限的政府对于超过一定年龄的人——比如说 83 岁左右——不应再提供医疗费用以延长其生命了。有人引用科罗拉多前州长 Richard Lamm 的话：年老体弱者应该死，以腾出位置让年轻、健康的人能实现其潜能。

我不会说得那样过分。精力充沛的人现在可以工作到 60 多岁而依然很活跃。Viacom 总裁 Sumner Redstone 通 78 岁时曾笑称自己 53 岁。最高法院法官 Sandra Day O'Connor 现在 70 多了。而前军医局局长 C·Everett Koop 80 多岁时还主持一家互联网公司。这些活生生的事实表明预防疾病是有效的，同时也表明人们能处理随自然衰老而产生的健康问题。作为一个 68 岁的老人，我希望自己老时仍然能像他们那样活跃。

然而，任何社会在保健方面费用的支出都是有限度的。作为一个内科医生，我知道费用最昂贵、最具特色的治疗措施也许是无效和令人痛苦的。同时我也了解，在日本、瑞典这些医疗费用支出比我们少的国家里，人们的寿命比我们长，生活得比我们健康。我们国家也许对那些不可能有效的疗法的探索投资过多，而对那些能提高生活质量的简单疗法的研究则投资太少了。

题目答案与解析

1. 第 1 句话暗指了什么？
   A. 与其他人相比，美国人为死亡所作的准备更充分。
   B. 美国人享受的生活质量比以前高。
   C. 美国人对他们的医疗技术过分自信。
   D. 美国人对其长寿盲目骄傲。
   【答案】C
   【解析】从文章第 1 段的第 1 句话可知，据说在英国，死亡是无法抗拒的；在加拿大，死亡是不可避免的；在加利福尼亚，死亡是可以选择的。接着讲道，过去一个世纪中，美国人的寿命已经延长了将近一半，像白内障这样的手术 30min 就可以完成。据此可知，美国人觉得自己国家的医疗技术十分先进。C 项与文意相符，因此 C 项为正确答案。

2. 作者列举癌症患者的例子，目的是为了说明 _____。
   A. 医疗资源经常被浪费　　　　　　B. 医生对于致命的疾病感到无能为力
   C. 一些治疗方法太大胆　　　　　　D. 医疗费用越来越让人承受不起
   【答案】A
   【解析】本题可参照文章的第 2 段。从中可知，由于第三方为我们支付医疗费用，我们便要求别人为我们做一切可能的事情，尽管有时候是徒劳的。最明显的例子便是晚期癌症的护理。由于不能治愈这种疾病所导致的沮丧以及害怕病人失去希望，医生经常提供大胆的医疗方法——这些方法远远超过科学上所证实的合理标准。从第 3 段的内容可知，1950 年，美国用于医疗保健的费用是 127 亿美元；2002 年，费用达到 15,400 亿美元。人人都知道这种趋势无法维持。有些学者断定——资源有限的政府完全应该停止为维持超过一定年龄的生命支付医疗保健费用。据此可知，美国没有利用好可利用的资源。A 项与文意相符，因此 A 项为正确答案。

3. 对 Richard Lamm 所作的评论，作者的态度是 _____。

   A. 强烈反对   B. 有保留的赞同   C. 有点蔑视   D. 热情支持

【答案】B

【解析】本题可参照文章的第 3 段。从中可知，有人引用前科罗拉多州州长 Richard Lamm 的话说，年老体弱者"有死亡的义务，应该让开位置"，以便更年轻、更健康者能够实现他们的潜能。第 4 段接着指出：我不会把话说得那么极端，如今，按照常规来说，精力充沛的人可以工作到 60 多岁，甚至更晚，而且其创造力令人惊讶。然后举例说明，指出这些领导者都是活生生的证据，证明预防是有效的，证明我们能够处理一些随着年龄自然而来的健康问题。据此可知，作者不太同意 Richard Lamm 的观点。B 项与文章的意思相符，因此 B 项为正确答案。

4. 比起美国，日本和瑞典的医疗保健投资 _____。

   A. 更灵活   B. 更过分   C. 更小心   D. 更合理

【答案】D

【解析】本题可参照文章的最后一段。从中可知，一个社会能够花在这项事业上的费用是有限的。作为一名内科医生，我知道，那些费用最昂贵、最引人注目的措施可能没有效果、令人痛苦。我也知道，在日本和瑞典这些医疗保健费用远低于我们的国家里，人们的寿命比我们长，生活得比我们健康。我们国家可能投于探索那些不可能的疗法的费用过多，而投于研究那些能够提高人们生活质量的简单疗法的费用太少。据此可知，美国人在医疗护理方面的投资不合理。D 项与文章的意思相符，因此 D 项为正确答案。

5. 本文想要表达的观点是 _____。

   A. 医学将进一步延长人的寿命

   B. 超出一定限度的生命不值得生存

   C. 死亡应该被看成是一种不可避免的事实

   D. 过度的要求提高了保健护理的费用

【答案】C

【解析】综观全文，可以推断出本文的主旨。从文章第 1 段的内容可知，在英国，死亡是无法抗拒的；在加拿大，死亡是不可避免的；在加利福尼亚，死亡则是可以选择的。这种说法不足为怪；在过去的一个世纪里，美国人的平均寿命增加了一倍；医学进步为老年人提供了一种以前不可想象的基本生活条件，但是，即使是先进的保健体系也不可能治愈死亡。从第 2 段的内容可知，死亡是正常的。我们的基因决定我们会衰变、会死亡，即使是在理想的条件下。第 3、4 段举例说明了一些人的观点和做法，即有人认为不必把有限的资源投入到延长人的寿命的医疗护理中，预防也可以起作用。他们还认为，他们能够应付随着年龄的增长而引发的健康问题。从文章的最后一段内容可知，我们国家投入到医疗护理的费用比日本和瑞典多得多，但日本人和瑞典人的寿命却比我们长，也比我们健康。据此可知，本文主要讲的是，因为死亡是正常的，我们没有必要把巨资投到医疗护理方面。C 项与文意相符，因此 C 项为正确答案。

Unit 14

If you intend using humor in your talk to make people smile, you must know how to identify shared experiences and problems. Your humor must be relevant to the audience and should help to show them that you are one of them or that you understand their situation and are in sympathy with their point of view. Depending on whom you are addressing, the problems will be different. If you are talking to a group of managers, you may refer to the disorganized methods of their secretaries; alternatively if you are addressing secretaries, you may want to comment on their disorganized bosses.

Here is an example, which I heard at a nurses' convention, of a story which works well because the audience all shared the same view of doctors. A man arrives in heaven and is being shown around by St. Peter. He sees wonderful accommodations, beautiful gardens, sunny weather, and so on. Everyone is very peaceful, polite and friendly until, waiting in a line for lunch, the new arrival is suddenly pushed aside by a man in a white coat, who rushes to the head of the line, grabs his food and stamps over to a table by himself. "Who is that?" the new arrival asked St. Peter. "Oh, that's God," came the reply, "but sometimes he thinks he's a doctor."

If you are part of the group which you are addressing, you will be in a position to know the experiences and problems which are common to all of you and it'll be appropriate for you to make a passing remark about the inedible canteen food or the chairman's notorious bad taste in ties. With other audiences you mustn't attempt to cut in with humor as they will resent an outsider making disparaging remarks about their canteen or their chairman. You will be on safer ground if you stick to scapegoats like the Post Office or the telephone system.

If you feel awkward being humorous, you must practice so that it becomes more natural. Include a few casual and apparently off-the-cuff remarks which you can deliver in a relaxed and unforced manner. Often it's the delivery which causes the audience to smile, so speak slowly and remember that a raised eyebrow or an unbelieving look may help to show that you are making a light-hearted remark.

Look for the humor. It often comes from the unexpected — a twist on a familiar quote "If at first you don't succeed, give up" or a play on words or on a situation. Search for exaggerations and understatements. Look at your talk and pick out a few words or sentences which you can turn about and inject with humor.

1. To make your humor work, you should _____.

   A. take advantage of different kinds of audience

   B. make fun of the disorganized people

   C. address different problems to different people

D.　show sympathy for your listeners

2.　The joke about doctors implies that, in the eyes of nurses, they are _____.
　　A.　impolite to new arrivals　　　　　B.　very conscious of their godlike role
　　C.　entitled to some privileges　　　　D.　very busy even during lunch hours

3.　It can be inferred from the text that public services _____.
　　A.　have benefited many people　　　　B.　are the focus of public attention
　　C.　are an inappropriate subject for humor　　D.　have often been the laughing stock

4.　To achieve the desired result, humorous stories should be delivered _____.
　　A.　in well-worded language　　　　　B.　as awkwardly as possible
　　C.　in exaggerated statements　　　　　D.　as casually as possible

5.　The best title for the text may be _____.
　　A.　Use Humor Effectively　　　　　　B.　Various Kinds of Humor
　　C.　Add Humor to Speech　　　　　　　D.　Different Humor Strategies

核心词汇注释

address　[ə'dres] *n.* 地址；致辞；演讲；说话的技巧
vt. 向……致辞；演说；写姓名地址；从事；忙于

disorganize　[dɪs'ɔːɡənaɪz] *v.* 扰乱；使紊乱；打乱

accommodation　[ə,kɒmə'deɪʃ(ə)n] *n.* 住处，膳宿，（车、船、飞机等的）预定铺位，（眼睛等的）适应性调节，（社会集团间的）迁就融合

stamp　[stæmp] *n.* 邮票；印花；印；图章；标志；印记；跺脚；顿足

v. 跺（脚）；顿（足）；压印
vi. 跺脚；践踏；重踏

inedible　[ɪn'edɪbl(ə)l] *adj.* 不适于食用的，不能吃的

notorious　[nəʊ'tɔːrɪəs] *adj.* 声名狼藉的

disparaging　[dɪs'pærɪdʒɪŋ] *adj.* 蔑视的；毁谤的；轻视的

scapegoat　['skeɪpɡəʊt] *n.* 替罪羊

understatement　[ʌndə'steɪtmənt] *n.* 节制的陈述；少说；少报

inject　[ɪn'dʒekt] *vt.* 注射；注入

长难句剖析

【文章难句】If you are part of the group which you are addressing, you will be in a position to know the experiences and problems which are common to all of you and it'll be appropriate for you to make a passing remark about the inedible canteen food or the chairman's notorious bad taste in ties.

【结构分析】本句中，主句是由 and 连接的两个并列句，其中，第一个句子中的固定搭配 in a position to do sth. 意思是"能够（做）"。which 引导的定语从句修饰 experiences and problems。第二个句子中 it 为形式主语，动词不定式 to make a passing remark about the inedible canteen food or the chairman's notorious bad taste in ties 为真正的主语。if you are part of the group 为条件状语从句，which you are addressing 为非限制性定语从句，修饰 group。

【参考译文】如果你是你说话对象中的一员，你就应该知道对于你们来说都再熟悉不过的经历和问题，这时，评论一下食堂难以下咽的饭菜或者众所周知的主席对领带极无品味，这些都将会是非常合适的话题。

全文参考译文

如果你想在交谈中运用幽默逗人发笑，那你必须知道怎样识别出和听众共同的经历和难题。你的幽默必须要与听众相关，能够向他们表明你是他们中的一员或者能够表明你理解他们的处境并且认同他们的观点。听众不同，你所谈的问题也应有所不同。如果你和经理们交谈，你可以谈论他们的秘书杂乱无序的工作方法；反过来，如果你和秘书们交谈，你也许会评论一下他们老板杂乱无章的作风。

举个例子来说，我曾在一次护士大会上听到一个很恰当的幽默故事，因为所有的听众对医生的看法相同。一位男士到了天堂，正由圣彼得带着四处观看。他看到华丽的房舍、美丽的花园、晴朗的天气等。每个人都十分和气、礼貌和友善。到排队吃中午饭时，新来的人突然被一个穿白大褂的人推到了一旁，他冲到队伍的前面，抓起自己的食物，骄横地走到桌边。"那是谁？"新来的人问圣彼得。"呃，那是上帝，"他回答，"但是有时候他以为自己是个医生。"

如果你是你的听众中的一员，你就会站在他们的角度了解对你们所有人来说都很普通的经历和难题，你可以评价一番难以下咽的食堂饭菜或主席领带的品位低下。当和其他听众交谈时，你一定不要试图介入此类幽默，因为，他们会对一个局外人对他们的食堂或主席的毁谤性的言论感到气愤。如果你一直都说些调侃像邮局或电信系统这种"替罪羊"话题的笑话，你就不会得罪任何人。

如果你觉得自己幽默起来感觉很生硬，那你必须不断练习以使其变得更加自然。你可以用一种轻松而不勉强的方式，夹带一些随意的或显然是临场发挥的评论。通常，幽默的表达过程使人发笑，所以，讲得慢一些，扬眉或摆出一幅不相信的脸孔容易让人知道你在开玩笑。

要善于发现幽默，它常常是在出其不意的时候出现。例如拿人们熟悉的谚语开玩笑，比如"假如一开始便不成功，那就放弃吧"，或者拿一出戏剧的对白或场景打趣。多思考一下夸大其词或者平铺直叙。看一下自己的语言，找出一些词汇或句子来，把它们反复琢磨，在其中注入幽默。

题目答案与解析

1. 要想让你的幽默奏效，你应该 _____。
   A. 利用不同的听众
   B. 取笑那些缺乏条理的人
   C. 和不同的人谈不同的话题
   D. 向你的听众表示同情

【答案】C

【解析】本题可参照文章的第 1 段。从中可知，如果你想在谈话中用幽默来使人发笑的话，你得先知道如何确定你与其他人有相同的经历和问题。你的幽默一定要和听众有关，应该有助于表明你是他们中间的一员，或者你了解他们的处境，赞同他们的观点。针对不同的谈话对象，你要谈的问题就应该有所不同。如果你和经理们交谈，你就可以指出其秘书的工作方法缺乏条理；反之，如果你跟秘书们交谈，你可能希望评论一下他们的老板毫无章法。

据此可知，为了使你的幽默使人发笑，你应该根据不同的谈话对象谈论不同的话题。C 项与文章的意思相符，因此 C 项为正确答案。

2．依照护士的观点，关于医生的笑话暗示了医生 _____。

　　A．对新来者不礼貌　　　　　　　　B．非常了解自己神圣的角色

　　C．被授予某些特权　　　　　　　　D．甚至午餐期间都非常忙

【答案】B

【解析】本题可参照文章的第 2 段。从中可知，我曾经在一次护士代表大会上听到一个效果很好的故事，因为听众都对医生持相同的看法——一个人来到天堂，圣彼得带他到四处参观；他看到了舒适的住房、美丽的花园、晴朗的天气等，所有人都非常和气、礼貌、友善；到排队吃午餐时，一个穿白大褂的人突然推开新来者，冲到队伍的最前面，夺过食物，跷着脚走到一张桌边自顾自地吃起来；新来者问圣彼得那人是谁；圣彼得答道，"那是上帝，但有时他认为自己是一名医生。"据此可知，护士认为医生自以为是上帝，可以耍威风、不讲道理。B 项与文章的意思相符，因此 B 项为正确答案。

3．从本文可以推知，公共服务 _____。

　　A．为许多人带来了利益　　　　　　B．是公众关注的焦点

　　C．不是幽默的合适话题　　　　　　D．常常被人当做笑料

【答案】D

【解析】从文章第 3 段的内容可知，如果你是你的听众中的一员的话，你就会了解你们所有人的共同经历或问题，你就可以随意评论食堂的饭菜难吃，或是评论领导的领带没有品味，这些都无可厚非。不过，同其他人交谈时，你千万不要尝试插入这类幽默，因为他们反感一个局外人对他们的食堂或领导发表蔑视性的评论；如果你一直说些调侃邮局或电信系统这类"替罪羊"的笑话，你就会平安无事。据此可知，邮局或电信系统等公共服务经常被人调侃。D 项与文章的意思相符，因此 D 项为正确答案。

4．要想达到想要的效果，应该 _____ 讲幽默故事。

　　A．用恰当的言语　　　　　　　　　B．以尽可能笨拙的表情

　　C．用夸张的陈述　　　　　　　　　D．以尽可能随意的表情

【答案】D

【解析】本题可参照文章的第 4 段。从中可知，如果你不擅长于使用幽默，你就必须练习，以使你的幽默显得更加自然。内容包括一些随意、显然是即兴的评论，你能够以悠闲、自然的方式发表这些评论。通常是幽默的表述过程使听众发笑，所以，要放慢语速，要记住——扬扬眉或露出一副难以置信的表情有助于让人知道你在开玩笑。据此可知，为了使幽默达到预期的效果，你应当显得随意、轻松、自然。D 项与文章的意思相符，因此 D 项为正确答案。

5．本篇文章的最佳标题也许是 _____。

　　A．有效地使用幽默　　　　　　　　B．各种各样的幽默

　　C．在言语中添加幽默　　　　　　　D．不同的幽默策略

【答案】A

【解析】从文章第 1 段的内容可知，如果你想在谈话中幽上一默，你就得先知道如何确定你与其他人有相同的经历和问题。你的幽默一定要和听众有关，应该有助于表明你是他们

中间的一员，或者你了解他们的处境，赞同他们的观点。针对不同的谈话对象，你要谈的问题就应该有所不同。文章第 2 段举例做了说明。从第 3 段的内容可知，如果你是你的听众中的一员的话，你就会了解你们所有人的共同经历或难题，你就可以随意评论食堂的饭菜难吃，或是评论领导的领带没有品味，这些都无可厚非；不过，同其他人交谈时，你千万不要尝试插入这类幽默。从文章第 4 段的内容可知，如果你不擅长于使用幽默，你就必须练习，以便你的幽默显得更加自然。从最后一段的内容可知，幽默常常是在出其不意的时候出现。不妨曲解人们熟知的引语，寻找夸张和掩饰用语。琢磨一下你的谈话，从中挑出你能够改动的几个字或几句话来，注入幽默。据此可知，本文主要谈的是如何利用幽默来使人发笑。A 项与文章的意思相符，因此 A 项为正确答案。

Text 2

Since the dawn of human ingenuity, people have devised ever more cunning tools to cope with work that is dangerous, boring, burdensome, or just plain nasty. That compulsion has resulted in robotics — the science of conferring various human capabilities on machines. And if scientists have yet to create the mechanical version of science fiction, they have begun to come close.

As a result, the modern world is increasingly populated by intelligent gizmos whose presence we barely notice but whose universal existence has removed much human labor. Our factories hum to the rhythm of robot assembly arms. Our banking is done at automated teller terminals that thank us with mechanical politeness for the transaction. Our subway trains are controlled by tireless robot-drivers. And thanks to the continual miniaturization of electronics and micro-mechanics, there are already robot systems that can perform some kinds of brain and bone surgery with submillimetre accuracy — far greater precision than highly skilled physicians can achieve with their hands alone.

But if robots are to reach the next stage of laborsaving utility, they will have to operate with less human supervision and be able to make at least a few decisions for themselves — goals that pose a real challenge. "While we know how to tell a robot to handle a specific error," says Dave Lavery, manager of a robotics program at NASA, "we can't yet give a robot enough 'common sense' to reliably interact with a dynamic world."

Indeed the quest for true artificial intelligence has produced very mixed results. Despite a spell of initial optimism in the 1960s and 1970s when it appeared that transistor circuits and microprocessors might be able to copy the action of the human brain by the year 2010, researchers lately have begun to extend that forecast by decades if not centuries.

What they found, in attempting to model thought, is that the human brain's roughly one hundred billion nerve cells are much more talented — and human perception far more complicated — than previously imagined. They have built robots that can recognize the error of a machine panel by a fraction of a millimeter in a controlled factory environment. But the human mind can glimpse a rapidly changing scene and immediately disregard the 98 percent that is irrelevant, instantaneously focusing on the monkey at the side of a winding forest road or the single suspicious face in a big crowd. The most advanced computer systems on Earth can't approach that kind of ability, and neuroscientists still don't know quite how we do it.

1. Human ingenuity was initially demonstrated in _____.
   A. the use of machines to produce science fiction
   B. the wide use of machines in manufacturing industry
   C. the invention of tools for difficult and dangerous work
   D. the elite's cunning tackling of dangerous and boring work

2. The word "gizmos" (Line 1, Para. 2) most probably means _____.
   A. programs　　　　B. experts　　　　C. devices　　　　D. creatures

3. According to the text, what is beyond man's ability now is to design a robot that can _____.
   A. fulfill delicate tasks like performing brain surgery
   B. interact with human beings verbally
   C. have a little common sense
   D. respond independently to a changing world

4. Besides reducing human labor, robots can also _____.
   A. make a few decisions for themselves
   B. deal with some errors with human intervention
   C. improve factory environments
   D. cultivate human creativity

5. The author uses the example of a monkey to argue that robots are _____.
   A. expected to copy human brain in internal structure
   B. able to perceive abnormalities immediately
   C. far less able than human brain in focusing on relevant information
   D. best used in a controlled environment

核心词汇注释

ingenuity [ɪn'dʒɪnjuːɪtɪ] *n.* 机灵；独创性；精巧；灵活性

nasty ['nɑːstɪ] *adj.* 污秽的；肮脏的；令人厌恶的；淫秽的；下流的；凶相的；威胁的

gizmo ['gɪzməu] *n.* 小发明

miniaturization [ˌmɪnɪətʃəraɪ'zeɪʃən] *n.* 小型化

submillimetre [sʌb'mɪlɪˌmiːtə(r)] *adj.* 亚毫米的；小于 1 毫米的

dynamic [daɪ'næmɪk] *adj.* 动力的；动力学的；动态的

transistor [træn'sɪstə(r)] *n.* [电子]晶体管

circuit ['sɜːkɪt] *n.* 电路；一圈；周游；巡回

microprocessor [ˌmaɪkrəu'prəusesə(r)] *n.* [计] 微处理器

instantaneous [ˌɪnstən'teɪnɪəs] *adj.* 瞬间的；即刻的；即时的

长难句剖析

【文章难句】And thanks to the continual miniaturization of electronics and micro-mechanics, there are already robot systems that can perform some kinds of brain and bone surgery with submillimeter accuracy — far greater precision than highly skilled physicians can achieve with their hands alone.

【结构分析】本句主干是 there are already robot systems，that 引导的定语从句修饰 robot systems。在这个定语从句中，that 做主语，far greater precision than highly skilled physicians can achieve with their hands alone 做状语起补充说明作用。前面的 and thanks to the continual miniaturization of electronics and micro-mechanics 做状语。

【参考译文】由于电子器材的不断微型化以及微机械制造学的不断发展，已经出现了能够以亚毫米的精确度实施某些脑部和骨科手术的机器人系统——这种精确度远远超过技术相当娴熟的医生只凭双手所能达到的精确度。

【文章难句】But the human mind can glimpse a rapidly changing scene and immediately disregard the 98 percent that is irrelevant, instantaneously focusing on the monkey at the side of a winding forest road or the single suspicious face in a big crowd.

【结构分析】本句中，the human mind 是主语，谓语动词为 glimpse 和 disregard，宾语分别是 a rapidly changing scene 和 the 98 percent，that 引导的定语从句修饰 the 98 percent，现在分词结构 instantaneously focusing on the monkey at the side of a winding forest road or the single suspicious face in a big crowd 做目的状语。

【参考译文】但是人类的大脑可以在一瞥之下就能够发现一个迅速变化的情景，随即忽视 98%的不相关部分，瞬间把注意力集中到蜿蜒的森林小路边上的猴子身上或一大群人中的一张可疑的面孔上。

全文参考译文

　　从人类最初有了智慧至今，人们一直在设计日益巧妙的工具来处理那些危险的、枯燥的、繁重的或者只是一般的肮脏的工作。这样一种需求导致了机器人技术的产生——赋予机器各种人的能力的科学。如果科学家还想设计出机械版的科幻小说，那他们已经开始接近这个目标了。

　　于是，当今世界出现了愈来愈多的智能设备。虽然我们几乎注意不到它们的存在，但是它们的广泛存在已经使人们摆脱了许多劳动。工厂随着机器人组装臂的韵律而转动；自动柜员机终端自动处理银行的业务，并用机器语言优雅地谢谢您的光顾；不知疲倦的机器人司机控制着我们的地铁。由于电子器材的不断微型化以及微机械制造学的不断发展，已经出现了能够以亚毫米的精确度实施某些脑部和骨科手术的机器人系统——这种精确度远远超过技术相当娴熟的医生只凭双手所能达到的精确度。

　　但如果机器人要延伸到下个省劳力的阶段，那它们必须能够在更少的人的监控下运行，并至少能够独立地做一些决定——那是真正具有挑战性的目标。（美国）国家航空航天局（NASA）的机器人项目经理 Dave Lavery 说："虽然我们知道告诉机器人如何处理一个特定的错误，但我们还不能给机器人足够的"常识"使其能够与动态的世界进行可靠的交流。

　　事实上，对真正人工智能的探索已经产生了各式各样的结果。尽管在 20 世纪 60 年代和 70 年代，人们刚开始乐观地认为晶体电路和微处理器可能在 2010 年前就能复制人脑的行为，但最近研究人员已经开始把这一预言延迟——数十年，甚至数百年。

　　在进行思维模拟时，他们发现人脑大约一千亿的神经细胞比从前想象的要能干得多，人类认知进程也更为繁杂。他们制造出的机器人能够识别在人工控制的工厂里的机器控制面板上不到一毫米的误差。但是人类的大脑可以在一瞥之下就能够发现一个迅速变化的情景，随即忽视 98% 的不相关部分，瞬间把注意力集中到蜿蜒的森林小路边上的猴子身上或一大群人中的一张可疑的面孔上。这一点即使是世界上最先进的计算机系统也无法具备。神经科学家们到如今也没弄明白人类是如何达到的。

题目答案与解析

1. 人类的独创性最开始被证实是在 _____。

　　A. 使用机器去创作科幻小说　　　　B. 制造业广泛使用机器

　　C. 发明工具以应付困难和危险的工作　　D. 精英对危险和乏味工作的巧妙处理

【答案】C

【解析】本题可参照文章的第 1 段。从中可知，从人类最初有了智慧至今，人们一直在设计日益巧妙的工具来处理那些危险的、枯燥的、繁重的或者只是一般的肮脏的工作。这样一种需求导致了机器人技术的产生。据此可知，C 项与文章的意思相符，因此 C 项为正确答案。

2. 单词 gizmos（第 2 段第 1 行）一词最可能意为 _____。

　　A. 项目　　　　B. 专家　　　　C. 发明　　　　D. 生物

【答案】C

【解析】本题可参照文章的第 2 段。从中可知，当今世界出现了越来越多的智能设备，虽然我们几乎注意不到它们，但是它们的广泛存在已经使人们摆脱了许多劳动。接着列举了机器人组装臂、自动柜员机终端、机器人司机以及以亚毫米的精确度做某些脑部和骨科手术的机器人系统。据此可知，gizmos 一词最可能指的是人们的发明。C 项与文章的意思相符，因此 C 项为正确答案。

3. 依照本文的观点，如今人类还无法做到的是设计一种能够 _____ 的机器人。

　　A. 完成像做脑部手术这样精细的任务　　B. 与人类进行语言交流

　　C. 有一点常识　　　　　　　　　　　　D. 独立应付不断变化的世界

【答案】D

【解析】本题可参照文章的第 3 段。从中可知，如果机器人想要进入下一个省劳力的阶段，那它们必须能在更少的人的监控下运行，并至少能够独立地做一些决定——那是真正具有挑战力的目标。Dave Lavery 说，"虽然我们知道告诉机器人如何去处理一个特定的错误，但我们还不能给机器人足够的'常识'使其能够与这个动态的世界进行可靠的交流"。据此可知，目前人类设计的机器人还不能单独发挥作用。D 项与文章的意思相符，因此 D 项为正确答案。

4. 机器人除了减少人类的劳动外，还能够 _____。

　　A. 为自己做一些决定　　　　　　　　B. 在人的干预下处理一些差错

　　C. 改善工厂的环境　　　　　　　　　D. 培养人类的创造力

【答案】B

【解析】本题可参照文章的第 3 段。从中可知，但是如果机器人想要进入下一个阶段，那么，它们必须能在更少的人的监控下运行，至少能够独立地做一些决定。根据文章最后一段的第 2 句话可知，人类制造的机器人能够识别在人工控制的工厂里的机器控制面板上不到一毫米的误差。由此可知，机器人除了减少人类的劳动，还可以在人的监控下处理具体错误。

B 项与文章的意思相符，因此 B 项为正确答案。

5．作者用猴子的例子来证明机器人 _____。

　　A．被期望复制人脑的内部结构　　　　　B．能够立即感知异常事物

　　C．远不如人脑能够关注相关的信息　　　D．在受控的环境中得到最好的利用

【答案】C

【解析】本题可参照文章的最后一段。从中可知，在进行思维模拟时，他们发现人脑大约一千亿的神经细胞比以前想象的要能干得多——人类的认知进程也更为复杂。人类制造的机器人能够识别在人工控制的工厂里的机器控制面板上不到一毫米的误差。但是人类的大脑可以在一瞥之下就能够发现一个迅速变化的情景，随即忽视 98%的不相关部分，瞬间把注意力集中到蜿蜒的森林小路边上的猴子身上或一大群人中的一张可疑的面孔上。世界上最先进的计算机系统也无法具备这种能力。据此可知，作者利用猴子这个例子是为了说明——机器人在注意迅速变化的场景方面没有人类强。C 项与文章的意思相符，因此 C 项为正确答案。

Text 3

Could the bad old days of economic decline be about to return? Since OPEC agreed to supply-cuts in March, the price of crude oil has jumped to almost $26 a barrel, up from less than $10 last December. This near-tripling of oil prices calls up scary memories of the 1973 oil shock, when prices quadrupled, and 1979-1980, when they also almost tripled. Both previous shocks resulted in double-digit inflation and global economic decline. So where are the headlines warning of gloom and doom this time?

The oil price was given another push up this week when Iraq suspended oil exports. Strengthening economic growth, at the same time as winter grips the northern hemisphere, could push the price higher still in the short term.

Yet there are good reasons to expect the economic consequences now to be less severe than in the 1970s. In most countries the cost of crude oil now accounts for a smaller share of the price of petrol than it did in the 1970s. In Europe, taxes account for up to four-fifths of the retail price, so even quite big changes in the price of crude have a more muted effect on pump prices than in the past.

Rich economies are also less dependent on oil than they were, and so less sensitive to swings in the oil price. Energy conservation, a shift to other fuels and a decline in the importance of heavy, energy-intensive industries have reduced oil consumption. Software, consultancy and mobile telephones use far less oil than steel or car production. For each dollar of GDP (in constant prices) rich economies now use nearly 50% less oil than in 1973. The OECD estimates in its latest Economic Outlook that, it oil prices averaged $22 a barrel for a full year, compared with $13 in 1998, this would increase the oil import bill in rich economies by only 0.25% — 0.5% of GDP. That is less than one-quarter of the income loss in 1974 or 1980. On the other hand, oil-importing emerging economies — to which heavy industry has shifted — have become more energy-intensive, and so could be more seriously squeezed.

One more reason not to lose sleep over the rise in oil prices is that, unlike the rises in the

1970s, it has not occurred against the background of general commodity-price inflation and global excess demand. A sizable portion of the world is only just emerging from economic decline. The Economist's commodity price index is broadly unchanging from a year ago. In 1973 commodity prices jumped by 70%, and in 1979 by almost 30%.

1. The main reason for the latest rise of oil price is _____.

    A. global inflation   B. reduction in supply

    C. fast growth in economy   D. Iraq's suspension of exports

2. It can be inferred from the text that the retail price of petrol will go up dramatically if _____.

    A. price of crude rises   B. commodity prices rise

    C. consumption rises   D. oil taxes rise

3. The estimates in Economic Outlook show that in rich countries _____.

    A. heavy industry becomes more energy-intensive

    B. income loss mainly results from fluctuating crude oil prices

    C. manufacturing industry has been seriously squeezed

    D. oil price changes have no significant impact on GDP

4. We can draw a conclusion from the text that _____.

    A. oil-price shocks are less shocking now

    B. inflation seems irrelevant to oil-price shocks

    C. energy conservation can keep down the oil prices

    D. the price rise of crude leads to the shrinking of heavy industry

5. From the text we can see that the writer seems _____.

    A. optimistic   B. sensitive   C. gloomy   D. scared

核心词汇注释

crude [kruːd] *adj.* 天然的；未加工的，粗糙的；拙劣的；粗鲁的
  n. 天然的物质

scary ['skærɪ] *adj.* 引起惊慌的

quadruple ['kwɒdrupl] *adj.* 四倍的；四重的；[乐] 每小节四拍的
  n. 四倍
  vt. 使成四倍
  vi. 成为四倍

glom [glɒm] *vt.* <俚>偷；抢；看；瞪

suspend [sə'spend] *vt.* 吊；悬挂

  v. 延缓

hemisphere ['hemɪsfɪə(r)] *n.* 半球

pump ['pʌmp] *n.* 泵；抽水机
  vt. （用泵）抽（水）；抽吸

conservation [ˌkɒnsə'veɪʃ(ə)n] *n.* 保存；保持；守恒

sizable ['saɪzəbl] *adj.* 相当大的；大小相当的

index ['ɪndeks] *n.* 索引；[数学] 指数；指标；（刻度盘上）指针
  vt. 编入索引中；指出
  vi. 做索引

长难句剖析

【文章难句】One more reason not to lose sleep over the rise in oil prices is that, unlike the rises in the 1970s, it has not occurred against the background of general commodity-price inflation and global excess demand.

【结构分析】本句中，One more reason not to lose sleep over the rise in oil prices 为主语，动词不定式 to lose…做定语，that 引导表语从句，unlike the rises in the 1970s 做状语。从句中，主干是 it has not occurred，介词短语 against the background of general commodity-price inflation and global excess demand 做从句的方式状语。against 的意思是"以……为背景，对照"。

【参考译文】不必担心油价上涨的另一个原因就是：与 70 年代不同，此次油价上涨并不是发生在物价普遍暴涨和全球的需求过剩的背景下。

全文参考译文

过去可怕的经济萧条的日子又要回来了么？自从欧佩克在 3 月份同意减产，原油价格已从去年 12 月的每桶不到 10 美元上涨到了 26 美元，攀升了几乎 3 倍。这使人想起 1973 年那次使人震惊、令人后怕的石油冲击（当时油价翻了 4 番）及 1979～1980 油价上涨的情况（那时也差不多翻了 3 番）。这两次油价暴涨导致了当时两位数的通货膨胀率和全球的经济萧条。这次警告人们经济衰退到来的头条新闻又在何处呢？

这个星期因伊拉克停止石油出口油价又一次被抬升。由于经济快速增长，加上冬季对北半球的强大影响，因而油价在短时间内仍会上升。

但是，人们有足够的理由预测现原油价格的上涨所引起的经济后果不会像 70 年代那样严重。因为在大多数国家里，如今原油价格在汽油价格中所占的比重比 70 年代原油价格所占的比重要少。但在欧洲，税收对石油零售价的作用占到 4/5，因此即使原油价格发生很大变动，但它对汽油价格的影响也比过去要小。

由于经济富裕的国家也不像以前那样依赖石油，因而对油价的涨幅也不是那样敏感。节约能源、转使别种燃料和能源集中型重工业的重要性的削弱，都减少了石油的消耗。软件、咨询和移动电话业消耗的石油要比钢铁或汽车业消耗的石油要少得多。相较于一美元的国内生产总值（GDP）（固定价格）来说，经济富裕的国家如今消耗的石油比 1973 年少 50%。经合组织（OECD）在新近的《经济展望》中预测，假如油价一年平均为每桶 22 美元（1998年为 13 美元）。在经济富裕的国家里，石油进口增加的开支只是国内生产总值的 0.25%～0.5%，还不到 1974 或 1980 年总收入消耗的 1/4。另外，那些进口石油的新兴国家——重工业已经转移到这些国家——已变得更加能源密集化，因而可能遭受更严重的打击。

不必担心油价上涨的另一个原因就是，与 70 年代不同，此次油价上升并不是发生在物价普遍暴涨和全球需求过剩的背景下。世界相当一部分国家才刚刚从经济萧条中复苏。《经济学家》商品价格指数从一年前就没有大的变化。但 1973 年物价上升 70%，1979 年上升近 30%。

题目答案与解析

1. 近来油价上涨的主要原因是 _____。
   A．全球性通货膨胀　　　　　　　　B．石油供应减少
   C．经济方面的快速增长　　　　　　D．伊拉克暂停石油出口
   【答案】B
   【解析】本题可参照文章的第 1 段。从中可知，自从 3 月份石油输出国组织同意减产以

来，原油的价格已经上涨到每桶 26 美元；油价近 3 倍的上涨使得人们回想起了以前的两次石油冲击，这两次石油冲击导致了两位数的通货膨胀率，并引发了全球性的经济衰退。据此可知，近期油价上涨的原因是石油输出国组织减少了石油的供应。B 项与文章的意思相符，因此 B 项为正确答案。

2. 从本文可以推知，若 _____，汽油的零售价会大幅上涨。

   A. 原油价格上涨　　B. 物价上涨　　　　C. 消费增加　　　　D. 油税上涨

【答案】D

【解析】本题可参照文章的第 1 段。从中可知，人们有充分的理由期望如今的油价上涨所产生的经济后果不会像 20 世纪 70 年代那样严重。如今，大多数国家的原油价格在汽油的价格中所占的份额比 20 世纪 70 年代所占的份额更小。在欧洲，税收占零售价的比例接近 4/5，所以，即使原油价格发生很大的波动，它对汽油价格的影响也比过去要小。据此可知，如今影响汽油零售价上涨的因素是税收。D 项与文章的意思相符，因此 D 项为正确答案。

3. 根据《经济展望》杂志的估计显示，在富裕国家，_____。

   A. 重工业更加能源密集化

   B. 收入损失主要起因于原油价格的波动

   C. 制造业已经受到严重打击

   D. 油价的波动对国内生产总值没有重要影响

【答案】D

【解析】本题可参照文章的第 4 段。从中可知，富裕国家也不像过去那样依赖石油，所以对油价的波动也不那么敏感了。节约能源、转用其他燃料以及重工业、能源密集型产业重要性的下降，这些都减少了石油的消费。富裕国家消耗的石油比 1973 年减少将近 50%；在最新的《经济展望》中，经合组织估计，如果全年的油价平均为每桶 22 美元的话，那么同 1998 年的每桶 13 美元相比，富裕国家进口石油的费用会增加，仅仅占国内生产总值的 0.25%～0.5%。这个比率不到 1974 年或 1980 年收入损失的 1/4。另一方面，那些进口石油的新兴国家——重工业已转至这些国家——变得更加能源密集化，所以可能遭受更严重的打击。据此可知，当前的油价波动对富裕国家的影响没有过去那样大了。D 项与文章的意思相符，因此 D 项为正确答案。

4. 依照本篇文章，我们可以得出这样的结论 _____。

   A. 油价冲击现在没有那么令人震惊了　　　B. 通货膨胀似乎与油价冲击没有关系

   C. 节约能源可以控制油价　　　　　　　　D. 原油价格的上涨导致重工业的萎缩

【答案】A

【解析】从文章第 1 段的内容可知，自从 3 月份石油输出国组织达成削减供应的协议以来，原油的价格已经上涨。油价接近 3 倍的上涨使得人们回想起了以前的两次石油冲击，这两次石油冲击导致通货膨胀，并引发了全球性经济衰退。从第 2 段的内容可知，伊拉克暂停石油出口和强劲的经济增长以及北半球进入冬季等因素仍然会在短期内促使油价涨得更高。随后几段分析了原因，指出：如今，大多数国家的原油价格在汽油的价格中所占的份额比 20 世纪 70 年代所占的份额更小，所以，即使原油价格发生很大的波动，对汽油价格的影响也比过去要小。富裕国家也不像过去那样依赖石油，所以对油价的波动也不那么敏感了。节约能源、转用其他燃料以及重工业、能源密集型产业重要性的下降减少了石油的消费。此次油价上涨并不是发生在物价普遍暴涨和全球的需求过剩的背景下。据此可知，我们得出的结论就是——目前的油价上涨所产生的经济后果不会像以前那样严重了。A 项与文章的意思相符，因此 A 项为正确答案。

5. 依照本篇文章，我们可以看出作者似乎 _____。

A. 乐观　　　　　B. 敏感　　　　　C. 忧郁　　　　　D. 害怕

【答案】A

【解析】从文章第 1 段的内容可知，可能要回到昔日经济衰退的日子吗？自从石油输出国组织达成削减供应的协议以来，原油的价格上涨了将近 3 倍，这使得人们回想起了以前的两次石油冲击，那次石油冲击导致了两位数的通货膨胀，并引发了全球性的经济衰退；那么，这次警告人们经济衰退的头条新闻在哪儿呢？从第 2 段的内容可知，油价这个星期因伊拉克停止石油出口又一次被抬升。由于经济快速增长，加上冬季对北半球的强大影响，因而油价在短时间内仍会上升。从第 3 段的内容可知，然而，人们有足够的理由预测现原油价格的上涨所引起的经济后果不会像 70 年代那样严重；即使原油价格发生很大的变动，对汽油价格的影响也比过去要小得多。第 4 段进一步说明了理由。从第 5 段的内容可知，不必担心油价上涨的另一个原因就是——此次油价上涨并不是发生在物价普遍暴涨和全球的需求过剩的背景下。据此可知，作者认为目前的油价上涨不会带来严重后果，没有必要为此担忧。A 项与文章的意思相符，因此 A 项为正确答案。

Text 4

The Supreme Court's decisions on physician-assisted suicide carry important implications for how medicine seeks to relieve dying patients of pain and suffering.

Although it ruled that there is no constitutional right to physician-assisted suicide, the Court in effect supported the medical principle of "double effect", a centuries-old moral principle holding that an action having two effects — a good one that is intended and a harmful one that is foreseen — is permissible if the actor intends only the good effect.

Doctors have used that principle in recent years to justify using high doses of morphine to control terminally ill patients' pain, even though increasing dosages will eventually kill the patient.

Nancy Dubler, director of Montefiore Medical Center, contends that the principle will shield doctors who "until now have very, very strongly insisted that they could not give patients sufficient mediation to control their pain if that might hasten death."

George Annas, chair of the health law department at Boston University, maintains that, as long as a doctor prescribes a drug for a legitimate medical purpose, the doctor has done nothing illegal even if the patient uses the drug to hasten death. "It's like surgery," he says, "We don't call those deaths homicides because the doctors didn't intend to kill their patients, although they risked their death. If you're a physician, you can risk your patient's suicide as long as you don't intend their suicide."

On another level, many in the medical community acknowledge that the assisted-suicide debate has been fueled in part by the despair of patients for whom modern medicine has prolonged the physical agony of dying.

Just three weeks before the Court's ruling on physician-assisted suicide, the National Academy of Science (NAS) released a two-volume report, *Approaching Death: Improving Care at the End of Life*. It identifies the undertreatment of pain and the aggressive use of "ineffectual and forced medical procedures that may prolong and even dishonor the period of dying" as the twin problems of end-of-life care.

The profession is taking steps to require young doctors to train in hospices, to test knowledge of aggressive pain management therapies, and to develop new standards for assessing and treating pain at the end of life.

Annas says lawyers can play a key role in insisting that these well-meaning medical initiatives translate into better care. "Large numbers of physicians seem unconcerned with the pain their patients are needlessly and predictably suffering," to the extent that it constitutes "systematic patient abuse". He says medical licensing boards "must make it clear that painful deaths are presumptively ones that are incompetently managed and should result in license suspension".

1. From the first three paragraphs, we learn that _____.
   A. doctors used to increase drug dosages to control their patients' pain
   B. it is still illegal for doctors to help the dying end their lives
   C. the Supreme Court strongly opposes physician-assisted suicide
   D. patients have no constitutional right to commit suicide

2. Which of the following statements its true according to the text?
   A. Doctors will be held guilty if they risk their patients' death.
   B. Modern medicine has assisted terminally ill patients in painless recovery.
   C. The Court ruled that high-dosage pain-relieving medication can be prescribed.
   D. A doctor's medication is no longer justified by his intentions.

3. According to the NAS's report, one of the problems in end-of-life care is _____.
   A. prolonged medical procedures   B. inadequate treatment of pain
   C. systematic drug abuse   D. insufficient hospital care

4. Which of the following best defines the word "aggressive" (Line 3, Para. 7)?
   A. Bold.   B. Harmful.   C. Careless.   D. Desperate.

5. George Annas would probably agree that doctors should be punished if they _____.
   A. manage their patients incompetently
   B. give patients more medicine than needed
   C. reduce drug dosages for their patients
   D. prolong the needless suffering of the patients

核心词汇注释

constitutional [ˌkɒnstɪˈtjuːʃ(ə)l] *adj.* 构成的；增强体质的；宪法的；拥护宪法的

foreseen [fɔːˈsiːn] *vbl.* foresee 的过去分词

dose [dəʊs] *n.* 剂量；（一）剂；（一）服 *v.* （给……）服药

morphine [ˈmɔːfiːn] *n.* 吗啡

dosage [ˈdəʊsɪdʒ] *n.* 剂量；配药；用量

hasten [ˈheɪs(ə)n] *v.* 催促；赶紧；促进；加速

homicide [ˈhɒmɪsaɪd] *n.* 杀人；杀人者

fuel [fjuːəl] *n.* 燃料	**hospice** [ˈhɒspɪs] *n.* 旅客住宿处；收容所；
vt. 加燃料；供以燃料；使感情更强烈	济贫院
vi. 得到燃料	**therapy** [ˈθerəpɪ] *n.* 治疗

长难句剖析

【文章难句】Although it ruled that there is no constitutional right to physician-assisted suicide, the Court in effect supported the medical principle of "double effect", a centuries-old moral principle holding that an action having two effects — a good one that is intended and a harmful one that is foreseen — is permissible if the actor intends only the good effect.

【结构分析】本句中，主句主干是 the Court supported the medical principle of "double effect", in effect 做状语，a centuries-old moral principle 做 the medical principle 的同位语。holding 和后面 that 引导的宾语从句一起作 a centuries-old moral principle 的定语。在这个定语从句中，主干是 an action is permissible，现在分词结构 having two effects — a good one that is intended and a harmful one that is foreseen 做定语修饰 an action，其中的两个 that 引导的均是定语从句，if the actor intends only the good effect 为条件状语从句。Although it ruled that there is no constitutional right to physician-assisted suicide 为状语从句，从句中 that 引导宾语从句，

【参考译文】尽管最高法院裁定宪法没有赋予医生协助病人自杀的权利，但是，最高法院实际上支持"双重效应"的医疗准则，这条履行了数百年的医学道德准则认为：假如一种行为具有两种效应——有以治病为目的的良好效应又有可预测的不利效应——但为了实现这一良好效应，医生被允许实施治疗而不用考虑其不利效应。

全文参考译文

最高法院对安乐死所做的裁定给正在探求减轻病危病人痛苦的医学界以重大影响。

尽管最高法院裁定宪法没有赋予医生协助病人自杀的权力。但是，最高法院事实上支持"双重效应"的医疗准则，这条履行了数百年的医疗道德准则认为：假如一种行为具有两种效应——有以治病为目的的良好效应又有可预测的不利效应——但为了实现这一良好效应，医生被允许实施治疗且不用考虑其不利效应。

最近几年来，医生们一直在用这一准则来为自己使用大剂量的吗啡来减轻濒危病人的病痛而辩护，尽管加大剂量会导致病人死亡。

Monte fiore 医疗中心主任 Nancy Dubler 认为，这一准则会为一些医生辩护，这些医生"直到现在还在坚决主张假如增加使用量可能使病人死亡加速，因而他们不能为了减小病人疼痛而大量用药"。

但波士顿大学健康法学系主任 George Annas 认为，医生开药方只要是为了应当的医疗目的，即使加速病人死亡，医生所做之事也不违法。他说："这就像外科手术，尽管医生可能导致病人死亡，但医生的目的并不想把病人治死，因而我们不可以称这种死亡为谋杀。假如你是位内科医生，假如你的出发点不是让别人自杀，你就可以冒险给病人看病。"

另外，医疗界很多人都承认安乐死的争论大部分是因为病人对治疗的绝望引发的。原因是现代医学使病人的疼痛延长。

在最高法院对安乐死做出裁决的三个星期之前，国家科学院发表了一部两册本的报告《临

近死亡：改善临终看护》，该报告认为，对病人的痛苦处理不力和盲目采用无实际功效的、刻板的医疗手段而导致病人垂死挣扎的时间延长是临终护理中并存的两个问题。

医学界正在采取措施，要求年轻医生到临终关怀所实习，要求他们测试有关大胆的疼痛处理疗法方面的知识，制定新标准评定和料理病人的临终苦痛。

Annas 说，在坚决要求这些善意的医疗动机应转化为更好的护理这方面，律师能够起关键作用。他说："很多医生好像对病人遭受到的不必要的，可以预见的痛苦视而不见，甚至到了有计划地虐待病人的程度"。他还说，医师执照颁发委员会"必须明确，痛苦的死亡如被推定为是治疗不得力而造成的，应当取消其行医资格"。

题目答案与解析

1. 我们从前三段了解到 _____。
   A. 医生过去常常增加药量来控制病人的痛苦
   B. 医生帮助垂死病人结束生命仍然是违法的
   C. 最高法院强烈反对医生协助的自杀
   D. 宪法没有赋予病人自杀的权利

【答案】B

【解析】从文章前三段的内容可知，最高法院对安乐死所做的裁决给正在探求减轻病危病人痛苦的医学界以重大影响。尽管最高法院裁定宪法没有赋予医生有协助病人自杀的权利，但是，最高法院实际上支持"双重效应"的医疗准则，这条履行了数百年的医疗道德准则认为：假如一种行为具有两种效应——有以治病为目的的良好效应又有可预测的不利效应——但为了实现这一良好效应，医生被允许实施治疗且不用考虑其不利效应。近几年来，医生已经利用这一原则来为自己使用大剂量的吗啡控制晚期病人的痛苦而辩护，尽管加大剂量最终会导致病人死亡。据此可知，最高法院认为医生没有协助病人自杀的权利。B 项与文章的意思相符，因此 B 项为正确答案。

2. 依照本篇文章的观点，以下说法正确的是哪项？
   A. 如果医生冒着导致病人死亡的危险施治，他们将被认为有罪。
   B. 现代医学已经帮助那些晚期病人在无痛苦中康复。
   C. 法院裁定，可以开大剂量减轻病痛的药物。
   D. 医生的用药是否恰当不再取决于他的目的。

【答案】C

【解析】本题可参照文章的第 2、3 段。从中可知，尽管最高法院裁定宪法没有赋予医生有协助病人自杀的权利，但是，最高法院实际上支持"双重效应"的医疗准则，这条履行了数百年的医疗道德准则认为：假如一种行为具有两种效应——有以治病为目的的良好效应又有可预测的不利效应——但为了实现这一良好效应，医生被允许实施治疗且不用考虑其不利效应。近几年来，医生已经利用这一原则来为自己使用大剂量的吗啡控制晚期病人的痛苦而辩护，尽管加大剂量最终会导致病人死亡。由此可知：最高法院认为，医生可以使用大剂量药物来减轻晚期病人的痛苦。C 项与文章的意思相符，因此 C 项为正确答案。

3. 依照国家科学院的报告，在临终护理中存在的问题之一是 _____。
   A. 延长的治疗过程　　　　　　　　　　B. 缺乏对痛苦的医治

C．有计划地滥用药物　　　　　　D．医院的护理不够

【答案】B

【解析】 本题可参照文章的第 7 段。从中可知，就在最高法院对医生协助病人自杀做出裁决的三个星期之前，国家科学院发表了一份两册的报告；该报告认为，对病人的痛苦处理不足以及大胆使用"可能延长甚至不尊重死亡时期的无效、强制性医疗手段"是临终护理中并存的两个问题。据此可知，报告认为，对病人的痛苦处理不足是临终护理存在的问题之一。B 项与文章的意思相符，因此 B 项为正确答案。

4．以下单词中，哪个最好地解释了单词"aggressive"（第 7 段第 3 行）的意思？

A．大胆的　　　　B．有害的　　　　C．粗心的　　　　D．不顾一切的

【答案】A

【解析】 从文章第 7 段的内容可知，就在最高法院对医生协助病人自杀做出裁决的三个星期之前，国家科学院发表了一份报告。该报告认为，对病人的痛苦处理不足以及大胆使用"可能延长甚至不尊重死亡时期的无效、强制性医疗手段"是临终护理中并存的两个问题。从第 8 段的内容可知，医学界正在采取措施，要求年轻医生到临终关怀所实习，要求他们测试有关大胆的疼痛处理疗法方面的知识。据此可知，aggressive 一词应意为"有闯劲的、大胆的"。A 项与文章的意思相符，因此 A 项为正确答案。

5．George Annas 可能赞成：如果医生 _____ 则应该受到惩罚。

A．治疗病人不得力　　　　　　B．给病人的药超过所需的量

C．减少病人的用药量　　　　　　D．延长病人不必要的痛苦

【答案】D

【解析】 本题可参照文章的最后一段。从中可知，Annas 认为，在坚决要求这些善意的医疗动机应该转化成更好的护理这个方面，律师能够起关键作用。他说"很多医生好像对病人遭受的不必要的、可以预见的痛苦视而不见，甚至到了有计划地虐待病人的程度。"他还说，医师执照颁发委员会必须明确—— 痛苦的死亡如被推定为是由于治疗不得力而造成的，应当取消其行医资格。据此可知，Annas 可能认为，如果医生造成病人痛苦的死亡，应当吊销他们的执照。D 项与文章的意思相符，因此 D 项为正确答案。

Unit 15

Text　1

Specialization can be seen as a response to the problem of an increasing accumulation of scientific knowledge. By splitting up the subject matter into smaller units, one man could continue to handle the information and use it as the basis for further research. But specialization was only one of a series of related developments in science affecting the process of communication. Another was the growing professionalisation of scientific activity.

No clear-cut distinction can be drawn between professionals and amateurs in science: exceptions can be found to any rule. Nevertheless, the word "amateur" does carry a connotation that the person concerned is not fully integrated into the scientific community and, in particular, may not fully share its values. The growth of specialization in the nineteenth century, with its consequent requirement of a longer, more complex training, implied greater problems for amateur participation in science. The trend was naturally most obvious in those areas of science based especially on a mathematical or laboratory training, and can be illustrated in terms of the development of geology in the United Kingdom.

A comparison of British geological publications over the last century and a half reveals not simply an increasing emphasis on the primacy of research, but also a changing definition of what constitutes an acceptable research paper. Thus, in the nineteenth century, local geological studies represented worthwhile research in their own right; but, in the twentieth century, local studies have increasingly become acceptable to professionals only if they incorporate, and reflect on, the wider geological picture. Amateurs, on the other hand, have continued to pursue local studies in the old way. The overall result has been to make entrance to professional geological journals harder for amateurs, a result that has been reinforced by the widespread introduction of refereeing, first by national journals in the nineteenth century and then by several local geological journals in the twentieth century. As a logical consequence of this development, separate journals have now appeared aimed mainly towards either professional or amateur readership. A rather similar process of differentiation has led to professional geologists coming together nationally within one or two specific societies, whereas the amateurs have tended either to remain in local societies or to come together nationally in a different way.

Although the process of professionalisation and specialization was already well under way in British geology during the nineteenth century, its full consequences were thus delayed until the twentieth century. In science generally, however, the nineteenth century must be reckoned as the crucial period for this change in the structure of science.

1. The growth of specialization in the 19th century might be more clearly seen in sciences such as _____.

A. sociology and chemistry　　　　B. physics and psychology

C. sociology and psychology　　　　D. physics and chemistry

2. We can infer from the passage that _____.

A. there is little distinction between specialization and professionalisation

B. amateurs can compete with professionals in some areas of science

C. professionals tend to welcome amateurs into the scientific community

D. amateurs have national academic societies but no local ones

3. The author writes of the development of geology to demonstrate _____.

A. the process of specialization and professionalisation

B. the hardship of amateurs in scientific study

C. the change of policies in scientific publications

D. the discrimination of professionals against amateurs

4. The direct reason for specialization is _____.

A. the development in communication

B. the growth of professionalisation

C. the expansion of scientific knowledge

D. the splitting up of academic societies

核心词汇注释

specialization [ˌspeʃəlaɪˈzeɪʃn] *n.* 特殊化，专门化

splitting [ˈsplɪtɪŋ] *adj.* 爆裂似的；极快的

amateur [ˈæmətə(r)] *n.* 业余爱好者，业余艺术家

connotation [ˌkɒnəˈteɪʃ(ə)n] *n.* 含蓄；储蓄的东西（词、语等）；内涵

integrated [ˈɪntɪɡreɪtɪd] *adj.* 综合的，完整的

reveal [rɪˈviːl] *vt.* 展现，显示；揭示，暴露

primacy [ˈpraɪməsɪ] *n.* 首位

reinforce [ˌriːɪnˈfɔːs] *vt.* 加强，增援，补充；增加……的数量；修补；加固

vi. 求援；得到增援

n. 加固物

referee [ˌrefəˈriː] *n.* 仲裁人，调解人；[体] 裁判员

v. 仲裁，裁判

reckon [ˈrekən] *vt.* 计算；总计；估计；猜想

vi. 数，计算；估计；依赖；料想

长难句剖析

【文章难句】A rather similar process of differentiation has led to professional geologists coming together nationally within one or two specific societies, whereas the amateurs have tended either to remain in local societies or to come together nationally in a different way.

【结构分析】本句是一个主从复合句。主句中的主语是 process，谓语是 has led to，professional geologists coming together nationally within one or two specific societies 做宾语。whereas 引导比较从句，从句中的主语是 the amateurs，谓语是 have tended，either to remain or to come together 做宾语。

【参考译文】一种很相似的分化进程是，全国专业地质学者会聚一堂，组成一两个专业协会，而业余人员要么倾向于占据地方学会，要么以其他方式在全国范围内联合。

全文参考译文

专业化是因科学知识的不断增加而产生的；通过把科学知识分成更小的单位，人们能够继续掌握这些知识，并把它作为进一步研究的基础。然而，专业分工仅是科学上影响交流进程的一系列相关科学发展的一个方面。另一方面则是科学活动的不断专业化。

专业人员和业余人员之间在科学上无法被明确地划分开来：因为任何规则都有例外。不过"业余人员"一词确实含有如此的意义：它并没有和科学界彻底综合，尤其是，可能不完全分享其实用价值。19 世纪专业分工的发展加上时间更长、内容更复杂的培训，暗示了业余人员参与科学研究将会碰到更多的问题。这一趋势在以数学或实验室培训为基础的科学领域里自然表现得尤为突出。英国地质学的发展可以阐明这种趋势。

比较一下英国最近一个半世纪的地质学方面的刊物，人们发现，不仅研究的重要性愈来愈受到强调，并且，学术论文的出版标准亦在不断改变。在 19 世纪，区域地质学研究本身象征着有价值的科研活动；但是，在 20 世纪，区域研究只有收编并仔细考虑更广泛的地质学问题，才会逐渐被专业人员接受。另一方面，业余人员继续以其熟悉的方式从事区域研究。其结果导致了业余人员在专业地质刊物上发表论文更加困难。19 世纪的国家级杂志和 20 世纪的几家地方地质杂志评审制度先后地广泛引进，促使该问题表现得更为明显。这一发展的必然结果是，导致分别出现了以专业读者或业余读者为主要对象的刊物。另一相似的分化进程是，全国专业地质学者会聚一堂，组成一两个专业协会，与之相反，业余人员要么倾向于占据地方学会，要么就以其他方式在全国范围内联合。

尽管在 19 世纪，专业化和专业分工进程在英国地质学领域里就早已开始形成，但直到 20 世纪其结果才充分显现。无论如何，从整个科学领域的范围来说，19 世纪必定被视为这种科学结构转变的至关重要的时期。

题目答案与解析

1. 在像 _____ 那样的科学领域，19 世纪专业化的发展可能看得更清晰。
   A．社会学与化学
   B．物理学与心理学
   C．社会学与心理学
   D．物理学与化学

【答案】D

【解析】本题可参照文章的第 2 段。从文章第 2 段倒数两句话可知，19 世纪专业分工的发展加上时间更长、内容更复杂的培训，暗示了业余人员参与科学研究将会碰到更多的问题。这一趋势在以数学或实验室训练为基础的科学领域里自然表现得尤为突出。英国地质学的发展可以阐明这种趋势。据此可知，19 世纪专业化的发展在那些以数学或实验室训练为基础的科学领域可能看得更清晰。D 项与文章的意思相符，因此 D 项为正确答案。

2. 我们可以从本文推知 _____。
   A．专业化和职业化之间几乎没有区别

B．业余人员能够在某些科学领域同专业人员竞争

C．专业人员往往欢迎业余研究人员加入科学团体

D．业余人员拥有全国性学术机构，但没有地方性学术机构

【答案】B

【解析】从文章第3段的内容可知，在19世纪，区域地质学研究本身象征着有价值的科研活动；但是，在20世纪，区域地质学研究只有收编并仔细考虑更广泛的地质学问题，才会逐渐被专业人员接受；另一方面，业余人员继续以其熟悉的方式从事地方地质学研究。据此可知，业余人员可以在某些研究领域同专业人员竞争。B项与文章的意思相符，因此B项为正确答案。

3．作者写地质学的发展是为了论证 ＿＿＿＿＿。

　　A．专业化与职业化的发展过程　　　B．业余人员在科学研究中的艰辛

　　C．科学出版政策上的变化　　　　　D．专业人员对业余人员的歧视

【答案】A

【解析】从文章第2段的最后一句话可知，这一趋势在以数学或实验室培训为基础的科学领域里自然表现得尤为突出。英国地质学的发展可以阐明这种趋势；从第3段的内容可知，比较一下英国最近一个半世纪的地质学方面的刊物，人们发现，不仅研究的重要性愈来愈受到强调，并且，学术论文的出版标准亦在不断改变。在19世纪，区域地质学研究本身象征着有价值的科研活动；但是，在20世纪，区域研究只有收编并仔细考虑更广泛地地质学问题，才会逐渐被专业人员接受。另一方面，业余人员继续以其熟悉的的方式从事区域研究。其结果导致了业余人员在专业地质刊物上发表论文更加困难。19世纪的国家级杂志和20世纪的几家地方地质杂志评审制度先后地广泛引进，促使该问题表现得更为明显。这一发展的必然结果是，导致分别出现了以专业读者或业余读者为主要对象的刊物。另一相似的分化进程是，全国专业地质学者会聚一堂，组成一两个专业协会，与之相反，业余人员要么倾向于占据地方学会，要么就以其他方式在全国范围内联合。据此可知，作者利用地质学发展的例子是为了说明业余人员与专业学者之间的分化过程。A项与文章的意思相符，因此A项为正确答案。

4．＿＿＿＿＿ 是专业化的直接原因。

　　A．交流的发展　　　　　　　　　　B．职业化的发展

　　C．科学知识的扩展　　　　　　　　D．学术团体的分化

【答案】C

【解析】本题可参照文章的第1段。从中可知，专业化可以被看做是对科学知识不断增加问题的应对之策；通过把科学知识分成更小的单位，人们能够继续掌握这些知识，并把它作为进一步研究的基础。据此可知，专业化的直接原因是科学知识的不断增加。C项与文章意思相符，因此C项为正确答案。

Text 2

A great deal of attention is being paid today to the so-called digital divide — the division of the world into the info (information) rich and the info poor. And that divide does exist today. My wife and I lectured about this looming danger twenty years ago. What was less visible then, however, were the new, positive forces that work against the digital divide. There are reasons to be optimistic.

There are technological reasons to hope the digital divide will narrow. As the Internet becomes more and more commercialized, it is in the interest of business to universalize access — after all, the more people online, the more potential customers there are. More and more governments, afraid their countries will be left behind, want to spread Internet access. Within the next decade or two, one to two billion people on the planet will be netted together. As a result, I now believe the digital divide will narrow rather than widen in the years ahead. And that is very good news because the Internet may well be the most powerful tool for combating world poverty that we've ever had.

Of course, the use of the Internet isn't the only way to defeat poverty. And the Internet is not the only tool we have. But it has enormous potential.

To take advantage of this tool, some impoverished countries will have to get over their outdated anti-colonial prejudices with respect to foreign investment. Countries that still think foreign investment is an invasion of their sovereignty might well study the history of infrastructure (the basic structural foundations of a society) in the United States. When the United States built its industrial infrastructure, it didn't have the capital to do so. And that is why America's Second Wave infrastructure — including roads, harbors, highways, ports and so on — were built with foreign investment. The English, the Germans, the Dutch and the French were investing in Britain's former colony. They financed them. Immigrant Americans built them. Guess who owns them now? The Americans. I believe the same thing would be true in places like Brazil or anywhere else for that matter. The more foreign capital you have helping you build your Third Wave infrastructure, which today is an electronic infrastructure, the better off you're going to be. That doesn't mean lying down and becoming fooled, or letting foreign corporations run uncontrolled. But it does mean recognizing how important they can be in building the energy and telecom infrastructures needed to take full advantage of the Internet.

1. Digital divide is something _____.
    A. getting worse because of the Internet
    B. the rich countries are responsible for
    C. the world must guard against
    D. considered positive today
2. Governments attach importance to the Internet because it _____.
    A. offers economic potentials
    B. can bring foreign funds
    C. can soon wipe out world poverty
    D. connects people all over the world
3. The writer mentioned the case of the United States to justify the policy of _____.
    A. providing financial support overseas
    B. preventing foreign capital's control
    C. building industrial infrastructure
    D. accepting foreign investment
4. It seems that now a country's economy depends much on _____.
    A. how well developed it is electronically
    B. whether it is prejudiced against immigrants
    C. whether it adopts America's industrial pattern
    D. how much control it has over foreign corporations

核心词汇注释

division [dɪ'vɪʒ(ə)n] *n.* 分开，分割；区分；除法；公司；（军事）师；分配；分界线

looming ['luːmɪŋ] *n.* 上现蜃景（光通过低层大气发生异常折射形成的一种海市蜃楼）
adj. 隐约可见的

universalize [,juːnɪ'vɜːsəlaɪz] *vt.* 使一般化，使普遍化

net [net] *n.* 网，网络，网状物；净利，实价
adj. 净余的；纯粹的
vt. 用网捕；净赚；得到
vi. 编网

impoverished [ɪm'pɒvərɪʃt] *adj.* 穷困的；无力的；用尽了的

outdated [aʊt'deɪtɪd] *adj.* 过时的，不流行的

prejudice ['predʒudɪs] *n.* 偏见，成见；损害，侵害
v. 损害

sovereignty ['sɒvrɪntɪ] *n.* 君主；主权；主权国家

infrastructure ['ɪnfrəstrʌktʃə(r)] *n.* 基础结构，基础设施

Brazil [brə'zɪl] *n.* 巴西

长难句剖析

【文章难句】Countries that still think foreign investment is an invasion of their sovereignty might well study the history of infrastructure (the basic structural foundations of a society) in the United States.

【结构分析】本句主干是 Countries might well study the history, that 引导的定语从句修饰 countries。在这个定语从句中，省略了 that 的宾语从句 foreign investment is an invasion of their sovereignty 做 think 的宾语。

【参考译文】那些至今依然认为外国投资是侵犯其主权的国家，最好学习一下美国基础设施（即一个社会基本的结构性的架构）的历史。

全文参考译文

　　如今，人们非常关注所谓的数字鸿沟问题——也就是把世界上的国家分成信息资源丰富的国家和信息资源贫乏的国家。这种差距在今天确实存在。20 年前我和妻子就针对这一隐约显示出危险做过演讲。可是，一些新的能够预防这种信息差出现的积极因素在那时并不像现在这样突出，但我们今天有理由对此持有乐观的看法。

　　从技术上看这种数字鸿沟有希望减小。伴随着互联网越来越商业化，其使用的普及符合商家的利益。毕竟，上网的人愈多，未来潜在的顾客就愈多。现在，愈来愈多的政府因为害怕自己的国家会落后于别国，所以想扩大互联网的使用范围。在以后的 10～20 年里，世界上将有一二十亿人口加入互联网。所以，我认为将来信息差距只会减小，而不会扩大。这是个好消息，因为互联网完全能够成为战胜目前我们所面对的世界贫困的强有力的工具。

　　当然，使用互联网并不是战胜贫困的唯一方法。互联网也不是我们拥有的唯一工具。但其具有无限潜力。

　　为了利用互联网这一工具的优势，一些贫困国家必须放弃对外国投资所持有的那种旧时的反殖民主义偏见。那些仍然认为外国投资是对本国主权的侵犯的国家不妨研究一下美国的基础设施建设史。美国当年建设自己的工业基础设施时没有丰厚的资金。这就是为什么美国

的第二浪潮——建设基础设施，包括道路、港口、交通干线、码头等都利用外国投资的原因。当时，英国、德国、荷兰和法国都在这块英国前殖民地上投资。这些国家给美国提供资金。美国移民建设了美国。猜猜看，如今这些设施归谁所有呢？是美国人。我相信在巴西和别的地方，此类情况亦是相似的。你拥有的，帮助你发展第三次基础设施建设浪潮——也就是当今的电子基础设施建设——的外国资本越多，你就会越富有但这并不意味着屈从和任人宰割，也不意味着让外国公司的经营不受控制。但是，这确实意味着——应该意识到在建设充分利用互联网所需的能源及电信基础设施的过程中，外国的资本可能有多么重要。

题目答案与解析

1. 数字差异是 _____ 的某种东西。
   A．因为因特网而变得更糟　　　　　B．富裕国家应该负责
   C．全世界必须提防　　　　　　　　D．如今被认为具有积极作用
   【答案】C
   【解析】从文章第 1 段的内容可知，如今，人们非常关注所谓的数字差距问题——也就是把世界上的国家分成信息资源丰富的国家与信息资源贫乏的国家。这种差距在今天确实存在；20 年前，我和妻子就针对这一隐约显示出的危险做过演讲；然而，一些新的能够预防这些信息差出现的积极因素在那时并不像现在这样突出。据此可知，数字差距是一个潜在的危险，应该提防。C 项与文章的意思相符，因此 C 项为正确答案。

2. 政府重视因特网是因为它 _____。
   A．提供经济潜力　　　　　　　　　B．能够带来外国投资
   C．能够很快消除世界贫穷　　　　　D．把世界各地的人们连接起来
   【答案】A
   【解析】本题可参照文章的第 2 段。从中可知，从技术上看这种数字差距有希望减小。伴随着互联网越来越商业化，其使用的普及符合商家的利益。毕竟，上网的人愈多，未来潜在的顾客就愈多。现在，愈来愈多的政府因为害怕自己的国家会落后于别国，所以想扩大互联网的使用范围。在以后的 10～20 年里，世界上将有一二十亿人口加入互联网。所以，我认为将来信息差距只会减小，而不会扩大。这是个好消息，因为互联网完全能够成为战胜目前我们所面对的世界贫困的强有力的工具。据此可知，人们之所以重视因特网，是因为它能够为人们带来商业利益。A 项与文章的意思相符，因此 A 项为正确答案。

3. 作者提及美国这个例子是用来证明 _____ 的政策是正确的。
   A．向国外提供经济援助　　　　　　B．防止外国资本的操纵
   C．建设工业基础结构　　　　　　　D．接受外国投资
   【答案】D
   【解析】本题可参照文章的第 4 段。从中可知，那些仍然认为外国的投资是对本国主权的侵犯的国家不妨研究一下美国的基础设施建设史；美国当年建设自己的工业基础设施时没有丰厚的资金。这就是为什么美国的第二次基础设施建设浪潮都是利用外国投资的原因。当时，英国、德国、荷兰以及法国都在这块英国的前殖民地上投资。这些国家给美国提供资金。美国移民建设了美国。现在，拥有美国的是美国人。你拥有的、帮助你发展第三次基础设施

建设浪潮的外国资本越多，你就会越富有。但这并不意味着屈从和任人宰割，也不意味着让外国公司的经营不受控制。但是，这确实意味着——应该意识到在建设充分利用互联网所需的能源及电信基础设施的过程中，外国的资本可能有多么重要。据此可知，作者提到美国是为了证明利用外国投资的重要性。D 项与文章的意思相符，因此 D 项为正确答案。

4． 如今来看，一个国家的经济特别依赖于 _____。

　　A．它在电子方面的发展程度有多高　　B．它是否歧视移民

　　C．它是否采用美国的产业模式　　D．它控制外国公司的力度有多大

　　【答案】A

　　【解析】从文章第 2 段的内容可知，伴随着互联网越来越商业化，其使用的普及符合商家的利益。毕竟，上网的人愈多，未来潜在的顾客就愈多。现在，愈来愈多的政府因为害怕自己的国家会落后于别国，所以想扩大互联网的使用范围。在以后的 10~20 年里，世界上将有一二十亿人口加入互联网。所以，我认为将来信息差距只会减小，而不会扩大。这是个好消息，因为互联网完全能够成为战胜目前我们所面对的世界贫困的强有力的工具。从第 3 段的内容可知，当然，使用互联网并不是战胜贫困的唯一方法。但其具有无限的潜力。从文章最后一段的内容可知，你拥有的、帮助你发展第三次基础设施建设浪潮——也就是当今的电子基础设施建设——的外国资本越多，你就会越富有。据此可知，一个国家的经济很大程度上取决于其电子基础设施的建设。A 项与文章的意思相符，因此 A 项为正确答案。

Text 3

Why do so many Americans distrust what they read in their newspapers? The American Society of Newspaper Editors is trying to answer this painful question. The organization is deep into a long self-analysis known as the journalism credibility project.

Sad to say, this project has turned out to be mostly low-level findings about factual errors and spelling and grammar mistakes, combined with lots of head-scratching puzzlement about what in the world those readers really want.

But the sources of distrust go way deeper. Most journalists learn to see the world through a set of standard templates (patterns) into which they plug each day's events. In other words, there is a conventional story line in the newsroom culture that provides a backbone and a ready-made narrative structure for otherwise confusing news.

There exists a social and cultural disconnect between journalists and their readers, which helps explain why the "standard templates" of the newsroom seem alien to many readers. In a recent survey, questionnaires were sent to reporters in five middle-size cities around the country, plus one large metropolitan area. Then residents in these communities were phoned at random and asked the same questions.

Replies show that compared with other Americans, journalists are more likely to live in upscale neighborhoods, have maids, own Mercedeses, and trade stocks, and they're less likely to go to church, do volunteer work, or put down roots in a community.

Reporters tend to be part of a broadly defined social and cultural elite, so their work tends to reflect the conventional values of this elite. The astonishing distrust of the news media isn't rooted in inaccuracy or poor reportorial skills but in the daily clash of world views between reporters and their readers.

This is an explosive situation for any industry, particularly a declining one. Here is a troubled business that keeps hiring employees whose attitudes vastly annoy the customers. Then it sponsors lots of symposiums and a credibility project dedicated to wondering why customers are annoyed and fleeing in large numbers. But it never seems to get around to noticing the cultural and class biases that so many former buyers are complaining about. If it did, it would open up its diversity program, now focused narrowly on race and gender, and look for reporters who differ broadly by outlook, values, education, and class.

1. What is the passage mainly about?
   A. Needs of the readers all over the world.
   B. Causes of the public disappointment about newspapers.
   C. Origins of the declining newspaper industry.
   D. Aims of a journalism credibility project.

2. The results of the journalism credibility project turned out to be _____.
   A. quite trustworthy   B. somewhat contradictory
   C. very illuminating   D. rather superficial

3. The basic problem of journalists as pointed out by the writer lies in their _____.
   A. working attitude   B. conventional lifestyle
   C. world outlook   D. educational background

4. Despite its efforts, he newspaper industry still cannot satisfy the readers owing to its _____.
   A. failure to realize its real problem   B. tendency to hire annoying reporters
   C. likeliness to do inaccurate reporting   D. prejudice in matters of race and gender

核心词汇注释

template ['templeɪt] *n.* (=templet) 模板

alien ['eɪlɪən] *n.* 外侨；外星生物
    adj. 外国的；不同的；背道而驰的

questionnaire [kwestʃə'neə(r)] *n.* 调查
    表，问卷

metropolitan [ˌmetrə'pɒlɪt(ə)n] *adj.* 首都
    的；主要都市的，大城市的

upscale ['ʌpskeɪl] *adj.* <美> 高消费阶层
    的，迎合高层次消费者的，（商品）质优
价高的

elite [eɪ'liːt] *n.* <法> [集合名词]精华；精
    锐，中坚分子

symposium [sɪm'pəʊzɪəm] *n.* 讨论会，座
    谈会

credibility [ˌkredɪ'bɪlɪtɪ] *n.* 可信性

dedicated ['dedɪkeɪtɪd] *adj.* 专注的；献身的

bias ['baɪəs] *n.* 偏见；偏爱；斜线
    vt. 使存偏见

长难句剖析

【文章难句】Sad to say, this project has turned out to be mostly low-level findings about factual errors and spelling and grammar mistakes, combined with lots of head-scratching puzzlement about what in the world those readers really want.

【结构分析】本句中，this project 是主语，has turned out to be 是谓语，过去分词短语 combined with…做伴随状语。what 引导的名词性从句做介词 about 的宾语。

【参考译文】令人遗憾的是，新闻可信度调查的最终结果是一种低水平的结论，它只是发现了一些报道与事实不符以及报道中存在的拼写和语法错误等问题，结论报告中还夹杂着许多关于读者究竟想要什么的困惑。

全文参考译文

为什么如此多的美国人不相信他们从报刊上看到的东西呢？美国报刊编辑协会正在尝试解释这一让人头疼的问题。该组织正在进行长期的自我分析，即人们所知的新闻可信度调查。

令人遗憾的是，新闻可信度调查的最终结果是一种低水平的结论，它只是发现了一些报道与事实不符以及报道中存在的拼写和语法错误等问题，结论报告中还夹杂着许多关于读者究竟想要什么的困惑。

但对报刊不信任有更深层的原因。第一是大部分记者通过一套标准模式来看世界，并用它衡量每天发生的事。也就是说，在报社的新闻编辑室文化氛围中有一种老套的故事生产线，它为那些不太显眼的新闻提供支持和现成的叙事框架。

第二是记者和读者之间存在社会和文化差异。这种差异对解释许多读者不能理解新闻界"标准模式"的原因是有帮助的。在最新的一项调查中，对国内五个中等城市和一个大城市的记者们做了问卷调查。随后，对这些地区的居民进行了随机电话访问，并对他们提出了一样的问题。

结果显示，和其他美国人相比，新闻记者更可能在高档社区居住，雇女佣、开奔驰、玩股票，而不大可能去做礼拜、当志愿者或在普通社区居住。

记者可以说是文化和社会方面的精英，因此他们的工作通常反映出上层的价值观。记者并不相信读者对新闻媒体令人惊讶的怀疑并不是由于报道有误或报道技术问题，而是因为记者和读者之间世界观的日常冲突。

对任何行业来说，这都是一种容易引起争论的情形，对于一个日趋衰落的行业来说尤其如此。新闻业是一个麻烦的行业，它一直雇着态度让读者讨厌的职员。现正，它又主办座谈，进行可信度调查，以便了解读者为什么恼怒、为什么大规模地消失。可新闻界好像从未注意到过去很多读者抱怨的文化和阶层偏见。如果新闻界注意到了这一点，就应该实施多样化计划，而不是只把焦点集中在种族和性别上，应该雇一些世界观、价值观、教育程度和社会阶层完全不同的记者。

题目答案与解析

1. 本篇文章主要讲的是什么？
   A．世界各地读者的需求　　　　　　B．公众对报纸失望的原因
   C．新闻业衰败的根源　　　　　　　D．新闻可信性调查的目的

   【答案】B

   【解析】本题实际是在问文章的主旨。从文章第 1 段的内容可知，为什么如此多的美

国人不相信他们从报刊上看到的信息呢？美国报刊编辑协会正在试图解释这个棘手的问题。该组织正在进行长期的自我分析，即人们所知的新闻可信度调查。第 2 段说明了项目的结果。在随后的几段中，作者分析了出现这种现象的原因——记者和读者之间存在社会和文化的差异，他们的标准模式不符合许多读者的要求。读者对新闻媒体令人惊讶的怀疑并不是由于报道有误或是报道技术的问题，而是因为记者与读者之间世界观的日常冲突。从文章最后一段的内容可知，对于任何产业来说，这都是一种容易引起争论的情形，对于一个日趋衰落的产业来说尤其如此。新闻业是一个麻烦不断的行业，它一直雇佣着那些态度让读者讨厌的职员。现在，它又主办座谈会，进行可信度调查，以便了解读者为什么恼怒，为什么大规模地消失。但是新闻界似乎从未注意到过去许多读者们所抱怨的文化与阶层偏见。如果新闻界注意到了这一点，它就应该实施多样化计划，应该雇佣那些世界观、价值观、教育背景以及社会阶层完全不同的记者。据此可知，本文主要探讨的是读者不相信报刊的原因。B 项与文章的意思相符，因此 B 项为正确答案。

2. 新闻可信度项目的结果证明是 _____。

　　A．非常可信　　　　B．有点矛盾　　　　C．很有启发性　　　　D．十分肤浅

【答案】D

【解析】从文章第 1 段的内容可知，美国报刊编辑协会正在进行长期的自我分析，即人们所知的新闻可信度调查；从第 2 段的内容可知，令人遗憾的是，新闻可信度调查的最终结果是一种低水平的结论，它只是发现了一些报道与事实不符以及报道中存在的拼写和语法错误等问题，结论报告中还夹杂着许多关于读者究竟想要什么的困惑。据此可知，新闻可信度调查结果只发现了一些低级问题。D 项与文章的意思相符，因此 D 项为正确答案。

3. 就像作者所指出的，新闻记者的根本问题存在于他们的 _____。

　　A．工作态度　　　B．传统的生活方式　　C．世界观　　　　　D．教育背景

【答案】C

【解析】从文章第 3 段的内容可知，大多数新闻记者学会了以一种标准模式去看世界，并用这种模式来宣传每天发生的事件。从第 4 段的内容可知，新闻记者和读者之间存在一种社会和文化断层。从第 5 段的内容可知，与其他美国人相比，新闻记者更可能在高级社区居住，雇女佣、开奔驰、玩股票，而不大可能做礼拜、当志愿者或者在一般社区居住。从第 6 段的内容可知，记者可以说是社会和文化精英，因此他们的工作往往反映出上层的价值观。读者对新闻媒体令人惊讶的怀疑并不是由于报道有误或报道技术的问题，而是因为记者与读者之间世界观的日常冲突。据此可知，作者认为，新闻记者的根本问题在于他们与读者的世界观不同。C 项与文章的意思相符，因此 C 项为正确答案。

4. 虽然新闻界作出了努力，但它仍然无法满足读者的需求，因为它 _____。

　　A．没有认识到它的真正问题　　　　　　B．雇佣令人恼怒的记者的倾向
　　C．可能做不准确的报道　　　　　　　　D．在种族和性别方面存在歧视

【答案】A

【解析】本题可参照文章的最后一段。从中可知，新闻业是一个麻烦不断的行业，它一直雇佣着那些态度令读者讨厌的职员。现在，它又主办许多座谈会，进行可信度调查，以便了解消费者为什么恼怒，为什么大规模地消失。但是新闻界似乎从未注意到过去许多读者所抱怨的文化与社会阶层偏见。如果新闻界注意到了这一点，它就应该实施多样化计划，应该

雇佣那些世界观、价值观、教育背景以及社会阶层完全不同的记者。据此可知，新闻界没有意识到它所面临的真正问题。A 项与文章的意思相符，因此 A 项为正确答案。

Text 4

The world is going through the biggest wave of mergers and acquisitions never witnessed. The process sweeps from hyperactive America to Europe and reaches the emerging countries with unsurpassed might. Many in these countries are looking at this process and worrying: "Won't the wave of business concentration turn into an uncontrollable anti-competitive force?"

There's no question that the big are getting bigger and more powerful. Multinational corporations accounted for less than 20% of international trade in 1982. Today the figure is more than 25% and growing rapidly. International affiliates account for a fast-growing segment of production in economies that open up and welcome foreign investment. In Argentina, for instance, after the reforms of the early 1990s, multinationals went from 43% to almost 70% of the industrial production of the 200 largest firms. This phenomenon has created serious concerns over the role of smaller economic firms, of national businessmen and over the ultimate stability of the world economy.

I believe that the most important forces behind the massive M&A wave are the same that underlie the globalization process: falling transportation and communication costs, lower trade and investment barriers and enlarged markets that require enlarged operations capable of meeting customer's demands. All these are beneficial, not detrimental, to consumers. As productivity grows, the world's wealth increases.

Examples of benefits or costs of the current concentration wave are scanty. Yet it is hard to imagine that the merger of a few oil firms today could recreate the same threats to competition that were feared nearly a century ago in the U.S., when the Standard Oil trust was broken up. The mergers of telecom companies, such as WorldCom, hardly seem to bring higher prices for consumers or a reduction in the pace of technical progress. On the contrary, the price of communications is coming down fast. In cars, too, concentration is increasing — witness Daimler and Chrysler, Renault and Nissan — but it does not appear that consumers are being hurt.

Yet the fact remains that the merger movement must be watched a few weeks ago, Alan Greenspan warned against the megamergers in the banking industry. Who is going to supervise, regulate and operate as lender of last resort with the gigantic banks that are being created? Won't multinationals shift production from one place to another when a nation gets too strict about infringements to fair competition? And should one country take upon itself the role of "defending competition" on issues that affect many other nations, as in the U.S. vs. Microsoft case?

1. What is the typical trend of businesses today?

   A. To take in more foreign funds   B. To invest more abroad

   C. To combine and become bigger   D. To trade with more countries

2. According to the author, one of the driving forces behind M&A wave is _____.

   A. the greater customer demands   B. a surplus supply for the market

   C. a growing productivity   D. the increase of the world's wealth

3. From Paragraph 4 we can infer that _____.

   A. the increasing concentration is certain to hurt consumers

   B. WorldCom serves as a good example of both benefits and costs

   C. the costs of the globalization process are enormous

   D. the Standard Oil trust might have threatened competition

4. Toward the new business wave, the writer's attitude can be said to be _____.

   A. optimistic   B. objective

   C. pessimistic   D. biased

核心词汇注释

acquisition [ˌækwɪˈzɪʃ(ə)n] *n.* 获得；获得物

witness [ˈwɪtnɪs] *n.* [律] 证人，目击者；证据，证明，证词
vt. 目击；为……作证；证明，表明
vi. 作证，成为证据

sweep [swiːp] *v.* 扫，打扫，清扫；席卷，冲光，扫过，掠过

hyperactive [ˌhaɪpəˈræktɪv] *adj.* 活动过度的，极度活跃的，活动亢奋的

unsurpassed [ˌʌnsəˈpɑːst] *adj.* 未被凌驾的；非常卓越的

multinational [ˌmʌltɪˈnæʃ(ə)n(ə)l] *adj.* 多国的；跨国公司的；多民族的
n. 跨国公司

affiliate [əˈfɪlɪeɪt] *v.* （使……）加入，接受为会员

Argentina [ˌɑːdʒənˈtiːnə] *n.* 阿根廷（南美洲南部国家）

underlie [ˌʌndəˈlaɪ] *vt.* 位于……之下；成为……的基础

detrimental [ˌdetrɪˈmentl] *adj.* 有害的

scanty [ˈskæntɪ] *adj.* 缺乏的，不足的；稀疏的，不充足的

supervise [ˈsuːpəvaɪz, ˈsjuː] *v.* 监督；管理；指导

gigantic [dʒaɪˈɡæntɪk] *adj.* 巨人般的，巨大的

infringement [ɪnˈfrɪndʒmənt] *n.* 违反；侵害

长难句剖析

【文章难句】Yet it is hard to imagine that the merger of a few oil firms today could recreate the same threats to competition that were feared nearly a century ago in the U.S., when the Standard Oil trust was broken up.

【结构分析】本句中，it 是形式主语，真正的主语是 to imagine。imagine 后面的 that 从句做其宾语。在这个宾语从句中，还有一个 that 引导的定语从句，用来修饰 threats。

【参考译文】然而，很难想象今天几家石油公司的合并会再现美国一个世纪以前的标准石油托拉斯解体时对竞争所产生的同样的威胁。

全文参考译文

　　全球正在经历一场有史以来最大的合并浪潮。这一合并浪潮从极度活跃的美国传到欧洲，随后，以一种无法抵挡的力量到达那些日渐富裕的国家。这些国家有许多人在关注着这一合并进程。他们担心：这种企业的合并会不会转变成一种无法控制的反竞争力量？

　　规模大的企业会愈大，实力会愈强，这是毋庸置疑的。1982 年，跨国公司在国际贸易中所占份额还不到 20%，可如今已超过 25%，并在急速增长。在开放的欢迎外国投资的国家里，跨国公司的分支机构已经成为经济领域中一个快速增长的生产部门。像阿根廷，90 年代改革后，在 200 家最大公司中，跨国公司的工业产值由 43%上升到几乎 70%。这种现象使人们对小型经济实体、民族企业家所扮演的角色以及世界经济的基本稳定性引发了极大关注。

　　我认为引发这场合并浪潮的最关键的力量与导致全球一体化的力量是相似的：即运输和通信费用降低；贸易和投资壁垒减小；市场扩大。这一切均需要扩大经营规模以满足消费者的需求。这对消费者来说有百利而无一害。随着生产力的发展，世界财富也会增加。

　　目前，这种合并是有利可图还是会付出代价，有关的实例并不多。然而，很难想象今天几家石油公司的合并，会再现美国一个世纪以前标准石油托拉斯解体时对竞争所产生的同样的威胁。像世界电信这类电讯公司的合并似乎不会给消费者带来更高的费用，或是减缓技术进步的速度。与之相反，通信费用在急速下跌。汽车行业，像戴姆勒汽车公司、克莱斯勒、雷诺和尼桑汽车公司，也在合并，可消费者的利益好像并未受到损害。

　　但我们必须密切关注这种合并浪潮。艾伦·格林斯潘几周前告诫人们警惕银行业的大合并现象。谁是正在出现的庞大银行的最后贷方并进行监督、规范和管理的领导者呢？若一个国家对侵害公平竞争现象管制过严时，跨国公司会不会把生产从一个国家转移到另一个国家呢？一个国家应不应像美国对待微软公司案例那样，在影响许多其他国家利益的问题上扮演"保护竞争"的角色呢？

题目答案与解析

1. 当今企业的典型趋势是什么？
　　A. 吸收更多的外国资金　　　　　　　B. 更多地投资海外
　　C. 联合并且变得更大　　　　　　　　D. 与更多的国家发展贸易
　　【答案】C
　　【解析】从文章的第 1 段可知，全世界正在经历一场有史以来最大的合并浪潮；这一合并浪潮从极度活跃的美国传到欧洲，随后，以一种无法抵挡的力量到达那些日渐富裕的国家。从第 2 段可知，规模大的企业会愈大，实力会愈强，这是毋庸置疑的。据此可知：当今企业的典型趋势是通过合并使自己变得更大。C 项与文章的意思相符，因此 C 项为正确答案。

2. 依照作者的观点，_____ 是一个隐藏于合并浪潮背后的推动力。
　　A. 更大的消费者需求　　　　　　　　B. 市场的供应过剩
　　C. 日益提高的生产力　　　　　　　　D. 世界财富的增加
　　【答案】A

【解析】本题可参照文章的第 3 段。从中可知，我认为引发这场合并浪潮的最关键的力量与导致全球一体化的力量是相似的：即运输与通信费用降低，贸易与投资壁垒减小；市场扩大这一切均需要扩大经营规模以满足消费者的需求；这对消费者来说有百利而无一害。随着生产力的发展，全世界的财富也会增加。据此可知，合并浪潮的推动力就是运输与通信费用降低、贸易与投资壁垒的减少以及市场扩大，这些市场需要能够满足消费者需求的、扩大了的经营规模。A 项与文章的意思相符，因此 A 项为正确答案。

3. 我们从第 4 段可以推知：_____。
　　A. 日益增多的行业集中肯定会损害消费者的利益
　　B. 世界电信的合并成为既有利可图又要付出代价的恰当实例
　　C. 全球化进程的代价高昂
　　D. 标准石油托拉斯可能给竞争带来过威胁
【答案】D
【解析】本题可参照文章的第 4 段。从中可知，目前的这种合并是有利可图还是要付出代价，有关的实例不多；然而，很难想象，今天几家石油公司的合并会再现美国一个世纪以前标准石油托拉斯解体时对竞争所产生的同样的威胁；像世界电信这类电信公司的合并似乎不会给消费者带来更高的费用，或是减缓技术进步的速度；与之相反，通信费用正在急速下降；汽车行业的合并也在逐渐增加，但是，消费者的利益好像并没有受到损害。据此可知，美国的标准石油托拉斯曾经给竞争带来过威胁。D 项与文章的意思相符，因此 D 项为正确答案。

4. 作者对于新的企业合并浪潮的态度可以说是 _____。
　　A. 乐观的　　　　B. 客观的　　　　C. 悲观的　　　　D. 有偏袒的
【答案】B
【解析】从文章第 1 段的内容可知，全世界正在经历一场有史以来最大的合并浪潮；从第 2 段的内容可知，毫无疑问，规模大的企业会愈大，实力也会愈强；从第 3 段的内容可知，我认为，引发这场大规模的合并的最重要的原因与导致全球化过程的原因相似；从文章第 4 段的内容可知，目前的这股行业集中浪潮是有利可图还是要付出代价，有关的实例不多；消费者的利益似乎并没有受到损害；从文章最后一段的内容可知，不过，存在的事实是我们必须关注这股合并浪潮；当一个国家对违反公平竞争的现象控制过于严格时，跨国公司难道不会把其生产从一个国家转到另一个国家去吗？在那些影响其他许多国家的问题上，一个国家应不应就像美国与微软公司的诉讼案那样承担起"保护竞争"的职责呢？据此可知，作者既分析了企业合并浪潮给人们带来的好处，又提出了应该注意的问题，说明作者比较客观。B 项与文章的意思相符，因此 B 项为正确答案。

Unit 16

Text 1

When I decided to quit my full time employment it never occurred to me that I might become a part of a new international trend. A lateral move that hurt my pride and blocked my professional progress prompted me to abandon my relatively high profile career although, in the manner of a disgraced government minister, I covered my exit by claiming "I wanted to spend more time with my family".

Curiously, some two-and-a-half years and two novels later, my experiment in what the Americans term "downshifting" has turned my tired excuse into an absolute reality. I have been transformed from a passionate advocate of the philosophy of "having it all", preached by Linda Kelsey for the past seven years in the page of *She* magazine, into a woman who is happy to settle for a bit of everything.

I have discovered, as perhaps Kelsey will after her much-publicized resignation from the editorship of *She* after a build up of stress, that abandoning the doctrine of "juggling your life" ,and making the alternative move into "downshifting" brings with it far greater rewards than financial success and social status. Nothing could persuade me to return to the kind of life Kelsey used to advocate and I once enjoyed: 12 hour working days, pressured deadlines, the fearful strain of office politics and the limitations of being a parent on "quality time".

In America, the move away from juggling to a simpler, less materialistic lifestyle is a well-established trend. Downshifting — also known in America as "voluntary simplicity" — has, ironically, even bred a new area of what might be termed anticonsumerism. There are a number of best-selling downshifting self-help books for people who want to simplify their lives; there are newsletters, such as *The Tightwad Gazette*, that give hundreds of thousands of Americans useful tips on anything from recycling their cling-film to making their own soap; there are even support groups for those who want to achieve the mid-'90s equivalent of dropping out.

While in America the trend started as a reaction to the economic decline — after the mass redundancies caused by downsizing in the late '80s — and is still linked to the politics of thrift, in Britain, at least among the middle-class down-shifters of my acquaintance, we have different reasons for seeking to simplify our lives.

For the women of my generation who were urged to keep juggling through the '80s, downshifting in the mid-'90s is not so much a search for the mythical good life — growing your own organic vegetables, and risking turning into one — as a personal recognition of your limitations.

1. Which of the following is true according to Paragraph 1?

   A. Full-time employment is a new international trend.

   B. The writer was compelled by circumstances to leave her job.

C. "A lateral move" means stepping out of full-time employment.

D. The writer was only too eager to spend more time with her family.

2. The writer's experiment shows that downshifting _____.

A. enables her to realize her dream

B. helps her mold a new philosophy of life

C. prompts her to abandon her high social status

D. leads her to accept the doctrine or *She* magazine

3. "Juggling one's life" probably means living a life characterized by _____.

A. non-materialistic lifestyle   B. a bit of everything

C. extreme stress   D. anti-consumerism

4. According to the passage, downshifting emerged in the U.S. as a result of _____.

A. the quick pace of modern life   B. man's adventurous spirit

C. man's search for mythical experiences   D. the economic situation

核心词汇注释

lateral ['lætər(ə)l] *n.* 侧部；支线；边音 *adj.* 横（向）的；侧面的

disgrace [dɪs'greɪs] *n.* 耻辱；失宠；丢脸的人（或事）*v.* 玷污

exit ['eksɪt] *n.* 出口；太平门；退场；去世 *vi.* 退出，脱离；去世；[计] 离开当前命令行

downshift ['daʊnʃɪft] *v.* （汽车等）调低速档

preach [priːtʃ] *v.* 鼓吹

publicize ['pʌblɪsaɪz] *v.* 宣扬

resignation [ˌrezɪg'neɪʃ(ə)n] *n.* 辞职；辞职书；放弃；顺从

editorship ['edɪtəʃɪp] *n.* 编辑的地位

doctrine ['dɒktrɪn] *n.* 教条；学说

juggling ['dʒʌɡlɪŋ] *n.* （=jugglery）欺骗，杂耍 *adj.* 欺骗的，欺诈的，变戏法（似）的

materialistic [məˌtɪərɪə'lɪstɪk] *adj.* 物质享乐主义的；唯物论的，唯物主义的

simplicity [sɪm'plɪsɪtɪ] *n.* 简单，简易；朴素；直率

ironically [aɪ'rɒnɪklɪ] *adv.* 说反话地，讽刺地

bred [bred] *vbl.* breed 的过去式和过去分词

newsletter ['njuːzˌletə(r)] *n.* 时事通讯

gazette [gə'zet] *n.* 报纸，政府的公报，（大学的）学报 *v.* 在公报上刊登，在公报上刊载

recycle [riː'saɪkl] *v.* 使再循环；反复应用 *n.* 再循环，再生，重复利用

equivalent [ɪ'kwɪvələnt] *adj.* 相等的；相当的；同意义的 *n.* 等价物，相等物

redundancy [rɪ'dʌndənsɪ] *n.* 冗余

downsize [daʊn'saɪz] *vt.* 以较小尺寸设计（或制造），缩小（汽车等）的外部尺寸

thrift [θrɪft] *n.* 节俭，节约；[植]海石竹

acquaintance [ə'kweɪntəns] *n.* 相识，熟人

长难句剖析

【文章难句】For the women of my generation who were urged to keep juggling through the '80s, downshifting in the mid-'90s is not so much a search for the mythical good life — growing your own organic vegetables, and risking turning into one — as a personal recognition of your limitations.

【结构分析】本句中，介词短语 For the women of my generation who were urged to keep juggling through the '80s 在句中做状语。who 引导的定语从句修饰 the women of my generation。not so much…as 是固定搭配，意思是"与其说……不如说……"。

【参考译文】对于我们这一代经历过 80 年代被督促着不停地应对生活的女人来说，90 年代中期放慢速度与其说是在寻找一种神话般的美好生活—— 自己种植有机绿色蔬菜，冒险转入这样的生活——不如说是对你自己局限的一种认识。

全文参考译文

在我决定辞去全职工作的时候，我从未想到过自己会成为国际新潮流的一分子。一次平级调动伤害了我的自尊，也妨碍了我业务上的进步，这件事促使我放弃了我那前途令人欣羡的职业。但我却以一位失宠的政府大臣的口气宣称"我想多陪陪家人"，以此来掩饰我辞职的真正原因。

令人惊讶的是，大约两年半的时间，我写了两部小说，随后，我的这种被美国人称为"慢节拍"的尝试已经将我那陈旧的借口转化成了彻底的事实。我已经由过去七年里 Linda Kelsey 在《女性》杂志上一再宣扬的"拥有一切"哲学的积极倡导者，演变成一个对一切浅尝辄止就感到喜悦的女人。

我已经发现，放弃那种"快节奏生活"的信念而选择"慢节拍"会带来比金钱和社会地位更大的回报。Kelsey 长期承受巨大压力后，由编辑《女性》杂志编辑部退下来之后，我恐怕她也将与我有相同的发现。什么事都不能劝服我重新回到那种 Kelsey 曾经倡导而我本人也曾钟爱的生活中：12 小时工作日，重压下的最后期限，工作中的尔虞我诈、提心吊胆、焦虑不安，在为人父人母的"最佳时期"受到约束。

而在美国，由忙碌的生活方式转向一种更朴素更远离物质的生活方式已是必然的趋势。颇具讽刺意义的是，放慢节拍，在美国被称为"宁愿朴素"的生活方式居然产生出一个被称为"反消费主义"的新领域。对那些想要过朴素生活的人来说，有很多关于"慢节拍"生活方式的畅销自助书；更有像《守财奴报》之类的通信报道，给数十万美国居民提供包罗万象而且实用的指导，从胶卷的再利用到自己制造肥皂；甚至还有支援小队，给想要实现 90 年代中期逃避社会现实的人提供帮助。

这一趋势在美国是对经济衰落的反映，它是在 80 年代后期企业缩小规模致使大规模裁员之后才开始，现在仍和节俭的观点密切相关；而在英国，至少在我所认识的那些过慢节拍生活的中产阶级当中，寻求朴素的生活方式却有着不同的原因。

对于我们这一代经历过 80 年代被督促着不停地应对生活的女人来说，90 年代中期放慢速度与其说是在寻找一种神话般的美好生活—— 自己种植有机绿色蔬菜，冒险转入这样的生活——不如说是对你自己局限的一种认识。

题目答案与解析

1.　依照文章的第 1 段，以下说法中哪项正确？

　　A．专职工作是一种新的国际潮流。

　　B．作者因环境所迫而辞去工作。

　　C．"一次平级调动"意味着退出专职工作。

　　D．作者只是太想多花时间与其家人在一起。

【答案】B

【解析】本题可参照文章的第 1 段。从中可知，当我决定辞去全职工作时，我从未想到自己可能成为国际新潮流的一分子；一次平级调动伤害了我的自尊，也妨碍了我的业务上的进步，这件事促使我放弃了我那前途令人欣羡的职业；但是，我以一种失宠的政府大臣的口气宣称，"我想多陪陪家人"，以此来掩饰我辞职的真正原因。据此可知，作者是因为形势所迫而辞职的。B 项与文章意思相符，因此 B 项为正确答案。

2．作者的实践说明了放缓节奏 ＿＿＿＿＿＿。

　　A．使她能够实现自己的梦想　　　　　B．帮助她形成了一种新的人生观

　　C．促使她放弃了很高的社会地位　　　D．导致她接受《女性》杂志的教条

【答案】B

【解析】从文章第 2 段的内容可知，令人惊讶的是，大约两年半的时间，我写了两部小说，随后，我的这种被美国人称为"慢节拍"的尝试已经将我那陈旧的借口变成了事实；我已经由过去七年里 Linda Kelsey 在《女性》杂志上一再宣扬的"拥有一切"哲学的积极倡导者，变成一个对一切浅尝辄止就感到喜悦的女人；从第 3 段的内容可知，我发现，放弃那种"快节奏生活"的教条而选择"放缓节奏"的做法带来的回报要比金融方面的成就和社会地位的提高丰厚得多。据此可知，"放缓节奏"的实践促使作者改变了人生观。B 项与文章的意思相符，因此 B 项为正确答案。

3．Juggling one's life 可能意味着过一种具有 ＿＿＿＿ 特性的生活。

　　A．非实利主义的生活方式　　　　　　B．很容易满足

　　C．极度紧张　　　　　　　　　　　　D．反消费主义

【答案】C

【解析】本题可参照文章的第 3 段。从中可知，我发现，放弃那种"快节奏生活"的教条而选择"放缓节奏"的做法带来的回报要比金融方面的成就和社会地位的提高丰厚得多，正如 Kelsey 在经受长期的巨大压力后，多次公开宣称辞去《女性》杂志编辑职位后可能发现的那样；什么也说服不了我重过 Kelsey 过去倡导的、我曾经喜爱过的那种生活了——每天工作 12 小时的工作日、令人觉得压抑的最后期限、办公室管理中令人胆怯的作风以及在"最佳年龄"成为父（母）的限制。据此可知，"Juggling one's life"可能指的是一种紧张、压抑的生活。C 项与文章的意思相符，因此 C 项为正确答案。

4．依照本篇文章的观点，＿＿＿＿＿＿ 是美国出现降低节奏的原因。

　　A．现代生活的快节奏　　　　　　　　B．人们的冒险精神

　　C．人们对神话般经历的追求　　　　　D．经济形势

【答案】D

【解析】本题可参照文章的第 5 段。从中可知，在美国，虽然这种趋势起初是对经济衰败的一种反应——80 年代晚期，由于企业缩减规模，导致大量的人员剩余——它还与节俭的政治策略有关，但是，在英国，至少在我所认识的那些过慢节拍生活的中产阶层中，我们寻

求简化生活的原因不尽相同。据此可知，美国出现降低节奏的生活方式与经济有关。D 项与文章的意思相符，因此 D 项为正确答案。

Text 2

A history of long and effortless success can be a dreadful handicap, but, if properly handled, it may become a driving force. When the United States entered just such a glowing period after the end of the Second World War, it had a market eight times larger than any competitor, giving its industries unparalleled economies of scale. Its scientists were the world's best, its workers the most skilled. America and Americans were prosperous beyond the dreams of the Europeans and Asians whose economies the war had destroyed.

It was inevitable that this primacy should have narrowed as other countries grew richer. Just as inevitably, the retreat from predominance proved painful. By the mid-1980s Americans had found themselves at a loss over their fading industrial competitiveness. Some huge American industries, such as consumer electronics, had shrunk or vanished in the face of foreign competition. By 1987 there was only one American television maker left, Zenith. (Now there is none: Zenith was bought by South Korea's LG Electronics in July.) Foreign-made cars and textiles were sweeping into the domestic market. America's machine-tool industry was on the ropes. For a while it looked as though the making of semiconductors, which America had invented and which sat at the heart of the new computer age, was going to be the next casualty.

All of this caused a crisis of confidence. Americans stopped taking prosperity for granted. They began to believe that their way of doing business was failing, and that their incomes would therefore shortly begin to fall as well. The mid-1980s brought one inquiry after another into the causes of America's industrial decline. Their sometimes sensational findings were filled with warnings about the growing competition from overseas.

How things have changed! In 1995 the United States can look back on five years of solid growth while Japan has been struggling. Few Americans attribute this solely to such obvious causes as a devalued dollar or the turning of the business cycle. Self-doubt has yielded to blind pride. "American industry has changed its structure, has gone on a diet, has learnt to be more quick-witted," according to Richard Cavanagh, executive dean of Harvard's Kennedy School of Management, "It makes me proud to be an American just to see how our businesses are improving their productivity," says Stephen Moore of the Cato Institute, a think-tank in Washington. And William Sahlman of the Harvard Business School believes that people will look back on this period as " a golden age of business management in the United States".

1. The U.S. achieved its predominance after World War II because _____.

   A. it had made painstaking efforts towards this goal

   B. its domestic market was eight times larger than before

   C. the war had destroyed the economies of most potential competitors

   D. the unparalleled size of its workforce had given an impetus to its economy

2. The loss of U.S. predominance in the world economy in the 1980s is manifested in the fact that the American _____.

    A. TV industry had withdrawn to its domestic market

    B. semiconductor industry had been taken over by foreign enterprises

    C. machine-tool industry had collapsed after suicidal actions

    D. auto industry had lost part of its domestic market

3. What can be inferred from the passage?

    A. It is human nature to shift between self-doubt and blind pried.

    B. Intense competition may contribute to economic progress.

    C. The revival of the economy depends on international cooperation.

    D. A long history of success may pave the way for further development.

4. The author seems to believe the revival of the U.S. economy in the 1990s can be attributed to the _____.

    A. turning of the business cycle   B. restructuring of industry

    C. improved business management   D. success in education

核心词汇注释

handicap [ˈhændɪkæp] *n.* 障碍，阻碍；障碍赛跑
v. 妨碍，使不利，阻碍

unparalleled [ʌnˈpærəleld] *adj.* 无比的，无双的；空前的

predominance [prɪˈdɒmɪnəns] *n.* 优势

textile [ˈtekstaɪl] *n.* 纺织品
adj. 纺织的

semiconductor [ˌsemɪkənˈdʌktə(r)] *n.* [物] 半导体

casualty [ˈkæʒʊəltɪ] *n.* 伤亡

sensational [senˈseɪʃənəl] *adj.* 使人感动的；非常好的

devalue [diːˈvæljuː] *v.* (=devaluate) 减值，贬值

yield [jiːld] *v.* 出产；生长；生产
vi. 屈服，屈从
n. 产量，收益

dean [ˈdiːn] *n.* (大学) 院长；主持牧师，（基督教）教长

长难句剖析

【文章难句】For a while it looked as though the making of semiconductors, which America had invented and which sat at the heart of the new computer age, was going to be the next casualty.

【结构分析】本句中，as though (=as if) 引导状语从句。在这个状语从句中，the making of semiconductors was going to be the next casualty 是句子的主干，which 引导非限制性定语从句，用来修饰从句中的主语。

【参考译文】美国发明的在计算机新时代占主要地位的半导体制造业，有段时间也好像一度濒临破产。

全文参考译文

拥有一段不用经过努力就获得成功的历史可能会成为一种可怕的不利因素，但是，如果恰当处理，也可能成为一种推动力。二战结束后，美国刚好进入了这样一段辉煌的时期，其市场是任何竞争者的 8 倍，这使得美国的经济达到了一个空前的规模。美国科学家是世界上最优秀的，美国的工人是世界上技术最熟练的。美国的繁荣和美国人的富有达到了那些经济被战争摧毁的欧亚诸国做梦也没有想到的程度。

但随着其他国家日趋富强，（美国）的领先地位不可避免地被削弱了。优势渐远的感觉让人痛苦也是必然的。到 80 年代中期，美国人对日趋衰退的工业竞争能力迷惑不解。一些像消费电子产品之类的大工业在面对国外的竞争时已经萎缩或逐渐消失。到 1987 年，仅剩下 Zenith 一家电视制造商。（而如今一家也没有了，Zenith 于当年 7 月被韩国的 LG 电器公司收购）。外国制造的轿车和纺织品正蜂拥进入美国国内市场。美国机床工业处于艰难发展时期。美国发明的在计算机新时代占主要地位的半导体制造业，有段时间也好像一度濒临破产。

所有这一切导致了一种信心危机。美国人不再把繁荣当做是理所当然的事。他们开始认为自己缺乏经济头脑，他们认为其收入不久也将下跌。在 80 年代中期，对美国工业走下坡路的原因作了一次又一次的调查。这些调查有时得出令人惊讶的结果，那就是告诫海外的竞争实力愈来愈强。

情况改变得多快呀！1995 年当日本还在奋力拼搏时，美国就可以追忆这五年来稳定发展的历史了。很少有美国人把这一巨变完全归咎于美元贬值和商业周期的循环这些明显原因。人们不再自我否定，取代的是盲目的骄傲。借用哈佛大学肯尼迪管理学院行政院长 Richard Cavanagh 的话说："美国的工业改变了结构，消除了臃肿，学得更加明智。"来自华盛顿特区的智囊团——卡托研究院的 Stephen Moore 说："我作为一个美国人看到我们的企业在提高生产率时，我感到骄傲。"哈佛商学院的 William Sahlman 认为人们将会把这个时期当做"美国企业管理的黄金时代"来追忆。

题目答案与解析

1. 美国于第二次世界大战后取得了领先地位的原因是哪一项？
   A. 它为实现这个目标付出了艰苦努力。
   B. 它的国内市场比以前大 8 倍。
   C. 第二次世界大战摧毁了大多数潜在竞争对手的经济。
   D. 它的空前规模的劳动大军促进了经济的发展。

【答案】C

【解析】本题可参照文章的第 1 段。从中可知，二战结束后，美国刚好进入了这样一段辉煌时期，其市场是任何竞争者的 8 倍，这使得美国的经济达到了一个空前的规模；美国科学家是世界上最优秀的，美国的工人是世界上技术最熟练的；美国的繁荣和美国人的富有达到了那些经济被战争摧毁的欧亚诸国做梦也没有想到的程度。据此可知，第二次世界大战结束后，美国之所以取得领先地位，是因为战争摧毁了其竞争对手的经济。C 项与文章意思相符，因此 C 项为正确答案。

2. 美国于 20 世纪 80 年代失去了在世界经济中的领先地位，美国的 _____ 的事实证实了这一点。

　　A．电视产业已经萎缩到国内市场　　　B．半导体产业已经被外国公司取代

　　C．机床产业在采取自杀行动后崩溃了　　D．汽车制造业失去了部分国内市场

【答案】D

【解析】本题可参照文章的第 2 段。从中可知，但随着其他国家日趋富强，（美国）的领先地位不可避免地被削弱了。优势渐远的感觉让人痛苦也是必然的。到 80 年代中期，美国人对日趋衰退的工业竞争能力迷惑不解。一些像消费电子产品之类的大工业在面对国外的竞争时已经萎缩或逐渐消失。到 1987 年，仅剩下 Zenith 一家电视制造商。（而如今一家也没有了，Zenith 于当年 7 月被韩国的 LG 电器公司收购）。外国制造的轿车和纺织品正蜂拥进入美国国内市场。美国机床工业处于艰难发展时期。美国发明的在计算机新时代占主要地位的半导体制造业，有段时间也好像一度濒临破产。据此可知，20 世纪 80 年代，美国失去了在世界经济中的领先地位，许多企业受到影响，外国制造的汽车和纺织品涌入美国国内市场，使其失去了部分国内市场。D 项与文章意思相符，因此 D 项为正确答案。

3. 我们从本文可以推知什么？

　　A．在自我怀疑和盲目骄傲之间来回转变是人的本性。

　　B．激烈竞争可以促进经济的发展。

　　C．经济的复苏取决于国际间的合作。

　　D．持续成功的历史可能为进一步的发展铺平道路。

【答案】B

【解析】从文章第 2 段的内容可知，随着其他国家日趋富强，（美国）的领先地位不可避免地被削弱了。优势渐远的感觉让人痛苦也是必然的。到 80 年代中期，美国人对日趋衰退的工业竞争能力迷惑不解；从第 3 段的内容可知，所有这一切导致了一种信心危机。美国人不再把繁荣当做是理所当然的事。他们开始认为自己缺乏经济头脑，他们认为其收入不久也将下跌。在 80 年代中期，对美国工业走下坡路的原因作了一次又一次的调查。这些调查有时得出令人惊讶的结果，那就是告诫海外的竞争实力愈来愈强。据此可知，一个国家的经济是衰退还是繁荣都是由于竞争所导致的。B 项与文章的意思相符，因此 B 项为正确答案。

4. 作者似乎认为，美国 20 世纪 90 年代经济的复兴可能归因于 _____。

　　A．商业周期循环的转变　　　　　　　B．产业重组

　　C．企业管理的改善　　　　　　　　　D．教育方面的成功

【答案】A

【解析】本题可参照文章的第 4 段。从中可知，1995 年当日本还在奋力拼搏时，美国就可以追忆这五年来稳定发展的历史了。很少有美国人把这一巨变完全归咎于美元贬值和商业周期的循环这些明显原因。人们不再自我否定，取代的是盲目的骄傲。借用哈佛大学肯尼迪管理学院行政院长 Richard Cavanagh 的话说：“美国的工业改变了结构，消除了臃肿，学得更加明智。”来自华盛顿特区的智囊团——卡托研究院的 Stephen Moore 说：“我作为一个美国人看到我们的企业在提高生产率时，我感到骄傲。”哈佛商学院的 William Sahlman 认为人们将会把这个时期当做“美国企业管理的黄金时代”来追忆。据此可知，作者认为美国经济的

复兴可能是因为美元的贬值或者商业周期的循环。A 项与文章的意思相符，因此 A 项为正确答案。

Text 3

Being a man has always been dangerous. There are about 105 males born for every 100 females, but this ratio drops to near balance at the age of maturity, and among 70-year-olds there are twice as many women as men. But the great universal of male mortality is being changed now, by babies survive almost as well as girls do. This means that, for the first time, there will be an excess of boys in those crucial years when they are searching for a mate. More important, another chance for natural selection has been removed. Fifty years ago, the chance of a baby (particularly a boy baby) surviving depended on its weight. A kilogram too light or too heavy meant almost certain death. Today it makes almost no difference. Since much of the variation is due to genes one more agent of evolution has gone.

There is another way to commit evolutionary suicide: stay alive, but have fewer children. Few people are as fertile as in the past. Except in some religious communities, very few women has 15 children. Nowadays, the number of births, like the age of death, has become average. Most of us have roughly the same number of offspring. Again, differences between people and the opportunity for natural selection to take advantage of it have diminished India shows what is happening. The country offers wealth for a few in the great cities and poverty for the remaining tribal peoples. The grand mediocrity of today everyone being the same in survival and number of offspring means that natural selection has lost 80% of its power in upper-middle-class India compared to the tribes.

For us, this means that evolution is over; the biological Utopia has arrived. Strangely, it has involved little physical change. No other species fills so many places in nature. But in the pass 100,000 years — even the pass 100 year our lives have been transformed but our bodies have not. We did not evolve, because machines and society did it for us. Darwin had a phrase to describe those ignorant of evolution: they "look at an organic being as average looks at a ship, as at something wholly beyond his comprehension." No doubt we will remember a 20th century way of life beyond comprehension for its ugliness. But however amazed our descendants may be at how far from Utopia we were, they will look just like us.

1. What used to be the danger in being a man according to the first paragraph?

    A. A lack of mates.   B. A fierce competition.

    C. A lower survival rate.   D. A defective gene.

2. What does the example of India illustrate?

    A. Wealthy people tend to have fewer children than poor people.

    B. Natural selection hardly works among the rich and the poor.

    C. The middle class population is 80% smaller than that of the tribes.

    D. India is one of the countries with a very high birth rate.

3. The author argues that our bodies have stopped evolving because _____.
   A. life has been improved by technological advance
   B. the number of female babies has been declining
   C. our species has reached the highest stage of evolution
   D. the difference between wealth and poverty is disappearing

4. Which of the following would be the best title for the passage?
   A. Sex Ration Changes in Human Evolution
   B. Ways of Continuing Man's Evolution
   C. The Evolutionary Future of Nature
   D. Human Evolution Going Nowhere

核心词汇注释

maturity [məˈtjʊərətɪ] *n.* 完备；（票据）到期；成熟

mortality [mɔːˈtælɪtɪ] *n.* 死亡率

excess [ˈekses] *n.* 过度；剩余；无节制；超过；超额
adj. 过度的；额外的

variation [ˌveərɪˈeɪʃ(ə)n] *n.* 变更；变化；变异；变种；[音]变奏；变调

fertile [ˈfɜːtaɪl] *adj.* 肥沃的；富饶的；能繁殖的

tribal [ˈtraɪbəl] *adj.* 部落的；种族的

mediocrity [ˌmiːdɪˈɒkrətɪ] *n.* 平常；平庸之才

Utopia [juːˈtəʊpɪə] *n.* 乌托邦；理想的完美境界；空想的社会改良计划

amazed [əˈmeɪzd] *adj.* 吃惊的；惊奇的

descendant [dɪˈsend(ə)nt] *n.* 子孙；后裔；后代

长难句剖析

【文章难句】Again, differences between people and the opportunity for natural selection to take advantage of it have diminished.

【结构分析】本句主干是 differences and the opportunity have diminished。介词短语 between people 做定语修饰 differences；for natural selection to take advantage of it 是定语，用来修饰 opportunity。

【参考译文】个体的差异以及利用自然淘汰的机会再一次变小。

全文参考译文

身为男人，总是有危险。男女出生比率大约为 105:100，但到成年时，这种比率下降，几乎达到平衡，在 70 岁的老年人中，女性比男性多一倍。可是男性死亡率普遍高的现象正在改变。如今的男婴和女婴的存活率一样。这意味着，男孩到了寻找伴侣的关键年龄，将第一时间出现男孩过剩现象。更重要的是，自然选择的另一个偶然性失去了作用。50 年前，婴儿（尤其是男婴）存活下来的几率取决于其体重。轻一公斤或重一公斤都几乎代表着必死无疑。体重在今天几乎不起作用。由于很多差别是由基因引起的，因而又一个进化因素消失了。

消灭进化因素的另一种方法就是高存活率，少生孩子。如今很少人像从前那样能生育了。

除了在一些宗教群体，很少有妇女生 15 个孩子。今天所生孩子的数目就像死亡年龄一样，人人都差不多。我们大多数人家的子女数量几乎都一样多。人与人之间的差异和利用差异进行自然选择的机会再次减小。印度的情况就是这样。该国为大城市的一部分人提供财富，而其余那些仍保持群居的部落民族依然贫困。今天最大的相同点——每个人的生存机会和子女数量都一样——意味着，与部落比较，自然选择在印度中上阶层已失去 80%的作用。

对于我们来说，这代表着进化已结束；生物学上的理想境界已经来临。令人奇怪的是，这种进化几乎不涉及身体的变化。没有另外的物种在大自然中占有这么多的地方。可在过去的 10 万年——甚或是 100 年中，我们的生活发生了改变，但我们的身体却没有。我们没有进化，是因为机器和社会代替我们进化了。达尔文有一句话描述了那些对进化一无所知的人；那些无知的人"看有机的生命就像野人看一条船，如看某种超出理解范围的东西"。不用怀疑，我们将会记住 20 世纪的生活方式，即使其丑态超出人们的理解，但是，不论我们的子孙对我们距理想状态的遥远感到多么迷惑不解，可他们会看起来和我们一样。

题目答案与解析

1. 依照文章第 1 段，作为男性过去面临的危险是什么？
    A．缺少配偶。　　　B．激烈的竞争。　　　C．更低的存活率。　　D．基因有缺陷。

【答案】C

【解析】本题可参照文章的第 1 段。身为男人，总是有危险。男女出生比率大约为 105:100，但到成年时，这种比率下降，几乎达到平衡，在 70 岁的老年人中，女性比男性多一倍。可是男性死亡率普遍高的现象正在改变。如今的男婴同女婴和存活率一样。这意味着，男孩到了寻找伴侣的关键年龄，将第一时间出现男孩过剩现象。更重要的是，自然选择的另一个偶然性失去了作用。50 年前，婴儿（尤其是男婴）存活下来的几率取决于其体重。轻一公斤或重一公斤都几乎代表着必死无疑。体重在今天几乎不起作用。由于很多差别是由基因引起的，因而又一个进化因素消失了。据此可知，以前，男性面临的危险是死亡率普遍高。C 项与文章的意思相符，因此 C 项为正确答案。

2. 举印度的例子是用来说明什么？
    A．富人生的子女往往比穷人少。
    B．自然选择在富人和穷人中几乎起不了作用。
    C．中产阶层的人口比部落人口少 80%。
    D．印度是人口出生率非常高的国家之一。

【答案】B

【解析】本题可参照文章的第 2 段。从中可知，如今很少人像从前那样能生育了。除了在一些宗教群体，很少有妇女生 15 个孩子。今天所生孩子的数目就像死亡年龄一样，人人都差不多。我们大多数人家的子女数量几乎都一样多。人与人之间的差异和利用差异进行自然选择的机会再次减小。印度的情况就是这样。该国为大城市的一部分人提供财富，而其余那些仍保持群居的部落民族依然贫困。今天最大的相同点——每个人的生存机会和子女数量都一样——意味着，与部落比较，自然选择在印度中上阶层已失去 80%的作用。据此可知，印度的例子说明——在印度，自然选择在穷人和富人之间所起的作用大大降低了。B 项与文章的意思相符，因此 B 项为正确答案。

3. 作者指出：我们的身体已经停止进化的原因是 _____。
   A. 技术的进步改善了人的生活　　　　B. 女婴的数量一直在减少
   C. 我们已经达到进化的最高境界　　　D. 贫富之间的差距正在消失

【答案】A

【解析】本题可参照文章的第 3 段。从中可知，对于我们来说，这意味着进化已结束；生物学上的理想境界已经来临；令人奇怪的是，这种进化几乎不涉及身体的变化；过去 10 万年——甚至过去 100 年中，我们的生活发生了改变，但我们的身体却没有；我们没有进化，因为机器和社会代替我们进化了。据此可知，我们的身体已经停止进化的原因是机器和社会代替我们进化了，也就是先进的技术代替我们进化了。A 项与文章的意思相符，因此 A 项为正确答案。

4. 以下各项中，哪项可以作为本文的最佳标题？
   A. 人类进化中性别比例的变化　　　　B. 延续人类进化的方法
   C. 自然的进化前景　　　　　　　　　D. 人类的进化停止了

【答案】D

【解析】从文章第 1 段的内容可知，如今的男婴和女婴的存活率几乎一样；这就意味着，自然选择的另一个偶然性已经被消除了；因为大部分的变异是由基因引起的，所以进化的又一个因素不存在了；从第 2 段的内容可知，如今，几乎没有人像过去那样能生育了；现在，出生的人数已经平均化；我们大多数人所生的子女数量几乎一样多；人与人之间的差别以及利用这种差别进行自然选择的机会都已经减少；每个人的寿命差不多，所生的子女数量也一样；从文章最后一段的内容可知，对于我们来说，这意味着进化已经结束了；生物学上的理想境界已经来临；过去 10 万年—— 甚至过去 100 年，我们的生活发生了变化，但我们的身体却没有改变；我们没有进化，因为机器和社会代替我们进化了；无论我们的后代感到多么惊奇，他们还是会看起来跟我们一样。据此可知，本文主要讲的是：由于一些进化因素的消失，人类的进化已经结束了。D 项与文章的意思相符，因此 D 项为正确答案。

Text 4

Aimlessness has hardly been typical of the postwar Japan whose productivity and social harmony are the envy of the United States and Europe. But increasingly the Japanese are seeing a decline of the traditional work-moral values. Ten years ago young people were hardworking and saw their jobs as their primary reason for being, but now Japan has largely fulfilled its economic needs, and young people don't know where they should go next.

The coming of age of the postwar baby boom and an entry of women into the male-dominated job market have limited the opportunities of teenagers who are already questioning the heavy personal sacrifices involved in climbing Japan's rigid social ladder to good schools and jobs. In a recent survey, it was found that only 24.5 percent of Japanese students were fully satisfied with school life, compared with 67.2 percent of students in the United States. In addition, far more Japanese workers expressed dissatisfaction with their jobs than did their counterparts in the 10 other countries surveyed.

While often praised by foreigners for its emphasis on the basics, Japanese education tends to stress test taking and mechanical learning over creativity and self-expression. "Those things that do not show up in the test scores personality, ability, courage or humanity are completely ignored," says Toshiki Kaifu, chairman of the ruling Liberal Democratic Party's education committee, "Frustration against this kind of thing leads kids to drop out and run wild." Last year Japan experienced 2,125 incidents of school violence, including 929 assaults on teachers. Amid the outcry, many conservative leaders are seeking a return to the prewar emphasis on moral education. Last year Mitsuo Setoyama, who was then education minister, raised eyebrows when he argued that liberal reforms introduced by the American occupation authorities after World War II had weakened the "Japanese morality of respect for parents".

But that may have more to do with Japanese life-styles. "In Japan," says educator Yoko Muro, "it's never a question of whether you enjoy your job and your life, but only how much you can endure." With economic growth has come centralization; fully 76 percent of Japan's 119 million citizens live in cities where community and the extended family have been abandoned in favor of isolated, two generation households. Urban Japanese have long endured lengthy commutes (travels to and from work) and crowded living conditions, but as the old group and family values weaken, the discomfort is beginning to tell. In the past decade, the Japanese divorce rate, while still well below that of the United States, has increased by more than 50 percent, and suicides have increased by nearly one-quarter.

1. In the Westerner's eyes, the postwar Japan was _____.
   A. under aimless development
   B. a positive example
   C. a rival to the West
   D. on the decline

2. According to the author, what may chiefly be responsible for the moral decline of Japanese society?
   A. Women's participation in social activities is limited.
   B. More workers are dissatisfied with their jobs.
   C. Excessive emphasis has been placed on the basics.
   D. The life-style has been influenced by Western values.

3. Which of the following is true according to the author?
   A. Japanese education is praised for helping the young climb the social ladder.
   B. Japanese education is characterized by mechanical learning as well as creativity.
   C. More stress should be placed on the cultivation of creativity.
   D. Dropping out leads to frustration against test taking.

4. The change in Japanese life-style is revealed in the fact that _____.
   A. the young are less tolerant of discomforts
   B. the divorce rate in Japan exceeds that in the U.S.
   C. the Japanese endure more than ever before
   D. the Japanese appreciate their present life

核心词汇注释

aimless [ˈeɪmlɪs] *adj.* 无目的的，没有目标的

harmony [ˈhɑːmənɪ] *n.* 协调；融洽

rigid [ˈrɪdʒɪd] *adj.* 刚硬的；死板的

counterpart [ˈkaʊntəpɑːt] *n.* 同仁；地位或作用相似的人或物

creativity [ˌkriːeɪˈtɪvətɪ] *n.* 创造力；创造

assault [əˈsɔːlt] *n.* 攻击；袭击
    v. 袭击

outcry [ˈaʊtkraɪ] *n.* 大声疾呼

conservative [kənˈsɜːvətɪv] *adj.* 保守的，守旧的
    n. 保守派

centralization [ˌsentrəlaɪˈzeɪʃən] *n.* 集中；中央集权化

commute [kəˈmjuːt] *v.* 交换；抵偿；减刑；<电工>整流

长难句剖析

【文章难句】The coming of age of the postwar baby boom and an entry of women into the male-dominated job market have limited the opportunities of teenagers who are already questioning the heavy personal sacrifices involved in climbing Japan's rigid social ladder to good schools and jobs.

【结构分析】本句主干是 The coming of age and an entry of women have limited the opportunities of teenagers。who 引导的定语从句修饰 teenagers。involved in climbing Japan's rigid social ladder 是过去分词短语做定语，修饰 sacrifices。固定搭配 sacrifices to sth. 的意思是"为……作出牺牲"。

【参考译文】战后生育高峰时期出生的人已成年以及女性进入以前由男性主导的工作领域，限制了日本青少年的机会。这些青少年本来就已经在质疑：为了爬上等级森严的社会阶梯而进入优秀的学校、找满意的工作，自己作出的巨大个人牺牲是否值得。

全文参考译文

日本在战后并非毫无目的地发展，它的高生产率和社会和睦让美国及欧洲各国羡慕不已。但是，日本人正在经历传统职业道德价值观的日益衰落。在十年前，年轻人工作努力，把工作当作存在的主要原因。可现在日本在很大程度上已满足了经济需求，结果导致年轻人不知道下一步该干什么。

战后生育高峰时期出生的人已成年以及女性进入以前由男性主导的工作领域，限制了日本青少年的机会，这些人本来就已经在质疑：为了爬上等级森严的社会阶梯而进入优秀的学校、找满意的工作，自己作出的巨大个人牺牲是否值得。最近的一项调查显示，仅有 24.5% 的日本学生对学校生活完全满意，与之相比，美国却有 67.2% 的学生对学校生活完全满意。此外，表示对工作不满意的日本人远远多于所调查的另外十个国家的工人。

虽然日本由于注重基本训练而受到外国人的称赞，可它的教育往往强调应试和机械性学习而不是强调创造性及能动性。执政的自民党教育委员会主席海部俊树（Toshiki Kaifu）说："考分无法展现学生的个性、能力、勇气或慈悲心，这些完全被忽略。由此引发的沮丧感导致学生辍学、放荡不羁。"去年，日本发生了 2,125 起校园暴力事件，其中包括 929 起是攻击老师的事件。在人们的强烈谴责声中，很多保守党领导人正尝试恢复到战前那样，强调道德教育。去年，当时的教育部长濑户山三男（Mitsuo Setoyama）令人大为震惊地说，二战后从

美国占领当局实施的自由主义改革淡化了"日本人尊敬父母的道德观"。

但是这也许与日本人的生活方式有更大关系。教育家室洋子（Yoko Muro）说："在日本，问题绝不是你是否喜欢自己的工作及生活，而是你能忍受到何种程度。"随着经济的发展实现了居住的集中化。在 1.19 亿日本人中，足有 76%住在城里。在城里，社区和大家庭已不复存在，取而代之的是独立的两代人的家庭。日本的城市居民长期忍受着漫长的上下班交通和拥挤的居住环境之苦，然而，随着传统群体和家庭观念的削弱，这种不便之处开始显现。在过去的十年中，日本的离婚率虽然仍远远低于美国，但却上升了 50%多，而自杀率上升了将近 25%。

题目答案与解析

1. 战后的日本在西方人看来 _____。
   A. 处于漫无目标的发展之中　　B. 是个正面例子
   C. 是西方国家的竞争者　　　　D. 在衰败

   【答案】B

   【解析】本题可参照文章的第 1 段。从中可知，日本在战后并非毫无目的的发展，它的高生产率和社会和睦让美国及欧洲各国羡慕不已。据此可知，西方人认为，战后的日本值得学习。B 项与文章的意思相符，因此 B 项为正确答案。

2. 依照作者的观点，什么是使日本社会道德水平下降的主要原因？
   A. 女性参加社会的活动受到限制。　　B. 更多的工人对其工作不满。
   C. 过多地重视基本训练。　　　　　　D. 生活方式受西方价值观的影响。

   【答案】D

   【解析】从文章第 1 段的第 2 句话可知，日本人正在经历传统职业道德价值观的日益衰落；从第 2 段的内容可知，战后生育高峰时期出生的人已成年以及女性进入以前由男性主导的工作领域，限制了日本青少年的机会；最近的一项调查显示，只有 24.5%的日本学生对学校生活完全满意，与之相比，美国却有 67.2%的学生对学校生活完全满意；此外，表示对工作不满意的日本工人远远多于所调查的另外十个国家的工人。从文章第 3 段的内容可知，虽然日本由于注重基本训练而受到外国人的称赞，但是，日本的教育往往强调的是应试和机械学习，而不是创造性和个性表现的培养；自民党教育委员会主席指出，考分无法展现学生的个性、能力、勇气或慈悲心，这些完全被忽略，由此引发的沮丧感导致孩子们辍学、放荡不羁；去年，日本发生了 2,125 起校园暴力事件，其中包括 929 起攻击老师的事件；在人们的谴责声中，保守派领导人正尝试恢复到战前那样，强调道德教育；当时的教育部长认为，二战后美国占领当局实施的自由主义改革淡化了日本人尊敬父母的道德观。从文章最后一段的内容可知，日本人的生活方式也发生了变化，人们逐渐放弃了社区和大家庭的观念，转而建立独立的两代人家庭；过去十年间，日本的离婚率虽然仍远低于美国，但是却上升了 50%多，自杀率上升了将近 25%。据此可知，作者认为，日本社会道德水平之所以下降，主要是因为日本人受了美国自由主义思想的影响。D 项与文章的意思相符，因此 D 项为正确答案。

3. 依照作者的观点，下面说法正确的是哪项？
   A. 人们称赞日本的教育有助于年轻人攀登社会阶梯。

B．日本的教育具有机械学习和创造力双重特征。

C．应该更注重创造力的培养。

D．辍学导致对应试教育的沮丧。

【答案】C

【解析】本题可参照文章的第 3 段。从中可知，虽然日本由于注重基本训练而受到外国人的称赞，但是，日本的教育往往强调的是应试和机械学习，而不是创造性和能动性的培养；自民党教育委员会主席指出，考试成绩反映不出的那些东西，比如个性、能力、勇气或人道等，全都被人们忽略了；由此而受到的挫折导致孩子们辍学、放荡不羁；去年，日本发生了 2,125 起校园暴力事件，其中包括 929 起攻击老师的事件；很多保守党领导甚至在寻求像战前一样，重新强调道德教育。据此可知，作者认为日本的教育应该注重创造性和能动性的培养。C 项与文章的意思相符，因此 C 项为正确答案。

4. ＿＿＿＿ 的事实显示出日本人的生活方式发生了变化。

A．年轻人更不能容忍生活中的不便之处　　B．离婚率超过了美国

C．日本人忍耐的东西甚至比以前更多　　D．日本人欣赏现在的生活

【答案】A

【解析】本题可参照文章的第 4 段。从中可知，这可能与日本人的生活方式关系更大；教育家室洋子（Yoko Muro）指出，在日本，问题绝不是你是否喜欢自己的工作或生活，而是你能够忍受到何种程度；在日本，人们逐渐放弃了社区和大家庭的观念，转而建立独立的两代人家庭；日本的城市居民长期忍受着漫长的乘车上、下班和拥挤的生活环境之苦，但是，随着传统的群体和家庭价值观念的淡薄，这些不便之处开始显露出来；过去十年间，日本的离婚率虽然仍远低于美国，但是却上升了 50% 多，自杀率上升了将近 25%。由此可知：日本人的生活方式发生变化的标志就是——他们忍受不了生活中的不便之处。A 项与文章的意思相符，因此 A 项为正确答案。

Unit 17

The relationship between formal education and economic growth in poor countries is widely misunderstood by economists and politicians alike. Progress in both areas is undoubtedly necessary for the social, political and intellectual development of these and all other societies, however, the conventional view that education should be one of the very highest priorities for promoting rapid economic development in poor countries is wrong. We are fortunate that it is, because building new educational systems there and putting enough people through them to improve economic performance would require two or three generations. The findings of a research institution have consistently shown that workers in all countries can be trained on the job to achieve radical higher productivity and, as a result, radically higher standards of living.

Ironically, the first evidence for this idea appeared in the United States. Not long ago, with the country entering a recession and Japan at its pre-bubble peak. The U.S. workforce was derided as poorly educated and one of primary cause of the poor U.S. economic performance. Japan was, and remains, the global leader in automotive-assembly productivity. Yet the research revealed that the U.S. factories of Honda, Nissan, and Toyota achieved about 95 percent of the productivity of their Japanese counterparts—a result of the training that U.S. workers received on the job.

More recently, while examining housing construction, the researchers discovered that illiterate, non-English-speaking Mexican workers in Houston, Texas, consistently met best-practice labor productivity standards despite the complexity of the building industry's work.

What is the real relationship between education and economic development? We have to suspect that continuing economic growth promotes the development of education even when governments don't force it. After all, that's how education got started. When our ancestors were hunters and gatherers 10,000 years ago, they didn't have time to wonder much about anything besides finding food. Only when humanity began to get its food in a more productive way was there time for other things.

As education improved, humanity's productivity potential increased as well. When the competitive environment pushed our ancestors to achieve that potential, they could in turn afford more education. This increasingly high level of education is probably a necessary, but not a sufficient, condition for the complex political systems required by advanced economic performance. Thus poor countries might not be able to escape their poverty traps without political changes that may be possible only with broader formal education. A lack of formal education, however, doesn't constrain the ability of the developing world's workforce to substantially improve productivity to the forested future. On the contrary, constraints on improving productivity explain why education isn't developing more quickly there than it is.

1. The author holds in paragraph 1 that the important of education in poor countries _____.

    A. is subject to groundless doubts

    B. has fallen victim of bias

    C. is conventional downgraded

    D. has been overestimated

2. It is stated in paragraph 1 that construction of a new education system _____.

    A. challenges economists and politicians

    B. takes efforts of generations

    C. demands priority from the government

    D. requires sufficient labor force

3. A major difference between the Japanese and U.S. workforces is that _____.

    A. the Japanese workforce is better disciplined

    B. the Japanese workforce is more productive

    C. the U.S. workforce has a better education

    D. the U.S. workforce is more organized

4. The author quotes the example of our ancestors to show that education emerged _____.

    A. when people had enough time

    B. prior to better ways of finding food

    C. when people on longer went hung

    D. as a result of pressure on government

5. According to the last paragraph, development of education _____.

    A. results directly from competitive environments

    B. does not depend on economic performance

    C. follows improved productivity

    D. cannot afford political changes

核心词汇注释

intellectual [,inti'lektjuəl] *n.* 知识分子
  adj. 智力的

assembly [ə'sembli] *n.* 集会，集合；集合
  的人们；立法机构，议会；装配，组装

consistent [kən'sistənt] *adj.* 一贯的，始终
  如一的；和……一致的（with）；坚实的，
  浓厚的；有节操的；相容的，相符的

constrain [kən'strein] *vt.* 强迫，强使；限

制，约束

counterpart ['kauntəpɑːt] *n.* 与对方地位
  相当的人，与另一方作用相当的物

priority [prai'ɒriti] *n.* 优先权，重点；优先
  考虑的事

suspect [səs'pekt] *vt.* 猜疑（是），怀疑（是），
  觉得（是）；怀疑，不信任；怀疑……有罪
  n. 嫌疑犯

长难句剖析

【文章难句】Progress in both areas is undoubtedly necessary for the social, political and intellectual development of these and all other societies; however, the conventional view that education should be one of the very highest priorities for promoting rapid economic development in poor countries is wrong.

【结构分析】该句由两个具有转折意味的分句构成。前面句子主干是 Progress is necessary for…，后面句子主干是 the conventional view should be one。that 引导同位语从句。

【参考译文】对这些贫困国家和其他所有国家来说，这两个领域的进步无疑是社会、政治和智力获得发展的必要前提。然而，那种为了促进贫困国家的经济迅速发展，将教育作为最优先考虑的事情之一的传统观点是错误的。

【文章难句】Not long ago, with the country entering a recession and Japan at its pre-bubble peak, the U.S. workforce was derided as poorly educated and one of the primary causes of the poor U.S. economic performance.

【结构分析】本句句子主干为：the U.S. workforce was derided as…，with 引导的独立主格结构为伴随状语。现在分词 entering 和介词短语 at its peak 两个并列部分构成了该句的独立主格结构。

【参考译文】不久之前，该国的经济步入衰退，日本的经济也达到泡沫前的顶峰。

【文章难句】Yet the research revealed that the U.S. factories of Honda Nissan, and Toyota achieved about 95 percent of the productivity of their Japanese counterpart—a result of the training that U.S. workers received on the job.

【结构分析】本句句子主干为：Yet the research revealed that…，第一个 that 引导宾语从句。第二个 that 引导定语从句，做 the training 的后置定语。

【参考译文】然而调查显示，美国的本田、尼桑和丰田工厂的生产率大约是日本同类工厂生产率的 95%，这是美国工人在工作中获得培训的结果。

【文章难句】More recently, while examining housing construction, the researchers discovered that illiterate, non-English-speaking Mexican workers in Houston, Texas, consistently met best-practice labor productivity standards despite the complexity of the building industry's work.

【结构分析】本句句子主干为：the researchers discovered that…，that 引导宾语从句，while… 时间状语相当于 when the researchers examined，despite 所引导的介词短语在此处充当让步状语。

【参考译文】最近在检验住宅建筑时，研究人员发现在休斯敦和得克萨斯，尽管建筑行业的工作很复杂，但没受过教育的、不会讲英语的墨西哥工人总是能达到最优劳动生产率的标准。

全文参考译文

经济学家和政治家们普遍误解了贫困国家的正规教育和经济发展之间的关系。对这些贫困国家和其他所有国家来说，这两个领域的进步无疑是社会、政治和民众文化水平获得发展的必要前提。然而，那种为了促进贫困国家的经济迅速发展，将教育作为最优先考虑的事情之一的传统观点是错误的。新的教育体制使我们觉得幸运，即让足够的人接受教育来提高经济绩效，但这需要两、三代人的共同努力。一家研究机构发现：每个国家的工人都可以进行在职培训以达到更高的生产力水平，从而达到更高的生活标准。

具有讽刺意味的是，美国是第一个正是此种想法的国家。不久前，美国经济步入衰退期，日本的经济也达到泡沫前的顶峰。美国的劳动力因缺乏教育而受到嘲笑，这也是美国经济绩效不佳的一个主要原因。在汽车装配生产率方面，日本占据着并且仍然保持着世界领先地位。然而调查显示，美国的本田、尼桑和丰田工厂的生产率大约是日本同类工厂生产率的 95%，这是美国工人在工作中进行培训的结果。

最近在检验住宅建筑时，研究人员发现在得克萨斯州休斯敦市，尽管建筑业的工作很复杂，但没受过教育、不会讲英语的墨西哥工人总是能达到最优劳动生产率的标准。

教育和经济发展之间的真正关系是什么？即使当政府没有强行干预，我们也不得不怀疑持续的经济增长促进了教育的发展。毕竟那是教育开始的原因。当我们的祖先在一万年前还是猎人和采集者时，除了寻找食物外，他们无暇思考其他事情。只有当人类开始用更有效率的方法来获取食物时，他们才有时间去做其他事情。

随着教育的改善，人类的生产潜能也得到提高。当竞争环境促使我们的祖先实现这一潜力时，他们反而又可以提供更多教育。对于高经济绩效所需求的复杂政治体制来说，教育水平的日益提高可能是必要而非充分条件。因此，如果不进行政治变革，贫困国家也许就不可能摆脱困境。这种政治变革只有在更广泛地普及正规教育的基础上才可能实现。然而，缺乏正规教育没有限制发展中国家的劳动力提高未来生产力的能力。相反，在提高生产力方面所受到的束缚解释了那里的教育为什么没有像它应该发展得那样快。

题目答案与解析

1. 作者于文章第一段表明：贫穷国家中教育的重要性 _____ 。

   A. 易受没有根据的怀疑

   B. 遭受偏见

   C. 惯例上被低估

   D. 被高估

   【答案】D

   【解析】本题可参照文章第 1 段。第 1 段表明传统观点认为促进贫困国家经济快速发展首要考虑的因素之一就是教育，然而这种观点是错误的。由此可见，作者不赞同贫困国家中的教育优先论，认为教育的重要性被高估了。因此 D 项为正确答案。

2. 首段所提新教育制度的建立 _____ 。

   A. 对经济学家以及政治学家形成挑战

   B. 需要几代人的共同努力

   C. 要求政府予以优先考虑

   D. 要求充足的劳动力

   【答案】B

   【解析】本题的依据句是文章第 1 段的第 3 句：We are fortunate that is it, because new educational systems there and putting enough people through them to improve economic performance would require two or three generations. 从中可知，B 项为正确答案。

3. 日本与美国的劳动力之间最大的区别在于 _____ 。

   A. 日本劳动工人更有纪律性

   B. 日本劳动力市场效率更高

   C. 美国劳动力教育背景更佳

   D. 美国劳动力更有组织性

   【答案】B

   【解析】本题的依据句是文章第 1 段的最后 1 句话：The findings of a research institution have consistently shown that workers in all countries can be trained on the job to achieve radical higher productivity and, as a result, radically higher standards of living. 从中可知，B 项为正确答案。

4. 作者引用祖先的例子为表明教育产生于 _____。
   A. 人类有足够多的时间时
   B. 在更好的寻找食物办法之前
   C. 人类不再挨饿时
   D. 政府施加的压力
   【答案】C
   【解析】本题可参照文章第 4 段。通过阅读第 4 段，我们了解到在人类祖先开始更有效地获取食物后，他们才有时间考虑猎取食物以外的其他事情。也就是在这个时候，教育才开始被人们纳入考虑范围并得以发展和重视。因此 C 项为正确答案。

5. 根据文章末段，教育的发展 _____。
   A. 由竞争的环境直接促成
   B. 不依赖于经济效益
   C. 伴随生产力的提高
   D. 无法带动政治变革
   【答案】C
   【解析】本题的依据句是文章第 5 段的第 2 句：This increasingly high level of education is probably a necessary, but not a sufficient, condition for the complex political systems required by advanced economic performance. 从中可知，C 项为正确答案。

Text 2

If ambition is to be well regarded, the rewards of ambition wealth, distinction, control over one's destiny must be deemed worthy of the sacrifices made on ambition's behalf. If the tradition of ambition is to have vitality, it must be widely shared; and it especially must be highly regarded by people who are themselves admired, the educated not least among them. In an odd way, however, it is the educated who have claimed to have give up on ambition as an ideal. What is odd is that they have perhaps most benefited from ambition — if not always their own then that of their parents and grandparents. There is heavy note of hypocrisy in this, a case of closing the barn door after the horses have escaped with the educated themselves riding on them.

Certainly people do not seem less interested in success and its signs now than formerly. Summer homes, European travel, BMWs. The locations, place names and name brands may change, but such items do not seem less in demand today than a decade or two years ago. What has happened is that people cannot confess fully to their dreams, as easily and openly as once they could, lest they be thought pushing, acquisitive and vulgar. Instead, we are treated to fine hypocritical spectacles, which now more than ever seem in ample supply: the critic of American materialism with a Southampton summer home; the publisher of radical books who takes his meals in three-star restaurants; the journalist advocating participatory democracy in all phases of life, whose own children are enrolled in private schools. For such people and many more perhaps not so exceptional, the proper formulation is, "Succeed at all costs but avoid appearing ambitious."

The attacks on ambition are many and come from various angles; its public defenders are few and unimpressive, where they are not extremely unattractive. As a result, the support for ambition as a healthy impulse, a quality to be admired and fixed in the mind of the young, is probably lower than it has ever been in the United States. This does not mean that ambition is at an end, that people no longer feel its stirrings and promptings, but only that, no longer openly honored, it is less openly underground, or made sly. Such, then, is the way things stand: on the left angry critics, on the right stupid supporters, and in the middle, as usual, the majority of earnest people trying to get on in life.

1. It is generally believed that ambition may be well regarded if _____.
   A. its returns well compensate for the sacrifices
   B. it is rewarded with money, fame and power
   C. its goals are spiritual rather than material
   D. it is shared by the rich and the famous

2. The last sentence of the first paragraph most probably implies that it is _____.
   A. customary of the educated to discard ambition in words
   B. too late to check ambition once it has been let out
   C. dishonest to deny ambition after the fulfillment of the goal
   D. impractical for the educated to enjoy benefits from ambition

3. Some people do not openly admit they have ambition because _____.
   A. they think of it as immoral
   B. their pursuits are not fame or wealth
   C. ambition is not closely related to material benefits
   D. they do not want to appear greedy and contemptible

4. From the last paragraph the conclusion can be drawn that ambition should be maintained _____.
   A. secretly and vigorously   B. openly and enthusiastically
   C. easily and momentarily   D. verbally and spiritually

核心词汇注释

deem [di:m] *v.* 认为；相信

vitality [vaɪˈtælɪtɪ] *n.* 活力；生命力；生动性

hypocrisy [hɪˈpɒkrɪsɪ] *n.* 伪善

spectacle [ˈspektək(ə)l] *n.* 展览物；公开展示；奇观；景象；光景

ample [ˈæmp(ə)l] *adj.* 充足的；丰富的

materialism [məˈtɪərɪəlɪz(ə)m] *n.* 唯物主义

participatory [pɑːˈtɪsɪpeɪtərɪ,pə-] *adj.* 供人分享的

formulation [ˌfɔːmjʊˈleɪʃən] *n.* 用公式表示；明确地表达；作简洁陈述

prompting [ˈprɒmptɪŋ] *n.* 促进；激励；提示

sly [slaɪ] *adj.* 狡猾的

长难句剖析

【文章难句】What has happened is that people cannot confess fully to their dreams, as easily and openly as once they could, lest they be thought pushing, acquisitive and vulgar.

【结构分析】主语从句 What has happened 在句中做主语。that 引导了一个表语从句。lest 引导的状语从句常用 should 或动词原形。

【参考译文】有所改变的就是，人们不能够再像以前那样轻松、公开地表露自己的理想，以免别人说自己爱出风头、贪得无厌以及没有品味。

全文参考译文

抱负若要受到重视，那它所带来的回报——财富、荣誉以及对命运的掌握——一定要被认为值得为之作出牺牲。抱负的传统若要激发活力，那它就应当得到人们的广泛认可；尤其应该得到那些受人羡慕之士的高度重视，特别是应得到那些受过良好教育的人们的高度重视。可正是那些受过良好教育的人却奇怪地声称，他们已经不再把抱负当做理想。但奇怪的是他们已从豪情壮志中获得了很大好处——如果不是自己的壮志雄心，就是他们父母的和祖父母的。这当中有很强的虚伪成分，如同马跑后再关上马房的门一样——但受过良好教育的人却正骑在那些逃跑的骏马上。

当然，现在人们对成功及其标志的兴趣好像并未比从前减少。避暑山庄、欧洲旅行及德国宝马汽车——它们的位置、地点和商标可能变化，但对这些东西的需求好像没比一二十年前减少。有所改变的是，人们不能像过去那样轻松地、公开地表露自己的理想，害怕别人认为自己爱出风头、贪得无厌以及没有品味。于是，我们如今看到的虚假情况比过去任何时候都多：美国物欲主义批评家在南安普敦拥有避暑山庄；激进的出版商到三星级宾馆吃饭；鼓吹分享民主制的新闻记者却把自己的孩子送入私立学校。对于这些人以及更多与之相似的人来说，恰当的解释是"要不惜一切换取成功，但避免表示出野心勃勃"。

对抱负的攻击很多，并来自不同的角度；它的公开捍卫者虽然并非特别没有吸引力，但由于人数很少，所以并未给人留下多深的印象。因此，在美国，人们不再像以前那样把抱负看成是一种健康的动力，看成是一种应该受到羡慕、应该深深扎根于年轻人心目中的品质。但这并不意味着人们没有了抱负，并不意味着人们感受不到它对人的鼓舞和启发了，只不过是人们不再公开以它为荣了，更不愿意公开表白它了；当然，由此产生了一些后果，其中有些就是抱负被迫转入地下，或是被暗藏心中；于是，情况就成了这样：左边是气愤的批评家，右边是愚蠢的支持者，而中间，正如平常一样，是大多数诚挚的人们，努力追求着成功。

题目答案与解析

1. 大众普遍认为，抱负会受到高度重视，如果 _____。
   A. 它带来的回报充分地补偿了它所做出的牺牲
   B. 它以金钱、名誉和权势作为回报
   C. 它的目标是精神上的，不是物质上的
   D. 它被富人和有名望者共同分享

【答案】A

【解析】本题可参照文章的第 1 段。从中可知，如果要人们高度重视抱负的话，那么它所带来的回报——财富、荣誉以及对自己命运的主宰必须让人们认为值得为它作出牺牲；抱负的传统若是要激发活力，那么它就应该得到人们的广泛认可；尤其应该得到那些受人羡慕之士的高度重视，特别是应该得到那些受过教育的人们的高度重视。据此可知，要想抱负受到高度重视，除非它所带来的回报值得为它作出牺牲。A 项与文章的意思相符，因此 A 项为正确答案。

2. 第 1 段最后一句话最可能暗示的是 _____。

A. 口头上摒弃抱负是受过教育者的习惯　　B. 一旦抱负被表露，要想抑制为时已晚

C. 达到目的后否认抱负是不诚实的　　D. 受过教育者享受抱负带来的好处不实际

【答案】C

【解析】本题可参照文章的第 1 段。从中可知，可正是那些受过良好教育的人却奇怪地声称，他们已经不再把抱负当做理想。但奇怪的是他们已从豪情壮志中获得了很大好处——如果不是自己的壮志雄心，就是他们父母的和祖父母的。这当中有很强的虚伪成分，如同马跑后再关上马房的门一样——但受过良好教育的人却正骑在那些逃跑的骏马上。据此可知，实现了理想后就否认自己有抱负，显然是虚伪之举。C 项与文章的意思相符，因此 C 项为正确答案。

3. 一些人不公开承认他们有抱负的原因是 _____。

A. 他们认为抱负不道德　　B. 他们追求的不是名誉或财富

C. 抱负与物质利益没有紧密的联系　　D. 他们不希望显得贪婪与可鄙

【答案】D

【解析】本题可参照文章的第 2 段。从中可知，与过去相比，现在的人们对成功以及成功标志的兴趣似乎并没有减少；别墅的位置、旅游的景点以及轿车的品牌可能会改变，但是，对这类东西的需求似乎并没有减少；有所改变的就是，人们不能够坦承自己的梦想，不能够再像以前那样轻松、公开地表露自己的理想，他们这样做是怕别人说自己爱出风头、贪得无厌以及没有品味；于是，我们现在看到的虚伪现象似乎比以前任何时候都多；对于这些人以及更多与之相似的人来说，恰当的解释是"不惜一切代价获得成功，但避免表现出野心勃勃"。据此可知，人们虽然有抱负，但却不敢表露出来，因为他们担心受到别人的指责。D 项与文章的意思相符，因此 D 项为正确答案。

4. 我们从最后一段可以总结出：应该 _____ 拥有抱负。

A. 秘密、精力充沛地　　B. 公开、热情地

C. 轻松、暂时地　　D. 口头、精神上地

【答案】B

【解析】本题可参照文章的最后一段。从中可知，对抱负的攻击很多，并来自不同的角度；因此，在美国，人们不再像以前那样把抱负看成是一种健康的动力，看成是一种应该受到羡慕、应该深深地扎根于年轻人心目中的品质，因而对它的支持可能比以前少了；但这并不意味着人们没有了抱负，并不意味着人们感受不到它对人的鼓舞和启发了，只不过是人们不再公开以它为荣了，更不愿意公开表白它了；当然，由此产生了一些后果，其中有些就是抱负被迫转入地下，或是被暗藏心中；于是，情况就成了这样——左边是愤怒的批评家，右边是愚笨的支持者，而中间，正如平常一样，是大多数诚挚的人们，努力追求着成功。据此可知，作者认为人们应该大胆、公开地追求自己的理想。B 项与文章的意思相符，因此 B 项为正确答案。

Text 3

It's a rough world out there. Step outside and you could break a leg slipping on your doormat. Light up the stove and you could burn down the house. Luckily, if the doormat or stove failed to warn of coming disaster, a successful lawsuit might compensate you for your troubles. Or so the thinking has gone since the early 1980s, when juries began holding more companies liable for their customers' misfortunes.

Feeling threatened, companies responded by writing ever-longer warning labels, trying to anticipate every possible accident. Today, stepladders carry labels several inches long that warn , among other things, that you might — surprise — fall off. The label on a child's Batman cape cautions that the toy "does not enable user to fly".

While warnings are often appropriate and necessary — the dangers of drug interactions, for example — and many are required by state or federal regulations, it isn't clear that they actually protect the manufacturers and sellers from liability if a customer is injured. About 50 percent of the companies lose when injured customers take them to court.

Now the tide appears to be turning. As personal injury claims continue as before, some courts are beginning to side with defendants, especially in cases where a warning label probably wouldn't have changed anything. In May, Julie Nimmons, president of Schutt Sports in Illinois, successfully fought a lawsuit involving a football player who was paralyzed in a game while wearing a Schutt helmet. "We're really sorry he has become paralyzed, but helmets aren't designed to prevent those kinds of injuries," says Nimmons. The jury agreed that the nature of the game, not the helmet, was the reason for the athlete's injury. At the same time, the American Law Institute — a group of judges, lawyers, and academics whose recommendations carry substantial weight — issued new guidelines for tort law stating that companies need not warn customers of obvious dangers or bombard them with a lengthy list of possible ones. "Important information can get buried in a sea of trivialities, " says a law professor at Cornell Law School who helped draft the new guidelines. If the moderate demand of the legal community has its way, the information on products might actually be provided for the benefit of customers and not as protection against legal liability.

1. What were things like in 1980s when accidents happened?

　A. Customers might be relieved of their disasters through lawsuits.

　B. Injured customers could expect protection from the legal system.

　C. Companies would avoid being sued by providing new warnings.

　D. Juries tended to find fault with the compensations companies promised.

2. Manufacturers as mentioned in the passage tend to _____.

　A. satisfy customers by writing long warnings on products

　B. become honest in describing the inadequacies of their products

　C. make the best use of labels to avoid legal liability

　D. feel obliged to view customers' safety as their first concern

3. The case of Schutt helmet demonstrated that _____.

　A. some injury claims were no longer supported by law

　B. helmets were not designed to prevent injuries

　C. product labels would eventually be discarded

　D. some sports games might lose popularity with athletes

4. The author's attitude towards the issue seems to be _____.

　A. biased　　　　B. indifferent　　　　C. puzzling　　　　D. objective

核心词汇注释

doormat ['dɔ:mæt] *n.*（放于门前的）擦鞋垫

lawsuit ['lɔ:su:t, 'lɔ:sju:t] *n.* 诉讼（尤指非刑事案件）

anticipate [æn'tɪsɪpeɪt] *vt.* 预期；期望；过早使用；先人一着；占先

　v. 预订；预见；可以预料

defendant [dɪ'fendənt] *n.* 被告

adj. 辩护的；为自己辩护的

Illinois [ˌɪlɪ'nɔɪ] *n.* 伊利诺伊州（美国州名）

paralyze ['pærəlaɪz] *vt.* 使瘫痪，使麻痹

tort [tɔ:t] *n.* [律]民事侵权行为

bombard [bɔm'bɑ:d] *vt.* 炮轰；轰击

triviality [ˌtrɪvɪ'ælɪtɪ] *n.* 琐事

长难句剖析

【文章难句】While warnings are often appropriate and necessary — the dangers of drug interactions, for example — and many are required by state or federal regulations, it isn't clear that they actually protect the manufacturers and sellers from liability if a customer is injured.

【结构分析】本句是一个主从复合句。it isn't clear that...是主句，it 是形式主语，真正的主语是 that 引导的从句。while 引导的状语从句由两个并列的句子组成。for example 在这里是对前面一句话的解释说明。

【参考译文】虽然警示标签通常是合理的和必需的，例如有关药物副作用可能产生危害的警示语，而且很多是州或联邦条例法律所要求的，但是，如果消费者受伤害，这些警示标签能否保护制造商和销售商免于赔偿，这还不清楚。

全文参考译文

外面的世界很危险。出门时，也许会滑倒在门口的擦鞋垫上，摔断一条腿。点炉时，也许会烧毁整幢房子。假如地垫或炉上没有警示字样来告诉你可能发生的危险，你或许可以幸运地就自己所受的伤害通过诉讼成功地获得赔偿。大概自20世纪80年代早期以来这种想法就一直延续着，20世纪80年代初陪审团成员开始持有这样的观点：认为更多的公司应该对他们的消费者遭受的不幸负责。

由于感到（赔偿的）威胁，公司便作出对策，写出的警告标签愈来愈冗长，以期预测出任何可能出现的意外。导致了现在的梯子上的警告标签有几英寸长，除了警告你可能发生的其他意外外，还警告你可能摔下来——这真是不可理喻的警告。孩子们的蝙蝠玩具的斗篷上的标签警告说：此玩具不能用来飞行。

虽然警示语经常是合理的和必需的，例如有关药物副作用可能产生的危害的警示语，而且很多是州或联邦法律所要求的，但是，如果消费者受伤，这些警示语能否保护产销商免于赔偿，这还不清楚。如果受伤的消费者把公司告上法庭，大约50%的公司会输掉官司。

今天看来这种趋势正在转变。虽然个人人身伤害索赔案件依然发生，但有些法院已开始站在被告一边，尤其是处理那些即使是有警示语亦无济于事的案例时，在5月份（美国）伊利诺伊州的 Schutt 体育用品公司被告，一位橄榄球队员戴着 Schutt 体育用品公司生产的头盔

挥球时受伤并瘫痪。该公司总裁 Julie Nimmons 先生辩解说。"我们对他的瘫痪深感遗憾，但我们设计这些防护头盔并不是为了防止那类伤害的。"陪审团也赞同造成球员受伤的不是头盔，而是橄榄球运动本身（的危险性）。公司因此胜诉。与此同时，美国法学会——该组织由一群举足轻重的法官、律师和学者组成——宣布的新民事侵害法纲要指出：公司没有必要警告消费者明显的危险，或者就可能产生的危险列出一串警示。康奈尔大学法学院的一位参与新纲要起草的法学教授说，"关键信息可能被埋没在浩如烟海的小细节里。"如果该法律组织的这一不太过分的要求能够实施，产品上提供的警示标语可能实际上是用来保护消费者利益的，而不只是为了保护公司摆脱法律责任。

题目答案与解析

1. 在 20 世纪 80 年代，当发生事故时情形会如何？
    A. 消费者可以通过诉讼而免受灾难。
    B. 受伤的消费者可望获得法律体制的保护。
    C. 公司会通过提供新警示而避免被起诉。
    D. 陪审团往往对公司答应的赔偿吹毛求疵。
    【答案】B
    【解析】本题可参照文章的第 1 段。从中可知，出门时，你可能会因为门前的擦鞋垫滑倒而摔断腿；点炉时，你可能会因此烧毁整幢房屋；幸运的是，如果垫子或炉子没有提醒你即将发生的灾难，一场成功的民事诉讼或许就可以补偿你所受的灾难；大约从 20 世纪 80 年代早期开始，这种观念就一直这么延续着—— 当时，陪审团开始认为，更多的公司应该对其消费者所遭受的不幸负责。据此可知，20 世纪 80 年代，如果消费者因使用商品而受伤，法律会保护他们，法庭会裁定公司应该对灾祸负责。B 项与文章的意思相符，因此 B 项为正确答案。

2. 在本篇文章中提到的制造商常常 _____。
    A. 通过在产品上注明长的警示来满足消费者的需要
    B. 在描述其产品的不足之处时很诚实
    C. 充分利用标签，以避免承担法律责任
    D. 被迫把消费者的安全看成他们最优先考虑的问题
    【答案】C
    【解析】从文章第 2 段的内容可知，由于感到（赔偿的）威胁，公司便想出对策——在产品上写上更长的警告标签，希望以此来预见各种可能的事故；从第 3 段的内容可知，虽然警示标签通常是合理的和必需的，而且许多警示标签是州或联邦法律所要求的，但是，如果消费者受伤，这些警示标签能否使制造商和销售商免担责任还不得而知；当受伤的消费者将制造商和销售商告上法庭时，大约一半的公司会输掉官司。据此可知，制造商和销售商们试图利用警示标签来避免承担责任。C 项与文章的意思相符，因此 C 项为正确答案。

3. 由 Schutt 体育用品公司制作的防护头盔的例子证明了 _____。
    A. 法律不再支持某些受伤索赔　　　　B. 防护头盔不是被设计用来预防伤害的
    C. 产品标签最终将会被抛弃　　　　　D. 某些体育项目可能失去运动员的欢迎
    【答案】A
    【解析】本题可参照文章的第 4 段。从中可知，这种趋势似乎正在扭转；个人伤害索赔案件如以往一样不断发生，但一些法庭开始支持被告，尤其在那些警示标签可能改变不了什么的案件中法庭会这样做；然后文章举例进一步说明，指出：Nimmons 说，"我们对他的瘫痪深感遗憾，但我们设计这些防护头盔并不是为了防止那类伤害的"；陪审团一致认为，造成运动员受伤的原因是橄榄球运动本身的性质，不是防护头盔；与此同时，美国法律协会发布了新的民事侵权行为法指导方针；如果法律界的这个适度目标能够实现的话，那么产品上所附的信息实际上就可能是用来保护消费者的利益的，而不是用来规避法律责任的。据此可知，"Schutt 体育用品公司"制作的防护头盔的例子证明——法庭不再支持那些警示标签可能改变不了什么的案件的受伤索赔。A 项与文章的意思相符，因此 A 项为正确答案。

4. 对（文中讨论的）问题，作者的态度像是 _____。

    A．有偏袒　　　B．漠不关心　　　C．感到困惑　　　D．客观

【答案】D

【解析】从文章第 1 段的内容可知，外面的世界很危险；出门时，你可能会摔断腿；点炉时，你可能会烧毁整幢房屋；幸运的是，一场成功的民事诉讼或许就可以补偿你所受的灾难；大约从 20 世纪 80 年代早期开始，这种观念就一直这么延续着；当时，陪审团开始认为，更多的公司应该对其客户的灾祸负责；从文章第 2 段的内容可知，觉得处境危险后，公司方面便做出反应，在产品上写上越来越长的警告标签，希望以此来预警各种可能的事故；从第 3 段的内容可知，虽然警示标签通常是合理的和必需的，而且许多警示标签是州或联邦法律所要求的，但是，如果消费者受了伤，这些警示标签能否使制造商和销售商免于责任还不得而知；当受伤的消费者将制造商和销售商告上法庭时，大约一半的公司会输掉官司；从文章最后一段的内容可知，现在，这种趋势似乎正在扭转；个人伤害索赔案如以往一样不断发生，但一些法庭开始支持被告，尤其在那些警示标签可能改变不了什么的案件中法庭会这样做；接着举例进一步作了说明；最后指出：美国法律协会发布了新的民事侵权行为法指导方针；如果法律界的这个不太过分的要求能够实现的话，那么产品上所附的信息实际上就可能是用来保护消费者的利益的，而不是用来规避法律责任的。据此可知，作者只是客观地分析、说明伤害索赔这个问题，并没有发表自己的观点，他的态度应该是客观的。D 项与文章的意思相符，因此 D 项为正确答案。

Text 4

In the first year or so of Web business, most of the action has revolved around efforts to tap the consumer market. More recently, as the Web proved to be more than a fashion, companies have started to buy and sell products and services with one another. Such business-to-business sales make sense because business people typically know what product they're looking for.

Nonetheless, many companies still hesitate to use the Web because of doubts about its reliability. "Businesses need to feel they can trust the pathway between them and the supplier," says senior analyst Blane Erwin of Forrester Research. Some companies are limiting the risk by conducting online transactions only with established business partners who are given access to the company's private internet.

Another major shift in the model for Internet commerce concerns the technology available for marketing. Until recently, Internet marketing activities have focused on strategies to "pull" customers into sites. In the past year, however, software companies have developed tools that allow companies to "push" information directly out to consumers, transmitting marketing messages directly to targeted customers. Most notably, the Pointcast Network uses a screen saver to deliver a continually updated stream of news and advertisements to subscribers' computer monitors. Subscribers can customize the information they want to receive and proceed directly to a company's Web site. Companies such as Virtual Vineyards are already starting to use similar technologies to push messages to customers about special sales, product offerings, or other events. But push technology has earned the contempt of many Web users. Online culture thinks highly of the notion that the information flowing onto the screen comes there by specific request. Once commercial promotion begins to fill the screen uninvited, the distinction between the Web and television fades. That's a prospect that horrifies Net purists.

But it is hardly inevitable that companies on the Web will need to resort to push strategies to make money. The examples of Virtual Vineyards, Amazon.com, and other pioneers show that a Web site selling the right kind of products with the right mix of interactivity, hospitality, and security will attract online customers. And the cost of computing power continues to free fall, which is a good sign for any enterprise setting up shop in silicon. People looking back 5 or 10 years from now may well wonder why so few companies took the online plunge.

1. We learn from the beginning of the passage that Web business _____.
   A. has been striving to expand its market
   B. intended to follow a fanciful fashion
   C. tried but in vain to control the market
   D. has been booming for one year or so

2. Speaking of the online technology available for marketing, the author implies that _____.
   A. the technology is popular with many Web users
   B. businesses have faith in the reliability of online transactions
   C. there is a radical change in strategy
   D. it is accessible limitedly to established partners

3. In the view of Net purists, _____.
   A. there should be no marketing messages in online culture
   B. money making should be given priority to on the Web
   C. the Web should be able to function as the television set
   D. there should be no online commercial information without requests

4. We learn from the last paragraph that _____.
   A. pushing information on the Web is essential to Internet commerce
   B. interactivity, hospitality and security are important to online customers
   C. leading companies began to take the online plunge decades ago
   D. setting up shops in silicon is independent of the cost of computing power

核心词汇注释

tap [tæp] *n.* 轻打；活栓；水龙头   流出；选择 *vi.* 轻叩，轻拍；轻声走
vt. 轻打；轻敲；敲打出；开发；分接，使   *n.* <美>（用复数）熄灯号

target [ˈtɑːɡɪt] *n.* 目标；对象；靶子

update [ʌpˈdeɪt] *v.* 使现代化；修正；校正；更新 *n.* 现代化；更新

subscriber [səbˈskraɪbə(r)] *n.* 订户；签署者；捐献者

customize [ˈkʌstəmaɪz] *v.* [计] 定制；用户化

vineyard [ˈvɪnjɑːd] *n.* 葡萄园

contempt [kənˈtempt] *n.* 轻视；轻蔑；耻辱；不尊敬；[律]藐视法庭（或国会）

purist [ˈpjʊərɪst] *n.* 纯化论者

resort [rɪˈzɔːt] *vi.* 求助；诉诸；采取；常去 *n.* 凭借；手段；常去之地；胜地

silicon [ˈsɪlɪkən] *n.* [化]硅，硅元素

长难句剖析

【文章难句】The examples of Virtual Vineyards, Amazon. com, and other pioneers show that a Web site selling the right kind of products with the right mix of interactivity, hospitality, and security will attract online customers.

【结构分析】本句主干是 The examples…show that…。that 引导了一个宾语从句。在这个宾语从句中，主语是 a Website，谓语是 will attract，宾语是 online customers。现在分词短语 selling the right kind of products with the right mix of interactivity, hospitality, and security 做定语修饰 a Website。

【参考译文】Virtual Vineyards、Amazon.com 网站以及其他开拓者的例子说明，一个网站销售对路的产品，同时具有互动性、热情周到、安全可靠等特点就能够吸引在线顾客。

全文参考译文

网上交易的头一两年中，大部分业务活动都围绕着开拓消费者市场而进行。最近，随着人们证明网络并不仅仅是一种时尚，公司间开始在网上交易产品和提供服务。公司间的这种交易方式能达成是因为商人一般都知道自己要寻找什么样的产品。

然而，由于怀疑网络的可靠性，许多公司仍然对网络的使用犹豫不决。Forrester 研究中心的资深分析家 Blane Erwin 说，"商家需要确定他们和供应商之间的交易通道值得信赖"。有些公司只向固定交易伙伴提供公司内部的局域网接点，从而通过这种在线交易手段来达到降低风险的目的。

网络商业模式的另一个重大转变是销售技术的进步。直到最近，互联网上的销售活动注重的仍是 "吸引"顾客到网站的策略。可就在去年，软件公司研制出新的技术，能让公司直接向用户 "推销"信息——将销售信息直接传送给特定的用户。最突出的例子是 Pointcast 网络，该网络使用一种屏幕保护系统，将最新的信息和广告不断地传送到用户的计算机显示器上。顾客可以定制他们想要的信息，可以直接进入某个公司的网站。像 Virtual Vineyards 这样的公司已经开始使用相似的策略将有关特价商品、产品推销或其他商业活动的信息"推"向用户。可是，推销策略让很多网上用户生厌。在线文化认为，信息应传送给那些提出需要的用户。一旦商业广告不请自来地充斥了电脑屏幕，那么网络与电视之间就没有区别了。这样的前景是网络净化者所恐惧的。

但是，网上公司即使不使用"推送"策略也肯定能赚钱。Virtual Vineyards、Amazon.com（两个网站的名称）以及其他开拓者的例子说明：如果一个网站销售的产品对路，再加上相互合作、热情周到、安全可靠这几点完好地结合，将同样能吸引网上客户。计算机的运算能力成本不断下跌，这对于企业在网上建立销售点是个好兆头。回顾一下过去 5～10 年的历史，人们可能会感到奇怪：尝试在线服务的公司为何这么少呢？

题目答案与解析

1. 我们从文章的开头了解到，网上业务 _____。
   A．一直在努力开拓其市场
   B．打算遵循一种奇异的风尚
   C．企图控制市场，但是徒劳无功
   D．已经蓬勃发展了大约一年的时间

   【答案】A

   【解析】本题可参照文章的第 1 段。从中可知，网上交易开始的头一两年中，大多数活动都围绕着开拓消费者市场而进行。据此可知，网上业务刚开始时，其业务活动主要是开拓消费者市场。A 项与文章的意思相符，因此 A 项为正确答案。

2. 作者谈到可用于营销的在线技术时暗示了 _____。
   A．这种技术受到许多网络用户的喜爱
   B．商家对在线交易的可靠性有信心
   C．交易的策略发生了根本变化
   D．在线技术只限于固定合作伙伴使用

   【答案】C

   【解析】本题可参照文章的第 3 段。从中可知，互联网商业模式的另一个重大变化是销售技术的进步；直到最近，互联网的营销活动注重的仍是"吸引"顾客到网站的策略；可就在去年，软件公司开发出了新的技术，这种技术可以使公司把信息直接"推销"给顾客，把市场信息直接传送给特定用户；用户可以定制他们想要的信息，可以直接进入某公司的网站。据此可知，过去一年里，在线的营销技术发生了变化。C 项与文章的意思相符，因此 C 项为正确答案。

3. 依照网络净化者的观点，_____。
   A．在线文化领域不应该有营销信息
   B．在网上赚钱应该被赋予优先权
   C．网络应该能够像电视那样起作用
   D．没有要求就不应该提供在线商业信息

   【答案】D

   【解析】本题可参照文章的第 3 段。从中可知，在线文化认为，信息应传送给那些提出需要的用户；一旦商业广告不请自来地充斥了计算机屏幕，那么网络和电视之间就没有区别了；这样的前景是网络净化者所恐惧的。据此可知，网络净化者们认为，商业促销信息不应该未经许可就充斥电脑屏幕，应该根据具体要求而提供信息。D 项与文章的意思相符，因此 D 项为正确答案。

4. 我们从最后一段了解到 _____。
   A．对于网络商业来说，在网上推销信息至关重要
   B．对于在线顾客来说，相互合作、热情周到以及安全可靠非常重要
   C．主导公司几十年前就开始涉足在线业务
   D．在网上建立专门零售部与计算机的成本没有关系

   【答案】B

   【解析】从文章最后一段的内容可知，网络公司并不是非得使用推销策略来赚钱不可；Virtual Vineyards，Amazon.com，以及其他开拓者的例子表明——如果一个网站销售对路的产品，再加上相互合作、热情周到、安全可靠等这些因素，将同样能吸引网上客户；并且电脑的成本不断自动下降，这对于任何在网上建立专门零售部的企业来说都是一个好兆头；只要回顾过去的 5 到 10 年的历史，人们或许会感到奇怪——尝试在线服务的公司为何这么少呢。据此可知，网络公司要想吸引网上顾客，除了使用推销策略之外，更重要的是对路的产品、相互合作、热情周到、安全可靠等这些因素。B 项与文章的意思相符，因此 B 项为正确答案。

Unit 18

In recent years many countries of the world have been faced with the problem of how to make their workers more productive. Some experts claim the answer is to make jobs more varied. But do more varied jobs lead to greater productivity? There is evidence to suggest that while variety certainly makes the workers' life more enjoyable, it does not actually make them work harder. As far as increasing productivity is concerned, then variety is not an important factor.

Other experts feel that giving the workers freedom to do their jobs in their own way is important and there is no doubt that this is true. The problem is that this kind of freedom cannot easily be given in the modern factory with its complicated machinery which must be used in a fixed way. Thus while freedom of choice may be important, there is usually very little that can be production lines rather than one large one, so that each worker contributes more to the production of the cars on his line. It would seem that not only is degree of worker contribution an important factor, but it is also one we can do something about.

To what extent does more money lead to greater productivity? The workers themselves certainly think this important. But perhaps they want more only because the work they do is so boring. Money just lets them enjoy their spare time more. A similar argument may explain demands for shorter working hours. Perhaps if we succeed in making their jobs more interesting, they will neither want more, nor will shorter working hours be so important to them.

1. Which of these possible factors leading to greater productivity is NOT true?
   A. To make jobs more varied.
   B. To give the workers freedom to do their jobs in their own way.
   C. Degree of worker contribution.
   D. Demands of longer working hours.
2. Why do workers want more money?
   A. Because their jobs are too boring.　　B. In order to enjoy more spare time.
   C. To make their jobs more interesting.　　D. To demand shorter working hours.
3. The last sentence in this passage means that if we succeed in making workers' jobs more interesting _____.
   A. they will want more money
   B. they will demand shorter working hours are important factors
   C. more money and shorter working hours are important factors
   D. more money and shorter working hours will not be so important to them

4. In this passage, the author tells us _____.

   A. how to make the workers more productive

   B. impossible factors leading to greater efficiency

   C. to what extent more money leads to greater productivity

   D. how to make workers' jobs more interesting

核心词汇注释

productive [prə'dʌktɪv] *adj.* 生产性的，生产的，能产的，多产的

expert ['eksp3:t] *n.* 专家，行家，[军]（特等）射手

   adj. 老练的，内行的，专门的

   vt. 在……中当行家，当专家

varied ['veərɪd] *adj.* 杂色的，各式各样的

productivity [ˌprɒdʌk'tɪvɪtɪ] *n.* 生产率

evidence ['evɪdəns] *n.* 明显，显著；明白；迹象，根据，[物]证据，证物

complicated ['kɒmplɪkeɪtɪd] *adj.* 复杂的，难解的

production [prə'dʌkʃ(ə)n] *n.* 生产，产品，作品，（研究）成果

contribution [kɒn'trɪbjuːʃn] *n.* 捐献，贡献，投稿

boring ['bɔːrɪŋ] *adj.* 令人厌烦的

argument ['ɑːgjuːmənt] （~for, against） *n.* 争论，辩论；论据，论点；意见

长难句剖析

【文章难句】In recent years many countries of the world have been faced with the problem of how to make their workers more productive.

【结构分析】本句中，in recent years 在句中作时间状语，主干是 "many countries…have been faced with the problem…of" 短语则是用来修饰 the problem，在这个 of 短语中，of 的宾语是由特殊疑问词 how 构成的复合式不定式。

【参考译文】近年来，世界上许多国家都面临着如何提高工人生产率的问题。

【文章难句】Other experts feel that giving the workers freedom to do their jobs in their own way is important and there is no doubt that this is true.

【结构分析】本句的主干是 "Other experts feel that…and there is no doubt…"。谓语动词是 feel，后面接的是由 that 引导的宾语从句。从句中主语是动名词 giving…way, is 是系动词。

【参考译文】其他专家认为重要的是要给工人自由让他们以自己的方式工作，无疑这是正确的。

【文章难句】The problem is that this kind of freedom cannot easily be given in the modern factory with its complicated machinery which must be used in a fixed way.

【结构分析】本句的主干是 "The problem is that…"，后面接的是由 that 引导的表语从句。在表语从句中主干是一个普通被动语气，with…machinery 是后置定语，用来修饰 the modern factory。which 引导的定语从句用来修饰 machinery。

【参考译文】问题是现代工厂有复杂的机器必须按固定的方法使用，在这样的工厂提供给工人自由并不容易。

全文参考译文

　　世界上许多国家近年来都面临着如何提高工人生产率的问题。有些专家声称，让工作更加富有变化是解决问题的方法。但更富有变化的工作能产生更高的生产效率吗？有证据显示，变化当然可以让工人的生活更加快乐，但它并不能使工人们更加努力工作。那么就提高生产效率而言，工作变化就不是一个重要的因素。

　　其他专家的见解是，重要的是要给工人自由，让他们以自己的方式工作，无疑这是正确的。问题是现代工厂有复杂的机器必须按固定的方法使用，在这样的工厂提供给工人自由并不容易。这样虽然选择的自由是很重要的，但通常无法创造这样的自由。另外一个很关键的考虑是每个工人可以给他所生产的产品起什么样的作用。在大多数工厂里老板试验使用多条小型生产线而非一整条大型生产线，这样的话每个工人就能为线上的汽车生产付出更多的劳动。看来好像不仅工人的劳动强度是一个重要的因素，而且也要看我们能够做点什么。

　　要想产生更高的生产效率，工资提高到什么程度呢？工人本人当然认为这一点很重要。但有可能他们想要更多的钱只是因为他们所做的工作非常令人厌烦。钱只会让他们更好地享受闲暇时光。缩短工作时间的要求也可以用这一论点解释。或许如果我们能够让他们的工作更加有趣，他们不仅不会要更多的薪水，而且缩短工作时间对他们也不是那么重要了。

题目答案与解析

1.　以下会导致更高生产率的因素中 _____ 是错误的？
　　A. 使工作细化　　　　　　　　　　B. 给工人们按自己的方式工作的自由
　　C. 劳动强度　　　　　　　　　　　D. 更长工作时间的需求
　　【答案】D
　　【解析】从文中内容可知，D 项（延长工作时间）在第三段最后提到，但文中提到的是缩短工作时间，与 D 项相反，因此 D 项为正确答案。

2.　工人们想要得到更多的钱是为什么？
　　A. 因为他们的工作太枯燥。　　　　B. 为了享受更多的空闲时间。
　　C. 为了使他们的工作更加有趣。　　D. 为了要求更短的工作时间。
　　【答案】A
　　【解析】本题的依据句是第三段的第三句 "But perhaps they want more only because the work they do is so boring（工人们想得到更多的报酬也许正是因为他们的工作太单调）"，因此 A 项为正确答案。

3.　文中最后一句话的含义是，如果我们成功地使工人的工作更加有趣，_____。
　　A. 他们将要更多的钱
　　B. 他们将要求缩短工作时间
　　C. 更多的钱和更少的工作时间都是重要因素
　　D. 更多的钱和更少的工作时间对他们都不那么重要了
　　【答案】D
　　【解析】本题的依据句是 "Perhaps if we succeed in making their jobs more interesting, they will neither want more, nor will shorter working hours be so important to them（或许如果我们能

够让他们的工作更加有趣，他们不仅不会要更多的薪水，而且缩短工作时间对他们也不是那么重要了）"，从中可知 D 项为正确答案。短语 neither…nor 的意思是"既不……也不……"。

4.　在这篇文章中，作者告诉我们 _____。

    A．怎样提高工人生产率　　　　　　　B．导致高生产率的不可能因素

    C．花的钱越多，生产率越高　　　　　D．怎样使工人的工作更加有趣

【答案】A

【解析】综观全文，这是一篇讨论如何使工人更加有效地工作的文章，因此 A 项为正确答案。B 项明显是错误的。而 C 和 D 两项仅是文章部分段落的中心思想，不是全文的中心思想。

Text　2

When a Scottish research team startled the world by revealing 3 months ago that it had cloned an adult sheep, President Clinton moved swiftly. Declaring that he was opposed to using this unusual animal husbandry technique to clone humans, he ordered that federal funds not be used for such an experiment — although no one had proposed to do so — and asked an independent panel of experts chaired by Princeton President Harold Shapiro to report back to the White House in 90 days with recommendations for a national policy on human cloning. That group — the National Bioethics Advisory Commission (NBAC) — has been working feverishly to put its wisdom on paper, and at a meeting on 17 May, members agreed on a near-final draft of their recommendations.

NBAC will ask that Clinton's 90-day ban on federal funds for human cloning be extended indefinitely, and possibly that it be made law. But NBAC members are planning to word the recommendation narrowly to avoid new restrictions on research that involves the cloning of human DNA or cells-routine in molecular biology. The panel has not yet reached agreement on a crucial question, however, whether to recommend legislation that would make it a crime for private funding to be used for human cloning. In a draft preface to the recommendations, discussed at the 17 May meeting, Shapiro suggested that the panel had found a broad consensus that it would be "morally unacceptable to attempt to create a human child by adult nuclear cloning." Shapiro explained during the meeting that the moral doubt stems mainly from fears about the risk to the health of the child. The panel then informally accepted several general conclusions , although some details have not been settled.

NBAC plans to call for a continued ban on federal government funding for any attempt to clone body cell nuclei to create a child because current federal law already forbids the use of federal funds to create embryos (the earliest stage of human offspring before birth) for research or to knowingly endanger an embryo's life, NBAC will remain silent on embryo research.

NBAC members also indicated that they will appeal to privately funded researchers and clinics not to try to clone humans by body cell nuclear transfer. But they were divided on whether to go further by calling for a federal law that would impose a complete ban on human cloning. Shapiro and most members favored an appeal for such legislation , but in a phone interview, he said this issue was still "up in the air".

1. We can learn from the first paragraph that _____.
   A. federal funds have been used in a project to clone humans
   B. the White House responded strongly to the news of cloning
   C. NBAC was authorized to control the misuse of cloning technique
   D. the White House has got the panel's recommendations on cloning

2. The panel agreed on all of the following except that _____.
   A. the ban on federal funds for human cloning should be made a law
   B. the cloning of human DNA is not to be put under more control
   C. it is criminal to use private funding for human cloning
   D. it would be against ethical values to clone a human being

3. NBAC will leave the issue of embryo research undiscussed because _____.
   A. embryo research is just a current development of cloning
   B. the health of the child is not the main concern of embryo research
   C. an embryo's life will not be endangered in embryo research
   D. the issue is explicitly stated and settled in the law

4. It can be inferred from the last paragraph that _____.
   A. some NBAC members hesitate to ban human cloning completely
   B. a law banning human cloning is to be passed in no time
   C. privately funded researchers will respond positively to NBAC's appeal
   D. the issue of human cloning will soon be settled

核心词汇注释

clone [kləʊn] *n.* 无性系；无性繁殖；克隆
v. 无性繁殖；复制

swift [swɪft] *n.* [鸟]雨燕；（梳棉机等的）大滚筒
adj. 迅速的；快的；敏捷的；立刻的
adv. 迅速地；敏捷地

husbandry [ˈhʌzbəndrɪ] *n.* 管理

feverish [ˈfiːvərɪʃ] *adj.* 发烧的；热病的；狂热的；兴奋的

indefinite [ɪnˈdefɪnɪt] *adj.* 模糊的；不确定的；[语]不定的

preface [ˈprefɪs] *n.* 序文；绪言；前言
vi. 作序；写前言
vt. 为……写序言；开始

consensus [kənˈsensəs] *n.* 一致同意；多数人的意见；舆论

nuclei [ˈnjuːklɪaɪ] *n.* nucleus 的复数形式

embryo [ˈembrɪəʊ] *n.* 胚胎，胎儿，胚芽
adj. 胚胎的，初期的

knowingly [ˈnəʊɪŋlɪ] *adv.* 有意地，心照不宣地

长难句剖析

【文章难句】Declaring that he was opposed to using this unusual animal husbandry technique to clone humans, he ordered that federal funds not be used for such an experiment — although no one had proposed to do so — and asked an independent panel of experts chaired by Princeton

President Harold Shapiro to report back to the White House in 90 days with recommendations for a national policy on human cloning.

【结构分析】本句主语是 he，两个并列的谓语是 ordered 和 asked。让步状语从句 although no one had proposed to do so 做补充成分，对前面的句子进一步加以限定，说明克林顿对此事极为重视。chaired by…做定语修饰 independent panel of experts。前面的 Declaring that he was opposed to using this unusual animal husbandry technique to clone humans 是现在分词短语做状语，表示原因。

【参考译文】他宣称反对利用这种特殊的畜牧业技术克隆人，同时下令禁止联邦基金用于此类实验——尽管还没有人打算这样做；他还要求成立一个由普林斯顿大学校长 Harold Shapiro 领导的独立专家小组，在 90 天内向白宫提交报告，为国家有关克隆人的政策提出建议。

全文参考译文

当苏格兰的一个研究小组透露 3 个月前他们已克隆了一只成年绵羊时，世界为之震惊，克林顿总统立即作出反应。他宣称他反对利用这种特殊的畜牧业技术去克隆人，同时下令禁止联邦基金用于此类实验——尽管还没有人打算这样做；他还要求成立一个由普林斯顿大学校长 Harold Shapiro 领导的独立专家小组，在 90 天内向白宫提交报告，为国家有关克隆人的政策提出建议。这个专家组名为"全国生物伦理道德顾问委员会（NBAC）"，此后它一直在积极而热情地为之工作，集众家所长，写出报告。在 5 月 17 日的一次会议上，委员们就接近定稿的报告书达成了共识。

NBAC 将要求克林顿总统将有关联邦基金不能用来克隆人的 90 天禁令无限期延长，并就此立法。可 NBAC 委员们计划在提案的言辞上更为严谨以防止给克隆人体 DNA（脱氧核糖核酸）或细胞等方面研究带来更多的限制——因为在分子生物学中这种研究属于常规研究项目。但是。这个专家组在一个关键问题上还未达成共识，即是否建议立法，规定将利用私人基金克隆人视为犯罪。

在 5 月 17 日开会讨论的报告序言草稿中 Shapiro 表示专家们已达成广泛的共识，认为"试图用成人细胞核去克隆婴儿是违背伦理道德的。"Shapiro 在会上解释说，伦理道德上禁止的主要原因是担心对婴儿的健康产生危害。随后，专家们非正式地达成几种一般的结论，尽管有些细节还未解决。

NBAC 计划号召持续禁止出于任何目的使用联邦政府基金利用人体细胞核来克隆婴孩。原因是现行联邦政府法律已经禁止使用联邦基金创造供研究用的胚胎（即人类后代出生前的萌芽阶段）或潜意识地危害胚胎的生命，但 NBAC 的报告将并不反对胚胎的研究。

NBAC 成员宣称：他们要呼吁由私人出资的研究人员和机构不要尝试通过利用人体细胞核克隆人。可他们在是否进一步要求联邦政府用法律强制执行完全禁止克隆人这一问题上存在分歧。Shapiro 和大多数委员赞成立法，可在电话采访中他透露，这仍是个"悬而未决"的问题。

题目答案与解析

1. 我们从第 1 段可以了解到_____。

   A. 联邦基金已经被用于一个克隆人的项目

B. 白宫对有关克隆的消息反应强烈

C. NBAC 被授权控制滥用克隆技术

D. 白宫已经得到专家小组有关克隆问题的建议

【答案】B

【解析】从文章第 1 段的内容可知，当苏格兰的一个研究小组透露，3 个月前他们已克隆了一只成年绵羊后，克林顿总统立即作出反应；他宣称他反对利用这种特殊的畜牧业技术去克隆人，同时下令禁止联邦基金用于此类实验；他还要求成立一个独立专家小组在 90 天内向白宫提交报告，为国家有关克隆人的政策提出建议；该小组将其明智的看法写成公文，在 5 月 17 日举行的会议上，委员们就这份接近定稿的报告书达成了共识。据此可知，美国总统对有关克隆的消息反应强烈，并迅速采取行动。B 项与文章的意思相符，因此 B 项为正确答案。

2. 专家小组除了 _____ 之外，对下面所有说法都同意。

A. 联邦基金不得用于克隆人的禁令应该被制定成为法律

B. 克隆人的 DNA 将不会受到更多控制

C. 使用私人基金克隆人的行为是犯罪行为

D. 克隆人将违背道德价值观

【答案】C

【解析】从文章第 2 段的内容可知，NBAC 将要求克林顿总统应该无限期延长联邦基金不得用于克隆人的 20 天禁令；如有可能，应该将此禁令定为法律；但是 NBAC 的成员正在计划准确表达建议报告，以避免对涉及人类 DNA 克隆或细胞克隆产生新的限制；不过，专家小组对是否建议将私人基金用于克隆人的行为法定为犯罪行为，尚未达成一致意见；从第 3 段的内容可知，Shapiro 暗示，"从道义上讲，试图用成人的细胞核克隆出婴儿的做法令人难以接受"，专家小组在这一点上已达成共识。据此可知，A、B 和 D 三项都是专家小组赞同的；只有 C 项与文章第 2 段最后一句话的意思不符，因此 C 项为正确答案。

3. NBAC 将不讨论胚胎研究问题的原因是 _____。

A. 胚胎研究只是克隆的流行发展

B. 婴儿的健康不是胚胎研究主要关心的问题

C. 在胚胎研究中，胚胎的生命不会有危险

D. 这个问题已经得到法律的清晰陈述，并被载入法律之中

【答案】D

【解析】本题可参照文章的第 4 段。从中可知，因为目前的联邦法律已经禁止联邦基金用于克隆胚胎以进行研究或故意危害胚胎的生命，所以 NBAS 将对胚胎研究不发表意见。据此可知，NBAC 之所以不讨论胚胎研究问题，是因为联邦法律已经禁止联邦基金用于胚胎研究。D 项与文章的意思相符，因此 D 项为正确答案。

4. 可以从最后一段推知 _____。

A. 一些 NBAC 成员对完全禁止克隆人犹豫不决

B. 一项禁止克隆人的法律将马上获通过

C. 受私人基金资助的研究人员将积极响应 NBAC 的呼吁

D. 克隆人的问题将很快得到解决

【答案】A

【解析】本题可参照文章的最后一段。从中可知，NBAC 的成员还暗示，他们将呼吁那些受私人基金资助的研究人员和专科医院不要尝试通过人体细胞核的移植来克隆人；但是，对于是否进一步要求制定一项完全禁止克隆人的联邦法律，NBAC 的成员意见不一致；Shapiro 和大多数成员赞成要求制定这样的法律，但在一次电话采访中，他说，这个问题仍然"悬而未决"。据此可知：并不是所有的 NBAC 成员都赞成完全禁止克隆人。A 项与文章的意思相符，因此 A 项为正确答案。

Text 3

Science, in practice, depends far less on the experiments it prepares than on the preparedness of the minds of the men who watch the experiments. Sir Isaac Newton supposedly discovered gravity through the fall of an apple. Apples had been falling in many places for centuries and thousands of people had seen them fall. But Newton for years had been curious about the cause of the orbital motion of the moon and planets. What kept them in place? Why didn't they fall out of the sky? The fact that the apple fell down toward the earth and not up into the tree answered the question he had been asking himself about those larger fruits of the heavens, the moon and the planets.

How many men would have considered the possibility of an apple falling up into the tree? Newton did because he was not trying to predict anything. He was just wondering. His mind was ready for the unpredictable. Unpredictability is part of the essential nature of research. If you don't have unpredictable things, you don' t have research. Scientists tend to forget this when writing their cut and dried reports for the technical journals, but history is filled with examples of it.

In talking to some scientists, particularly younger ones, you might gather the impression that they find the "scientific method" — a substitute for imaginative thought. I've attended research conferences where a scientist has been asked what he thinks about the advisability of continuing a certain experiment. The scientist has frowned, looked at the graphs, and said "the data are still inconclusive." "We know that," the men from the budget office have said, "but what do you think? Is it worthwhile going on? What do you think we might expect?" The scientist has been shocked at having even been asked to speculate.

What this amounts to, of course, is that the scientist has become the victim of his own writings. He has put forward unquestioned claims so consistently that he not only believes them himself, but has convinced industrial and business management that they are true. If experiments are planned and carried out according to plan as faithfully as the reports in the science journals indicate, then it is perfectly logical for management to expect research to produce results measurable in dollars and cents. It is entirely reasonable for auditors to believe that scientists who know exactly where they are going and how they will get there should not be distracted by the necessity of keeping one eye on the cash register while the other eye is on the microscope. Nor, if regularity and conformity to a standard pattern are as desirable to the scientist as the writing of his papers would appear to reflect , is management to be blamed for discriminating against the "odd balls" among researchers in favor of more conventional thinkers who "work well with the team".

1. The author wants to prove with the example of Isaac Newton that _____.
    A. inquiring minds are more important than scientific experiments
    B. science advances when fruitful researches are conducted
    C. scientists seldom forget the essential nature of research
    D. unpredictability weighs less than prediction in scientific research

2. The author asserts that scientists _____.
    A. shouldn't replace "scientific method" with imaginative thought
    B. shouldn't neglect to speculate on unpredictable things
    C. should write more concise reports for technical journals
    D. should be confident about their research findings

3. It seems that some young scientists _____.
    A. have a keen interest in prediction   B. often speculate on the future
    C. think highly of creative thinking   D. stick to "scientific method"

4. The author implies that the results of scientific research _____.
    A. may not be as profitable as they are expected
    B. can be measured in dollars and cents
    C. rely on conformity to a standard pattern
    D. are mostly underestimated by management

核心词汇注释

preparedness [prɪ'peədnɪs] *n.* 有准备；已准备

gravity ['ɡrævɪtɪ] *n.* 地心引力；重力

unpredictable [ˌʌnprɪ'dɪktəb(ə)l] *adj.* 不可预知的

graph [ɡrɑːf] *n.* 图表；曲线图

speculate ['spekjuleɪt] *vi.* 推测；思索；做投机买卖

consistent [kən'sɪst(ə)nt] *adj.* 一致的；调和的；坚固的；[数、统]相容的

auditor ['ɔːdɪtə(r)] *n.* 计员；核数师

distracted [dɪs'træktɪd] *adj.* 心烦意乱的

microscope ['maɪkrəskəup] *n.* 显微镜

discriminating [dɪ'skrɪmɪneɪtɪŋ] *adj.* 识别的；有差别的；有识别力的

长难句剖析

【文章难句】Nor, if regularity and conformity to a standard pattern are as desirable to the scientist as the writing of his papers would appear to reflect, is management to be blamed for discriminating against the "odd balls" among researchers in favor of more conventional thinkers who "work well with the team".

【结构分析】本句是一个主从复合句。主句是一个倒装句，主语是 management，谓语是 is。由于 nor 放在句首，所以句子倒装。who 引导的定语从句修饰 thinkers。前面的 if 引导了一个条件状语从句，其中包含一个 as…as…句型。

【参考译文】如果正像他们的论文所反映的那样，规律性和符合标准模式是那位科学家的理想的话，我们也不能指责管理部门歧视研究人员中的那些"思维另类"，而青睐那些以更传统方式思维的"擅长团队协作"的思考者。

全文参考译文

在实践中，科学与其说是依赖有准备的实践，不如说是依赖实验观察者有准备的头脑。艾萨克·牛顿爵士通过对苹果落地现象进行推理，发现了万有引力定律。多少个世纪以来许多地方一直都有苹果坠落，成千上万的人看到苹果落地。而牛顿多年来一直对月球和行星绕轨道运行的原因感到好奇。是什么力量使得它们处在现在的位置？它们为何不落到天空之外呢？苹果向下跌落到地上而不是向上飞到树上的这一事实，回答了牛顿长期以来对月球和行星所持有的疑惑。月球和行星是天空中更大的果实。

有多少人考虑过苹果向上飞到树上的可能性呢？牛顿考虑过，因为他不愿对任何事情作预料。他只是喜欢思索。他的头脑随时为思考不可预料的事做准备。不可预知性是科学研究不可或缺的一个重要特征。如果没有无法预言的东西，你就不会去研究。在为科学杂志撰写枯燥乏味的报告时，科学家们经常忘记这一点，可是历史上却不乏这样的实例。

在和一些科学家，尤其是青年科学家交谈时，你可能会形成这样一种印象：他们找到了"科学的方法"——一种替代想象思维的方法。我曾出席过一些科研会议。在会上有人问一位科学家继续某项实验是否明智。这位科学家皱了皱眉头，看了看图表，然后说："数据还不是太充分"。主管预算的人员说："这点我们知道，但你是怎么想的？值得继续进行吗？你认为我们可以期待发生什么呢？"这位科学家感到很震惊，他没想到他们会叫他作出预测。

当然，这几乎等于说：这位科学家成了他自己论文的受害者。他们对实验结果所下的结论是如此不用质疑、如此的一致，以至于不仅让他们本人，而且也让工商管理部门相信其预料的准确性。假使实验完全依照科学杂志报告中所说的那样按事先的计划去执行，那么管理部门期待研究成果可以用美元、美分来衡量，这完全符合逻辑。审计员完全有理由相信，那些确切地了解自己的目标，并且知道如何实现这一目标的科学家完全没有必要分心，一边关注经费，一边关注实验了。如果正像他们的论文所反映的那样，规律性和与符合标准模式是那位科学家的理想的话，我们也不能指责管理部门歧视研究人员中的"思维另类"，而青睐那些以更传统方式思维的"擅长团队协作"的思考者。

题目答案与解析

1. 作者引用艾萨克·牛顿的例子是想要证明 ＿＿＿＿＿。
   A．爱追根究底的头脑比科学实验更重要
   B．当进行富有成效的探索时，科学就会向前发展
   C．科学家很少忽略研究的本质特性
   D．在科学研究中，不可预知性没有可预知性重要
   【答案】A
   【解析】从文章第 1 段的内容可知，在实践中，科学与其说是依赖有准备的实践，不如

说是依赖实验观察者有准备的头脑。艾萨克·牛顿爵士通过对苹果落地现象进行推理，发现了万有引力定律。多少个世纪以来许多地方一直都有苹果坠落，成千上万的人看到苹果落地。而牛顿多年来一直对月球和行星绕轨道运行的原因感到好奇。"苹果向下跌落到地上而不是向上飞到树上的这一事实回答了牛顿长期以来对月球和行星所持的疑惑。从第2段的内容可知，有多少人会考虑过苹果飞落到树上的可能呢？牛顿这样做了，因为他不是在打算预言什么。他只是对此感到奇怪。他的大脑乐于接受那些无法预言的东西；不可预知性是探索的一个重要特性。如果没有无法预言的东西，你就不会去研究。据此可知，作者引用艾萨克·牛顿的例子是想证明—— 虽然科学依赖实验，但它更依赖实验观察者的心理准备状态，不可预知性是探索的一个重要特性。A项与文意相符，因此A项为正确答案。

2. 作者声称，科学家们 _____。

　　A．不应该用想象思维代替"科学方法" 　　B．不应该忽视对不可预知事物的推测

　　C．应该为学术杂志写更简洁的报告 　　D．应该对他们的研究发现有信心

【答案】B

【解析】从文章第2段的内容可知，不可预知性是探索的一个重要特性。如果没有无法预言的东西，你就不会去研究。在为学术刊物撰写枯燥乏味的报告时，科学家往往会忽略这一点，但是，历史上不乏这类实例。从第3段的内容可知，在与一些科学家交谈时，你可能会形成这种印象—— 科学家觉得，"科学方法"是想象思维的替代品。对于有人竟然要求那位科学家作出推测这种事情，他感到震惊；从文章最后一段的内容可知，这说明这位科学家已经成为他自己写的报告的受害者。据此可知，作者认为，科学家不喜欢推测不可预知的事物，这种作法会害人害己。B项与文章的意思相符，因此B项为正确答案。

3. 一些年轻的科学家似乎 _____。

　　A．对预测很感兴趣 　　B．常常预测未来

　　C．高度重视创造性思维 　　D．坚持"科学方法"

【答案】D

【解析】本题可参照文章的第3段。从中可知，在与一些科学家，尤其是年轻科学家交谈时，你可能会形成这样一种印象—— 科学家觉得，"科学方法"是想象思维的替代品；在一次研讨会上，有人问一位科学家继续某项实验是否明智；这位科学家皱了皱眉头，看了看图表，然后说，"数据还不是太充分"；对于有人竟然要求他做推测这种事情，该科学家感到震惊。据此可知，年轻科学家认为，"科学方法"可以代替想象思维。D项与文意相符，因此D项为正确答案。

4. 作者暗示了科学研究的成果 _____。

　　A．可能不如人们预期的那样有利可图 　　B．能够以美元来衡量

　　C．依赖于符合一种标准模式 　　D．大都被管理部门低估了

【答案】A

【解析】本题可参照文章的第4段。从中可知，假如实验完全依照科学杂志上的报告所说的那样按事先的计划去执行，那么管理部门期望研究能够带来可用美元衡量的成果是完全合理的；审计员完全有理由相信，那些确切地了解自己的目标并且知道如何实现目标的科学家没有必要分心走神——不必一边关注经费，一边关注实验；如果正像他们的论文所反映的那样，正规和符合标准模式是那位科学家的理想的话，那么我们也不能责备管理部门区别

对待研究人员中的那些"思维另类",而青睐那些"擅长团队协作"、以更传统的方式思维的思考者。据此可知,作者认为科学研究所取得的成果并没有如预期的那样带来很大利润。A项与文章的意思相符,因此 A 项为正确答案。

Text 4

Few creations of big technology capture the imagination like giant dams. Perhaps it is humankind's long suffering at the mercy of flood and drought that makes the ideal of forcing the waters to do our bidding so fascination. But to be fascinated is also, sometimes, to be blind Several giant dam projects threaten to do more harm than good.

The lesson from dams is that big is not always beautiful. It doesn't help that building a big, powerful dam has become a symbol of achievement for nations and people striving to assert themselves. Egypt's leadership in the Arab world was cemented by the Aswan High Dam. Turkey's bid for First World status includes the giant Ataturk Dam.

But big dams tend not to work as intended. The Aswan Dam, for example stopped the Nile flooding but deprived Egypt of the fertile silt that floods left—all in return for a giant reservoir of disease which is now so full of silt that it barely generates electricity.

And yet, the myth of controlling the waters persists. This week, in the heart of civilized Europe, Slovaks and Hungarians stopped just short of sending in the troops in their contention over a dam on the Danube. The huge complex will probably have all the usual problems of big dams. But Slovakia is bidding for independence from the Czechs, and now needs a dam to prove itself.

Meanwhile, in India, the World Bank has given the go ahead to the even more wrong headed Narmada Dam. And the bank has done this even though its advisors say the dam will cause hardship for the powerless and environmental destruction. The benefits are for the powerful, but they are far from guaranteed.

Proper scientific study of the impacts of dams and of the cost and benefits of controlling water can help to resolve these conflicts. Hydroelectric power and flood control and irrigation are possible without building monster dams. But when you are dealing with myths, it is hard to be either proper, or scientific. It is time that the world learned the lessons of Aswan. You don't need a dam to be saved.

1. The third sentence of paragraph 1 implies that _____.
   A. people would be happy if they shut their eyes to reality
   B. the blind could be happier than the sighted
   C. over-excited people tend to neglect vital things
   D. fascination makes people lose their eyesight

2. In Paragraph 5, "the powerless" probably refers to _____.
   A. areas short of electricity   B. dams without power stations
   C. poor countries around India   D. common people in the Narmada Dam area

3. What is the myth concerning giant dams?
   A. They bring in more fertile soil.   B. They help defend the country.

C. They strengthen international ties.　　D. They have universal control of the waters.

4. What the author tries to suggest may best be interpreted as "_____".

A. It's no use crying over spilt milk　　B. More haste, less speed

C. Look before you leap　　D. He who laughs last laughs best

核心词汇注释

dam [dæm] *n.* 水坝；障碍
　v. 控制；筑坝

drought [draʊt] *n.* 干旱；缺乏

bidding ['bɪdɪŋ] *n.* 命令；出价；邀请

cement [sɪ'ment] *n.* 水泥；接合剂
　vt. 接合；用水泥涂；巩固
　vi. 粘牢

turkey ['tɜːkɪ] *n.* 火鸡；无用的东西
　Turkey　*n.* 土耳其

Nile [naɪl] *n.* 尼罗河（非洲东北部河流）

deprive [dɪ'praɪv] *vt.* 剥夺；使丧失

reservoir ['rezəvwɑː(r)] *n.* 水库；蓄水池

persist [pə'sɪst] *vi.* 坚持；持续

Hungarian [hʌŋ'geərɪən] *adj.* 匈牙利的
　n. 匈牙利人

contention [kən'tenʃ(ə)n] *n.* 争夺；争论；争辩；论点

Danube ['dænjuːb] *n.* 多瑙河（欧洲南部河流）

Czech [tʃek] *n.* 捷克人（语）
　adj. 捷克斯洛伐克的，捷克斯洛伐克人（语）的

irrigation [ˌɪrɪ'geɪʃ(ə)n] *n.* 灌溉；冲洗

长难句剖析

【文章难句】The Aswan Dam, for example stopped the Nile flooding but deprived Egypt of the fertile silt that floods left — all in return for a giant reservoir of disease which is now so full of silt that it barely generates electricity.

【结构分析】本句的主干是 The Aswan Dam stopped…deprived…。that floods left 修饰的是 the fertile silt。破折号后面的内容表示结果，由 in return for 引出，句末是一个由 which 引导的定语从句，修饰 disease。

【参考译文】比如，阿斯旺水坝虽然防止了尼罗河的洪水泛滥，但埃及失去了洪水留下的肥沃淤泥。取而代之的却是一个病态的大水库，水库里满是淤泥，几乎发不了电。

全文参考译文

重大技术的创造中很少有哪个比巨型大坝更让人神往。可能正是因为人类久受旱涝之苦，才使得"让洪水听从人的调遣"这种理想如此令人痴迷。但令人痴迷有时也会令人盲目。有好几个巨型大坝工程有弊大于利的预兆。

大的并不总是美的，这是修建大坝的教训。建一个功能巨大的大水坝象征着国家和人民在努力显示自身力量已取得的成功，但对于国家和人民却没有好处。埃及在阿拉伯世界的领导地位由于阿斯旺大坝得以巩固和加强；土耳其为争取跻身于第一世界所做的努力中也包括修建阿塔特克大坝。

可巨型水坝不一定会像预想的那样发挥作用。例如阿斯旺大坝，它抵挡住了尼罗河的洪

水。但也使埃及失去了洪水冲击后留下的肥沃土壤,取而代之的却是一个病态的大水库。如今的水库积满泥沙,几乎发不出电来。

可是控制洪水的神话还在继续传播。这星期,在文明欧洲的中心地区,斯洛伐克人和匈牙利人为在多瑙河建坝问题上发生争执,差一点儿就要调遣军队了。在这一大型工程上,可能会出现大坝修建上所有的常见问题。但是,斯洛伐克人正在搞独立,要脱离捷克,他们需要建大坝来证实自己的强大。

与此同时,在印度,世界银行已经给那个更离谱的纳尔马达水坝发放了许可证。尽管世界银行的顾问认为那个水坝会给那里的平民百姓带来灾难,会破坏那里的生态环境,但是世界银行还是发放了许可证。这样做是在为那些有权势的人带来好处,但这些好处也没有保障。

对建坝造成的危害以及治水的耗资和收益进行合理的科学研究,有助于解决这些矛盾。进行水力发电、治洪,以及灌溉并非一定要修建巨型大坝。但如果你迷信神话,就很难做到合理或科学。如今是世界各国从阿斯旺大坝的事例中吸取教训的时候了。人们并不需要大坝来拯救自己。

题目答案与解析

1. 第 1 段第 3 句话暗示了 _____。
   A. 如果人们无视现实,他们就会感到幸福
   B. 盲人可能比看得见的人更幸福
   C. 过于兴奋的人往往忽视至关重要的东西
   D. 迷恋使人们丧失视力

   【答案】C

   【解析】从文章第 1 段的内容可知,重大的科技创造中很少有哪个比巨型水坝更让人神往;可能正是因为人类久受旱涝之苦,才使得"让洪水听从人的调遣"这种理想如此令人痴迷;但是,令人痴迷有时也会令人盲目;好几个巨型水坝工程有弊大于利的预兆。据此可知,人们往往因为盲目乐观而失去理智,缺乏对关系重大事情的判断力。C 项与文章的意思相符,因此 C 项为正确答案。

2. 第 5 段中的 powerless 可能是指 _____。
   A. 缺电的地区
   B. 没有发电站的水坝
   C. 印度周边的贫穷国家
   D. 纳玛达水坝地区的普通人民

   【答案】D

   【解析】从文章第 5 段的内容可知,在印度,世界银行已经给那个更离谱的纳尔马达水坝发放了许可证;尽管世界银行的顾问认为那个水坝会给平民百姓带来苦难,会破坏那里的环境,但是世界银行还是发放了许可证;这样做是在给那些有权势的人带来好处。据此可知,powerless 可能的意思应该与 powerful(有权势的人)之意相反,也就是"没有权势的人",即平民百姓。D 项与文章的意思相符,因此 D 项为正确答案。

3. 什么是关于大型水坝的神话?
   A. 大型水坝带来更多肥沃的泥土。
   B. 大型水坝帮助保卫国家。
   C. 大型水坝巩固了国际关系。
   D. 大型水坝完全控制了洪水。

   【答案】D

【解析】从文章第 1 段的内容可知，好几个巨型水坝工程有弊大于利的预兆；从文章第 3 段的内容可知，但是巨型水坝不一定会像预想的那样发挥作用；从文章第 4 段的内容可知，控制洪水的神话仍在延续；从文章最后一段的内容可知，进行水力发电、治洪，以及灌溉并非一定要修建巨型大坝。但如果你迷信神话，就很难做到合理或科学。如今是世界各国从阿斯旺大坝的事例中吸取教训的时候了。人们并不需要大坝来拯救自己。据此可知，有关大型水坝的神话是——人们相信大型水坝控制了洪水，但事实证明这种神话不对。D 项与文章的意思相符，因此 D 项为正确答案。

4. 作者尽力暗示的意思可以最恰当地解释为 "_____"。

    A. 覆水难收   B. 欲速则不达

    C. 三思而后行   D. 笑到最后者笑得最开心

【答案】C

【解析】从文章第 1 段的内容可知，很少有重大的科技创造物像巨型水坝那样激发人的想象力；可能正是由于人类久受旱涝之苦，才使得 "让水听从人的调遣" 这种理想如此令人痴迷；但是，令人着迷有时也使人盲目；好几个巨型水坝工程有弊大于利的预兆；从第 2 段的内容可知，从修建水坝得到的教训是——大的并不总是美的；从文章第 3 段的内容可知，但是巨型水坝往往不如预期的那样发挥作用；从第 4 段的内容可知，然而，控制洪水的神话仍在延续；第 5 段举例说明了这一点；从文章最后一段的内容可知，彻底、科学地研究大坝将造成的影响，研究控制洪水的成本和效益，有助于人们解决这些问题；是整个世界从阿斯旺水坝中吸取教训的时候了；人类并不需要水坝来拯救自己。据此可知，作者想提醒人们不要再相信大型水坝可以完全控制洪水的神话，不能因为盲目乐观而失去理智，应该彻底、科学地研究问题，从阿斯旺水坝中吸取教训，解决面临的实际困难。C 项与作者的意图相符，因此 C 项为正确答案。

Unit 19

Well, no gain without pain, they say. But what about pain without gain? Everywhere you go in America, you hear tales of corporate revival. What is harder to establish is whether the productivity revolution that businessmen assume they are presiding over is for real.

The official statistics are mildly discouraging. They show that, if you lump manufacturing and services together, productivity has grown on average by 1.2% since 1987. That is somewhat faster than the average during the previous decade. And since 1991, productivity has increased by about 2% a year, which is more than twice the 1978-1987 average. The trouble is that part of the recent acceleration is due to the usual rebound that occurs at this point in a business cycle, and so is not conclusive evidence of a revival in the underlying trend. There is, as Robert Rubin, the treasury secretary, says, a "disjunction" between the mass of business anecdote that points to a leap in productivity and the picture reflected by the statistics.

Some of this can be easily explained. New ways of organizing the workplace all that reengineering and downsizing — are only one contribution to the overall productivity of an economy, which is driven by many other factors such as joint investment in equipment and machinery, new technology, and investment in education and training. Moreover, most of the changes that companies make are intended to keep them profitable, and this need not always mean increasing productivity: switching to new markets or improving quality can matter just as much.

Two other explanations are more speculative. First, some of the business restructuring of recent years may have been ineptly done. Second, even if it was well done, it may have spread much less widely than people suppose.

Leonard Schlesinger, a Harvard academic and former chief executive of Au Bong Pain, a rapidly growing chain of bakery cafes, says that much "reengineering" has been crude. In many cases, he believes, the loss of revenue has been greater than the reductions in cost. His colleague, Michael Beer, says that far too many companies have applied reengineering in a mechanistic fashion, chopping out costs without giving sufficient thought to long term profitability. BBDO's Al Rosenshine is blunter. He dismisses a lot of the work of reengineering consultants as mere rubbish — "the worst sort of ambulance cashing".

1. According to the author, the American economic situation is _____.
   A. not as good as it seems   B. at its turning point
   C. much better than it seems   D. near to complete recovery
2. The official statistics on productivity growth _____.
   A. exclude the usual rebound in a business cycle

    B.　fall short of businessmen's anticipation

    C.　meet the expectation of business people

    D.　fail to reflect the true state of economy

3.　The author raises the question "what about pain without gain?" because _____.

    A.　he questions the truth of "no gain without pain"

    B.　he does not think the productivity revolution works

    C.　he wonders if the official statistics are misleading

    D.　he has conclusive evidence for the revival of businesses

4.　Which of the following statements is NOT mentioned in the passage?

    A.　Radical reforms are essential for the increase of productivity.

    B.　New ways of organizing workplaces may help to increase productivity.

    C.　The reduction of costs is not a sure way to gain long term profitability.

    D.　The consultants are a bunch of good for nothings.

核心词汇注释

preside [prɪˈzaɪd] *v.* 主持

lump [lʌmp] *n.* 块（尤指小块）；肿块；笨人
  vt. 使成块状；混在一起；忍耐；笨重地移动
  vi. 结块

rebound [ˈriːbaʊnd] *n.* 回弹
  v. 回弹

treasury [ˈtreʒərɪ] *n.* 财政部；国库

disjunction [dɪsˈdʒʌŋkʃ(ə)n] *n.* 分离；分裂；折断

anecdote [ˈænɪkdəʊt] *n.* 轶事；奇闻

downsize [daʊnˈsaɪz] *vt.* 以较小尺寸设计（或制造）；缩小（汽车等）的外部尺寸

speculative [ˈspekjʊlətɪv] *adj.* 投机的

inept [ɪˈnept] *adj.* 不适当的；无能的；不称职的

chopping [ˈtʃɒpɪŋ] 波浪汹涌的；硕大强健的

长难句剖析

【文章难句】What is harder to establish is whether the productivity revolution that businessmen assume they are presiding over is for real.

【结构分析】本句中，What is harder to establish 是主语。that 引导的定语从句修饰 the productivity revolution。本句的难点在于理解 whether...is for real 意为 "是否是真实的"。

【参考译文】更难以证明的是企业家自认为是他们引领的这场生产力革命是否名副其实。

全文参考译文

    人们说，不劳则不获。但是，要是劳而无获呢？不管走到美国任何地方，你都将能听到公司复兴的故事。然而，更加难以证明的是企业家自认为是他们引领的这场生产力革命是否名副其实。

    官方的统计数字多少有些令人失望。数据显示，如果把制造业和服务业合在一块计算的话，那么，从 1987 年以来，生产力平均每年提高 1.2%，这比在上一个十年期内的平均增幅大。而且，从 1991 年起，生产力每年约增长 2%，这一比率是 1978～1987 年度平均增长指数的两倍。然而，近期的增长一定程度上是由于商业周期运行至这个阶段所出现的常见反弹所引发的。因此，还不能以此作为确凿的证据来证实这一潜在趋势中会出现经济复苏。正像财政部长 Robert Rubin 所说的那样，商业界大量神话似乎说明生产力大幅度提高，这同官方的统计数字所反映出的情况"有分歧"。

有些还容易解释。组织工作场所的新办法——包括机构重组和缩减规模的所有方法——仅仅是促进某一经济实体的综合生产力水平的一项措施，还有许多其他因素推动生产力的提高。例如，联合投资机械设备、采用新技术，以及人才教育培训投资等。此外，公司进行的大部分改革是以赢利为目的，这一前提并不总是意味着提高生产力；转入新的市场或提高产品质量能够达到一样的效果。

另外两种解释理论性较强。有的说，近年来一些企业的改组并未奏效；有的说，即使奏效了，也没有像人们想象的那样大量推广。

哈佛大学学者 Leonard Schlesinger 是急速扩大的美味面包连锁店的前任总裁。他说，大多数的"企业改组"都相当粗糙。他还认为，多数企业效益上的损失大大超出成本的降低。他的同事 Michael Beer 说，为数更多的公司以简单机械的方式进行机构重组，降低了成本，可对长期赢利缺乏长远考虑。BBDO 公司的 Al Rosenshine 的说法更加不留情面，他对重组顾问们做的大量工作视而不见，认为那些完全是垃圾——典型的"劳而无获"。

题目答案与解析

1. 依照作者的观点，美国的经济状况 _____。
   A. 不如看起来那么好　　　　　B. 处于转折点
   C. 比看起来的好得多　　　　　D. 即将全面恢复
   【答案】A
   【解析】从文章第 1 段的内容可知，在美国，无论你到什么地方，你都会听到有关公司复兴的故事；更难以证实的是企业家自以为是他们在引领的这场生产力革命是否名副其实；从文章第 2 段的内容可知，官方的统计数字多少有些令人失望；统计表明，生产力平均每年增长 1.2%，但近期的增长一定程度上是由于商业周期运行至这个时段所出现的常见反弹引发的，因此，不能证实会出现经济复苏；正如财政部长 Robert Rubin 所说的那样，大量的商业神话似乎说明生产力剧增，这同官方的统计数字所反映出的情况"有分歧"；在随后的两段中，文章分析了造成这种现象的原因；从文章最后的内容可知，一些企业的重组没有达到预期目的。据此可知，美国目前的经济形势不如表现的那样好。A 项与文章的意思相符，因此 A 项为正确答案。

2. 官方关于生产力增长的统计 _____。
   A. 没有包括商业循环中通常出现的反弹　B. 没有达到商业人士的预期目的
   C. 达到了商业人士的预期目标　　　　　D. 没有反映出经济的真实状况
   【答案】B
   【解析】本题可参照文章的第 2 段。从中可知，官方的统计数字有些令人失望；数据显示，如果把制造业和服务业合在一起计算的话，那么，从 1987 年以来，生产力平均每年增长 1.2%；这比在上一个十年期内的平均增幅大；从 1991 年起，生产力每年约增长 2%，这一比率是 1978～1987 年平均增长指数的两倍；问题是，近期的增长一定程度上是由于商业周期运行至这个时段所出现的常见反弹所引发的，因此，不能以此作为确凿的证据来证实在这一潜在的趋势中会出现经济复苏；正如财政部长所说的那样，大量的商业奇闻显示生产力剧增，这同官方的统计数字所反映出的情况"有分歧"。据此可知，有关生产力增长的官方统计数据与商业界人士的传说不符，说明生产力并没有如官方人士所说的那样增长了。B 项与文章的意思相符，因此 B 项为正确答案。

3. 作者提出"劳而无获又会怎样？"这一问题的原因是 _____。

    A. 他怀疑"不劳无获"这一说法的真实性

    B. 他认为生产力革命没有成效

    C. 他怀疑官方的统计是否在误导人们

    D. 他有经济复兴确凿的证据

【答案】B

【解析】从文章第 1 段的内容可知，有人说，不劳无获；但若是劳而无获又会怎样呢？在美国，无论你到什么地方，你都会听到公司复兴的故事；更难以证实的是企业家自以为是他们在引领的这场生产力革命是否名副其实；从第 4 段的内容可知，有人认为，近几年，一些企业的改组可能并未奏效；另一些人认为，即使改组奏效了，也不如人们所想象的那样大量推广；作者最后引用专家的话进一步说明目前采取的措施没有成效。据此可知，作者认为当前的生产力革命没有什么成效。B 项与文章的意思相符，因此 B 项为正确答案。

4. 下面各项说法中，本文没有提到哪项？

    A. 彻底的改革对生产力的增长至关重要。

    B. 统筹安排工作场所的新方法可能有助于提高生产力。

    C. 降低成本并不是获得长期效益的可靠办法。

    D. 顾问是一群无用之辈。

【答案】A

【解析】从文章第 3 段第 2 句话的内容可知，组织工作场所的新方法——包括机构重组和缩减规模的所有方法——仅仅是促进某一经济实体综合生产力提高的一个因素，还有许多其他因素推动生产力的提高；这说明文中提到了 B 项；文章最后一段第 2、3 句话证实了文中提到了 C 项；从文章最后一段最后一句话的内容可知，Al Rosenshine 对重组顾问的许多工作不屑一顾，认为那只不过是荒唐的事情——典型的"劳而无获"；这证明了文中提到了 D 项；只有 A 项文中没有提到，因此 A 项为正确答案。

Text 2

Science has long had an uneasy relationship with other aspects of culture. Think of Gallileo's 17th century trial for his rebelling belief before the Catholic Church or poet William Blake's harsh remarks against the mechanistic worldview of Isaac Newton. The schism between science and the humanities has, if anything, deepened in this century.

Until recently, the scientific community was so powerful that it could afford to ignore its critics—but no longer. As funding for science has declined, scientists have attacked "antiscience" in several books, notably Higher Superstition, by Paul R.Gross, a biologist at the University of Verginia, and Norman Levitt, a mathematician at Rutgers University; and The Demon Haunted World, by Carl Sagan of Cornell University. Defenders of science have also voiced their concerns at meetings such as "The Flight from Science and Reason," held in New York City in 1995, and "Science in the Age of (Mis) information," which assembled last June near Buffalo.

Antiscience clearly means different things to different people. Gross and Levitt find fault primarily with sociologists, philosophers and other academics who have questioned science's objectivity. Sagan is more concerned with those who believe in ghosts, creationism and other phenomena that contradict the scientific worldview.

A survey of news stories in 1996 reveals that the antiscience tag has been attached to many other groups as well, from authorities who advocated the elimination of the last remaining stocks of smallpox virus to Republicans who advocated decreased funding for basic research.

Few would dispute that the term applies to the Unbomber, those manifesto, published in 1995, scorns science and longs for return to a pretechnological utopia. But surely that does not mean environmentalists concerned about uncontrolled industrial growth are antiscience, as an essay in U.S. News & World Report last May seemed to suggest.

The environmentalists, inevitably, respond to such critics. The true enemies of science, argues Paul Ehrlich of Stanford University, a pioneer of environmental studies, are those who question the evidence supporting global warming, the depletion of the ozone layer and other consequences of industrial growth.

Indeed, some observers fear that the antiscience epithet is in danger of becoming meaningless. "The term 'antiscience' can lump together too many, quite different things," notes Harvard University philosopher Gerald Holton in his 1993 work Science and Anti Science. "They have in common only one thing that they tend to annoy or threaten those who regard themselves as more enlightened."

1. The word "schism" (Line 3, Para. 1) in the context probably means _____.

   A. confrontation   B. dissatisfaction   C. separation   D. contempt

2. Paragraphs 2 and 3 are written to _____.

   A. discuss the cause of the decline of science's power

   B. show the author's sympathy with scientists

   C. explain the way in which science develops

   D. exemplify the division of science and the humanities

3. Which of the following is true according to the passage?

   A. Environmentalists were blamed for antiscience in an essay.

   B. Politicians are not subject to the labeling of antiscience.

   C. The "more enlightened" tend to tag others as antiscience

   D. Tagging environmentalists as "antiscience" is justifiable

4. The author's attitude toward the issue of "science vs. antiscience" is _____.

   A. impartial   B. subjective   C. biased   D. puzzling

核心词汇注释

schism [ˈsɪz(ə)m] *n.*（政治组织等的）分裂；教派

humanity [hjuːˈmænɪtɪ] *n.* 人性；人类；博爱；仁慈

antiscience [ˌæntɪˈsaɪəns] *n.* 科学无用论 *adj.* 反对（或摒弃）科学的

mathematician [ˌmæθəməˈtɪʃ(ə)n] *n.* 数学家

creationism [kriːˈeɪʃənɪzəm] *n.* 创造宇宙说；特别创造说

smallpox [ˈsmɔːlpɒks] *n.* [医] 天花

manifesto [ˌmænɪˈfestəʊ] *n.* 宣言；声明

depletion [dɪˈpliːʃ n] *n.* 损耗

epithet [ˈepɪθet] *n.* 绰号；称号

enlightened [ɪnˈlaɪt(ə)nd] *v.* 启迪 *adj.* 开明的；有知识的

长难句剖析

【文章难句】A survey of news stories in 1996 reveals that the antiscience tag has been attached to many other groups as well, from authorities who advocated the elimination of the last remaining stocks of smallpox virus to Republicans who advocated decreased funding for basic research.

【结构分析】本句主干是 a survey reveals that…，that 引导宾语从句。在这个宾语从句中，主语是 the antiscience tag, from…to…用来补充说明 groups。两个以 who 为连接词引导的是定语从句，分别修饰的是 authorities 和 Republicans。

【参考译文】1996 年新闻报道的调查显示：反科学的标签也已贴在其他许多的群体身上，从提倡消灭残留天花病毒的专家到倡议削减基础研究经费的共和党人。

全文参考译文

科学和文化的其他方面关系一向紧张。想一想，17 世纪的伽利略为他叛逆性的信仰而遭到天主教会的审判；还有诗人威廉·布莱克对艾萨克·牛顿的机械论世界观所发表的尖锐批判。在本世纪，如果说有什么不同的话，那就是科学和人文科学间的裂痕更深了。

以前，科学界势力如此强大，以致可以对批评者置之不理——但现在不一样了。因为科研经费减少，科学家推出几本书来反击"反科学"的倾向。其中，值得关注的有弗吉尼亚大学生物学家 Paul R. Gross 与拉特格斯大学数学家 Norman Levitt 合著的《高级迷信》以及康奈尔大学的 Carl Sagan 著的《鬼怪世界》。

科学捍卫者还在集会上发表他们的忧虑，例如，1995 年在纽约城举行的"从科学和理性逃亡"大会上，以及去年 6 月在布法罗附近召开的"信息（迷信）时代的科学"集会上。

对于不同的人来说，反科学显然有不同的含义。Gross 和 Levitt 主要挑那些质疑科学客观性的社会学家、哲学家以及其他学者的毛病。萨根更关注那些相信鬼怪、上帝造物以及其他与科学世界观背道而驰的人。

1996 年新闻报道的调查显示：反科学的标签也已贴在其他许多群体身上，从提倡消灭残留天花病毒的官员到倡议削减基础研究经费的共和党人。

如把该词用到反原子弹组织身上也不会引起很大争议。该组织在 1995 年公开发表声明藐视科学，渴望回到前技术时代的理想社会。可这绝不是说，对不加制止的工业发展表示担忧的环保主义者也是反科学的，而去年 5 月份刊登在《美国新闻与世界报道》上的一篇文章好像含有此种暗示。

环保主义者不可避免地要对这种抨击作出回应。居于环境研究前沿的斯坦福大学的 Paul Ehrlich 认为，科学的真正敌人是那些对工业增长使全球变暖、臭氧层日渐稀薄及其他严重后果的证据提出质疑的人。

确实如此，一些观察家担忧反科学这个词语会变得没有意义。哈佛大学的哲学家 Gerald Holton 在他 1993 年发表的《科学与反科学》的著作中写道："'反科学'一词能够包含太多的完全不同的东西，而它们只有一个共同点那就是会激怒或威胁那些自以为是、自恃清高的人。"

题目答案与解析

1. 在上下文中，单词"schism"（第 1 段第 3 行）的意思可能是 _____。
   A. 对峙　　　　　　B. 不满　　　　　　C. 分离　　　　　　D. 轻视
   【答案】C
   【解析】本题可参照文章的第 1 段。从中可知，科学与文化的其他方面关系一向紧张；然后列举了伽利略的受审和威廉·布莱克对艾萨克·牛顿的尖刻批评这两个例子来说明这一问题；最后一句话指出：在本世纪，如果说有什么不同的话，那就是，科学与人文科学之间的裂痕更加深了。据此可知，"schism"一词在上下文中的意思应该是"分裂"。C 项与文章的意思相符，因此 C 项为正确答案。

2. 写第 2 段和第 3 段的目的是 _____。
   A. 讨论科学影响力下降的原因　　　　B. 表明作者同情科学家
   C. 解释科学发展的方式　　　　　　　D. 例证科学与人文学科的分裂
   【答案】D
   【解析】从文章第 1 段的内容可知，自然科学与人文科学之间的裂痕甚至加深了；文章第 2、3 段对此作了具体说明：以前，科学界的势力非常强大，以致可以对批评者置之不理——但现在不一样了；因为科研经费减少，科学家推出几本书来反击"反科学"的倾向；科学捍卫者还在集会上发表了他们的忧虑。据此可知，第 2 段和第 3 段是用来具体说明"自然科学与人文科学之间的裂痕加深了"这一主题的。D 项与文章的意思相符，因此 D 项为正确答案。

3. 依照本文的观点，以下哪项说法是正确的？
   A. 环保人士被一篇文章斥责为反科学。
   B. 政客不容易被贴上反科学的标签。
   C. 那些"更开明的人"往往把别人称为反科学。
   D. 把环保人士当做"反科学"是有理由的。
   【答案】A
   【解析】A 项与文章的意思相符，依据是文章第 6 段的第 2 句话"可这绝不是说，对不加制止的工业发展表示担忧的环保主义者也是反科学的，而去年 5 月份刊登在《美国新闻与世界报道》上的一篇文章好像含有此种暗示"；B 项不正确，从文章第 5 段的内容可知，1996 年新闻报道的调查显示，反科学的标签也贴到了其他许多团体的身上，从倡导消灭最后残留的天花病毒群的专家到倡议缩基础研究基金的共和党人；C 项不正确，依据是文章最后一段最后一句话，即"反科学"一词可以包含太多完全不同的东西，而它们唯一的共同之处就是——它们往往会激怒那些自以为是、自恃清高的人；D 项明显与文章的意思不符。

4.　对于"科学与反科学"的这场争端，作者的态度是 _____。

　　A．公平的　　　　　　B．主观的　　　　　　C．有偏见的　　　　　D．令人困惑的

【答案】A

【解析】本题可参照文章的第 1 段。从中可知，科学与文化其他方面关系一直紧张；本世纪，科学与人文科学之间的裂痕更深了；随后两段举例说明了科学家的做法——抨击他人，把别人说成是反科学；最后两段谈了一些人对此的反应。据此可知，作者只是客观地叙述了自然科学与人文科学（即"科学与反科学"）之间的争论，并没有发表自己的观点，说明他是公正的。因此 A 项为正确答案。

Text　3

Emerging from the 1980 census is the picture of a nation developing more and more regional competition, as population growth in the Northeast and Midwest reaches a near standstill.

This development — and its strong implications for U.S. politics and economy in years ahead — has enthroned the South as America's most densely populated region for the first time in the history of the nation's head counting.

Altogether, the U.S. population rose in the 1970s by 23.2 million people — numerically the third largest growth ever recorded in a single decade. Even so, that gain adds up to only 11.4 percent, lowest in American annual records except for the Depression years.

Americans have been migrating south and west in larger number since World War Ⅱ, and the pattern still prevails.

Three sun belt states — Florida, Texas and California — together had nearly 10 million more people in 1980 than a decade earlier. Among large cities, San Diego moved from 14th to 8th and San Antonio from 15th to 10th — with Cleveland and Washington .D.C, dropping out of the top 10.

Not all that shift can be attributed to the movement out of the snow belt, census officials say, Nonstop waves of immigrants played a role, too — and so did bigger crops of babies as yesterday's "baby boom" generation reached its child bearing years.

Moreover, demographers see the continuing shift south and west as joined by a related but newer phenomenon: More and more, Americans apparently are looking not just for places with more jobs but with fewer people, too. Some instances:

Regionally, the Rocky Mountain states reported the most rapid growth rate — 37.1 percent since 1970 in a vast area with only 5 percent of the U.S. population.

Among states, Nevada and Arizona grew fastest of all: 63.5 and 53.1 percent respectively. Except for Florida and Texas, the top 10 in rate of growth is composed of Western states with 7.5 million people — about 9 per square mile.

The flight from over crowdedness affects the migration from snow belt to more bearable climates.

Nowhere do 1980 census statistics dramatize more the American search for spacious living than in the Far West. There, California added 3.7 million to its population in the 1970s, more than any other state.

In that decade, however, large numbers also migrated from California, mostly to other parts of the West. Often they chose — and still are choosing — somewhat colder climates such as Oregon, Idaho and Alaska in order to escape smog, crime and other plagues of urbanization in the Golden State.

As a result, California's growth rate dropped during the 1970s, to 18.5 percent — little more than two thirds the 1960s growth figure and considerably below that of other Western states.

1. Discerned from the perplexing picture of population growth the 1980 census provided, America in 1970s _____.

    A. enjoyed the lowest net growth of population in history

    B. witnessed a southwestern shift of population

    C. underwent an unparalleled period of population growth

    D. brought to a standstill its pattern of migration since World War II

2. The census distinguished itself from previous studies on population movement in that _____.

    A. it stresses the climatic influence on population distribution

    B. it highlights the contribution of continuous waves of immigrants

    C. it reveals the Americans' new pursuit of spacious living

    D. it elaborates the delayed effects of yesterday's "baby boom"

3. We can see from the available statistics that _____.

    A. California was once the most thinly populated area in the whole U.S.

    B. the top 10 states in growth rate of population were all located in the West

    C. cities with better climates benefited unanimously from migration

    D. Arizona ranked second of all states in its growth rate of population

4. The word "demographers" (Line 1, Para. 7) most probably means _____.

    A. people in favor of the trend of democracy

    B. advocates of migration between states

    C. scientists engaged in the study of population

    D. conservatives clinging to old patterns of life

核心词汇注释

census ['sensəs] *n.* 人口普查

standstill ['stændstɪl] *n.* 停止，停顿

enthrone [ɪn'θrəʊn] *vt.* 立……为王；使登基；崇拜
vi. 热心

numerical [njuː'merɪk(ə)l] *adj.* 数字的；用数字表示的

prevail [prɪ'veɪl] *vi.* 流行，盛行；获胜，成功

demographer [di:'mɒɡrəfə(r)] *n.* 人口统计学家

respectively [rɪ'spektɪvlɪ] *adv.* 分别地，各
个地

dramatize ['dræmətaɪz] *vt.* 改编成为戏
剧；编写剧本　*vi.* 戏剧地表现

plague [pleɪg] *n.* 瘟疫；麻烦；苦恼；灾祸
vt. 折磨；使苦恼；使得灾祸

urbanization [ˌɜːb(ə)naɪ'zeɪʃ(ə)n] *n.* 都
市化

长难句剖析

【文章难句】Nonstop waves of immigrants played a role, too — and so did bigger crops of babies as yesterday's "baby boom" generation reached its child bearing years.

【结构分析】本句主干是 immigrants played a role…so did babies。as 引导的是原因状语从句。

【参考译文】持续的移民潮也起了一定的作用，"生育高峰"时期出生的一代人如今到了生育年龄，他们生育的大批婴儿也起了作用。

全文参考译文

1980 年的人口普查表明，随着东北部和中西部人口增长几乎停顿，区域性的竞争已愈演愈烈。

这一发展趋势及其对以后美国在制定政策和经济上的重大影响使得南方首次成了美国人口普查史上人口最稠密的地区。

总体上看，20 世纪 70 年代，美国人口共增加了 2 320 万——从数字上看，这是有记录以来十年期人口增长的第三高峰。即便如此，人口总数也只增加了 11.4%。除了大萧条时期，这是美国最低的年增长率。

自从第二次世界大战以来，美国人口一直大幅度向南部和西部地区迁移，到目前为止，这一趋势仍然不减。

在佛罗里达、得克萨斯和加利福尼亚这三个阳光充裕的州，1980 年的人口几乎比 10 年前增加了将近 1 000 万。在大城市排行榜上，圣地亚哥从第 14 位上升到第 8 位，圣安东尼奥从第 15 位上升到第 10 位，而克利夫兰和华盛顿特区却被挤出前十名之列。

人口普查官员说，并不是所有的迁移都是因为人们想搬出寒带地区，持续的移民潮加上还有当年"生育高峰"时期出生的孩子已经到了生育年龄，这些原因都在起着作用。

另外，人口统计学家发现，向南部和西部的不断迁移还伴随着一种与此相关却又与从前不同的现象：愈来愈多的美国人明显不再只寻找有更多就业机会的地方，他们还在寻找人口较少的地方。有以下例子为证；

从区域上看，落基山脉地区各州的人口增长率最高——有报告说，在这片幅员辽阔地带居住的人口仅占美国总人口的 5%，但自 1970 年开始，其增长率却上升到了 37.1%。

在各个州中，内华达州与亚利桑那州是增长率最高的两个州，分别为 63.5% 和 53.1%。除了佛罗里达州和得克萨斯州外，人口增长率排名前十位的是西部各州，共有 750 万人口——大约每平方英里有 9 个人。

逃离人口拥挤地区的做法影响了过去一味要离开寒带地区到气候暖和的地方居住的趋势。

1980 年人口普查的统计数字最精确地描绘出美国人迁移到最西部是为了找到更广阔的

居住空间。如此一来，70 年代加利福尼亚州人口增长最快，增长了 370 万。

同时也有大批的人在 70 年代离开加利福尼亚州，但是，大部分人的目的地是西部的其他地方。他们那时——现在也是如此——要去的地方是气候比较寒冷的俄勒冈、爱达荷和阿拉斯加等地，目的是躲开"黄金州"（加利福尼亚）的烟雾、犯罪以及其他都市化进程中出现的问题。

结果导致了 70 年代加利福尼亚州的人口增长率下降到了 18.5%。这个数字比 60 年代增长率的 2/3 稍高一点，但显然比其他西部各州要低。

题目答案与解析

1. 从 1980 年人口统计提供的人口增长的复杂图表可以看出，美国在 20 世纪 70 年代 _____。

    A．享有历史上最低的人口净增长　　B．经历了人口向西南地区的迁移

    C．经历了一段空前的人口增长期　　D．终止了自二战以来的迁移模式

    【答案】B

    【解析】从文章第 1 段的内容可知，1980 年的人口普查表明，随着东北部和中西部地区的人口增长几乎停顿，区域性的竞争已愈演愈烈；从文章第 2 段的内容可知，这一发展趋势使得南方首次成了美国人口普查史上人口最稠密的地区；文章第 3 段具体说明了增长的人口数量；从文章第 4 段的内容可知，自二战以来，美国人口一直大幅度向南部和西部地区迁移，而且这种趋势仍然盛行。据此可知，1980 年人口统计的结果显示——二战后，美国人口大量移居南部和西部地区。B 项与文章的意思相符，因此 B 项为正确答案。

2. 此次人口普查与以前的人口流动研究有所不同的原因是 _____。

    A．它强调了气候对人口分布的影响

    B．它强调了无休止的移民潮造成的影响

    C．它揭示了美国人对宽敞的生活空间的新追求

    D．它详尽阐述了昔日"生育高峰"的滞后影响

    【答案】C

    【解析】从文章第 6 段的内容可知，人口普查官员说，并不是所有的迁移都是因为人们想搬出寒带地区；从第 7 段的内容可知，人口统计学家发现，向南部、西部地区的不断迁移还伴随着一种与此相关却又与从前不同的现象：愈来愈多的美国人明显不再只寻找有更多就业机会的地方，他们还在寻找人口较少的地区；从文章第 11 段的第 1 句话可知，1980 年人口普查的数据戏剧性地显示，美国人主要是到西部地区寻找宽敞的生活空间。据此可知，如今的美国人注重的是宽敞的生活空间。C 项与文章的意思相符，因此 C 项为正确答案。

3. 我们从能得到的统计资料可以看出 _____。

    A．加利福尼亚曾经是全美国人口最稀少的地区

    B．人口增长率排名前十位的州都位于西部地区

    C．气候条件更好的城市无一例外地从移民中获得效益

    D．亚利桑那州的人口增长率在所有州中排名第二

    【答案】D

    【解析】本题可参照文章的第 8、9 段。从中可知，从区域上来看，落基山脉地区各州成

为人口增长最快的地方；从各州的情况来看，内华达州和亚利桑那州是增长率最高的两个州——分别为 63.5% 和 53.1%；除了佛罗里达州和德克萨斯州以外，人口增长率排名前十位是西部各州。据此可知，内华达州的人口增长速度最快，亚利桑那州的人口增长速度第二。D 项与文章的意思相符，因此 D 项为正确答案。

4．单词"demographers"（第 7 段第 1 行）最有可能的意思为 _____。

    A．赞成民主倾向的人   B．提倡州与州之间迁移的人

    C．从事人口研究的科学家   D．坚持旧生活模式的保守主义者

【答案】C

【解析】从文章第 6 段的内容可知，人口普查官员说，并不是所有的迁移都是因为人们想搬出寒带；持续的移民潮也起了一定的作用，当年"生育高峰"时期出生的一代到了生育年龄，这些人生育了大批婴儿，这也起了作用；从第 7 段的第一句话可知，人口统计学家发现，向南部、西部地区的持续迁移伴随着一种与之相关却与从前不同的现象。据此可知，"demographer"所做的工作与人口统计有关，所以它最可能的意思应该是"研究人口问题的科学家"。C 项与文章的意思相符，因此 C 项为正确答案。

Text 4

    Scattered around the globe are more than 100 small regions of isolated volcanic activity known to geologists as hot spots. Unlike most of the world's volcanoes, they are not always found at the boundaries of the great drifting plates that make up the earth's surface; on the contrary, many of them lie deep in the interior of a plate. Most of the hot spots move only slowly, and in some cases the movement of the plates past them has left trails of dead volcanoes. The hot spots and their volcanic trails are milestones that mark the passage of the plates.

    That the plates are moving is not beyond dispute. Africa and South America, for example, are moving away from eath other as new material is injected into the sea floor between them. The complementary coastlines and certain geological features that seem to span the ocean are reminders of where the two continents were once joined. The relative motion of the plates carrying these continents has been constructed in detail, but the motion of one plate with respect to another cannot readily be translated into motion with respect to the earth's interior. It is not possible to determine whether both continents are moving in opposite directions or whether one continent is stationary and the other is drifting away from it. Hot spots, anchored in the deeper layers of the earth, provide the measuring instruments needed to resolve the question. From an analysis of the hot spot population it appears that the African plate is stationary and that it has not moved during the past 30 million years.

    The significance of hot spots is not confined to their role as a frame of reference. It now appears that they also have an important influence on the geophysical processes that propel the plates across the globe. When a continental plate come to rest over a hot spot, the material rising from deeper layer creates a broad dome. As the dome grows, it develops seed fissures (cracks) ; in at least a few cases the continent may break entirely along some of these fissures, so that the hot spot initiates the formation of a new ocean. Thus just as earlier theories have explained the mobility of the continents, so hot spots may explain their mutability (inconstant).

1. The author believes that _____.

    A. the motion of the plates corresponds to that of the earth's interior

    B. the geological theory about drifting plates has been proved to be true

    C. the hot spots and the plates move slowly in opposite directions

    D. the movement of hot spots proves the continents are moving apart

2. That Africa and South America were once joined can be deduced from the fact that _____.

    A. the two continents are still moving in opposite directions

    B. they have been found to share certain geological features

    C. the African plates has been stable for 30 million years

    D. over 100 hot spots are scattered all around the globe

3. The hot spot theory may prove useful in explaining _____.

    A. the structure of the African plates   B. the revival of dead volcanoes

    C. the mobility of the continents   D. the formation of new oceans

4. The passage is mainly about _____.

    A. the features of volcanic activities

    B. the importance of the theory about drifting plates

    C. the significance of hot spots in geophysical studies

    D. the process of the formation of volcanoes

核心词汇注释

milestone ['maɪlstəʊn] n. 里程碑，里程标；重要事件；转折点

dispute [dɪ'spjuːt] v. 争论；辩论；怀疑；抗拒；阻止；争夺　n. 争论；辩论；争吵

span [spæn] n. 跨度；跨距；范围　v. 横越

geophysical [ˌdʒiːəʊ'fɪzɪkəl] adj. 地球物理学的

propel [prə'pel] vt. 推进；驱使

fissure ['fɪʃə(r)] n. 裂缝；裂沟；（思想、观点等的）分歧　v.（使）裂开；（使）分裂

initiate [ɪ'nɪʃɪeɪt] vt. 开始；发动；传授　v. 开始；发起

mobile ['məʊbaɪl, məʊ'biːl] adj. 可移动的；易变的；机动的　n. 运动物体

mutability [ˌmjuːtə'bɪlɪtɪ] n. 易变性；性情不定

inconstancy [ɪn'kɒnstənsɪ] n. 反复无常

长难句剖析

【文章难句】Unlike most of the world's volcanoes, they are not always found at the boundaries of the great drifting plates that make up the earth's surface; on the contrary, many of them lie deep in the interior of a plate.

【结构分析】本句主干是 they are not found…on the contrary…many of them lie。unlike 引导的是状语，由 that 引导的主语从句修饰 the great drifting plates。on the contrary 为连接词，

把两个句子连接在一起。

【参考译文】与地球上大多数火山不同的是，它们并不总是在形成地球表面的巨大漂移板块的连接点，反而有很多位于板块的深处。

全文参考译文

地球上散布着一百多个相互独立并且面积不大的火山活动区，地质学家称之为热点区。与世界上大多数火山不同的是，它们并不总是在形成地球表面的巨大漂移板块的连接点，反而有很多位于板块的深处。大部分热点区移动极其缓慢，在某些情况下，板块滑过这些热点区，便留下死火山的痕迹。热点区加上其火山痕迹是板块移动的象征。

如今，板块漂移学说是无需质疑的了。例如非洲和南美洲，因为有新物质深入洋底，两个大陆距离愈来愈远。即使远隔大洋，可互补的海岸线和似乎横跨海洋的地质地貌特征提示人们：这两个大陆曾是相连的。带着两个大陆漂移的板块做相对运动，这已得到具体解释，但不能把一个板块相对于另一板块的运动简单地解释为板块与地球内部之间的运动。由于人们还没法肯定两个大陆是否在朝相反的方向运动，也没法肯定是否是一个大陆原地不动，而另一个大陆正在远它而去。因而位于地壳深处的热点区提供了解决这一问题的测量仪。根据热点密度分析可以看出，非洲板块静止不动了 3,000 万年。

热点区的重要意义并不仅仅在于它们所起到的参照物的作用。如今它们还对推动板块在地球表面漂移这一地球物理进程有重要作用。当大陆板块漂移到热点区上方时，地壳深处涌出的物质便会使板块凸起，形成一个宽阔的穹顶，随着穹顶不断生长，就会产生小裂缝。如此作用几次以后，大陆可能会沿着这些小裂缝完全裂开，这样热点地区就导致了新大洋的诞生。这样一来，就像早些时候的一些理论已经解释了大陆的流动性一样，热点区理论或许能解释大陆板块的不稳定性。

题目答案与解析

1. 作者相信 _____。
   A. 板块的运动与地球内部的运动相似
   B. 有关板块漂移的地质理论已经被证实是正确的
   C. 热点与板块向相反的方向缓慢移动
   D. 热点的运动证明大陆正在逐渐分离

   【答案】B

   【解析】从文章第 1 段的内容可知，地球上散布着一百多个热点；大部分热点区移动极其缓慢，某些情况下，板块滑过这些热点区，便留下死火山的痕迹；热点区及其火山痕迹是板块移动的象征。从文章第 2 段的内容可知，如今，板块漂移学说已是无需质疑的了；然后举例进一步说明。从文章最后一段的内容可知，热点的重要性并不仅限于作为参照体系这一作用上；现在看来，它们对推动板块在地球上移动的地球物理学的过程也产生了重大影响；因此，正如早期的理论解释了大陆的移动那样，热点或许可以解释大陆的易变性。据此可知，作者认为有关大陆移动的理论是正确的。B 项与文章的意思相符，因此 B 项为正确答案。

2. 非洲和南美洲曾经连在一起这种说法可以依据 _____ 这一事实推论出来。

A．这两个洲仍然在向相反的方向移动

B．人们发现，这两个洲具有引人注目的地质特征

C．非洲板块已经稳定了 3,000 万年

D．地球各地散布着一百多个热点

【答案】B

【解析】本题可参照文章的第 2 段。从中可知，因为有新物质深入洋底，两个大陆距离愈来愈远；互补的海岸线以及似乎横跨海洋的地质地貌特征提示人们——这两块大陆曾经连接在一起；人们既不能确定是否这两块大陆在向相反的方向移动，也不能确定是否其中的一块大陆静止不动，而另一块大陆正在远它而去；根据热点密度的分析可以看出，非洲板块静止不动了的 3,000 万年。据此可知，人们之所以认为非洲和南美洲曾经连在一起，是因为它们的某些地质特征相似。B 项与文章的意思相符，因此 B 项为正确答案。

3．热点理论在解释 _____ 时可能被证实有用。

A．非洲板块的结构　　B．死火山的复活　　C．大陆的漂移　　D．新海洋的形成

【答案】D

【解析】本题可参照文章的第 3 段。从中可知，热点区的重要性并不仅在于它们所起到的参照物作用；现在看来，它们还对推动板块在地球上移动的地球物理学的过程也产生了重大影响；当大陆板块漂移到热点区上方时，地壳深处涌出的物质会形成一个巨大的穹顶；随着穹顶不断增长，它会出现深深的裂缝；如此作用几次后，大陆可能会沿着这些小裂缝完全裂开，这样热点地区就导致了新大洋的诞生。于是，该热点便开始形成一个新海洋；因此，正如早期的理论解释了大陆的移动那样，热点或许可以解释大陆的易变性。据此可知，热点理论可以用于解释大陆的不稳定性，即热点可以促使形成新海洋。D 项与文章的意思相符，因此 D 项为正确答案。

4．本篇文章主要是叙述 _____。

A．火山运动的特点　　　　　　　　　　B．有关板块漂移理论的重要性

C．地质物理研究中热点的重要性　　　　D．火山形成的过程

【答案】C

【解析】从文章第 1 段的内容可知，地球上散布着一百多个相互独立并且面积不大的火山活动区，地质学家称之为热点。随后说明了热点的特点。文章第 2 段说明了板块漂移理论，最后一句话指出：根据热点密度的分析可以看出——非洲板块静止不动了 3,000 万年；从文章第 3 段的内容可知，热点的重要性并不仅限于作为参照体系这一作用上，它们对推动板块地球上移动的地质物理过程也产生了重大影响；然后具体说明了热点如何促使形成了新海洋；从文章的最后一句话可知，正如早期的理论解释了大陆的移动那样，热点理论或许可以解释大陆的易变性。据此可知，本文主要讲的是热点理论在地质物理研究中的重要作用。C 项与文章的意思相符，因此 C 项为正确答案。

Unit 20

Text 1

It was 3:45 in the morning when the vote was finally taken. After six months of arguing and final 16 hours of hot parliamentary debates, Australia's Northern Territory became the first legal authority in the world to allow doctors to take the lives of incurably ill patients who wish to die. The measure passed by the convincing vote of 15 to 10. Almost immediately word flashed on the Internet and was picked up, half a world away, by John Hofsess, executive director of the Right to Die Society of Canada. He sent it on via the group's on line service, Death NET. Says Hofsess: "We posted bulletins all day long, because of course this isn't just something that happened in Australia. It's world history."

The full import may take a while to sink in. The NT Rights of the Terminally Ⅲ law has left physicians and citizens alike trying to deal with its moral and practical implications. Some have breathed sighs of relief, others, including churches, right to life groups and the Australian Medical Association, bitterly attacked the bill and the haste of its passage. But the tide is unlikely to turn back. In Australia — where an aging population, life extending technology and changing community attitudes have all played their part — other states are going to consider making a similar law to deal with euthanasia In the U.S. and Canada, where the right to die movement is gathering strength, observers are waiting for the dominoes to start falling.

Under the new Northern Territory law, an adult patient can request death — probably by a deadly injection or pill — to put an end to suffering. The patient must be diagnosed as terminally ill by two doctors. After a "cooling off" period of seven days, the patient can sign a certificate of request. After 48 hours the wish for death can be met. For Lloyd Nickson, a 54 year old Darwin resident suffering from lung cancer, the NT Rights of Terminally Ⅲ law means he can get on with living without the haunting fear of his suffering: a terrifying death from his breathing condition. "I'm not afraid of dying from a spiritual point of view, but what I was afraid of was how I'd go, because I've watched people die in the hospital fighting for oxygen and clawing at their masks," he says.

1. From the second paragraph we learn that _____.
   A. the objection to euthanasia is slow to come in other countries
   B. physicians and citizens share the same view on euthanasia
   C. changing technology is chiefly responsible for the hasty passage of the law
   D. it takes time to realize the significance of the law's passage

2. When the author says that observers are waiting for the dominoes to start falling, he means _____.
   A. observers are taking a wait and see attitude towards the future of euthanasia
   B. similar bills are likely to be passed in the U.S., Canada and other countries

    C. observers are waiting to see the result of the game of dominoes

    D. the effect taking process of the passed bill may finally come to a stop

3. When Lloyd Nickson dies, he will _____.

    A. face his death with calm characteristic of euthanasia

    B. experience the suffering of a lung cancer patient

    C. have an intense fear of terrible suffering

    D. undergo a cooling off period of seven days

4. The author's attitude towards euthanasia seems to be that of _____.

    A. opposition   B. suspicion   C. approval   D. indifference

核心词汇注释

parliamentary [ˌpɑːlə'mentərɪ] *adj.* 议会的

territory ['terɪtərɪ] *n.* 领土；版图；地域

convincing [kən'vɪnsɪŋ] *adj.* 令人信服的；有力的；令人心悦诚服的

bulletin ['bʊlətɪn] *n.* 公告，报告

euthanasia [ˌjuːθə'neɪzɪə] *n.* 安乐死

domino ['dɒmɪnəʊ] *n.* 骨牌；多米诺骨牌；面具；戴面罩及头巾的外衣

diagnose ['daɪəgnəʊz,ˌdaɪəg'nəʊz] *v.* 诊断

haunting ['hɔːntɪŋ] *adj.* 常浮现于脑海中的；不易忘怀的

oxygen ['ɒksɪdʒ(ə)n] *n.* [化]氧

claw [klɔː] *n.* 爪，脚爪；*v.* 抓

长难句剖析

【文章难句】Almost immediately word flashed on the Internet and was picked up, half a world away, by John Hofsess, executive director of the Right to Die Society of Canada.

【结构分析】本句主干是 word flashed and was picked up by John Hofsess。half a world away 以及 executive director of the Right to Die Society of Canada 是两个同位语,修饰 John Hofsess。

【参考译文】这一消息几乎立即出现在互联网上,并被远在地球另一端的加拿大死亡权利协会执行主席 John Hofsess 看到了。

全文参考译文

    清晨 3:45 进行了最后的投票表决。经过 6 个月的争论和最后 16 个小时的国会激烈辩论,澳大利亚北部省成了世界上第一个允许医生根据病人意愿结束绝症患者生命的合法当局。这一法案是以 15:10 的令人信服的投票结果通过的。这一消息几乎立即出现在互联网上。并被远在地球另一端的加拿大死亡权利协会执行主席 John Hofsess 看到了。他随即通过协会的网络服务站"死亡网络"发了公告。他说:"我们一整天都在发布公告,这当然不只是因为澳大利亚发生的事情,还因为这是要载入世界史册的。"

    这一立法的深刻意义可能要过一段时间才能为人们所理解。北部省所通过的晚期病人权益法使得无论是内科医生还是普通市民都同样地努力从道义和实际意义两方面来对待这一问题。有些人如释重负,而包括教会人士、生存权利组织成员以及澳大利亚医学会成员在内的其他人则猛烈抨击了这一法案及其草率的通过。而这种潮流将不太可能逆转。在澳大利亚,

人口老龄化、寿命延长技术以及公众态度的变化都在各自发挥着作用。其他州也准备考虑制定类似的法规来对待安乐死问题。在美国和加拿大，死亡权利运动正在逐渐兴起，观察家正等待着多米诺骨牌开始倒下。

根据澳北州所通过的这个新法案，成年病人可要求安乐死——可能通过注射致死针剂或服用致死药物——以结束痛苦。但须由两名医生诊断其已病入膏肓。病人经过七天"冷静思考"时间，方可签署一份申请证明。48 小时后，其安乐死愿望才能得到实现。对于居住在达尔文的现年 54 岁的肺癌患者 Nickson 来说，这个法案意味着他可以平静地生活下去而无须惧怕因呼吸困难而死去。"从精神上说，我并不怕死，害怕的是怎样死。"他说，"我曾看见医院里的病人死前用手抓他们的供氧面罩，与氧气抗争。"

题目答案与解析

1. 我们从第 2 段了解到 _____。
   A. 在其他国家，对安乐死的反对意见出现的较慢
   B. 医生和市民对安乐死所持的观点一致
   C. 变化的技术应该对这项法律的草率通过负主要责任
   D. 要认识这项法律通过的意义需要时间

   【答案】D

   【解析】从文章第 2 段的内容可知，这一立法的深刻意义可能要过一段时间才能为人们所理解。澳北州所通过的晚期病人权益法使得无论是内科医生还是普通市民都同样地努力从道义和实际意义两方面来对待这一问题。有些人如释重负，而包括教会人士、生存权利组织成员以及澳大利亚医学会成员在内的其他人则猛烈抨击了这一法案及其草率的通过。而这种潮流将不太可能逆转。在澳大利亚，人口老龄化、寿命延长技术以及公众态度的变化都在各自发挥着作用。其他国家也准备考虑制定类似的法规来对待安乐死问题。在美国和加拿大，死亡权利运动正在逐渐兴起，观察家正等待着多米诺骨牌开始倒下。据此可知，由于人们对安乐死的看法有异，要充分领会安乐死法案通过的全部意义需要时间。D 项与文章的意思相符，因此 D 项为正确答案。

2. 当作者说"观察家在等待多米诺骨牌开始倒下"时，他意指 _____。
   A. 观察家对安乐死的未来持观望态度
   B. 类似的法律很可能在美国、加拿大和其他国家通过
   C. 观察家在等着看多米诺骨牌游戏的结果
   D. 已经通过的这项法律产生影响的过程可能最终会停止

   【答案】B

   【解析】本题中，"domino"意为"多米诺骨牌"，指引发连锁反应。从文章第 2 段的最后一句话可知，在美国和加拿大，死亡权利运动正在逐渐兴起，观察家们正在等待多米诺骨牌开始倒下。据此可知，作者认为，由于澳大利亚通过了安乐死法案，这对美国和加拿大产生了影响，使得这两个国家的死亡权利运动逐渐兴起，从而会产生连锁反应。B 项与文章的意思相符，因此 B 项为正确答案。

3. 当 Lloyd Nickson 死时，他将 _____。

A．以安乐死的平静心态面对死亡　　　B．体验肺癌患者所受的痛苦

C．非常惧怕可怕的痛苦　　　　　　　D．经历七天的冷静期

【答案】A

【解析】从文章第 2 段的后半部分可知，对于居住在达尔文的现年 54 岁的肺癌患者 Nickson 来说，这个法案意味着他可以平静地生活下去而无须惧怕因呼吸困难而死去。"从精神上说，我并不怕死，害怕的是怎样死。"他说，"我曾看见医院里的病人死前用手抓他们的供氧面罩，与氧气抗争。"据此可知，Lloyd Nickson 在去世时，将不会像其他病人那样有恐惧感和折磨感。A 项与文章的意思相符，因此 A 项为正确答案。

4．作者对安乐死好像持 _____ 态度。

A．反对　　　　　B．怀疑　　　　　C．赞成　　　　　D．漠不关心

【答案】C

【解析】从文章第 1 段的内容可知，经过 6 个月的争论和 16 个小时议会的最后激烈辩论，澳大利亚北部地区成为第一个允许医生结束那些无药可救、但求一死的病人的生命的合法地区；这一法案的通过不只是澳大利亚发生的事情，它是世界上的一件历史大事；从文章第 2 段的内容可知，这一法案的深刻意义可能需要过一段时间才能为人们所理解；有些人如释重负，而另一些人都对这一法案以及它的草率通过进行了猛烈抨击；但是这一趋势不可能逆转；在美国和加拿大，死亡权利运动正在逐渐兴起，观察家们正在等待多米诺骨牌开始倒下；从文章最后一段的内容可知，根据澳大利亚北部地区的新法，成年病人可以要求安乐死来结束痛苦；对于饱受肺癌煎熬的 Lloyd Nickson 来说，北部地区的晚期病人权利法案意味着他可以平静地生活下去而无需惧怕因呼吸困难而死去。据此可知，作者支持安乐死。C 项与文章的意思相符，因此 C 项为正确答案。

Text 2

A report consistently brought back by visitors to the U.S. is how friendly, courteous, and helpful most Americans were to them. To be fair, this observation is also frequently made of Canada and Canadians, and should best be considered North American. There are, of course, exceptions. Small minded officials, rude waiters, and ill mannered taxi drivers are hardly unknown in the U.S.. Yet it is an observation made so frequently that it deserves comment.

For a long period of time and in many parts of the country, a traveler was a welcome break in an otherwise dull existence. Dullness and loneliness were common problems of the families who generally lived distant from one another. Strangers and travelers were welcome sources of diversion, and brought news of the outside world.

The harsh realities of the frontier also shaped this tradition of hospitality. Someone traveling alone, if hungry, injured, or ill, often had nowhere to turn except to the nearest cabin or settlement. It was not a matter of choice for the traveler or merely a charitable impulse on the part of the settlers. It reflected the harshness of daily life: if you didn't take in the stranger and take care of him, there was no one else who would, and someday, remember, you might be in the same situation.

Today there are many charitable organizations which specialize in helping the weary traveler. Yet, the old tradition of hospitality to strangers is still very strong in the U.S., especially in the smaller cities and towns away from the busy tourist trails. "I was just traveling through, got talking with this American, and pretty soon he invited me home for dinner—amazing." Such observations reported by visitors to the U.S. are not uncommon, but are not always understood properly. The casual friendliness of many Americans should be interpreted neither as superficial nor as artificial, but as the result of a historically developed cultural tradition.

As is true of any developed society, in America a complex set of cultural signals, assumptions, and conventions underlies all social interrelationships. And, of course, speaking a language does not necessarily meant that someone understands social and cultural patterns. Visitors who fail to "translate" cultural meanings properly often draw wrong conclusions. For example, when an American uses the word "friend", the cultural implications of the word may be quite different from those it has in the visitor's language and culture. It takes more than a brief encounter on a bus to distinguish between courteous convention and individual interest. Yet, being friendly is a virtue that many American value highly and expect from both neighbors and strangers.

1.　In the eyes of visitors from the outside world, _____.

　　A.　rude taxi drivers are rarely seen in the U.S.

　　B.　small minded officials deserve a serious comment

　　C.　Canadians are not so friendly as their neighbors

　　D.　most Americans are ready to offer help

2.　It could be inferred from the last paragraph that _____.

　　A.　culture exercises an influence over social interrelationship

　　B.　courteous convention and individual interest are interrelated

　　C.　various virtues manifest themselves exclusively among friends

　　D.　social interrelationships equal the complex set of cultural conventions

3.　Families in frontier settlements used to entertain strangers _____.

　　A.　to improve their hard life　　　　　　B.　in view of their long distance travel

　　C.　to add some flavor to their own daily life　　D.　out of a charitable impulse

4.　The tradition of hospitality to strangers _____.

　　A.　tends to be superficial and artificial

　　B.　is generally well kept up in the United States

　　C.　is always understood properly

　　D.　was something to do with the busy tourist trails

核心词汇注释

minded　['maɪndɪd] *adj.* 有思想的

dull　[dʌl] *adj.* 感觉或理解迟钝的；无趣的；呆滞的；阴暗的
　　vt. 使迟钝；使阴暗；缓和

　　vi. 变迟钝；减少

diversion　[daɪ'vɜːʃ(ə)n] *n.* 转移；转换；牵制；解闷；娱乐

frontier　['frʌntɪə(r)] *n.* 国境；边疆；边境

charitable [ˈtʃærɪtəb(ə)l] *adj.* 仁慈的；（为）慈善事业的；宽恕的

specialize [ˈspeʃəlaɪz] *vi.* 专攻；专门研究；使适应特殊目的；使专用于

weary [ˈwɪərɪ] *adj.* 疲倦的；厌倦的；令人厌烦的；疲劳的
v. 疲倦；厌倦；厌烦

complex [ˈkɒmpleks] *adj.* 复杂的；合成

的；综合的
n. 联合体

assumption [əˈsʌmpʃ(ə)n] *n.* 假定；设想；担任；承担；假装；作态；圣母升天

encounter [ɪnˈkaʊntə(r)] *v.* 遭遇；遇到；相遇
n. 遭遇；遭遇战

长难句剖析

【文章难句】For example, when an American uses the word "friend", the cultural implications of the word may be quite different from those it has in the visitor's language and culture.

【结构分析】本句中，the cultural implications of the word 是主句的主语，宾语是 those，定语从句 it has in the visitor's language and culture 用来修饰 those，those 指代 the cultural implications of the word。前面的关系代词 when 引导条件状语从句。

【参考译文】比如，美国人在使用"朋友"这个词的时候，它的文化内涵可能完全不同于这个词在游客的本国语和文化中的内涵。

全文参考译文

去过美国的人回来说，大多数美国人对他们友好、谦恭、乐于助人。公平地讲，人们对加拿大和加拿大人也有同样的观察报告。最好应当看作这在整个北美都普遍存在。当然也有例外，在美国，心胸狭窄的官员、粗鲁的服务生以及缺乏教养的出租车司机也不少。但由于人们常得出上面的结论，那就值得议论一番了。

长时间以来，在美国很多地方，旅行者打破了当地沉闷的生活，所以受到欢迎。那时人们一般住在相距遥远的地方，沉闷、孤独是家庭普遍存在的问题。陌生人和旅行者很受欢迎，因为他们带来了消遣娱乐，还带来了外部世界的消息。

边境上的残酷现实也促进了这一好客传统的发展。当一个人独自旅行时，如果饿了，受了伤或生了病，通常无处可去，只能向最近的小屋或村落求助。对旅行者来说，这不是选择的问题，对当地人来说，这也并非出于一时的仁慈冲动。它反映了日常生活的残酷：如果你不接纳陌生人，并照顾他，那他就再找不到别人了。请记住，也许某一天你也会面临相同的处境。

现在有很多慈善组织，专门帮助那些疲倦的旅行者。不过，款待陌生人的传统在美国仍很盛行，在那些远离热门旅游线路的小市镇尤其如此。"我刚转了一圈，同这个美国人聊了聊，很快，他就邀请我到他家吃饭——不可思议。"在来美国旅行的游客中碰到过这类事的很普遍，但对此并不都能正确理解。许多美国人随意表现出的友好不应被看做是表面应付或矫揉造作，而应视为历史发展形成的一种文化传统。

美国同任何发达国家一样，文化、信念以及习俗是社会关系的基础。当然，一个人会说一种语言并不一定意味着他了解该语言所代表的社会和文化模式。那些不能正确"解读"文化含义的游客经常会得出错误的结论。比如，美国人在使用"朋友"一词的时候，它的文化内涵可能完全不同于该词在游客母语和文化中的内涵。仅凭借在汽车上偶遇时说声"朋友"并不能区分这是出于礼貌还是个人兴趣。不过，友好待人是许多美国人都看重的一种美德，他们希望邻居和陌生人也能如此。

题目答案与解析

1. 在外国游客的眼中，_____。
   A. 在美国很少见到粗鲁无礼的出租车司机
   B. 心胸狭窄的政府官员应该受到严肃批评
   C. 加拿大人不如他们的邻国人友好
   D. 大多数美国人乐于提供帮助

【答案】D

【解析】本题可参照文章第 1 段的第 1 句话。从中可知，去过美国的人回来说，大多数美国人友好、谦恭、乐于助人。据此可知，游客认为大多数美国人对人友好。D 项与文章的意思相符。A 项不正确，依据是第 1 段的第 3 句话；B 项不正确，文中只是说政府官员心胸狭窄、服务员粗鲁无礼以及出租车司机态度恶劣，但并没有说游客认为应该严肃批评他们。C 项与文章第 1 段第 2 句话的意思不符。综上所述，只有 D 项为正确答案。

2. 从最后一段可以推知 _____。
   A. 文化对社会相互关系有影响
   B. 谦恭的习俗和个人的爱好是相关的
   C. 各种美德只在朋友间的交往中体现
   D. 社会相互关系等同于文化习俗的复合体

【答案】A

【解析】从文章最后一段的内容可知，在美国同任何发达国家一样，文化、信念以及习俗是社会关系的基础；当然，一个人会说一种语言并不意味着他了解该语言所代表的社会和文化模式；那些没有正确"解读"文化含义的游客经常会得出错误的结论；仅凭借在汽车上偶遇时说声"朋友"并不能区分出这是出于礼貌还是个人兴趣；不过，友好待人是许多美国人都看重的美德，他们希望邻居和陌生人也能如此。据此可知，又化、思维方式（文化复合体关系）决定或影响社会相互交往的方式。A 项与文章的意思相符；B 项与文章最后一段倒数第 2 句话的意思不符；C 项不正确，依据是文章最后一段倒数第一句话；D 项与文章的意思明显不符。只有 A 项为正确答案。

3. 居住在边界的家庭过去经常款待陌生人，_____。
   A. 以便改善他们的艰难生活
   B. 是出于对他们长途旅行的考虑
   C. 为他们自己的日常生活增添一些情趣
   D. 出于一时行善的冲动

【答案】C

【解析】从文章第 2 段的最后一句话可知，陌生人和旅行者带来了欢乐，因而受到人们的欢迎；从文章第 3 段的内容可知，边界上严酷的现实也促进了这一好客传统的发展；独自旅行的人，如果饿了、受伤了或是生病了，常常只能求助于距离最近的小屋或居民点；对于旅行者来说，这不是选择的问题，对当地人来说，也不仅仅是一时的仁慈冲动，这反映了日常生活的严酷性——如果你不接纳并照顾陌生人，那么也没有人会这么做。据此可知，在边界居住的人们之所以常常招待陌生人，是因为这样做可以为自己枯燥乏味和孤独寂寞的生活解闷。C 项与文章的意思相符。A 项不正确，文中只是说可以解闷，并没有说可以改善艰难的生活。B 项不正确，文中没有提到；D 项明显与文章第 3 段第 3 句话的意思不符。综上所述，只有 C 项为正确答案。

4. 招待陌生人的传统 _____。
   A. 往往是表面的、虚伪的
   B. 在美国普遍得到很好的继承
   C. 总是被正确理解
   D. 与旅游热线有关系

【答案】B

【解析】从文章第 4 段的内容可知，现在有许多慈善机构专门帮助那些疲倦的旅行者；不过，款待陌生人的传统在美国仍然盛行，在那些远离旅游热线的小城市和城镇尤其如此；到美国旅行过的游客有这样的感受很常见，但人们并不总是能够正确理解这样的感受；很多美国人随意表现出的友好既不应被看做是表面应付和矫揉造作，而应被看成是一种文化传统历史发展的结果；文章最后一段还指出：友好待人是许多美国人都看重的美德。由此可知：在美国，人们看重款待陌生人的传统，这一传统也一直得到人们的继承。B 项与文章的意思相符。A 项和 C 项明显与文章的意思不符。D 项不正确，依据是文中的“在那些远离繁忙旅游线路的小城市和城镇，人们更是款待陌生人”。综上所述，只有 B 项为正确答案。

Text 3

Technically, any substance other than food that alters our bodily or mental functioning is a drug. Many people mistakenly believe the term drug refers only to some sort of medicine or an illegal chemical taken by drug addicts. They don't realize that familiar substances such as alcohol and tobacco are also drugs. This is why the more neutral term substance is now used by many physicians and psychologists. The phrase "substance abuse" is often used instead of "drug abuse" to make clear that substances such as alcohol and tobacco can be just as harmfully misused as heroin and cocaine.

We live a society in which the medicinal and social use of substances (drugs) is pervasive: an aspirin to quiet a headache, some wine to be sociable, coffee to get going in the morning, a cigarette for the nerves. When do these socially acceptable and apparently constructive uses of a substance become misuses? First of all, most substances taken in excess will produce negative effects such as poisoning or intense perceptual distortions. Repeated use of a substance can also lead to physical addiction or substance dependence. Dependence is marked first by an increased tolerance, with more and more of the substance required to produce the desired effect, and then by the appearance of unpleasant withdrawal symptoms when the substance is discontinued.

Drugs (substances) that affect the central nervous system and alter perception, mood, and behavior are known as psychoactive substances. Psychoactive substances are commonly grouped according to whether they are stimulants, depressants, or hallucinogens. Stimulants initially speed up or activate the central nervous system, whereas depressants slow it down. Hallucinogens have their primary effect on perception, distorting and altering it in a variety of ways including producing hallucinations. These are the substances often called psychedelic (from the Greek word meaning "mind manifesting") because they seemed to radically alter one's state of consciousness.

1. "Substance abuse" (Line 5, Para. 1) is preferable to "drug abuse" in that _____.

A. substances can alter our bodily or mental functioning if illegally used

B. "drug abuse" is only related to a limited number of drug takers

C. alcohol and tobacco are as fatal as heroin and cocaine

D. many substances other than heroin or cocaine can also be poisonous

2. The word "pervasive" (Line 1, Para. 2) might mean _____.

A. widespread　　　B. overwhelming　　　C. piercing　　　D. fashionable

3. Physical dependence on certain substances results from _____.

A. uncontrolled consumption of them over long periods of time

B. exclusive use of them for social purposes

C. quantitative application of them to the treatment of diseases

D. careless employment of them for unpleasant symptoms

4. From the last paragraph we can infer that _____.

A. stimulants function positively on the mind

B. hallucinogens are in themselves harmful to health

C. depressants are the worst type of psychoactive substances

D. the three types of psychoactive substances are commonly used in groups

核心词汇注释

addict [ə'dɪkt] *vt.* 使沉溺；使上瘾
　　n. 入迷的人；有瘾的人

neutral ['njuːtrəl] *n.* 中立者；中立国；非
彩色；齿轮的空当
　　adj. 中立的；中立国的；中性的；无确定
性质的；（颜色等）不确定的

misuse [mɪs'juːz] *v.* 误用；错用；滥用；虐
待
　　n. 误用；错用；滥用；误用之实例

cocaine [kəʊ'keɪn] *n.* 可卡因

pervasive [pə'veɪsɪv] *adj.* 普遍深入的

perceptual [pə'septjuəl;-tʃuəl] *adj.* 知觉
的；有知觉的

psychoactive [ˌsaɪkəʊ'æktɪv] *adj.* 作用于
精神的；影响（或改变）心理状态的

stimulant ['stɪmjulənt] *n.* 刺激物

hallucinogen [hə'luːsɪnədʒ(ə)n] *n.* 迷幻剂

psychedelic [ˌsaɪkɪ'delɪk] *adj.* 引起幻觉
的；迷幻的
　　n. 迷幻剂

长难句剖析

【文章难句】Technically, any substance other than food that alters our bodily or mental functioning is a drug.

【结构分析】本句主干是 any substance other than food is a drug。副词 technically 是插入语，　other than 的意思是"而不是"。由 that 引导的定语从句修饰 food。

【参考译文】从技术的角度讲，除食品外，任何能改变我们的生理或心理机能的物质均是药物。

全文参考译文

从技术的角度讲，除食品外，任何能改变我们生理或心理机能的物质均是药物。很多人错误地认为"药物"这个词仅指某些药品或嗜毒者服用的违禁化学品。他们没有意识到像酒精、烟草这类常见物质也是药物。这也就是为何很多医生和心理学家现在使用了一个更为折中的词——物质，他们经常用"物质滥用"而不是"药物滥用"来明确表明酒精和烟草这样的物质有可能像海洛因和可卡因一样因滥用而对人造成危害。

在我们居住的社会里，物质（药物）被广泛地应用于社交和治疗：服用阿斯匹林来减轻头痛，喝点儿酒以增进友谊，早晨喝咖啡以提神，吸烟以消除紧张情绪等。这些物质的使用得到了社会认可，而且明显具有积极的一面，可何时被滥用了呢？首先，大多数物质使用过量都会产生副作用，例如中毒或反复使用一种物质可引起上瘾或对该物质（药物）产生依赖。依赖的起初症状为耐受力增强，用量愈来愈大才能达到预期效果，一旦停用就会产生不舒服的症状。

通过影响中枢神经系统来改变人的感觉、情绪及行为的药物（物质）被称为精神活性物质。这类物质一般分为兴奋剂、镇静剂或致幻剂。兴奋剂主要有加速或刺激中枢神经系统活动的效用，而镇静剂刚好与之相反：使其活动减缓。致幻剂主要作用于人的感觉，以多样的方式对感觉加以扭曲和变形，其中包括产生幻觉。这些物质常被称为"迷幻药"（psychedelic 一词源自希腊语，意思是"精神显现"）。因为它们好像能够使人的感觉状态发生改变。

题目答案与解析

1. "物质滥用"（第 1 段第 5 行）比"药物滥用"的说法更可取的原因是 _____。
   A. 如果非法使用，物质能够改变我们的身体和心理机能
   B. "药物滥用"只指数量有限的服药者
   C. 酒精和烟草同海洛因和可卡因一样致命
   D. 除了海洛因和可卡因以外，许多物质也可能有毒

【答案】D

【解析】本题可参照文章的第 1 段。从中可知，从技术的角度讲，除食品外，任何能改变我们生理或心理机能的物质都是药物；许多人错误地认为，药物这个词只指某些药品或嗜毒者服用的违禁化学药品，他们没有意识到像酒精和烟草这类常见物质也是药物；医生和心理学家们经常用 "物质滥用"取代"药物滥用"，来明确表明像酒精和烟草这样的物质也会像海洛因和可卡因一样因滥用而造成危害。据此可知，能够对人造成伤害的不只是海洛因和可卡因这类药物，其他许多物质都可以对人造成伤害。D 项与文章的意思相符；A 项与文章第 1 段第 2 句话的意思不符；B 项与文章第 1 段第 2、3 句话的意思不符；C 项不正确，文章只是说"酒精和烟草也能像海洛因和可卡因一样因滥用而对人造成危害"，并没有说使人致命。综上所述，只有 D 项为正确答案。

2. 单词"pervasive"（第 2 段第 1 行）的意思可能是指 _____。
   A. 普遍的   B. 压倒性的   C. 敏锐的   D. 时髦的

【答案】A

【解析】本题可参照文章第 2 段的第 1 句话。从中可知，在我们生活的社会，物质（药物）被广泛地应用于社交和医疗——服用阿司匹林以减缓头痛，喝点酒以增进友谊，早上喝咖啡以提神，吸烟以消除紧张情绪。据此可知，阿司匹林、酒、咖啡和烟等都是常用物品，因此"pervasive"的意思应该是"使用广泛的"。因此 A 项为正确答案。

3. 对某些物质的生理依赖的原因是 _____。

A. 长时期对这些物质无节制的使用

B. 出于社交目的而专门使用这些物质

C. 为了治病而定量使用这些物质

D. 为了消除令人不愉快的症状而草率地使用这些物质

【答案】A

【解析】本题可参照文章第 2 段的倒数两句话。从中可知，反复使用一种物质也会导致对该物质的生理上瘾或对药物依赖；依赖性起初表现为耐受性不断增强，需要越来越多的药物才能获得所需的效果，一旦停用，就会产生不舒服的症状。据此可知，对某些物质的生理依赖，是由于人们长时间、大量使用这些物质所造成的。A 项与文章的意思相符；B 项不正确，文中是说"喝一点酒以增进友谊"，但并没有说这会导致对酒的生理依赖；C 项和 D 项明显不是对某些物质生理依赖的原因。综上所述，只有 A 项为正确答案。

4. 我们从最后一段可以推知 _____。

A. 兴奋剂肯定对智力有影响

B. 幻觉剂本质上对健康有害

C. 镇静剂是对神经系统起作用的物质中最坏的一种物质

D. 三种对神经系统起作用的物质通常一起使用

【答案】B

【解析】从文章最后一段的内容可知，通过影响中枢神经系统来改变人的感觉、情绪和行为的药物（物质）被称作精神活性物质；这类物质一般分为兴奋剂、镇静剂和幻觉剂；兴奋剂主要有加快或激活中枢神经系统的作用，而镇静剂却刚好于之相反：使其减缓；幻觉剂主要作用于人的感觉，以多种方式（包括制造幻觉）扭曲和改变知觉；这些就是通常被称作迷幻剂的物质，因为它们似乎彻底改变了一个人的意识状态。据此可知，在三种对神经系统起作用的物质中，兴奋剂和镇静剂影响人的中枢神经系统，而幻觉剂却改变人的知觉、情绪和行为，显然对人的身体更有害。B 项与文章的意思相符；A 项不正确，文中是说"兴奋剂主要有加快或激活中枢神经系统的作用"，并没有说对智力有影响；文中没有提到 C 项；D 项不正确，文中是说"兴奋剂主要有加快或激活中枢神经系统的作用，而镇静剂却刚好于之相反：使其减缓，幻觉剂主要作用于人的感觉"，并没有说把三种对神经系统起作用的物质一起使用。综上所述，只有 B 项为正确答案。

Text 4

No company likes to be told it is contributing to the moral decline of a nation. "Is this what you intended to accomplish with your careers?" Senator Robert Dole asked Time Warner executives last week. "You have sold your souls, but must you corrupt our nation and threaten our children as well?" At Time Warner, however, such questions are simply the latest manifestation of the soul searching that has involved the company ever since the company was born in 1990. It's a self-examination that has, at various times, involved issues of responsibility, creative freedom and the corporate bottom line.

At the core of this debate is chairman Gerald Levin, 56, who took over for the late Steve Ross in 1992. On the financial front, Levin is under pressure to raise the stock price and reduce the company's mountainous debt, which will increase to 17.3 billion after two new cable deals close. He has promised to sell off some of the property and restructure the company, but investors are waiting impatiently.

The flap over rap is not making life any easier for him. Levin has consistently defended the company's rap music on the grounds of expression. In 1992, when Time Warner was under fire for releasing Ice T's violent rap song Cop Killer, Levin described rap as a lawful expression of street culture, which deserves an outlet. "The test of any democratic society," he wrote in a *Wall Street Journal* column, "lies not in how well it can control expression but in whether it gives freedom of thought and expression the widest possible latitude, however disputable or irritating the results may sometimes be. We won't retreat in the face of any threats."

Levin would not comment on the debate last week, but there were signs that the chairman was backing off his hard line stand, at least to some extent. During the discussion of rock singing verses at last month's stockholders' meeting, Levin asserted that "music is not the cause of society's ills" and even cited his son, a teacher in the Bronx, New York, who uses rap to communicate with students. But he talked as well about the "balanced struggle" between creative freedom and social responsibility, and he announced that the company would launch a drive to develop standards for distribution and labeling of potentially objectionable music.

The 15 member Time Warner board is generally supportive of Levin and his corporate strategy. But insiders say several of them have shown their concerns in this matter. "Some of us have known for many, many years that the freedoms under the First Amendment are not totally unlimited," says Luce. "I think it is perhaps the case that some people associated with the company have only recently come to realize this."

1. Senator Robert Dole criticized Time Warner for _____.
    A. its raising of the corporate stock price   B. its self-examination of soul
    C. its neglect of social responsibility   D. its emphasis on creative freedom

2. According to the passage, which of the following is TRUE?
    A. Luce is a spokesman of Time Warner.
    B. Gerald Levin is liable to compromise.
    C. Time Warner is united as one in the face of the debate.
    D. Steve Ross is no longer alive

3. In face of the recent attacks on the company, the chairman _____.
    A. stuck to a strong stand to defend freedom of expression
    B. softened his tone and adopted some new policy
    C. changed his attitude and yielded to objection
    D. received more support from the 15 member board

4. The best title for this passage could be _____.
    A. A Company under Fire   B. A Debate on Moral Decline

C. A Lawful Outlet of Street Culture　　D. A Form of Creative Freedom

核心词汇注释

senator ['senətə(r)] *n.* 参议员；（大学的）评议员；（古罗马的）元老院议员

corrupt [kə'rʌpt] *adj.* 腐败的；贪污的；被破坏的；混浊的；（语法）误用的
vt. 使腐烂；腐蚀；使恶化
vi. 腐烂；堕落

rap [ræp] *n.* 叩击；轻拍；轻敲；斥责
vt. 敲；拍；打；厉声说出；斥责；使着迷
vi. 敲击；交谈

deserve [dɪ'zɜ:v] *vt.* 应受；值得
v. 应受

latitude ['lætɪtju:d] *n.* 纬度；范围；（用复数）地区；行动或言论的自由（范围）

disputable [dɪ'spju:təb(ə)l] *adj.* 有讨论余地的；真假可疑的

retreat [rɪ'tri:t] *vi.* 撤退；退却
n. 撤退；退却

verse [vɜ:s] *n.* 韵文；诗；诗节；诗句；诗篇

objectionable [əb'dʒekʃənəbl] *adj.* 引起反对的，讨厌的

insider [ɪn'saɪdə(r)] *n.* 内部的人；会员；知道内情的人；权威人士

长难句剖析

【文章难句】On the financial front, Levin is under pressure to raise the stock price and reduce the company's mountainous debt, which will increase to 17.3 billion after two new cable deals close.

【结构分析】本句主干是 Levin is under pressure to raise the stock price and reduce，是由两个并列动词构成的简单句。连接词 which 引导的是非限制性定语从句，在这个定语从句中有一个以 after 引导的时间状语从句。介宾短语 on the financial front 做状语。

【参考译文】面对着财政危机，Levin 承受着抬高股价、减少公司巨额债务的压力，在经过两笔新的有线电视买卖后，债务将上升到 173 亿美元。

全文参考译文

没有一家公司乐意被别人说它导致了社会风气的败坏。上周参议员 Robert Dole 问时代华纳公司管理者时说，"你们的事业就要达到这样的结果吗？你们已经出卖了自己的灵魂，难道还要腐化我们的民族，威胁我们的孩子吗？"不过，对于时代华纳公司来说，这样的问题只不过是公司自 1990 年建立以来的灵魂解析的最新表白，它是在不同时期有关责任、创作自由和利润最低限等问题的自我检查。

56 岁的董事长 Gerald Levin 是这次争论的核心。他在 1992 年取代已故董事长 Steve Ross 接管公司。面对着财政危机，他承受着抬高股价、减少公司巨额债务的压力，在经过两笔新的有线电视买卖后，债务将上升到 173 亿美元。他已允诺出售部分财产，并重组公司，但投资者还在焦急地等待着。

提高说唱音乐的影响一点都未使他的日子好过一些。Levin 始终如一地以表达情感为理由维护公司的说唱音乐。1992 年，公司因发布冰特乐队的猛烈的说唱歌曲《警察杀手》而备受攻击时，Levin 把它描述成街头文化的合法表达形式，认为它应该有自己的表现形式。他在《华尔街日报》一篇专栏中写道："看一个社会是否民主，不是看它控制言论自由的程度，

而是看它能否给人们思考和表达自由提供尽可能宽松的范围——不管其结果有时可能会引起多么大的争议和愤怒。面对任何威胁，我们都不会退却。"

　　Levin 对上周的评论保持沉默，但有迹象表明这位总裁的强硬立场正在弱化，至少在一定程度上如此。在上个月的股东大会上，进行了摇滚乐唱词的讨论。Levin 强调说："音乐不是社会病的根源"，甚至还以在纽约布朗克斯任教的教师儿子为例，他的儿子以说唱音乐的形式与学生交流。但他也谈到了创作自由与社会责任之间要"努力保持平衡"的问题。他宣布，公司将开始对可能引起人们反对的音乐制定各种发行和标志的标准。

　　总的来说，时代华纳公司董事会的 15 名成员是支持他和他的公司经营策略的。但内部人士透露，他们中一些人对此表示担忧。Luce 说，"许多年之前，我们中有些人已知道宪法第一修正案规定的自由不是完全无限制的。我认为公司里和公司有关联的一些人可能最近才开始意识到这一点。"

题目答案与解析

1. 参议员 Robert Dole 批评时代华纳公司的原因是 _____。
　　A．该公司抬高本公司的股票价格　　　　B．该公司良心上的自我反省
　　C．该公司忽视其社会责任　　　　　　　D．该公司强调创作自由
　　【答案】C
　　【解析】从文章第 1 段的内容可知，参议员 Robert Dole 上个星期质问时代华纳公司的管理人员，"你们的事业就是要达到这样的结果吗？你们已经出卖了自己的灵魂，难道还要腐化我们的国家、威胁我们的孩子吗？"自 1990 年时代华纳公司创建以来，良心上的自我反省问题就一直困扰着它，这样的质问只不过是这一问题的最新表现而已。据此可知，参议员 Robert Dole 认为时代华纳公司没有承担应有的社会责任，因此批评他们，C 项与文章的意思相符；A 项不正确，Robert Dole 的话中并没有提到经济问题；B 项不正确，时代华纳公司创建以来一直在对自己所做的事进行良心上的自我反省，但这并不是 Robert Dole 批评他们的原因；D 项不正确，强调创作自由是时代华纳公司进行良心上的自我反省所涉及的内容，也不是 Robert Dole 批评他们的原因。综上所述，只有 C 项为正确答案。

2. 依据本文的观点，以下说法中正确的是哪项？
　　A．Luce 是时代华纳公司的一名发言人。
　　B．Gerald Levin 易于妥协。
　　C．面对辩论，时代华纳公司团结一致。
　　D．Steve Ross 已经去世了。
　　【答案】D
　　【解析】A 项不正确，从文章最后一段的内容可知，有 15 名成员的时代华纳公司董事会普遍支持 Levin 以及他有关公司的发展战略；但知情人士透露，有几位成员对此事表示担忧；Luce 说，"我们中有些人早就知道宪法第一修正案中规定的自由不是完全没有限制，我认为一些与公司有关的人士可能直到最近才开始意识到这一点。"这只能说明 Luce 是董事会成员，并不能证明他是时代华纳公司的发言人；B 项不正确，从文章第 3 段的内容可知，Levin 一直以言论自由为由替公司的说唱音乐辩护；他说他们不会在任何威胁面前退却；从第 4 段的内

容可知，有迹象表明这位董事长正在放弃他的强硬立场，至少在某种程度上是这样；但这并不能说明他容易妥协，C 项不正确，依据是文章最后一段的第 2 句话；从文章第 2 段的第 1 句话可知，这场辩论的核心人物是 56 岁的 Gerald Levin，他于 1992 年接替已故的 Steve Ross 任董事长；这说明 D 项正确。因此正确答案为 D。

3. 面对公司近来受到的攻击，董事长 _____。

  A. 坚持强硬立场，维护言论自由　　　B. 缓和语气，采取某项新的策略
  C. 改变态度，屈从于反对意见　　　　D. 得到 15 人董事会的更多支持

【答案】B

【解析】本题中，A 项和 C 项明显与文章的意思不符；D 项也与文章最后一段第 2 句话的意思不符。从文章第 4 段可知，Levin 不想对上个星期的辩论发表评论，但有迹象表明这位董事长正在放弃他的强硬立场，至少在某种程度上是这样；Levin 宣称，"音乐不是引发社会病的根源"，公司将采取措施，为可能引起异议的音乐制定各种发行和标志的标准。据此可知，Levin 在逐渐放弃他的强硬立场，准备采取新的措施。B 项与文章的意思相符，因此 B 项为正确答案。

4. 本篇文章的最佳标题可能是 _____。

  A. 一个受到攻击的公司　　　　　　　B. 一场有关道德败坏的辩论
  C. 一种街头文化的合法宣泄机会　　　D. 一种创作自由方式

【答案】A

【解析】本题中，B 项不能表达文章的中心意思，文中并没有辩论过道德败坏问题；C 项以及 D 项只是文章第 3 段中 Levin 为公司的新音乐辩护和为《华尔街日报》的专栏写文章时所持的观点，也不能表达文章的中心意思。本文第 1 段提到了时代华纳公司因为发行新音乐专辑而被谴责缺乏社会责任这一问题，随后几段具体说明了该公司对此所作的反应。据此可知，本文主要讲的是时代华纳公司受到的谴责和他们对谴责作出的反应。A 项与文章的意思相符，因此 A 项为正确答案。

第三部分 冲刺演练 20 篇

Unit 21

Text 1

What accounts for the great outburst of major inventions in early America-breakthroughs such as the telegraph, the steamboat and the weaving machine?

Among the many shaping factors, I would single out the country's excellent elementary schools; a labor force that welcomed the new technology; the practice of giving premiums to inventors; and above all the American genius for nonverbal, "spatial" thinking about things technological .

Why mention the elementary schools? Because thanks to these schools our early mechanics, especially in the New England and Middle Atlantic states, were generally literate and at home in arithmetic and in some aspects of geometry and trigonometry.

Acute foreign observers related American adaptiveness and inventiveness to this educational advantage. As a member of a British commission visiting here in 1853 reported, "With a mind prepared by thorough school discipline, the American boy develops rapidly into the skilled workman."

A further stimulus to invention came from the "premium" system, which preceded our patent system and for years ran parallel with it. This approach, originated abroad, offered inventors medals, cash prizes and other incentives.

In the United States, multitudes of premiums for new devices were awarded at country fairs and at the industrial fairs in major cities. Americans flocked to these fairs to admire the new machines and thus to renew their faith in the beneficence of technological advance.

Given this optimistic approach to technological innovation, the American worker took readily to that special kind of nonverbal thinking required in mechanical technology. As Eugene Ferguson has pointed out, "A technologist thinks about objects that cannot be reduced to unambiguous verbal descriptions; they are dealt with in his mind by a visual, nonverbal process... The designer and the inventor... are able to assemble and manipulate in their minds devices that as yet do not exist."

This nonverbal "spatial" thinking can be just as creative as painting and writing. Robert Fulton once wrote, "The mechanic should sit down among levers, screws, wedges, wheels, etc., like a poet among the letters of the alphabet, considering them as an exhibition of his thoughts, in which a new arrangement transmits a new idea."

When all these shaping forces — schools, open attitudes, the premium system, a genius for spatial thinking — interacted with one another on the rich U.S. mainland, they produced that American characteristic, emulation. Today that word implies mere imitation. But in earlier times it meant a friendly but competitive striving for fame and excellence.

1. According to the author, the great outburst of major inventions in early America was in a large part due to _____.

    A. elementary schools   B. enthusiastic workers

    C. the attractive premium system   D. a special way of thinking

2. It is implied that adaptiveness and inventiveness of the early American mechanics _____.

    A. benefited a lot from their mathematical knowledge

    B. shed light on disciplined school management

    C. was brought about by privileged home training

    D. owed a lot to the technological development

3. A technologist can be compared to an artist because _____.

    A. they are both winners of awards   B. they are both experts in spatial thinking

    C. they both abandon verbal description   D. they both use various instruments

4. The best title for this passage might be _____.

    A. Inventive Mind   B. Effective Schooling

    B. Ways of Thinking   D. Outpouring of Inventions

核心词汇注释

premium ['priːmɪəm] *n.* 额外费用；奖金；奖赏；保险费；（货币兑现的）贴水

geometry [dʒɪ'ɒmɪtrɪ] *n.* 几何学

trigonometry [ˌtrɪgə'nɒmɪtrɪ] *n.* 三角法

patent ['peɪt(ə)nt] *n.* 专利权；执照；专利品

   adj. 特许的；专利的；显著的；明白的；新奇的

   vt. 取得……的专利权

incentive [ɪn'sentɪv] *n.* 动机

   adj. 激励的

multitude ['mʌltɪtjuːd] *n.* 多数；群众

flock [flɒk] *n.* 羊群；大量；众多

   v. 聚结

beneficence [bɪ'nefɪsəns] *n.* 行善；慈善；捐款；捐赠物；仁慈

unambiguous [ˌʌnæm'bɪgjuəs] *adj.* 不含糊的；明确的

imitation [ˌɪmɪ'teɪʃ(ə)n] *n.* 模仿；效法；冒充；赝品；仿造物

长难句剖析

【文章难句】The mechanic should sit down among levers, screws, wedges, wheels, etc., like a poet among the letters of the alphabet, considering them as an exhibition of his thoughts, in which a new arrangement transmits a new idea.

【结构分析】本句主干是 The mechanic should sit down，like a poet among the letters of the alphabet 做句子的状语，其中 like 为介词。现在分词结构 considering them as an exhibition of his thoughts 做状语。非限制性定语从句 in which a new arrangement transmits a new idea 修饰 an exhibition of his thoughts。

【参考译文】一个机械师会坐在杠杆、螺丝、楔子和轮子等之中，就像一个诗人沉浸在字母表的字母中，把这些字母看成自己思想的展示，展示中的每一个新组合都传达了一种新的思路。

全文参考译文

什么原因导致了早期美国的重大发明——如电报、汽船和织布机——的大量出现？

在许多形成因素中，我想强调的是这个国家优秀的初等学校、劳动者对新技术的热情、奖励发明者的做法；最重要的是，美国人的天赋——处理技术性事务的非语言的"立体"思维。

为什么提到初等学校呢？因为多亏了这些学校，我们早期的机械工人，特别是在新英格兰和大西洋沿岸中部各州，才普及了文化知识，通晓了算术和一定的几何、三角知识。

敏锐的外国观察家把美国人的适应能力和创造能力与这种教育优势联系起来。正如一个 1853 年到这儿访问的英国访问团成员报道说："有了在学校彻底训练过的思维，美国孩子很快成为技术熟练的工人。"

发明的另一个刺激因素来自"奖赏"制度，这个制度先于专利制度存在，且若干年来与专利制度同时运作。这种做法起源于国外，给发明者提供奖章、奖金和其他奖励。

在美国，乡村博览会和大城市的工业博览会都设有诸多奖项。美国人聚集到这些博览会，对新机器赞叹不绝，也因此使他们更加坚信技术进步所带来的利益。

有了这种对技术革新的乐观态度，美国工人轻易地学会了机械技术需要的那种非语言的思维方式。就像 Eugene Ferguson 指出的那样："技术专家在思考那些不能进行明确的口头描述的物体时，将它们在头脑中以直观的、非语言方式来处理……设计者和发明者能把这些还没有实际存在的设备在头脑中组装和操作。"

这一非语言的空间思维像绘画、写作一样富有创造力。Robert Fulton 曾经写道："一个机械师会坐在杠杆、螺丝、楔子和轮子等之中，就像一个诗人沉浸在字母表的字母中，把这些字母看成自己思想的展示，展示中的每一个新组合都传达了一种新思路。"

当所有这些形成因素——学校、开放态度、奖赏制度、空间思维的天赋——同富饶的美国大陆相互作用时，便产生了美国特色的"emulation"。现在这个词仅表示"模仿"的意思。但在早期的美国，它却意味着为名誉和优秀而进行友好但竞争性的拼搏。

题目答案与解析

1. 依照作者的观点，早期美国之所以涌现出一些重大发明的主要原因是 _____。
   A. 小学
   B. 满腔热情的工人
   C. 富有吸引力的奖励机制
   D. 一种特殊的思考方式

【答案】D

【解析】本题中，A、B、C 三项都只是一般原因，不是主要原因。从文章第 2 段的内容可知，在许多决定性因素中，作者特别提到美国优秀的初等学校、欢迎新技术的劳动力以及奖励发明者的做法这些因素；最重要的是美国人的天赋——处理技术性事务的非语言的"立体"思维。据此可知，D 项与文中的意思相符，因此 D 项为正确答案。

2. 文章暗示早期美国技工的适应能力和独创能力 _____。
   A. 从他们的数学知识中获益匪浅
   B. 阐明了严格的学校管理
   C. 产生于享有特权的家庭训练
   D. 主要归因于技术的发展

【答案】A

【解析】本题中，B 项不正确，文中没有提到学校管理。C 项不正确，文章第 3 段第 2 句话中提到了 at home in arithmetic and...，但句子中的 at home in 是词组，意为"通晓"，并不是"在家"之意。D 项不正确，是适应能力和创造能力的发展推动了技术的发展，并不是技术的发展推动了适应能力和创造能力的发展。从文章第 4 段的第 1 句话可知，敏锐的外国观察家把美国人的适应能力以及创造能力与这种教育优势联系起来；而这种教育优势指的就是第 3 段第 2 句话中的"通晓了算术以及部分几何和三角知识"，这些都是数学知识。据此可知，早期美国技工的适应能力和创造能力得益于数学知识。A 项符合文章的意思，因此 A 项为正确答案。

3. 能把技术专家比作是艺术家，是因为 _____。

    A．他们都是奖品的获得者   B．他们都是立体思维方面的专家

    C．他们都不用语言描述   D．他们都使用各种各样的工具

【答案】B

【解析】本题中，A 项不正确，文中没有提到。C 项明显与第 8 段第 2 句话的意思不符。D 项不正确，文中没有提到。从文章第 7 段的第 2 句话可知，技术专家在思考那些不能用明确的语言描述的东西时，在头脑中以直观的、非语言的过程处理这些东西；从文章第 8 段的第 1 句话可知，这种非语言的"立体"思维能够像绘画和写作一样具有创造性；随后文章指出：技术工人应该坐在杠杆、螺杆、楔子和轮子等之间，像诗人沉浸于字母表中的字母一样，把这些东西看做他们的思想展示，展示中的每一种新组合都会传达一种新思想。据此可知，技术专家同艺术家一样，具有非语言"立体"思维。B 项与文章的意思相符，因此 B 项为正确答案。

4. 本篇文章的最佳标题可能是 _____。

    A．创造性头脑   B．有效的学校教育   C．思维的方式   D．发明的涌现

【答案】A

【解析】本题中，B 项和 C 项只是文章两个段落的意思，不能代表文章的中心意思。D 项"发明的涌现"之意也不能代表文章的意思，本文只是以"早期的美国为何发明涌现"这一问题引出文章，并没有刻意说明发明的涌现。文章询问早期的美国涌现出一些重大发明的主要原因。文章第 2 段对此作了分析，指出了几个因素，学校教育、劳动者对新技术的热情、奖励制度，最主要的是具有发明创造的思想；在随后的几段中，作者分别探讨了初级学校教育带来的影响、奖励制度带来的影响、美国人特有的立体思维方式所起的作用；最后一段得出结论：这些因素相互影响，形成了创造性意识，因而早期的美国涌现出一些重大发明。据此可知，本文主要讲的就是美国人的创造性意识及其根源。A 项与文章的意思相符，因此 A 项为正确答案。

Text 2

The most thoroughly studied intellectuals in the history of the New World are the ministers and political leaders of seventeenth-century New England. According to the standard history of American philosophy, nowhere else in colonial America was "so much important attached to intellectual pursuits". According to many books and articles, New England's leaders established the basic themes and preoccupations of an unfolding, dominant Puritan tradition in American intellectual life.

To take this approach to the New Englanders normally means to start with the Puritans' theological innovations and their distinctive ideas about the church—important subjects that we may not neglect. But in keeping with our examination of southern intellectual life, we may consider the original Puritans as carriers of European culture, adjusting to New World circumstances. The New England colonies were the scenes of important episodes in the pursuit of widely understood ideals of civility and virtuosity.

The early settlers of Massachusetts Bay included men of impressive education and influence in England. Besides the ninety or so learned ministers who came to Massachusetts churches in the decade after 1629, there were political leaders like John Winthrop, an educated gentleman, lawyer, and official of the Crown before he journeyed to Boston. There men wrote and published extensively, reaching both New World and Old World audiences, and giving New England an atmosphere of intellectual earnestness.

We should not forget, however, that most New Englanders were less well educated. While few crafts men or farmers, let alone dependents and servants, left literary compositions to be analyzed. Their thinking often had a traditional superstitions quality. A tailor named John Dane, who emigrated in the late 1630s, left an account of his reasons for leaving England that is filled with signs. Sexual confusion, economic frustrations, and religious hope — all name together in a decisive moment when he opened the Bible, told his father the first line he saw would settle his fate, and read the magical words: "come out from among them, touch no unclean thing, and I will be your God and you shall be my people." One wonders what Dane thought of the careful sermons explaining the Bible that he heard in puritan churched.

Meanwhile, many settles had slighter religious commitments than Dane's, as one clergyman learned in confronting folk along the coast who mocked that they had not come to the New World for religion. "Our main end was to catch fish."

1. The author notes that in the seventeenth-century New England _____.

　　A. Puritan tradition dominated political life

　　B. intellectual interests were encouraged

　　C. politics benefited much from intellectual endeavors

　　D. intellectual pursuits enjoyed a liberal environment

2. It is suggested in paragraph 2 that New Englanders _____.

　　A. experienced a comparatively peaceful early history

　　B. brought with them the culture of the Old World

　　C. paid little attention to southern intellectual life

　　D. were obsessed with religious innovations

3. The early ministers and political leaders in Massachusetts Bay _____.

　　A. were famous in the New World for their writings

　　B. gained increasing importance in religious affairs

　　C. abandoned high positions before coming to the New World

　　D. created a new intellectual atmosphere in New England

4. The story of John Dane shows that less well-educated New Englanders were often _____.

　　A. influenced by superstitions　　　　B. troubled with religious beliefs

　　C. puzzled by church sermons　　　　D. frustrated with family earnings

5. The text suggests that early settlers in New England _____.

　　A. were mostly engaged in political activities

　　B. were motivated by an illusory prospect

　　C. came from different backgrounds.

　　D. left few formal records for later reference

核心词汇注释

thorough ['θʌrə] *adj.* 彻底的，完全的；精心的

minister ['ministə] *n.* 部长，大臣；牧师；公使；外交使节
v.（与 to 连用）照料，帮助
相信罗素的哲学。

confront [kən'frʌnt] *v.* 面对，（使）面临

episode ['episəud] *n.* 插曲，片段

unfold [ʌn'fəuld] *v.* 展开，打开；逐渐表露；说明

sermon ['sə:mən] *n.* 训诫，说教，布道

dominant ['dɒminənt] *adj.* 支配的，统治的，居高临下的；显性的

长难句剖析

【文章难句】But in keeping with our examination of southern intellectual life, we may consider the original Puritans as carriers of European culture, adjusting to New World circumstances.

【结构分析】本句句子主干为：we may consider the original Puritans as carriers of European culture。主语是 we，谓语部分是 consider sb as sth，as 介词引出宾语补足语；现在分词短语 adjusting to…修饰名词 carriers，做其后置定语；介词短语 in keeping with…为目的状语。

【参考译文】但是要与南部精神生活的考查一致，我们可认为他们是欧洲文化的传递者，以适应新世界的环境。

【文章难句】Besides the ninety or so learned ministers who came to Massachusetts churches in the decade after 1629, there were political leaders like John Winthrop, an educated gentleman, lawyer, and official of the Crown before he journeyed to Boston.

【结构分析】本句句子主干为 there be 句型。John Winthrop 的同位语是名词词组 an educated…Boston，起到补充说明该人物身份的作用；句首的介词短语 Besides…在句子中充当状语，其中 who 引导的定语从句是名词 ministers 的后置定语。

【参考译文】除了大约 90 个博学的牧师外——他们在 1629 年后的十年内到达了马萨诸塞教堂，还有像约翰·温思罗普这样的政治领导人。

【文章难句】While few craftsmen or farmers, let alone dependents and servants, left literary compositions to be analyzed, it is obvious that their views were less fully intellectualized.

【结构分析】分析本句结构不难发现本句是一个主从复合句。该复合句中主句主干为 it is obvious that…，其中 it 为形式主语，真正的主语是 that 引导的主语从句。while 引导让步状语从句。

【参考译文】很少有手艺工人和农夫，更不用说附庸者和仆人会留下一些文学作品被后人分析，很明显他们的想法往往不是很理智。

【文章难句】Sexual confusion, economic frustrations, and religious hope — all came together in a decisive moment when he opened the Bible, told his father that the first line he saw would settle his fate, and read the magical words…

【结构分析】本句为主从复合句。主句主干是 Sexual confusion, economic frustrations, and religious hope came together in a moment。when 引导定语从句，做 moment 的后置定语；he saw 为省略引导词 that 的定语从句，修饰 the first line 动词 told 的宾语是 that 引导的宾语从句。

【参考译文】性混乱、经济挫败和宗教希望，这所有的一切在他打开圣经那个决定性的时刻都出现了。

全文参考译文

在新世界历史中，人们研究得最透彻的知识分子就是 17 世纪时期英格兰的牧师和政治领袖。据美国标准哲学史记载，在美洲殖民地中，任何其他地方都没有这儿更重视知识的追求。根据很多书籍和文章所载内容可知，新英格兰的统治者们在美国精神生活中确立了以清教传统为主的基本主题。

对于英格兰人来说，采用这种方式通常意味着开启清教徒神学上的革新，还有他们对教会所具有的独特思想，这是我们不可忽视的重要主题。但是要与南部精神生活的考查一致，我们可认为他们是欧洲文化的传递者，以适应新世界的环境。在追求广义的文明和艺术鉴别力方面，新英格兰殖民地是众多场景中重要的一个。

马萨诸塞湾的早期定居者包括那些在英格兰受到良好教育，并且影响广泛的人。除了大约 90 个博学的牧师外——他们在 1629 年后的十年内到达了马萨诸塞教堂，还有像约翰·温思罗普这样的政治领导人。在去波士顿之前，约翰·温思罗普是受过教育的绅士、律师和官员。这些人进行大量写作和出版，对新世界和旧世界的读者都产生影响，还在新英格兰创造出一种渴求知识的氛围。

然而我们应该记住一点，多数新英格兰人都未受过良好教育。很少有手艺工人和农夫，更不用说附庸者和仆人会留下一些文学作品被后人分析，很明显他们的想法往往不是很理智。他们的思想常常带有传统的迷信性。一位名叫约翰·丹奈的裁缝，他在 15 世纪 30 年代末移民，离开英格兰的理由是因为那里充满各种迹象。性混乱、经济挫败和宗教希望，这所有的一切在他打开圣经那个决定性的时刻都出现了。他告诉父亲，他看到的第一行文字将决定了他的命运。他看到了充满神奇的句子："离开他们，别触摸不洁的东西，我将是你的上帝，你将成为我的信徒。"人们想知道丹奈在清教徒教堂里听到对圣经进行讲解的布道词时将作何感想。

同时，就像一位牧师所了解的情况那样，很多移民的宗教信仰并不如丹奈那样强烈。他在海岸见到的移民嘲笑说，自己不是为了宗教信仰来到新大陆，而是"为了捕鱼"。

题目答案与解析

1. 作者表明 17 世纪的新英格兰地区的 _____。
   A．清教传统统领政治生活　　　　　B．学术兴趣得到鼓励
   C．政治从学术当中受益颇丰　　　　D．求知环境轻松自由
   【答案】B
   【解析】本题的依据句是文章第 1 段的第 2 句：According to the standard history of American philosophy, nowhere else in colonial America was "So much important attached to intellectual pursuits". 从中可知，B 项为正确答案。

2. 第二段暗示新英格兰人 _____。
   A．早期历史相对和平　　　　　　　B．将旧世界文化带到新英格兰
   C．很少关注美国南部地区的精神生活　　D．热衷宗教革新
   【答案】B
   【解析】本题可参照文章第 2 段。第 2 段中提到：我们可以将这些最初的清教徒移民视为欧洲文化的使者，他们在适应新大陆的环境。相对于北美新大陆而言，欧洲是旧大陆。考查文中事实细节。因此 B 项为正确答案。

3．早期时，生活在马萨诸塞湾的牧师和政治领袖 ＿＿＿＿。

　　A．因其作品而闻名于新大陆　　　　　B．在宗教事务中变得日益重要

　　C．在来新大陆之前辞去高官要职　　　D．在新英格兰营造一种新的知识氛围

【答案】D

【解析】本题的依据句是第 3 段的最后 1 句：There men wrote and published extensively, reaching both New World and Old World audiences, and giving New England an atmosphere of intellectual earnestness. 从中可知，D 项为正确答案。

4．约翰·丹奈的故事表明：那些受教育程度较低的新英格兰人经常 ＿＿＿＿＿

　　A．受迷信的影响　　　　　　　　　　B．受宗教信仰的困扰

　　C．困惑于教会的布道词　　　　　　　D．受挫于家庭收入

【答案】A

【解析】本题可参照文章第 4 段。第 4 段前面部分的内容指出，未受到良好教育的新英格兰人的思想往往带有传统的宗教迷信色彩。接着，后半部分举出约翰·丹奈的例子。约翰·丹奈因为受到宗教感召而移民新大陆。因此 A 项为正确答案。

5．文章表明早期新英格兰定居者 ＿＿＿＿＿＿。

　　A．主要参与政治活动　　　　　　　　B．受虚幻前景驱使

　　C．都来自不同知识背景　　　　　　　D．很少有正式记录资料可供后人参考

【答案】C

【解析】本题可参照文章第 3、4、5 段。第 3 段介绍早期移民受过良好教育并具有相当的影响力；第 4 段表明大多数新英格兰移民并未受过良好的教育，他们的思想常常带有传统的宗教迷信；第 5 段指出，还有很多移民没有虔诚的宗教信仰。因此 C 项为正确答案。

Text　3

Money spent on advertising is money spent as well as any I know of. It serves directly to assist a rapid distribution of goods at reasonable price, thereby establishing a firm home market and so making it possible to provide for export at competitive prices. By drawing attention to new ideas it helps enormously to raise standards of living. By helping to increase demand it ensures an increased need for labour, and is therefore an effective way to fight unemployment. It lowers the costs of many services: without advertisements your daily newspaper would cost four times as much, the price of your television licence would need to be doubled, and travel by bus or tube would cost 20 percent more.

And perhaps most important of all, advertising provides a guarantee of reasonable value in the products and services you buy. Apart from the fact that twenty-seven acts of Parliament govern the terms of advertising, no regular advertiser dare promote a product that fails to live up to the promise of his advertisements. He might fool some people for a little while through misleading advertising. He will not do so for long, for mercifully the public has the good sense not to buy the inferior article more than once. If you see an article consistently advertised, it is the surest proof I know that the article does what is claimed for it, and that it represents good value.

Advertising does more for the material benefit of the community than any other force I can think of. There is one more point I feel I ought to touch on. Recently I heard a well-known television personality declare that he was against advertising because it persuades rather than informs. He was drawing excessively fine distinctions. Of course advertising seeks to persuade.

If its message were confined merely to information — and that in itself would be difficult if not impossible to achieve, for even a detail such as the choice of the colour of a shirt is subtly persuasive — advertising would be so boring that no one would pay any attention. But perhaps that is what the well-known television personality wants.

1. By the first sentence of the passage the author means that _____.
   A. he is fairly familiar with the cost of advertising
   B. everybody knows well that advertising is money consuming
   C. advertising costs money like everything else
   D. it is worthwhile to spend money on advertising

2. In the passage, which of the following is NOT included in the advantages of advertising?
   A. Securing greater fame.　　　　　　B. Providing more jobs.
   C. Enhancing living standards.　　　　D. Reducing newspaper cost.

3. The author deems that the well-known TV personality is _____.
   A. very precise in passing his judgement on advertising
   B. interested in nothing but the buyers' attention
   C. correct in telling the difference between persuasion and information
   D. obviously partial in his views on advertising

4. In the author's opinion, _____.
   A. advertising can seldom bring material benefit to man by providing information
   B. advertising informs people of new ideas rather than wins them over
   C. there is nothing wrong with advertising in persuading the buyer
   D. the buyer is not interested in getting information from an advertisement

核心词汇注释

competitive [kəmˈpetɪtɪv] *adj.* 竞争的

enormously [ɪˈnɔːməslɪ] *adv.* 非常地；巨大地

licence [ˈlaɪsəns] *n.* 执照；许可证；特许
　　vt. 许可；特许；认可；发给执照

guarantee [ˌgærənˈtiː] *n.* 保证；保证书；担保；抵押品
　　vt. 保证；担保

inferior [ɪnˈfɪərɪə(r)] *adj.* 下等的；下级的，差的；次的；自卑的；劣等的

excessively [ɪkˈsesɪvlɪ] *adv.* 过分地；非常地

distinction [dɪˈstɪŋkʃ(ə)n] *n.* 区别；差别；级别；特性；声望；显赫

confined [kənˈfaɪnd] *adj.* 被限制的；狭窄的；分娩的

subtle [ˈsʌt(ə)l] *adj.* 狡猾的；敏感的；微妙的；精细的；稀薄的

persuasive [pəˈsweɪsɪv] *n.* 说服者；劝诱
　　adj. 善说服的

长难句剖析

【文章难句】Recently I heard a well-known television personality declare that he was against advertising because it persuades rather than informs.

【结构分析】本句主干是 I heard a well-known television personality declare，that 引导的是宾语从句，句中 because it persuades rather than informs 是原因状语从句。副词 recently 做状语。

【参考译文】近来，我听到一位电视名人声称，他反对广告，因为广告是在说服人而不是提供信息。

全文参考译文

把钱花在做广告上是我知道的最好的花钱方式。广告直接帮助货物以合理价格快速销售，由此建立稳定的国内市场，并有可能以有竞争力的价格出口。通过把人们的注意力吸引到新观念上来，它有助于极大提高生活水平。通过促进需求的增加，它确保对劳动力的需求，因此是应对失业的有效方法。它降低许多服务的成本，没有广告，日报价格就会增加四倍，电视收视费将变成两倍，乘公交车或地铁会多花 20%。

最重要的也许是，广告为你所买的产品和服务提供合理的价值保证。除了 27 个国会法案控制着广告条款这一事实外，没有一家广告商敢于促销与广告内容不符的产品。他可能会通过令人误解的广告，暂时愚弄某些人。但他这样做的时间不会很长，因为，庆幸的是，公众有很好的判断力，他们不会第二次购买质量低下的产品。如果你看到一件物品被连续地做广告，那么这是我知道的最确信的证明，这件物品名副其实，表现出很好的价值。

广告比我所能想起的任何其他手段都更能带给人们物质利益。

还有一点我觉得应该涉及一下。近来，我听到一位电视名人声称，他反对广告，因为广告是在说服人而不是提供信息。他在过分地区分这些差异。当然，广告目的就是力求去说服人。

如果广告仅限于提供信息，其本身即使可能，也会很难实现，因为即使是衬衫颜色的选择这种细节也带有说服性——广告将会令人厌烦，以至于没有人会注意。但也许那正是那位电视名人所想要的。

题目答案与解析

1. 作者在文章的第一句话中指出 _____。
   A. 他对广告的费用非常了解　　　　　B. 人人都知道做广告耗费金钱
   C. 做广告像其他事一样需要花钱　　　D. 花钱做广告值得

【答案】D

【解析】作者在第 1 句话指出："把钱花在做广告上是我知道的最好的花钱方式"。故正确答案为 D 项。

2. 根据本文，下面哪项不是广告的优点？
   A. 获得更大声誉。　　　　　　　　　B. 提供更多的工作。
   C. 提高生活水平。　　　　　　　　　D. 降低报纸成本。

【答案】A

【解析】从文章第 1、2 段可以得出正确答案。B 项与文章第 1 段第 4 句"通过促进需求的增加，它确保对劳动力的需求，因此是抵制失业的有效方法"一致。C 项与第 1 段第 3 句内容一致。D 项与第 1 段最后一句内容一致。A 项在文中未涉及，因此 A 项正确。

3. 作者认为电视名人 _____。
   A. 对广告的评价非常精确

B. 只想引起购买者的注意

C. 对说服和提供信息之间的区别的讲述是正确的

D. 对广告的看法明显有偏见

【答案】D

【解析】见文章最后两段。电视名人的观点在第 4 段第 2 句话，他反对广告，认为，广告是在说服人而不是在提供信息。第 3、4 句话中，作者提出了自己的观点："他在过分地区分这些差异。当然，广告的目的就是力求去说服人"。这表明作者不同意电视名人的观点。由此可知，D 项为正确答案。

4. 根据作者的观点，_____。

A. 广告不可能通过提供信息给人带来物质利益

B. 广告给人们提供新的观念而不是争取购买者

C. 广告劝购物者购物并没有错

D. 购买者对从广告中获取信息不感兴趣

【答案】C

【解析】从第 4 段最后一句话和最后一段第 1 句话可以得出答案。C 项为正确答案。A 项与第 3 段作者的观点相反。B 项与作者观点明显不符。D 项文章未曾提及。

Text 4

There are two basic ways to see growth: one as a product, the other as a process. People have generally viewed personal growth as an external result or product that can easily be identified and measured. The worker who gets a promotion, the student whose grades improve, the foreigner who learns a new language — all these are examples of people who have measurable results to show for their efforts.

By contrast, the process of personal growth is much more difficult to determine, since by definition it is a journey and not the specific signposts or landmarks along the way. The process is not the road itself, but rather the attitudes and feelings people have, their caution or courage, as they encounter new experiences and unexpected obstacles. In this process, the journey never really ends; there are always new ways to experience the world, new ideas to try, new challenges to accept .

In order to grow, to travel new roads, people need to have a willingness to take risks, to confront the unknown, and to accept the possibility that they may "fail" at first. How we see ourselves as we try a new way of being is essential to our ability to grow. Do we perceive ourselves as quick and curious? If so, then we tend to take more chances and to be more open to unfamiliar experiences. Do we think we're shy and indecisive? Then our sense of timidity can cause us to hesitate, to move slowly, and not to take a step until we know the ground is safe. Do we think we're slow to adapt to change or that we're not smart enough to cope with a new challenge? Then we are likely to take a more passive role or not try at all.

These feelings of insecurity and self-doubt are both unavoidable and necessary if we are to change and grow. If we do not confront and overcome these internal fears and doubts, if we protect ourselves too much, then we cease to grow. We become trapped inside a shell of our own making.

1. A person is generally believed to achieve personal growth when _____.

A. he has given up his smoking habit

B. he has made great efforts in his work

C. he is keen on learning anything new

D. he has tried to determine where he is on his journey

2. In the author's eyes, one who views personal growth as a process would _____.

   A. succeed in climbing up the social ladder

   B. judge his ability to glow from his own achievements

   C. face difficulties and take up challenges

   D. aim high and reach his goal each time

3. When the author says "a new way of being" (Line 3, Para. 3) he is referring to _____.

   A. a new approach to experiencing the world   B. a new way of taking risks

   C. a new method of perceiving ourselves   D. a new system of adaptation to change

4. For personal growth, the author advocates all of the following except _____.

   A. curiosity about more chances   B. promptness in self-adaptation

   C. open-mindedness to new experiences   D. avoidance of internal fears and doubts

核心词汇注释

external [ekˈstɜːn(ə)l] *adj.* 外部的；客观的；[医] 外用的；外国的；表面的 *n.* 外部；外面

measurable [ˈmeʒərəbl] *adj.* 可测量的

definition [ˌdefɪˈnɪʃ(ə)n] *n.* 定义；解说；精确度；（轮廓影像等的）清晰度

signpost [ˈsaɪnpəust] *n.* 路标

obstacle [ˈɒbstək(ə)l] *n.* 障碍；妨害物

willing [ˈwɪlɪŋ] *adj.* 乐意的；自愿的；心甘情愿的

perceive [pəˈsiːv] *vt.* 察觉 *v.* 感知；感到；认识到

indecisive [ˌɪndɪˈsaɪsɪv] *adj.* 优柔寡断的；非决定性的

timidity [tɪˈmɪdətɪ] *n.* 胆怯

insecurity [ˌɪnsɪˈkjuərətɪ] *n.* 不安全；不安全感

长难句剖析

【文章难句】If we do not confront and overcome these internal fears and doubts, if we protect ourselves too much, then we cease to grow.

【结构分析】本句主干是 we cease to grow。两个 if 引导的都是条件从句，它们是并列关系。

【参考译文】如果我们不去面对、不去克服这些内在的恐惧和疑虑，如果我们过分地保护自己，那么我们就会停止成长。

全文参考译文

对于成长，人们有两种基本看法：一种是看做结果；另一种是看做过程。人们通常把个人成长看作很容易识别和衡量的外在结果。工人获得晋升，学生的成绩有了提高，外国人掌握了一门新语言，这些都是人们付出之后取得可衡量成绩的例子。

相比之下，对个人成长过程的测定就难得多了。因为从定义上讲，它是一种旅程，而不是路途中特定的路标或里程碑。过程不是道路本身，而是当人遇到新体验或意料之外的障碍时所持的态度和情感，谨慎小心或者勇气十足。在这个过程中，旅程从来没有真正的尽头；总是存在要体验世界的新方式，要尝试的新思路，要接受的新挑战。

为了成长，为了游历新的道路，人们需乐于去冒险，去面对未知世界，去接受开始阶段失败的可能性。当我们尝试新的生存方式时，如何看待自己，这对我们能力的提高是至关重要的。我们认为自己反应敏捷又好奇心强吗？如果那样，我们会抓住更多的机会，会更勇于面对陌生的经历。我们是否认为自己害羞而优柔寡断呢？那么这种胆怯感会使我们犹豫不前、行动缓慢，直到我们确信安全才会更进一步。我们是否认为自己适应改变很缓慢，或是应对新挑战不够精明呢？那样的话，我们可能会更加消极，或者根本不去尝试。

如果我们要改变、要成长，不安全感和自我怀疑的感觉是不可避免和必要的。如果我们不去面对、不去克服这些内在的恐惧和疑虑，如果我们过分地保护自己，那么我们就会停止成长。我们就会作茧自缚。

题目答案与解析

1. 当一个人 _____，通常认为他取得了个人的成长。
   A. 他克服掉了吸烟的习惯
   B. 他在工作中很努力
   C. 他渴望学习任何新的事物
   D. 他努力确定自己的人生目标
   【答案】A
   【解析】从第 1 段第 2 句话"人们通常把个人成长看作很容易识别和衡量的外在结果"可知，A 项为正确答案。A 项表达的内容原文并未提到，但我们知道，戒烟是非常不易的，它需要坚定的决心与毅力。正像是一个学生要取得好成绩必须做出努力，最后才能取得成功。

2. 在作者的眼中，将个人成长视作一个过程的人会 _____。
   A. 提高社会地位
   B. 判断自己从个人成就中得到的能力
   C. 面对困难，迎接挑战
   D. 要求高，并且每次都实现自己的目标
   【答案】C
   【解析】从第 2 段可以得出答案，C 项为正确答案。A 项、B 项、D 项均属于结果。

3. 当作者说"为人处世的新方法"（第 3 段第 3 行）时，他指的是 _____。
   A. 一种体验世界的新方法
   B. 一种冒险的新方法
   C. 一种自我感知的新方法
   D. 一种适应改变的新方法
   【答案】A
   【解析】本题中的 new way 指第 2 段最后一句话 there are always new ways to experience the world，new ideas to try, new challenges to accept，因此答案为 A 项。

4. 对于个人成长，以下几项除了 _____ 之外作者都提倡。
   A. 对更多机会充满好奇
   B. 自我适应迅速
   C. 对新的经历能够接受
   D. 回避内心的恐惧和疑虑
   【答案】D
   【解析】从最后两段可以得出正确答案。A 项、B 项、C 项均可以从文章中找到，只有 D 项没有提及。

Unit　22

Text　1

In such a changing, complex society formerly simple solutions to informational needs become complicated. Many of life's problems which were solved by asking family members, friends or colleagues are beyond the capability of the extended family to resolve. Where to turn for expert information and how to determine which expert advice to accept are questions facing many people today.

In addition to this, there is the growing mobility of people since World War Ⅱ. As families move away from their stable community, their friends of many years, their extended family relationships, the informal flow of information is cut off, and with it the confidence that information will be available when needed and will be trustworthy and reliable. The almost unconscious flow of information about the simplest aspects of living can be cut off. Thus, things once learned subconsciously through the casual communications of the extended family must be consciously learned.

Adding to societal changes today is an enormous stockpile of information. The individual now has more information available than any generation, and the task of finding that one piece of information relevant to his or her specific problem is complicated, time-consuming and sometimes even overwhelming .

Coupled with the growing quantity of information is the development of technologies which enable the storage and delivery of more information with greater speed to more locations than has ever been possible before. Computer technology makes it possible to store vast amounts of data in machine-readable files, and to program computers to locate specific information. Telecommunication developments enable the sending of messages via television, radio, and very shortly, electronic mail to bombard people with multitudes of messages.

Satellites have extended the power of communications to report events at the instant of occurrence. Expertise can be shared world wide through teleconferencing, and problems in dispute can be settled without the participants leaving their homes and/or jobs to travel to a distant conference site. Technology has facilitated the sharing of information and the storage and delivery of information, thus making more information available to more people.

In this world of change and complexity, the need for information is of greatest importance. Those people who have accurate, reliable up-to-date information to solve the day-to-day problems, the critical problems of their business, social and family life, will survive and succeed. "Knowledge is power" may well be the truest saying and access to information may be the most critical requirement of all people.

1.　The word "it" (Line 3, Para. 2) most probably refers to _____.

　　A.　the lack of stable communities

　　B.　the breakdown of informal information channels

C. the increased mobility of families

D. the growing number of people moving from place to place

2. The main problem people may encounter today arises from the fact that _____.

A. they have to learn new things consciously

B. they lack the confidence of securing reliable and trustworthy information

C. they have difficulty obtaining the needed information readily

D. they can hardly carry out casual communications with an extended family

3. From the passage we can infer that _____.

A. electronic mail will soon play a dominant role in transmitting messages

B. it will become more difficult for people to keep secrets in an information era

C. people will spend less time holding meetings or conferences

D. events will be reported on the spot mainly through satellites

4. We can learn from the last paragraph that _____.

A. it is necessary to obtain as much

B. people should make the best use of the information

C. we should realize the importance of accumulating information

D. it is of vital importance to acquire needed information efficiently

核心词汇注释

mobility [məʊˈbɪlɪtɪ] *n.* 活动性；灵活性；迁移率；机动性

subconscious [sʌbˈkɒnʃəs] *adj.* 下意识的

societal [səˈsaɪətəl] *adj.* 社会的

stockpile [ˈstɒkpaɪl] *n.* 积蓄；库存 *vt.* 储蓄；贮存

bombard [bɒmˈbɑːd] *vt.* 炮轰；轰击

multitude [ˈmʌltɪtjuːd] *n.* 多数；群众

occurrence [əˈkʌrəns; -ˈkɜː-] *n.* 发生；出现；事件；发生的事情

expertise [ˌekspɜːˈtiːz] *n.* 专家的意见；专门技术

teleconferencing [ˈtelɪˌkɒnfərənsɪŋ] 电信会议

facilitation [fəˌsɪlɪˈteɪʃən] *n.* 简易化；助长

长难句剖析

【文章难句】Coupled with the growing quantity of information is the development of technologies which enable the storage and delivery of more information with greater speed to more locations than has ever been possible before.

【结构分析】本句主干是 Coupled with the growing quantity of information is the development of technologies。which 引导的是定语从句，在这个定语从句中用了比较级。

【参考译文】伴随着信息量的大量增加，各种技术发展开来。这些技术的发展可以更快地储存和传递更多的信息到更多的地方去，这在以前是不可能的。

全文参考译文

在这样一个不断变化的复杂社会中，对信息的需求由从前的简单变得复杂。许多过去可以通过询问家庭成员、朋友或同事就能解决的生活难题现在却超出了这个大家庭的能力范围。去哪儿找专家，如何确定哪些专家的建议应该接受，成了今天许多人面对的问题。

此外，二战以来，人口流动性越来越大。随着家庭搬出其稳定的社区，离开了多年的朋友，脱离了大家庭的关系，日常的信息交流被切断了，需要时就可以获得可靠信息的信心也随之而去了。生活中最简单方面的无意识的信息交流也被切断。所以，过去通过大家庭随意交流就能学到的东西现在必须有意识地去学。

除了当今的社会变化之外，信息量剧增也是一个问题。现在个人可获得的信息比任何一代人都多，然而，找到一条与自己的特定问题相关的信息是很复杂、很耗时的，有时甚至很困难。

伴随着信息量的大量增加，各种技术快速发展起来。这些技术的发展使人们可以更快地储存更多的信息，并传递到更多的地方去，这在以前是不可能的。计算机技术可以在机读文件中储存大量的信息，人们通过计算机编程定位特定信息。电信技术的发展使人们可以通过电视、广播传送信息，不久电子邮件会不间断地给人们送来大量信息。

卫星拓展了通信能力，可以对事件进行实时报道。专门知识可以通过电话会议在全球范围内共享。参加会议者不必离开家或工作岗位去遥远的会场，就可以解决有争议的问题。技术使信息的共享、储存和传递更加便利，也因此使更多的人得到更多的信息。

在这个多变和复杂的世界里，对信息的需求是最重要的。那些能够利用准确可靠的最新信息解决日常问题以及生意、社会与家庭生活的关键问题的人就能生存下去并取得成功。"知识就是力量"是再正确不过的谚语，对信息的获取也许是所有人最迫切的需求了。

题目答案与解析

1．单词"it"（第 2 段第 3 行）最可能指的是 _____。
   A．社区缺乏稳定　　　　　　　　　B．日常的信息交流被切断了
   C．家庭的流动性增强　　　　　　　D．人口流动不断增长
   【答案】B
   【解析】从文中"随着家庭搬出稳定的社区，离开多年的好友，脱离了大家庭的关系，日常的信息交流被切断，需要时就可以获得可靠信息的信心也随之而去了。"可知 it 指的"日常的信息交流被切断了"。

2．今天人们可能遭遇的主要问题来自于 _____。
   A．他们得自觉学习新的事物
   B．他们对获得可靠的、可信的信息缺乏信心
   C．他们很难轻易得到所需的信息
   D．他们几乎无法与大家庭随意交流
   【答案】C
   【解析】从第 3 段第 2 句话"今天，个人可获得的信息比任何一代人都多，然而，找到一条与自己问题相关的信息既复杂又耗时，有时甚至很困难"可知，C 项为正确答案。

3．根据本文我们可以推知 _____。
   A．电子邮件不久可以在传递信息中起主导作用
   B．对人们来说，在信息时代保密将变得更加困难

C. 人们将花很少的时间来开会

D. 现场事件将主要通过卫星报道

【答案】A

【解析】从第 4 段第 3 句话 "计算机技术使人们能把大量的信息储存在机读文件中，人们通过计算机编程找到某一信息。电信技术的发展使人们可以通过电视、广播发送信息，不久电子邮件会不断地给人们送来大量信息" 可知，A 项为正确答案。

4. 从最后一段我们可知 _____。

    A. 获取尽量多的信息是必要的   B. 人们应充分利用信息

    C. 我们应该意识到积累信息的必要性   D. 有效地获取所需信息是非常重要的

【答案】D

【解析】从第 4 段第 3 句话可知答案。最后一段第 1 句话指出在这个变化和复杂的世界里，对信息的需求最为重要，第 2 句话进行了具体说明 "那些利用准确、可靠、最新信息解决日常问题、企业的关键问题及社会与家庭问题的人就能生存下去并获得成功"。D 项总结了最后一段的内容。

Text 2

Personality is to a large extent inherent — A-type parents usually bring about A-type offspring. But the environment must also have a profound effect, since if competition is important to the parents, it is likely to become a major factor in the lives of their children.

One place where children soak up A-characteristics is school, which is, by its very nature, a highly competitive institution. Too many schools adopt "the win at all costs" moral standard and measure their success by sporting achievements. The current passion for making children compete against their classmates or against the clock produces a two-layer system, in which competitive A-types seem in some way better than their B-type fellows. Being too keen to win can have dangerous consequences: remember that Pheidippides, the first marathon runner, dropped dead seconds after saying: "Rejoice, we conquer!"

By far the worst form of competition in schools is the disproportionate emphasis on examinations. It is a rare school that allows pupils to concentrate on those things they do well. The merits of competition by examination are somewhat questionable, but competition in the certain knowledge of failure is positively harmful.

Obviously, it is neither practical nor desirable that all A-youngsters change into B's. The world needs A-types, and schools have an important duty to try to fit a child's personality to his possible future employment. It is top management.

If the preoccupation of schools with academic work was lessened, more time might be spent teaching children surer values. Perhaps selection for the caring professions, especially medicine could be made less by good grades in chemistry and more by such considerations as sensitivity and sympathy. It is surely a mistake to choose our doctors exclusively from A-type stock. B's are important and should be encouraged.

1. According to the passage, A-type individuals are usually _____.
   A. impatient　　　B. considerate　　　C. aggressive　　　D. agreeable
2. The author is strongly opposed to the practice of examinations at schools because _____.
   A. the pressure is too great on the students　B. some students are bound to fail
   C. failure rates are too high　D. the results of examinations are doubtful
3. The selection of medical professionals are currently based on _____.
   A. candidates' sensitivity　B. academic achievements
   C. competitive spirit　D. surer values
4. From the passage we can draw the conclusion that _____.
   A. the personality of a child is well established at birth
   B. family influence dominates the shaping of one's characteristics
   C. the development of one's personality is due to multiple factors
   D. B-type characteristics can find no place in competitive society

核心词汇注释

inherent [ɪnˈhɪərənt] *adj.* 固有的；内在的；与生俱来的

soak [səʊk] *v.* 浸，泡；浸透 *n.* 浸透

consequence [ˈkɒnsɪkwəns] *n.* 结果；[逻] 推理，推论；因果关系；重要的地位

marathon [ˈmærəθɒn, -θən] *n.* [体]马拉松赛跑（全长 421,954 米）；耐力的考验

disproportionate [ˌdɪsprəˈpɔːʃənet] *adj.* 不成比例的

merit [ˈmerɪt] *n.* 优点；价值 *v.* 有益于

preoccupation [priːˌɒkjʊˈpeɪʃ(ə)n] *n.* 当务之急

caring [ˈkeərɪŋ] *adj.* 人的，人道的；有同情心的

sensitivity [ˌsensɪˈtɪvɪtɪ] *n.* 敏感；灵敏（度），灵敏性

exclusively [ɪkˈskluːsɪvlɪ] *adv.* 排外地；专有地

长难句剖析

【文章难句】The current passion for making children compete against their classmates or against the clock produces a two-layer system , in which competitive A-types seem in some way better than their B-type fellows.

【结构分析】本句主干是 The current passion…produces a two-layer system。主句中，for 与后面的现在分词短语构成介宾短语，做定语；in which 引导的是非限制性定语从句，其中还有一个比较级 better than。

【参考译文】目前热衷于让孩子们与同学们或与时间竞争产生了一种双层机制，在这种机制中，竞争型的 A 型性格的学生在某种程度上似乎比 B 型性格的学生表现要好。

全文参考译文

性格在很大程度上是与生俱来的。A 型性格的父母通常会有 A 型性格的后代，但是环境

也有深远的影响，因为如果竞争对父母来说很重要，那么竞争很可能成为孩子成长中的一个重要因素。

孩子吸收 A 型性格的地方之一是学校，学校就其本质而言是一个高度竞争的机构。有太多学校采纳"不惜一切取得成功"作为道德标准，并用成绩衡量孩子的成败。目前热衷于让孩子们与同学们或与时间竞争产生了一种双层机制，在这种机制中，竞争型的 A 型性格的学生在某种程度上似乎比 B 型性格的学生表现要好。太想获胜可能导致危险的结局：记得第一个跑马拉松的人费迪皮迪兹，说完"欢呼吧，我们胜利啦！"之后几秒便倒地而死。

到目前为止，学校里最糟糕的竞争形式就是不恰当地强调考试。让学生集中精力做他们能做好的事，这类学校已很少见了。用考试来竞争的优点有点令人质疑，但明知会失败却还要竞争则是肯定有害的。

显然，把所有 A 型性格变成 B 型性格既不现实也不合理。世界也需要 A 型性格的人，学校的一个重要职责就是使孩子的个性适合未来可能从事的职业。这是最佳管理模式。

如果学校对学业的重视减少一些，或许有更多的时间教孩子们一些更有价值的东西，也许对护理行业，特别是医务人员的选择少看重化学成绩，多关注一些其敏感性及同情心会更合理一些。只从 A 型性格的人中挑选医生肯定是不对的。B 型性格的人同样重要，应当受到鼓励。

题目答案与解析

1. 根据本文，A 型性格的人通常 _____。
   A. 没有耐心   B. 考虑周到   C. 有进取心的   D. 使人愉快
   【答案】C
   【解析】从第 2 段第 1 句话"孩子吸收 A 性格的地方之一是学校，学校就其本质而言是一个高度竞争的机构"，可知 C 项为正确答案。

2. 作者对学校考试的做法强烈反对的原因是 _____。
   A. 对学生压力太大   B. 一些学生必定会失败（不及格）
   C. 不及格率太高   D. 考试结果令人怀疑
   【答案】B
   【解析】本题问作者强烈反对学校考试的做法的原因。参看第 3 段第 3 句话"用考试来竞争的优点有点令人质疑，但明知失败却还要竞争是肯定有害的"，即作者认为学校的考试是一种竞争，有人会成功，有人会失败。这和 B 项一致。A 项和 C 项在文中未提及。D 项与原文不一致。

3. 目前对医务人员的选择是根据 _____。
   A. 候选人的敏感性   B. 学术成就
   C. 竞争精神   D. 更高的价值
   【答案】A
   【解析】从最后一段第 2 句话"也许对护理行业特别是医务人员的选择少侧重于化学成绩，更多考虑其敏感性及同情心会更好一些"可知 A 项为正确答案。

4. 从文中我们能够得出结论 _____。

　　A．孩子的个性在出生时就已确定

　　B．家庭的影响控制一个人性格的塑造

　　C．一个人个性的发展受多种因素的影响

　　D．B 型性格的人在竞争性社会无法立足

【答案】C

【解析】本题为推论题。本文主要谈论了学校教育对学生性格形成的影响。综观全文，我们知道性格的发展受先天和环境等多种因素影响。因此 C 项为正确答案。

Text　3

That experiences influence subsequent behaviour is evidence of an obvious but nevertheless remarkable activity called remembering. Learning could not occur without the function popularly named memory. Constant practice has such as effect on memory as to lead to skillful performance on the piano, to recitation of a poem, and even to reading and understanding these words. So-called intelligent behaviour demands memory, remembering being a primary requirement for reasoning. The ability to solve any problem or even to recognize that a problem exists depends on memory. Typically, the decision to cross a street is based on remembering many earlier experiences .

Practice (or review) tends to build and maintain memory for a task or for any learned material. Over a period of no practice what has been learned tends to be forgotten; and the adaptive consequences may not seem obvious. Yet, dramatic instances of sudden forgetting can seem to be adaptive. In this sense, the ability to forget can be interpreted to have survived through a process of natural selection in animals. Indeed, when one's memory of an emotionally painful experience lead to serious anxiety, forgetting may produce relief. Nevertheless, an evolutionary interpretation might make it difficult to understand how the commonly gradual process of forgetting survived natural selection.

In thinking about the evolution of memory together with all its possible aspects, it is helpful to consider what would happen if memories failed to fade. Forgetting clearly aids orientation in time, since old memories weaken and the new tend to stand out, providing clues for inferring duration. Without forgetting, adaptive ability would suffer, for example, learned behaviour that might have been correct a decade ago may no longer be. Cases are recorded of people who (by ordinary standards) forgot so little that their everyday activities were full of confusion. This forgetting seems to serve that survival of the individual and the species.

Another line of thought assumes a memory storage system of limited capacity that provides adaptive flexibility specifically through forgetting. In this view, continual adjustments are made between learning or memory storage (input) and forgetting (output) . Indeed, there is evidence that the rate at which individuals forget is directly related to how much they have learned.Such data offers gross support of contemporary models of memory that assume an input-output balance.

1. From the evolutionary point of view, _____.

　　A．forgetting for lack of practice tends to be obviously inadaptive

    B. if a person gets very forgetful all of a sudden he must be very adaptive

    C. the gradual process of forgetting is an indication of an individual's adaptability

    D. sudden forgetting may bring about adaptive consequences

2. According to the passage, if a person never forgot , _____.

    A. he would survive best   B. he would have a lot of trouble

    C. his ability to learn would be enhanced   D. the evolution of memory would stop

3. From the last paragraph we know that _____.

    A. forgetfulness is a response to learning

    B. the memory storage system is an exactly balanced input-output system

    C. memory is a compensation for forgetting

    D. the capacity of a memory storage system is limited because forgetting occurs

4. In this article, the author tries to interpret the function of _____.

    A. remembering   B. forgetting   C. adapting   D. experiencing

核心词汇注释

constant [ˈkɒnstənt] n. [数、物]常数，恒量
adj. 不变的，持续的；坚决的

recitation [ˌresɪˈteɪʃ(ə)n] n. 朗诵，背诵；叙述；背诵的东西

evolutionary [ˌiːvəˈluːʃənərɪ] 进化的

interpretation [ɪnˌtɜːprɪˈteɪʃ(ə)n] n. 解释，阐明；口译，通译

orientation [ˌɔːrɪənˈteɪʃ(ə)n] n. 方向，方位；定位；倾向性；向东方

duration [djʊəˈreɪʃ(ə)n] n. 持续时间，为期

survival [səˈvaɪv(ə)l] n. 生存；幸存，残存；幸存者，残存物

flexibility [ˌfleksəˈbɪlɪtɪ] n. 弹性；适应性，机动性

gross [ɡrəʊs] adj. 总的；毛重的
n. 总额

contemporary [kənˈtempərərɪ] n. 同时代的人
adj. 当代的，同时代的

长难句剖析

【文章难句】Nevertheless, an evolutionary interpretation might make it difficult to understand how the commonly gradual process of forgetting survived natural selection.

【结构分析】本句主语是 an evolutionary interpretation，谓语是 might make，it 是形式宾语，to 引导的不定式做宾语补足语，其中疑问副词 how 引导的句子做 understand 的宾语。

【参考译文】然而，进化论的解释可能会让人难以理解这个一般的逐渐遗忘过程是如何经自然选择而幸存下来的。

全文参考译文

过去的经历会影响日后的行为，这一现象表明一种明显却又非凡的脑力活动，我们称之为记忆。没有记忆这种功能，学习便不可能发生。不断练习对记忆有这样一种效果，它可以使人们在演奏钢琴、背诵诗歌，甚至阅读和理解这些话方面有熟练表现。这种所谓的智力行为需要记忆，记忆是推理的主要条件。解决任何问题甚至识别某个问题是否存在的能力都倚

赖于记忆。举个典型的例子，作出穿越马路的决定就是建立在此前经历的记忆的基础之上的。

实践（或复习）往往能建立和维持对某项任务或任何已学内容的记忆。所学的东西，如果一段时间不运用，往往会忘记；其适应性结果可能看起来就不明显。但是，戏剧性的突然遗忘的事例好像具有适应性。在这种意义上，遗忘的能力可以解释为动物通过自然选择过程幸存下来的结果。的确，当一个人记忆某种情感上伤痛的经历并给他带来严重焦虑时，遗忘可以使他获得解脱。然而，进化论的解释可能会让人难以理解这个一般的逐渐遗忘过程是如何经自然选择后幸存下来的。

在思考记忆的进化和它所有的可能方面时，考虑一下如果记忆不会消失会怎样是很有用的。很明显，遗忘有助于时间的定位，因为过去的记忆淡忘了，新的记忆往往就会显现出来，同时这就为推断延续时间提供了线索。没有遗忘，适应能力就会受影响，例如，10 年前也许正确的行为现在可能不再正确了。在一些病历中，有的人遗忘的太少（和普通人相比），以至于他们的日常活动充满了混乱。遗忘好像有助于个体及物种生存。

另一种想法假定，有限容量的记忆存储系统通过遗忘提供了适应的灵活性。按照这种观点，人们可以在学习或记忆存储（输入）和遗忘（输出）之间不断进行调整。实际上，有证据表明，个人的遗忘速度与学习东西的多少直接相关。这些数据为输入与输出平衡的当代记忆模式提供了有力的支持。

题目答案与解析

1. 从进化观点来说，_____。
   A. 因缺乏练习而遗忘往往有明显的不适应性
   B. 如果一个人突然变得非常健忘，他一定非常具有适应性
   C. 逐渐的遗忘过程表明了一个人的适应能力
   D. 突然遗忘可以产生适应性的结果

【答案】D

【解析】从第 2 段第 2、3 句话"所学的东西，如果一段时间不运用，往往会遗忘；其适应性结果可能就不太明显，然而，戏剧性的突然遗忘的例子好像具有适应性"可知，D 项为正确答案。A 项、B 项、C 项均与原文不符。

2. 根据本文，如果一个人从未遗忘过，_____。
   A. 他会生活得最好　　　　　　　B. 他会有许多麻烦
   C. 他学习的能力会提高　　　　　D. 记忆的进化会停止

【答案】B

【解析】从第 3 段倒数第 2 句话"在一些病历中，有的人遗忘的太少（和普通人相比），以至于他们的日常活动充满了混乱"可知，B 项为正确答案。

3. 从最后一段我们可知 _____。
   A. 遗忘是对学习的响应
   B. 记忆储存系统是绝对平衡的输入与输出系统
   C. 记忆是对遗忘的弥补
   D. 记忆储存系统的容量有限是因为发生了遗忘

【答案】A

【解析】从最后一段第 2 句话"根据这种观点，在学习或记忆储存（输入）及遗忘（输出）之间不断进行调整"可知，A 项正确。B 项、C 项、D 项均不正确。

4.　本文中，作者试图说明 _____ 的作用。

　　A．记忆　　　　　　　B．遗忘　　　　　　　C．适应　　　　　　　D．体验

【答案】B

【解析】本题为主旨题。B 项正确。

Text　4

　　The American economic system is organized around a basically private-enterprise, market-oriented economy in which consumers largely determine what shall be produced by spending their money in the marketplace for those goods and services that they want most. Private businessmen, striving to make profits, produce these goods and services in competition with other businessmen; and the profit motive, operating under competitive pressures, largely determines how these goods and services are produced. Thus, in the American economic system it is the demand of individual consumers, coupled with the desire of businessmen to maximize profits and the desire of individuals to maximize their incomes, that together determine what shall be produced and how resources are used to produce it.

　　An important factor in a market-oriented economy is the mechanism by which consumer demands can be expressed and responded to by producers. In the American economy, this mechanism is provided by a price system, a process in which prices rise and fall in response to relative demands of consumers and supplies offered by seller-producers. If the product is in short supply relative to the demand, the price will be bid up and some consumers will be eliminated from the market. If, on the other hand, producing more of a commodity results in reducing its cost, this will tend to increase the supply offered by seller-producers, which in turn will lower the price and permit more consumers to buy the product. Thus, price is the regulating mechanism in the American economic system.

　　The important factor in a private-enterprise economy is that individuals are allowed to own productive resources (private property), and they are permitted to hire labor, gain control over natural resources, and produce goods and services for sale at a profit. In the American economy, the concept of private property embraces not only the ownership of productive resources but also certain rights, including the right to determine the price of a product or to make a free contract with another private individual.

1.　In Line 7, Paragraph 1, "the desire of individuals to maximize their incomes" means _____.

　　A．Americans are never satisfied with their incomes

　　B．Americans tend to overstate their incomes

　　C．Americans want to have their incomes increased

　　D．Americans want to increase the purchasing power of their incomes

2.　The first two sentences in the second paragraph tell us that _____.

　　A．producers can satisfy the consumers by mechanized production

B. consumers can express their demands through producers

C. producers decide the prices of products

D. supply and demand regulate prices

3. According to the passage, a private-enterprise economy is characterized by _____.

A. private property and rights concerned　　B. manpower and natural resources control

C. ownership of productive resources　　D. free contracts and prices

4. The passage is mainly about _____.

A. how American goods are produced

B. how American consumers buy their goods

C. how American economic system works

D. how American businessmen make their profits

核心词汇注释

oriented ['ɔːrɪentɪd,'-ʊe-] *adj.* 导向的

marketplace ['mɑːkɪtpleɪs] *n.* 集会场所，·市场，商场

motive ['məʊtɪv] *n.* 动机，目的 *adj.* 发动的；运动的

maximize ['mæksɪmaɪz] *vt.* 取……最大值；最佳化

resource [rɪ'sɔːs] *n.* (*pl.*) 资源；财力；办法；智谋

mechanism ['mekənɪz(ə)m] *n.* 机械装置；机构；机制

bid [bɪd] *vt.* 出价，投标；祝愿；命令，吩咐 *n.* 出价，投标 *v.* 支付

eliminate [ɪ'lɪmɪneɪt] *vt.* 排除，消除 *v.* 除去

embrace [ɪm'breɪs] *vt.* 拥抱，互相拥抱；包含；收买；信奉 *vi.* 拥抱 *n.* 拥抱

长难句剖析

【文章难句】The American economic system is organized around a basically private-enterprise, market-oriented economy in which consumers largely determine what shall be produced by spending their money in the marketplace for those goods and services that they want most.

【结构分析】本句主干是 The American economic system is organized。介词短语 around…做状语。其中，in which 引导的是定语从句；what 引导的从句做 determine 的宾语；介词 by 和后面的现在分词短语共同做状语；最后还有一个 that 引导的定语从句，用来修饰 goods and services。

【参考译文】美国经济体制根本上是围绕私有企业、市场经济组织起来的。这种体制很大程度上是根据消费者到市场购买他们最需要的商品和服务来决定生产什么。

全文参考译文

美国经济体制根本上是围绕私有企业、市场经济组织起来的。这种体制很大程度上是根据消费者到市场购买他们最需要的商品和服务来决定生产什么。为了极力获取利润，私有企业主在与其他企业主竞争中提供这些产品和服务。在竞争的压力下追逐利润的动机在很大程度上决定提

供这些商品和服务的方式。所以，在美国经济体制中，个人消费者的需求、商人获取最大利润的欲望和消费者想尽可能提高收入的愿望三者共同决定该生产什么和怎样利用资源生产产品。

市场经济中的一个重要因素是反映消费者需求以及生产者响应消费者需求的机制。在美国经济中，这种机制是通过价格体系决定的。在这种价格体系中，价格根据消费者的相对需求与生产者的供应情况或升或降。如果产品供不应求，价格就上涨，有些消费者就被排挤出市场。另一方面，如果一种产品生产过量导致成本下降，生产者提供的产品就会增加，这就相应地导致了价格下跌，这就允许更多的消费者购买该产品。因此，价格是美国经济系统的调节机制。

私有企业经济的一个重要因素是个人被允许拥有生产资料（私有财产），允许雇佣劳动力、控制自然资源、生产产品、提供服务获得利润。在美国经济中，私有财产的概念不仅包括生产资料的所有权，也包括决定产品价格或与其他私有个体自由签订合同的权利。

题目答案与解析

1. 在第 1 段的第 7 行，"the desire of individuals to maximize their incomes" 的意思是 _____。

   A．美国人从未对他们的收入满意过　　B．美国人往往夸大他们的收入

   C．美国人想让他们的收入增加　　　　D．美国人想提高收入的购买力

   【答案】D

   【解析】maximize：把……增加到最大限度；充分利用。maximize their income：充分利用他们的收入。D 项为正确答案。

2. 第 2 段的前两句话告诉我们 _____。

   A．生产者可以通过机械化生产来满足消费者的需求

   B．消费者通过生产者表达他们的要求

   C．生产者决定产品的价格

   D．供求调节价格

   【答案】D

   【解析】A 项文中没有提及。B 项与文章内容不符。C 项也没有提及，D 选项正确。

3. 根据本文，私企经济的特色是由 _____ 表现出来的。

   A．私有财产及相关的权利　　　　　B．人力和自然资源的支配

   C．生产资料的所有权　　　　　　　D．自由的签约权和价格决定权

   【答案】A

   【解析】从文章最后一段最后一句话 "在美国经济中，私有财产的概念不仅包括生产资料的所有权，也包括决定产品价格的或与其他私有个体自由签订合同的权利" 可以得出答案。由此可知 A 项为正确答案。

4. 本文主要是叙述 _____。

   A．美国的产品是如何生产的　　　　B．美国消费者是如何购买产品的

   C．美国的经济体制是如何运作的　　D．美国商人是如何赚取利润的

   【答案】C

   【解析】本题是主旨题。第 1 段讲述美国经济体系的构成；第 2 段讲市场调节的作用；第 3 段讲私有企业的特征。C 项概括了全文的主旨。A、B、D 项均属于细节。

Unit 23

Text 1

One hundred and thirteen million Americans have at least one bank-issued credit card. They give their owners automatic credit in stores, restaurants, and hotels, at home, across the country, and even abroad, and they make many banking services available as well. More and more of these credit cards can be read automatically, making it possible to withdraw or deposit money in scattered locations, whether or not the local branch bank is open. For many of us the "cashless society" is not on the horizon—it's already here.

While computers offer these conveniences to consumers, they have many advantages for sellers too. Electronic cash registers can do much more than simply ring up sales. They can keep a wide range of records, including who sold what, when, and to whom. This information allows businessmen to keep track of their list of goods by showing which items are being sold and how fast they are moving. Decisions to reorder or return goods to suppliers can then be made. At the same time these computers record which hours are busiest and which employees are the most efficient, allowing personnel and staffing assignments to be made accordingly. And they also identify preferred customers for promotional campaigns. Computers are relied on by manufacturers for similar reasons. Computer-analyzed marketing reports can help to decide which products to emphasize now, which to develop for the future, and which to drop. Computers keep track of goods in stock, of raw materials on hand, and even of the production process itself.

Numerous other commercial enterprises, from theaters to magazine publishers, from gas and electric utilities to milk processors , bring better and more efficient services to consumers through the use of computers.

1. According to the passage, the credit card enables its owner to _____.
    A. withdraw as much money from the bank as he wishes
    B. obtain more convenient services than other people do
    C. enjoy greater trust from the storekeeper
    D. cash money wherever he wishes to

2. From the last sentence of the first paragraph we learn that _____.
    A. in the future all the Americans will use credit cards
    B. credit cards are mainly used in the United States today
    C. nowadays many Americans do not pay in cash
    D. it is now more convenient to use credit cards than before

3. The phrase "ring up sales" (Line 2, Para. 2) most probably means " _____ ".
    A. make an order of goods
    C. call the sales manager
    B. record sales on a cash register
    D. keep track of the goods in stock

4. What is this passage mainly about?
   A. Approaches to the commercial use of computers.
   B. Conveniences brought about by computers in business.
   C. Significance of automation in commercial enterprises.
   D. Advantages of credit cards in business.

核心词汇注释

automatically [ˌɔːtə'mætɪklɪ] *adv.* 自动地；机械地

withdraw [wɪð'drɔː] *vt.* 收回，撤销 *vi.* 缩回；退出；撤退

scatter ['skætə(r)] *v.* 分散，散开，撒开，驱散

branch [brɑːntʃ] *n.* 枝，分枝；分部，分店，（学科）分科；部门；支流，支脉 *v.* 出现分歧

cashless ['kæʃlɪs] *adj.* 无现款的，无现金的，无钱的

horizon [hə'raɪz(ə)n] *n.* 地平线；（知识、思想等的）范围，视野

track [træk] *n.* 轨迹，车辙；跟踪，航迹，足迹；路，磁轨，途径 *vt.* 循路而行，追踪，通过，用纤拉 *vi.* 追踪，留下足迹，走

reorder [riː'ɔːdə(r)] *vt.* 再订购；重新安排 *vi.* 再订购；重新排序 *n.* 再订购

accordingly [ə'kɔːdɪŋlɪ] *adv.* 因此，从而

preferred [prɪ'fɜːd] *adj.* 首选的

长难句剖析

【文章难句】Computer-analyzed marketing reports can help to decide which products to emphasize now, which to develop for the future , and which to drop.

【结构分析】本句主语是 Computer-analyzed marketing reports，谓语是 can help to decide，三个并列的 which 引导的句子做宾语。

【参考译文】计算机分析的营销报告有助于决定目前哪些商品应重点生产，哪些将要开发，哪些应放弃生产。

全文参考译文

1 亿 1300 万美国人手中至少持有一种银行信用卡。信用卡持有者可在商场、餐厅、宾馆、当地、整个国内甚至国外结账，同时他们还能得到银行提供的许多服务。越来越多的信用卡可以自动读取，使持卡人可以在不同地方存取款，无论本地支行是否营业。对于我们中的许多人来说，"无现金社会"不是刚刚开始，而是早已存在。

计算机为消费者提供这些便利的同时，也给销售者带来很多优势。电子收款机能做的事远不止仅仅记录销售额，它们可进行更广领域的记录，包括何人何时卖给何人什么东西。这些信息使商人们通过了解正在销售商品种类和销售速度来跟踪其销售的商品列表。然后就能决定是再进货还是把商品退还给供应商。同时，这些计算机记录哪些时段销售最忙，哪些职员工作效率最高，并据此进行相应的人事和人员安排。他们还能确定首选的顾客群进行促销活动。同样，生产者也依赖计算机。计算机分析的营销报告有助于决定目前哪些商品应重点

生产，哪些将要开发，哪些应放弃生产。计算机还能跟踪库存商品，现有原材料甚至生产过程本身。

许多其他商业性企业，从剧场到杂志出版社，从煤气、供电公司到牛奶加工厂，都通过使用计算机为消费者提供更好、更有效率的服务。

题目答案与解析

1. 根据本文，信用卡能让它的使用者 _____。
   A. 提取他想要的钱数
   B. 比其他人享有更多的便利服务
   C. 享有店主的更多信任
   D. 无论在哪里都可以兑换金钱

   【答案】B

   【解析】本题是细节题，从第 1 段可以得出答案。信用卡持有者可以在商店、饭店、宾馆，在当地、整个国内甚至国外结账，同时他们还能得到银行提供的许多服务。越来越多的信用卡可以自动读取，使持卡人可以在不同地方存取款，无论本地支行是否营业。因此 B 项为正确答案。

2. 从第 1 段的最后一句话，我们可知 _____。
   A. 将来所有美国人都将使用信用卡
   B. 目前信用卡主要在美国使用
   C. 如今很多美国人不用现金支付
   D. 现在比过去使用信用卡更方便

   【答案】C

   【解析】A 项、B 项、D 项均不正确。第 1 段最后一句话指出：对于我们中的许多人来说，"无现金社会"不是刚刚兴起，而是早已存在。故 C 是正确答案。

3. 短语"ring up sales"（第 2 段第 2 行）最可能的意思是 _____。
   A. 定购货物
   B. 在收银机上记录销售额
   C. 给销售经理打电话
   D. 了解库存

   【答案】B

   【解析】ring up sales：记录销售额。故 B 项为正确答案。

4. 本文主题是关于什么的？
   A. 商业使用计算机的方法。
   B. 商业使用计算机所带来的好处。
   C. 自动化在商业企业中的重要性。
   D. 信用卡在商业中的优势。

   【答案】B

   【解析】本题是主旨题。三段文章中，有两段讲述计算机的应用，故 B 项是正确答案。A 项、C 项、D 项均不恰当。

Text 2

Exceptional children are different in some significant way from others of the same age. For these children to develop to their full adult potential, their education must be adapted to those differences.

Although we focus on the needs of exceptional children, we find ourselves describing their environment as well. While the leading actor on the stage captures our attention, we are aware of the importance of the supporting players and the scenery of the play itself. Both the family and the society in which exceptional children live are often the key to their growth and development. And it is in the public schools that we find the full expression of society's understanding — the knowledge, hopes, and fears that are passed on to the next generation.

Education in any society is a mirror of that society. In that minor we can see the strengths, the weaknesses, the hopes, the prejudices, and the central values of the culture itself. The great interest in exceptional children shown in public education over the past three decades indicates the strong feeling in our society that all citizens, whatever their special conditions, deserve the opportunity to fully develop their capabilities.

"All men are created equal." We've heard it many times, but it still has important meaning for education in a democratic society. Although the phrase was used by this country's founders to denote equality before the law, it has also been interpreted to mean equality of opportunity. That concept implies educational opportunity for all children — the right of each child to receive help in learning to the limits of his or her capacity, whether that capacity be small or great. Recent court decisions have confirmed the right of all children — disabled or not — to an appropriate education, and have ordered that public schools take the necessary steps to provide that education. In response, schools are modifying their programs, adapting instruction to children who are exceptional, to those who cannot profit substantially from regular programs.

1. In Paragraph 2, the author cites the example of the leading actor on the stage to show that _____.
   A. the growth of exceptional children has much to do with their family and the society
   B. exceptional children are more influenced by their families than normal children are
   C. exceptional children are the key interest of the family and society
   D. the needs of the society weigh much heavier than the needs of the exceptional children

2. The reason that the exceptional children receive so much concern in education is that _____.
   A. they are expected to be leaders of the society
   B. they might become a burden of the society
   C. they should fully develop their potentials
   D. disabled children deserve special consideration

3. This passage mainly deals with _____.
   A. the differences of children in their learning capabilities
   B. the definition of exceptional children in modern society
   C. the special educational programs for exceptional children
   D. the necessity of adapting education to exceptional children

4. From this passage we learn that the educational concern for exceptional children _____.
   A. is now enjoying legal support
   B. disagrees with the tradition of the country
   C. was clearly stated by the country's founders
   D. will exert great influence over court decisions

核心词汇注释

exceptional [ɪkˈsepʃən(ə)l] *adj.* 例外的，异常的

capture [ˈkæptʃə(r)] *n.* 捕获，战利品 *vt.* 俘获，捕获，夺取

deserve [dɪˈzɜːv] *vt.* 应受，值得 *v.* 应受

democratic [ˌdeməˈkrætɪk] *adj.* 民主的，民主主义的，民主政体的，平民的

denote [dɪˈnəʊt] *vt.* 指示，表示

disabled [dɪsˈeɪb(ə)ld] *adj.* 伤残的 *v.* 丧失能力

response [rɪˈspɒns] *n.* 回答，响应，反应

modify [ˈmɒdɪfaɪ] *vt.* 更改，修改 *v.* 修改

instruction [ɪnˈstrʌkʃ(ə)n] *n.* 指示，用法说明（书），教育，指导，指令

substantially [səbˈstænʃ(ə)lɪ] *adv.* 充分地

长难句剖析

【文章难句】Both the family and the society in which exceptional children live are often the key to their growth and development.

【结构分析】本句主语是 Both the family and the society。both... and... 的意思是"不但……而且……；既……又……"。in which 引导的是定语从句。are often the key to their growth and development 是系表结构。

【参考译文】特殊儿童生活的家庭与社会环境常常是他们成长与发展的关键。

全文参考译文

特殊儿童与其他同龄人在一些重要方面有所不同。要使这些儿童能够长大成熟，他们所受的教育必须适应这些差异。

尽管我们专注于特殊儿童的需要，但我们不经意间也在谈论他们所处的环境。尽管舞台上的主角吸引我们的注意力，我们也意识到了配角以及舞台布景的重要性。特殊儿童生活的家庭与社会环境常常是他们成长与发展的关键。并且，在公立学校里，我们发现社会的理解得到了充分的体现—— 知识、希望、恐惧都传给了下一代。

任何社会的教育都是那个社会的一面镜子。在镜中，我们能够看到力量、劣势、希望、偏见以及文化的核心价值。在过去的 30 年中，公共教育对特殊儿童显示出的极大兴趣表明了我们社会的强烈情感，即所有公民，无论他们的条件如何特殊，都应该有机会全面发展自己的能力。

"人人生来平等。"这句话我们已听了很多遍了，但是它对于民主社会里的教育仍然具有重要意义。虽然这句话被这个国家的建立者们用来指在法律面前的平等，但也被解释为机会均等。这一观念揭示了所有儿童都有接受教育的机会——即每个儿童，无论其能力大小，都有权在最大限度地提高学习能力上得到帮助。近来法院的裁决已经认可所有儿童——无论残疾与否——都有权接受适当教育，并且命令公立学校采取必要措施提供这种教育。相应地，学校正在修改教学计划，调整教学适应特殊儿童，适应那些不能从正常教学中充分获益的学生。

题目答案与解析

1. 在第 2 段，作者引用舞台上主角的例子是用来说明 _____。
   A．特殊儿童的成长与家庭和社会有很重要的关系
   B．特殊儿童比正常儿童受家庭影响要大
   C．家庭和社会最感兴趣的是特殊儿童
   D．社会的需要比特殊儿童的需要更为重要

   【答案】A

   【解析】作者把特殊儿童比做舞台上的主角，把家庭和社会比做配角和戏剧布景。这一比喻表明，家庭、社会对特殊儿童的成长和发展所起的作用如同配角和戏剧场景对主要演员所起的作用一样。A 项是正确答案。B 项、C 项、D 项均不正确。

2. 特殊儿童在教育方面受到极大关注的原因是 _____。
   A．他们被期待成为社会的领导者　　B．他们可能成为社会的负担
   C．他们应该充分发展自身潜力　　　D．应特别体谅残疾儿童

   【答案】C

   【解析】从文章第 3 段最后一句话"在过去的 30 年中，公共教育对特殊儿童显示出的极大兴趣表明了我们社会的强烈情感，即所有公民，无论他们的条件如何特殊，都应该有机会全面发展自己的能力"可知，C 项为正确答案。

3. 本文主要是关于 _____。
   A．儿童学习能力的差异　　　　　　B．现代社会中特殊儿童的定义
   C．为特殊儿童制定的特别教育计划　D．使教育适应特殊儿童的必要性

   【答案】D

   【解析】本题为主旨题。D 项为正确答案。A、B、C 项均属于细节，不是主旨。

4. 我们从本文可知，对特殊儿童的教育关注 _____。
   A．正在得到法律的支持
   B．与本国传统不符
   C．当初国家缔造者们已清楚地说明了这一点
   D．对法院的裁决将施加很大影响

   【答案】A

   【解析】从最后一段第 5 句话"近来法院的裁决已经认可所有儿童——无论残疾与否——都有权接受适当教育，并且命令公立学校采取必要措施提供这种教育"可知，A 项为正确答案。

Text　3

"I have great confidence that by the end of the decade we'll know in vast detail how cancer cells arise," says microbiologist Robert Weinberg, an expert on cancer. "But," he cautions, "some people have the idea that once one understands the causes, the cure will rapidly follow. Consider Pasteur, he discovered the causes of many kinds of infections, but it was fifty or sixty years before cures were available."

This year, 50 percent of the 910,000 people who suffer from cancer will survive at least five years. In the year 2000, the National Cancer Institute estimates, that figure will be 75 percent.

For some skin cancers, the five-year survival rate is as high as 90 percent. But other survival statistics are still discouraging — 13 percent for lung cancer, and 2 percent for cancer of the pancreas.

With as many as 120 varieties in existence, discovering how cancer works is not easy. The researchers made great progress in the early 1970s, when they discovered that oncogenes, which are cancer-causing genes, are inactive in normal cells. Anything from cosmic rays to radiation to diet may activate a dormant oncogene, but how remains unknown. If several oncogenes are driven into action, the cell, unable to turn them off, becomes cancerous.

The exact mechanisms involved are still mysterious, but the likelihood that many cancers are initiated at the level of genes suggests that we will never prevent all cancers. "Changes are a normal part of the evolutionary process," says oncologist William Hayward. Environmental factors can never be totally eliminated; as Hayward points out, "We can't prepare a medicine against cosmic rays."

The prospects for cure, though still distant, are brighter.

"First, we need to understand how the normal cell controls itself. Second, we have to determine whether there are a limited number of genes in cells which are always responsible for at least part of the trouble. If we can understand how cancer works, we can counteract its action."

1. The example of Pasteur in the passage is used to _____.
   A. predict that the secret of cancer will be disclosed in a decade
   B. indicate that the prospects for curing cancer are bright
   C. prove that cancer will be cured in fifty to sixty years
   D. warn that there is still a long way to go before cancer can be conquered

2. The author implies that by the year 2000, _____.
   A. there will be a drastic rise in the five-year survival rate of skin-cancer patients
   B. 90 percent of the skin-cancer patients today will still be living
   C. the survival statistics will be fairly even among patients with various cancers
   D. there won't be a drastic increase of survival rate of all cancer patients

3. Oncogenes are cancer-causing genes _____.
   A. that are always in operation in a healthy person
   B. which remain unharmful so long as they are not activated
   C. that can be driven out of normal cells
   D. which normal cells can't turn off

4. The word "dormant" in the third paragraph most probably means _____.
   A. dead   B. ever-present   C. inactive   D. potential

核心词汇注释

estimate ['estɪmət] *v.* 估计，估价，评估   *n.* 估计，估价，评估

discouraging [dɪsˈkʌrɪdʒɪŋ] *adj.* 令人气馁的

pancreas [ˈpæŋkrɪəs] *n.* [解]胰腺

oncogene [ˈɒŋkədʒiːn] *n.* 致癌基因

radiation [ˌreɪdɪˈeɪʃ(ə)n] *n.* 发散，发光，发热，辐射，放射，放射线，放射物

cancerous [ˈkænsərəs] *adj.* 癌的

likelihood [ˈlaɪklɪhʊd] *n.* 可能，可能性

initiate [ɪˈnɪʃɪeɪt] *vt.* 开始，发动，传授 *v.* 开始，发起

counteract [ˌkaʊntəˈrækt] *vt.* 抵消，中和，阻碍

长难句剖析

【文章难句】The researchers made great progress in the early 1970s, when they discovered that oncogenes, which are cancer-causing genes , are inactive in normal cells.

【结构分析】本句主干是 The researchers made great progress。when 引导的是非限制性定语从句，修饰前面的时间。在这个定语从句中，that...是宾语从句。which are cancer-causing genes 为非限制性定语从句，修饰 oncogenes。

【参考译文】在 20 世纪 70 年代初，研究者们取得了重大进展，那时他们发现在普通细胞中，致癌基因并不活跃。

全文参考译文

"我深信，在本年代末，我们将对癌细胞的产生有更详细的了解。"微生物学家及癌症专家 Robert Weinberg 说。"但是"，他警告说："有些人认为，一旦人们找到了病因，治疗办法很快就会找到。想一想 Pasteur 吧，他发现了许多传染病病因，但是过了五六十年才有了治疗方法。"

今年，91 万癌症患者中，50%的人可生存至少 5 年。国家癌症研究所估计，到 2000 年，这个数字将会是 75%。对于一些皮肤癌患者，存活 5 年的几率高达 90%。但是其他生存几率统计数字仍令人失望——肺癌患者 13%，胰腺癌患者 2%。

由于存在着 120 多种不同的癌症，发现癌症的机理并不容易。在 20 世纪 70 年代初，研究者们取得了重大进展，当时他们发现，在普通细胞中，致癌基因并不活跃。从宇宙射线辐射到饮食的任何东西都可能激活处于休眠状态的致癌基因，但如何激活仍不为人知。如果一些致癌基因被激活，而细胞不能消灭它们，细胞就变成癌细胞。

包含其中的准确机理仍然是一个未知之数。但是许多癌症起因于基因这一可能性，表明我们永远不可能预防所有的癌症。"变化是进化过程的正常组成部分。"肿瘤学家 William Hayward 说。环境因素永远不可完全排除在外；正如 Hayward 指出的那样："我们无法准备一种对付宇宙射线的药物。"

治疗前景虽然还很遥远，但越加光明起来。

"首先，我们需要知道普通细胞是如何控制自己的。其次，我们必须确定细胞中是否有有限数量的基因经常成为癌症的起因或至少部分起因。如果我们知道了癌症发作机理，我们就能防止其发生。"

题目答案与解析

1. 文中举用 Pasteur 的例子是用来 _____。

A. 预言 10 年后癌症的秘密将被揭开

B. 预示治疗癌症的前景是光明的

C. 证明五六十年后癌症将被治愈

D. 告诫说，在征服癌症之前还有很长的路要走

【答案】D

【解析】从第 1 段最后一句话 "想一想 Pasteur 吧，他发现了许多传染病病因，但是过了五六十年才有了治疗方法" 可知，D 项为正确答案。

2. 作者暗示说到 2000 年 _____。

A. 皮肤癌患者存活 5 年的几率会有大幅度的增加

B. 今天 90% 的皮肤癌病人仍然活着

C. 各种癌症患者之间的生存率统计数字将会持平

D. 所有癌症患者生存率不会有大的提高

【答案】D

【解析】本题为推断题。A、B、C 项均不正确。D 项正确。

3. 致癌基因就是引起癌症的基因，它们 _____。

A. 总是活跃在健康人体内   B. 只要不被激活，就不会有害

C. 可以从正常细胞中驱赶出去   D. 无法被正常细胞消灭

【答案】B

【解析】从第 3 段第 2 句话可知：70 年代初，研究者们取得了重大进展，当时他们发现，在正常细胞中，致癌基因并不活跃。从宇宙射线辐射到饮食的任何东西都可能激活休眠的致癌基因，但如何激活仍然不为人知。如果一些致癌基因被激活，而细胞不能消灭他们，细胞就会变成癌细胞，可知 B 为正确答案。A、C、D 项均不正确。

4. 第 3 段中的单词 "dormant" 最有可能的意思是 _____。

A. 死的   B. 经常存在的   C. 不活动的   D. 潜在的

【答案】C

【解析】activate：激活。dormant：*adj.* 睡眠状态的；静止的；隐匿的。inactive：*adj.* 无行动的；不活动的；停止的。由上一句 "当时他们发现，在正常细胞中，致癌基因并不活跃" 可知，答案为 C。

Text 4

Discoveries in science and technology are thought by "untaught minds" to come in blinding flashes or as the result of dramatic accidents. Sir Alexander Fleming did not, as legend would have it, look at the mold on a piece of cheese and get the idea for penicillin there and then. He experimented with antibacterial substances for nine years before he made his discovery. Inventions and innovations almost always come out of laborious trial and error. Innovation is like soccer; even the best players miss the goal and have their shots blocked much more frequently than they score.

The point is that the players who score most are the ones who take most shots at the goal and so it goes with innovation in any field of activity. The prime difference between innovators and others is one of approach. Everybody gets ideas, but innovators work consciously on theirs, and they follow them through until they prove practicable or otherwise. What ordinary people see as fanciful abstractions, professional innovators see as solid possibilities.

"Creative thinking may mean simply the realization that there's no particular virtue in doing things the way they have always been done," wrote Rudolph Flesch, a language authority, this accounts for our reaction to seemingly simple innovations like plastic garbage bags and suitcases on wheels that make life more convenient: "How come nobody thought of that before?"

The creative approach begins with the proposition that nothing is as it appears. Innovators will not accept that there is only one way to do anything. Faced with getting from A to B, the average person will automatically set out on the best-known and apparently simplest route. The innovators will search for alternate courses, which may prove easier in the long run and are bound to be more interesting and challenging even if they lead to dead ends.

Highly creative individuals really do march to a different drummer.

1. What does the author probably mean by "untaught mind" in the first paragraph?

　　A. A person ignorant of the hard work involved in experimentation.

　　B. A citizen of a society that restricts personal creativity.

　　C. A person who has had no education.

　　D. An individual who often comes up with new ideas by accident.

2. According to the author, what distinguishes innovators from non-innovators?

　　A. The variety of ideas they have.　　　　B. The intelligence they possess.

　　C. The way they deal with problems.　　　D. The way they present their findings.

3. The author quotes Rudolph Flesch in Paragraph 3 because _____.

　　A. Rudolph Flesch is the best-known expert in the study of human creativity

　　B. the quotation strengthens the assertion that creative individuals look for new ways of doing things

　　C. the reader is familiar with Rudolph Flesch's point of view

　　D. the quotation adds a new idea to the information previously presented

4. The phrase "march to a different drummer" (the last line of the passage) suggests that highly creative individuals are _____.

　　A. diligent in pursuing their goals

　　B. reluctant to follow common ways of doing things

　　C. devoted to the progress of science

　　D. concerned about the advance of society

核心词汇注释

flash　[flæʃ] *n.* 闪光；闪现，一瞬间，[计]Macromedia 公司开发的动画编辑工具

　　vi. 闪光；闪现；反射；使迅速传递

　　vt. 使闪光；反射

　　adj. 闪光的；火速的

mold　[məuld] *n.* 模子，铸型

　　vt. 浇铸，塑造

penicillin　[ˌpenɪ'sɪlɪn] *n.* [微] 青霉素（一种抗生素，音译名为盘尼西林）

antibacterial　[ˌæntɪbæk'tɪərɪəl] *adj.* 抗菌的

n. 抗菌药

innovation [ˌɪnəˈveɪʃ(ə)n] *n.* 改革，创新

laborious [ləˈbɔːrɪəs] *adj.* （指工作）艰苦的，费力的；（指人）勤劳的

error [ˈerə(r)] *n.* 错误，过失；误差

block [blɒk] *n.* 木块，石块，块；街区；印版；滑轮；阻滞；（一）批

vt. 妨碍，阻塞

fanciful [ˈfænsɪful] *adj.* 爱空想的；奇怪的，稀奇的；想象的

abstraction [əbˈstrækʃ(ə)n] *n.* 提取；抽象概念

drummer [ˈdrʌmə(r)] *n.* 鼓手；<美> 旅行推销员

长难句剖析

【文章难句】The innovators will search for alternate courses, which may prove easier in the long run and are bound to be more interesting and challenging even if they lead to dead ends.

【结构分析】本句主干是 The innovator will search for alternate courses，which 引导的是非限制性定语从句，还有一个 if...条件状语在这个非限制性定语从句中。

【参考译文】创新家们会寻找其他路线，这些道路从长远看可能更容易，即使它们通向死胡同，但必定会更有趣、更富挑战性。

全文参考译文

科技发明总是被"无知"的人们认为是产生于头脑中的灵光一现或是戏剧性的事件的结果。Alexander Fleming 爵士并不如传说中所说，看到一块奶酪上的霉，就有了青霉素的概念。他用了 9 年时间对抗菌物质进行实验才发现了青霉素。发明与创新几乎总是产生于艰苦的反复实验。创新就像足球比赛，即使最好的球员也有射不中的时候，也可能射门被阻次数比进球的次数多得多。

关键一点是进球最多的球员也是射门次数最多的球员——任何活动领域里的创新也是如此。创新者与其他人主要的区别在于处理问题的方法不同。每个人都有想法，但创新者自觉地将想法付诸实践。他们把这些想法一直坚持下来，直到证明这些想法可行或不可行。普通人视为凭空想象的抽象概念，在职业创新者眼里却是极其可能的东西。

"创新思维也许只不过意味着意识到按老办法办事没有什么特别可取之处。"语言权威 Rudolph Flesch 曾写道。这解释了我们看到像塑料垃圾袋、带轮子的箱子这些使生活更便利，但看似简单的发明时的反应："为什么以前没人想到呢？"

创造方法起源于这样一个命题：现象不等于本质。创新家们从不认为做任何事只有一种方法。面对从 A 地到 B 地，普通人自动沿着最熟悉、表面上最简单的路线。创新家们会寻找其他路线，这些道路从长远看可能更容易，即使它们通向死胡同，但必定会更有趣、更富挑战性。

极富创造力的人实际是合着不同鼓手打出的鼓点行进的。

题目答案与解析

1. 在第 1 段中，作者可能用"untaught mind"来指什么？
   A. 对与实验有关的艰巨工作无知的人。
   B. 限制了个人创造力的社会的公民。
   C. 没有受过教育的人。
   D. 由于意外事件而经常提出新见解的人。

【答案】A

【解析】untaught mind：未受过教育的，无知的。A 项为正确答案。

2. 根据作者的观点，创新者与非创新者的区别是什么？

A．他们所拥有的各种各样的方法。   B．他们拥有的智慧。

C．他们处理问题的方法。   D．他们陈述其发现的方法。

【答案】C

【解析】第 2 段第 2 句话指出创新者与其他人主要区别在于处理问题的方法不同。此处的方法指的是处理解决问题的方法，不是陈述其发现的方法。故 C 项正确。A、B 和 D 项均未提及。

3. 在第 3 段中，作者引用 Rudolph Flesch 的话的原因是 _____。

A．Rudolph Flesch 是研究人类创造性的专家

B．引文强调了富有创造性的人寻找新方法来做事这个论点

C．读者熟悉 Rudolph Flesch 的观点

D．引文对以前提出的信息提供新的观点

【答案】B

【解析】日常生活中有许多小发明，这些小发明给人们的生活带来了极大的便利。但是"为什么以前没人想到呢？"其意义在于说明，有些人能想到这些小发明就是因为他们勇于进行创造性思维，喜欢从新的角度去考虑问题，而不是按老方法去做事。这和 B 项一致。A 项与文章内容不符。C 项文章未提。D 项与文章内容不符，因为文章并无新观点出现。

4. 短语 "march to a different drummer"（文中的最后一行）提出富有创造性的人 _____。

A．勤于追寻他们的目标   B．不愿意按常规去做事

C．专心于科学的发展   D．关于社会的进步

【答案】B

【解析】march to a different drummer：按不同的鼓点前进。按一个鼓点行军，就显得单调。搞研究如只按传统方法，则很难有创新。B 项为正确答案。

Unit 24

Text 1

Is language, like food, a basic human need without which a child at a critical period of life can be starved and damaged? Judging from the drastic experiment of Frederick II in the thirteenth century, it may be. Hoping to discover what language a child would speak if he heard no mother tongue, he told the nurses to keep silent.

All the infants died before the first year. But clearly there was more than lack of language here. What was missing was good mothering. Without good mothering, in the first year of life especially, the capacity to survive is seriously affected.

Today no such severe lack exists as that ordered by Frederick. Nevertheless, some children are still backward in speaking. Most often the reason for this is that the mother is insensitive to the signals of the infant, whose brain is programmed to learn language rapidly. If these sensitive periods are neglected, the ideal time for acquiring skills passes and they might never be learned so easily again. A bird learns to sing and to fly rapidly at the right time, but the process is slow and hard once the critical stage has passed.

Experts suggest that speech stages are reached in a fixed sequence and at a constant age, but there are cases where speech has started late in a child who eventually turns out to be of high IQ. At twelve weeks a baby smiles and makes vowel-like sounds; at twelve months he can speak simple words and understand simple commands; at eighteen months he has a vocabulary of three to fifty words. At three he knows about 1,000 words which he can put into sentences, and at four his language differs from that of his parents in style rather than grammar.

Recent evidence suggests that an infant is born with the capacity to speak. What special about man's brain, compared with that of the monkey, is the complex system which enables a child to connect the sight and feel of, say, a toy-bear with the sound pattern "toy-bear". And even more incredible is the young brain's ability to pick out an order in language from the mixture of sound around him, to analyse, to combine and recombine the parts of a language in new ways.

But speech has to be induced, and this depends on interaction between the mother and the child, where the mother recognizes the signals in the child's babbling, grasping and smiling, and responds to them. Insensitivity of the mother to these signals dulls the interaction because the child gets discouraged and sends out only the obvious signals. Sensitivity to the child's non-verbal signals is essential to the growth and development of language.

1. The purpose of Frederick II's experiment was _____.

    A. to prove that children are born with the ability to speak

    B. to discover what language a child would speak without hearing any human speech

    C. to find out what role careful nursing would play in teaching a child to speak

D. to prove that a child could be damaged without learning a language

2. The reason some children are backward in speaking is most probably that _____.

    A. they are incapable of learning language rapidly

    B. they are exposed to too much language at once

    C. their mothers respond inadequately to their attempts to speak

    D. their mothers are not intelligent enough to help them

3. What is exceptionally remarkable about a child is that _____.

    A. he is born with the capacity to speak

    B. he has a brain more complex than an animal's

    C. he can produce his own sentences

    D. he owes his speech ability to good nursing

4. Which of the following can NOT be inferred from the passage?

    A. The faculty of speech is inborn in man.

    B. Encouragement is anything but essential to a child in language learning.

    C. The child's brain is highly selective.

    D. Most children learn their language in definite stages.

5. If a child starts to speak later than others, he will _____.

    A. have a high IQ   B. be less intelligent

    C. be insensitive to verbal signals   D. not necessarily be backward

核心词汇注释

critical ['krɪtɪk(ə)l] *adj.* 评论的，鉴定的；批评的；危急的，临界的；决定性的，关键的

drastic ['dræstɪk] *adj.* 激烈的，（药性等）猛烈的

insensitive [ɪn'sensɪtɪv] *adj.* 对……没有感觉的，感觉迟钝的

neglected [nɪ'glektɪd] *adj.* 被忽视的

sequence ['siːkwəns] *n.* 次序，顺序，序列

vowel ['vauəl] *n.* 元音
    adj. 元音的

recombine [ˌriːkəm'baɪn] *vt.* 再结合，重组

interaction [ˌɪntər'ækʃ(ə)n] *n.* 交互作用，交感

babbling ['bæblɪŋ] *n.* 胡说；婴儿发出的咿呀声
    adj. 胡说的

dull [dʌl] *adj.* 感觉或理解迟钝的；无趣的，呆滞的；阴暗的
    vt. 使迟钝，使阴暗；缓和
    vi. 变迟钝；减少

长难句剖析

【文章难句】But speech has to be induced, and this depends on interaction between the mother and the child, where the mother recognizes the signals in the child's babbling, grasping and smiling, and responds to them.

【结构分析】本句的主干是 But speech has to be induced, and this depends on interaction between the mother and the child。where 引导的是非限制性定语从句。

【参考译文】但是，学习语言必须加以引导，这取决于母子之间的互动效果。在他们的互动中，母亲识别出婴儿咿呀学语、抓挠及微笑的信号，并对这些信号作出反应。

全文参考译文

语言是否像食物一样，是人类的一种基本需要，没有它，孩子可能会在成长关键时期挨饿和受到损害吗？根据 13 世纪 Frederick II 所做的大量实验可推断出，事实的确如此。为了发现孩子在听不到母语的情况下会讲什么语言，他要求保育员保持沉默。

所有的婴儿在一年内都死亡了。但很明显，夭折的原因不只是缺少语言，缺少的还有良好的母爱。没有良好的母爱，尤其是在生命的第一年内，婴儿的生存能力会受到严重影响。

今天已不存在像 Frederick 所安排的那样极端的情况。尽管如此，一些孩子在语言学习方面仍很迟钝。主要原因是由于母亲对大脑已作好快速学习语言准备的孩子所发出的信号不敏感。如果错过这些敏感时期，那么获取技巧的理想时期就会被错过，他们再也不能如此轻松学习。鸟在恰当的时期能很快学会歌唱和飞翔，但一旦这样的关键时期被错过，学习过程就会缓慢而困难。

专家们认为，不同语言阶段都有其固定的顺序和年龄，但是，也存在这样的情形，开始说话晚的婴儿长大后却智商很高。婴儿在 12 周时，开始会笑并会发出类似元音的声音；在 12 个月时，他能讲简单的话并能理解简单的命令；18 个月时，就能有 3～50 的词汇量。到 3 岁时，约认识 1000 个单词，并能用这些单词造句；4 岁时，他的语言与其父母的差异仅表现在风格上而不是语法上面。

最新资料显示，婴儿生来就有说话的能力。与猴子的大脑相比，人脑的特殊之处就在于其组成大脑的复杂系统所具有的功能。该系统能使婴儿把所见所感联系起来，例如，把玩具熊及其发音模式联系起来。更加令人难以置信的是婴儿的大脑能从其周围混杂的声音中识别出语言的顺序，能够分析并按新的方法组合与重组语言各个组成部分。

但是，学习语言必须加以引导，这取决于母子之间的互动效果。在他们的互动中，母亲识别出婴儿咿呀学语、抓挠及微笑的信号，并对这些信号作出反应。母亲对这些信号的不敏感会削弱母子间的互动效果，因为孩子不能得到鼓励就会只发出这些明显的信号。对婴儿非言语信号的敏感性对婴儿语言的形成和发展是极其必要的。

题目答案与解析

1. Frederick II 的实验目的是 _____。
   A. 用来证实婴儿天生具有语言的能力
   B. 弄清楚听不到任何人类语言时孩子会讲什么语言
   C. 弄清楚保育员教婴儿说话所起的作用
   D. 用来证实不学语言的婴儿会受到损害
   【答案】B
   【解析】从文中第 1 段最后一句话"为了发现婴儿有听不到母语的情况下会讲什么语言，他要求保育员保持沉默"可以得出答案。B 项正好与之一致。
2. 一些孩子在讲话方面迟钝最可能的原因是 _____。

A．他们不能快速地学习语言

B．他们立刻接触了太多的语言

C．对孩子说话所作的努力没有充分的反应

D．他们母亲的才智不足以帮助他们

【答案】C

【解析】从第 3 段第 3 句话"母亲对大脑已作好快速学习语言准备的婴儿所发出的信号不敏感"可以得出正确答案。由此可知 C 项为正确答案。

3．婴儿的非凡之处在于 _____。

A．他天生具有语言的能力

B．他的大脑比动物的大脑复杂

C．他能发出自己的句子

D．他的语言能力归功于良好的看护

【答案】C

【解析】从第 5 段最后一句话"更加令人难以置信的是婴儿的大脑能从其周围杂乱的声音中识别出语言的顺序，能够分析并按新的方法组合与重新组合语言各个组成部分"可以得出答案。C 项正好与之一致。

4．以下哪项无法从文中推出？

A．人类的语言才能是天生的。

B．在婴儿学习语言的过程中，鼓励一点儿也不重要。

C．婴儿的大脑具有高度的选择性。

D．多数的婴儿在特定的阶段学习语言。

【答案】B

【解析】本题为推论题。B 项正好与文章内容相反。

5．如果一个婴儿开始讲话比其他婴儿晚，他将 _____。

A．具有高智商   B．不聪明

C．对语言信号感觉迟钝   D．未必迟钝

【答案】D

【解析】从第 4 段第 1 句话中"但是，也存在这样的情形，开始说话晚的婴儿长大后却智商很高"可知，D 项为正确答案。

Text 2

In general, our society is becoming one of giant enterprises directed by a bureaucratic management in which man becomes a small, well-oiled cog in the machinery. The oiling is done with higher wages, well-ventilated factories and piped music, and by psychologists and "human-relations" experts; yet all this oiling does not alter the fact that man has become powerless, that he does not wholeheartedly participate in his work and that he is bored with it. In fact, the blue and the white-collar workers have become economic puppets who dance to the tune of automated machines and bureaucratic management.

The worker and employee are anxious, not only because they might find themselves out of a job; they are anxious also because they are unable to acquire any real satisfaction or interest in life. They live and die without ever having confronted the fundamental realities of human existence as emotionally and intellectually independent and productive human beings.

Those higher up on the social ladder are no less anxious. Their lives are no less empty than those of their subordinates. They are even more insecure in some respects. They are in a highly competitive race. To be promoted or to fall behind is not a matter of salary but even more a matter of self-respect. When they apply for their first job, they are tested for intelligence as well as for the tight mixture of submissiveness and independence. From that moment on they are tested again and again by the psychologists, for whom testing is a big business, and by their superiors, who judge their behavior, sociability, capacity to get along , etc. This constant need to prove that one is as good as or better than one's fellow-competitor creates constant anxiety and stress, the very causes of unhappiness and illness.

Am I suggesting that we should return to the preindustrial mode of production or to nineteenth-century "free enterprise" capitalism? Certainly not. Problems are never solved by returning to a stage which one has already outgrown. I suggest transforming our social system from a bureaucratically managed industrialism in which maximal production and consumption are ends in themselves into a humanist industrialism in which man and full development of his potentialities—those of love and of reason—are the aims of all social arrangements. Production and consumption should serve only as means to this end, and should be prevented from ruling man.

1. By "a well-oiled cog in the machinery" the author intends to render the idea that man is _____.
   A. a necessary part of the society though each individual's function is negligible
   B. working in complete harmony with the rest of the society
   C. an unimportant part in comparison with the rest of the society, though functioning smoothly
   D. a humble component of the society, especially when working smoothly

2. The real cause of the anxiety of the workers and employees is that _____.
   A. they are likely to lose their jobs
   B. they have no genuine satisfaction or interest in life
   C. they are faced with the fundamental realities of human existence
   D. they are deprived of their individuality and independence

3. From the passage we can infer that real happiness of life belongs to those _____.
   A. who are at the bottom of the society
   B. who are higher up in their social status
   C. who prove better than their fellow-competitors
   D. who could keep far away from this competitive world

4. To solve the present social problems the author suggests that we should _____.
   A. resort to the production mode of our ancestors
   B. offer higher wages to the workers and employees
   C. enable man to fully develop his potentialities

D. take the fundamental realities for granted

5. The author's attitude towards industrialism might best be summarized as one of _____.

    A. approval   B. dissatisfaction   C. suspicion   D. tolerance

核心词汇注释

bureaucratic [ˌbjʊərəʊˈkrætɪk] *adj.* 官僚政治的

cog [kɒg] *n.* [机]嵌齿；小船
    vt. 上齿轮；欺骗

ventilated [ˈventɪleɪtɪd] *adj.* 通风的

piped [paɪpt] *adj.*（服装）拷边的，滚边的

wholehearted [ˈhəʊlˈhɑːtɪd] *adj.* 一心一意的，诚恳的，整整的，全神贯注的

puppet [ˈpʌpɪt] *n.* 傀儡，木偶

subordinate [səˈbɔːdɪnət] *adj.* 次要的，从属的，下级的
    n. 下属
    v. 服从

submissiveness [səbˈmɪsɪvnəs] *n.* 柔顺，服从

sociability [ˌsəʊʃəˈbɪlɪtɪ] *n.* 好交际，社交性，善于交际

preindustrial [ˌpriːɪnˈdʌstrɪəl] *adj.* 未工业化的，工业化前的

长难句剖析

【文章难句】In general, our society is becoming one of giant enterprises directed by a bureaucratic management in which man becomes a small , well-oiled cog in the machinery.

【结构分析】本句的主干是 our society is becoming one of giant enterprises。句首的 in general 做状语。directed…是过去分词引导的状语，其中的 in which…是限制性定语从句。

【参考译文】总的看来，我们的社会正变成一个由官僚主义管理方式所控制的巨大企业。在这个企业中，人成为机器中润滑良好的小齿轮。

全文参考译文

    总的看来，我们的社会正变成一个由官僚主义管理方式所控制的巨大企业。在这个企业中，人成为机器中润滑良好的小齿轮。这种润滑，是通过高薪、通风良好的工厂和管弦乐创造，并由心理学者和研究人类关系的专家进行的，但整个润滑并没有改变这样一个事实，人类已变得力不从心；他不能全身心地投入他的工作，他已厌烦他的工作。实际上，蓝领和白领工人已变成伴随着自动化机器和官僚主义管理节奏起舞的经济木偶。

    工人和受雇佣者不仅因担心自己失业而忧虑，他们也因为不能在生活中找到任何真正的满足和兴趣而犯愁。他们从生到死甚至不能作为一个情感上、智力上独立，并能自由发挥创造力的人去面对人类生存的基本现实。

    那些处于社会高层的人也不乏忧虑。他们的生活同他们的下属一样空虚。在某些方面他们甚至更加不安全。他们处于高度竞争的境地。得到提升或降职不是工资的问题，而是自尊的问题。当他们应聘第一份工作时，他们的服从性和独立性的综合表现以及智力都要受到测试。从那时开始，他们一次又一次地被心理学家和他们的上司测试。对心理学家而言，测试是他们的重要工作；上司则通过测试判断他们的处事能力、社交能力和与他人相处能力等等。

这种不断证明自己与竞争对手同样优秀或者超过对手从而不断地产生忧虑和压力，正是不快乐和疾病的根源。

我是在建议我们应回到工业化前的生产模式或 19 世纪的"自由企业"资本主义时期吗？当然不是。问题决不能通过返回已经历时期的方法来解决。我建议转变我们的社会生产体制，从以追求最大限度的生产和消费为目的的官僚主义管理方式的工业体制转变为一个以充分发挥人的潜能（如爱与理性）为目的的人性化工业体制。生产和消费都是实现这个终极目标的一种手段，要防止它们控制人类。

题目答案与解析

1. 作者通过 "a well-oiled cog in the machinery" 来试图表达 _____ 。
   A．尽管每个人的作用微不足道，人仍然是社会不可分割的一部分
   B．人与社会的其余部分完全和睦相处
   C．尽管平稳地发挥着作用，人与社会其余部分相比并不重要
   D．人是社会中一个地位卑贱的零件，特别是工作顺利的时候
   【答案】C
   【解析】a well-oiled cog in the machinery：机器中润滑良好的齿轮，指人在社会中所发挥的作用是微不足道的。C 选项正好与之相一致。A、B、D 项均与文章不符。

2. 工人们和雇员们忧虑的真正原因是 _____ 。
   A．他们可能失业
   B．他们在生活中不能得到真正的满足和兴趣
   C．他们面对着人类生存的基本现实
   D．他们被剥夺了个性和独立性
   【答案】D
   【解析】从文章第 2 段可以得出答案。工人们和雇员们忧虑的原因是可能失业；生活不能得到真正的满足和兴趣；被剥夺了个性和独立性。D 项做了很好的概括。

3. 从文中我们可以推出生活中真正的幸福属于 _____ 。
   A．处于社会底层的人   B．社会地位高的人
   C．证明比竞争者优秀的人   D．远离竞争世界的人
   【答案】D
   【解析】本题是细节题。第 3 段最后一句话指出这种不断证明自己与竞争对手同样优秀或者超过对手从而不断地产生忧虑和压力，正是不快乐和疾病的起因。可知 D 项为正确答案。

4. 为解决目前的社会问题，作者建议我们应该 _____ 。
   A．采用祖先的生产方式
   B．付给工人们和雇员们更高的工资
   C．使人能充分发挥自己的潜能
   D．认为基础现实是正确的
   【答案】C
   【解析】第 4 段第 4 句话指出，我建议转变我们的社会生产体制，从以追求最大限度的生产和消费为目的的官僚主义管理工业体制转变成一个以充分发挥人的潜能（如爱和理性的潜能）为

目的的人性化工业体制。C 项为正确答案。

5. 作者对产业主义的态度的最好概括是 _____。

　　A. 赞许　　　　　B. 不满　　　　　C. 怀疑　　　　　D. 容忍

【答案】B

【解析】本题问作者对工业体制的态度。本文作者指出了现代工业社会的种种弊端；第 1 段指出人的地位微不足道；第 2 段指出工人们与雇员们都感到忧虑；第 3 段指出上层社会的人们也感到忧虑。最后作者提出了改变这种社会体制的建议。因此不难得出，作者认为现行的 industrialism 不好。正确答案是 B 项。

Text　3

When an invention is made, the inventor has three possible courses of action open to him: he can give the invention to the world by publishing it, keep the idea secret, or patent it.

A granted patent is the result of a bargain struck between an inventor and the state, by which the inventor gets a limited period of monopoly and publishes full details of his invention to the public after that period terminates.

Only in the most exceptional circumstances is the lifespan of a patent extended to alter this normal process of events.

The longest extension ever granted was to Georges Valensi; his 1939 patent for color TV receiver circuitry was extended until 1971 because for most of the patent's normal life there was no colour TV to receive and thus no hope of reward for the invention.

Because a patent remains permanently public after it has terminated, the shelves of the library attached to the patent office contain details of literally millions of ideas that are free for anyone to use and, if older than half a century, sometimes even re-patent. Indeed, patent experts often advise anyone wishing to avoid the high cost of conducting a search through live patents that the one sure way of avoiding violation of any other inventor's right is to plagiarize a dead patent. Likewise, because publication of an idea in any other form permanently invalidates further patents on that idea, it is traditionally safe to take ideas from other areas of print. Much modern technological advance is based on these presumptions of legal security.

Anyone closely involved in patents and inventions soon learns that most "new" ideas are, in fact, as old as the hills. It is their reduction to commercial practice, either through necessity or dedication, or through the availability of new technology, that makes news and money. The basic patent for the theory of magnetic recording dates back to 1886. Many of the original ideas behind television originate from the late 19th and early 20th century. Even the Volkswagen rear engine car was anticipated by a 1904 patent for a cart with the horse at the rear.

1. The passage is mainly about _____.

　　A. an approach to patents　　　　　　B. the application for patents

　　C. the use of patents　　　　　　　　D. the access to patents

2. Which of the following is TRUE according to the passage?

　　A. When a patent becomes out of effect, it can be re-patented or extended if necessary.

B. It is necessary for an inventor to apply for a patent before he makes his invention public.

C. A patent holder must publicize the details of his invention when its legal period is over.

D. One can get all the details of a patented invention from a library attached to the patent office .

3. George Valensi's patent lasted until 1971 because _____.

A. nobody would offer any reward for his patent prior to that time

B. his patent could not be put to use for an unusually long time

C. there were not enough TV stations to provide colour programmes

D. the colour TV receiver was not available until that time

4. The word "plagiarize" (Line 5 , Para.5) most probably means "_____".

A. steal and use   B. give reward to

C. make public   D. take and change

5. From the passage we learn that _____.

A. an invention will not benefit the inventor unless it is reduced to commercial practice

B. products are actually inventions which were made a long time ago

C. it is much cheaper to buy an old patent than a new one

D. patent experts often recommend patents to others by conducting a search through dead patents

核心词汇注释

patent ['peɪt(ə)nt] *n.* 专利权，执照，专利品
adj. 特许的，专利的，显著的，明白的，新奇的
vt. 取得……的专利权

monopoly [mə'nɒpəlɪ] *n.* 垄断，垄断者，专利权，专利事业

terminate ['tɜːmɪneɪt] *v.* 停止，结束，终止

circuitry ['sɜːkɪtrɪ] *n.* 电路，线路

violation [ˌvaɪə'leɪʃən] *n.* 违反，违背，妨碍，侵害，[体] 违例，强奸

plagiarize ['pleɪdʒəraɪz] *v.* 剽窃，抄袭

invalidate [ɪn'vælɪdeɪt] *vt.* 使无效

presumption [prɪ'zʌmpʃ(ə)n] *n.* 假定

dedication [ˌdedɪ'keɪʃ(ə)n] *n.* 贡献，奉献

anticipate [æn'tɪsɪpeɪt] *vt.* 预期，期望；过早使用，先人一着，占先
v. 预订，预见，可以预料

长难句剖析

【文章难句】Because a patent remains permanently public after it has terminated, the shelves of the library attached to the patent office contain details of literally millions of ideas that are free for anyone to use and, if older than half a century, sometimes even re-patent.

【结构分析】本句主干是 the shelves of the library attached to the patent office contain details of literally millions of ideas。attached 是过去分词做状语。后面的 that are…是定语从句，修饰 ideas。if 引导的是条件状语从句，主语被省略。前面的 because 引导的是原因状语从句，其中 after 引导的是时间状语从句。

【参考译文】因为一项专利在终止期限后保持长期公开，专利局所属的图书馆的架子上

有数百万个专利设想的书面细节，任何人都可使用，如果超过半个世纪，有时甚至可以重新申请专利。

全文参考译文

当一项发明成功时，发明者有三种可能的行为方针供选择：通过出版把成果公布于世、对这项发明保密，或取得专利。

一项授予的专利是发明者和国家之间形成的一种契约。根据契约，发明者对自己的发明获得了一定时期的垄断权，并应在垄断期结束后把发明的完整细节公布于众。仅在极特殊情形下，才可延长一项专利的生命周期，改变事情的通常过程。

延长时间最长的专利批准给了 Georges Valensi，他 1939 年的彩色电视接收机线路的专利一直延续到 1971 年，因为专利期内大部分时间没有彩色电视节目可以接收，所以这项专利没有得到回报的希望。

因为一项专利在到期后将永久公开，所以专利局所属的图书馆的架子上有数百万个专利设想的书面细节，任何人都可自由使用，如果超过半个世纪，有时甚至可以重新申请专利。实际上，专利专家们常建议希望使用可用专利而又不愿付出高额费用的人使用过期专利，避免侵犯他人专利权。同样，因为用任何其他一种方式公布一种专利设想都会使该设想的专利权永久失效，所以使用其他印刷材料上的专利设想一般来讲是安全的。很多现代技术的进步都是基于这些法律安全的认定。

任何与专利及发明密切相关的人很快就知道，多数"新"的设想实际上已相当古老。只有把握时代的需求，通过使用新技术，专利才能转化为商业实践，做到名利双收。利用电磁录音这一理论的最初专利可追溯到 1886 年。电视背后的许多原始思路都开始于 19 世纪末 20 世纪初。甚至 1904 年马在车后的马车专利已经预见到了发动机后置的"大众"汽车的出现。

题目答案与解析

1. 这篇文章主要是关于 _____。
   - A．申请专利的方法
   - B．申请专利
   - C．专利的用途
   - D．获得专利的途径

【答案】D

【解析】本题是主旨题。文章主要是谈如何利用已有的技术进行新的发明创造和取得专利的途径。D 项为正确答案，A、B、C 项不是文章的主题，

2. 根据本文，以下说法中哪项是正确的？
   - A．当一项专利失效时，如果有必要，可以再申请或者延期。
   - B．发明者向公众宣告他的发明前，有必要先申请专利。
   - C．当专利的法律有效期结束时，专利持有者必须公布发明的细节。
   - D．人们可以从专利局所属的图书馆获得一项已申请专利的发明的所有细节。

【答案】C

【解析】C 项为正确答案。文章第 2 段指出一项授予的专利是发明者和国家之间形成的一种契约。根据契约，发明者对自己的发明获得了一定时期的垄断权，并应在垄断期结束后

把发明的完整细节公布于众。由此可知 C 项正确。

3. Georges Valensi 的专利权一直延续到 1971 年，原因是 _____。
  A. 在那之前没人付报酬给他的这项专利　B. 他的专利在相当长的时间内都无法采用
  C. 没有足够多的电视台来提供彩电节目　D. 彩色电视机直到那时才能使用
  【答案】B
  【解析】文章第 4 段指出，延续时间最长的专利经批准给了 George Valensi。他 1939 年的彩色电视机线路的专利一直延续到 1971 年，因为专利期内大部分时间没有彩电节目可以接收，所以这项专利没有得到回报的希望。由此可知 B 项为正确答案。

4. 单词 "plagiarize"（第 5 段第 5 行）最可能的意思是 "_____"。
  A. 偷窃并使用　　　B. 付给报酬　　　C. 使公开　　　D. 取得并改变
  【答案】A
  【解析】本题为词义推测题。从第 5 段第 2 句话可知 A 项为正确答案。plagiarize：剽窃，偷来加以利用。

5. 从文中我们得知 _____。
  A. 除非将发明转化为商业行为，发明不会对发明者有任何益处
  B. 产品实际上就是很久之前的发明
  C. 购买旧专利比购买新专利便宜得多
  D. 专利专家常建议通过使用过期的专利来获取他人的专利
  【答案】A
  【解析】文章第 6 段第 2 句话指出，只有把握时代的需求，通过使用新技术，专利才能转化为商业实践，做到名利双收。A 项为正确答案。

Text 4

A recent study examined men's attitudes to women, life goals and gender roles and the findings indicate that the popular image of men as insensitive, macho slobs has almost disappeared. The report found that modern British men have accepted the feminist revolution and have become more feminine in the process. "Men have turned into metrosexuals."

Paradoxically, the term "metrosexual", which is now being embraced by marketers, was coined in the mid-90's to mock everything marketers stand for. Mark Simpson used the word to satirize what he saw as consumerism's toll on traditional masculinity. Men didn't go to shopping malls, buy glossy magazines or load up on grooming products, Mr. Simpson argued, so consumer culture promoted the idea of a sensitive guy — who went to malls, bought magazines and spent freely to improve his personal appearance.

Within a few years, British advertisers and newspapers picked up the term. In 2001, Britain's Channel Four brought out a show about sensitive guys called "metrosexuality". And in recent years the European media found a metrosexual icon in David Beckham, the English soccer star, who paints his fingernails, braids his hair and poses for gay magazines, all while maintaining a manly profile on the pitch.

The challenge of the marketers is still to convince men that it is perfectly normal to groom.

What separates the modern-day metrosexual is a care-free attitude toward the inevitable suspicion that a man who dresses well, has good manners, or has opinions on women's fashion is gay. Some metrosexuals may simply be indulging in pursuits they had avoided for fear of being suspected as gay.

1. According to the text, men _____.

   A. have rejected the feminist view of themselves

   B. accept the need to groom

   C. now have new attitudes of themselves and women

   D. have adopted many characteristics formerly thought of as women's

2. The best definition of the term "metrosexual" would be _____.

   A. a consumer who shops for feminine products

   B. a man who grooms himself the same way as a woman

   C. a man who is halfway between a heterosexual and a homosexual

   D. a heterosexual who has feminine sensitivities and habits

3. From the second paragraph we can conclude that the term "metrosexual" _____.

   A. was not originally a marketing term

   B. only became popular in the mid-nineties

   C. was invented by marketers

   D. was actually meant to describe gay men

4. According to the text, the metrosexual's attitude towards fashion _____.

   A. is only a way of distinguishing themselves

   B. is a consequence of a new tolerance for pursuits that were though of as gay

   C. is a carefree attitude that seems unconcerned about society's reaction

   D. is connected to hip-hop culture

5. What is the text mainly about?

   A. A new emerging type of fashion trend.

   B. A new way of classifying the modern man.

   C. How a metrosexual differs form a heterosexual.

   D. The background and description of the "metrosexual".

核心词汇注释

macho ['mætʃəʊ] *adj.* 雄壮的，男子气概的

feminist ['femɪnɪst] *n.* 男女平等主义者，女权主义者

feminine ['femɪnɪn] *adj.* 妇女（似）的，娇柔的，阴性的，女性的

mock [mɒk] *v.* 嘲笑，嘲弄；骗；挫败
  adj. 假的

n. 嘲弄；模仿，仿制品

satirize ['sætɪraɪz] *v.* 讽刺性描写

consumerism [kən'sjuːmərɪz(ə)m] *n.* 用户至上主义，商品的消费和销售性服务

masculinity [ˌmæskjʊ'lɪnɪtɪ] *n.* 男性，阳性，雄性

fingernail ['fɪŋgəneɪl] *n.* 手指甲

braid [breɪd] *v.* 编织

　　　　　　 n. 编织物

groom [grum] *n.* 马夫；新郎；男仆

vt. 喂马；推荐；修饰

vi. 修饰

长难句剖析

【文章难句】The report found that "modern British men have accepted the feminist revolution and have become more feminine in the process.

【结构分析】本句中，the report 做主语，found 做谓语，that 引导的是宾语从句。have accepted the feminist revolution 和 have become more feminine in the process 是并列关系。

【参考译文】这份报告发现，现代英国男人接受了女性革命，并且在此过程中变得较为女性化。

全文参考译文

　　最近一项调查研究了男人对女人的态度、生活目标以及性别作用。结果表明，感觉迟钝、不修边幅这种普遍的男人形象不见了。这份报告发现，现代英国男人接受了女性革命，并且在此过程中变得较为女性化。"男人已经转变为城市玉男。"

　　矛盾的是，"城市玉男"这个词是 20 世纪 90 年代中期创造的，用来嘲弄商家所代表的一切，但正在为商家欣然接受。描写同性恋的作家马克•辛普森用这个词讥讽他所看到的消费主义对传统男人气概的重创。辛普森先生说，男人不去购物中心，不买有光纸杂志，不买化妆品，于是消费文化就宣传了感性男人的理念——逛商场，买杂志，慷慨解囊，改善个人形象。

　　没过几年，英国广告商和报纸用起了这个词。2001 年，英国的第四频道推出一个关于感性男人的节目，叫做"城市玉男风度"。近年来，欧洲媒体发现英国足球明星大卫•贝克汉姆是城市玉男偶像，他染指甲，给同性恋杂志拍照，同时在足球场上仍保持刚健的男人形象。

　　商家的难题仍然是让男人确信装饰打扮完全正常。人们不可避免地怀疑一个穿着讲究、举止温文，或者对女性时装有见地的男人是同性恋者，对此，现代城市玉男有的持满不在乎的态度，只管我行我素，不再像以往那样由于担心被怀疑为同性恋者而谨慎行事。

题目答案与解析

1. 根据本文，男人 _____。

　　A. 自己否决了男女平等观点

　　B. 接受了修饰的需要

　　C. 对自己和女人有了新的态度

　　D. 已采用了很多从前被认为是女人的特征

【答案】C

【解析】根据本文的第 1 段可知：现代英国男人接受了女性革命，并且在此过程中变得较为女性化。这说明男人对自己和女人有了新的态度。

2. 术语"metrosexual"最恰当的定义是 _____。

　　A. 购买女性产品的消费者

　　B. 像女人一样修饰自己的男人

　　C. 一个介于异性恋和同性恋之间的男人

　　D．一个有着女性敏感性和习惯的男异性恋者

【答案】D

【解析】本题可参照文章的第3段。从举贝克汉姆为例可以判断，所谓的metrosexual是指具有女性情感和习惯，但又不是同性恋的男人，即女性化的男异性恋者。

3．从第2段我们可以推断出术语"metrosexual"_____。

　　A．最初并不是营销术语　　　　　B．仅仅在90年代中期流行

　　C．是市场商人发明的　　　　　　D．实际上意指男同性恋者

【答案】A

【解析】从第2段可知，metrosexual这个词在创造之初是用来嘲弄商家所代表的一切，所以该词最初不是营销术语。

4．根据本文，城市玉男对时尚的态度_____。

　　A．只有区别他们自己的一种方式

　　B．是对被认为是同性恋者这种攻击的新的忍耐的结果

　　C．是对社会反应不关心的我行我素的态度

　　D．与前卫文化相关联

【答案】C

【解析】最后一段讲到，有些metrosexual对社会的反应满不在乎，我行我素。据此可知，C项为正确答案。

5．本文的主旨是什么？

　　A．一种新出现的时尚趋势的类型　　B．一种给现代男人分类的新方法

　　C．城市玉男与异性恋男人的区别　　D．城市玉男的背景和含义

【答案】D

【解析】属主旨思想题。文章主要介绍metrosexual这个概念的背景并描述它现在的含义。

Unit 25

Text 1

The close relationship between poetry and music scarcely needs to be argued. Both are aural modes which employ rhythm, rime, and pitch as major devices; to these the one adds linguistic meaning, connotation, and various traditional figures, and the other can add, at least in theory, all of these plus harmony, counterpoint, and orchestration techniques. In English the two are closely bound historically. Anglo-Saxon heroic poetry seems certainly to have been read or chanted to a harpist's accompaniment; the verb used in *Beowulf* for such a performance, the Finn episode, is singan, to sing, and the noun gyd, song. A major source of the lyric tradition in English poetry is the songs of the troubadours.

The distance between the gyd in *Beowulf* and the songs of Leonard Cohen or Bob Dylan may seem great, but is one of time rather than aesthetics. The lyric poem as a literary work and the lyrics of a popular song are both still essentially the same thing: poetry. Whether the title of the work be "Gerontion", or "Hound Dog", our criteria for evaluating the work must remain the same.

The most important prerequisite for both a significant poem and significant lyrics in a popular song is that the writer be faithful to his own personal vision or to the vision of the poem he is writing. Skill and craft for writing poetry are indeed necessary because these are the only means by which a poet can preserve the integrity of this vision in the poem. A poet must not, either because of lack of skill or because of worship of popularity, wealth, or critical acclaim, go outside of his own or his own poem's vision — on pain of writing only the derivative or the trivial. Historically, the writers and singers of the lyrics of popular songs have seemed often to be incapable of personal vision, and to have confused both originality and morality with a servile compliance to popular taste.

1. According to the writer, the relationship between poetry and music _____.
   A. is a debatable topic
   B. can be made but in a limited way
   C. is indisputable if you analyse history
   D. needs to be acknowledged more by poets

2. The author cites *Beowulf* in order to show that _____.
   A. the distance between song and poetry is not so great
   B. a song like *Beowulf* can sound like a poem
   C. English poetry is highly connected to songs
   D. songs generally evolve into poetry over time

3. Which of the following statements is true, according to the text?
   A. The lyrics of a song are no different from the lyrics of poetry.
   B. Song lyrics and poetry must be treated analytically as the same.

C. The differences between poetry and song lyrics have been overstated.

D. It is the time not the aesthetics that is different in most poems and song lyrics.

4. A poem or a song can be significant when _____.

A. it is done by a faithful writer

B. the writer has a personal vision of the poem or song

C. it is written within the vision of the poem, song, poet or songwriter

D. the writer is willing to go outside of the vision

5. In the text, the author focuses on _____.

A. the shared, most important evaluation criteria in songwriting and poetry

B. the various ways songs and poems are similar

C. the difference between good poetry and songs and mediocre ones

D. how to evaluate a poem and a song's value from a lyrical standpoint

核心词汇注释

aural ['ɔːr(ə)l] *adj.* 听觉的

counterpoint ['kaʊntəpɔɪnt] *n.* [音]对位法，旋律配合；对应物

orchestration [ˌɔːkɪ'streɪʃən] *n.* 管弦乐编曲，管弦乐作曲法

harpist ['hɑːpɪst] *n.* 弹竖琴者，竖琴师

episode ['epɪsəʊd] *n.* 一段情节，[音]插曲，插话；有趣的事件

troubadour ['truːbədɔː(r)] *n.* 行吟诗人，民谣歌手

prerequisite [priː'rekwɪzɪt] *n.* 先决条件 *adj.* 首要必备的

integrity [ɪn'tegrɪtɪ] *n.* 正直，诚实；完整，完全；完整性

derivative [dɪ'rɪvətɪv] *adj.* 引出的，系出的 *n.* 派生的事物，派生词

长难句剖析

【文章难句】The most important prerequisite for both a significant poem and significant lyrics in a popular song is that the writer be faithful to his own personal vision or to the vision of the poem he is writing.

【结构分析】本句中，The most important prerequisite 做主语，介语 for 引导的介宾短语做定语，修饰主语。that 引导的是表语从句。he is writing 做定语从句修饰 poem。

【参考译文】意义深长的诗歌和流行歌曲的歌词二者最为重要的前提都是，作者忠实于自己的个人眼界或者所写诗歌的境界。

全文参考译文

毋庸置疑，诗歌与音乐密切相关。二者皆运用节律、谐韵和抑扬顿挫为重要手段，悦人听觉；前者加之以语言意义、内涵和各种传统人物，后者至少在理论上加之以和声、对位以及配器技法。在英语中，二者自古就密不可分。似乎确定无疑的是，盎格鲁—撒克逊的英雄史诗，当初是在竖琴的伴奏下朗读或吟唱；《贝奥武夫》中描写芬恩插曲的动词 singan 意思为唱，名词 gyd 意思为歌。英语诗歌适用歌唱的传统的一个重要来源是吟游诗人的歌曲。

《贝奥武夫》中的 gyd 和 Leonard Cohen 或者 Bob Dylan 的歌曲之间或许差异巨大，但只是时代的差别，而不是美学的差别。作为文学作品的抒情诗和流行歌曲的歌词实质上仍然是一回事：诗歌。不管作品题目是《小老头》还是《猎犬》，我们评价作品的尺度必须始终如一。

意义深长的诗歌和流行歌曲的歌词二者最为重要的前提都是，作者忠实于自己的个人眼界或者所写诗歌的境界。写诗的技巧和手法的确必不可少，因为这是诗人在诗中保存眼界完整的唯一手段。诗人绝不能因为缺乏技巧或是因为崇拜名声、财富或者赞誉而游离自己的或自己诗歌的眼界之外——那样写出的只是缺乏独创、无足轻重的东西。历史上，通俗歌曲歌词的作者和演唱者似乎时常丧失个人眼界，哗众媚俗，混淆独创性和道德观。

题目答案与解析

1. 根据作者，诗和音乐之间的关系 _____。
   - A. 是一个有争议的话题
   - B. 可以在一个有限的范围内建立
   - C. 通过分析历史可知是无可争议的
   - D. 需要诗人们更多地认可

   【答案】C

   【解析】作者在第 1 段指出，诗歌与音乐自古就密不可分。据此可知，C 项为正确答案。

2. 作者引用《贝奥武夫》是为了说明 _____。
   - A. 歌曲和诗之间的差距并不是很大
   - B. 《贝奥武夫》的歌听起来像诗
   - C. 英国诗歌与歌曲联系紧密
   - D. 随着时间的推移，歌曲发展成为诗歌

   【答案】C

   【解析】本文第 1 段中，从历史角度说明诗歌与音乐密切相关，其中，以《贝奥武夫》为例是为了说明本段主题，即英国诗歌与歌曲联系紧密。据此可知 C 项为正确答案。

3. 根据本文，以下陈述中正确的是哪项？
   - A. 歌词与诗歌没有区别。
   - B. 诗歌与歌曲的歌词实质上是一回事。
   - C. 诗和歌词之间的区别被过分夸大。
   - D. 在多数诗和歌词之间的差别是时代而不是美学的差别。

   【答案】B

   【解析】从第 2 段可知，诗歌与歌曲的歌词实质上是一回事。因此 B 项为正确答案。

4. 当 _____ 时，一首诗或一首歌有着重大意义。
   - A. 由一名忠实的作者来创作
   - B. 作者对诗或歌曲有着个人的眼界
   - C. 诗人或歌曲作家忠实于自己的眼界来创作
   - D. 作者愿意超出眼界创作

   【答案】C

   【解析】从文中第 3 段可知，意义深长的诗歌和流行歌曲的歌词二者最为重要的前提都是，作者忠实于自己的个人眼界或者所写诗歌的境界。因此 C 项为正确答案。

5. 文章中作者的主要意思是 _____。
   - A. 对作曲和作诗共同的、最重要的评估标准

B．歌曲和诗相似的不同方面

C．优秀的诗和歌曲与普通的诗和歌曲之间的区别

D．如何从诗的角度来评估诗和歌曲的价值

【答案】A

【解析】综观全文，本文说明诗歌和音乐密切的关系，主要涉及二者共同的重要评价标准。因此 A 项为正确答案。

Text　2

Whatever their chosen method, Americans bathe zealously. A study conducted found that we take an average of 4.5 baths and 7.5 showers each week and in the ranks of non-edible items purchased by store customers, bar soap ranks second, right after toilet paper. We spend more than $700 million annually on soaps, but all work the same way. Soap is composed of molecules that at one end attract water and at the other end attract oil and dirt, while repelling water. With a kind of pushing and pulling action, the soap loosens the bonds holding dirt to the skin.

Unless you're using a germicidal soap, it usually doesn't kill the bacteria — soap simply removes bacteria along with dirt and oil. Neither baths nor showers are all that necessary and unless you're in a Third World country where infectious diseases are common, or you have open sores on your skin, the dirt and bacteria aren't going to hurt. The only reason for showering or bathing is to feel clean and refreshed. There is a physiological basis for this relaxed feeling. Your limbs become slightly buoyant in bathwater, which takes a load off muscles and tension. Moreover, if the water is hotter than normal body temperature, the body attempts to shed heat by expanding the blood vessels near the surface of the skin, lessening the circulatory system's resistance to blood flow, and dropping blood pressure gently. A bath is also the most effective way to hydrate the skin. The longer you soak, the more water gets into the skin and because soap lowers the surface tension of the water, it helps you hydrate rapidly and remove dry skin flakes.

However, in a bath, all the dirt and grime and the soap in which it's suspended float on the surface. So when you stand up, it covers your body like a film. The real solution is to take a bath and then rinse off with a shower, however, after leaving a tub or freshly exposed skin becomes a playground for microbes. In two hours, you probably have as many bacteria on certain parts of the body, such as the armpits, as before the bath.

1．The statement "Americans bathe zealously" (Line 1, Para. 1) is closest to saying _____.

A．Americans bathe wastefully

B．Americans are rather ambivalent to bathing

C．Americans bathe with intense enthusiasm

D．Americans bathe too much

2．Which of the following is mentioned as one of the benefits of bathing?

A．Dry skins flakes will disappear from the body once you get out of the bathtub.

B．It kills bacteria better than showering.

C．It reduces your blood circulation if it is nice and warm.

D. The floating action can reduce the stress on your muscles.

3. According to the text, bathing removes dry skin flakes because _____.
   A. the soap draw it off the body
   B. the skin hydrates
   C. the circulation of blood expands skin particles
   D. the change in blood pressure releases the film

4. A bath will not kill the bacteria from your body even if _____.
   A. you use a germicidal soap   B. use an anti-bacterial soap
   C. you use soap to scrub it vigorously   D. you are under special treatment for it

5. We can infer from this text that the author believes _____.
   A. the real benefits of bathing are psychological not hygienic
   B. bathing is superior to taking shower
   C. buying soap is a waste of money
   D. we do not need to bathe as much as we do currently

核心词汇注释

zealous ['zeləs] *adj.* 热心的

molecule ['mɒlɪkjuːl] *n.* [化] 分子；些微

germicidal [ˌdʒɜːmɪ'saɪdəl] *adj.* 杀菌的，有杀菌力的

limb [lɪm] *n.* 肢，翼；分支

buoyant ['bɔɪənt] *adj.* 有浮力的；轻快的

vessel ['ves(ə)l] *n.* 船；容器，器皿；脉管，导管

hydrate ['haɪdreɪt] *n.* 氢氧化物
   v. 与水化合

flake [fleɪk] *n.* 薄片
   v. 使成薄片，剥落，雪片般落下

grime [graɪm] *n.* 尘垢，污点；煤尘
   vt. 使污秽，污浊

rinse [rɪns] *v.* 漱口，（用清水）刷，冲洗掉，漂净
   n. 嗽洗，漂洗，漂清，冲洗

长难句剖析

【文章难句】Moreover, if the water is hotter than normal body temperature, the body attempts to shed heat by expanding the blood vessels near the surface of the skin, lessening the circulatory system's resistance to blood flow, and dropping blood pressure gently.

【结构分析】本句主干是 the body attempts to shed heat by expanding the blood vessels near the surface of the skin。前面 if 引导的是条件状语从句。lessening the circulatory system's resistance to blood flow 和 dropping blood pressure gently 是并列现在分词短语做状语。

【参考译文】而且，如果水温高于正常体温，身体会舒张皮下血管来散热，从而减少循环系统对血流的阻力，慢慢地降低血压。

全文参考译文

不论选择何种方式，美国人对洗澡有种狂热。一项研究发现，我们每周平均洗澡 4.5

次，淋浴 7.5 次，并且在商店顾客购买的非食物商品中，条形肥皂位居第二，仅次于卫生纸。我们每年买肥皂的花费超过 7 亿美元，但是用途都一样。肥皂的分子一端吸水，一端吸油、吸尘，排斥水分。由于斥力和引力的双重作用，肥皂缓释了污垢在皮肤上的附着。

除非使用除菌皂，否则肥皂通常不杀菌，只是让细菌和污垢、油渍一起洗掉。洗澡和淋浴都没有那么必要，如果你不是在传染病流行的第三世界国家，或者皮肤上没有外露的疮口，污垢和细菌不会伤人。淋浴或洗澡的唯一理由是感觉清爽。这种放松的感觉有生理基础。在洗澡水中四肢微微浮起，使肌肉和身体的紧张状态得到松弛。而且，如果水温高于正常体温，身体会舒张皮下血管来散热，从而减少循环系统对血流的阻力，慢慢地降低血压。洗澡也是让皮肤吸水的最为有效的方式。在水中浸泡时间越长，进入皮肤的水分就越多。因为肥皂能减轻水的表面张力，所以有助于皮肤迅速水合，从而去除干燥的皮屑。

但是，在洗澡时，所有污垢和悬浮着污垢的肥皂都浮于水面。所以当你起身时，这些东西像一层薄膜一样覆盖全身。真正的解决方法是，先洗澡，出浴缸后用淋浴冲洗，否则出浴的皮肤就成了微生物的活动场所。两小时后，在身体的某些部位，如腋窝处细菌数量可能和洗澡前一样多了。

题目答案与解析

1. 与句子 "Americans bathe zealously"（第 1 段第 1 行）最接近的意思是 _____。
   A. 美国人洗澡不经济　　　　　　　B. 美国人对洗澡相当矛盾
   C. 美国人对洗澡极其狂热　　　　　D. 美国人洗澡太频繁
   【答案】C
   【解析】从第 1 段可知，美国人对洗澡狂热，对肥皂的消费巨大，因此题中该词应理解为"狂热地"。

2. 以下提及的项目中，哪项是洗澡有益的一面？
   A. 当你出浴缸时干燥的皮屑会从身上消失。
   B. 比起沐浴来，洗澡更能杀菌。
   C. 如果水温良好，洗澡可减少血液循环。
   D. 漂浮动作能够减少肌肉的压力。

   【答案】D
   【解析】A 项的说法不正确，第 3 段开头提到：在洗澡时，所有污垢和悬浮着污垢的肥皂都浮于水面。所以当你起身时，这些东西像一层薄膜一样覆盖全身。B 项不正确，第 2 段指出：除非使用除菌皂，否则肥皂通常不杀菌，只是让细菌和污垢、油渍一起洗掉。可见，洗澡和淋浴都不杀菌。C 项不正确，第 2 段同时指出：洗澡能减少循环系统对血流的阻力，慢慢地降低血压，说明洗澡可增加血液循环。只有 D 项正确，因为第 2 段指出：在水中四肢微微浮起，使肌肉和身体的紧张状态得到松弛。

3. 根据本文，洗澡能够去掉皮屑的原因是 _____。
   A. 肥皂把它从身体上去掉　　　　　B. 皮肤与水化合
   C. 血液循环使皮肤粒子扩张　　　　D. 血液压力的改变去掉了薄膜
   【答案】B

【解析】从第 2 段末尾一句话可知，因为肥皂能减轻水的表面张力，所以有助于皮肤迅速水合，从而去除干燥的皮屑。因此 B 项为正确答案。

4.　洗澡不能将人体上的细菌杀死，即使 _____。
　　A．你用了杀菌肥皂　　　　　　　　B．你用了抗菌肥皂
　　C．你用力地用肥皂擦身体　　　　　D．你处于特殊的治疗之下

【答案】C

【解析】从第 2 段可知，肥皂通常不杀菌。因此 C 项为正确答案。

5.　我们从文中可以推出，作者认为 _____。
　　A．洗澡的益处不在于卫生方面而在于心理方面
　　B．洗澡比淋浴好
　　C．购买肥皂浪费钱
　　D．我们洗澡并不需要像现在这样频繁

【答案】A

【解析】从第 2 段可知，洗澡不能杀菌，而且污垢和细菌一般情况下不会伤人。同时又谈到：淋浴或洗澡的唯一理由是感觉清爽。所以，作者认为洗澡的真正好处不在卫生方面，而在心理方面。因此 A 项为正确答案。

Text 3

Very soon, unimaginably powerful technologies will remake our lives. This could have dangerous consequences, especially because we may not even understand the basic science underlying them. There's a growing gap between our technological capability and our underlying scientific understanding. We can do very clever things with the technology of the future without necessarily understanding some of the science underneath, and that is very dangerous.

The technologies that are particularly dangerous over the next hundred years are nanotechnology, artificial intelligence and biotechnology. The benefits they will bring are beyond doubt but they are potentially very dangerous. In the field of artificial intelligence there are prototype designs for something that might be 50,000 million times smarter than the human brain by the year 2010. The only thing not feasible in the film *Terminator* is that the people win. If you're fighting against technology that is that much smarter than you, you probably will not win. We've all heard of the grey goo problem that self-replicating nanotech devices might keep on replicating until the world has been reduced to sticky goo, and certainly in biotechnology, we've really got a big problem because it's converging with nanotechnology. Once you start mixing nanotech with organisms and you start feeding nanotech — enabled bacteria, we can go much further than the Borg in *Star Trek*, and those superhuman organisms might not like us very much.

We are in a world now where science and commerce are increasingly bedfellows. The development of technology is happening in the context of global free trade regimes which see technological diffusion embedded with commerce as intrinsically a good. We should prepare for new and unfamiliar forms of argument around emerging technologies.

1. From the text, we know that the author's greatest worry is _____.
   A. our lack of technological understanding of the process involved
   B. our lack of technological capability
   C. creating technology without really understanding the issues
   D. our refusal to face the consequences of the technology we create

2. It can be inferred from the text that the author _____.
   A. thinks people overestimate the capabilities of technology
   B. is not optimistic that artificial intelligence will always be used positively
   C. thinks that we should take science fiction movies more seriously
   D. believes artificial intelligence is the greatest threat we face technologically

3. Why does the author say it is not feasible in the film Terminator that the humans win?
   A. Because the power of the technology was exaggerated.
   B. Because the strength of the machines would be much greater.
   C. Because machines with that much intelligence would not allow it.
   D. Because even heroic humans would achieve nothing from such a battle.

4. The mixing of nanotech with organisms may _____.
   A. produce dangerous viruses capable of killing many people
   B. produce creatures that are unfriendly to humans
   C. upset our balance of nature
   D. reduce the world to sticky glue

5. The author's attitude toward the emerging technologies is _____.
   A. critical　　　　　　B. skeptical　　　　　C. provocative　　　　D. alarmist

核心词汇注释

unimaginable [ˌʌnɪˈmædʒɪnəbl] *adj.* 想不到的，不可思议的

remake [ˈriːmeɪk] *v.* 重制

biotechnology [ˌbaɪəʊtekˈnɒlədʒɪ] *n.* 生物工艺学

prototype [ˈprəʊtəʊtaɪp] *n.* 原型

sticky [ˈstɪkɪ] *adj.* 黏的，黏性的

converge [kənˈvɜːdʒ] *v.* 聚合，集中于一点 *vt.* 会聚

organism [ˈɔːgənɪz(ə)m] *n.* 生物体，有机体

bedfellow [ˈbedˌfeləʊ] *n.* 同床者；伙伴

regime [reɪˈʒiːm] *n.* 政体；政权；政权制度

长难句剖析

【文章难句】The development of technology is happening in the context of global free trade regimes which see technological diffusion embedded with commerce as intrinsically a good.

【结构分析】本句中，the development of technology 做主语，in the context of global free trade regimes 是介宾短语做状语。which 引导定语从句修饰 regimes。

【参考译文】在全球自由贸易体制的环境中，技术正在发展。这种体制认为技术的传播

与商业结合实质上是件好事。

全文参考译文

　　无比强大的科技很快就将完全改变我们的生活。这可能会产生危险的后果，尤其是因为我们可能不懂背后的基础科学。我们的科技能力和对科学的基本理解之间的差距愈发加大。我们借助于未来科技可以从事非常巧妙的事情，而不必理解基本的科学，这是很危险的。

　　未来的一百年中特别危险的技术是纳米技术、人工智能和生物技术。它们带来的好处不容置疑，但它们潜在的危险很大。在人工智能领域，到 2010 年比人脑聪明 500 亿倍的东西其原型设计已经出现。电影《终结者》中唯一不可能实现的事，是人类获胜。假如你在和比自己聪明得多的技术对抗，你可能不会取胜。我们都听说过灰色黏质问题，能自我复制的纳米技术装置不停地复制，直到世界沦为黏糊糊的质体。无疑在生物技术方面，我们真的有个大问题，因为它在与纳米技术合流。一旦把纳米技术和有机体相结合，就有了纳米技术制造的细菌，我们能够比《星际迷航》中的博格飞船旅行得更远，但那些超人生物体可能对我们并不太友好。

　　我们所处的世界科学与商业日益结盟。在全球自由贸易体制的环境中，技术正在发展。这种体制认为技术的传播与商业结合实质上是件好事。我们应该做好准备，迎接围绕新兴技术而展开的前所未有的争论。

题目答案与解析

1. 我们从文中可知，作者最大的担忧是 _____。
   A. 我们对相关过程的技术缺乏了解
   B. 我们对技术能力的缺乏
   C. 在创造技术的同时没有真正懂得问题
   D. 我们拒绝面对我们所创造的技术所产生的后果
   【答案】C
   【解析】从第 1 段可知，作者先后指出：无比强大的科技很快就将完全改变我们的生活。这可能会产生危险的后果，尤其是因为我们可能不懂背后的基本科学；我们借助于未来科技可以从事非常巧妙的事情，而不必理解基本的科学，这是很危险的。可见，作者的最大担心是在创造技术的同时没有真正懂得问题。因此 C 项为正确答案。

2. 从文中可以推出作者 _____。
   A. 认为人们对科技的能力估计过高
   B. 对人工智能的积极应用并不乐观
   C. 认为我们应更加严肃地对待科学虚构电影
   D. 认为我们在科技上所面对的最大威胁是人工智能
   【答案】B
   【解析】文中第 2 段具体分析探讨了人工智能、纳米技术和生物技术的潜在危险。从中可知，作者对人工智能的积极应用并不乐观。因此 B 项为正确答案。

3. 为什么作者说在电影《终结者》中人类是不会获胜的？

    A. 因为科技的力量被夸大了。

    B. 因为机器的力量会大得多。

    C. 因为拥有很高智能的机器使人类无法获胜。

    D. 因为从这样一场战役中，即使是英勇的人类也会一无所获。

【答案】C

【解析】从第 2 段可知，电影《终结者》中唯一不可能实现的是人类会胜出。假如你在和比自己聪明得多的技术对抗，你可能不会取胜。这两句话的关系是前果后因。因此 C 项为正确答案。

4. 纳米技术和有机体的结合会 _____。

    A. 产生使人致命的危险病毒

    B. 产生对人不太友好的生物

    C. 打破自然的平衡

    D. 使世界陷入黏液之中

【答案】B

【解析】从第 2 段可知，纳米技术与有机体相结合可能产生对人类不太友好的生物。因此 B 项为正确答案。

5. 作者对新兴技术的态度是 _____。

    A. 批评   B. 怀疑   C. 煽动   D. 大惊小怪

【答案】B

【解析】从第 2 段开头可知，未来一百年中特别危险的技术是纳米技术、人工智能和生物技术。它们带来的好处不容置疑，但它们潜在的危险很大。据此可知，B 项为正确答案。

Text 4

The long, wet summer here in the northeastern U.S. notwithstanding, there's a world shortage of pure, fresh water. As demand for water hits the limits of finite supply, potential conflicts are brewing between nations that share transboundary freshwater reserves.

Many people ask why we cannot simply take it from the sea, using our sophisticated technology of desalinization. But a good water supply must be hygienically safe and pleasant tasting and water containing salt would corrode machinery used in manufacturing in addition to producing chemical impurities. Since more than 95% of our water sits in the salty seas, man is left to face the reality that most water on the surface of the earth is not available for us.

One very feasible way of sustaining our supply of freshwater is to protect the ecology of our mountains. Mountains and water go together, a fact to which Secretary General Kofi Annan has drawn attention more than once. From 30% to 60% of downstream fresh water in humid areas and up to 95% in arid and semi-arid environments are supplied by mountains. Without interference nature has its own way of purifying water — even though chlorination and filtration are still necessary as a precaution. In a mountainous area, aeration, due to turbulent flow and waterfalls, causes an exchange of gases between the atmosphere and the water. Agriculture, industry, hydroelectric generators and homes that need water to drink and for domestic use depend on these resources and, thus, we must protect mountainous areas as a means of survival.

1. The author of this text states that _____.
   A. the problem of obtaining good drinking water has plagued man throughout time
   B. palatability is synonymous with purity of water
   C. most of the world's water is unusable as a water supply
   D. man no longer depends on desalinization for his water supply

2. The author believes that industry avoids salt water because _____.
   A. water is needed for livestock
   B. crops must be considered before man-made products
   C. it is used in desalinization plants
   D. it causes corrosion

3. Streams would purify themselves if not for _____.
   A. human beings   B. nature
   C. chlorination   D. mountains

4. By saying that nature "has its own way of purifying water" (Line 5, Para. 3) the author is referring to _____.
   A. aeration   B. filtration
   C. chlorination   D. absorption

5. The best title for this text is _____.
   A. The Water Problem: The Dangers Ahead
   B. The Water Supply Problem: Our Options
   C. The Mountains: Our Only Hope for Water
   D. Water Conservation: The Challenges Ahead

核心词汇注释

notwithstanding [ˌnɒtwɪð'stændɪŋ] *prep.*
虽然，尽管 *adv.* 尽管，还是
conj. 虽然，尽管

finite ['faɪnaɪt] *adj.* 有限的，[数]有穷的，限定的

desalinization [diːˌsælɪnaɪ'zeɪʃən] *n.* <美>
减少盐分，脱盐作用

hygienically [ˌhaɪdʒɪ'enɪklɪ] *adv.* 卫生地

corrode [kə'rəud] *v.* 使腐蚀，侵蚀

humid ['hjuːmɪd] *adj.* 潮湿的，湿润的，多湿气的

chlorination [ˌklɔːrɪ'neɪʃən] *n.* [化]氯化，用氯处理

filtration [fɪl'treɪʃən] *n.* 过滤，筛选

precaution [prɪ'kɔːʃ(ə)n] *n.* 预防，警惕，防范

长难句剖析

【文章难句】Since more than 95% of our water sits in the salty seas, man is left to face the reality that most water on the surface of the earth is not available for us.

【结构分析】本句主干是 man is left to face the reality。that 引导的是同位语从句，修饰 reality。前面的 since 引导的是原因状语从句。

【参考译文】由于我们 95%以上的水资源都存在于含盐的海洋，人类只得面对现实：地球表面的大部分水资源我们无法获得。

全文参考译文

　　尽管美国东北部的夏季漫长而湿润，但在世界范围内纯净淡水却很短缺。随着水的需求达到有限供应的极限，共享跨边界淡水资源的国家之间正在酝酿着潜在的争端。

　　许多人问道，我们为何不利用先进的脱盐技术向海洋获取淡水呢？但是，良好的水资源必须健康安全，味道适宜，而且盐水除了产生化学杂质外，还会腐蚀生产设备。由于我们 95%以上的水资源都存在于含盐的海洋，人类只得面对现实：地球表面的大部分水资源我们无法获得。

　　维持淡水供应的一个非常可行的方法是，保护我们山区的生态。山水相伴而生，科菲·安南秘书长不止一次提醒过这一事实。湿润地区 30%～60%的，以及干旱、半干旱环境多达 95%的下游淡水，都是由山脉提供。在没有干预的情况下，大自然用自己的方式净化水源——尽管氯化和过滤仍是必要的预防措施。在山区，由于湍急的水流和瀑布产生的空气净化作用导致大气和水之间作气的置换。工农业、水力发电机以及家庭需要饮用和使用的水都依赖这些资源，因此，我们必须把山区作为生存手段加以保护。

题目答案与解析

1. 本文中作者指出 _____。
　　A．获得良好的饮用水的问题一直困扰着人们
　　B．palatability 与纯净水同义
　　C．地球表面的大部分水资源无法使用
　　D．人类不再依靠脱盐作用来获得水的供应
　　【答案】C
　　【解析】从第 2 段的末尾可知，地球表面的大部分水资源我们无法获得。因此 C 项为正确答案。
2. 作者认为工业避免使用盐水的原因是 _____。
　　A．家畜需要水　　　　　　　　　　　B．比起人造产品，应优先考虑农作物
　　C．它被有脱盐作用的工厂所使用　　　D．它能引起腐蚀
　　【答案】D
　　【解析】从第 2 段可知，海水腐蚀生产设备。因此 D 项为正确答案。
3. 如果不是因为 _____，河流会自己净化。
　　A．人类　　　　　B．大自然　　　　　C．用氯处理　　　　　D．山脉
　　【答案】A
　　【解析】从第 3 段可知，在没有干预的情况下，大自然用自己的方式净化水源。因此 A

项为正确答案。

4. 文中说大自然"有自己的方式净化水源"（第 3 段第 5 行），作者指的是 _____。

   A．充气　　　　　　B．过滤　　　　　　C．氯化　　　　　　D．吸收

【答案】A

【解析】本题中大自然净化水源的方式指的是后文提到的充气。因此 A 项为正确答案。

5. 本文最恰当的标题是 _____。

   A．水的问题：前面的危险　　　　　　B．水供给的问题：我们的选择

   C．山：我们获取水的唯一希望　　　　D．水的保护：前面的挑战

【答案】B

【解析】综观全文，本文探讨淡水资源的获取并且给出解决办法，因此 B 项为正确答案。

检
4